2/30/02

To Brendan,

Our extremely intelligent
god-son!

Happy Birthday,

Love,
Uncle Doug +.
Aunt Laurie

ALSO BY HAROLD BLOOM

# Stories and Poems
# for Extremely Intelligent Children
# of All Ages

SELECTED BY

## Harold Bloom

SCRIBNER

New York   London   Toronto   Sydney   Singapore

SCRIBNER
1230 Avenue of the Americas
New York, NY 10020

For information regarding special discounts for bulk purchases,
please contact Simon & Schuster Special Sales at 1-800-456-6798 or
*business@simonandschuster.com*

DESIGNED BY ERICH HOBBING

Set in Granjon

Manufactured in the United States of America

1    3    5    7    9    10    8    6    4    2

Library of Congress Cataloging-in-Publication Data
Stories and poems for extremely intelligent children of all ages / selected by Harold Bloom.
p. cm.
Summary: A collection of stories and poems, arranged in
four sections corresponding to the four seasons.
1. Children's literature. [1. Literature—Collections.] I. Bloom, Harold.

PZ5.S87919 2001
808.8'99282—dc21    2001042839

ISBN 0-684-86873-3

*Art Permissions*
Page 23: courtesy of Mary Evans Picture Library;
67: courtesy of Mary Evans Picture Library/Thomas Gillmor;
223: courtesy of Culver Pictures; 359: courtesy of
The Granger Collection, New York

# ACKNOWLEDGMENTS

My research assistants Tara Mohr and Kate Cambor helped greatly in putting together this anthology. I have a particular debt to the erudition of my assistant, Emmy Chang, in choosing stories and advising me on arrangement. My agents, Glen Hartley and Lynn Chu, and my editor, Gillian Blake, helped sustain me throughout this project.

# CONTENTS

## *Book II*    *Summer*

# Contents   9

## Book III      Autumn

## *Book IV*    *Winter*

# Contents 11

# Stories and Poems
## for Extremely Intelligent Children
## of All Ages

# INTRODUCTION

Here are forty-one stories and tales (many of them quite short) and eighty-three poems (only Christina Rossetti's *Goblin Market* is at all long). Since there are eight poems and tales by Lewis Carroll, which is more than by anyone else except Anonymous (by whom I count seventeen), I begin with Carroll. Some of my favorite poems by him are here ("A Pig-Tale" goes on ever improving, after hundreds of readings), but not the one I love best, *The Hunting of the Snark*, because it is fifteen pages long, and I cannot bear to cut it. Few poems ever have opened so splendidly:

> "Just the place for a Snark!" the Bellman cried,
> As he landed his crew with care;
> Supporting each man on the top of the tide
> By a finger entwined in his hair.
>
> "Just the place for a Snark! I have said it twice:
> That alone should encourage the crew.
> Just the place for a Snark! I have said it thrice:
> What I tell you three times is true."

The crew, besides the Bellman (a town crier) is very motley, but the hero is the courageous and overspecialized Baker (who can only bake wedding cake). He will sacrifice himself in the quest for the Snark (evidently a snail-like shark), who turns out to be a dread Boojum. Lewis Carroll somewhat defensively called his *Alice* books and the *Snark* "nonsense" writing, but they are masterful visions of the imagination murdering time. Such a murder amounts to a warding-off gesture, a prolongation of the time all of us still wish to possess. Time is a realistic continuity in which one thing must happen after another, but in nonsense writing, continuity can become a thousand things.

Anyone, of any age, reading this volume will see quickly that I do not accept the category of "Children's Literature," which had some use and distinction a century ago, but now all too often is a mask for the dumbing-down that is destroying our literary culture. Most of what is now commercially offered as children's literature would be inadequate fare for any reader of any age at any time. I myself first read nearly everything I have gathered together in this book between the ages of five and fifteen, and I have gone on reading these stories and poems from fifteen to seventy. My title is meant to be precise: What is between these covers is for extremely intelligent children of all ages. Rudyard Kipling, Lewis Carroll, and Edward Lear are blended with Nathaniel Hawthorne, Nicolai Gogol, and Ivan Turgenev, because all of them—in the poems and stories I have chosen—make themselves open to authentic readers of any age. There is nothing here that is difficult or obscure, nothing that will not both illuminate and entertain. If anyone finds a work here that does not yield immediately to their understanding, I would urge them to persevere. It is by extending oneself, by exercising some capacity previously unused that you come to a better knowledge of your own potential. I forbear suggesting any particular story or poem for one age or another because I would like to think of this book as an open field in which the reader will wander and find, for himself or herself, what seems appropriate. These selections offer and will confer delight, and many of them will bring even the most solitary reader a sense of companionship.

There are many convenient explanations as to why many children (of all ages) no longer read, or find it difficult to be challenged by what they read. The Age of Information emphasizes the screen—motion picture, television, and personal computer—and the e-book begins to be an alternative to the printed book. My own students at Yale, where I have taught for almost half a century, are as gifted as their forerunners, and yet they have read less. The obstacles to reading are, to some extent, merely a matter of fashion, or of inadequate examples set by parents for children. What is read remains the pragmatic question, the difference that will make a difference.

This book has a forty-year history for me, since I edited, in 1961, a volume called *The Wind and the Rain: An Anthology of Poems for Young People,* with John Hollander. *The Wind and the Rain* is now long out of print, as is a similar work I greatly admire, Walter de la Mare's *Come Hither.*

*The Wind and the Rain* was organized on a seasonal scheme, and I have adapted that for this book also, though many stories are gathered here, as well as poems. A seasonal scheme is universally applicable, at least in all climes that have four seasons! While a number of the poems and some of the stories have dominant seasonal settings, their placement is generally thematic rather than a reflection of tradition that associates spring with comedy, summer with romance, autumn with tragedy, and winter with different modes of irony.

Most immediately, the idea of *Stories and Poems for Extremely Intelligent Children of All Ages* came to me as I started work upon *How to Read and Why.* I first thought of a companion volume, to be called *The Solitary Reader,* but increasingly came to see that I wanted a book for younger readers.

Most of this book is nineteenth century or earlier because I wanted to maintain a coherence of tone and vision in these fantasies, narratives, lyrics, and meditations. After the First World War, various waves of what then was called "Modernism" ended the visionary speculation and wonder that makes *Stories and Poems for Extremely Intelligent Children* a harmony, at least in its editor's intention.

In general, I have chosen lyric poems of directness and relative simplicity, avoiding the difficulties of some of the strongest poets in the language, such as Donne and Dickinson, and including only one poem by Blake. These great poets are complex ironists, and too easily misread at any age. The superb Christina Rossetti is well represented here, because her finely tuned laments so directly express her passion for renunciation, which in turn is set aside in her astonishing, fantastic *Goblin Market.*

Fantasy, which is the nineteenth-century form of the ancient genre of romance, is the most characteristic mode of the stories I have selected, including the animal fables of Kipling, the fairy tales of the remarkable Edwardian writers Catherine Sinclair and Mary de Morgan, and scary imaginings by E. Nesbit and Edith Wharton, both manifesting extraordinary versatility. Lewis Carroll is my (and everyone's) favorite fantasist, but I have particular love for John Ruskin's *The King of the Golden River,* which appropriately leads off the Book of Summer here.

Comedy is represented throughout, with concentrated zest in Mark Twain's outrageous "Journalism in Tennessee" and Saki's "The Recessional," but the primary tonality of this book is a certain rich plangency, a "dying fall" (Orsino on music in Shakespeare's *Twelfth Night*), as evident in Hawthorne's tales as in Tennyson's lyrics. As we grow older, even when chronologically we remain quite young, we are likely to look back at our past selves with intense nostalgia. That nostalgia is not so much for the unlived life but for certain moments so rich in feeling and joy that we wonder if they can come again. After much reflection, I reluctantly excluded Chekhov, best of all short-story writers, because he will not blend with tones that accommodate fantasy. Subtle beyond any writer (except his model, Shakespeare), Chekhov deals entirely with the unlived life and so he demands to be read in his own company, which is a paradox since he has influenced nearly every story-writer after him.

I have placed nothing in this book that has not sustained me through many rereadings, the test being whether there is not always more to discover. The poet Wallace Stevens's tests for a fiction, verse or prose, were: it must change, it must give pleasure, and it must be abstract. Stevens did not mean "abstract" as opposed to "real," but "withdrawn from," taken out from something, from the stale coverings that masquerade as reality. Every lyric and tale in this volume has scrubbed the varnish off the commonplace in order to reveal hidden magic.

I am old-fashioned and romantic enough to believe that many children, given the right circumstances, are natural readers until this instinct is destroyed by the media. The tyranny of the screen threatens any order in which literary value or human wisdom can be preferred to the steady flow of information. It may be an illusion to believe that the magical connection of solitary children to the best books can endure, but such a relationship does go so long a way back that it will not easily expire. The romance of reading, like all experiential romance, depends upon enchantment, and enchantment relies upon the potential of power rather than upon complete knowledge. You are unlikely to fall in love with someone, however charming such a person may be, if you have known one another all your lives. What you can know fully will not induce you to fall in love, so that falling in love with a book is not wholly unlike falling in love with a person.

In Ovid's Pygmalion myth, adapted by George Bernard Shaw for his play and motion picture (which later became the musical *My Fair Lady*), the sculptor Pygmalion is unable to bring his beautiful statue, Galatea, to life. The goddess Venus does that for him. I take this (as Shaw did not) as a parable for reading: The poem or story will not come alive for you if you do not fall in love with it. If asked my favorite story or poem in this book, I would become bewildered in attempting a reply. In some moods I might vote for Hawthorne's "Feathertop" among the stories, and for Shelley's poem "The Two Spirits." "Feathertop" is so light it seems almost delicate, like the fragile scarecrow who gives the tale its title. And yet its reverberations take us all the way from the creation of Adam to the kind of despair that leads Feathertop to immolate himself. Shelley's "The Two Spirits" haunts one with the memories of first love, and the endless wonder as to how that could have turned out. But moods vary, and today I prefer Pushkin's "The Queen of Spades" and Edward Lear's "The Dong with a Luminous Nose." In "The Queen of Spades" horror suddenly erupts in the most decorous of contexts while "The Dong with a Luminous Nose" both satirizes and yet more piercingly laments the dreadful sadness of what it means to suffer an unrequited love.

One young man, in the middle of the journey, surprised me over the phone by telling me how immensely moved and chagrined he was by reading the little poem "Sorrow" by the Victorian minor poet Aubrey de Vere that I have reprinted in this volume. Our era of melancholia or depression has brought forth little as germane as this:

> When I was young, I said to Sorrow,
> "Come I will play with thee"—
> He is near me now all day;
> And at night returns to say,
> "I will come again to-morrow,
> I will come and stay with thee."
>
> Through the woods we walk together;
> His soft footsteps rustle nigh me.
> To shield an unregarded head,
> He hath built a wintry shed;
> And all night in rainy weather,
> I hear his gentle breathings by me.

The speaker begins by confessing that *he* chose sorrow as his playmate, and never has been able to evade that choice. One need not house Sorrow; he will build for himself, and he will be faithful, all too faithful. The self-indulgence of an early melancholy develops into a haunting hardly mitigated by the "gentle" nature of this particular depression.

When I am tired, my way of reading returns, across three score years and some, to the pleasure of reading like a child again. When I was a child, each time I fell in love with a poem, I read it again and again until I had it by heart. Then I would go off by myself, whether indoor or outdoor, in order to have the pleasure of chanting it endlessly to myself. I have seen children do that still. I have just spent several days rereading everything in this book, from John Keats's celebratory sonnet "The Human Seasons" to Christina Rossetti's spiritual triumph in the lyric "Up-Hill." Some of the fresh delights of poetry were William Morris's "The Message of the March Wind" and Elizabeth Barrett Browning's "A Musical Instrument," Kipling's "The Way Through the Woods," and Algernon Charles Swinburne's ecstatic "August." Among the stories, I was newly startled by G. K.

Chesterton and Robert Louis Stevenson, by H. G. Wells and Ivan Turgenev. Such reactions rise out of momentary needs and feelings; at other times, there is nothing in this volume that has not moved me out of apathy or weariness into wonder and joy.

My lifelong passion for reading or chanting poetry aloud often leads me back to E. A. Robinson's "Luke Havergal" and "Roaring Mad Tom," the magnificent, anonymous Tom O'Bedlam song that I wish we could attribute to Shakespeare. (The date is possible, and who else could write so miraculous a poem?) Many of the prose sketches and stories in this book are appropriate for recitation, to yourself or others, as are nearly all of the poems. Though I urge possession-by-memory of poems, through repeated readings, I suspect that reading aloud is also a valid test for poetry and fictional prose alike. Reciting a bad poem is a distressing experience, reading aloud a poor story is scarcely better. But it can be astonishing how an excellent story or poem suddenly expands into a cosmos of absolute illumination when one listens to its recitation. I remember then that the Homeric epics were chanted aloud to audiences, and that Geoffrey Chaucer wrote in order to read his work at the royal court and in the houses of the great nobles. I would regard the fortunes of this book with most satisfaction if it could help lead to a revival of people reading aloud to one another whether singly or in groups.

Reading well makes children more interesting both to themselves and others, a process in which they will develop a sense of being separate and distinct selves. To be alone with a true book is to be able to see more about who you are. To reread Carroll's *Alice* books is to be reminded of how strong Alice herself is, and can be a path to sharing her independence:

> "Hold your tongue!" said the Queen, turning purple.
> "I won't!" said Alice.
> "Off with her head!" the Queen shouted at the top of her voice.
> Nobody moved.
> "Who cares for *you*?" said Alice (she had grown to her full size by this time).
> "You're nothing but a pack of cards!"

The seven-year-old Alice is supremely courageous, and like Hamlet is only mad north-northwest. Hamlet, perhaps the most fascinating person in all literature, is a dangerous role model, but Alice is both outrageous and prudential, and well worth imitating. More than once in her or his life every reader will grow to full size by crying out, to the right auditors: "Who cares for *you*? You're nothing but a pack of cards!"

My older sisters, when I was very young, took me to the library, and thus transformed my life. After awhile, I found my own way there, and became twice-born, transported by poetry and by prose fiction. If readers are to come to Shakespeare and to Chekhov, to Henry James and to Jane Austen, then they are best prepared if they have read Lewis Carroll and Edward Lear, Robert Louis Stevenson and Rudyard Kipling.

Where shall we find ourselves more truly and more strange? Ideally, in family and in friends, or at last, if possible, in life partnerships. Yet there are so many shadows, so many difficulties, in all human love that something deep within us may go on feeling lonely. As intelligence and awareness increase in us, we can believe that what is best and oldest in us cannot be known by others. I was a very lonely child, despite a loving family circle, and remain solitary after a lifetime of teaching, rereading, and writing. But how much more isolated I would be if poems and stories had not nurtured me, and if they did not go on fostering me. The child alone with her or his book is, for me, the true image of potential happiness, of something evermore about to be. A child, lonely and gifted, will employ a marvelous story or poem to create a companion for himself or myself. Such an invisible friend is not an unhealthy phantasmagoria, but the mind learning to exercise itself in all its powers. Perhaps it is also the mysterious moment in which a new poet or storyteller comes to birth.

# BOOK I

# Spring

# THE HUMAN SEASONS

## John Keats

Four seasons fill the measure of the year;
    Four seasons are there in the mind of man.
He hath his lusty spring when fancy clear
    Takes in all beauty with an easy span:
He hath his summer, when luxuriously
    He chews the honied cud of fair spring thoughts,
Till, in his soul dissolv'd they come to be
    Part of himself. He hath his autumn ports
And havens of repose, when his tired wings
    Are folded up, and he content to look
On mists in idleness: to let fair things
    Pass by unheeded as a threshold brook.
        He hath his winter too of pale misfeature,
        Or else would forget his mortal nature.

# THE SONG OF THE FOUR WINDS

## Thomas Love Peacock

Wind from the north: the young spring day
Is pleasant on the sunny mead;
The merry harps at evening play:
The dance gay youths and maidens lead:
The thrush makes chorus from the thorn:
The mighty drinker fills his horn.

Wind from the east: the shore is still;
The Mountain-clouds fly tow'rds the sea;

The ice is on the winter-rill;
The great hall fire is blazing free:
The prince's circling feast is spread:
Drink fills with fumes the brainless head.
Wind from the south: in summer shade

'Tis sweet to hear the loud harp ring;
Sweet is the step of comely maid,
Who to the bard a cup doth bring:
The black crow flies where carrion lies:
Where pig-nuts lurk, the swine will work.

Wind from the west: the autumnal deep
Rolls on the shore its billowy pride:
He, who the rampart's watch must keep,
Will mark with awe the rising tide:
The high spring-tide, that bursts its mound,
May roll o'er miles of level ground.

Wind from the west: the mighty wave
Of ocean bounds o'er rock and sand;
The foaming surges roar and rave
Against the bulwarks of the land:
When waves are rough, and winds are high,
Good is the land that's high and dry.

Wind from the west: the storm-clouds rise;
The breakers rave; the whirl-blasts roar,
The mingled rage of seas and skies
Bursts on the low and lonely shore:
When safety's far, and danger nigh,
Swift feet the readiest aid supply.

## THE WIND AND THE RAIN

### *William Shakespeare*

When that I was and a little tiny boy,
    With hey, ho, the wind and the rain:
A foolish thing was but a toy,
    For the rain it raineth every day.

But when I came to man's estate,
    With hey, ho, the wind and the rain:
'Gainst Knaves and Thieves men shut their gate,
    For the rain it raineth every day.

But when I came, alas, to wive,
    With hey, ho, the wind and the rain:
By swaggering could I never thrive,
    For the rain it raineth every day.

But when I came unto my beds,
    With hey, ho, the wind and the rain,
With toss-pots still had drunken heads,—
    For the rain it raineth every day.

A great while ago the world begun,
    With hey, ho, the wind and the rain,
But that's all one, our Play is done,
    And we'll strive to please you every day.

## THE ASS EATING THISTLES

*Aesop*

An Ass was loaded with good provisions of several sorts, which, in time of harvest, he was carrying into the field, for his master and the reapers to dine upon. By the way, he met with a fine large thistle, and being very hungry, began to mumble it; which, while he was doing, he entered into this reflection: How many greedy epicures would think themselves happy, amidst such a variety of delicate viands as I now carry! but to me, this bitter, prickly thistle is more savoury and relishing than the most exquisite and sumptuous banquet.

*Translated by Samuel Croxall*

❧

## A CRAZY TALE

*Gilbert Keith Chesterton*

*"Hey, diddle, diddle,*
*The cat and the fiddle,*
*The cow jumped over the moon."*

It is incredible, but true, that a young man sat opposite me in a restaurant and spoke as is hereafter set down.

He was a tall, spare man, carefully dressed in a formal frock-coat and silk hat. His tone was low and casual, his manner simple and very slow, and his bleak blue eyes never changed. Anyone just out of earshot of the words would have supposed that he was describing, in a rather leisurely way, an opera or a cycling tour. I alone heard the words; and ever since that day I have gone about ready for the Apocalypse, expecting the news of some incalculable revolution in human affairs. For I know that we have reached a new era in the history of our planet: the creation of a second Adam.

He spoke as follows, between the puffs of a cigar:

"I do not ask anyone to believe this story. Only in some wild hour of a windy night, when we could believe anything, when the craziest of a knot of old wives is wiser than all the schools of reason, when the blood is lawless and the brain dethroned, when we could see the windmills grind the wind, and the sea drag the moon, the apple-tree grow lemons, and the cow lay eggs, as a wild half-holiday of nature; then, in the ear and coarsely, let this tale be told.

"When my story begins, I was walking in a still green place. The words sound strange and abrupt even in my own ears; but there is a reason for their abruptness.

"At that point the record of my life breaks off. The day, hour, or second before some stunning blow, some tremendous event befell me, and I awoke without a memory.

"Of the lost knowledge thus sealed within me I have a kind of half-witted fear. I move trembling in the close proximity of something huge, yet hidden in the darkness of my brain. Only of two things I am convinced. The first is, that this event, which I cannot recall, was the greatest of my life, that all my after adventures, wild as they were, were dwarfed in its unapproachable presence. The second comes of a certain hour, when sud-denly, and for a second, the veil was lifted and I knew all. It had gone in a flash, but I am profoundly convinced that if I tell to another all the cir-cumstances that led up to that instantaneous revelation, to him also, as he studies them, the words will suddenly give up their meaning, and their simplicity strike him with an awful laughter.

"This, then, is the story.

"The greenness, that I walked like one in a dream, stretched away on all sides to the edges of the sky. Sleepily, I let my eyes fall and woke, with a stunning thrill, to clearness. I stood shrunken with the shock, clutching myself in the smallest compass.

"Every inch of the green place was a living thing, a spire or tongue, rooted in the ground for those fantastic armies. The silence deafened me with a sense of busy eating, working, and breeding. I thought of that mul-titudinous life, and my brain reeled.

"Treading fearfully amid the growing fingers of the earth, I raised my eyes, and at the next moment shut them, as at a blow. High in the empty air blazed and streamed a great fire, which burnt and blinded me every time I raised my eyes to it. I have lived many years under this meteor of a fixed Apocalypse, but I have never survived the feelings of that moment. Men eat and drink, buy and sell, marry, are given in marriage, and all the time there is something in the sky at which they cannot look. They must be very brave.

"Again, a little while after, as in one of the changes in a dream, I found myself looking at something standing in the fields, something which looked at first like a man, and then like two men, and then like two men joined, till, after dizzy turning and tramping round it like the searching of a maze, I found it was some great abortion of nature with two legs at each end, calmly cropping the grass under the staring sun. I have said that I ask no one to believe this story.

"So I travelled along a road of portents, like undeciphered parables. There was no twilight as in a dream; everything was clear cut in the sunlight, standing out in defiant plainness and infantile absurdity. All was in simple colours, like the landscape of a child's alphabet, but to a child who had not learnt the meaning.

"At one time I seemed to come to the end of the earth; to a place where it fell into space. A little beyond, the land re-commenced, but between the two I looked down into the sky. As I bent over I saw another bending over under me, hanging head downwards in those fallen heavens, a little child with round eyes. It was some strange mercy of God assuredly that the child did not fall far into hopeless eternity."

The young man paused reflectively. I tried to say "a pool," but the words would not come. I seemed to have forgotten it. I seemed to have forgotten everything except his terrible blue eyes, big with unsupportable significance. Then I realised that he was speaking again. "I heard a great noise out of the sky, and I turned and saw a giant. Stories and legends there are of those who, in the morning of the world, strayed also into the borders of the land of giants. But it is impossible for any tongue to utter the overpowering sense of anarchy and portent felt in seeing so much of the landscape moving upon two legs, of looking up and seeing a face like my own, colossal, filling the heavens.

"He lifted me like a flying bird through space and set me upon his shoulder. I shall never forget the sight of his huge bare features growing larger as I came nearer to them; the sun shining on them as they smiled and smiled; a sight to give one dreams."

The young man paused again. I seemed to feel the whole sane universe of custom and experience slipping from me, and with an effort like a drowning man's I cried out desperately. "But it was a man—it was your father."

He raised his eyebrows, as at a coincidence. "So they said," he observed. "Do you know what it means?"

I found myself broken and breathless, as Job might have been, battered with the earthquake question of Omniscience.

He went on, smoking slowly.

"With the giant was a woman. When I saw her something stirred within me like the memory of a previous existence. And after I had lived some little while with them, I began to have an idea of what the truth must be. Instead of killing me, the giant and giantess fed and tended me like servants. I began to understand that in that lost epic of adventures which led up to the greatest event of my life, I must have done some great service for these good people. What it was, I had, by a quaint irony, myself forgotten. But I loved to see it shining with inscrutable affection in the woman's eyes like the secret of the stars. There are few things more beautiful than gratitude.

"One day, as I stood beside her knee, she spoke to me; but I was speechless. A new and dreadful fancy had me by the throat. The woman was smaller than before. The house was smaller: the ceiling was nearer. Heaven and earth, even to the remotest star, were closing in to crush me.

"The next moment I had realised the truth, fled from the house, and plunged into the thickets like a thing possessed. A disease of transformation too monstrous for nightmare had quickened within me. I was growing larger and larger whether I would or no.

"I rolled in the gravel, revolving wild guesses as to whether I should grow to fill the sky, a giant with my head in heaven, bewildered among the golden plumage of Cherubim. This, as a matter of fact, I never did.

"It will always fill me with awe to think that no sign or premonition gave me warning of what I saw next. I merely raised my eyes—and saw it.

"Within a few feet of me was kneeling one of my own size, a little girl with big blue eyes and hair black as crows.

"The landscape behind her was the same in every hedge and tree that I had left; yet I felt sure I had come into a new world.

"I had got to my feet and made her a kind of bow, looking a fantastic figure enough; but a red star came into her cheek.

" 'Why, you are quite nice,' she said.

"I looked at her enquiringly.

" 'They say you are the mad boy,' she said, 'who stares at everything. But I think I like them mad.'

"I said nothing. I only stood up straight, and thanked God for every turn of my rambling path through that elvish topsey-turveydom, which had led at length to this. Although I had not asked for a miracle in answer, two or three drops of clear water fell out of the open sky.

" 'There will be a storm,' cried the girl hastily.

"She seemed quite frightened of the dark that had come over the wood, and the shocks of sound that shook the sky now and again. This fear surprised me, for she had not seemed afraid of the grass.

"She seemed so broken with the noise and dark and driving rain that I put my arm round her. As I did so, something new came over me: a feeling less alien, and disturbed, more responsible and strangely strong; as if I had inherited a trust and privilege. For the first time I felt a kinship with the monstrous landscape; I knew that I had been sent to the right place.

" 'You are very brave,' she said, as the deafening skies seemed bowed about us and shouting in our ears; 'Do you not hear it?'

" 'I hear the daisies growing,' I said.

"Her answer was lost in the thunder.

"We were miles further on before she said, 'But are you not mad?'

"I spoke; but it seemed as if another spoke in my ear.

" 'I am the first that ever saw in the world. Prophets and sages there have been, out of whose great hearts came schools and churches. But I am the first that ever saw a dandelion as it is.'

"Wind and dark rain swept round, swathing in a cloud the place of that awful proclamation."

The young man paused once more. Some one near me moved his chair against mine. I remember with what a start I realised that I was in a crowded room; not in a desert with an insane hermit.

"But you have not told me," I said, "of the great moment: when you seemed to have discovered all."

"It is soon told," he said. "Ten years afterwards the girl and I stood in one room together: we were man and wife. Other men and women went in and out, all of my own stature. There were no more giants; it was as though I had dreamed of them. I seemed to have come back among my own people.

"Just then my wife, who was bending over a kind of couch, lifted a coverlet, and I saw that for which, haply, I have been sent to this fantastic borderland of things.

"It was a little human creature hardly bigger than a bird. And when I saw it, I—knew everything. I knew what was the greatest event of my life: the event I had forgotten."

I said "Being born" in a low voice.

I did not dare to look at his face.

The next consciousness I had was that he had risen to his feet, and was putting on his gloves very carefully.

I sprang erect also and spoke quickly.

"What does it mean? Are you a man? What thing are you? Are you a savage, or a spirit, or a child? You wear the dress and speak the language of a cultivated pupil of this over-cultivated time: yet you see everything as if you saw it for the first time. What does it mean?"

After a silence he spoke in his quiet way.

"Have you ever said some simple word over and over till it became unmeaning, a scrap of an unknown tongue, till you seem to be opening and shutting your mouth with a cry like an animal's? So it is with the great world in which we live: it begins familiar: it ends unfamiliar. When first men began to think and talk and theorise and work the world over and over with phrases and associations, then it was involved and fated, as a psychological necessity, that some day a creature should be produced, corresponding to the twentieth pronunciation of the word, a new animal with eyes to see and ears to hear; with an intellect capable of performing a new function never before conceived truly; thanking God for his creation. I tell you religion is in its infancy; dervish and anchorite, Crusader and Ironside, were not fanatical enough, or frantic enough, in their adoration. A new type has arrived. You have seen it."

He moved towards the door. Then I noticed he had come to a standstill again, and was gazing at the floor apparently in deep thought.

"I have never understood them," he said. "Those two creatures I see everywhere, stumping along the ground, first one and then the other. I have never been content with the current explanation that they were my feet."

And he passed out, still carefully buttoning his gloves.

I went back to the table and sat down. About four minutes after he was gone I felt a kind of mental shock, like something resuming its place in my brain.

It occurred to me that the man was mad. I am almost ashamed to admit with what suddenness it came. For so long as I was in his presence, I had believed him and his whole attitude to be sane, normal, complete, and that it was the rest, the whole human race, that were half-witted, since the making of the world.

∾

# HOW THE RHINOCEROS GOT HIS SKIN

## *Rudyard Kipling*

Once upon a time, on an uninhabited island on the shores of the Red Sea, there lived a Parsee from whose hat the rays of the sun were reflected in more-than-oriental splendour. And the Parsee lived by the Red Sea with nothing but his hat and his knife and a cooking-stove of the kind that you must particularly never touch. And one day he took flour and water and currants and plums and sugar and things, and made himself one cake which was two feet across and three feet thick. It was indeed a Superior Comestible (*that's* magic), and he put it on the stove because *he* was allowed to cook on that stove, and he baked it and he baked it till it was all done brown and smelt most sentimental. But just as he was going to eat it there came down to the beach from the Altogether Uninhabited Interior one Rhinoceros with a horn on his nose, two piggy eyes, and few manners. In those days the Rhinoceros's skin fitted him quite tight. There were no wrinkles in it anywhere. He looked exactly like a Noah's Ark Rhinoceros, but of course much bigger. All the same, he had no manners then, and he has no manners now, and he never will have any manners. He said, "How!" and the Parsee left that cake and climbed to the top of a palm tree with nothing on but his hat, from which the rays of the sun were always reflected in more-than-oriental splendour. And the Rhinoceros upset the oil-stove with his nose, and the cake rolled on the sand, and he spiked that cake on the horn of his nose, and he ate it, and he went away, waving his tail, to the desolate and Exclusively Uninhabited Interior which abuts on the islands of Mazanderan, Socotra, and the Promontories of the Larger Equinox. Then the Parsee came down from his palm-tree and put the stove on its legs and recited the following *Sloka,* which, as you have not heard, I will now proceed to relate:—

> Them that takes cakes
> Which the Parsee-man bakes
> Makes dreadful mistakes.

And there was a great deal more in that than you would think.

*Because,* five weeks later, there was a heat-wave in the Red Sea, and everybody took off all the clothes they had. The Parsee took off his hat; but the Rhinoceros took off his skin and carried it over his shoulder as he came down to the beach to bathe. In those days it buttoned underneath with three buttons and looked like a waterproof. He said nothing whatever about the Parsee's cake, because he had eaten it all; and he never had any manners, then, since, or henceforward. He waddled straight into the water and blew bubbles through his nose, leaving his skin on the beach.

Presently the Parsee came by and found the skin, and he smiled one smile that ran all round his face two times. Then he danced three times round the skin and rubbed his hands. Then he went to his camp and filled his hat with cake-crumbs, for the Parsee never ate anything but cake, and never swept out his camp. He took that skin, and he shook that skin, and he scrubbed that skin, and he rubbed that skin just as full of old, dry, stale, tickly cake-crumbs and some burned currants as ever it could *possibly* hold. Then he climbed to the top of his palm-tree and waited for the Rhinoceros to come out of the water and put it on.

And the Rhinoceros did. He buttoned it up with the three buttons, and it tickled like cake-crumbs in bed. Then he wanted to scratch, but that made it worse; and then he lay down on the sands and rolled and rolled and rolled, and every time he rolled the cake crumbs tickled him worse and worse and worse. Then he ran to the palm-tree and rubbed and rubbed and rubbed himself against it. He rubbed so much and so hard that he rubbed his skin into a great fold over his shoulders, and another fold underneath, where the buttons used to be (but he rubbed the buttons off), and he rubbed some more folds over his legs. And it spoiled his temper, but it didn't make the least difference to the cake-crumbs. They were inside his skin and they tickled. So he went home, very angry indeed and horribly scratchy; and from that day to this every rhinoceros has great folds in his skin and a very bad temper, all on account of the cake-crumbs inside.

But the Parsee came down from his palm-tree, wearing his hat, from which the rays of the sun were reflected in more-than-oriental splendour, packed up his cooking-stove, and went away in the direction of Orotavo, Amygdala, the Upland Meadows of Anantarivo, and the Marshes of Sonaput.

# THE MESSAGE OF THE MARCH WIND

### *William Morris*

Fair now is the springtide, now earth lies beholding
With the eyes of a lover, the face of the sun;
Long lasteth the daylight, and hope is enfolding
The green-growing acres with increase begun.

Now sweet, sweet it is through the land to be straying
'Mid the birds and the blossoms and the beasts of the field;
Love mingles with love, and no evil is weighing
On thy heart or mine, where all sorrow is healed.

From township to township, o'er down and by tillage
Fair, far have we wandered and long was the day;
But now cometh eve at the end of the village,
Where over the grey wall the church riseth grey.

There is wind in the twilight; in the white road before us
The straw from the ox-yard is blowing about;
The moon's rim is rising, a star glitters o'er us,
And the vane on the spire-top is swinging in doubt.

Down there dips the highway, toward the bridge crossing over
The brook that runs on to the Thames and the sea.
Draw closer, my sweet, we are lover and lover;
This eve art thou given to gladness and me.

Shall we be glad always? Come closer and hearken:
Three fields further on, as they told me down there,
When the young moon has set, if the March sky should darken,
We might see from the hill-top the great city's glare.

Hark, the wind is in the elm-boughs! From London it bloweth,
And telleth of gold, and of hope and unrest;
Of power that helps not; of wisdom that knoweth,
But teacheth not aught of the worst and the best.

Of the rich men it telleth, and strange is the story
How they have, and they hanker, and grip far and wide;
And they live and they die; and the earth and its glory
Have been but a burden they scarce might abide.

Hark! the March wind again of a people is telling;
Of the life that they live there, so haggard and grim,
That if we and our love amidst them had been dwelling
My fondness had faltered, thy beauty grown dim.

This land we have loved in our love and our leisure
For them hangs in heaven, high out of their reach;
The wide hills o'er the sea plain for them have no pleasure,
The grey homes of their fathers no story to teach.

The singers have sung and the builders have builded,
The painters have fashioned their tales of delight;
For what and for whom hath the world's book been gilded,
When all is for these but the blackness of night?

How long, and for what is their patience abiding?
How oft and how oft shall their story be told,
While the hope that none seeketh in darkness is hiding
And in grief and in sorrow the world groweth old?

Come back to the inn, love, and the lights and the fire,
And the fiddler's old tune and the shuffling of feet;
For there in a while shall be rest and desire,
And there shall the morrow's uprising be sweet.

Yet, love, as we wend, the wind bloweth behind us,
And beareth the last tale it telleth to-night,
How here in the springtide the message shall find us;
For the hope that none seeketh is coming to light.

So the hope of the people now buddeth and groweth,
Rest fadeth before it, and blindness and fear;
It biddeth us learn all the wisdom it knoweth;
It hath found us and held us, and biddeth us hear:

For it beareth the message: "Rise up on the morrow
And go on your ways toward the doubt and the strife;
Join hope to our hope and blend sorrow with sorrow,
And seek for men's love in the short days of life."

But lo, the old inn, and the lights, and the fire,
And the fiddler's old tune and the shuffling of feet;
Soon for us shall be quiet and rest and desire,
And to-morrow's uprising to deeds shall be sweet.

# A MUSICAL INSTRUMENT

*Elizabeth Barrett Browning*

What was he doing, the great god Pan,
    Down in the reeds by the river?
Spreading ruin and scattering ban,
Splashing and paddling with hoofs of a goat,
And breaking the golden lilies afloat
    With the dragon-fly on the river.

He tore out a reed, the great god Pan,
    From the deep cool bed of the river;
The limpid water turbidly ran,
And the broken lilies a-dying lay,
And the dragon-fly had fled away,
    Ere he brought it out of the river.

High on the shore sat the great god Pan,
    While turbidly flow'd the river;
And hack'd and hew'd as a great god can
With his hard bleak steel at the patient reed,
Till there was not a sign of the leaf indeed
    To prove it fresh from the river.

He cut it short, did the great god Pan
    (How tall it stood in the river!),
Then drew the pith, like the heart of a man,
Steadily from the outside ring,
And notch'd the poor dry empty thing
    In holes, as he sat by the river.

"This is the way," laugh'd the great god Pan
    (Laugh'd while he sat by the river),
"The only way, since gods began
To make sweet music, they could succeed."
Then dropping his mouth to a hole in the reed,
    He blew in power by the river.

Sweet, sweet, sweet, O Pan!
    Piercing sweet by the river!
Blinding sweet, O great god Pan!
The sun on the hill forgot to die,
And the lilies revived, and the dragon-fly
    Came back to dream on the river.

Yet half a beast is the great god Pan,
    To laugh as he sits by the river,
Making a poet out of a man:
The true gods sigh for the cost and pain—
For the reed which grows nevermore again
    As a reed with the reeds of the river.

                ॐ

## LITTLE BIRDS OF THE NIGHT

### Stephen Crane

Little birds of the night
Aye, they have much to tell
Perching there in rows

Blinking at me with their serious eyes
Recounting of flowers they have seen and loved
Of meadows and groves of the distance
And pale sands at the foot of the sea
And breezes that fly in the leaves.
They are vast in experience
These little birds that come in the night.

∾

# THERE WAS A CHILD WENT FORTH

## *Walt Whitman*

There was a child went forth every day,
And the first object he look'd upon, that object he
     became,
And that object became part of him for the day or a
     certain part of the day,
Or for many years or stretching cycles of years.

The early lilacs became part of this child,
And grass and white and red morning-glories, and
     white and red clover, and the song of the
     phœbe-bird,
And the Third-month lambs and the sow's pink-faint
     litter, and the mare's foal and the cow's calf,
And the noisy brood of the barnyard or by the mire of
     the pondside,
And the fish suspending themselves so curiously below
     there, and the beautiful curious liquid,
And the water-plants with their graceful flat heads, all
     became part of him.

The field-sprouts of Fourth-month and Fifth-month
     became part of him,
Winter-grain sprouts and those of the light-yellow
     corn, and the esculent roots of the garden,

And the apple-trees cover'd with blossoms and the
  fruit afterward, and wood-berries, and the
  commonest weeds by the road,
And the old drunkard staggering home from the
  outhouse of the tavern whence he had lately risen,
And the schoolmistress that pass'd on her way to the
  school,
And the friendly boys that pass'd, and the quarrelsome
  boys,
And the tidy and fresh-cheek'd girls, and the barefoot
  negro boy and girl,
And all the changes of city and country wherever he
  went.

His own parents, he that had father'd him and she that
  had conceiv'd him in her womb and birth'd him,
They gave this child more of themselves than that,
They gave him afterward every day, they became part
  of him.

The mother at home quietly placing the dishes on the
  supper-table,
The mother with mild words, clean her cap and gown,
  a wholesome odor falling off her person and
  clothes as she walks by,
The father, strong, self-sufficient, manly, mean,
  anger'd, unjust,
The blow, the quick loud word, the tight bargain, the
  crafty lure,
The family usages, the language, the company, the
  furniture, the yearning and swelling heart,
Affection that will not be gainsay'd, the sense of what
  is real, the thought if after all it should prove
  unreal,
The doubts of day-time and the doubts of night-time,
  the curious whether and how,
Whether that which appears so is so, or is it all flashes
  and specks?
Men and women crowding fast in the streets, if they
  are not flashes and specks what are they?

The streets themselves and the façades of houses, and
    goods in the windows,
Vehicles, teams, the heavy-plank'd wharves, the huge
    crossing at the ferries,
The village on the highland seen from afar at sunset,
    the river between,
Shadows, aureola and mist, the light falling on roofs
    and gables of white or brown two miles off,
The schooner near by sleepily dropping down the tide,
    the little boat slack-tow'd astern,
The hurrying tumbling waves, quick-broken crests,
    slapping,
The strata of color'd clouds, the long bar of maroon-
    tint away solitary by itself, the spread of purity it
    lies motionless in,
The horizon's edge, the flying sea-crow, the fragrance
    of salt marsh and shore mud,
These became part of that child who went forth every
    day, and who now goes, and will always go forth
    every day.

❧

# REFLECTIONS

## Lafcadio Hearn

Long enough ago there dwelt within a day's journey of the city of Kioto a gentleman of simple mind and manners, but good estate. His wife, rest her soul, had been dead these many years, and the good man lived in great peace and quiet with his only son. They kept clear of women-kind, and knew nothing at all either of their winning or their bothering ways. They had good steady men-servants in their house, and never set eyes on a pair of long sleeves or a scarlet *obi* from morning till night.

The truth is that they were as happy as the day is long. Sometimes they labored in the rice-fields. Other days they went a-fishing. In the spring, forth they went to admire the cherry flower or the plum, and later they set out to view the iris or the peony or the lotus, as the case might be. At these times they would drink a little *saké,* and twist their blue and white *tenegui* about their heads and be as jolly as you please, for there was no one to say them nay. Often enough they came home by lantern light. They wore their oldest clothes, and were mighty irregular at their meals.

But the pleasures of life are fleeting—more's the pity!—and presently the father felt old age creeping upon him.

One night, as he sat smoking and warming his hands over the charcoal, "Boy," says he, "it's high time you got married."

"Now the gods forbid!" cries the young man. "Father, what makes you say such terrible things? Or are you joking? You must be joking," he says.

"I'm not joking at all," says the father. "I never spoke a truer word, and that you'll know soon enough."

"But, father, I am mortally afraid of women."

"And am I not the same?" says the father. "I'm sorry for you, my boy."

"Then what for must I marry?" says the son.

"In the way of nature I shall die before long, and you'll need a wife to take care of you."

Now the tears stood in the young man's eyes when he heard this, for he was tender-hearted; but all he said was, "I can take care of myself very well."

"That's the very thing you cannot," says his father.

The long and short of it was that they found the young man a wife. She was young, and as pretty as a picture. Her name was Tassel, just that, or Fusa, as they say in her language.

After they had drunk down the "Three Times Three" together and so became man and wife, they stood alone, the young man looking hard at the girl. For the life of him he did not know what to say to her. He took a bit of her sleeve and stroked it with his hand. Still he said nothing and looked mighty foolish. The girl turned red, turned pale, turned red again, and burst into tears.

"Honorable Tassel, don't do that, for the dear gods' sake," says the young man.

"I suppose you don't like me," sobs the girl. "I suppose you don't think I'm pretty."

"My dear," he says, "you're prettier than the bean-flower in the field; you're prettier than the little bantam hen in the farm-yard; you're prettier than the rose carp in the pond. I hope you'll be happy with my father and me."

At this she laughed a little and dried her eyes. "Get on another pair of *hakama,*" she says, "and give me those you've got on you; there's a great hole in them—I was noticing it all the time of the wedding!"

Well, this was not a bad beginning, and taking one thing with another they got on pretty well, though of course things were not as they had been in that blessed time when the young man and his father did not set eyes upon a pair of long sleeves or an *obi* from morning till night.

By and by, in the way of nature, the old man died. It is said he made a very good end, and left that in his strong-box which made his son the richest man in the country-side. But this was no comfort at all to the poor young man, who mourned his father with all his heart. Day and night he paid reverence to the tomb. Little sleep or rest he got, and little heed he gave to his wife, Mistress Tassel, and her whimsies, or even to the delicate dishes she set before him. He grew thin and pale, and she, poor maid, was at her wits' end to know what to do with him. At last she said, "My dear, and how would it be if you were to go to Kioto for a little?"

"And what for should I do that?" he says.

It was on the tip of her tongue to answer, "To enjoy yourself," but she saw it would never do to say that.

"Oh," she says, "as a kind of a duty. They say every man that loves his country should see Kioto; and besides, you might give an eye to the fashions, so as to tell me what like they are when you get home. My things," she says, "are sadly behind the times! I'd like well enough to know what people are wearing!"

"I've no heart to go to Kioto," says the young man, "and if I had, it's the planting-out time of the rice, and the thing's not to be done, so there's an end of it."

All the same, after two days he bids his wife get out his best *hakama* and *haouri,* and to make up his *bento* for a journey. "I'm thinking of going to Kioto," he tells her.

"Well, I am surprised," says Mistress Tassel. "And what put such an idea into your head, if I may ask?"

"I've been thinking it's a kind of duty," says the young man.

"Oh, indeed," says Mistress Tassel to this, and nothing more, for she had some grains of sense. And the next morning as ever was she packs her husband off bright and early for Kioto, and betakes herself to some little matter of house cleaning she has on hand.

The young man stepped out along the road, feeling a little better in his spirits, and before long he reached Kioto. It is likely he saw many things to wonder at. Amongst temples and palaces he went. He saw castles and gardens, and marched up and down fine streets of shops, gazing about him with his eyes wide open, and his mouth too, very like, for he was a simple soul.

At length, one fine day he came upon a shop full of metal mirrors that glittered in the sunshine.

"Oh, the pretty silver moons!" says the simple soul to himself. And he dared to come near and take up a mirror in his hand.

The next minute he turned as white as rice and sat him down on the seat in the shop door, still holding the mirror in his hand and looking into it.

"Why, father," he said, "how did you come here? You are not dead, then? Now the dear gods be praised for that! Yet I could have sworn—But no matter, since you are here alive and well. You are something pale still, but how young you look. You move your lips, father, and seem to speak, but I do not hear you. You'll come home with me, dear, and live with us just as you used to do? You smile, you smile, that is well."

"Fine mirrors, my young gentleman," said the shopman, "the best that can be made, and that's one of the best of the lot you have there. I see you are a judge."

The young man clutched his mirror tight and sat staring stupidly enough no doubt. He trembled. "How much?" he whispered. "Is it for sale?" He was in a taking lest his father should be snatched from him.

"For sale it is, indeed, most noble sir," said the shopman, "and the price is a trifle, only two *bu*. It's almost giving it away I am, as you'll understand."

"Two *bu*— only two *bu*! Now the gods be praised for this their mercy!" cried the happy young man. He smiled from ear to ear, and he had the purse out of his girdle, and the money out of his purse, in a twinkling.

Now it was the shopman who wished he had asked three *bu* or even five. All the same he put a good face upon it, and packed the mirror in a fine white box and tied it up with green cords.

"Father," said the young man, when he had got away with it, "before we set out for home we must buy some gauds for the young woman there, my wife, you know."

Now, for the life of him, he could not have told why, but when he came to his home the young man never said a word to Mistress Tassel about buying his old father for two *bu* in the Kioto shop. That was where he made his mistake, as things turned out.

She was as pleased as you like with her coral hair-pins, and her fine new *obi* from Kioto. "And I'm glad to see him so well and so happy," she said to herself. "But I must say he's been mighty quick to get over his sorrow after all. But men are just like children." As for her husband, unbeknown to her he took a bit of green silk from her treasure-box and spread it in the cupboard of the *toko no ma*. There he placed the mirror in its box of white wood.

Every morning early and every evening late, he went to the cupboard of the *toko no ma* and spoke with his father. Many a jolly talk they had and many a hearty laugh together, and the son was the happiest young man of all that countryside, for he was a simple soul.

But Mistress Tassel had a quick eye and a sharp ear, and it was not long before she marked her husband's new ways.

"What for does he go so often to the *toko no ma*," she asked herself, "and what has he got there? I should be glad enough to know." Not being one to suffer much in silence, she very soon asked her husband these same things.

He told her the truth, the good young man. "And now I have my dear old father home again, I'm as happy as the day is long," he says.

"H'm," she says.

"And wasn't two *bu* cheap," he says, "and wasn't it a strange thing altogether?"

"Cheap, indeed," says she, "and passing strange; and why, if I may ask," she says, "did you say naught of all this at the first?"

The young man grew red.

"Indeed, then, I cannot tell you, my dear," he says. "I'm sorry, but I don't know," and with that he went out to his work.

Up jumped Mistress Tassel the minute his back was turned, and to the *toko no ma* she flew on the wings of the wind and flung open the doors with a clang.

"My green silk for sleeve-linings!" she cried at once. "But I don't see any old father here, only a white wooden box. What can he keep in it?"

She opened the box quickly enough.

"What an odd flat shining thing!" she said, and, taking up the mirror, looked into it.

For a moment she said nothing at all, but the great tears of anger and jealousy stood in her pretty eyes, and her face flushed from forehead to chin.

"A woman!" she cried, "a woman! So that is his secret! He keeps a woman in this cup-board. A woman, very young and very pretty—no, not pretty at all, but she thinks herself so. A dancing-girl from Kioto, I'll be bound; ill-tempered too—her face is scarlet; and oh, how she frowns, nasty little spitfire. Ah, who could have thought it of him? Ah, it's a miserable girl I am—and I've cooked his *daikon* and mended his *hakama* a hundred times. Oh! oh! oh!"

With that, she threw the mirror into its case, and slammed-to the cupboard door upon it. Herself she flung upon the mats, and cried and sobbed as if her heart would break.

In comes her husband.

"I've broken the thong of my sandal," says he, "and I've come to—But what in the world?" and in an instant he was down on his knees beside Mistress Tassel doing what he could to comfort her, and to get her face up from the floor where she kept it.

"Why, what is it, my own darling?" says he.

"*Your* own darling!" she answers very fierce through her sobs; and "I want to go home," she cries.

"But, my sweet, you are at home, and with your own husband."

"Pretty husband!" she says, "and pretty goings-on, with a woman in the cupboard! A hateful, ugly woman that thinks herself beautiful; and she has *my* green sleeve-linings there with her to boot."

"Now, what's all this about women and sleeve-linings? Sure you wouldn't grudge poor old father that little green rag for his bed? Come, my dear, I'll buy you twenty sleeve-linings."

At that she jumped to her feet and fairly danced with rage.

"Old father! old father! old father!" she screamed. "Am I a fool or a child? I saw the woman with my own eyes."

The poor young man didn't know whether he was on his head or his heels. "Is it possible that my father is gone?" he said, and he took the mirror from the *toko no ma*.

"That's well; still the same old father that I bought for two *bu*. You seem worried, father; nay, then, smile as I do. There, that's well."

Mistress Tassel came like a little fury and snatched the mirror from his hand. She gave but one look into it and hurled it to the other end of the room. It made such a clang against the woodwork, that servants and neighbors came rushing in to see what was the matter.

"It is my father," said the young man. "I bought him in Kioto for two *bu*."

"He keeps a woman in the cupboard who has stolen my green sleeve-linings," sobbed the wife.

After this there was a great to-do. Some of the neighbors took the man's part and some the woman's, with such a clatter and chatter and noise as never was; but settle the thing they could not, and none of them would look into the mirror, because they said it was bewitched.

They might have gone on the way they were till doomsday, but that one of them said, "Let us ask the Lady Abbess, for she is a wise woman." And off they all went to do what they might have done sooner.

The Lady Abbess was a pious woman, the head of a convent of holy nuns. She was the great one at prayers and meditations and at mortifyings of the flesh, and she was the clever one, none the less, at human affairs. They took her the mirror, and she held it in her hands and looked into it for a long time. At last she spoke:

"This poor woman," she said, touching the mirror, "for it's as plain as daylight that it is a woman—this poor woman was so troubled in her mind at the disturbance that she caused in a quiet house, that she has taken vows, shaved her head, and become a holy nun. Thus she is in her right place here. I will keep her, and instruct her in prayers and meditations. Go you home, my children; forgive and forget, be friends."

Then all the people said, "The Lady Abbess is the wise woman."

And she kept the mirror in her treasure.

Mistress Tassel and her husband went home hand in hand.

"So I was right, you see, after all," she said.

"Yes, yes, my dear," said the simple young man, "of course. But I am wondering how my old father is going to get on at the holy convent. He was never much of a one for religion."

∾

# THE OWL AND THE PUSSY-CAT

*Edward Lear*

## I

The Owl and the Pussy-cat went to sea
   In a beautiful pea-green boat,
They took some honey, and plenty of money,
   Wrapped up in a five-pound note.
The Owl looked up to the stars above,
   And sang to a small guitar,
"O lovely Pussy! O Pussy, my love,
   What a beautiful Pussy you are,
     You are,
     You are!
What a beautiful Pussy you are!"

## II

Pussy said to the Owl, "You elegant fowl!
   How charmingly sweet you sing!
O let us be married! too long we have tarried:
   But what shall we do for a ring?"
They sailed away, for a year and a day,
   To the land where the Bong-tree grows
And there in a wood a Piggy-wig stood
   With a ring at the end of his nose,
     His nose,
     His nose,
With a ring at the end of his nose.


## III

"Dear Pig, are you willing to sell for one shilling
   Your ring?" Said the Piggy, "I will."
So they took it away, and were married next day
   By the Turkey who lives on the hill.
They dined on mince, and slices of quince,
   Which they ate with a runcible spoon;
And hand in hand, on the edge of the sand,
   They danced by the light of the moon,
     The moon,
     The moon,
They danced by the light of the moon.

## OLD MAY SONG

*Anonymous*

All in this pleasant evening, together come are we,
  *For the summer springs so fresh, green, and gay;*
We tell you of a blossoming and buds on every tree,
  *Drawing near unto the merry month of May.*

Rise up, the master of this house, put on your charm of gold,
  *For the summer springs so fresh, green, and gay;*
Be not in pride offended with your name we make so bold,
  *Drawing near unto the merry month of May.*

Rise up, the mistress of this house, with gold along your
      breast;
  *For the summer springs so fresh, green, and gay;*
And if your body be asleep, we hope your soul's at rest,
  *Drawing near unto the merry month of May.*

Rise up, the children of this house, all in your rich attire,
  *For the summer springs so fresh, green, and gay;*
And every hair upon your heads shines like the silver wire:
  *Drawing near unto the merry month of May.*

God bless this house and arbour, your riches and your store,
  *For the summer springs so fresh, green, and gay;*
We hope the Lord will prosper you, both now and evermore,
  *Drawing near unto the merry month of May.*

And now comes we must leave you, in peace and plenty here,
  *For the summer springs so fresh, green, and gay;*
We shall not sing you May again until another year,
  *To draw you these cold winters away.*

&

## "HOME NO MORE HOME TO ME"

*Robert Louis Stevenson*

Home no more home to me, whither must I wander?
 Hunger my driver, I go where I must.
Cold blows the winter wind over hill and heather;
 Thick drives the rain, and my roof is in the dust.
Loved of wise men was the shade of my roof-tree.
 The true word of welcome was spoken in the door—
Dear days of old, with the faces in the firelight,
 Kind folks of old, you come again no more.

Home was home then, my dear, full of kindly faces,
 Home was home then, my dear, happy for the child,
Fire and the windows bright glittered on the moorland;
 Song, tuneful song, built a palace in the wild.
Now, when day dawns on the brow of the moorland,
 Lone stands the house, and the chimney-stone is cold.
Lone let it stand, now the friends are all departed,
 The kind hearts, the true hearts, that loved the place
  of old.

Spring shall come, come again, calling up the moor-fowl,
 Spring shall bring the sun and rain, bring the bees and
  flowers;
Red shall the heather bloom over hill and valley,
 Soft flow the stream through the even-flowing hours;
Fair the day shine as it shone on my childhood—
 Fair shine the day on the house with open door;
Birds come and cry there and twitter in the chimney—
 But I go for ever and come again no more.

## THE FAIRIES

*William Allingham*

Up the airy mountain,
   Down the rushy glen,
We daren't go a-hunting
   For fear of little men;
Wee folk, good folk,
   Trooping all together;
Green jacket, red cap,
   And white owl's feather!

Down along the rocky shore
   Some make their home,
They live on crispy pancakes
   Of yellow tide-foam;
Some in the reeds
   Of the black mountain-lake,
With frogs for their watch-dogs,
   All night awake.

High on the hill-top
   The old King sits;
He is now so old and gray
   He's nigh lost his wits.

With a bridge of white mist
   Columbkill he crosses,
On his stately journeys
   Fom Slieveleague to Rosses;
Or going up with music
   On cold starry nights,
To sup with the Queen
   Of the gay Northern Lights.

They stole little Bridget
   For seven years long;

When she came down again
  Her friends were all gone.
They took her lightly back,
  Between the night and morrow,

They thought that she was fast asleep,
  But she was dead with sorrow.
They have kept her ever since
  Deep within the lake,
On a bed of flag-leaves,
  Watching till she wake.

By the craggy hill-side,
  Through the mosses bare,
They have planted thorn-trees
  For pleasure here and there.
Is any man so daring
  As to dig one up in spite,
He shall find the thornies set
  In his bed at night.

Up the airy mountain,
  Down the rushy glen,
We daren't go a-hunting
  For fear of little men;
Wee folk, good folk,
  Trooping all together;
Green jacket, red cap,
  And white owl's feather!

## GREEN GRASS

*Anonymous*

*A dis, a dis, a green grass,*
  *A dis, a dis, a dis;*
Come all you pretty fair maids
  And dance along with us.

For we are going roving,
  A roving in this land;
We take this pretty fair maid,
  We take her by the hand.

She shall get a duke, my dear,
  As duck do get a drake;
And she shall have a young prince,
  For her own fair sake.

And if this young prince chance to die,
  She shall get another;
The bells will ring, and the birds will sing,
  And we clap hands together.

❧

## "BEAUTIFUL SOUP, SO RICH AND GREEN"

*Lewis Carroll*

Beautiful Soup, so rich and green,
  Waiting in a hot tureen!
Who for such dainties would not stoop?
Soup of the evening, beautiful Soup!
Soup of the evening, beautiful Soup!
  Beau-ootiful Soo-oop!

Beau-ootiful Soo-oop!
Soo-oop of the e-e-evening,
　　Beautiful, beautiful Soup!

Beautiful Soup! Who cares for fish,
Game, or any other dish?
Who would not give all else for two p
ennyworth only of beautiful Soup?
Pennyworth only of beautiful Soup?
　　Beau ootiful Soo oop!
　　Beau-ootiful Soo-oop!
Soo-oop of the e-e-evening,
　　Beautiful, beauti-FUL SOUP!

∾

## "GAY GO UP, AND GAY GO DOWN"

*Anonymous*

Gay go up, and gay go down,
To ring the bells of London town.

Bull's eyes and targets,
Say the bells of St. Marg'ret's.

Brickbats and tiles,
Say the bells of St. Giles'.

Halfpence and farthings,
Say the bells of St. Martin's.

Oranges and lemons,
Say the bells of St. Clement's.

Pancakes and fritters,
Say the bells of St. Peter's.

Two sticks and an apple,
Say the bells at Whitechapel.

Old Father Baldpate,
Say the slow bells at Aldgate.

You owe me ten shillings,
Say the bells at St. Helen's.

Pokers and tongs,
Say the bells at St. John's.

Kettles and pans,
Say the bells at St. Ann's.

When will you pay me?
Say the bells at Old Bailey.

When I grow rich,
Say the bells at Shoreditch.

Pray when will that be?
Say the bells at Stepney.

I am sure I don't know,
Says the great bell at Bow.

Here comes a candle to light you to bed,
And here comes a chopper to chop off
      your head.

## "HERE WE COME A PIPING"

*Anonymous*

Here we come a piping
First in spring, and then in May;
The queen she sits upon the sand,
Fair as a lily, white as a wand:
King John has sent you letters three,
And begs you'll read them unto me.—
We can't read one without them all,
So pray, Miss Bridget, deliver the ball!

## "HEY NONNY NO!"

*Anonymous*

Hey nonny no!
Men are fools that wish to die!
Is't not fine to dance and sing
When the bells of death do ring?
Is't not fine to swim in wine,
And turn upon the toe
And sing hey nonny no;
When the winds do blow,
And the seas do flow?
Hey nonny no!

## "I HAD A LITTLE NUT-TREE"

*Anonymous*

I had a little nut-tree, nothing would it bear
But a silver nutmeg and a golden pear;
The King of Spain's daughter came to visit me,
And all was because of my little nut-tree.
I skipp'd over water, I danced over sea,
And all the birds in the air couldn't catch me.

∾

## THE LINCOLNSHIRE POACHER

*Anonymous*

When I was bound apprentice in famous Lincolnshire,
Full well I served my master for more than seven year,
Till I took up to poaching—as you shall quickly hear:
    Oh, 'tis my delight on a shining night
    In the season of the year!

As mé and my cómrade were setting of a snare,
Twas then we spied the gamekeeper, for him we did not care,
For we can wrestle and fight, my boys, and jump o'er anywhere:
    Oh, 'tis my delight on a shining night
    In the season of the year!

As me and my comrade were setting four or five,
And taking on 'em up again we caught a hare alive,
We took the hare alive, my boys, and through the woods did steer:
    Oh, 'tis my delight on a shining night
    In the season of the year!

I threw him on my shoulder, and then we trudged home,
We took him to a neighbour's house and sold him for a crown
We sold him for a crown, my boys, but I did not tell you where:
      Oh, 'tis my delight on a shining night
      In the season of the year!

Success to every gentleman that lives in Lincolnshire,
Success to every poacher that wants to sell a hare,
Bad luck to every gamekeeper that will not sell his deer:
      Oh, 'tis my delight on a shining night
      In the season of the year!

# COMPLEMENTS

*Emile Zola*

## I

In Paris they have everything for sale—silly girls and wise, lies and truth, tears and smiles. You surely know that in this land of business beauty is a commodity in which they deal on a tremendous scale. They buy and sell large eyes and small mouths; noses and chins are valued down to a fine point. This dimple or that mole represents a certain price. And since imitation is always going on, they often counterfeit God's merchandise; artificial eyebrows traced with burnt matches or false switches stuck on with long hairpins are more highly prized than the genuine article.

All of which is perfectly reasonable. We are a civilized people, and of what use is civilization if it doesn't help us to deceive and to be deceived in order to make life more worth the living?

But I was really surprised when I learned yesterday that a business man, old Durandeau, whom you know as well as I do, had hit upon the ingenious and astounding inspiration of dealing in ugliness. That they should sell beauty is perfectly comprehensible; that they should sell false beauty is quite natural—it is a sign of progress. But beyond the shadow of a doubt Durandeau has earned the gratitude of all France by putting on the market the commodity, deadwood until now, called ugliness. Understand me, I am speaking of ugliness that is ugly—frank ugliness, honestly sold as ugliness.

You have surely often met women traveling in pairs on the principal avenues. They walk slowly, stopping at the shop-windows with stifled laughter and carrying their clothes gracefully. They lock arms like two old friends with an air of intimacy; almost of the same age, costumed with equal elegance. But you will always find one of them fairly good looking— one of those faces which call for no especial remark. You wouldn't think of turning around to get a better view, but if by chance you should notice her you could look without displeasure. The other is always atrociously ugly— irritatingly so, an ugliness which catches the eye, which compels passersby to make comparisons between her and her companion. Confess that you have been ensnared, and that sometimes you have started to follow the two women. The monster alone on the avenue would have frightened you. The fairly good-looking young woman would have left you quite indifferent. But they were together, and the ugliness of the one heightened the beauty of the other.

Well, I can tell you: the monster, the atrociously ugly woman, belongs to Durandeau's Agency. She is one of his "Complements." The great Durandeau has let her to the insignificant face at five francs an hour.

## II

Here is the story. Durandeau is a business man of originality and invention, a millionaire who can afford to be something of an artist in trade. For many years he bewailed the fact that one had never been able to make a cent out of ugly girls. As for speculating in the pretty ones, it is a delicate business, and Durandeau, who has all the scruples of a rich man, would never think of it. One day he was suddenly inspired. He conceived his original idea in a twinkling, just as all great inventors do. He was walking on the Avenue when he saw in front of him two girls, one pretty and the other ugly. And as he looked he understood that the ugly one was an adjustment which complemented the pretty one. Just as ribbons, rice powder and false tresses are to be had for sale, so it was right and proper, he reasoned, that beauty should be able to purchase ugliness like an ornament which should be becoming.

Durandeau went home to reflect at leisure. The venture which he was meditating must be conducted with the greatest tact. He did not wish to jump pell-mell into an enterprise which would prove a bonanza if it succeeded, but ridiculous if it miscarried. He passed the night in calculations and reading the philosophers who have said the cleverest things about man's folly and woman's vanity. Next morning, at dawn, he had come to a decision. Calculation had borne him out: the philosophers had said so much about the vileness of humanity that he counted upon a large patronage.


### III

Would I had the inspiration; I would write the epic of the foundation of Durandeau's Agency. It would be an epic farcical and sad, full of tears and bursts of laughter.

Durandeau had more trouble than he anticipated in laying in a stock of wares. Wishing to act directly, he contented himself at first with posting on pipes and on the trees in by-places little placards which bore the following legend, written by hand: "Wanted—Ugly girls to do easy work." He waited eight days, and not a single ugly girl applied. Five or six pretty ones came and begged for work, sobbing. They were just hovering between hunger and vice, and still hoped to save themselves by work. Durandeau, much embarrassed, told them over and over again that they were pretty and wouldn't do. But they insisted that they were ugly, that it was pure gallantry and quite wrong on his part if he called them pretty. And now, being unable to sell the ugliness which they had not, they are selling the good-looks which they have.

Durandeau, in the face of this result, understood that only pretty girls have the courage of owning imaginary ugliness. As for the really ugly ones, they would never come of their own will and admit the unmeasurable size of their mouths nor the extraordinary smallness of their eyes. Advertise by hand-bills that you will give ten francs to every ugly girl who will present herself, and you will not be impoverished.

Durandeau gave up advertising. He hired half-a-dozen emissaries and turned them loose on the city in quest of monstrosities. There was a general recruiting of the ugliness of Paris. The emissaries, men of tact and taste, had ticklish business. Their methods depended upon the character and position of those they approached; brusque when the subject was in dire need of money, more gentle when they were dealing with some girl not yet on the brink of starvation. It is impossible for a polite man to say to a woman: "Madam, you are ugly. I will pay you for your ugliness so much a day."

Some memorable episodes occurred in this hunt for the poor girls who weep before their mirrors. Sometimes the emissaries were hot upon the scent. They had seen in the street a woman of ideal ugliness, and they did their best to bring her before Durandeau, to earn the thanks of the master. Some of them had recourse to extreme methods.

Every morning Durandeau received and inspected the stock gathered the day before. Comfortably ensconced in an armchair, in yellow housecoat and black satin cap, he had the new recruits file past him, each with the emissary who had captured her. Then he would turn away, blink his eyes, and look like a fancier—displeased or satisfied. He would pause and hesitate; then to get a better view he would have the goods turned around and would examine them on all sides. Sometimes he would even rise, touch their hair and examine their faces, as a merchant feels of a woolen or as a grocer satisfies himself about candles or pepper. When the ugliness was unquestionable, when the expression was stupid and dull, Durandeau would rub his hands gleefully and congratulate the emissary; he would even have embraced the monster. But he was chary of new kinds of ugliness. When the eyes glistened and the lips had sharp smiles, he frowned and mumbled to himself that such a type of ugliness, if it was not exactly fit for love, might do for passion. He showed marked coldness to the emissary, and told the woman to come back again, later on, when she was older.

It is not as easy as one might think to be an expert on ugliness, to make a collection of women truly ugly, quite harmless to pretty girls. Durandeau proved his genius in the selections he made, for he showed how deep a knowledge he had of the heart and of the emotions. The great criterion for him, of course, was the face, and he accepted only discouraging faces—those which froze by their grossness and stupidity.

The day on which the agency was finally opened, when it placed at the disposal of pretty women ugly ones suited to their complexions and their particular styles of beauty, he issued the following prospectus:

IV

Paris, 1st May, 18—

AGENCY FOR COMPLEMENTS,
L. DURANDEAU,
18 Rue M—, Paris
Office Hours:
10 to 4.

MADAM:—

I have the honor of advising you that I have just established this house, which must be of the greatest service for the maintenance of woman's beauty. I am the inventor of an article which will set off with a new glory nature's graces.

Heretofore adornment has been patent. Laces and jewels are obvious. You can easily detect a false switch in the coiffure, and whether the purple of the lips and the delicate pink of the cheeks are tinted.

Now, I have set myself to the solution of this problem—impossible at first blush—to beautify women, leaving everyone to guess whence comes the added touch. Without an extra ribbon, without touching the skin, my purpose has been to find for them an infallible means of attracting all eyes, and yet not overdoing nature's tender grace.

I believe I flatter myself that I have completely solved the apparently insoluble problem to which I addressed myself.

And to-day every lady who will honor me with her confidence can secure, at a low figure, the admiration of all eyes.

My device is extremely simple and reliable. I need only describe it, Madam, and you will understand at once exactly how it acts.

Have you ever noticed a poor woman in close proximity with a beauty in silks and laces, who is giving her alms from her gloved hand? Did you mark how the silk shone in contrast with the tatters; how well all that richness was set off and how it gained from contrast with the misery?

Madam, I have to offer to handsome faces the most complete line of ugly ones that can be found anywhere. Seedy garments set off new. My ugly faces set off pretty ones.

No more false teeth; no more false switches; no more false necks! No more make-up, costly costumes, enormous expenditures for colors and laces!—Only "Complements," which one takes by the arm and leads along the Avenue, to set off one's beauty, and win the tender glances of the gentlemen.

Your patronage is respectfully solicited, Madam. You will find here the ugliest and most varied assortment. You are at liberty to select and suit your beauty with the type of ugliness which best becomes it.

Rates: 5 francs an hour; 50 francs a day.

I am, Madam, most respectfully,

Durandeau.

N.B.—The Agency supplies likewise well-trained mothers, fathers, uncles, and aunts. Charges moderate.

## V

The success was great. Next day the Agency was opened for business. The office was crowded with customers, each of whom chose her "Complement," and marched her off in a sort of ferocious joy. Can you imagine what a pleasure it is for a handsome woman to lean on the arm of an ugly one? She enhances her own beauty, and thoroughly enjoys the ugliness of the other. Durandeau was a great philosopher.

It must not be supposed, however, that the working of the Agency was perfectly easy. A thousand unforseen obstacles arose. The difficulty of acquiring a stock in trade was nothing beside that of satisfying customers.

A lady would come in and ask for a "Complement." They showed the stock and bade her choose, presuming only to give a hint of advice now and then. Thereupon, the lady would flit from one "Complement" to another, disdainful, finding the poor girls too ugly or not ugly enough, complaining that not one of the uglinesses suited her own style of beauty. The clerks pointed out to her the crooked nose of this one, the receding forehead of another; they were put to their wits' end.

At other times the lady herself was frightfully ugly—so much so that Durandeau, had he been there, would have been possessed of a mad desire to procure her at any price. She came to have her beauty heightened, she would say; she wanted a young "Complement"—not too ugly, since she needed only slight adornment. The clerks, in despair, stationed her before a large mirror and paraded behind her the entire stock. But she herself would have taken the prize. Then she would sweep out, indignant that they had the presumption to offer her such looking objects.

Little by little, however, the patronage settled down. Each "Complement" had her regular customers. Durandeau could rest assured in his heart of having helped humanity take a great step in advance.

I doubt whether the position of the "Complement" is thoroughly appreciated. It has its joys, which are shown to the world; but it has also its tears, which are hidden. The "Complement" is ugly. She is a slave; she draws her salary for being a slave and for being ugly. As for the rest, she is well-dressed, she shakes hands with celebrities, she lives in carriages, she luncheons and dines at the famous restaurants, she passes her evenings at the theatre. She is apparently on terms of intimacy with famous beauties; and the uninitiated think her of the inner circle at the races and at first nights. All day she is in a whirl of gaiety. At night she eats her heart out, in tears. She has taken off her finery, which belongs to the Agency; she is alone in her attic room, before her little mirror, which tells the truth. She is face to face with all her ugliness, and she realizes that she will never be loved. She whose business it is to kindle emotion for others will never taste a kiss herself.


## VI


My present purpose has been only to outline the establishment of the Agency, and to transmit the name of Durandeau to posterity. Such men have their positions well defined in history. Some day perhaps I will write the "Confessions of a Complement." I knew one of the unfortunates, and her sufferings touched me to the quick. She used to enjoy the patronage of some women whom all Paris knows; and they were pretty hard on her. Have pity, my ladies! Do not tear the laces which bedeck you; be gentle to the ugly, without whom you would not be so engaging.

My "Complement" was a spirited creature, who, I imagine, had read a great deal of Walter Scott. I can think of nothing sadder than a cripple in love or an ugly woman yearning for the ideal. The poor girl fell in love with all the men whose eyes her dreadful face deflected to her patronesses. She has lived many a little drama. She was frightfully jealous of those women who paid for the use of her, as one pays for a pot of pommade or a pair of boots. She was a thing let for so much an hour, and it always turned out a good bargain. Can you imagine her bitterness, all the while she was smiling and prattling with those women who were stealing the love that should have been hers? And those very pretty women who took a spiteful delight in cajoling her intimately before the world treated her like a servant when alone; they would have liked to crush her for fun, as they might break the ornaments on their *étagères*.

But of what account is a suffering soul to the progress of the world? Humanity marches on. Durandeau will be blessed by generations yet unborn for having put on the market a line of goods unheard of before, for having invented a device to make woman's conquest easier.

*Translated by Alison M. Lederer*

∾

# BOOK II

## Summer

# THE KING OF THE GOLDEN RIVER
# OR THE BLACK BROTHERS

*John Ruskin*

I

How the Agricultural System of the Black Brothers
Was Interfered with by South West Wind, Esquire

In a secluded and mountainous part of Stiria, there was, in old time, a valley of the most surprising and luxuriant fertility. It was surrounded, on all sides, by steep and rocky mountains, rising into peaks, which were always covered with snow, and from which a number of torrents descended in constant cataracts. One of these fell westward, over the face of a crag so high, that, when the sun had set to everything else, and all below was darkness, his beams still shone full upon this waterfall, so that it looked like a shower of gold. It was, therefore, called by the people of the neighbourhood, the Golden River. It was strange that none of these streams fell into the valley itself. They all descended on the other side of the mountains, and wound away through broad plains and by populous cities. But the clouds were drawn so constantly to the snowy hills, and rested so softly in the circular hollow, that in time of drouth and heat, when all the country round was burnt up, there was still rain in the little valley; and its crops were so heavy, and its hay so high, and its apples so red, and its grapes so blue, and its wine so rich, and its honey so sweet, that it was a marvel to every one who beheld it, and was commonly called the Treasure Valley. The whole of this little valley belonged to three brothers, called Schwartz, Hans, and Gluck. Schwartz and Hans, the two elder brothers, were very ugly men, with overhanging eyebrows and small dull eyes, which were always half shut, so that you couldn't see into *them,* and always fancied they saw very far into *you.* They lived by farming the Treasure Valley, and very good farmers they were. They killed everything that did not pay for its eating. They shot the blackbirds, because they pecked the fruit; and killed the hedgehogs, lest they should suck the cows; they poisoned the crickets for eating the crumbs in the kitchen, and smothered the cicadas, which used to sing all summer in

69

the lime-trees. They worked their servants without any wages, till they would not work any more, and then quarrelled with them, and turned them out of doors without paying them. It would have been very odd, if with such a farm, and such a system of farming, they hadn't got very rich; and very rich they *did* get. They generally contrived to keep their corn by them till it was very dear, and then sell it for twice its value; they had heaps of gold lying about on their floors, yet it was never known that they had given so much as a penny or a crust in charity; they never went to mass; grumbled perpetually at paying tithes; and were, in a word, of so cruel and grinding a temper, as to receive from all those with whom they had any dealings, the nick-name of the "Black Brothers." The youngest brother, Gluck, was as completely opposed, in both appearance and character, to his seniors as could possibly be imagined or desired. He was not above twelve years old, fair, blue-eyed, and kind in temper to every living thing. He did not, of course, agree particularly well with his brothers, or rather, they did not agree with *him*. He was usually appointed to the honourable office of turnspit, when there was anything to roast, which was not often; for, to do the brothers justice, they were hardly less sparing upon themselves than upon other people. At other times he used to clean the shoes, floors, and sometimes the plates, occasionally getting what was left on them, by way of encouragement, and a wholesome quantity of dry blows, by way of education.

Things went on in this manner for a long time. At last came a very wet summer, and everything went wrong in the country round. The hay had hardly been got in, when the haystacks were floated bodily down to the sea by an inundation; the vines were cut to pieces with the hail; the corn was all killed by a black blight; only in the Treasure Valley, as usual, all was safe. As it had rain when there was rain nowhere else, so it had sun when there was sun nowhere else. Every body came to buy corn at the farm, and went away pouring maledictions on the Black Brothers. They asked what they liked, and got it, except from the poor people, who could only beg, and several of whom were starved at their very door, without the slightest regard or notice.

It was drawing towards winter, and very cold weather, when one day the two elder brothers had gone out, with their usual warning to little Gluck, who was left to mind the roast, that he was to let nobody in, and give nothing out. Gluck sat down quite close to the fire, for it was raining very hard, and the kitchen walls were by no means dry or comfortable-looking. He turned and turned, and the roast got nice and brown. "What a pity," thought Gluck, "my brothers never ask anybody to dinner. I'm sure, when they've got such a nice piece of mutton as this, and nobody else has got so much as a piece of dry bread, it would do their hearts good to have somebody to eat it with them."

Just as he spoke, there came a double knock at the house door, yet heavy and dull, as though the knocker had been tied up—more like a puff than a knock. "It must be the wind," said Gluck; "nobody else would venture to knock double knocks at our door." No it wasn't the wind: there it came again very hard, and what was particularly astounding, the knocker seemed to be in a hurry, and not to be in the least afraid of the consequences. Gluck went to the window, opened it, and put his head out to see who it was. It was the most extraordinary-looking little gentleman he had ever seen in his life. He had a very long nose, slightly brass-coloured, and expanding towards its termination into a development not unlike the lower extremity of a key bugle. His cheeks were very round, and very red, and might have warranted a supposition that he had been blowing a refractory fire for the last eight-and-forty hours. His eyes twinkled merrily through long silky eyelashes, his moustaches curled twice round like a cork-screw on each side of his mouth, and his hair, of a curious mixed pepper-and-salt colour, descended far over his shoulders. He was about four feet six in height, and wore a conical pointed cap of nearly the same altitude, decorated with a black feather some three feet long. His doublet was prolonged behind into something resembling a violent exaggeration of what is now termed a "swallow-tail," but was much obscured by the swelling folds of an enormous black, glossy-looking cloak, which must have been very much too long in calm weather, as the wind, whistling round the old house, carried it clear out from the wearer's shoulders to about four times his own length.

Gluck was so perfectly paralyzed by the singular appearance of his visitor, that he remained fixed without uttering a word, until the old gentleman, having performed another and a more energetic concerto on the knocker, turned round to look after his fly-away cloak. In so doing he caught sight of Gluck's little yellow head jammed in the window, with its mouth and eyes very wide open indeed.

"Hollo!" said the little gentleman, "that's not the way to answer the door: I'm wet, let me in."

To do the little gentleman justice, he *was* wet. His feather hung down between his legs like a beaten puppy's tail, dripping like an umbrella; and from the ends of his moustaches the water was running into his waistcoat pockets, and out again like a mill-stream.

"I beg pardon, sir," said Gluck, "I'm very sorry, but I really can't."

"Can't what?" said the old gentleman.

"I can't let you in, sir,—I can't indeed; my brothers would beat me to death, sir, if I thought of such a thing. What do you want, sir?"

"Want?" said the old gentleman petulantly. "I want fire, and shelter; and there's your great fire there blazing, crackling, and dancing on the walls, with nobody to feel it. Let me in, I say; I only want to warm myself."

Gluck had had his head, by this time, so long out of the window, that he began to feel it was really unpleasantly cold, and when he turned, and saw the beautiful fire rustling and roaring, and throwing long bright tongues up the chimney, as if it were licking its chops at the savoury smell of the leg of mutton, his heart melted within him that it should be burning away for nothing. "He does look *very* wet," said little Gluck; "I'll just let him in for a quarter of an hour." Round he went to the door, and opened it; and as the little gentleman walked in, there came a gust of wind through the house, that made the old chimneys totter.

"That's a good boy," said the little gentleman. "Never mind your brothers. I'll talk to them."

"Pray, sir, don't do any such thing," said Gluck. "I can't let you stay till they come; they'd be the death of me."

"Dear me," said the old gentleman, "I'm very sorry to hear that. How long may I stay?"

"Only till the mutton's done, sir," replied Gluck, "and it's very brown."

Then the old gentleman walked into the kitchen, and sat himself down on the hob, with the top of his cap accommodated up the chimney, for it was a great deal too high for the roof.

"You'll soon dry there, sir," said Gluck, and sat down again to turn the mutton. But the old gentleman did *not* dry there, but went on drip, drip, dripping among the cinders, and the fire fizzed, and sputtered, and began to look very black, and uncomfortable; never was such a cloak; every fold in it ran like a gutter.

"I beg pardon, sir," said Gluck at length, after watching the water spreading in long, quick-silver-like streams over the floor for a quarter of an hour; "mayn't I take your cloak?"

"No, thank you," said the old gentleman.

"Your cap, sir?"

"I am all right, thank you," said the old gentleman rather gruffly.

"But—sir,—I'm very sorry," said Gluck, hesitatingly; "but—really, sir,—you're—putting the fire out."

"It'll take longer to do the mutton then," replied his visitor drily.

Gluck was very much puzzled by the behaviour of his guest; it was such a strange mixture of coolness and humility. He turned away at the string meditatively for another five minutes.

"That mutton looks very nice," said the old gentleman at length. "Can't you give me a little bit?"

"Impossible, sir," said Gluck.

"I'm very hungry," continued the old gentleman. "I've had nothing to eat yesterday, nor to-day. They surely couldn't miss a bit from the knuckle!"

He spoke in so very melancholy a tone, that it quite melted Gluck's heart. "They promised me one slice to-day, sir," said he. "I can give you that, but not a bit more."

"That's a good boy," said the old gentleman again.

Then Gluck warmed a plate, and sharpened a knife. "I don't care if I do get beaten for it," thought he. Just as he had cut a large slice out of the mutton, there came a tremendous rap at the door. The old gentleman jumped off the hob, as if it had suddenly become inconveniently warm. Gluck fitted the slice into the mutton again, with desperate efforts at exactitude, and ran to open the door.

"What did you keep us waiting in the rain for?" said Schwartz, as he walked in, throwing his umbrella in Gluck's face. "Ay! what for, indeed, you little vagabond?" said Hans, administering an educational box on the ear, as he followed his brother into the kitchen.

"Bless my soul!" said Schwartz when he opened the door.

"Amen," said the little gentleman, who had taken his cap off, and was standing in the middle of the kitchen, bowing with the utmost possible velocity.

"Who's that?" said Schwartz, catching up a rolling-pin, and turning to Gluck with a fierce frown.

"I don't know, indeed, brother," said Gluck in great terror.

"How did he get in?" roared Schwartz.

"My dear brother," said Gluck, deprecatingly, "he was so *very* wet!"

The rolling-pin was descending on Gluck's head; but, at the instant, the old gentleman interposed his conical cap, on which it crashed with a shock that shook the water out of it all over the room. What was very odd, the rolling-pin no sooner touched the cap, than it flew out of Schwartz's hand, spinning like a straw in a high wind, and fell into the corner at the further end of the room.

"Who are you, sir?" demanded Schwartz, turning upon him.

"What's your business?" snarled Hans.

"I'm a poor old man, sir," the little gentleman began very modestly, "and I saw your fire through the window, and begged shelter for a quarter of an hour."

"Have the goodness to walk out again, then," said Schwartz. "We've quite enough water in our kitchen, without making it a drying-house."

"It is a cold day to turn an old man out in, sir; look at my grey hairs." They hung down to his shoulders, as I told you before.

"Ay!" said Hans, "there are enough of them to keep you warm. Walk!"

"I'm very, very hungry, sir; couldn't you spare me a bit of bread before I go?"

"Bread, indeed!" said Schwartz; "do you suppose we've nothing to do with our bread, but to give it to such red-nosed fellows as you?"

"Why don't you sell your feather?" said Hans, sneeringly. "Out with you."

"A little bit," said the old gentleman.

"Be off!" said Schwartz.

"Pray, gentlemen."

"Off, and be hanged!" cried Hans, seizing him by the collar. But he had no sooner touched the old gentleman's collar, than away he went after the rolling-pin, spinning round and round, till he fell into the corner on the top of it. Then Schwartz was very angry, and ran at the old gentleman to turn him out; but he also had hardly touched him, when away he went after Hans and the rolling-pin, and hit his head against the wall as he tumbled into the corner. And so there they lay, all three.

Then the old gentleman spun himself round with velocity in the opposite direction; continued to spin until his long cloak was all wound neatly about him; clapped his cap on his head, very much on one side (for it could not stand upright without going through the ceiling), gave an additional twist to his cork-screw moustaches, and replied with perfect coolness: "Gentlemen, I wish you a very good morning. At twelve o'clock to-night, I'll call again; after such a refusal of hospitality as I have just experienced, you will not be surprised if that visit is the last I ever pay you."

"If ever I catch you here again," muttered Schwartz, coming half frightened out of the corner—but, before he could finish his sentence, the old gentleman had shut the house-door behind him with a great bang: and there drove past the window, at the same instant, a wreath of ragged cloud, that whirled and rolled away down the valley in all manner of shapes; turning over and over in the air; and melting away at last in a gush of rain.

"A very pretty business, indeed, Mr. Gluck!" said Schwartz. "Dish the mutton, sir. If ever I catch you at such a trick again—bless me, why the mutton's been cut!"

"You promised me one slice, brother, you know," said Gluck.

"Oh! and you were cutting it hot, I suppose, and going to catch all the gravy. It'll be long before I promise you such a thing again. Leave the room, sir; and have the kindness to wait in the coal-cellar till I call you."

Gluck left the room, melancholy enough. The brothers ate as much mutton as they could, locked the rest in the cupboard, and proceeded to get very drunk after dinner.

Such a night as it was! Howling wind, and rushing rain, without intermission. The brothers had just sense enough left to put up all the shutters, and double-bar the door, before they went to bed. They usually slept in the same room. As the clock struck twelve, they were both awakened by a tremendous crash. Their door burst open with a violence that shook the house from top to bottom.

"What's that?" cried Schwartz, starting up in his bed.

"Only I," said the little gentleman

The two brothers sat up on their bolster, and stared into the darkness. The room was full of water, and by a misty moonbeam, which found its way through a hole in the shutter, they could see in the midst of it an enormous foam globe, spinning round, and bobbing up and down like a cork, on which, as on a most luxurious cushion, reclined the little old gentleman, cap and all. There was plenty of room for it now, for the roof was off.

"Sorry to incommode you," said their visitor, ironically. "I'm afraid your beds are dampish; perhaps you had better go to your brother's room: I've left the ceiling on, there."

They required no second admonition, but rushed into Gluck's room, wet through, and in an agony of terror.

"You'll find my card on the kitchen table," the old gentleman called after them. "Remember, the *last* visit."

"Pray Heaven it may!" said Schwartz, shuddering. And the foam globe disappeared.

Dawn came at last, and the two brothers looked out of Gluck's little window in the morning. The Treasure Valley was one mass of ruin, and desolation. The inundation had swept away trees, crops, and cattle, and left in their stead, a waste of red sand, and grey mud. The two brothers crept shivering and horror-struck into the kitchen. The water had gutted the whole first floor; corn, money, almost every moveable thing had been swept away, and there was left only a small white card on the kitchen table. On it, in large, breezy, long-legged letters, were engraved the words:— SOUTH WEST WIND, ESQUIRE.


## II


OF THE PROCEEDINGS OF THE THREE BROTHERS AFTER THE VISIT
OF SOUTH WEST WIND, ESQUIRE; AND HOW LITTLE GLUCK HAD AN
INTERVIEW WITH THE KING OF THE GOLDEN RIVER

South West Wind, Esquire, was as good as his word. After the momentous visit above related, he entered the Treasure Valley no more; and, what was worse, he had so much influence with his relations, the West Winds in general, and used it so effectually, that they all adopted a similar line of conduct. So no rain fell in the valley from one year's end to another. Though everything remained green and flourishing in the plains below, the inheritance of the Three Brothers was a desert. What had once been the richest soil in the kingdom became a shifting heap of red sand; and the brothers, unable longer to contend with the adverse skies, abandoned their valueless patrimony in despair, to seek some means of gaining a livelihood among the cities and people of the plains. All their money was gone, and they had nothing left but some curious old-fashioned pieces of gold plate, the last remnants of their ill-gotten wealth.

"Suppose we turn goldsmiths?" said Schwartz to Hans, as they entered the large city. "It is a good knave's trade; we can put a great deal of copper into the gold, without any one's finding it out."

The thought was agreed to be a very good one; they hired a furnace, and turned goldsmiths. But two slight circumstances affected their trade: the first, that people did not approve of the coppered gold; the second, that the two elder brothers, whenever they had sold anything, used to leave little Gluck to mind the furnace, and go and drink out the money in the alehouse next door. So they melted all their gold, without making money enough to buy more, and were at last reduced to one large drinking-mug, which an uncle of his had given to little Gluck, and which he was very fond of, and would not have parted with for the world; though he never drank anything out of it but milk and water. The mug was a very odd mug to look at. The handle was formed of two wreaths of flowing golden hair, so finely spun that it looked more like silk than metal, and these wreaths descended into and mixed with a beard and whiskers, of the same exquisite workmanship, which surrounded and decorated a very fierce little face, of the reddest gold imaginable, right in the front of the mug, with a pair of eyes in it which seemed to command its whole circumference. It was impossible to drink out of the mug without being subjected to an intense gaze out of the side of these eyes; and Schwartz positively averred that once, after emptying it full of Rhenish seventeen times, he had seen them wink! When it came to the mug's turn to be made into spoons, it half broke poor little Gluck's heart; but the brothers only laughed at him, tossed the mug into the melting-pot, and staggered out to the ale-house; leaving him, as usual, to pour the gold into bars, when it was all ready.

When they were gone, Gluck took a farewell look at his old friend in the melting-pot. The flowing hair was all gone; nothing remained but the red nose, and the sparkling eyes, which looked more malicious than ever. "And no wonder," thought Gluck, "after being treated that way." He sauntered disconsolately to the window, and sat himself down to catch the fresh evening air, and escape the hot breath of the furnace. Now this window commanded a direct view of the range of mountains, which as I told you before, overhung the Treasure Valley, and more especially of the peak from which fell the Golden River. It was just at the close of the day, and, when Gluck sat down at the window, he saw the rocks of the mountain-tops, all crimson and purple with the sunset; and there were bright tongues of fiery cloud burning and quivering about them; and the river, brighter than all, fell, in a waving column of pure gold, from precipice to precipice, with the double arch of a broad purple rainbow stretched across it, flushing and fading alternately in the wreaths of spray.

"Ah!" said Gluck aloud, after he had looked at it for a little while, "if that river were really all gold, what a nice thing it would be."

"No it wouldn't, Gluck," said a clear metallic voice, close at his ear.

"Bless me, what's that?" exclaimed Gluck, jumping up. There was nobody there. He looked round the room, and under the table, and a great many times behind him, but there was certainly nobody there, and he sat down again at the window. This time he didn't speak, but he couldn't help thinking again that it would be very convenient if the river were really all gold.

"Not at all, my boy," said the same voice, louder than before.

"Bless me!" said Gluck again, "what *is* that?" He looked again into all the corners, and cupboards, and then began turning round and round, as fast as he could, in the middle of the room, thinking there was somebody behind him, when the same voice struck again on his ear. It was singing now very merrily "Lala-lira-la"; no words, only a soft running effervescent melody, something like that of a kettle on the boil. Gluck looked out of the window. No, it was certainly in the house. Up stairs, and down stairs. No, it was certainly in that very room, coming in quicker time, and clearer notes, every moment. "Lala-lira-la." All at once it struck Gluck that it sounded louder near the furnace. He ran to the opening, and looked in: yes, he saw right, it seemed to be coming, not only out of the furnace, but out of the pot. He uncovered it, and ran back in a great fright, for the pot was certainly singing! He stood in the farthest corner of the room, with his hands up, and his mouth open, for a minute or two, when the singing stopped, and the voice became clear, and pronunciative.

"Hollo!" said the voice.

Gluck made no answer.

"Hollo! Gluck, my boy," said the pot again.

Gluck summoned all his energies, walked straight up to the crucible, drew it out of the furnace, and looked in. The gold was all melted, and its surface as smooth and polished as a river; but instead of reflecting little Gluck's head, as he looked in, he saw meeting his glance, from beneath the gold, the red nose and sharp eyes of his old friend of the mug, a thousand times redder and sharper than ever he had seen them in his life.

"Come Gluck, my boy," said the voice out of the pot again, "I'm all right; pour me out."

But Gluck was too much astonished to do anything of the kind.

"Pour me out, I say," said the voice rather gruffly.

Still Gluck couldn't move.

"*Will* you pour me out?" said the voice passionately. "I'm too hot."

By a violent effort, Gluck recovered the use of his limbs, took hold of the crucible, and sloped it, so as to pour out the gold. But instead of a liquid stream, there came out, first, a pair of pretty little yellow legs, then some coat-tails, then a pair of arms stuck akimbo, and, finally, the well-known head of his friend the mug; all which articles, uniting as they rolled out, stood up energetically on the floor, in the shape of a little golden dwarf, about a foot and a half high.

"That's right!" said the dwarf, stretching out first his legs, and then his arms, and then shaking his head up and down, and as far round as it would go, for five minutes, without stopping; apparently with the view of ascertaining if he were quite correctly put together, while Gluck stood contemplating him in speechless amazement. He was dressed in a slashed doublet of spun gold, so fine in its texture, that the prismatic colours gleamed over it, as if on a surface of mother-of-pearl; and, over this brilliant doublet, his hair and beard fell full half-way to the ground, in waving curls, so exquisitely delicate, that Gluck could hardly tell where they ended; they seemed to melt into air. The features of the face, however, were by no means finished with the same delicacy; they were rather coarse, slightly inclining to coppery in complexion, and indicative, in expression, of a very pertinacious and intractable disposition in their small proprietor. When the dwarf had finished his self-examination, he turned his small sharp eyes full on Gluck, and stared at him deliberately for a minute or two. "No it wouldn't, Gluck, my boy," said the little man.

This was certainly rather an abrupt and unconnected mode of commencing conversation. It might indeed be supposed to refer to the course of Gluck's thoughts, which had first produced the dwarf's observations out of the pot; but whatever it referred to, Gluck had no inclination to dispute the dictum.

"Wouldn't it, sir?" said Gluck, very mildly and submissively indeed.

"No," said the dwarf, conclusively. "No it wouldn't." And with that, the dwarf pulled his cap hard over his brows, and took two turns, of three feet long, up and down the room, lifting his legs up very high, and setting them down very hard. This pause gave time for Gluck to collect his thoughts a little, and, seeing no great reason to view his diminutive visitor with dread, and feeling his curiosity overcome his amazement, he ventured on a question of peculiar delicacy.

"Pray, sir," said Gluck, rather hesitatingly, "were you my mug?"

On which the little man turned sharp round, walked straight up to Gluck, and drew himself up to his full height. "I," said the little man, "am the King of the Golden River." Whereupon he turned about again, and took two more turns, some six feet long, in order to allow time for the consternation which this announcement produced in his auditor to evaporate. After which, he again walked up to Gluck and stood still, as if expecting some comment on his communication.

Gluck determined to say something at all events. "I hope your Majesty is very well," said Gluck.

"Listen!" said the little man, deigning no reply to this polite inquiry. "I am the King of what you mortals call the Golden River. The shape you saw me in was owing to the malice of a stronger king, from whose enchantments you have this instant freed me. What I have seen of you, and your conduct to your wicked brothers, renders me willing to serve you; therefore attend to what I tell you. Whoever shall climb to the top of that mountain from which you see the Golden River issue, and shall cast into the stream, at its source, three drops of holy water, for him, and for him only, the river shall turn to gold. But no one failing in his first can succeed in a second attempt;

and if any one shall cast unholy water into the river, it will overwhelm him, and he will become a black stone." So saying, the King of the Golden River turned away, and deliberately walked into the centre of the hottest flame of the furnace. His figure became red, white, transparent, dazzling—a blaze of intense light—rose, trembled, and disappeared. The King of the Golden River had evaporated.

"Oh!" cried poor Gluck, running to look up the chimney after him. "Oh, dear, dear, dear me! My mug! my mug! my mug!"

## III

How Mr. Hans Set Off on an Expedition to the Golden River, and How He Prospered Therein

The King of the Golden River had hardly made the extraordinary exit related in the last chapter, before Hans and Schwartz came roaring into the house, very savagely drunk. The discovery of the total loss of their last piece of plate had the effect of sobering them just enough to enable them to stand over Gluck, beating him very steadily for a quarter of an hour; at the expiration of which period they dropped into a couple of chairs, and requested to know what he had got to say for himself. Gluck told them his story, of which of course they did not believe a word. They beat him again, till their arms were tired, and staggered to bed. In the morning, however, the steadiness with which he adhered to his story obtained him some degree of credence; the immediate consequence of which was, that the two brothers, after wrangling a long time on the knotty question, which of them should try his fortune first, drew their swords, and began fighting. The noise of the fray alarmed the neighbours, who, finding they could not pacify the combatants, sent for the constable.

Hans, on hearing this, contrived to escape, and hid himself; but Schwartz was taken before the magistrate, fined for breaking the peace, and, having drunk out his last penny the evening before, was thrown into prison till he should pay.

When Hans heard this, he was much delighted, and determined to set out immediately for the Golden River. How to get the holy water, was the question. He went to the priest, but the priest could not give any holy water to so abandoned a character. So Hans went to vespers in the evening for the first time in his life, and, under pretence of crossing himself, stole a cupful, and returned home in triumph.

Next morning he got up before the sun rose, put the holy water into a strong flask, and two bottles of wine and some meat in a basket, slung them over his back, took his alpine staff in his hand, and set off for the mountains.

On his way out of the town he had to pass the prison, and as he looked in at the windows, whom should he see but Schwartz himself peeping out of the bars, and looking very disconsolate.

"Good morning, brother," said Hans; "have you any message for the King of the Golden River?"

Schwartz gnashed his teeth with rage, and shook the bars with all his strength; but Hans only laughed at him, and, advising him to make himself comfortable till he came back again, shouldered his basket, shook the bottle of holy water in Schwartz's face till it frothed again, and marched off in the highest spirits in the world.

It was, indeed, a morning that might have made any one happy, even with no Golden River to seek for. Level lines of dewy mist lay stretched along the valley, out of which rose the massy mountains—their lower cliffs in pale grey shadow, hardly distinguishable from the floating vapour, but gradually ascending till they caught the sunlight, which ran in sharp touches of ruddy colour along the angular crags, and pierced, in long level rays, through their fringes of spear-like pine. Far above, shot up red splintered masses of castellated rock, jagged and shivered into myriads of fantastic forms, with here and there a streak of sunlit snow, traced down their chasms like a line of forked lightning; and, far beyond, and far above all these, fainter than the morning cloud, but purer and changeless, slept, in the blue sky, the utmost peaks of the eternal snow.

The Golden River, which sprang from one of the lower and snowless elevations, was now nearly in shadow; all but the uppermost jets of spray, which rose like slow smoke above the undulating line of the cataract, and floated away in feeble wreaths upon the morning wind.

On this object, and on this alone, Hans' eyes and thoughts were fixed; forgetting the distance he had to traverse, he set off at an imprudent rate of walking, which greatly exhausted him before he had scaled the first range of the green and low hills. He was, moreover, surprised, on surmounting them, to find that a large glacier, of whose existence, notwithstanding his previous knowledge of the mountains, he had been absolutely ignorant, lay between him and the source of the Golden River. He entered on it with the boldness of a practised mountaineer; yet he thought he had never traversed so strange or so dangerous a glacier in his life. The ice was excessively slippery, and out of all its chasms came wild sounds of gushing water; not monotonous or low, but changeful and loud, rising occasionally into drifting passages of wild melody, then breaking off into short melancholy tones, or sudden shrieks, resembling those of human voices in distress or pain. The ice was broken into thousands of confused shapes, but none, Hans thought, like the ordinary forms of splintered ice. There seemed a curious *expression* about all their outlines—a perpetual resemblance to living features, distorted and scornful. Myriads of deceitful shadows, and lurid lights, played and floated about and through the pale blue pinnacles, dazzling and confusing the sight of the traveller; while his ears grew dull and his head giddy with the constant gush and roar of the concealed waters. These painful circumstances increased upon him as he advanced; the ice crashed and yawned into fresh chasms at his feet, tottering spires nodded around him, and fell thundering across his path; and thought he had repeatedly faced these dangers on the most terrific glaciers, and in the wildest weather, it was with a new and oppressive feeling of panic terror that he leaped the last chasm, and flung himself, exhausted and shuddering, on the firm turf of the mountain.

He had been compelled to abandon his basket of food, which became a perilous incumbrance on the glacier, and had now no means of refreshing himself but by breaking off and eating some of the pieces of ice. This, however, relieved his thirst; an hour's repose recruited his hardy frame, and, with the indomitable spirit of avarice, he resumed his laborious journey.

His way now lay straight up a ridge of bare red rocks, without a blade of grass to ease the foot, or a projecting angle to afford an inch of shade from the south sun. It was past noon, and the rays beat intensely upon the steep path, while the whole atmosphere was motionless, and penetrated with heat. Intense thirst was soon added to bodily fatigue with which Hans was now afflicted; glance after glance he cast on the flask of water which hung at his belt. "Three drops are enough," at last thought he; "I may, at least, cool my lips with it."

He opened the flask, and was raising it to his lips, when his eye fell on an object lying on the rock beside him; he thought it moved. It was a small dog, apparently in the last agony of death from thirst. Its tongue was out, its jaws dry, its limbs extended lifelessly, and a swarm of black ants were crawling about its lips and throat. Its eye moved to the bottle which Hans held in his hand. He raised it, drank, spurned the animal with his foot, and passed on. And he did not know how it was, but he thought that a strange shadow had suddenly come across the blue sky.

The path became steeper and more rugged every moment; and the high hill air, instead of refreshing him, seemed to throw his blood into a fever. The noise of the hill cataracts sounded like mockery in his ears: they were all distant, and his thirst increased every moment. Another hour passed, and he again looked down to the flask at his side; it was half empty, but there was much more than three drops in it. He stopped to open it, and again, as he did so, something moved in the path above him. It was a fair child, stretched nearly lifeless on the rock, it breast heaving with thirst, its eyes closed, and its lips parched and burning. Hans eyed it deliberately, drank, and passed on. And a dark grey cloud came over the sun, and long, snake-like shadows crept up along the mountain-sides. Hans struggled on. The sun was sinking, but its descent seemed to bring no coolness; the leaden weight of the dead air pressed upon his brow and heart, but the goal was near. He saw the cataract of the Golden River springing from the hill-side, scarcely five hundred feet above him. He paused for a moment to breathe, and sprang on to complete his task.

At this instant a faint cry fell on his ear. He turned, and saw a grey-haired old man extended on the rocks. His eyes were sunk, his features deadly pale, and gathered into an expression of despair. "Water!" he stretched his arms to Hans, and cried feebly. "Water! I am dying."

"I have none," replied Hans; "thou hast had thy share of life." He strode over the prostate body, and darted on. And a flash of blue lightning rose out of the East, shaped like a sword; it shook thrice over the whole heaven, and left it dark with one heavy, impenetrable shade. The sun was setting; it plunged towards the horizon like a red-hot ball.

The roar of the Golden River rose on Hans' ear. He stood at the brink of the chasm through which it ran. Its waves were filled with the red glory of the sunset: they shook their crests like tongues of fire, and flashes of bloody light gleamed along their foam. Their sound came mightier and mightier on his senses; his brain grew giddy with the prolonged thunder. Shuddering, he drew the flask from his girdle, and hurled it into the centre of the torrent. As he did so, an icy chill shot through his limbs; he staggered, shrieked, and fell. The waters closed over his cry. And the moaning of the river rose wildly into the night, as it gushed over THE BLACK STONE.

IV

HOW MR. SCHWARTZ SET OFF ON AN EXPEDITION
TO THE GOLDEN RIVER, AND HOW HE PROSPERED THEREIN

Poor little Gluck waited very anxiously alone in the house, for Hans' return. Finding he did not come back, he was terribly frightened, and went and told Schwartz in the prison all that had happened. Then Schwartz was very much pleased, and said that Hans must certainly have been turned into a black stone, and he should have all the gold to himself. But Gluck was very sorry, and cried all night. When he got up in the morning, there was no bread in the house, nor any money; so Gluck went, and hired himself to another goldsmith, and he worked so hard, and so neatly, and so long every day, that he soon got enough money together to pay his brother's fine, and he went, and gave it all to Schwartz, and Schwartz got out of prison. Then Schwartz was quite pleased, and said he should have some of the gold of the river. But Gluck only begged he would go and see what had become of Hans.

Now when Schwartz had heard that Hans had stolen the holy water, he thought to himself that such a proceeding might not be considered altogether correct by the King of the Golden River, and determined to manage matters better. So he took some more of Gluck's money, and went to a bad priest, who gave him some holy water very readily for it. Then Schwartz was sure it was all quite right. So Schwartz got up early in the morning before the sun rose, and took some bread and wine in a basket, and put his holy water in a flask, and set off for the mountains. Like his brother, he was much surprised at the sight of the glacier, and had great difficulty in crossing it, even after leaving his basket behind him. The day was cloudless, but not bright: there was a heavy purple haze hanging over the sky, and the hills looked lowering and gloomy. And as Schwartz climbed the steep rock path, the thirst came upon him, as it had upon his brother, until he lifted his flask to his lips to drink. Then he saw the fair child lying near him on the rocks, and it cried to him, and moaned for water.

"Water indeed," said Schwartz; "I haven't half enough for myself," and passed on. And as he went he thought the sunbeams grew more dim, and he saw a low bank of black cloud rising out of the West; and, when he had climbed for another hour, the thirst overcame him again, and he would have drunk. Then he saw the old man lying before him on the path, and heard him cry out for water. "Water, indeed," said Schwartz, "I haven't half enough for myself," and on he went.

Then again the light seemed to fade from before his eyes, and he looked up, and, behold, a mist, of the colour of blood, had come over the sun; and the bank of black cloud had risen very high, and its edges were tossing and tumbling like the waves of the angry sea. And they cast long shadows, which flickered over Schwartz's path.

Then Schwartz climbed for another hour, and again his thirst returned; and as he lifted his flask to his lips, he thought he saw his brother Hans lying exhausted on the path before him, and, as he gazed, the figure stretched its arms to him, and cried for water. "Ha, ha," laughed Schwartz, "are you there? remember the prison bars, my boy. Water, indeed! do you suppose I carried it all the way up here for *you*?" And he strode over the figure; yet, as he passed, he thought he saw a strange expression of mockery about its lips. And, when he had gone a few yards further, he looked back; but the figure was not there.

And a sudden horror came over Schwartz, he knew not why; but the thirst for gold prevailed over his fear, and he rushed on. And the bank of black cloud rose to the zenith, and out of it came bursts of spiry lightning, and waves of darkness seemed to heave and float, between their flashes, over the whole heavens. And the sky where the sun was setting was all level, and like a lake of blood; and a strong wind came out of that sky, tearing its crimson clouds into fragments, and scattering them far into the darkness. And when Schwartz stood by the brink of the Golden River, its waves were black, like thunderclouds, but their foam was like fire; and the roar of the waters below and the thunder above met, as he cast the flask into the stream. And, as he did so, the lightning glared in his eyes, and the earth gave way beneath him, and the waters closed over his cry. And the moaning of the river rose wildly into the night, as it gushed over the Two Black Stones.

V

HOW LITTLE GLUCK SET OFF ON AN EXPEDITION
TO THE GOLDEN RIVER, AND HOW HE PROSPERED THEREIN;
WITH OTHER MATTERS OF INTEREST

When Gluck found that Schwartz did not come back, he was very sorry, and did not know what to do. He had no money, and was obliged to go and hire himself again to the goldsmith, who worked him very hard, and gave him very little money. So, after a month, or two, Gluck grew tired, and made up his mind to go and try his fortune with the Golden River. "The little king looked very kind," thought he. "I don't think he will turn me into a black stone." So he went to the priest, and the priest gave him some holy water as soon as he asked for it. Then Gluck took some bread in his basket, and the bottle of water, and set off very early for the mountains.

If the glacier had occasioned a great deal of fatigue to his brothers, it was twenty times worse for him, who was neither so strong nor so practised on the mountains. He had several very bad falls, lost his basket and bread, and was very much frightened at the strange noises under the ice. He lay a long time to rest on the grass, after he had got over, and began to climb the hill just in the hottest part of the day. When he had climbed for an hour, he got dreadfully thirsty, and was going to drink like his brothers, when he saw an old man coming down the path above him, looking very feeble, and leaning on a staff. "My son," said the old man, "I am faint with thirst, give me some of that water." Then Gluck looked at him, and when he saw that he was pale and weary, he gave him the water: "Only pray don't drink it all," said Gluck. But the old man drank a great deal, and gave him back the bottle two-thirds empty. Then he bade him good-speed, and Gluck went on again merrily. And the path became easier to his feet, and two or three blades of grass appeared upon it, and some grasshoppers began singing on the bank beside it; and Gluck thought he had never heard such merry singing.

Then he went on for another hour, and the thirst increased on him so that he thought he should be forced to drink. But, as he raised the flask, he saw a little child lying panting by the road-side, and it cried out piteously for water. Then Gluck struggled with himself, and determined to bear the thirst a little longer; and he put the bottle to the child's lips, and it drank all but a few drops. Then it smiled on him, and got up, and ran down the hill; and Gluck looked after it, till it became as small as a little star, and then turned, and began climbing again. And then there were all kinds of sweet flowers growing on the rocks, bright green moss, with pale pink starry flowers, and soft belled gentians, more blue than the sky at its deepest, and pure white transparent lilies. And crimson and purple butterflies darted hither and thither, and the sky sent down such pure light, that Gluck had never felt so happy in his life.

Yet, when he had climbed for another hour, his thirst became intolerable again; and, when he looked at his bottle, he saw that there were only five or six drops left in it, and he could not venture to drink. And, as he was hanging the flask to his belt again, he saw a little dog lying on the rocks, gasping for breath—just as Hans had seen it on the day of his ascent. And Gluck stopped and looked at it, and then at the Golden River, not five hundred yards above; and he thought of the dwarf's words, "that no one could succeed, except in their first attempt"; and he tried to pass the dog, but it whined piteously, and Gluck stopped again. "Poor beastie," said Gluck, "it'll be dead when I come down again, if I don't help it." Then he looked closer and closer at it, and its eye turned on him so mournfully, that he could not stand it. "Confound the King and his gold too," said Gluck; and he opened the flask, and poured all the water into the dog's mouth.

The dog sprang up and stood on its hind legs. Its tail disappeared; its ears became long, longer, silky, golden; its nose became very red; its eyes became very twinkling; in three seconds the dog was gone, and before Gluck stood his old acquaintance, the King of the Golden River.

"Thank you," said the monarch, "but don't be frightened, it's all right"; for Gluck showed manifest symptoms of consternation at this unlooked-for reply to his last observation. "Why didn't you come before," continued the dwarf, "instead of sending me those rascally brothers of yours, for me to have the trouble of turning into stones? Very hard stones they make too."

"Oh dear me!" said Gluck, "have you really been so cruel?"

"Cruel!" said the dwarf, "they poured unholy water into my stream: do you suppose I'm going to allow that?"

"Why," said Gluck, "I am sure, sir—your Majesty, I mean—they got the water out of the church font."

"Very probably," replied the dwarf; "but," and his countenance grew stern as he spoke, "the water which has been refused to the cry of the weary and dying is unholy, though it had been blessed by every saint in heaven; and the water which is found in the vessel of mercy is holy, though it had been defiled with corpses."

So saying, the dwarf stooped and plucked a lily that grew at his feet. On its white leaves there hung three drops of clear dew. And the dwarf shook them into the flask which Gluck held in his hand. "Cast these into the river," he said, "and descend on the other side of the mountains into the Treasure Valley. And so good-speed."

As he spoke, the figure of the dwarf became indistinct. The playing colours of his robe formed themselves into a prismatic mist of dewy light: he stood for an instant veiled with them as with the belt of a broad rainbow. The colours grew faint, the mist rose into the air; the monarch had evaporated.

And Gluck climbed to the brink of the Golden River, and its waves were as clear as crystal, and as brilliant as the sun. And, when he cast the three drops of dew into the stream, there opened where they fell a small circular whirlpool, into which the waters descended with a musical noise. Gluck stood watching it for some time, very much disappointed, because not only the river was not turned into gold, but its waters seemed much diminished in quantity. Yet he obeyed his friend the dwarf, and descended the other side of the mountains, towards the Treasure Valley; and, as he went, he thought he heard the noise of water working its way under the ground. And, when he came in sight of the Treasure Valley, behold, a river, like the Golden River, was springing from a new cleft of the rocks above it, and was flowing in innumerable streams along the dry heaps of red sand. And as Gluck gazed, fresh grass sprang beside the new streams, and creeping plants grew and climbed among the moistening soil. Young flowers opened suddenly along the river-sides, as stars leap out when twilight is deepening, and thickets of myrtle, and tendrils of vine, cast lengthening shadows over the valleys as they grew. And thus the Treasure Valley became a garden again, and the inheritance, which had been lost by cruelty, was regained in love. And Gluck went in, and dwelt in the valley, and the poor were never driven from his door; so that his barns became full of corn, and his house of treasure. And, for him, the river had, according to the dwarf's promise, become a River of Gold. And, to this day, the inhabitants of the valley point out the place where the three drops of holy dew were cast into the stream, and trace the course of the Golden River under the ground, until it emerges in the Treasure Valley. And, at the top of the cataract of the Golden River, are still to be seen two BLACK STONES, round which the waters howl mournfully every day at sunset; and these stones are still called by the people of the valley, THE BLACK BROTHERS.

# THE JUMBLIES

*Edward Lear*

## I

They went to sea in a Sieve, they did,
    In a Sieve they went to sea:
In spite of all their friends could say,
On a winter's morn, on a stormy day,
    In a Sieve they went to sea!
And when the Sieve turned round and round,
And every one cried, "You'll all be drowned!"
They called aloud, "Our Sieve ain't big,

But we don't care a button! we don't care a fig!
  In a Sieve we'll go to sea!"
    Far and few, far and few,
      Are the lands where the Jumblies live;
     Their heads are green, and their hands are blue,
      And they went to sea in a Sieve.


## II

They sailed away in a Sieve, they did,
  In a Sieve they sailed so fast,
With only a beautiful pea-green veil
Tied with a riband by way of a sail,
  To a small tobacco-pipe mast;
And every one said, who saw them go,
"O won't they be soon upset, you know!
For the sky is dark, and the voyage is long,
And happen what may, it's extremely wrong
  In a Sieve to sail so fast!"
    Far and few, far and few,
      Are the lands where the Jumblies live;
     Their heads are green, and their hands are blue,
      And they went to sea in a Sieve.


## III

The water it soon came in, it did,
  The water it soon came in;
So to keep them dry, they wrapped their feet
In a pinky paper all folded neat,
  And they fastened it down with a pin.
And they passed the night in a crockery-jar,
And each of them said, "How wise we are!
Though the sky be dark, and the voyage be long,
Yet we never can think we were rash or wrong,
  While round in our Sieve we spin!"
    Far and few, far and few,
      Are the lands where the Jumblies live;

Their heads are green, and their hands are blue,
And they went to sea in a Sieve.


## IV

And all night long they sailed away;
    And when the sun went down,
They whistled and warbled a moony song
To the echoing sound of a coppery gong,
    In the shade of the mountains brown.
"O Timballo! How happy we are,
When we live in a sieve and a crockery-jar,
And all night long in the moonlight pale,
We sail away with a pea-green sail,
    In the shade of the mountains brown!"
        Far and few, far and few,
            Are the lands where the Jumblies live;
            Their heads are green, and their hands are blue,
            And they went to sea in a Sieve.


## V

They sailed to the Western Sea, they did,
    To a land all covered with trees,
And they bought an Owl, and a useful Cart,
And a pound of Rice, and a Cranberry Tart,
    And a hive of silvery Bees.
And they bought a Pig, and some green Jack-daws,
And a lovely Monkey with lollipop paws,
And forty bottles of Ring-Bo-Ree,
    And no end of Stilton Cheese.
        Far and few, far and few,
            Are the lands where the Jumblies live;
            Their heads are green, and their hands are blue,
            And they went to sea in a Sieve.

## VI

And in twenty years they all came back,
   In twenty years or more,
And every one said, "How tall they've grown!
For they've been to the Lakes, and the Torrible Zone,
   And the hills of the Chankly Bore";
And they drank their health, and gave them a feast
Of dumplings made of beautiful yeast;
And every one said, "If we only live,
We too will go to sea in a Sieve, —
   To the hills of the Chankly Bore!"
      Far and few, far and few,
         Are the lands where the Jumblies live;
         Their heads are green, and their hands are blue,
         And they went to sea in a Sieve.

॰॰

## A RUNNABLE STAG

### *John Davidson*

When the pods went pop on the broom, green broom,
   And apples began to be golden-skinned,
We harboured a stag in the Priory coomb,
   And we feathered his trail up-wind, up-wind,
   We feathered his trail up-wind—
      A stag of warrant, a stag, a stag,
      A runnable stag, a kingly crop,
      Brow, bay and tray and three on top,
      A stag, a runnable stag.

Then the huntsman's horn rang yap, yap, yap,
   And "Forwards" we heard the harbourer shout;
But 'twas only a brocket that broke a gap
   In the beechen underwood, driven out,

From the underwood antlered out
     By warrant and might of the stag, the stag,
     The runnable stag, whose lordly mind
     Was bent on sleep, though beamed and tined
     He stood, a runnable stag.

So we tufted the covert till afternoon
     With Tinkerman's Pup and Bell-of-the-North;
And hunters were sulky and hounds out of tune
     Before we tufted the right stag forth,
     Before we tufted him forth,
          The stag of warrant, the wily stag,
          The runnable stag with his kingly crop,
          Brow, bay and tray and three on top,
          The royal and runnable stag.

It was Bell-of-the-North and Tinkerman's Pup
     That stuck to the scent till the copse was drawn.
"Tally ho! tally ho!" and the hunt was up,
     The tufters whipped and the pack laid on,
     The resolute pack laid on,
          And the stag of warrant away at last,
          The runnable stag, the same, the same,
          His hoofs on fire, his horns like flame
          A stag, a runnable stag.

"Let your gelding be: if you check or chide
     He stumbles at once and you're out of the hunt;
For three hundred gentlemen, able to ride,
     On hunters accustomed to bear the brunt,
     Accustomed to bear the brunt,
          Are after the runnable stag, the stag,
          The runnable stag with his kingly crop,
          Brow, bay and tray and three on top,
          The right, the runnable stag."

By perilous paths in coomb and dell,
     The heather, the rocks, and the river-bed,
The pace grew hot, for the scent lay well,
     And a runnable stag goes right ahead,

The quarry went right ahead—
    Ahead, ahead, and fast and far;
    His antlered crest, his cloven hoof,
    Brow, bay and tray and three aloof,
    The stag, the runnable stag.

For a matter of twenty miles and more,
    By the densest hedge and the highest wall,
Through herds of bullocks he baffled the lore
    Of harbourer, huntsmen, hounds and all,
    Of harbourer, hounds and all—
    The stag of warrant, the wily stag,
    For twenty miles, and five and five,
    He ran, and he never was caught alive,
    This stag, this runnable stag.

When he turned at bay in the leafy gloom,
    In the emerald gloom where the brook ran deep,
He heard in the distance the rollers boom,
    And he saw in a vision of peaceful sleep,
    In a wonderful vision of sleep,
    A stag of warrant, a stag, a stag,
    A runnable stag in a jewelled bed,
    Under the sheltering ocean dead,
    A stag, a runnable stag.

So a fateful hope lit up his eye,
    And he opened his nostrils wide again,
And he tossed his branching antlers high
    As he headed the hunt down Charlock glen,
    As he raced down the echoing glen
    For five miles more, the stag, the stag,
    For twenty miles, and five and five,
    Not to be caught now, dead or alive,
    The stag, the runnable stag.

Three hundred gentlemen, able to ride,
    Three hundred horses as gallant and free,
Beheld him escape on the evening tide,
    Far out till he sank in the Severn Sea,

Till he sank in the depths of the sea—
    The stag, the buoyant stag, the stag
    That slept at last in a jewelled bed
    Under the sheltering ocean spread,
    The stag, the runnable stag.

ॐ

## A PIG-TALE

### *Lewis Carroll*

There was a Pig that sat alone
    Beside a ruined Pump:
By day and night he made his moan—
It would have stirred a heart of stone
To see him wring his hoofs and groan,
    Because he could not jump.

A certain Camel heard him shout—
    A Camel with a hump.
"Oh, is it Grief, or is it Gout?
What is this bellowing about?"
That Pig replied, with quivering snout,
    "Because I cannot jump!"

That Camel scanned him, dreamy-eyed.
    "Methinks you are too plump.
I never knew a Pig so wide—
That wobbled so from side to side—
Who could, however much he tried,
    Do such a thing as jump!

"Yet mark those trees, two miles away,
    All clustered in a clump:
If you could trot there twice a day,

Not ever pause for rest or play,
In the far future—Who can say?—
    You may be fit to jump."

That Camel passed, and left him there,
    Beside the ruined Pump.
Oh, horrid was that Pig's despair!
His shrieks of anguish filled the air.
He wrung his hoofs, he rent his hair,
    Because he could not jump.

There was a Frog that wandered by—
    A sleek and shinning lump:
Inspected him with fishy eye,
And said "O Pig, what makes you cry?"
And bitter was that Pig's reply,
    "Because I cannot jump!"

That Frog he grinned a grin of glee,
    And hit his chest a thump.
"O Pig," he said, "be ruled by me,
And you shall see what you shall see.
This minute, for a trifling fee,
    I'll teach you how to jump!

"You may be faint from many a fall,
    And bruised by many a bump:
But, if you persevere through all,
And practise first on something small,
Concluding with a ten-foot wall,
    You'll find that you can jump!"

That Pig looked up with joyful start:
    "Oh Frog, you are a thump!
Your words have healed my inward smart—
Come, name your fee and do your part:
Bring comfort to a broken heart,
    By teaching me to jump!"

"My fee shall be a mutton-chop,
My goal this ruined Pump.
Observe with what an airy flop
I plant myself upon the top!
Now bend your knees and take a hop,
For that's the way to jump!"

Uprose that Pig, and rushed, full whack,
Against the ruined Pump:
Rolled over like an empty sack,
And settled down upon his back,
While all his bones at once went "Crack!"
It was a fatal jump.

That Camel passed, as Day grew dim
Around the ruined Pump.
"O broken heart! O broken limb!
It needs," that Camel said to him,
"Something more fairy-like and slim,
To execute a jump!".

That Pig lay still as any stone,
And could not stir a stump:
Nor ever, if the truth were known,
Was he again observed to moan,
Nor ever wring his hoofs and groan,
Because he could not jump.

That Frog made no remark, for he
Was dismal as a dump:
He knew the consequence must be
That he would never get his fee—
And still he sits, in miserie,
Upon that ruined Pump!

☙

# THE ELEPHANT'S CHILD

## Rudyard Kipling

In the High and Far-Off Times the Elephant, O Best Beloved, had no trunk. He had only a blackish, bulgy nose, as big as a boot, that he could wriggle about from side to side; but he couldn't pick up things with it. But there was one Elephant—a new Elephant—an Elephant's Child—who was full of 'satiable curtiosity, and that means he asked ever so many questions. *And* he lived in Africa, and he filled all Africa with his 'satiable curtiosities. He asked his tall aunt, the Ostrich, why her tail-feathers grew just so, and his tall aunt the Ostrich spanked him with her hard, hard claw. He asked his tall uncle, the Giraffe, what made his skin spotty, and his tall uncle, the Giraffe, spanked him with his hard, hard hoof. And still he was full of 'satiable curtiosity! He asked his broad aunt, the Hippopotamus, why her eyes were red, and his broad aunt, the Hippopotamus, spanked him with her broad, broad hoof; and he asked his hairy uncle, the Baboon, why melons tasted just so, and his hairy uncle, the Baboon, spanked him with his hairy, hairy paw. And *still* he was full of 'satiable curtiosity! He asked questions about everything that he saw, or heard, or felt, or smelt, or touched, and all his uncles and his aunts spanked him. And still he was full of 'satiable curtiosity!

One fine morning in the middle of the Precession of the Equinoxes this 'satiable Elephant's Child asked a new fine question that he had never asked before. He asked, "What does the Crocodile have for dinner?" Then everybody said, "Hush!" in a loud and dretful tone, and they spanked him immediately and directly, without stopping, for a long time.

By and by, when that was finished, he came upon Kolokolo Bird sitting in the middle of a wait-a-bit thorn-bush, and he said, "My father has spanked me, and my mother has spanked me; all my aunts and uncles have spanked me for my 'satiable curtiosity; and *still* I want to know what the Crocodile has for dinner!"

Then Kolokolo Bird said, with a mournful cry, "Go to the banks of the great grey-green, greasy Limpopo River, all set about with fever-trees, and find out."

That very next morning, when there was nothing left of the Equinoxes, because the Precession had preceded according to precedent, this 'satiable Elephant's Child took a hundred pounds of bananas (the little short red kind), and a hundred pounds of sugar-cane (the long purple kind), and seventeen melons (the greeny-crackly kind), and said to all his dear families, "Good-bye. I am going to the great grey-green, greasy Limpopo River, all set about with fever-trees, to find out what the Crocodile has for dinner." And they all spanked him once more for luck, though he asked them most politely to stop.

Then he went away, a little warm, but not at all astonished, eating melons, and throwing the rind about, because he could not pick it up.

He went from Graham's Town to Kimberley, and from Kimberley to Khama's Country, and from Khama's Country he went east by north, eating melons all the time, till at last he came to the banks of the great grey-green, greasy Limpopo River, all set about with fever-trees, precisely as Kolokolo Bird had said.

Now you must know and understand, O Best Beloved, that till that very week, and day, and hour, and minute, this 'satiable Elephant's Child had never seen a Crocodile, and did not know what one was like. It was all his 'satiable curtiosity.

The first thing that he found was a Bi-Coloured-Python-Rock-Snake curled round a rock.

"'Scuse me," said the Elephant's Child most politely, "but have you seen such a thing as a Crocodile in these promiscuous parts?"

"*Have* I seen a Crocodile?" said the Bi-Coloured-Python-Rock-Snake, in a voice of dretful scorn. "What will you ask me next?"

"'Scuse me," said the Elephant's Child, "but could you kindly tell me what he has for dinner?"

Then the Bi-Coloured-Python-Rock-Snake uncoiled himself very quickly from the rock, and spanked the Elephant's Child with his scalesome, flailsome tail.

"That is odd," said the Elephant's Child, "because my father and my mother, and my uncle and my aunt, not to mention my other aunt, the Hippopotamus, and my other uncle, the Baboon, have all spanked me for my 'satiable curtiosity—and I suppose this is the same thing."

So he said good-bye very politely to the Bi-Coloured-Python-Rock-Snake, and helped to coil him up on the rock again, and went on, a little warm, but not at all astonished, eating melons, and throwing the rind about, because he could not pick it up, till he trod on what he thought was a log of wood at the very edge of the great grey-green, greasy Limpopo River, all set about with fever-trees.

But it was really the Crocodile, O Best Beloved, and the Crocodile winked one eye—like this!

"'Scuse me," said the Elephant's Child most politely, "but do you happen to have seen a Crocodile in these promiscuous parts?"

Then the Crocodile winked the other eye, and lifted half his tail out of the mud; and the Elephant's Child stepped back most politely, because he did not wish to be spanked again.

"Come hither, Little One," said the Crocodile. "Why do you ask such things?"

"'Scuse me," said the Elephant's Child most politely, "but my father has spanked me, my mother has spanked me, not to mention my tall aunt, the Ostrich, and my tall uncle, the Giraffe, who can kick ever so hard, as well as my broad aunt, the Hippopotamus, and my hairy uncle, the Baboon, *and* including the Bi-Coloured-Python-Rock-Snake, with the scalesome, flailsome tail, just up the bank, who spanks harder than any of them; and *so,* if it's quite all the same to you, I don't want to be spanked any more."

"Come hither, Little One," said the Crocodile, "for I am the Crocodile," and he wept crocodile-tears to show it was quite true.

Then the Elephant's Child grew all breathless, and panted, and kneeled down on the bank and said, "You are the very person I have been looking for all these long days. Will you please tell me what you have for dinner?"

"Come hither, Little One," said the Crocodile, "and I'll whisper."

Then the Elephant's Child put his head down close to the Crocodile's musky, tusky mouth, and the Crocodile caught him by his little nose, which up to that very week, day, hour, and minute, had been no bigger than a boot, though much more useful.

"I think," said the Crocodile—and he said it between his teeth, like this—"I think to-day I will begin with Elephant's Child!"

At this, O Best Beloved, the Elephant's Child was much annoyed, and he said, speaking through his nose, like this, "Led go! You are hurtig be!"

Then the Bi-Coloured-Python-Rock-Snake scuffled down from the bank and said, "My young friend, if you do not now, immediately and instantly, pull as hard as ever you can, it is my opinion that your acquaintance in the large-pattern leather ulster" (and by this he meant the Crocodile) "will jerk you into yonder limpid stream before you can say Jack Robinson."

This is the way Bi-Coloured-Python-Rock-Snakes always talk.

Then the Elephant's Child sat back on his little haunches, and pulled, and pulled, and pulled, and his nose began to stretch. And the Crocodile floundered into the water, making it all creamy with great sweeps of his tail, and *he* pulled, and pulled, and pulled.

And the Elephant's Child's nose kept on stretching; and the Elephant's Child spread all his little four legs and pulled, and pulled, and pulled, and his nose kept on stretching; and the Crocodile threshed his tail like an oar, and *he* pulled, and pulled, and pulled, and at each pull the Elephant's Child's nose grew longer and longer—and it hurt him hijjus!

Then the Elephant's Child felt his legs slipping, and he said through his nose, which was now nearly five feet long, "This is too butch for be!"

Then the Bi-Coloured-Python-Rock-Snake came down from the bank, and knotted himself in a double-clove-hitch round the Elephant's Child's hind legs, and said, "Rash and inexperienced traveller, we will now seriously devote ourselves to a little high tension, because if we do not, it is my impression that yonder self-propelling man-of-war with the armour-plated upper deck" (and by this, O Best Beloved, he meant the Crocodile), "will permanently vitiate your future career."

That is the way all Bi-Coloured-Python-Rock-Snakes always talk.

So he pulled, and the Elephant's Child pulled, and the Crocodile pulled; but the Elephant's Child and the Bi-Coloured-Python-Rock-Snake pulled hardest; and at last the Crocodile let go of the Elephant's Child's nose with a plop that you could hear all up and down the Limpopo.

Then the Elephant's Child sat down most hard and sudden; but first he was careful to say "Thank you" to the Bi-Coloured-Python-Rock-Snake; and next he was kind to his poor pulled nose, and wrapped it all up in cool banana leaves, and hung it in the great grey-green, greasy Limpopo to cool.

"What are you doing that for?" said the Bi-Coloured-Python-Rock-Snake.

"'Scuse me," said the Elephant's Child, "but my nose is badly out of shape, and I am waiting for it to shrink."

"Then you will have to wait a long time," said the Bi-Coloured-Python-Rock-Snake. "Some people do not know what is good for them."

The Elephant's Child sat there for three days waiting for his nose to shrink. But it never grew any shorter, and, besides, it made him squint. For, O Best Beloved, you will see and understand that the Crocodile had pulled it out into a really truly trunk same as all Elephants have to-day.

At the end of the third day a fly came and stung him on the shoulder, and before he knew what he was doing he lifted up his trunk and hit that fly dead with the end of it.

"'Vantage number one!" said the Bi-Coloured-Python-Rock-Snake. "You couldn't have done that with a mere-smear nose. Try and eat a little now."

Before he thought what he was doing the Elephant's Child put out his trunk and plucked a large bundle of grass, dusted it clean against his fore-legs, and stuffed it into his own mouth.

"'Vantage number two!" said the Bi-Coloured-Python-Rock-Snake. "You couldn't have done that with a mere-smear nose. Don't you think the sun is very hot here?"

"It is," said the Elephant's Child, and before he thought what he was doing he schlooped up a schloop of mud from the banks of the great grey-green, greasy Limpopo, and slapped it on his head, where it made a cool schloopy-sloshy mud-cap all trickly behind his ears.

"'Vantage number three!" said the Bi-Coloured-Python-Rock-Snake. "You couldn't have done that with a mere-smear nose. Now how do you feel about being spanked again?"

"'Scuse me," said the Elephant's Child, "but I should not like it at all."

"How would you like to spank somebody?" said the Bi-Coloured-Python-Rock-Snake.

"I should like it very much indeed," said the Elephant's Child.

"Well," said the Bi-Coloured-Python-Rock-Snake, "you will find that new nose of yours very useful to spank people with."

"Thank you," said the Elephant's Child, "I'll remember that; and now I think I'll go home to all my dear families and try."

So the Elephant's Child went home across Africa frisking and whisk-ing his trunk. When he wanted fruit to eat he pulled fruit down from a tree, instead of waiting for it to fall as he used to do. When he wanted grass he plucked grass up from the ground, instead of going on his knees as he used to do. When the flies bit him he broke off the branch of a tree and used it as a fly-whisk; and he made himself a new, cool, slushy-squshy mud-cap whenever the sun was hot. When he felt lonely walking through Africa he sang to himself down his trunk, and the noise was louder than several brass bands. He went especially out of his way to find a broad Hippopotamus (she was no relation of his), and he spanked her very hard, to make sure that the Bi-Coloured-Python-Rock-Snake had spoken the truth about his new trunk. The rest of the time he picked up the melon rinds that he had dropped on his way to the Limpopo—for he was a Tidy Pachyderm.

One dark evening he came back to all his dear families, and he coiled up his trunk and said, "How do you do?" They were very glad to see him, and immediately said, "Come here and be spanked for your 'satiable cur-tiosity."

"Pooh," said the Elephant's Child. "I don't think you peoples know anything about spanking; but I do, and I'll show you."

Then he uncurled his trunk and knocked two of his dear brothers head over heels.

"O Bananas!" said they, "Where did you learn that trick, and what have you done to your nose?"

"I got a new one from the Crocodile on the banks of the great grey-green, greasy Limpopo River," said the Elephant's Child. "I asked him what he had for dinner, and he gave me this to keep."

"It looks very ugly," said his hairy uncle, the Baboon.

"It does," said the Elephant's Child. "But it's very useful," and he picked up his hairy uncle, the Baboon, by one hairy leg, and hove him into a hornets' nest.

Then that bad Elephant's Child spanked all his dear families for a long time, till they were very warm and greatly astonished. He pulled out his tall Ostrich aunt's tail-feathers; and he caught his tall uncle, the Giraffe, by the hindleg, and dragged him through a thorn-bush; and he shouted at his broad aunt, the Hippopotamus, and blew bubbles into her ear when she was sleeping in the water after meals; but he never let any one touch Kolokolo Bird.

At last things grew so exciting that his dear families went off one by one in a hurry to the banks of the great grey-green, greasy Limpopo River, all set about with fever-trees, to borrow new noses from the Crocodile. When they came back nobody spanked anybody any more; and ever since that day, O Best Beloved, all the Elephants you will ever see, besides all those that you won't, have trunks precisely like the trunk of the 'satiable Elephant's Child.

∾

# THE BOTTLE IMP

## *Robert Louis Stevenson*

There was a man of the Island of Hawaii, whom I shall call Keawe; for the truth is, he still lives, and his name must be kept secret; but the place of his birth was not far from Honaunau, where the bones of Keawe the Great lie hidden in a cave. This man was poor, brave, and active; he could read and write like a schoolmaster; he was a first-rate mariner besides, sailed for some time in the island steamers, and steered a whale-boat on the Hamakua coast.

At length it came in Keawe's mind to have a sight of the great world and foreign cities, and he shipped on a vessel bound to San Francisco.

This is a fine town, with a fine harbour, and rich people uncountable; and, in particular, there is one hill which is covered with palaces. Upon this hill Keawe was one day taking a walk with his pocket full of money, viewing the great houses upon either hand with pleasure. "What fine houses these are!" he was thinking, "and how happy must those people be who dwell in them, and take no care for the morrow!" The thought was in his mind when he came abreast of a house that was smaller than some others, but all finished and beautiful like a toy; the steps of that house shone like silver, and the borders of the garden bloomed like garlands, and the windows were bright like diamonds; and Keawe stopped and wondered at the excellence of all he saw. So stopping, he was aware of a man that looked forth upon him through a window so clear that Keawe could see him as you see a fish in a pool upon the reef. The man was elderly, with a bald head and a black beard, and his face was heavy with sorrow, and he bitterly sighed. And the truth of it is, that as Keawe looked in upon the man, and the man looked out upon Keawe, each envied the other.

All of a sudden, the man smiled and nodded, and beckoned Keawe to enter, and met him at the door of the house.

"This is a fine house of mine," said the man, and bitterly sighed. "Would you not care to view the chambers?"

So he led Keawe all over it, from the cellar to the roof, and there was nothing there that was not perfect of its kind, and Keawe was astonished.

"Truly," said Keawe, "this is a beautiful house; if I lived in the like of it, I should be laughing all day long. How comes it, then, that you should be sighing?"

"There is no reason," said the man, "why you should not have a house in all points similar to this, and finer, if you wish. You have some money, I suppose?"

"I have fifty dollars," said Keawe; "but a house like this will cost more than fifty dollars."

The man made a computation. "I am sorry you have no more," said he, "for it may raise you trouble in the future; but it shall be yours at fifty dollars."

"The house?" asked Keawe.

"No, not the house," replied the man; "but the bottle. For, I must tell you, although I appear to you so rich and fortunate, all my fortune, and this house itself and its garden, came out of a bottle not much bigger than a pint. This is it."

And he opened a lockfast place, and took out a round-bellied bottle with a long neck; the glass of it was white like milk, with changing rainbow colours in the grain. Within-sides something obscurely moved, like a shadow and a fire.

"This is the bottle," said the man; and, when Keawe laughed, "You do not believe me?" he added. "Try, then, for yourself. See if you can break it."

So Keawe took the bottle up and dashed it on the floor till he was weary; but it jumped on the floor like a child's ball, and was not injured.

"This is a strange thing," said Keawe. "For by the touch of it, as well as by the look, the bottle should be of glass."

"Of glass it is," replied the man, sighing more heavily than ever; "but the glass of it was tempered in the flames of hell. An imp lives in it, and that is the shadow we behold there moving: or so I suppose. If any man buy this bottle the imp is at his command; all that he desires—love, fame, money, houses like this house, ay, or a city like this city—all are his at the word uttered. Napoleon had this bottle, and by it he grew to be the king of the world; but he sold it at the last, and fell. Captain Cook had this bottle, and by it he found his way to so many islands; but he, too, sold it, and was slain upon Hawaii. For once it is sold, the power goes and the protection; and unless a man remain content with what he has, ill will befall him."

"And yet you talk of selling it yourself?" Keawe said.

"I have all I wish, and I am growing elderly," replied the man. "There is one thing the imp cannot do—he cannot prolong life; and, it would not be fair to conceal from you, there is a drawback to the bottle; for if a man die before he sells it, he must burn in hell for ever."

"To be sure, that is a drawback and no mistake," cried Keawe. "I would not meddle with the thing. I can do without a house, thank God; but there is one thing I could not be doing with one particle, and that is to be damned."

"Dear me, you must not run away with things," returned the man. "All you have to do is to use the power of the imp in moderation, and then sell it to someone else, as I do to you, and finish your life in comfort."

"Well, I observe two things," said Keawe. "All the time you keep sighing like a maid in love, that is one; and, for the other, you sell this bottle very cheap."

"I have told you already why I sigh," said the man. "It is because I fear my health is breaking up; and, as you said yourself, to die and go to the devil is a pity for anyone. As for why I sell so cheap, I must explain to you there is a peculiarity about the bottle. Long ago, when the devil brought it first upon earth, it was extremely expensive, and was sold first of all to Prester

John for many millions of dollars; but it cannot be sold at all, unless sold at a loss. If you sell it for as much as you paid for it, back it comes to you again like a homing pigeon. It follows that the price has kept falling in these centuries, and the bottle is now remarkably cheap. I bought it myself from one of my great neighbours on this hill, and the price I paid was only ninety dollars. I could sell it for as high as eighty-nine dollars and ninety-nine cents, but not a penny dearer, or back the thing must come to me. Now, about this there are two bothers. First, when you offer a bottle so singular for eighty odd dollars people suppose you to be jesting. And second—but there is no hurry about that—and I need not go into it. Only remember it must be coined money that you sell it for."

"How am I to know that this is all true?" asked Keawe.

"Some of it you can try at once," replied the man. "Give me your fifty dollars, take the bottle, and wish your fifty dollars back into your pocket. If that does not happen, I pledge you my honour I will cry off the bargain and restore your money."

"You are not deceiving me?" said Keawe.

The man bound himself with a great oath.

"Well, I will risk that much," said Keawe, "for that can do no harm." And he paid over his money to the man, and the man handed him the bottle.

"Imp of the bottle," said Keawe, "I want my fifty dollars back." And sure enough he had scarce said the word before his pocket was as heavy as ever.

"To be sure this is a wonderful bottle," said Keawe.

"And now good morning to you, my fine fellow, and the devil go with you for me!" said the man.

"Hold on," said Keawe, "I don't want any more of this fun. Here, take your bottle back."

"You have bought it for less than I paid for it," replied the man, rubbing his hands. "It is yours now; and, for my part, I am only concerned to see the back of you." And with that he rang for his Chinese servant, and had Keawe shown out of the house.

Now, when Keawe was in the street with the bottle under his arm, he began to think. "If all is true about this bottle, I may have made a losing bargain," thinks he. "But perhaps the man was only fooling me." The first thing he did was to count his money; the sum was exact—forty-nine dollars American money, and one Chili piece. "That looks like the truth," said Keawe. "Now I will try another part."

The streets in that part of the city were as clean as a ship's decks, and though it was noon, there were no passengers. Keawe set the bottle in the gutter and walked away. Twice he looked back, and there was the milky, round-bellied bottle where he left it. A third time he looked back, and turned a corner; but he had scarce done so, when something knocked upon his elbow, and, behold! it was the long neck sticking up; and as for the round belly, it was jammed into the pocket of his pilot-coat.

"And that looks like the truth," said Keawe.

The next thing he did was to buy a corkscrew in a shop, and go apart into a secret place in the fields. And there he tried to draw the cork, but as often as he put the screw in, out it came again, and the cork as whole as ever.

"This is some new sort of cork," said Keawe, and all at once he began to shake and sweat, for he was afraid of that bottle.

On his way back to the port-side, he saw a shop where a man sold shells and clubs from the wild islands, old heathen deities, old coined money, pictures from China and Japan, and all manner of things that sailors bring in their sea-chests. And here he had an idea. So he went in and offered the bottle for a hundred dollars. The man of the shop laughed at him at the first, and offered him five; but, indeed, it was a curious bottle—such glass was never blown in any human glassworks, so prettily the colours shone under the milky white, and so strangely the shadow hovered in the midst; so, after he had disputed awhile after the manner of his kind, the shopman gave Keawe sixty silver dollars for the thing, and set it on a shelf in the midst of his window. "Now," said Keawe, "I have sold that for sixty which I bought for fifty—or, to say truth, a little less, because one of my dollars was from Chili. Now I shall know the truth upon another point."

So he went back on board his ship, and, when he opened his chest, there was the bottle, and had come more quickly than himself. Now Keawe had a mate on board whose name was Lopaka.

"What ails you," said Lopaka, "that you stare in your chest?"

They were alone in the ship's forecastle, and Keawe bound him to secrecy, and told all.

"This is a very strange affair," said Lopaka; "and I fear you will be in trouble about this bottle. But there is one point very clear—that you are sure of the trouble, and you had better have the profit in the bargain. Make up your mind what you want with it; give the order, and if it is done as you desire, I will buy the bottle myself; for I have an idea of my own to get a schooner, and go trading through the islands."

"That is not my idea," said Keawe; "but to have a beautiful house and garden on the Kona Coast, where I was born, the sun shining in at the door, flowers in the garden, glass in the windows, pictures on the walls, and toys and fine carpets on the tables, for all the world like the house I was in this day—only a storey higher, and with balconies all about like the King's palace; and to live there without care and make merry with my friends and relatives."

"Well," said Lopaka, "let us carry it back with us to Hawaii; and if all comes true, as you suppose, I will buy the bottle, as I said, and ask a schooner."

Upon that they were agreed, and it was not long before the ship returned to Honolulu, carrying Keawe and Lopaka and the bottle. They were scarce come ashore when they met a friend upon the beach who began at once to condole with Keawe.

"I do not know what I am to be condoled about," said Keawe.

"Is it possible you have not heard," said the friend, "your uncle—that good old man—is dead, and your cousin—that beautiful boy—was drowned at sea?"

Keawe was filled with sorrow, and, beginning to weep and to lament, he forgot about the bottle. But Lopaka was thinking to himself, and presently when Keawe's grief was a little abated, "I have been thinking," said Lopaka. "Had not your uncle lands in Hawaii, in the district of Kaü?"

"No," said Keawe, "not in Kaü; they are on the mountainside—a little way south of Hookena."

"These lands will now be yours?" asked Lopaka.

"And so they will," says Keawe, and began again to lament for his relatives.

"No," said Lopaka, "do not lament at present. I have a thought in my mind. How if this should be the doing of the bottle? For here is the place ready for your house."

"If this be so," cried Keawe, "it is a very ill way to serve me by killing my relatives. But it may be, indeed; for it was in just such a station that I saw the house with my mind's eye."

"The house, however, is not yet built," said Lopaka.

"No, nor like to be!" said Keawe; "for though my uncle has some coffee and ava and bananas, it will not be more than will keep me in comfort; and the rest of that land is the black lava."

"Let us go to the lawyer," said Lopaka; "I have still this idea in my mind."

Now, when they came to the lawyer's, it appeared Keawe's uncle had grown monstrous rich in the last days, and there was a fund of money.

"And here is the money for the house!" cries Lopaka.

"If you are thinking of a new house," said the lawyer, "here is the card of a new architect, of whom they tell me great things."

"Better and better!" cried Lopaka. "Here is all made plain for us. Let us continue to obey orders."

So they went to the architect, and he had drawings of houses on his table.

"You want something out of the way," said the architect. "How do you like this?" and he handed a drawing to Keawe.

Now, when Keawe set eyes on the drawing, he cried out aloud, for it was the picture of his thought exactly drawn.

"I am in for this house," thought he. "Little as I like the way it comes to me, I am in for it now, and I may as well take the good along with the evil."

So he told the architect all that he wished, and how he would have that house furnished, and about the pictures on the wall and the knick-knacks on the tables; and he asked the man plainly for how much he would undertake the whole affair.

The architect put many questions, and took his pen and made a computation; and when he had done he named the very sum that Keawe had inherited.

Lopaka and Keawe looked at one another and nodded.

"It is quite clear," thought Keawe, "that I am to have this house, whether or no. It comes from the devil, and I fear I will get little good by that; and of one thing I am sure, I will make no more wishes as long as I have this bottle. But with the house I am saddled, and I may as well take the good along with the evil."

So he made his terms with the architect, and they signed a paper; and Keawe and Lopaka took ship again and sailed to Australia; for it was concluded between them they should not interfere at all, but leave the architect and the bottle imp to build and to adorn that house at their own pleasure.

The voyage was a good voyage, only all the time Keawe was holding in his breath, for he had sworn he would utter no more wishes, and take no more favours from the devil. The time was up when they got back. The architect told them that the house was ready, and Keawe and Lopaka took a passage in the *Hall,* and went down Kona way to view the house, and see if all had been done fitly according to the thought that was in Keawe's mind.

Now, the house stood on the mountain-side, visible to ships. Above, the forest ran up into the clouds of rain; below, the black lava fell in cliffs, where the kings of old lay buried. A garden bloomed about that house with every hue of flowers; and there was an orchard of papaia on the one hand and an orchard of breadfruit on the other, and right in front, toward the sea, a ship's mast had been rigged up and bore a flag. As for the house, it was three storeys high, with great chambers and broad balconies on each. The windows were of glass, so excellent that it was as clear as water and as bright as day. All manner of furniture adorned the chambers. Pictures hung upon the wall in golden frames: pictures of ships, and men fighting, and of the most beautiful women, and of singular places; nowhere in the world are there pictures of so bright a colour as those Keawe found hanging in his house. As for the knick-knacks, they were extraordinary fine; chiming clocks and musical boxes, little men with nodding heads, books filled with pictures, weapons of price from all quarters of the world, and the most elegant puzzles to entertain the leisure of a solitary man. And as no one would care to live in such chambers, only to walk through and view them, the balconies were made so broad that a whole town might have lived upon them in delight; and Keawe knew not which to prefer, whether the back porch, where you got the land breeze, and looked upon the orchards and the flowers, or the front balcony, where you could drink the wind of the sea, and look down the steep wall of the mountain and see the *Hall* going by once a week or so between Hookena and the hills of Pele, or the schooners plying up the coast for wood and ava and bananas.

When they had viewed all, Keawe and Lopaka sat on the porch.

"Well," asked Lopaka, "is it all as you designed?"

"Words cannot utter it," said Keawe. "It is better than I dreamed, and I am sick with satisfaction."

"There is but one thing to consider," said Lopaka; "all this may be quite natural, and the bottle imp have nothing whatever to say to it. If I were to buy the bottle, and got no schooner after all, I should have put my hand in the fire for nothing. I gave you my word, I know; but yet I think you would not grudge me one more proof."

"I have sworn I would take no more favours," said Keawe. "I have gone already deep enough."

"This is no favour I am thinking of," replied Lopaka. "It is only to see the imp himself. There is nothing to be gained by that, and so nothing to be ashamed of; and yet, if I once saw him, I should be sure of the whole matter. So indulge me so far, and let me see the imp; and, after that, here is the money in my hand, and I will buy it."

"There is only one thing I am afraid of," said Keawe. "The imp may be very ugly to view; and if you once set eyes upon him you might be very undesirous of the bottle."

"I am a man of my word," said Lopaka. "And here is the money betwixt us."

"Very well," replied Keawe. "I have a curiosity myself. So come, let us have one look at you, Mr. Imp."

Now as soon as that was said, the imp looked out of the bottle, and in again, swift as a lizard; and there sat Keawe and Lopaka turned to stone. The night had quite come, before either found a thought to say or voice to say it with; and then Lopaka pushed the money over and took the bottle.

"I am a man of my word," said he, "and had need to be so, or I would not touch this bottle with my foot. Well, I shall get my schooner and a dollar or two for my pocket; and then I will be rid of this devil as fast as I can. For, to tell you the plain truth, the look of him has cast me down."

"Lopaka," said Keawe, "do not you think any worse of me than you can help; I know it is night, and the roads bad, and the pass by the tombs an ill place to go by so late, but I declare since I have seen that little face, I cannot eat or sleep or pray till it is gone from me. I will give you a lantern, and a basket to put the bottle in, and any picture or fine thing in all my house that takes your fancy;—and be gone at once, and go sleep at Hookena with Nahinu."

"Keawe," said Lopaka, "many a man would take this ill; above all, when I am doing you a turn so friendly, as to keep my word and buy the bottle; and for that matter, the night and the dark, and the way by the tombs, must be all tenfold more dangerous to a man with such a sin upon his conscience, and such a bottle under his arm. But for my part, I am so extremely terrified myself, I have not the heart to blame you. Here I go then; and I pray God you may be happy in your house, and I fortunate with my schooner, and both get to Heaven in the end in spite of the devil and his bottle."

So Lopaka went down the mountain; and Keawe stood in his front balcony, and listened to the clink of the horse's shoes, and watched the lantern go shining down the path, and along the cliff of caves where the old dead are buried; and all the time he trembled and clasped his hands, and prayed for his friend, and gave glory to God that he himself was escaped out of that trouble.

But the next day came very brightly, and that new house of his was so delightful to behold that he forgot his terrors. One day followed another, and Keawe dwelt there in perpetual joy. He had his place on the back porch; it was there he ate and lived, and read the stories in the Honolulu newspapers; but when anyone came by they would go in and view the chambers and the pictures. And the fame of the house went far and wide; it was called *Ka-Hale Nui*—the Great House—in all Kona; and sometimes the Bright

House, for Keawe kept a Chinaman, who was all day dusting and fur-
bishing; and the glass, and the gilt, and the fine stuffs, and the pictures,
shone as bright as the morning. As for Keawe himself, he could not walk
in the chambers without singing, his heart was so enlarged; and when ships
sailed by upon the sea, he would fly his colours on the mast.

So time went by, until one day Keawe went upon a visit as far as
Kailua to certain of his friends. There he was well feasted; and left as soon
as he could the next morning, and rode hard, for he was impatient to
behold his beautiful house; and, besides, the night then coming on was the
night in which the dead of old days go abroad in the sides of Kona; and
having already meddled with the devil, he was the more chary of meeting
with the dead. A little beyond Honaunau, looking far ahead, he was
aware of a woman bathing in the edge of the sea; and she seemed a well-
grown girl, but he thought no more of it. Then he saw her white shift flutter as she put it on, and then her red holoku; and by the time he came
abreast of her she was done with her toilet, and had come up from the sea,
and stood by the track-side in her red holoku, and she was all freshened
with the bath, and her eyes shone and were kind. Now Keawe no sooner
beheld her than he drew rein.

"I thought I knew every one in this country," said he. "How comes it
that I do not know you?"

"I am Kokua, daughter of Kiano," said the girl, "and I have just
returned from Oahu. Who are you?"

"I will tell you who I am in a little," said Keawe, dismounting from his
horse, "but not now. For I have a thought in my mind, and if you knew who
I was, you might have heard of me, and would not give me a true answer.
But tell me, first of all, one thing: Are you married?"

At this Kokua laughed out aloud. "It is you who ask questions," she
said. "Are you married yourself?"

"Indeed, Kokua, I am not," replied Keawe, "and never thought to be
until this hour. But here is the plain truth. I have met you here at the road-
side, and I saw your eyes which are like the stars, and my heart went to you
as swift as a bird. And so now, if you want none of me, say so, and I will go
to my own place; but if you think me no worse than any other young man,
say so, too, and I will turn aside to your father's for the night, and tomorrow I will talk with the good man."

Kokua said never a word, but she looked at the sea and laughed.

"Kokua," said Keawe, "if you say nothing, I will take that for the
good answer; so let us be stepping to your father's door."

She went on ahead of him, still without speech; only sometimes she glanced back and glanced away again, and she kept the strings of her hat in her mouth.

Now, when they had come to the door, Kiano came out on his veranda, and cried out and welcomed Keawe by name. At that the girl looked over, for the fame of the great house had come to her ears; and, to be sure, it was a great temptation. All that evening they were very merry together; and the girl was as bold as brass under the eyes of her parents, and made a mock of Keawe, for she had a quick wit. The next day he had a word with Kiano, and found the girl alone.

"Kokua," said he, "you made a mock of me all the evening; and it is still time to bid me go. I would not tell you who I was, because I have so fine a house, and I feared you would think too much of that house and too little of the man who loves you. Now you know all, and if you wish to have seen the last of me, say so at once."

"No," said Kokua; but this time she did not laugh, nor did Keawe ask for more.

This was the wooing of Keawe; things had gone quickly; but so an arrow goes, and the ball of a rifle swifter still, and yet both may strike the target. Things had gone fast, but they had gone far also, and the thought of Keawe rang in the maiden's head; she heard his voice in the breach of the surf upon the lava, and for this young man that she had seen but twice she would have left father and mother and her native islands. As for Keawe himself, his horse flew up the path of the mountain under the cliff of tombs, and the sound of the hoofs, and the sound of Keawe singing to himself for pleasure, echoed in the caverns of the dead. He came to the Bright House, and still he was singing. He sat and ate in the broad balcony, and the Chinaman wondered at his master, to hear how he sang between the mouthfuls. The sun went down into the sea, and the night came; and Keawe walked the balconies by lamplight, high on the mountains, and the voice of his singing startled men on ships.

"Here am I now upon my high place," he said to himself. "Life may be no better; this is the mountain top: and all shelves about me toward the worse. For the first time I will light up the chambers, and bathe in my fine bath with the hot water and the cold, and sleep alone in the bed of my bridal chamber."

So the Chinaman had word, and he must rise from sleep and light the furnaces; and as he wrought below, beside the boilers, he heard his master singing and rejoicing above him in the lighted chambers. When the water began to be hot the Chinaman cried to his master; and Keawe went into the bathroom; and the Chinaman heard him sing as he filled the marble basin;

and heard him sing, and the singing broken, as he undressed; until of a sudden, the song ceased. The Chinaman listened, and listened; he called up the house to Keawe to ask if all were well, and Keawe answered him "Yes," and bade him go to bed; but there was no more singing in the Bright House; and all night long, the Chinaman heard his master's feet go round and round the balconies without repose.

Now the truth of it was this: as Keawe undressed for his bath, he spied upon his flesh a patch like a patch of lichen on a rock, and it was then that he stopped singing. For he knew the likeness of that patch, and knew that he was fallen in the Chinese Evil.[*]

Now, it is a sad thing for any man to fall into this sickness. And it would be a sad thing for any one to leave a house so beautiful and so commodious, and depart from all his friends to the north coast of Molokai between the mighty cliff and the sea-breakers. But what was that to the case of the man Keawe, he who had met his love but yesterday, and won her but that morning, and now saw all his hopes break, in a moment, like a piece of glass?

Awhile he sat upon the edge of the bath; then sprang, with a cry, and ran outside; and to and fro, to and fro, along the balcony, like one despairing.

"Very willingly could I leave Hawaii, the home of my fathers," Keawe was thinking. "Very lightly could I leave my house, the high-placed, the many-windowed, here upon the mountains. Very bravely could I go to Molokai, to Kalaupapa by the cliffs, to live with the smitten and to sleep there, far from my fathers. But what wrong have I done, what sin lies upon my soul, that I should have encountered Kokua coming cool from the seawater in the evening? Kokua, the soul ensnarer! Kokua, the light of my life! Her may I never wed, her may I look upon no longer, her may I no more handle with my loving hand; and it is for this, it is for you, O Kokua! that I pour my lamentations!"

Now you are to observe what sort of a man Keawe was, for he might have dwelt there in the Bright House for years, and no one been the wiser of his sickness; but he reckoned nothing of that, if he must lose Kokua. And again, he might have wed Kokua even as he was; and so many would have done, because they have the souls of pigs; but Keawe loved the maid manfully, and he would do her no hurt and bring her in no danger.

A little beyond the midst of the night, there came in his mind the recollection of that bottle. He went round to the back porch, and called to memory the day when the devil had looked forth; and at the thought ice ran in his veins.

[*]Leprosy

"A dreadful thing is the bottle," thought Keawe, "and dreadful is the imp, and it is a dreadful thing to risk the flames of hell. But what other hope have I to cure my sickness or to wed Kokua? What!" he thought, "would I beard the devil once, only to get me a house, and not face him again to win Kokua?"

Thereupon he called to mind it was the next day the *Hall* went by on her return to Honolulu. "There must I go first," he thought," and see Lopaka. For the best hope that I have now is to find that same bottle I was so pleased to be rid of."

Never a wink could he sleep; the food stuck in his throat; but he sent a letter to Kiano, and about the time when the steamer would be coming, rode down beside the cliff of the tombs. It rained; his horse went heavily; he looked up at the black mouths of the caves, and he envied the dead that slept there and were done with trouble; and called to mind how he had galloped by the day before, and was astonished. So he came down to Hookena, and there was all the country gathered for the steamer as usual. In the shed before the store they sat and jested and passed the news; but there was no matter of speech in Keawe's bosom, and he sat in their midst and looked without on the rain falling on the houses, and the surf beating among the rocks, and the sighs arose in his throat.

"Keawe of the Bright House is out of spirits," said one to another. Indeed, and so he was, and little wonder.

Then the *Hall* came, and the whale-boat carried him on board. The after-part of the ship was full of Haoles* who had been to visit the volcano, as their custom is; and the midst was crowded with Kanakas, and the fore-part with wild bulls from Hilo and horses from Kaü; but Keawe sat apart from all in his sorrow, and watched for the house of Kiano. There it sat, low upon the shore in the black rocks, and shaded by the cocoa-palms, and there by the door was a red holoku, no greater than a fly, and going to and fro with a fly's busyness. "Ah, queen of my heart," he cried, "I'll venture my dear soul to win you!"

Soon after, darkness fell, and the cabins were lit up, and the Haoles sat and played at the cards and drank whisky as their custom is; but Keawe walked the deck all night; and all the next day, as they steamed under the lee of Maui or of Molokai, he was still pacing to and fro like a wild animal in a menagerie.

Towards evening they passed Diamond Head, and came to the pier of Honolulu. Keawe stepped out among the crowd and began to ask for

*Whites

Lopaka. It seemed he had become the owner of a schooner—none better in the islands—and was gone upon an adventure as far as Pola-Pola or Kahiki; so there was no help to be looked for from Lopaka. Keawe called to mind a friend of his, a lawyer in the town (I must not tell his name), and inquired of him. They said he had grown suddenly rich, and had a fine new house upon Waikiki shore; and this put a thought in Keawe's head, and he called a hack and drove to the lawyer's house.

The house was all brand new, and the trees in the garden no greater than walking-sticks, and the lawyer, when he came, had the air of a man well pleased.

"What can I do to serve you?" said the lawyer.

"You are a friend of Lopaka's," replied Keawe, "and Lopaka purchased from me a certain piece of goods that I thought you might enable me to trace."

The lawyer's face became very dark. "I do not profess to misunderstand you, Mr. Keawe," said he, "though this is an ugly business to be stirring in. You may be sure I know nothing, but yet I have a guess, and if you would apply in a certain quarter I think you might have news."

And he named the name of a man, which, again, I had better not repeat. So it was for days, and Keawe went from one to another, finding everywhere new clothes and carriages, and fine new houses and men everywhere in great contentment, although to be sure, when he hinted at his business their faces would cloud over.

"No doubt I am upon the track," thought Keawe. "These new clothes and carriages are all the gifts of the little imp, and these glad faces are the faces of men who have taken their profit and got rid of the accursed thing in safety. When I see pale cheeks and hear sighing, I shall know that I am near the bottle."

So it befell at last that he was recommended to a Haole in Beritania Street. When he came to the door, about the hour of the evening meal, there were the usual marks of the new house, and the young garden, and the electric light shining in the windows; but when the owner came, a shock of hope and fear ran through Keawe; for here was a young man, white as a corpse, and black about the eyes, the hair shedding from his head, and such a look in his countenance as a man may have when he is waiting for the gallows.

"Here it is, to be sure," thought Keawe, and so with this man he noways veiled his errand. "I am come to buy the bottle," said he.

At the word, the young Haole of Beritania Street reeled against the wall.

"The bottle!" he gasped. "To buy the bottle!" Then he seemed to choke, and seizing Keawe by the arm carried him into a room and poured out wine in two glasses.

"Here is my respects," said Keawe, who had been much about with Haoles in his time. "Yes," he added, "I am come to buy the bottle. What is the price by now?"

At that word the young man let his glass slip through his fingers, and looked upon Keawe like a ghost.

"The price," says he; "the price! You do not know the price?"

"It is for that I am asking you," returned Keawe. "But why are you so much concerned? Is there anything wrong about the price?"

"It has dropped a great deal in value since your time, Mr. Keawe," said the young man, stammering.

"Well, well, I shall have the less to pay for it," says Keawe. "How much did it cost you?"

The young man was as white as a sheet. "Two cents," said he.

"What?" cried Keawe, "two cents? Why, then, you can only sell it for one. And he who buys it—" The words died upon Keawe's tongue; he who bought it could never sell it again, the bottle and the bottle imp must abide with him until he died, and when he died must carry him to the red end of hell.

The young man of Beritania Street fell upon his knees. "For God's sake buy it!" he cried. "You can have all my fortune in the bargain. I was mad when I bought it at that price. I had embezzled money at my store; I was lost else; I must have gone to jail."

"Poor creature," said Keawe, "you would risk your soul upon so desperate an adventure, and to avoid the proper punishment of your own disgrace; and you think I could hesitate with love in front of me. Give me the bottle, and the change which I make sure you have all ready. Here is a five-cent piece."

It was as Keawe supposed; the young man had the change ready in a drawer; the bottle changed hands, and Keawe's fingers were no sooner clasped upon the stalk than he had breathed his wish to be a clean man. And, sure enough, when he got home to his room, and stripped himself before a glass, his flesh was whole like an infant's. And here was the strange thing: he had no sooner seen this miracle than his mind was changed within him, and he cared naught for the Chinese Evil, and little enough for Kokua; and had but the one thought, that here he was bound to the bottle imp for time and for eternity, and had no better hope but to be a cinder for ever in the flames of hell. Away ahead of him he saw them blaze with his mind's eye, and his soul shrank, and darkness fell upon the light.

When Keawe came to himself a little, he was aware it was the night when the band played at the hotel. Thither he went, because he feared to be alone; and there, among happy faces, walked to and fro, and heard the tunes go up and down, and saw Berger beat the measure, and all the while he heard the flames crackle, and saw the red fire burning in the bottomless pit. Of a sudden the band played *Hiki-ao-ao,* that was a song that he had sung with Kokua, and at the strain courage returned to him.

"It is done now," he thought, "and once more let me take the good along with the evil."

So it befell that he returned to Hawaii by the first steamer, and as soon as it could be managed he was wedded to Kokua, and carried her up the mountain-side to the Bright House.

Now it was so with these two, that when they were together, Keawe's heart was stilled; but so soon as he was alone, he fell into a brooding horror, and heard the flames crackle, and saw the red fire burn in the bottomless pit. The girl, indeed, had come to him wholly; her heart leapt in her side at sight of him, her hand clung to his; and she was so fashioned from the hair upon her head to the nails upon her toes that none could see her without joy. She was pleasant in her nature. She had the good word always. Full of song she was, and went to and fro in the Bright House, the brightest thing in its three storeys, carolling like the birds. And Keawe beheld and heard her with delight, and then must shrink upon one side, and weep and groan to think upon the price that he had paid for her; and then he must dry his eyes, and wash his face, and go and sit with her on the broad balconies, joining in her songs, and, with a sick spirit, answering her smiles.

There came a day when her feet began to be heavy and her songs more rare; and now it was not Keawe only that would weep apart, but each would sunder from the other and sit in opposite balconies with the whole width of the Bright House betwixt. Keawe was so sunk in his despair, he scarce observed the change and was only glad he had more hours to sit alone and brood upon his destiny, and was not so frequently condemned to pull a smiling face on a sick heart. But one day, coming softly through the house, he heard the sound of a child sobbing, and there was Kokua rolling her face upon the balcony floor, and weeping like the lost.

"You do well to weep in this house, Kokua," he said. "And yet I would give the head off my body that you (at least) might have been happy."

"Happy!" she cried. "Keawe, when you lived alone in your Bright House, you were the word of the island for a happy man; laughter and song were in your mouth, and your face was as bright as the sunrise. Then you wedded poor Kokua; and the good God knows what is amiss in her—but from that day you have not smiled. Oh!" she cried, "what ails me? I thought I was pretty, and I knew I loved him. What ails me that I throw this cloud upon my husband?"

"Poor Kokua," said Keawe. He sat down by her side, and sought to take her hand; but that she plucked away. "Poor Kokua," he said, again. "My poor child—my pretty. And I had thought all this while to spare you! Well, you shall know all. Then, at least, you will pity poor Keawe; then you will understand how much he loved you in the past—that he dared hell for your possession—and how much he loves you still (the poor condemned one), that he can yet call up a smile when he beholds you."

With that, he told her all, even from the beginning.

"You have done this for me?" she cried. "Ah, well, then what do I care!"—and she clasped and wept upon him.

"Ah, child!" said Keawe, "and yet, when I consider of the fire of hell, I care a good deal!"

"Never tell me," said she; "no man can be lost because he loved Kokua, and no other fault. I tell you, Keawe, I shall save you with these hands, or perish in your company. What! you loved me, and gave your soul, and you think I will not die to save you in return?"

"Ah, my dear! you might die a hundred times, and what difference would that make?" he cried, "except to leave me lonely till the time comes of my damnation?"

"You know nothing," said she, "I was educated in a school in Honolulu; I am no common girl. And I tell you, I shall save my lover. What is this you say about a cent? But all the world is not American. In England they have a piece they call a farthing, which is about half a cent. Ah! sorrow!" she cried, "that makes it scarcely better, for the buyer must be lost, and we shall find none so brave as my Keawe! But, then, there is France; they have a small coin there which they call a centime, and these go five to the cent or thereabout. We could not do better. Come, Keawe, let us go to the French islands; let us go to Tahiti, as fast as ships can bear us. There we have four centimes, three centimes, two centimes, one centime; four possible sales to come and go on; and two of us to push the bargain. Come, my Keawe! kiss me, and banish care. Kokua will defend you."

"Gift of God!" he cried. "I cannot think that God will punish me for desiring aught so good! be it as you will, then; take me where you please: I put my life and my salvation in your hands."

Early the next day Kokua was about her preparations. She took

Keawe's chest that he went with sailoring; and first she put the bottle in a corner; and then packed it with the richest of their clothes and the bravest of the knick-knacks in the house. "For," said she, "we must seem to be rich folks, or who will believe in the bottle?" All the time of her preparation she was as gay as a bird; only when she looked upon Keawe, the tears would spring in her eye, and she must run and kiss him. As for Keawe, a weight was off his soul; now that he had his secret shared, and some hope in front of him, he seemed like a new man, his feet went lightly on the earth, and his breath was good to him again. Yet was terror still at his elbow; and ever and again, as the wind blows out a taper, hope died in him, and he saw the flames toss and the red fire burn in hell.

It was given out in the country they were gone pleasuring to the States, which was thought a strange thing, and yet not so strange as the truth, if any could have guessed it. So they went to Honolulu in the *Hall,* and thence in the *Umatilla* to San Francisco with a crowd of Haoles, and at San Francisco took their passage by the mail brigantine, the *Tropic Bird,* for Papeete, the chief place of the French in the south islands. Thither they came, after a pleasant voyage, on a fair day of the Trade Wind, and saw the reef with the surf breaking, and Motuiti with its palms, and the schooner riding withinside, and the white houses of the town low down along the shore among green trees, and overhead the mountains and the clouds of Tahiti, the wise island.

It was judged the most wise to hire a house, which they did accordingly, opposite the British Consul's, to make a great parade of money, and themselves conspicuous with carriages and horses. This it was very easy to do, so long as they had the bottle in their possession; for Kokua was more bold than Keawe, and, whenever she had a mind, called on the imp for twenty or a hundred dollars. At this rate they soon grew to be remarked in the town; and the strangers from Hawaii, their riding and their driving, the fine holokus and the rich lace of Kokua, became the matter of much talk.

They got on well after the first with the Tahitian language, which is indeed like to the Hawaiian, with a change of certain letters; and as soon as they had any freedom of speech, began to push the bottle. You are to consider it was not an easy subject to introduce it; it was not easy to persuade people you were in earnest, when you offered to sell them for four centimes the spring of health and riches inexhaustible. It was necessary besides to explain the dangers of the bottle; and either people disbelieved the whole thing and laughed, or they thought the more of the darker part, became overcast with gravity, and drew away from Keawe and Kokua, as from persons who had dealings with the devil. So far from gaining ground, these two began to find they were avoided in the town; the children ran away from them screaming, a thing intolerable to Kokua; Catholics crossed themselves as they went by, and all persons began with one accord to disengage themselves from their advances.

Depression fell upon their spirits. They would sit at night in their new house, after a day's weariness, and not exchange one word, or the silence would be broken by Kokua bursting suddenly into sobs. Sometimes they would pray together; sometimes they would have the bottle out upon the floor, and sit all the evening watching how the shadow hovered in the midst. At such times they would be afraid to go to rest. It was long ere slumber came to them, and if either dozed off, it would be to wake and find the other silently weeping in the dark, or, perhaps, to wake alone, the other having fled from the house and the neighbourhood of that bottle, to pace under the bananas in the little garden, or to wander on the beach by moonlight.

One night it was so when Kokua awoke. Keawe was gone. She felt in the bed and his place was cold. Then fear fell upon her and she sat up in bed. A little moonshine filtered through the shutters. The room was bright, and she could spy the bottle on the floor. Outside it blew high, the great trees of the avenue cried aloud, and the fallen leaves rattled in the veranda. In the midst of this Kokua was aware of another sound; whether of a beast or of a man she could scarce tell, but it was as sad as death, and cut her to the soul. Softly she arose, set the door ajar, and looked forth into the moonlit yard. There, under the bananas, lay Keawe, his mouth in the dust, and as he lay he moaned.

It was Kokua's first thought to run forward and console him; her second potently withheld her. Keawe had borne himself before his wife like a brave man; it became her little in the hour of weakness to intrude upon his shame. With the thought she drew back into the house.

"Heaven!" she thought, "how careless have I been—how weak! It is he, not I, that stands in this eternal peril; it was he not I, that took the curse upon his soul. It is for my sake, and for the love of a creature of so little worth and such poor help, that he now beholds so close to him the flames of hell—ay, and smells the smoke of it, lying without there in the wind and moonlight. Am I so dull of spirit that never till now I have surmised my duty, or have I seen it before and turned aside? But now, at least, I take up my soul in both the hands of my affection; now I say farewell to the white steps of heaven and the waiting faces of my friends. A love for a love, and let mine be equalled with Keawe's! A soul for a soul, and be it mine to perish!"

She was a deft woman with her hands, and was soon apparelled. She took in her hands the change—the precious centimes they kept ever at their side; for this coin is little used, and they had made provision at a Government office. When she was forth in the avenue, clouds came on the wind and the moon was blackened. The town slept, and she knew not whither to turn till she heard one coughing in the shadow of the trees.

"Old man," said Kokua, "what do you here abroad in the cold night?"

The old man could scarce express himself for coughing, but she made out that he was old and poor, and a stranger in the island.

"Will you do me a service?" said Kokua. "As one stranger to another, and as an old man to a young woman, will you help a daughter of Hawaii?"

"Ah," said the old man. "So you are the witch from the Eight Islands, and even my old soul you seek to entangle. But I have heard of you, and defy your wickedness."

"Sit down here," said Kokua, "and let me tell you a tale." And she told him the story of Keawe from the beginning to the end.

"And now," said she, "I am his wife, whom he bought with his soul's welfare. And what should I do? If I went to him myself and offered to buy it, he would refuse. But if you go, he will sell it eagerly; I will await you here: you will buy it for four centimes, and I will buy it again for three. And the Lord strengthen a poor girl!"

"If you meant falsely," said the old man, "I think God would strike you dead."

"He would!" cried Kokua. "Be sure he would. I could not be so treacherous— God would not suffer it."

"Give me the four centimes and await me here," said the old man.

Now, when Kokua stood alone in the street, her spirit died. The wind roared in the trees, and it seemed to her the rushing of the flames of hell; the shadows tossed in the light of the street lamp, and they seemed to her the snatching hands of evil ones. If she had had the strength, she must have run away, and if she had had the breath she must have screamed aloud; but, in truth, she could do neither, and stood and trembled in the avenue, like an affrighted child.

Then she saw the old man returning, and he had the bottle in his hand.

"I have done your bidding," said he. "I left your husband weeping like a child; tonight he will sleep easy." And he held the bottle forth.

"Before you give it me," Kokua panted. "take the good with the evil—ask to be delivered from your cough."

"I am an old man," replied the other, "and too near the gate of the grave to take a favour from the devil. But what is this? Why do you not take the bottle? Do you hesitate?"

"Not hesitate!" cried Kokua. "I am only weak. Give me a moment. It is my hand resists, my flesh shrinks back from the accursed thing. One moment only!"

The old man looked upon Kokua kindly. "Poor child!" said he, "you fear; your soul misgives you. Well, let me keep it. I am old, and can never more be happy in this world, and as for the next——"

"Give it me!" gasped Kokua. "There is your money. Do you think I am so base as that? Give me the bottle."

"God bless you, child," said the old man.

Kokua concealed the bottle under her holoku, said farewell to the old man, and walked off along the avenue, she cared not whither. For all roads were now the same to her, and led equally to hell. Sometimes she walked, and sometimes ran; sometimes she screamed out loud in the night, and sometimes lay by the wayside in the dust and wept. All that she had heard of hell came back to her; she saw the flames blaze, and she smelt the smoke, and her flesh withered on the coals.

Near day she came to her mind again, and returned to the house. It was even as the old man said—Keawe slumbered like a child. Kokua stood and gazed upon his face.

"Now, my husband," said she, "it is your turn to sleep. When you wake it will be your turn to sing and laugh. But for poor Kokua, alas! that meant no evil—for poor Kokua no more sleep, no more singing, no more delight, whether in earth or Heaven."

With that she lay down in the bed by his side, and her misery was so extreme that she fell in a deep slumber instantly.

Late in the morning her husband woke her and gave her the good news. It seemed he was silly with delight, for he paid no heed to her distress, ill though she dissembled it. The words stuck in her mouth, it mattered not; Keawe did the speaking. She ate not a bite, but who was to observe it? for Keawe cleared the dish. Kokua saw and heard him, like some strange thing in a dream; there were times when she forgot or doubted, and put her hands to her brow; to know herself doomed and hear her husband babble, seemed so monstrous.

All this while Keawe was eating and talking, and planning the time of their return, and thanking her for saving him, and fondling her, and calling her the true helper after all. He laughed at the old man that was fool enough to buy that bottle.

"A worthy old man he seemed," Keawe said. "But no one can judge by appearances. For why did the old reprobate require the bottle?"

"My husband," said Kokua humbly, "his purpose may have been good."

Keawe laughed like an angry man.

"Fiddle-de-dee!" cried Keawe. "An old rogue, I tell you; and an old ass to boot. For the bottle was hard enough to sell at four centimes; and at three it will be quite impossible. The margin is not broad enough, the thing begins to smell of scorching—brrr!" said he, and shuddered. "It is true I bought it myself at a cent, when I knew not there were smaller coins. I was a fool for my pains; there will never be found another: and whoever has that bottle now will carry it to the pit."

"O my husband!" said Kokua. "Is it not a terrible thing to save oneself by the eternal ruin of another? It seems to me, I could not laugh. I would be humbled. I would be filled with melancholy. I would pray for the poor holder."

Then Keawe, because he felt the truth of what she said, grew the more angry. "Heighty-teighty!" cried he. "You may be filled with melancholy if you please. It is not the mind of a good wife. If you thought at all of me, you would sit shamed."

Thereupon he went out, and Kokua was alone.

What chance had she to sell that bottle at two centimes? None, she perceived. And if she had any, here was her husband hurrying her away to a country where there was nothing lower than a cent. And here—on the morrow of her sacrifice—was her husband leaving her and blaming her.

She would not even try to profit by what time she had, but sat in the house, and now had the bottle out and viewed it with unutterable fear, and now, with loathing, hid it out of sight.

By and by, Keawe came back, and would have her take a drive.

"My husband, I am ill," she said. "I am out of heart. Excuse me, I can take no pleasure."

Then was Keawe more wroth than ever. With her, because he thought she was brooding over the case of the old man; and with himself, because he thought she was right, and was ashamed to be so happy.

"This is your truth," cried he, "and this your affection! Your husband is just saved from eternal ruin, which he encountered for the love of you—and you can take no pleasure! Kokua, you have a disloyal heart."

He went forth again furious, and wandered in the town all day. He met friends, and drank with them; they hired a carriage and drove into the country, and there drank again. All the time Keawe was ill at ease, because he was taking his pastime while his wife was sad, and because he knew in his heart that she was more right than he; and the knowledge made him drink the deeper.

Now there was an old brutal Haole drinking with him, one that had been a boatswain of a whaler, a runaway, a digger in gold mines, a convict in prisons. He had a low mind and a foul mouth; he loved to drink and to see others drunken; and he pressed the glass upon Keawe. Soon there was no more money in the company.

"Here you!" says the boatswain, "you are rich, you have been always saying. You have a bottle or some foolishness."

"Yes," says Keawe, "I am rich; I will go back and get some money from my wife, who keeps it."

"That's a bad idea, mate," says the boatswain. "Never you trust a petticoat with dollars. They're all as false as water; you keep an eye on her."

Now, this word stuck in Keawe's mind; for he was muddled with what he had been drinking.

"I should not wonder but she was false, indeed," thought he. "Why else should she be so cast down at my release? But I will show her I am not the man to be fooled. I will catch her in the act."

Accordingly, when they were back in town, Keawe bade the boatswain wait for him at the corner, by the old calaboose, and went forward up the avenue alone to the door of his house. The night had come again; there was a light within, but never a sound, and Keawe crept about the corner, opened the back door softly, and looked in.

There was Kokua on the floor, the lamp at her side; before her was a milk-white bottle, with a round belly and a long neck; and as she viewed it, Kokua wrung her hands.

A long time Keawe stood and looked in the doorway. At first he was struck stupid; and then fear fell upon him that the bargain had been made amiss, and the bottle had come back to him as it came at San Francisco; and at that his knees were loosened, and the fumes of the wine departed from his head like mists off a river in the morning. And then he had another thought; and it was a strange one, that made his cheeks to burn.

"I must make sure of this," thought he.

So he closed the door, and went softly round the corner again, and then came noisily in, as though he were but now returned. And lo! by the time he opened the front door no bottle was to be seen; and Kokua sat in a chair and started up like one awakened out of sleep.

"I have been drinking all day and making merry," said Keawe. "I have been with good companions, and now I only come back for money, and return to drink and carouse with them again."

Both his face and voice were as stern as judgment, but Kokua was too troubled to observe.

"You do well to use your own, my husband," said she, and her words trembled.

"Oh, I do well in all things," said Keawe, and he went straight to the chest and took out money. But he looked besides in the corner where they kept the bottle, and there was no bottle there. At that the chest heaved upon the floor like a sea-billow, and the house span about him like a wreath of smoke, for he saw he was lost now, and there was no escape. "It is what I feared," he thought; "it is she who has bought it."

And then he came to himself a little and rose up; but the sweat streamed on his face as thick as the rain and as cold as the well-water.

"Kokua," said he, "I said to you today what ill became me. Now I return to carouse with my jolly companions," and at that he laughed a little quietly. "I will take more pleasure in the cup if you forgive me."

She clasped his knees in a moment; she kissed his knees with flowing tears.

"Oh," she cried, "I asked but a kind word!"

"Let us never one think hardly of the other," said Keawe, and was gone out of the house.

Now, the money that Keawe had taken was only some of that store of centime pieces they had laid in at their arrival. It was very sure he had no mind to be drinking. His wife had given her soul for him, now he must give his for her; no other thought was in the world with him.

At the corner, by the old calaboose, there was the boatswain waiting.

"My wife has the bottle," said Keawe, "and, unless you help me to recover it, there can be no more money and no more liquor to-night."

"You do not mean to say you are serious about that bottle?" cried the boatswain.

"There is the lamp," said Keawe. "Do I look as if I was jesting?"

"That is so," said the boatswain. "You look as serious as a ghost."

"Well, then," said Keawe, "here are two centimes; you must go to my wife in the house, and offer her these for the bottle, which (if I am not much mistaken) she will give you instantly. Bring it to me here, and I will buy it back from you for one; for that is the law with this bottle, that it still must be sold for a less sum. But whatever you do, never breathe a word to her that you have come from me."

"Mate, I wonder are you making a fool of me?" asked the boatswain.

"It will do you no harm if I am," returned Keawe.

"That is so, mate," said the boatswain.

"And if you doubt me," added Keawe, "you can try. As soon as you are clear of the house, wish to have your pocket full of money, or a bottle of the best rum, or what you please, and you will see the virtue of the thing."

"Very well, Kanaka," says the boatswain. "I will try; but if you are having your fun out of me, I will take my fun out of you with a belaying pin."

So the whaler-man went off up the avenue; and Keawe stood and waited. It was near the same spot where Kokua had waited the night before; but Keawe was more resolved, and never faltered in his purpose; only his soul was bitter with despair.

It seemed a long time he had to wait before he heard a voice singing in the darkness of the avenue. He knew the voice to be the boatswain's; but it was strange how drunken it appeared upon a sudden.

Next, the man himself came stumbling into the light of the lamp. He had the devil's bottle buttoned in his coat; another bottle was in his hand; and even as he came in view he raised it to his mouth and drank.

"You have it," said Keawe. "I see that."

"Hands off!" cried the boatswain, jumping back. "Take a step near me, and I'll smash your mouth. You thought you could make a cat's-paw of me, did you?"

"What do you mean?" cried Keawe.

"Mean?" cried the boatswain. "This is a pretty good bottle, this is; that's what I mean. How I got it for two centimes I can't make out; but I'm sure you shan't have it for one."

"You mean you won't sell?" gasped Keawe.

"No, *sir*!" cried the boatswain. "But I'll give you a drink of the rum, if you like."

"I tell you," said Keawe, "the man who has that bottle goes to hell."

"I reckon I'm going anyway," returned the sailor: "and this bottle's the best thing to go with I've struck yet. No, sir!" he cried again, "this is my bottle now, and you can go and fish for another."

"Can this be true?" Keawe cried. "For your own sake, I beseech you, sell it me!"

"I don't value any of your talk," replied the boatswain. "You thought I was a flat; now you see I'm not; and there's an end. If you won't have a swallow of the rum, I'll have one myself. Here's your health, and good-night to you!"

So off he went down the avenue towards town, and there goes the bottle out of the story.

But Keawe ran to Kokua light as the wind; and great was their joy that night; and great, since then, has been the peace of all their days in the Bright House.

## "I SAW A PEACOCK WITH A FIERY TAIL"

### Anonymous

I saw a peacock with a fiery tail
I saw a blazing comet drop down hail
I saw a cloud wrapped with ivy round
I saw an oak creep upon the ground
I saw a pismire swallow up a whale
I saw the sea brimful of ale
I saw a Venice glass full fifteen feet deep
I saw a well full of men's tears that weep
I saw red eyes all of a flaming fire
I saw a house bigger than the moon and higher
I saw the sun at twelve o'clock at night
I saw the man that saw this wondrous sight.

## "IN WINTER, WHEN THE FIELDS ARE WHITE"

### Lewis Carroll

[THE ASTERISKS INDICATE ALICE'S INTERRUPTIONS.]
In winter, when the fields are white,
I sing this song for your delight—

\*          \*          \*

In spring, when woods are getting green,
I'll try and tell you what I mean—

\*          \*          \*

In summer, when the days are long,
Perhaps you'll understand the song:

In autumn, when the leaves are brown,
Take pen and ink, and write it down.

\*          \*          \*

I sent a message to the fish:
I told them "This is what I wish."

The little fishes of the sea
They sent an answer back to me.
The little fishes' answer was
"We cannot do it, Sir, because—"

\*          \*          \*

I sent to them again to say
"It will be better to obey."

The fishes answered with a grin
"Why what a temper you are in!"

I told them once, I told them twice:
They would not listen to advice.

I took a kettle large and new,
Fit for the deed I had to do.

My heart went hop, my heart went thump;
I filled the kettle at the pump.

Then some one came to me and said
"The little fishes are in bed."

I said to him, I said it plain,
"Then you must wake them up again."

I said it very loud and clear;
I went and shouted in his ear.

\*          \*          \*

But he was very stiff and proud;
He said "You needn't shout so loud!"

I took a corkscrew from the shelf:
I went to wake them up myself.

And when I found the door was locked,
I pulled and pushed and kicked and knocked.

And when I found the door was shut
I tried to turn the handle, but—

There was a long pause.
"Is that all?" Alice timidly asked.
"That's all," said Humpty Dumpty.
"Good-bye."

❧

## ECHO'S LAMENT FOR NARCISSUS

### *Ben Jonson*

Slow, slow, fresh fount, keep time with my salt tears;
    Yet, slower yet; O faintly, gentle springs;
List to the heavy part the music bears;
    Woe weeps out her division when she sings.
            Droop herbs and flowers;
            Fall grief in showers,
            Our beauties are not ours;
                O, I could still,
Like melting snow upon some craggy hill,
            Drop, drop, drop, drop,
Since nature's pride is now a withered daffodil.

❧

## THE WAY THROUGH THE WOODS

### *Rudyard Kipling*

They shut the road through the woods
Seventy years ago.
Weather and rain have undone it again,
And now you would never know

There was once a road through the woods
Before they planted the trees.
It is underneath the coppice and heath,
And the thin anemones.
Only the keeper sees
That, where the ring-dove broods,
And the badgers roll at ease,
There was once a road through the woods.

Yet, if you enter the woods
Of a summer evening late,
When the night-air cools on the trout-ringed pools
Where the otter whistles his mate
(They fear not men in the woods,
Because they see so few),
You will hear the beat of a horse's feet
And the swish of a skirt in the dew,
Steadily cantering through
The misty solitudes,
As though they perfectly knew
The old lost road through the woods . . .
But there is no road through the woods!

❧

# THE REMARKABLE ROCKET

## Oscar Wilde

The King's son was going to be married, so there were general rejoicings. He had waited a whole year for his bride, and at last she had arrived. She was a Russian Princess, and had driven all the way from Finland in a sledge drawn by six reindeer. The sledge was shaped like a great golden swan, and between the swan's wings lay the little Princess herself. Her long ermine cloak reached right down to her feet, on her head was a tiny cap of silver tissue, and she was as pale as the Snow Palace in which she had always lived. So pale was she that as she drove through the streets all the people wondered. "She is like a white rose!" they cried, and they threw down flowers on her from the balconies.

At the gate of the Castle the Prince was waiting to receive her. He had dreamy violet eyes, and his hair was like fine gold. When he saw her he sank upon one knee, and kissed her hand.

"Your picture was beautiful," he murmured, "but you are more beautiful than your picture," and the little Princess blushed.

"She was like a white rose before," said a young page to his neighbour, "but she is like a red rose now"; and the whole Court was delighted.

For the next three days everybody went about saying, "White rose, Red rose, Red rose, White rose" and the King gave orders that the page's salary was to be doubled. As he received no salary at all this was not of much use to him, but it was considered a great honour, and was duly published in the Court Gazette.

When the three days were over the marriage was celebrated. It was a magnificent ceremony, and the bride and bridegroom walked hand in hand under a canopy of purple velvet embroidered with little pearls. Then there was a State Banquet, which lasted for five hours. The Prince and Princess sat at the top of the Great Hall and drank out of a cup of clear crystal. Only true lovers could drink out of this cup, for if false lips touched it, it grew grey and dull and cloudy.

"It is quite clear that they love each other," said the little page, "as clear as crystal!" and the King doubled his salary a second time.

"What an honour!" cried all the courtiers.

After the banquet there was to be a Ball. The bride and bridegroom were to dance the Rose-dance together, and the King had promised to play the flute. He played very badly, but no one had ever dared to tell him so, because he was the King. Indeed, he knew only two airs, and was never quite certain which one he was playing; but it made no matter, for, whatever he did, everybody cried out, "Charming! charming!"

The last item on the programme was a grand display of fireworks, to be let off exactly at midnight. The little Princess had never seen a firework in her life, so the King had given orders that the Royal Pyrotechnist should be in attendance on the day of her marriage.

"What are fireworks like?" she had asked the Prince, one morning, as she was walking on the terrace.

"They are like the Aurora Borealis," said the King, who always answered questions that were addressed to other people, "only much more natural. I prefer them to stars myself, as you always know when they are going to appear, and they are as delightful as my own flute-playing. You must certainly see them."

So at the end of the King's garden a great stand had been set up, and as soon as the Royal Pyrotechnist had put everything in its proper place, the fireworks began to talk to each other.

"The world is certainly very beautiful," cried a little Squib. "Just look at those yellow tulips. Why! if they were real crackers they could not be lovelier. I am very glad I have travelled. Travel improves the mind wonderfully, and does away with all one's prejudices."

"The King's garden is not the world, you foolish Squib," said a big Roman Candle; "the world is an enormous place, and it would take you three days to see it thoroughly."

"Any place you love is the world to you," exclaimed the pensive Catherine Wheel, who had been attached to an old deal box in early life, and prided herself on her broken heart; "but love is not fashionable any more, the poets have killed it. They wrote so much about it that nobody believed them, and I am not surprised. True love suffers, and is silent. I remember myself once—But no matter now. Romance is a thing of the past."

"Nonsense!" said the Roman Candle. "Romance never dies. It is like the moon, and lives for ever. The bride and bridegroom, for instance, love each other very dearly. I heard all about them this morning from a brown-paper cartridge, who happened to be staying in the same drawer as myself, and he knew the latest Court news."

But the Catherine Wheel shook her head. "Romance is dead, Romance is dead, Romance is dead," she murmured. She was one of those people who think that, if you say the same thing over and over a great many times, it becomes true in the end.

Suddenly, a sharp, dry cough was heard, and they all looked round.

It came from a tall, supercilious-looking Rocket, who was tied to the end of a long stick. He always coughed before he made any observations, so as to attract attention.

"Ahem! ahem!" he said, and everybody listened except the poor Catherine Wheel, who was still shaking her head, and murmuring, "Romance is dead."

"Order! order!" cried out a Cracker. He was something of a politician, and had always taken a prominent part in the local elections, so he knew the proper Parliamentary expressions to use.

"Quite dead," whispered the Catherine Wheel, and she went off to sleep.

As soon as there was perfect silence, the Rocket coughed a third time and began. He spoke with a very slow, distinct voice, as if he were dictating his memoirs, and always looked over the shoulder of the person to whom he was talking. In fact, he had a most distinguished manner.

"How fortunate it is for the King's son," he remarked, "that he is to be married on the very day on which I am to be let off! Really, if it had not been arranged beforehand, it could not have turned out better for him; but Princes are always lucky."

"Dear me!" said the little Squib, "I thought it was quite the other way, and that we were to be let off in the Prince's honour."

"It may be so with you," he answered; "indeed, I have no doubt that it is, but with me it is different. I am a very remarkable Rocket, and come of remarkable parents. My mother was the most celebrated Catherine Wheel of her day, and was renowned for her graceful dancing. When she made her great public appearance she spun round nineteen times before she went out, and each time that she did so she threw into the air seven pink stars. She was three feet and a half in diameter, and made of the very best gunpowder. My father was a Rocket like myself, and of French extraction. He flew so high that the people were afraid that he would never come down again. He did, though, for he was of a kindly disposition, and he made a most brilliant descent in a shower of golden rain. The newspapers wrote about his performance in very flattering terms. Indeed, the Court Gazette called him a triumph of Pylotechnic art."

"Pyrotechnic, Pyrotechnic, you mean," said a Bengal Light; "I know it is Pyrotechnic, for I saw it written on my own canister."

"Well, I said Pylotechnic," answered the Rocket, in a severe tone of voice, and the Bengal Light felt so crushed that he began at once to bully the little squibs, in order to show that he was still a person of some importance.

"I was saying," continued the Rocket, "I was saying—What was I saying?"

"You were talking about yourself," replied the Roman Candle.

"Of course; I knew I was discussing some interesting subject when I was so rudely interrupted. I hate rudeness and bad manners of every kind, for I am extremely sensitive. No one in the whole world is so sensitive as I am, I am quite sure of that."

"What is a sensitive person?" said the Cracker to the Roman Candle.

"A person who, because he has corns himself, always treads on other people's toes," answered the Roman Candle in a low whisper; and the Cracker nearly exploded with laughter.

"Pray, what are you laughing at?" inquired the Rocket; "I am not laughing."

"I am laughing because I am happy," replied the Cracker.

"That is a very selfish reason," said the Rocket angrily. "What right have you to be happy? You should be thinking about others. In fact, you should be thinking about me. I am always thinking about myself, and I expect everybody to do the same. That is what is called sympathy. It is a beautiful virtue, and I possess it in a high degree. Suppose, for instance, anything happened to me tonight, what a misfortune that would be for everyone! The Prince and Princess would never be happy again, their whole married life would be spoiled; and as for the King, I know he would not get over it. Really, when I begin to reflect on the importance of my position, I am almost moved to tears."

"If you want to give pleasure to others," cried the Roman Candle, "you had better keep yourself dry."

"Certainly," exclaimed the Bengal Light, who was now in better spirits; "that is only common sense."

"Common sense, indeed!" said the Rocket indignantly; "you forget that I am very uncommon, and very remarkable. Why, anybody can have common sense, provided that they have no imagination. But I have imagination, for I never think of things as they really are; I always think of them as being quite different. As for keeping myself dry, there is evidently no one here who can at all appreciate an emotional nature. Fortunately for myself, I don't care. The only thing that sustains one through life is the consciousness of the immense inferiority of everybody else, and this is a feeling I have always cultivated. But none of you have any hearts. Here you are laughing and making merry just as if the Prince and Princess had not just been married."

"Well, really," exclaimed a small Fire-balloon, "why not? It is a most joyful occasion, and when I soar up into the air I intend to tell the stars all about it. You will see them twinkle when I talk to them about the pretty bride."

"Ah! what a trivial view of life!" said the Rocket; "but it is only what I expected. There is nothing in you; you are hollow and empty. Why, perhaps the Prince and Princess may go to live in a country where there is a deep river, and perhaps they may have one only son, a little fair-haired boy with violet eyes like the Prince himself; and perhaps some day he may go out to walk with his nurse; and perhaps the nurse may go to sleep under a great elder-tree; and perhaps the little boy may fall into the deep river and be drowned. What a terrible misfortune! Poor people, to lose their only son! It is really too dreadful! I shall never get over it."

"But they have not lost their only son," said the Roman Candle; "no misfortune has happened to them at all."

"I never said that they had," replied the Rocket; 'I said that they might. If they had lost their only son there would be no use in saying any more about the matter. I hate people who cry over spilt milk. But when I think that they might lose their only son, I certainly am very much affected."

"You certainly are!" cried the Bengal Light. "In fact, you are the most affected person I ever met."

"You are the rudest person I ever met," said the Rocket, "and you cannot understand my friendship for the Prince."

"Why, you don't even know him," growled the Roman Candle.

"I never said I knew him," answered the Rocket. "I dare say that if I knew him I should not be his friend at all. It is a very dangerous thing to know one's friends."

"You had really better keep yourself dry," said the Fire-balloon. "That is the important thing."

"Very important for you, I have no doubt," answered the Rocket, "but I shall weep if I choose"; and he actually burst into real tears, which flowed down his stick like rain-drops, and nearly drowned two little beetles, who were just thinking of setting up house together, and were looking for a nice dry spot to live in.

"He must have a truly romantic nature," said the Catherine Wheel, "for he weeps when there is nothing at all to weep about"; and she heaved a deep sigh and thought about the deal box.

But the Roman Candle and the Bengal Light were quite indignant, and kept saying, "Humbug! humbug!" at the top of their voices. They were extremely practical, and whenever they objected to anything they called it humbug.

Then the moon rose like a wonderful silver shield; and the stars began to shine, and a sound of music came from the palace.

The Prince and Princess were leading the dance. They danced so beautifully that the tall white lilies peeped in at the window and watched them, and the great red poppies nodded their heads and beat time.

Then ten o'clock struck, and then eleven, and then twelve, and at the last stroke of midnight everyone came out on the terrace, and the King sent for the Royal Pyrotechnist.

"Let the fireworks begin," said the King; and the Royal Pyrotechnist made a low bow, and marched down to the end of the garden. He had six attendants with him, each of whom carried a lighted torch at the end of a long pole.

It was certainly a magnificent display.

Whizz! Whizz! went the Catherine Wheel, as she spun round and round. Boom! Boom! went the Roman Candle. Then the Squibs danced all over the place, and the Bengal Lights made everything look scarlet. "Good-bye," cried the Fire-balloon, as he soared away, dropping tiny blue sparks. Bang! Bang! answered the Crackers, who were enjoying themselves immensely. Every one was a great success except the Remarkable Rocket. He was so damped with crying that he could not go off at all. The best thing in him was the gunpowder, and that was so wet with tears that it was of no use. All his poor relations, to whom he would never speak, except with a sneer, shot up into the sky like wonderful golden flowers with blossoms of fire. Huzza! Huzza! cried the Court; and the little Princess laughed with pleasure.

"I suppose they are reserving me for some grand occasion," said the Rocket; "no doubt that is what it means," and he looked more supercilious than ever.

The next day the workmen came to put everything tidy. "This is evidently a deputation," said the Rocket; "I will receive them with becoming dignity": so he put his nose in the air, and began to frown severely, as if he were thinking about some very important subject. But they took no notice of him at all till they were just going away. Then one of them caught sight of him. "Hallo!" he cried, "what a bad rocket!" and he threw him over the wall into the ditch.

"BAD ROCKET? BAD ROCKET?" he said, as he whirled through the air; "impossible! GRAND ROCKET, that is what the man said. BAD and GRAND sound very much the same, indeed they often are the same"; and he fell into the mud.

"It is not comfortable here," he remarked, "but no doubt it is some fashionable watering-place, and they have sent me away to recruit my health. My nerves are certainly very much shattered, and I require rest."

Then a little Frog, with bright jewelled eyes, and a green mottled coat, swam up to him.

"A new arrival, I see!" said the Frog. "Well, after all there is nothing like mud. Give me rainy weather and a ditch, and I am quite happy. Do you think it will be a wet afternoon? I am sure I hope so, but the sky is quite blue and cloudless. What a pity!"

"Ahem! ahem!" said the Rocket, and he began to cough.

"What a delightful voice you have!" cried the Frog. "Really it is quite like a croak, and croaking is, of course, the most musical sound in the world. You will hear our glee-club this evening. We sit in the old duck-pond close by the farmer's house, and as soon as the moon rises we begin. It is so entrancing that everybody lies awake to listen to us. In fact, it was only yesterday that I heard the farmer's wife say to her mother that she could not get a wink of sleep at night on account of us. It is most gratifying to find oneself so popular."

"Ahem! ahem!" said the Rocket angrily. He was very much annoyed that he could not get a word in.

"A delightful voice, certainly," continued the Frog; "I hope you will come over to the duck-pond. I am off to look for my daughters. I have six beautiful daughters, and I am so afraid the Pike may meet them. He is a perfect monster, and would have no hesitation in breakfasting off them. Well, good-bye; I have enjoyed our conversation very much, I assure you."

"Conversation, indeed!" said the Rocket. "You have talked the whole time yourself. That is not conversation."

"Somebody must listen," answered the Frog, "and I like to do all the talking myself. It saves time, and prevents arguments."

"But I like arguments," said the Rocket.

"I hope not," said the Frog complacently. "Arguments are extremely vulgar, for everybody in good society holds exactly the same opinions. Good bye a second time; I see my daughters in the distance"; and the little Frog swam away.

"You are a very irritating person," said the Rocket, "and very ill-bred. I hate people who talk about themselves, as you do, when one wants to talk about oneself, as I do. It is what I call selfishness, and selfishness is a most detestable thing, especially to anyone of my temperament, for I am well known for my sympathetic nature. In fact, you should take example by me; you could not possibly have a better model. Now that you have the chance you had better avail yourself of it, for I am going back to Court almost immediately. I am a great favourite at Court; in fact, the Prince and Princess were married yesterday in my honour. Of course, you know nothing of these matters, for you are a provincial."

"There is no good talking to him," said a Dragonfly, who was sitting on the top of a large brown bulrush; "no good at all, for he has gone away."

"Well, that is his loss, not mine," answered the Rocket. "I am not going to stop talking to him merely because he pays no attention. I like hearing myself talk. It is one of my greatest pleasures. I often have long conversations all by myself, and I am so clever that sometimes I don't understand a single word of what I am saying."

"Then you should certainly lecture on Philosophy," said the Dragonfly, and he spread a pair of lovely gauze wings and soared away into the sky.

"How very silly of him not to stay here!" said the Rocket. "I am sure that he has not often got such a chance of improving his mind. However, I don't care a bit. Genius like mine is sure to be appreciated some day"; and he sank down a little deeper into the mud.

After some time a large White Duck swam up to him. She had yellow legs, and webbed feet, and was considered a great beauty on account of her waddle.

"Quack, quack, quack," she said. "What a curious shape you are! May I ask were you born like that, or is it the result of an accident?"

"It is quite evident that you have always lived in the country," answered the Rocket, "otherwise you would know who I am. However, I excuse your ignorance. It would be unfair to expect other people to be as remarkable as oneself. You will no doubt be surprised to hear that I can fly up into the sky, and come down in a shower of golden rain."

"I don't think much of that," said the Duck, "as I cannot see what use it is to anyone. Now, if you could plough the fields like the ox, or draw a cart like the horse, or look after the sheep like the collie-dog, that would be something."

"My good creature," cried the Rocket in a very haughty tone of voice, "I see that you belong to the lower orders. A person of my position is never useful. We have certain accomplishments, and that is more than sufficient. I have no sympathy myself with industry of any kind, least of all with such industries as you seem to recommend. Indeed, I have always been of the opinion that hard work is simply the refuge of people who have nothing whatever to do."

"Well, well," said the Duck, who was of a very peaceful disposition, and never quarrelled with anyone, "everybody has different tastes. I hope, at any rate, that you are going to take up your residence here."

"Oh! dear no," cried the Rocket. "I am merely a visitor, a distinguished visitor. The fact is that I find this place rather tedious. There is neither society here, nor solitude. In fact, it is essentially suburban. I shall probably go back to Court, for I know that I am destined to make a sensation in the world."

"I had thoughts of entering public life once myself," remarked the Duck; "there are so many things that need reforming. Indeed, I took the chair at a meeting some time ago, and we passed resolutions condemning everything that we did not like. However, they did not seem to have much effect. Now I go in for domesticity, and look after my family."

"I am made for public life," said the Rocket, "and so are all my relations, even the humblest of them. Whenever we appear we excite great attention. I have not actually appeared myself, but when I do so it will be a magnificent sight. As for domesticity, it ages one rapidly, and distracts one's mind from higher things."

"Ah! the higher things of life, how fine they are!" said the Duck; "and that reminds me how hungry I feel"; and she swam away down the stream, saying, "Quack, quack, quack."

"Come back! come back!" screamed the Rocket, "I have a great deal to say to you"; but the Duck paid no attention to him. "I am glad that she has gone," he said to himself, "she has a decidedly middle-class mind"; and he sank a little deeper still into the mud, and began to think about the loneliness of genius, when suddenly two little boys in white smocks came running down the bank with a kettle and some faggots.

"This must be the deputation," said the Rocket, and he tried to look very dignified.

"Hallo!" cried one of the boys, "look at this old stick; I wonder how it came here"; and he picked the rocket out of the ditch.

"OLD STICK!" said the Rocket, "impossible! GOLD STICK, that is what he said. Gold Stick is very complimentary. In fact, he mistakes me for one of the Court dignitaries!"

"Let us put it into the fire!" said the other boy, "it will help to boil the kettle."

So they piled the faggots together, and put the Rocket on top, and lit the fire.

"This is magnificent," cried the Rocket, "they are going to let me off in broad daylight, so that everyone can see me."

"We will go to sleep now," they said, "and when we wake up the kettle will be boiled"; and they lay down on the grass, and shut their eyes.

The Rocket was very damp, so he took a long time to burn. At last, however, the fire caught him.

"Now I am going off!" he cried, and he made himself very stiff and straight. "I know I shall go much higher than the stars, much higher than the moon, much higher than the sun. In fact, I shall go so high that—"

Fizz! Fizz! Fizz! and he went straight up into the air.

"Delightful!" he cried, "I shall go on like this for ever. What a success I am!"

But nobody saw him.

Then he began to feel a curious tingling sensation all over him.

"Now I am going to explode," he cried. "I shall set the whole world on fire, and make such a noise that nobody will talk about anything else for a whole year." And he certainly did explode. Bang! Bang! Bang! went the gunpowder. There was no doubt about it.

But nobody heard him, not even the two little boys, for they were sound asleep.

Then all that was left of him was the stick, and this fell down on the back of a Goose who was taking a walk by the side of the ditch.

"Good heavens!" cried the Goose. "It is going to rain sticks"; and she rushed into the water.

"I knew I should create a great sensation," gasped the Rocket, and he went out.

∾

# JOURNALISM IN TENNESSEE

## Mark Twain

*The editor of the Memphis* Avalanche *swoops thus mildly down upon a correspondent who posted him as a Radical:— "While he was writing the first word, the middle, dotting his i's, crossing his t's, and punching his period, he knew he was concocting a sentence that was saturated with infamy and reeking with falsehood."*

—Exchange.

I was told by the physician that a Southern climate would improve my health, and so I went down to Tennessee, and got a berth on the *Morning Glory and Johnson County War-Whoop* as associate editor. When I went on duty I found the chief editor sitting tilted back in a three-legged chair with his feet on a pine table. There was another pine table in the room and another afflicted chair, and both were half buried under newspapers and scraps and sheets of manuscript. There was a wooden box of sand, sprinkled with cigar stubs and "old soldiers," and a stove with a door hanging by its upper hinge. The chief editor had a long-tailed black cloth frock-coat on, and white linen pants. His boots were small and neatly blacked. He wore a ruffled shirt, a large seal-ring, a standing collar of obsolete pattern, and a checkered neckerchief with the ends hanging down. Date of costume about 1848. He was smoking a cigar, and trying to think of a word, and in pawing his hair he had rumpled his locks a good deal. He was scowling fearfully, and I judged that he was concocting a particularly knotty editorial. He told me to take the exchanges and skim through them and write up the "Spirit of the Tennessee Press," condensing into the article all of their contents that seemed of interest.

I wrote as follows:

### SPIRIT OF THE TENNESSEE PRESS

The editors of the *Semi-Weekly Earthquake* evidently labor under a misapprehension with regard to the Ballyhack railroad. It is not the object of the company to leave Buzzardville off to one side. On the contrary, they consider it one of the most important points along the line, and consequently can have no desire to slight it. The gentlemen of the *Earthquake* will, of course, take pleasure in making the correction.

John W. Blossom, Esq., the able editor of the Higginsville *Thunderbolt and Battle Cry of Freedom,* arrived in the city yesterday. He is stopping at the Van Buren House.

We observe that our contemporary of the Mud Springs *Morning Howl* has fallen into the error of supposing that the election of Van Werter is not an established fact, but he will have discovered his mistake before this reminder reaches him, no doubt. He was doubtless misled by incomplete election returns.

It is pleasant to note that the city of Blathersville is endeavoring to contract with some New York gentlemen to pave its well-nigh impassable streets with the Nicholson pavement. The *Daily Hurrah* urges the measure with ability, and seems confident of ultimate success.

I passed my manuscript over to the chief editor for acceptance, alteration, or destruction. He glanced at it and his face clouded. He ran his eye down the pages, and his countenance grew portentous. It was easy to see that something was wrong. Presently he sprang up and said:

"Thunder and lightning! Do you suppose I am going to speak of those cattle that way? Do you suppose my subscribers are going to stand such gruel as that? Give me the pen!"

I never saw a pen scrape and scratch its way so viciously, or plow through another man's verbs and adjectives so relentlessly. While he was in the midst of his work, somebody shot at him through the open window, and marred the symmetry of my ear.

"Ah," said he, "that is that scoundrel Smith, of the *Moral Volcano*—he was due yesterday." And he snatched a navy revolver from his belt and fired. Smith dropped, shot in the thigh. The shot spoiled Smith's aim, who was just taking a second chance, and he crippled a stranger. It was me. Merely a finger shot off.

Then the chief editor went on with his erasures and interlineations. Just as he finished them a hand-grenade came down the stove-pipe, and the explosion shivered the stove into a thousand fragments. However, it did no further damage, except that a vagrant piece knocked a couple of my teeth out.

"That stove is utterly ruined," said the chief editor.

I said I believed it was.

"Well, no matter—don't want it this kind of weather. I know the man that did it. I'll get him. Now, *here* is the way this stuff ought to be written."

I took the manuscript. It was scarred with erasures and interlineations till its mother wouldn't have known it if it had had one. It now read as follows:

### SPIRIT OF THE TENNESSEE PRESS

The inveterate liars of the *Semi-Weekly Earthquake* are evidently endeavoring to palm off upon a noble and chivalrous people another of their vile and brutal falsehoods with regard to that most glorious conception of the nineteenth century, the Ballyhack railroad. The idea that Buzzardville was to be left off at one side originated in their own fulsome brains—or rather in the settlings which *they* regard as brains. They had better swallow this lie if they want to save their abandoned reptile carcasses the cowhiding they so richly deserve.

That ass, Blossom, of the Higginsville *Thunderbolt and Battle Cry of Freedom,* is down here again sponging at the Van Buren.

We observe that the besotted blackguard of the Mud Springs *Morning Howl* is giving out, with his usual propensity for lying, that Van Werter is not elected. The heaven-born mission of journalism is to disseminate truth; to eradicate error; to educate, refine, and elevate the tone of public morals and manners, and make all men more gentle, more virtuous, more charitable, and in all ways better, and holier, and happier; and yet this black-hearted scoundrel degrades his great office persistently to the dissemination of falsehood, calumny, vituperation, and vulgarity.

Blathersville wants a Nicholson pavement—it wants a jail and a poorhouse more. The idea of a pavement in a one-horse town composed of two gin-mills, a blacksmith shop, and that mustard-plaster of a news-paper, the *Daily Hurrah*! The crawling insect, Buckner, who edits the *Hurrah,* is braying about his business with his customary imbecility, and imagining that he is talking sense.

"Now *that* is the way to write—peppery and to the point. Mush-and-milk journalism gives me the fan-tods."

About this time a brick came through the window with a splintering crash, and gave me a considerable of a jolt in the back. I moved out of range—I began to feel in the way.

The chief said, "That was the Colonel, likely. I've been expecting him for two days. He will be up now right away."

He was correct. The Colonel appeared in the door a moment after-ward with a dragoon revolver in his hand.

He said, "Sir, have I the honor of addressing the poltroon who edits this mangy sheet?"

"You have. Be seated, sir. Be careful of the chair, one of its legs is gone. I believe I have the honor of addressing the putrid liar, Colonel Blather-skite Tecumseh?"

"Right, sir. I have a little account to settle with you. If you are at leisure we will begin."

"I have an article on the 'Encouraging Progress of Moral and Intellec-tual Development in America' to finish, but there is no hurry. Begin."

Both pistols rang out their fierce clamor at the same instant. The chief lost a lock of his hair, and the Colonel's bullet ended its career in the fleshy part of my thigh. The Colonel's left shoulder was clipped a little. They fired again. Both missed their men this time, but I got my share, a shot in the arm. At the third fire both gentlemen were wounded slightly, and I had a knuckle chipped. I then said, I believed I would go out and take a walk, as this was a private matter, and I had a delicacy about participating in it fur-ther. But both gentlemen begged me to keep my seat, and assured me that I was not in the way.

They then talked about the elections and the crops while they reloaded, and I fell to tying up my wounds. But presently they opened fire again with animation, and every shot took effect—but it is proper to remark that five out of the six fell to my share. The sixth one mortally wounded the Colonel, who remarked, with fine humor, that he would have to say good morning now, as he had business uptown. He then inquired the way to the under-taker's and left.

The chief turned to me and said, "I am expecting company to dinner, and shall have to get ready. It will be a favor to me if you will read proof and attend to the customers."

I winced a little at the idea of attending to the customers, but I was too bewildered by the fusillade that was still ringing in my ears to think of anything to say.

He continued, "Jones will be here at three—cowhide him. Gillespie will call earlier, perhaps—throw him out of the window. Ferguson will be along about four—kill him. That is all for to-day, I believe. If you have any odd time, you may write a blistering article on the police—give the chief inspector rats. The cowhides are under the table; weapons in the drawer—ammunition there in the corner—lint and bandages up there in the pigeonholes. In case of accident, go to Lancet, the surgeon, down-stairs. He advertises—we take it out in trade."

He was gone. I shuddered. At the end of the next three hours I had been through perils so awful that all peace of mind and all cheerfulness were gone from me. Gillespie had called and thrown *me* out of the window. Jones arrived promptly, and when I got ready to do the cowhiding he took the job off my hands. In an encounter with a stranger, not in the bill of fare, I had lost my scalp. Another stranger, by the name of Thompson, left me a mere wreck and ruin of chaotic rags. And at last, at bay in the corner, and beset by an infuriated mob of editors, blacklegs, politicians, and desperadoes, who raved and swore and flourished their weapons about my head till the air shimmered with glancing flashes of steel, I was in the act of resigning my berth on the paper when the chief arrived, and with him a rabble of charmed and enthusiastic friends. Then ensued a scene of riot and carnage such as no human pen, or steel one either, could describe. People were shot, probed, dismembered, blown up, thrown out of the window. There was a brief tornado of murky blasphemy, with a confused and frantic war-dance glimmering through it, and then all was over. In five minutes there was silence, and the gory chief and I sat alone and surveyed the sanguinary ruin that strewed the floor around us.

He said, "You'll like this place when you get used to it."

I said, "I'll have to get you to excuse me; I think maybe I might write to suit you after a while; as soon as I had had some practice and learned the language I am confident I could. But, to speak the plain truth, that sort of energy of expression has its inconveniences, and a man is liable to interruption. You see that yourself. Vigorous writing is calculated to elevate the public, no doubt, but then I do not like to attract so much attention as it calls forth. I can't write with comfort when I am interrupted so much as I have been to-day. I like this berth well enough, but I don't like to be left here to wait on the customers. The experiences are novel, I grant you, and entertaining, too, after a fashion, but they are not judiciously distributed. A gentleman shoots at you through the window and cripples *me;* a bomb-shell comes down the stove-pipe for your gratification and sends the stove door down *my* throat; a friend drops in to swap compliments with you, and freckles *me* with bullet-holes till my skin won't hold my principles; you go to dinner, and Jones comes with his cowhide, Gillespie throws me out of the window, Thompson tears all my clothes off, and an entire stranger takes my scalp with the easy freedom of an old acquaintance; and in less than five minutes all the blackguards in the country arrive in their war-paint, and proceed to scare the rest of me to death with their tomahawks. Take it altogether, I never had such a spirited time in all my life as I have had to-day. No; I like you, and I like your calm unruffled way of explaining things to the customers, but you see I am not used to it. The Southern heart is too impulsive; Southern hospitality is too lavish with the stranger. The paragraphs which I have written to-day, and into whose cold sentences your masterly hand has infused the fervent spirit of Tennesseean journalism, will wake up another nest of hornets. All that mob of editors will come—and they will come hungry, too, and want somebody for breakfast. I shall have to bid you adieu. I decline to be present at these festivities. I came South for my health, I will go back on the same errand, and suddenly. Tennesseean journalism is too stirring for me."

After which we parted with mutual regret, and I took apartments at the hospital.

∾

# ROARING MAD TOM

*Anonymous*

I

From the hag and hungry goblin
    That into rags would rend ye,
The spirit that stands by the naked man
    In the Book of Moons defend ye,
That of your five sound senses

You never be forsaken
Nor wander from yourselves, with Tom,
    Abroad to beg your bacon.
While I do sing "Any food, any feeding
    Feeding, drink or clothing?"
Come dame or maid, be not afraid:
    Poor Tom will injure nothing.


## II

Of thirty bare years have I
    Twice twenty been enraged,
And of forty been three times fifteen
    In durance soundly caged,
On the lordly lofts of Bedlam
    With stubble soft and dainty,
Brave bracelets strong, sweet whips ding-dong,
    And wholesome hunger plenty.
And now I sing "Any food, any feeding
    Feeding, drink or clothing?"
Come dame or maid, be not afraid:
    Poor Tom will injure nothing.


## III

A thought I took for Maudlin
    With a cruse of cockle pottage—
A thing thus tall, sky bless you all!—
    When I fell into this dotage.
I've slept not since the Conquest,
    Ere then I never waked
Till the roguish boy of love where I lay
    Me found and stripped me naked.
And now I sing "Any food, any feeding
    Feeding, drink or clothing?"
Come dame or maid, be not afraid:
    Poor Tom will injure nothing.

## IV

When I short have shorn my sow's-face
    And swigged my horny barrel,
At an oaken inn I impound my skin
    In a suit of gilt apparel.
The Moon's my constant mistress
    And the lovely owl my marrow,
The flaming drake and the night-crow make
    Me music to my sorrow.
While I do sing "Any food, any feeding
    Feeding, drink or clothing?"
Come dame or maid, be not afraid:
    Poor Tom will injure nothing.

## V

The palsy plague my pulses
    If I prig your pigs or pullen,
Your culvers take, or matchless make
    Your Chanticlere or Solan!
When I want provant, with Humphry
    I sup, and when benighted
I repose in Paul's with waking souls
    Yet never am affrighted.
But I do sing "Any food, any feeding
    Feeding, drink or clothing?"
Come dame or maid, be not afraid:
    Poor Tom will injure nothing.

## VI

I know more than Apollo,
    For oft when he lies sleeping
I see the stars at bloody wars
    And the wounded welkin weeping,
The moon embrace her shepherd

And the Queen of Love her warrior,
While the first doth horn the Star of Morn
And the next, the Heavenly Farrier.
While I do sing "Any food, any feeding
Feeding, drink or clothing?"
Come dame or maid, be not afraid:
Poor Tom will injure nothing.


## VII

The gipsies, Snap and Pedro
Are none of Tom's comradoes;
The punk I scorn and the cut-purse sworn
And the roaring-boy's bravadoes:
The meek, the white, the gentle
Me handle, touch and spare not,
But those that cross Tom Rhinosceros
Do what the Panther dare not.
Although I sing "Any food, any feeding
Feeding, drink or clothing?"
Come dame or maid, be not afraid:
Poor Tom will injure nothing.


## VIII

With an host of furious fancies
Whereof I am commander,
With a burning spear, and a horse of air
To the wilderness I wander.
By a knight of ghosts and shadows
I summoned am to Tourney,
Ten leagues beyond the wide world's end—
Methinks it is no journey.
Yet will I sing "Any food, any feeding
Feeding, drink or clothing?"
Come dame or maid, be not afraid:
Poor Tom will injure nothing.

## THE MAD GARDENER'S SONG

*Lewis Carroll*

He thought he saw an Elephant,
    That practised on a fife:
He looked again, and found it was
    A letter from his wife.
"At length I realize," he said,
    "The bitterness of Life!"

He thought he saw a Buffalo
    Upon the chimney-piece;
He looked again, and found it was
    His Sister's Husband's Niece,
"Unless you leave this house," he said,
    "I'll send for the Police!"

He thought he saw a Rattlesnake
    That questioned him in Greek:
He looked again, and found it was
    The Middle of Next Week.
"The one thing I regret," he said,
    "Is that it cannot speak!"

He thought he saw a Banker's Clerk
    Descending from the 'bus:
He looked again, and found it was
    A Hippopotamus.
"If this should stay to dine," he said
    "There won't be much for us!"

He thought he saw a Kangaroo
    That worked a coffee-mill:
He looked again, and found it was
    A Vegetable-Pill.
"Were I to swallow this," he said,
    "I should be very ill!"

He thought he saw a Coach-and-Four
        That stood beside his bed:
He looked again, and found it was
        A Bear without a Head.
"Poor thing," he said, "poor silly thing!
        It's waiting to be fed!"

He thought he saw an Albatross
        That fluttered around the lamp:
He looked again, and found it was
        A Penny-Postage-Stamp.
"You'd best be getting home," he said,
        "The nights are very damp!"

He thought he saw a Garden-Door
        That opened with a key:
He looked again, and found it was
        A Double Rule of Three:
"And all its mystery," he said
        "Is clear as day to me!"

He thought he saw an Argument
        That proved he was the Pope:
He looked again, and found it was
        A Bar of Mottled Soap.
"A fact so dread," he faintly said,
        "Extinguishes all hope!"

# THE WAR-SONG OF DINAS VAWR

## Thomas Love Peacock

The mountain sheep are sweeter,
But the valley sheep are fatter;
We therefore deemed it meeter

To carry off the latter,
We made an expedition;
We met a host, and quelled it;
We forced a strong position,
And killed the men who held it.

On Dyfed's richest valley,
Where herds of kine were browsing,
We made a mighty sally,
To furnish our carousing.
Fierce warriors rushed to meet us;
We met them, and o'erthrew them:
They struggled hard to beat us;
But we conquered them, and slew them.

As we drove our prize at leisure,
The king marched forth to catch us;
His rage surpassed all measure,
But his people could not match us.
He fled to his hall-pillars;
And, ere our force we led off,
Some sacked his house and cellars,
While others cut his head off.

We there, in strife bewild'ring,
Spilt blood enough to swim in:
We orphaned many children,
And widowed many women.
The eagles and the ravens
We glutted with our foemen;
The heroes and the cravens,
The spearmen and the bowmen.

We brought away from battle,
And much their land bemoaned them,
Two thousand head of cattle,
And the head of him who owned them:
Ednyfed, king of Dyfed,
His head was borne before us;

His wine and beasts supplied our feasts,
And his overthrow, our chorus.

∽

## "RIKKI-TIKKI-TAVI"

### *Rudyard Kipling*

This is the story of the great war that Rikki-tikki-tavi fought single-handed, through the bath-rooms of the big bungalow in Segowlee cantonment. Darzee, the tailor-bird, helped him, and Chuchundra, the muskrat, who never comes out into the middle of the floor, but always creeps round by the wall, gave him advice; but Rikki-tikki did the real fighting.

He was a mongoose, rather like a little cat in his fur and his tail, but quite like a weasel in his head and his habits. His eyes and the end of his restless nose were pink; he could scratch himself anywhere he pleased, with any leg, front or back, that he chose to use; he could fluff up his tail till it looked like a bottle-brush, and his war-cry as he scuttled through the long grass, was: "*Rikk-tikk-tikki-tikki-tchk!*"

One day, a high summer flood washed him out of the burrow where he lived with his father and mother, and carried him, kicking and clucking, down a roadside ditch. He found a little wisp of grass floating there, and clung to it till he lost his senses. When he revived, he was lying in the hot sun on the middle of a garden path, very draggled indeed, and a small boy was saying: "Here's a dead mongoose. Let's have a funeral."

"No," said his mother; "let's take him in and dry him. Perhaps he isn't really dead."

They took him into the house, and a big man picked him up between his finger and thumb and said he was not dead but half choked; so they wrapped him in cotton-wool, and warmed him, and he opened his eyes and sneezed.

"Now," said the big man (he was an Englishman who had just moved into the bungalow); "don't frighten him, and we'll see what he'll do."

It is the hardest thing in the world to frighten a mongoose, because he is eaten up from nose to tail with curiosity. The motto of all the mongoose family is, "Run and find out"; and Rikki-tikki was a true mongoose. He looked at the cotton-wool, decided that it was not good to eat, ran all round the table, sat up and put his fur in order, scratched himself, and jumped on the small boy's shoulder.

"Don't be frightened, Teddy," said his father. "That's his way of making friends."

"Ouch! He's tickling under my chin," said Teddy.

Rikki-tikki looked down between the boy's collar and neck, snuffed at his ear, and climbed down to the floor, where he sat rubbing his nose.

"Good gracious," said Teddy's mother, "and that's a wild creature! I suppose he's so tame because we've been kind to him."

"All mongooses are like that," said her husband. "If Teddy does n't pick him up by the tail, or try to put him in a cage, he'll run in and out of the house all day long. Let's give him something to eat."

They gave him a little piece of raw meat. Rikki-tikki liked it immensely, and when it was finished he went out into the veranda and sat in the sunshine and fluffed up his fur to make it dry to the roots. Then he felt better.

"There are more things to find out about in this house," he said to himself, "than all my family could find out in all their lives. I shall certainly stay and find out."

He spent all that day roaming over the house. He nearly drowned himself in the bath-tubs, put his nose into the ink on a writing-table, and burned it on the end of the big man's cigar, for he climbed up in the big man's lap to see how writing was done. At nightfall he ran into Teddy's nursery to watch how kerosene lamps were lighted, and when Teddy went to bed Rikki-tikki climbed up too; but he was a restless companion, because he had to get up and attend to every noise all through the night, and find out what made it. Teddy's mother and father came in, the last thing, to look at their boy, and Rikki-tikki was awake on the pillow. "I don't like that," said Teddy's mother; "he may bite the child." "He'll do no such thing," said the father. "Teddy's safer with that little beast than if he had a bloodhound to watch him. If a snake came into the nursery now—"

But Teddy's mother would n't think of anything so awful.

Early in the morning Rikki-tikki came to early breakfast in the veranda riding on Teddy's shoulder, and they gave him banana and some boiled egg; and he sat on all their laps one after the other, because every well-brought-up mongoose always hopes to be a house-mongoose some day and have rooms to run about in, and Rikki-tikki's mother (she used to live in the General's house at Segowlee) had carefully told Rikki what to do if ever he came across white men.

Then Rikki-tikki went out into the garden to see what was to be seen.

It was a large garden, only half cultivated, with bushes as big as summer-houses of Marshal Niel roses, lime and orange trees, clumps of bamboos, and thickets of high grass. Rikki-tikki licked his lips. "This is a splendid hunting-ground," he said, and his tail grew bottle-brushy at the thought of it, and he scuttled up and down the garden, snuffing here and there till he heard very sorrowful voices in a thorn-bush.

It was Darzee, the tailor-bird, and his wife. They had made a beautiful nest by pulling two big leaves together and stitching them up the edges with fibers, and had filled the hollow with cotton and downy fluff. The nest swayed to and fro, as they sat on the rim and cried.

"What is the matter?" asked Rikki-tikki.

"We are very miserable," said Darzee. "One of our babies fell out of the nest yesterday and Nag ate him."

"H'm!" said Rikki-tikki, "that is very sad—but I am a stranger here. Who is Nag?"

Darzee and his wife only cowered down in the nest without answering, for from the thick grass at the foot of the bush there came a low hiss—a horrid cold sound that made Rikki-tikki jump back two clear feet. Then inch by inch out of the grass rose up the head and spread hood of Nag, the big black cobra, and he was five feet long from tongue to tail. When he had lifted one-third of himself clear of the ground, he stayed balancing to and fro exactly as a dandelion-tuft balances in the wind, and he looked at Rikki-tikki with the wicked snake's eyes that never change their expression, whatever the snake may be thinking of.

"Who is Nag?" he said. "*I* am Nag. The great god Brahm put his mark upon all our people when the first cobra spread his hood to keep the sun off Brahm as he slept. Look, and be afraid!"

He spread out his hood more than ever, and Rikki-tikki saw the spectacle-mark on the back of it that looks exactly like the eye part of a hook-and-eye fastening. He was afraid for the minute; but it is impossible for a mongoose to stay frightened for any length of time, and though Rikki-tikki had never met a live cobra before, his mother had fed him on dead ones, and he knew that all a grown mongoose's business in life was to fight and eat snakes. Nag knew that too, and at the bottom of his cold heart he was afraid.

"Well," said Rikki-tikki, and his tail began to fluff up again, "marks or no marks, do you think it is right for you to eat fledglings out of a nest?"

Nag was thinking to himself, and watching the least little movement in the grass behind Rikki-tikki. He knew that mongooses in the garden meant death sooner or later for him and his family; but he wanted to get

Rikki-tikki off his guard. So he dropped his head a little, and put it on one side.

"Let us talk," he said. "You eat eggs. Why should not I eat birds?"

"Behind you! Look behind you!" sang Darzee.

Rikki-tikki knew better than to waste time in staring. He jumped up in the air as high as he could go, and just under him whizzed by the head of Nagaina, Nag's wicked wife. She had crept up behind him as he was talking, to make an end of him; and he heard her savage hiss as the stroke missed. He came down almost across her back, and if he had been an old mongoose he would have known that then was the time to break her back with one bite; but he was afraid of the terrible lashing return-stroke of the cobra. He bit, indeed, but did not bite long enough, and he jumped clear of the whisking tail, leaving Nagaina torn and angry.

"Wicked, wicked Darzee!" said Nag, lashing up as high as he could reach toward the nest in the thorn-bush; but Darzee had built it out of reach of snakes, and it only swayed to and fro.

Rikki-tikki felt his eyes growing red and hot (when a mongoose's eyes grow red, he is angry), and he sat back on his tail and hind legs like a little kangaroo, and looked all around him, and chattered with rage. But Nag and Nagaina had disappeared into the grass. When a snake misses its stroke, it never says anything or gives any sign of what it means to do next. Rikki-tikki did not care to follow them, for he did not feel sure that he could manage two snakes at once. So he trotted off to the gravel path near the house, and sat down to think. It was a serious matter for him.

If you read the old books of natural history, you will find they say that when the mongoose fights the snake and happens to get bitten, he runs off and eats some herb that cures him. That is not true. The victory is only a matter of quickness of eye and quickness of foot,—snake's blow against mongoose's jump,—and as no eye can follow the motion of a snake's head when it strikes, that makes things much more wonderful than any magic herb. Rikki-tikki knew he was a young mongoose, and it made him all the more pleased to think that he had managed to escape a blow from behind. It gave him confidence in himself, and when Teddy came running down the path, Rikki-tikki was ready to be petted.

But just as Teddy was stooping, something flinched a little in the dust, and a tiny voice said: "Be careful. I am death!" It was Karait, the dusty brown snakeling that lies for choice on the dusty earth; and his bite is as dangerous as the cobra's. But he is so small that nobody thinks of him, and so he does the more harm to people.

Rikki-tikki's eyes grew red again, and he danced up to Karait with the peculiar rocking, swaying motion that he had inherited from his family. It looks very funny, but it is so perfectly balanced a gait that you can fly off from it at any angle you please; and in dealing with snakes this is an advantage. If Rikki-tikki had only known, he was doing a much more dangerous thing than fighting Nag, for Karait is so small, and can turn so quickly, that unless Rikki bit him close to the back of the head, he would get the return-stroke in his eye or lip. But Rikki did not know: his eyes were all red, and he rocked back and forth, looking for a good place to hold. Karait struck out. Rikki jumped sideways and tried to run in, but the wicked little dusty gray head lashed within a fraction of his shoulder, and he had to jump over the body, and the head followed his heels close.

Teddy shouted to the house: "Oh, look here! Our mongoose is killing a snake"; and Rikki-tikki heard a scream from Teddy's mother. His father ran out with a stick, but by the time he came up, Karait had lunged out once too far, and Rikki-tikki had sprung, jumped on the snake's back, dropped his head far between his fore legs, bitten as high up the back as he could get hold, and rolled away. That bite paralyzed Karait, and Rikki-tikki was just going to eat him up from the tail, after the custom of his family at dinner, when he remembered that a full meal makes a slow mongoose, and if he wanted all his strength and quickness ready, he must keep himself thin.

He went away for a dust-bath under the castor-oil bushes, while Teddy's father beat the dead Karait. "What is the use of that?" thought Rikki-tikki. "I have settled it all"; and then Teddy's mother picked him up from the dust and hugged him, crying that he had saved Teddy from death, and Teddy's father said that he was a providence, and Teddy looked on with big scared eyes. Rikki-tikki was rather amused at all the fuss, which, of course, he did not understand. Teddy's mother might just as well have petted Teddy for playing in the dust. Rikki was thoroughly enjoying himself.

That night, at dinner, walking to and fro among the wine-glasses on the table, he could have stuffed himself three times over with nice things; but he remembered Nag and Nagaina, and though it was very pleasant to be patted and petted by Teddy's mother, and to sit on Teddy's shoulder, his eyes would get red from time to time, and he would go off into his long war-cry of *"Rikk-tikk-tikki-tikki-tchk!"*

Teddy carried him off to bed, and insisted on Rikki-tikki sleeping under his chin. Rikki-tikki was too well bred to bite or scratch, but as soon as Teddy was asleep he went off for his nightly walk round the house, and in the dark he ran up against Chuchundra, the muskrat, creeping round by the wall. Chuchundra is a broken-hearted little beast. He whimpers and cheeps all the night, trying to make up his mind to run into the middle of the room, but he never gets there.

"Don't kill me," said Chuchundra, almost weeping. "Rikki-tikki, don't kill me."

"Do you think a snake-killer kills muskrats?" said Rikki-tikki scornfully.

"Those who kill snakes get killed by snakes," said Chuchundra, more sorrowfully than ever. "And how am I to be sure that Nag won't mistake me for you some dark night?"

"There's not the least danger," said Rikki-tikki; "but Nag is in the garden, and I know you don't go there."

"My cousin Chua, the rat, told me—" said Chuchundra, and then he stopped.

"Told you what?"

"H'sh! Nag is everywhere, Rikki-tikki. You should have talked to Chua in the garden."

"I did n't—so you must tell me. Quick, Chuchundra, or I'll bite you!"

Chuchundra sat down and cried till the tears rolled off his whiskers. "I am a very poor man," he sobbed. "I never had spirit enough to run out into the middle of the room. H'sh! I must n't tell you anything. Can't you *hear*, Rikki-tikki?"

Rikki-tikki listened. The house was as still as still, but he thought he could just catch the faintest *scratch-scratch* in the world,— a noise as faint as that of a wasp walking on a window-pane,—the dry scratch of a snake's scales on brickwork.

"That's Nag or Nagaina," he said to himself; "and he is crawling into the bath-room sluice. You're right, Chuchundra; I should have talked to Chua."

He stole off to Teddy's bath-room, but there was nothing there, and then to Teddy's mother's bath-room. At the bottom of the smooth plaster wall there was a brick pulled out to make a sluice for the bath-water, and as Rikki-tikki stole in by the masonry curb where the bath is put, he heard Nag and Nagaina whispering together outside in the moonlight.

"When the house is emptied of people," said Nagaina to her husband, "*he* will have to go away, and then the garden will be our own again. Go in quietly, and remember that the big man who killed Karait is the first one to bite. Then come out and tell me, and we will hunt for Rikki-tikki together."

"But are you sure that there is anything to be gained by killing the people?" said Nag.

"Everything. When there were no people in the bungalow, did we have any mongoose in the garden? So long as the bungalow is empty, we are king and queen of the garden; and remember that as soon as our eggs in the melon-bed hatch (as they may to-morrow), our children will need room and quiet."

"I had not thought of that," said Nag. "I will go, but there is no need that we should hunt for Rikki-tikki afterward. I will kill the big man and his wife, and the child if I can, and come away quietly. Then the bungalow will be empty, and Rikki-tikki will go."

Rikki-tikki tingled all over with rage and hatred at this, and then Nag's head came through the sluice, and his five feet of cold body followed it. Angry as he was, Rikki-tikki was very frightened as he saw the size of the big cobra. Nag coiled himself up, raised his head, and looked into the bathroom in the dark, and Rikki could see his eyes glitter.

"Now, if I kill him here, Nagaina will know; and if I fight him on the open floor, the odds are in his favor. What am I to do?" said Rikki-tikki-tavi.

Nag waved to and fro, and then Rikki-tikki heard him drinking from the biggest water-jar that was used to fill the bath. "That is good," said the snake. "Now, when Karait was killed, the big man had a stick. He may have that stick still, but when he comes in to bathe in the morning he will not have a stick. I shall wait here till he comes. Nagaina—do you hear me?—I shall wait here in the cool till daytime."

There was no answer from outside, so Rikki-tikki knew Nagaina had gone away. Nag coiled himself down, coil by coil, round the bulge at the bottom of the water-jar, and Rikki-tikki stayed still as death. After an hour he began to move, muscle by muscle, toward the jar. Nag was asleep, and Rikki-tikki looked at his big back, wondering which would be the best place for a good hold. "If I don't break his back at the first jump," said Rikki, "he can still fight; and if he fights—O Rikki!" He looked at the thickness of the neck below the hood, but that was too much for him; and a bite near the tail would only make Nag savage.

"It must be the head," he said at last; "the head above the hood; and, when I am once there, I must not let go."

Then he jumped. The head was lying a little clear of the water-jar, under the curve of it; and, as his teeth met, Rikki braced his back against the bulge of the red earthenware to hold down the head. This gave him just one second's purchase, and he made the most of it. Then he was battered to and fro as a rat is shaken by a dog—to and fro on the floor, up and down, and round in great circles; but his eyes were red, and he held on as the body cart-whipped over the floor, upsetting the tin dipper and the soap-dish and the flesh-brush, and banged against the tin side of the bath. As he held he closed his jaws tighter and tighter, for he made sure he would be banged to death, and, for the honor of his family, he preferred to be found with his teeth locked. He was dizzy, aching, and felt shaken to pieces when something went off like a thunderclap just behind him; a hot wind knocked him senseless and red fire singed his fur. The big man had been wakened by the noise, and had fired both barrels of a shot-gun into Nag just behind the hood.

Rikki-tikki held on with his eyes shut, for now he was quite sure he was dead; but the head did not move, and the big man picked him up and said: "It's the mongoose again, Alice; the little chap has saved *our* lives now." Then Teddy's mother came in with a very white face, and saw what was left of Nag, and Rikki-tikki dragged himself to Teddy's bedroom and spent half the rest of the night shaking himself tenderly to find out whether he really was broken into forty pieces, as he fancied.

When morning came he was very stiff, but well pleased with his doings. "Now I have Nagaina to settle with, and she will be worse than five Nags, and there's no knowing when the eggs she spoke of will hatch. Goodness! I must go and see Darzee," he said.

Without waiting for breakfast, Rikki-tikki ran to the thorn-bush where Darzee was singing a song of triumph at the top of his voice. The news of Nag's death was all over the garden, for the sweeper had thrown the body on the rubbish-heap.

"Oh, you stupid tuft of feathers!" said Rikki-tikki, angrily. "Is this the time to sing?"

"Nag is dead—is dead—is dead!" sang Darzee. "The valiant Rikki-tikki caught him by the head and held fast. The big man brought the bang-stick and Nag fell in two pieces! He will never eat my babies again."

"All that's true enough; but where's Nagaina?" said Rikki-tikki, looking carefully round him.

"Nagaina came to the bath-room sluice and called for Nag," Darzee went on; "and Nag came out on the end of a stick—the sweeper picked him up on the end of a stick and threw him upon the rubbish-heap. Let us sing about the great, the red-eyed Rikki-tikki!" and Darzee filled his throat and sang.

"If I could get up to your nest, I'd roll all your babies out!" said Rikki-tikki. "You don't know when to do the right thing at the right time. You're safe enough in your nest there, but it's war for me down here. Stop singing a minute, Darzee."

"For the great, the beautiful Rikki-tikki's sake I will stop," said Darzee. "What is it, O Killer of the terrible Nag!"

"Where is Nagaina, for the third time?"

"On the rubbish-heap by the stables, mourning for Nag. Great is Rikki-tikki with the white teeth."

"Bother my white teeth! Have you ever heard where she keeps her eggs?"

"In the melon-bed, on the end nearest the wall, where the sun strikes nearly all day. She had them there weeks ago."

"And you never thought it worth while to tell me? The end nearest the wall, you said?"

"Rikki-tikki, you are not going to eat her eggs?"

"Not eat exactly; no. Darzee, if you have a grain of sense you will fly off to the stables and pretend that your wing is broken, and let Nagaina chase you away to this bush? I must get to the melon-bed, and if I went there now she'd see me."

Darzee was a feather-brained little fellow who could never hold more than one idea at a time in his head; and just because he knew that Nagaina's children were born in eggs like his own, he did n't think at first that it was fair to kill them. But his wife was a sensible bird, and she knew that cobra's eggs meant young cobras later on; so she flew off from the nest, and left Darzee to keep the babies warm, and continue his song about the death of Nag. Darzee was very like a man in some ways.

She fluttered in front of Nagaina by the rubbish-heap, and cried out, "Oh, my wing is broken! The boy in the house threw a stone at me and broke it." Then she fluttered more desperately than ever.

Nagaina lifted up her head and hissed, "You warned Rikki-tikki when I would have killed him. Indeed and truly, you've chosen a bad place to be lame in." And she moved toward Darzee's wife, slipping along over the dust.

"The boy broke it with a stone!" shrieked Darzee's wife.

"Well! It may be some consolation to you when you're dead to know that I shall settle accounts with the boy. My husband lies on the rubbish-heap this morning, but before night the boy in the house will lie very still. What is the use of running away? I am sure to catch you. Little fool, look at me!"

Darzee's wife knew better than to do *that,* for a bird who looks at a snake's eyes gets so frightened that she cannot move. Darzee's wife fluttered on, piping sorrowfully, and never leaving the ground, and Nagaina quickened her pace.

Rikki-tikki heard them going up the path from the stables, and he raced for the end of the melon-patch near the wall. There, in the warm litter about the melons, very cunningly hidden, he found twenty-five eggs, about the size of a bantam's eggs, but with whitish skin instead of shell.

"I was not a day too soon," he said; for he could see the baby cobras curled up inside the skin, and he knew that the minute they were hatched they could each kill a man or a mongoose. He bit off the tops of the eggs as fast as he could, taking care to crush the young cobras, and turned over the litter from time to time to see whether he had missed any. At last there were only three eggs left, and Rikki-tikki began to chuckle to himself, when he heard Darzee's wife screaming:

"Rikki-tikki, I led Nagaina toward the house, and she has gone into the veranda, and—oh, come quickly—she means killing!"

Rikki-tikki smashed two eggs, and tumbled backward down the melon-bed with the third egg in his mouth, and scuttled to the veranda as hard as he could put foot to the ground. Teddy and his mother and father were there at early breakfast; but Rikki-tikki saw that they were not eating anything. They sat stone-still, and their faces were white. Nagaina was coiled up on the matting by Teddy's chair, within easy striking distance of Teddy's bare leg, and she was swaying to and fro singing a song of triumph.

"Son of the big man that killed Nag," she hissed, "stay still. I am not ready yet. Wait a little. Keep very still, all you three. If you move I strike, and if you do not move I strike. Oh, foolish people, who killed my Nag!"

Teddy's eyes were fixed on his father, and all his father could do was to whisper, "Sit still, Teddy. You mustn't move. Teddy, keep still."

Then Rikki-tikki came up and cried: "Turn round, Nagaina; turn and fight!"

"All in good time," said she, without moving her eyes. "I will settle my account with *you* presently. Look at your friends, Rikki-tikki. They are still and white; they are afraid. They dare not move, and if you come a step nearer I strike."

"Look at your eggs," said Rikki-tikki, "in the melon-bed near the wall. Go and look, Nagaina."

The big snake turned half round, and saw the egg on the veranda. "Ah-h! Give it to me," she said.

Rikki-tikki put his paws one on each side of the egg, and his eyes were blood-red. "What price for a snake's egg? For a young cobra? For a young king-cobra? For the last—the very last of the brood? The ants are eating all the others down by the melon-bed."

Nagaina spun clear round, forgetting everything for the sake of the one egg; and Rikki-tikki saw Teddy's father shoot out a big hand, catch Teddy by the shoulder, and drag him across the little table with the tea-cups, safe and out of reach of Nagaina.

"Tricked! Tricked! Tricked! *Rikk-tck-tck!*" chuckled Rikki-tikki. "The boy is safe, and it was I—I—I that caught Nag by the hood last night in the bath-room." Then he began to jump up and down, all four feet together, his head close to the floor. "He threw me to and fro, but he could not shake me off. He was dead before the big man blew him in two. I did it. *Rikki-tikki-tck-tck!* Come then, Nagaina. Come and fight with me. You shall not be a widow long."

Nagaina saw that she had lost her chance of killing Teddy, and the egg lay between Rikki-tikki's paws. "Give me the egg, Rikki-tikki. Give me the last of my eggs, and I will go away and never come back," she said, lowering her hood.

"Yes, you will go away, and you will never come back; for you will go to the rubbish-heap with Nag. Fight, widow! The big man has gone for his gun! Fight!"

Rikki-tikki was bounding all round Nagaina, keeping just out of reach of her stroke, his little eyes like hot coals. Nagaina gathered herself together, and flung out at him. Rikki-tikki jumped up and backward. Again and again and again she struck, and each time her head came with a whack on the matting of the veranda and she gathered herself together like a watch-spring. Then Rikki-tikki danced in a circle to get behind her, and Nagaina spun round to keep her head to his head, so that the rustle of her tail on the matting sounded like dry leaves blown along by the wind.

He had forgotten the egg. It still lay on the veranda, and Nagaina came nearer and nearer to it, till at last, while Rikki-tikki was drawing breath, she caught it in her mouth, turned to the veranda steps, and flew like an arrow down the path, with Rikki-tikki behind her. When the cobra runs for her life, she goes like a whiplash flicked across a horse's neck.

Rikki-tikki knew that he must catch her, or all the trouble would begin again. She headed straight for the long grass by the thorn-bush, and as he was running Rikki-tikki heard Darzee still singing his foolish little song of triumph. But Darzee's wife was wiser. She flew off her nest as Nagaina came along, and flapped her wings about Nagaina's head. If Darzee had helped they might have turned her; but Nagaina only lowered her hood and went on. Still, the instant's delay brought Rikki-tikki up to her, and as she plunged into the rat-hole where she and Nag used to live, his little white teeth were clenched on her tail, and he went down with her—and very few mongooses, however wise and old they may be, care to follow a cobra into its hole. It was dark in the hole; and Rikki-tikki never knew when it might open out and give Nagaina room to turn and strike at him. He held on savagely, and struck out his feet to act as brakes on the dark slope of the hot, moist earth.

Then the grass by the mouth of the hole stopped waving, and Darzee said: "It is all over with Rikki-tikki! We must sing his death-song. Valiant Rikki-tikki is dead! For Nagaina will surely kill him underground."

So he sang a very mournful song that he made up all on the spur of the minute, and just as he got to the most touching part the grass quivered again, and Rikki-tikki, covered with dirt, dragged himself out of the hole leg by leg, licking his whiskers. Darzee stopped with a little shout. Rikki-tikki shook some of the dust out of his fur and sneezed. "It is all over," he said. "The widow will never come out again." And the red ants that live between the grass stems heard him, and began to troop down one after another to see if he had spoken the truth.

Rikki-tikki curled himself up in the grass and slept where he was—slept and slept till it was late in the afternoon, for he had done a hard day's work.

"Now," he said, when he awoke, "I will go back to the house. Tell the Coppersmith, Darzee, and he will tell the garden that Nagaina is dead."

The Coppersmith is a bird who makes a noise exactly like the beating of a little hammer on a copper pot; and the reason he is always making it is because he is the town-crier to every Indian garden, and tells all the news to everybody who cares to listen. As Rikki-tikki went up the path, he heard his "attention" notes like a tiny dinner-gong; and then the steady "*Ding-dong-tock!* Nag is dead—*dong!* Nagaina is dead! *Ding-dong-tock!*" That set all the birds in the garden singing, and the frogs croaking; for Nag and Nagaina used to eat frogs as well as little birds.

When Rikki got to the house, Teddy and Teddy's mother (she looked very white still, for she had been fainting) and Teddy's father came out and almost cried over him; and that night he ate all that was given him till he could eat no more, and went to bed on Teddy's shoulder, where Teddy's mother saw him when she came to look late at night.

"He saved our lives and Teddy's life," she said to her husband. "Just think, he saved all our lives."

Rikki-tikki woke up with a jump, for all the mongooses are light sleepers.

"Oh, it's you," said he. "What are you bothering for? All the cobras are dead; and if they were n't, I'm here."

Rikki-tikki had a right to be proud of himself; but he did not grow too proud, and he kept that garden as a mongoose should keep it, with tooth and jump and spring and bite, till never a cobra dared show its head inside the walls.

## DARZEE'S CHAUNT

### (SUNG IN HONOR OF RIKKI-TIKKI-TAVI)

Singer and tailor am I—
　　Doubled the joys that I know—
Proud of my lilt through the sky,
　　Proud of the house that I sew—
Over and under, so weave I my music—so weave I
　　the house that I sew.

Sing to your fledglings again,
　　Mother, oh lift up your head!
Evil that plagued us is slain,
　　Death in the garden lies dead.
Terror that hid in the roses is impotent—flung on
　　the dung-hill and dead!

Who hath delivered us, who?
　　Tell me his nest and his name.
Rikki, the valiant, the true,
　　Tikki, with eyeballs of flame.
Rik-tikki-tikki, the ivory-fanged, the hunter with eye-
　　balls of flame.

Give him the Thanks of the Birds,
　　Bowing with tail-feathers spread!
Praise him with nightingale words—
　　Nay, I will praise him instead.
Hear! I will sing you the praise of the bottle-tailed
　　Rikki, with eyeballs of red!

*(Here Rikki-tikki interrupted, and the rest of the song*
　　*is lost.)*

## UNCLE DAVID'S NONSENSICAL STORY
## ABOUT GIANTS AND FAIRIES

*Catherine Sinclair*

*Pie-crust, and pastry-crust, that was the wall;*
*The windows were made of black-puddings and white,*
*And slated with pancakes — you ne'er saw the like!*

In the days of yore, children were not all such clever, good, sensible people as they are now! Lessons were then considered rather a plague—sugar-plums were still in demand—holidays continued yet in fashion—and toys were not then made to teach mathematics, nor story-books to give instruction in chemistry and navigation. These were very strange times, and there existed at that period, a very idle, greedy, naughty boy, such as we never hear of in the present day. His papa and mamma were—no matter who, and he lived,—no matter where. His name was Master No-book, and he seemed to think his eyes were made for nothing but to stare out of the windows, and his mouth for no other purpose but to eat. This young gentleman hated lessons like mustard, both of which brought tears into his eyes, and during school-hours he sat gazing at his books, pretending to be busy, while his mind wandered away to wish impatiently for dinner, and to consider where he could get the nicest pies, pastry, ices and jellies, while he smacked his lips at the very thoughts of them. I think he must have been first cousin to Peter Grey; but that is not perfectly certain.

Whenever Master No-book spoke, it was always to ask for something, and you might continually hear him say, in a whining tone of voice, "Papa! may I take this piece of cake? Aunt Sarah! will you give me an apple? Mamma! do end me the whole of that plum-pudding!" Indeed, very frequently, when he did not get permission to gormandize, this naughty glutton helped himself without leave. Even his dreams were like his waking hours, for he had often a horrible nightmare about lessons, thinking he was smothered with Greek Lexicons, or pelted out of the school with a shower of English Grammars; while one night he fancied himself sitting down to devour an enormous plum-cake, and all on a sudden it became transformed into a Latin Dictionary!

One afternoon, Master No-book, having played truant all day from school, was lolling on his mamma's best sofa in the drawing-room, with his leather boots tucked up on the satin cushions, and nothing to do but to suck a few oranges, and nothing to think of but how much sugar to put upon them, when suddenly an event took place, which filled him with astonishment.

A sound of soft music stole into the room, becoming louder and louder the longer he listened, till at length, in a few moments afterwards, a large hole burst open in the wall of his room, and there stepped into his presence two magnificent fairies, just arrived from their castles in the air, to pay him a visit. They had travelled all the way on purpose to have some conversation with Master No-book, and immediately introduced themselves in a very ceremonious manner.

The fairy Do-nothing was gorgeously dressed with a wreath of flaming gas round her head, a robe of gold tissue, a necklace of rubies, and a bouquet in her hand of glittering diamonds. Her cheeks were rouged to the very eyes, her teeth were set in gold, and her hair was of a most brilliant purple; in short, so fine and fashionable-looking a fairy never was seen in a drawing-room before.

The fairy Teach-all, who followed next, was simply dressed in white muslin, with bunches of natural flowers in her light brown hair, and she carried in her hand a few neat small books, which Master No-book looked at with a shudder of aversion.

The two fairies now informed him, that they very often invited large parties of children to spend some time at their palaces, but as they lived in quite an opposite direction, it was necessary for their young guests to choose which it would be best to visit first; therefore now they had come to inquire of Master No-book whom he thought it would be most agreeable to accompany on the present occasion.

"In my house," said the fairy Teach-all, speaking with a very sweet smile, and a soft, pleasing voice, "you shall be taught to find pleasure in every sort of exertion; for I delight in activity and diligence. My young friends rise at seven every morning, and amuse themselves with working in a beautiful garden of flowers,—rearing whatever fruit they wish to eat,—visiting among the poor,—associating pleasantly together,—studying the arts and sciences,—and learning to know the world in which they live, and to fulfil the purposes for which they have been brought into it. In short, all our amusements tend to some useful object, either for our own improvement or the good of others, and you will grow wiser, better, and happier every day you remain in the palace of Knowledge."

"But in Castle Needless, where I live," interrupted the fairy Do-nothing, rudely pushing her companion aside, with an angry, contemptuous look, "we never think of exerting ourselves for anything. You may put your head in your pocket, and your hands in your sides as long as you choose to stay. No one is ever even asked a question, that he may be spared the trouble of answering. We lead the most fashionable life imaginable, for nobody speaks to anybody! Each of my visitors is quite an exclusive, and sits with his back to as many of the company as possible, in the most comfortable arm-chair that can be contrived. There, if you are only so good as to take the trouble of wishing for anything, it is yours, without even turning an eye round to look where it comes from. Dresses are provided of the most magnificent kind, which go on themselves, without your having the smallest annoyance with either buttons or strings,—games which you can play without an effort of thought,—and dishes dressed by a French cook, smoking hot under your nose, from morning till night,—while any rain we have is either made of sherry, brandy, lemonade, or lavender water, and in winter it generally snows iced-punch for an hour during the forenoon."

Nobody need be told which fairy Master No-book preferred; and quite charmed at his own good fortune in receiving so agreeable an invitation, he eagerly gave his hand to the splendid new acquaintance who promised him so much pleasure and ease, and gladly proceeded in a carriage lined with velvet, stuffed with downy pillows, and drawn by milk-white swans, to that magnificent residence, Castle Needless, which was lighted by a thousand windows during the day, and by a million of lamps every night.

Here Master No-book enjoyed a constant holiday and a constant feast, while a beautiful lady covered with jewels was ready to tell him stories from morning till night, and servants waited to pick up his playthings if they fell, or to draw out his purse or his pocket-handkerchief when he wished to use them.

Thus Master No-book lay dozing for hours and days on richly embroidered cushions, never stirring from his place, but admiring the view of trees covered with the richest burned almonds, grottoes of sugar-candy, a *jet d'eau* of champagne, a wide sea which tasted of sugar instead of salt, and a bright clear pond, filled with gold-fish, that let themselves be caught whenever he pleased. Nothing could be more complete; and yet, very strange to say, Master No-book did not seem particularly happy! This appears exceedingly unreasonable, when so much trouble was taken to please him, but the truth is, that every day he became more fretful and peevish. No sweetmeats were worth the trouble of eating, nothing was pleasant to play at, and in the end he wished it were possible to sleep all day, as well as all night.

Not a hundred miles from the fairy Do-nothing's palace, there lived a most cruel monster called the giant Snap-'em-up, who looked, when he stood up, like the tall steeple of a great church, raising his head so high that he could peep over the loftiest mountains, and was obliged to climb up a ladder to comb his own hair!

Every morning regularly, this prodigiously great giant walked round the world before breakfast for an appetite, after which he made tea in a large lake, used the sea as a slop-basin, and boiled his kettle on Mount Vesuvius. He lived in great style, and his dinners were most magnificent, consisting very often of an elephant roasted whole, ostrich patties, a tiger smothered in onions, stewed lions, and whale soup; but for a side dish his greatest favourite consisted of little boys, as fat as possible, fried in crumbs of bread, with plenty of pepper and salt.

No children were so well fed, or in such good condition for eating, as those in the fairy Do-nothing's garden, who was a very particular friend of the giant Snap-'em-up's, and who sometimes laughingly said she would give him a licence, and call her own garden his "preserve," because she allowed him to help himself, whenever he pleased, to as many of her visitors as he chose, without taking the trouble even to count them, and in return for such extreme civility, the giant very frequently invited her to dinner.

Snap-em-up's favourite sport was to see how many brace of little boys he could bag in a morning; so in passing along the streets, he peeped into all the drawing-rooms without having occasion to get upon tiptoe, and picked up every young gentleman who was idly looking out of the windows, and even a few occasionally who were playing truant from school; but busy children seemed always somehow quite out of his reach.

One day, when Master No-book felt even more lazy, more idle, and more miserable than ever, he lay beside a perfect mountain of toys and cakes, wondering what to wish for next, and hating the very sight of everything and everybody. At last he gave so loud a yawn of weariness and disgust, that his jaw very nearly fell out of joint, and then he sighed so deeply, that the giant Snap-'em-up heard the sound as he passed along the road after breakfast, and instantly stepped into the garden, with his glass at his eye, to see what was the matter. Immediately on observing a large, fat, over-grown boy, as round as a dumpling, lying on a bed of roses, he gave a cry of delight, followed by a gigantic peal of laughter, which was heard three miles off, and picking up Master No-book between his finger and thumb, with a pinch that very nearly broke his ribs, he carried him rapidly towards his own castle, while the fairy Do-nothing laughingly shook her head as he passed, saying, "That little man does me great credit! he has only been fed for a week, and is as fat already as a prize ox! What a dainty morsel he will be. When do you dine to-day, in case I should have time to look in upon you?"

On reaching home the giant immediately hung up Master No-book, by the hair of his head, on a prodigious hook in the larder, having first taken some large lumps of nasty suet, forcing them down his throat to make him become still fatter, and then stirring the fire, that he might be almost melted with heat, to make his liver grow larger. On a shelf quite near, Master No-book perceived the dead bodies of six other boys, whom he remembered to have seen fattening in the fairy Do-nothing's garden, while he recollected how some of them had rejoiced at the thoughts of leading a long, useless, idle life, with no one to please but themselves.

The enormous cook now seized hold of Master No-book, brandishing her knife, with an aspect of horrible determination, intending to kill him, while he took the trouble of screaming and kicking in the most desperate manner, when the giant turned gravely round and said, that as pigs were considered a much greater dainty when whipped to death than killed in any other way, he meant to see whether children might not be improved by it also; therefore she might leave that great hog of a boy till he had time to try the experiment, especially as his own appetite would be improved by the exercise. This was a dreadful prospect for the unhappy prisoner; but meantime it prolonged his life a few hours, as he was immediately hung up again in the larder, and left to himself. There, in torture of mind and body,—like a fish upon a hook,—the wretched boy began at last to reflect seriously upon his former ways, and to consider what a happy home he might have had, if he could only have been satisfied with business and pleasure succeeding each other, like day and night, while lessons might have come in as a pleasant sauce to his play-hours, and his play-hours as a sauce to his lessons.

In the midst of many reflections, which were all very sensible, though rather too late, Master No-book's attention became attracted by the sound of many voices laughing, talking, and singing, which caused him to turn his eyes in a new direction, when, for the first time, he observed that the fairy Teach-all's garden lay upon a beautiful sloping bank not far off. There a crowd of merry, noisy, rosy-cheeked boys were busily employed, and seemed happier than the day was long; while poor Master No-book watched them during his own miserable hours, envying the enjoyment with which they raked the flower-borders, gathered the fruit, carried baskets of vegetables to the poor, worked with carpenters' tools, drew pictures, shot with bows and arrows, played at cricket, and then sat in the sunny arbours learning their tasks, or talking agreeably together, till at length, a dinner-bell having been rung, the whole party sat merrily down with hearty appetites, and cheerful good humour, to an entertainment of plain roast meat and pudding, where the fairy Teach-all presided herself, and helped her guests moderately, to as much as was good for each.

Large tears rolled down the cheeks of Master No-book while watching this scene; and remembering that if he had known what was best for him, he might have been as happy as the happiest of these excellent boys, instead of suffering *ennui* and weariness, as he had done at the fairy Do-nothing's, ending in a miserable death; but his attention was soon after most alarmingly roused by hearing the giant Snap-'em-up again in conversation with his cook; who said, that if he wished for a good large dish of scalloped children at dinner, it would be necessary to catch a few more, as those he had already provided would scarcely be a mouthful.

As the giant kept very fashionable hours, and always waited dinner for himself till nine o'clock, there was still plenty of time; so, with a loud grumble about the trouble, he seized a large basket in his hand, and set off at a rapid pace towards the fairy Teach-all's garden. It was very seldom that Snap-'em-up ventured to think of foraging in this direction, as he never once succeeded in carrying off a single captive from the enclosure, it was so well fortified and so bravely defended; but on this occasion, being desperately hungry, he felt as bold as a lion, and walked, with outstretched hands, straight towards the fairy Teach-all's dinner-table, taking such prodigious strides, that he seemed almost as if he would trample on himself.

A cry of consternation arose the instant this tremendous giant appeared; and as usual on such occasions, when he had made the same attempt before, a dreadful battle took place. Fifty active little boys bravely flew upon the enemy, armed with their dinner knives, and looked like a nest of hornets, stinging him in every direction, till he roared with pain, and would have run away, but the fairy Teach-all, seeing his intention, rushed forward with the carving-knife, and brandishing it high over her head, she most courageously stabbed him to the heart!

If a great mountain had fallen to the earth, it would have seemed like nothing in comparison with the giant Snap-'em-up, who crushed two or three houses to powder beneath him, and upset several fine monuments that were to have made people remembered for ever; but all this would have seemed scarcely worth mentioning, had it not been for a still greater event which occurred on the occasion, no less than the death of the fairy Do-nothing, who had been indolently looking on at this great battle, without taking the trouble to interfere, or even to care who was victorious; but being also lazy about running away, when the giant fell, his sword came with so violent a stroke on her head, that she instantly expired.

Thus, luckily for the whole world, the fairy Teach-all got possession of immense property, which she proceeded without delay to make the best use of in her power.

In the first place, however, she lost no time in liberating Master No-book from his hook in the larder, and gave him a lecture on activity, moderation, and good conduct, which he never afterwards forgot; and it was astonishing to see the change that took place immediately in his whole thoughts and actions. From this very hour, Master No-book became the most diligent, active, happy boy in the fairy Teach-all's garden; and on returning home a month afterwards, he astonished all the masters at school by his extraordinary reformation. The most difficult lessons were a pleasure to him,—he scarcely ever stirred without a book in his hand,—never lay on a sofa again,—would scarcely even sit on a chair with a back to it, but preferred a three-legged stool,—detested holidays,—never thought any exertion a trouble,—preferred climbing over the top of a hill to creeping round the bottom,—always ate the plainest food in very small quantities,—joined a Temperance Society!—and never tasted a morsel till he had worked very hard and got an appetite.

Not long after this, an old uncle, who had formerly been ashamed of Master No-book's indolence and gluttony, became so pleased at the wonderful change, that, on his death, he left him a magnificent estate, desiring that he should take his name; therefore, instead of being any longer one of the No-book family, he is now called Sir Timothy Bluestocking,—a pattern to the whole country round, for the good he does to every one, and especially for his extraordinary activity, appearing as if he could do twenty things at once. Though generally very good-natured and agreeable, Sir Timothy is occasionally observed in a violent passion, laying about him with his walking-stick in the most terrific manner, and beating little boys within an inch of their lives; but on inquiry, it invariably appears that he has found them out to be lazy, idle, or greedy, for all the industrious boys in the parish are sent to get employment from him, while he assures them that they are far happier breaking stones on the road, than if they were sitting idly in a drawing-room with nothing to do. Sir Timothy cares very little for poetry in general; but the following are his favourite verses, which he has placed over the chimney-piece at a school that he built for the poor, and every scholar is obliged, the very day he begins his education, to learn them:—

Some people complain they have nothing to do,
    And time passes slowly away;
They saunter about, with no object in view,
    And long for the end of the day.

In vain are the trifles and toys they desire,
    For nothing they truly enjoy;
Of trifles, and toys, and amusements they tire,
    For want of some useful employ.

Although for transgression the ground was accursed,
    Yet gratefully man must allow,
'Twas really a blessing which doomed him, at first,
    To live by the sweat of his brow.

"Thank you a hundred times over, Uncle David!" said Harry, when the story was finished. "I shall take care not to be found hanging any day on a hook in the larder! Certainly, Frank, you must have spent a month with the good fairy; and I hope she will some day invite me to be made a scholar of too, for Laura and I still belong to the No-book family."

"It is very important, Harry, to choose the best course from the beginning," observed Lady Harriet. "Good or bad habits grow stronger and stronger every minute, as if an additional string were tied on daily, to keep us in the road where we walked the day before; so those who mistake the path of duty at first, find hourly increasing difficulty in turning round."

"But, grandmamma!" said Frank, "you have put up some finger-posts to direct us right; and whenever I see 'No passage this way,' we shall all wheel about directly."

"As Mrs. Crabtree has not tapped at the door yet, I shall describe the progress of a wise and a foolish man, to see which Harry and you would prefer copying," replied Lady Harriet, smiling. "The fool begins when he is young, with hating lessons, lying long in bed, and spending all his money on trash. Any books he will consent to read are never about what is true or important; but he wastes all his time and thoughts on silly stories that never could have happened. Thus he neglects to learn what was done and thought by all the great and good men who really lived in former times; while even his Bible, if he has one, grows dusty on the shelf. After so bad a beginning, he grows up with no useful or interesting knowledge; therefore his whole talk is to describe his own horses, his own dogs, his own guns, and his own exploits; boasting of what a high wall his horse can leap over, the number of little birds he can shoot in a day, and how many bottles of wine he can swallow without tumbling under the table. Thus 'glorying in his shame,' he thinks himself a most wonderful person, not knowing that men are born to do much better things than merely to find selfish pleasure and amusement for themselves. Presently he grows old, gouty, and infirm—no longer able to do such prodigious achievements; therefore now his great delight is to sit with his feet upon the fender, at a club, all day, telling what a famous rider, shooter, and drinker he was long ago: but nobody cares to hear such old stories: therefore he is called a 'proser,' and every person avoids him. It is no wonder a man talks about himself, if he has never read or thought about any one else. But at length his precious time has all been wasted, and his last hour comes, during which he can have nothing to look back upon but a life of folly and guilt. He sees no one around who loves him, or will weep over his grave; and when he looks forward, it is towards an eternal world, which he has never prepared to enter, and of which he knows nothing."

"What a terrible picture, grandmamma!" said Frank, rather gravely. "I hope there are not many people like that, or it would be very sad to meet with them. Now pray let us have a pleasanter description of the sort of persons you would like Harry and me to become."

"The first foundation of all is, as you already know, Frank, to pray that you may be put in the right course, and kept in it; for of ourselves we are so sinful and weak, that we can do no good thing. Then feeling a full trust in the Divine assistance, you must begin and end every day with studying your Bible; not merely reading it, but carefully endeavouring to understand and obey what it contains. Our leisure should be bestowed on reading of wiser and better people than ourselves, which will keep us humble while it instructs our understandings, and thus we shall be fitted to associate with persons whose society is even better than books. Christians who are enlightened and sanctified in the knowledge of all good things will show us an example of carefully using our time, which is the most valuable of all earthly possessions. If we waste our money, we may perhaps get more; if we lose our health, it may be restored; but time squandered on folly must hereafter be answered for, and can never be regained. Whatever be your station in life, waste none of your thoughts upon fancying how much better you might have acted in some other person's place, but see what duties belong to that station in which you live, and do what that requires with activity and diligence. When we are called to give an account of our stewardship, let us not have to confess at the last that we wasted our one talent, because we wished to have been trusted with ten; but let us prepare to render up what was given to us with joy and thankfulness, perfectly satisfied that the best place in life is where God appoints, and where He will guide us to a safe and peaceful end."

"Yes!" added Major Graham, "we have two eyes in our minds as well as in our bodies. With one of these we see all that is good or agreeable in our lot—with the other we see all that is unpleasant or disappointing; and you may generally choose which eye to keep open. Some of my friends always peevishly look at the troubles and vexations they endure, but they might turn them into good, by considering that every circumstance is sent from the same hand, with the same merciful purpose—to make us better now, and happier hereafter."

"Well! my dear children," said Lady Harriet, "it is time now for retiring to Bedfordshire; so good-night."

"If you please, grandmamma! not yet," asked Harry anxiously. "Give us five minutes longer!"

"And then in the morning you will want to remain five minutes more in bed. That is the way people learn to keep such dreadfully late hours at last, Harry! I knew one very rich old gentleman formerly, who always wished to sit up a little later in the morning, till at length, he ended by hiring a set of servants to rise at nine in the evening, as he did himself, and to remain in bed all day."

"People should regulate their sleep very conscientiously," added Major Graham, "so as to waste as little time as possible; and our good king George III set us the example, for he remarked, that six hours in the night were quite enough for a man, seven hours for a woman, and eight for a fool. Or perhaps, Harry, you might like to live by Sir William Jones' rule:

'Six hours to read, to soothing slumber seven,
Ten to the world allot—and all to Heaven.'"

&

## THE FOX AND THE HEDGEHOG

*Aesop*

A Fox was swimming across a river; and, when he came to the other side, he found the bank so steep and slippery, that he could not get up it. But this was not all the misfortune; for, while he stood in the water deliberating what to do, he was attacked by a swarm of flies, who, settling upon his head and eyes, stung and plagued him grievously. A Hedgehog, who stood upon the shore, beheld and pitied his condition, and withal, offered to drive away the flies, which molested and teased him in that manner. Friend, replies the Fox, I thank you for your kind offer, but must desire you by no means to destroy these honest bloodsuckers, that are now quartered upon me, and whose bellies are, I fancy, pretty well filled; for, if they should leave me, a fresh swarm would take their places, and I should not have a drop of blood left in my whole body.

*Translated by Samuel Croxull*

## THE GOOSE-GIRL

*Jakob and Wilhelm Grimm*

There was once upon a time an old Queen whose husband had been dead for many years, and she had a beautiful daughter. When the princess grew up she was betrothed to a prince who lived at a great distance. When the time came for her to be married, and she had to journey forth into the distant kingdom, the aged Queen packed up for her many costly vessels of silver and gold, and trinkets also of gold and silver; and cups and jewelry— in short, everything which appertained to a royal dowry, for she loved her child with all her heart. She likewise sent her maid-in-waiting, who was to ride with her, and hand her over to the bridegroom, and each had a horse for the journey, but the horse of the King's daughter was called Falada, and could speak. So when the hour of parting had come, the aged mother went into her bedroom, took a small knife and cut her finger with it until it bled, then she held a white handkerchief to it into which she let three drops of blood fall, gave it to her daughter and said, "Dear child, preserve this carefully, it will be of service to you on your way."

So they took a sorrowful leave of each other; the princess put the piece of cloth in her bosom, mounted her horse, and then went away to her bridegroom. After she had ridden for a while she felt a burning thirst, and said to her waiting-maid, "Dismount, and take my cup which thou hast brought with thee for me, and get me some water from the stream, for I should like to drink." "If you are thirsty," said the waiting-maid, "get off your horse yourself, and lie down and drink out of the stream, I don't choose to be your servant." So in her great thirst the princess alighted, bent down over the water in the stream and drank and was not allowed to drink out of the golden cup. Then she said, "Ah, Heaven!" and the three drops of blood answered, "If thy mother knew this, her heart would break." But the King's daughter was humble, said nothing, and mounted her horse again. She rode some miles farther, but the day was warm, the sun scorched her, and she was thirsty once more, and when they came to a stream of water, she again cried to her waiting-maid, "Dismount, and give me some water in my golden cup," for she had long ago forgotten the girl's ill words. But the waiting-maid said still more haughtily, "If you wish to drink, drink as you can; I don't choose to be your maid." Then in her great thirst the King's daughter alighted, bent over the flowing stream, wept and said, "Ah, Heaven!" and the drops of blood again replied, "If thy mother knew this, her heart would break." And as she was thus drinking and leaning right over the stream, the handkerchief with the three drops of blood fell out of her bosom, and floated away with the water without her observing it, so great was her trouble. The waiting-maid, however, had seen it, and she rejoiced to think that she had now power over the bride, for since the princess had lost the drops of blood, she had become weak and powerless. So now when she wanted to mount her horse again, the one that was called Falada, the waiting-maid said, "Falada is more suitable for me, and my nag will do for thee," and the princess had to be content with that. Then the waiting-maid, with many hard words, bade the princess exchange her royal apparel for her own shabby clothes; and at length she was compelled to swear by the clear sky above her, that she would not say one word of this to any one at the royal court, and if she had not taken this oath she would have been killed on the spot. But Falada saw all this, and observed it well.

The waiting-maid now mounted Falada, and the true bride the bad horse, and thus they traveled onwards, until at length they entered the royal palace. There were great rejoicings over her arrival, and the prince sprang forward to meet her, lifted the waiting-maid from her horse, and thought she was his consort. She was conducted upstairs, but the real princess was left standing below. Then the old King looked out of the window and saw her standing in the courtyard, and how dainty and delicate and beautiful she was, and instantly went to the royal apartment, and asked the bride about the girl she had with her who was standing down below in the courtyard, and who she was. "I picked her up on my way for a companion; give the girl something to work at, that she may not stand idle." But the old King had no work for her, and knew of none, so he said, "I have a little boy who tends the geese; she may help him." The boy was called Conrad, and the true bride had to help him to tend the geese. Soon afterwards the false bride said to the young King, "Dearest husband, I beg you to do me a favor." He answered, "I will do so most willingly." "Then send for the knacker, and have the head of the horse on which I rode here cut off, for it vexed me on the way." In reality, she was afraid that the horse might tell how she had behaved to the King's daughter. Then she succeeded in making the King promise that it should be done, and the faithful Falada was to die. This came to the ears of the real princess, and she secretly promised the knacker a piece of gold if he would perform a small service for her. There was a great dark-looking gateway in the town, through which morning and evening she had to pass with the geese; would he be so good as to nail up Falada's head on it, so that she might see him again, more than once? The knacker's man promised to do that, and cut off the head, and nailed it fast beneath the dark gateway.

Early in the morning, when she and Conrad drove out their flock beneath this gateway, she said in passing,

"Alas, Falada, hanging there!"

Then the head answered,

"Alas, young Queen, how ill you fare!
If this your tender mother knew,
Her heart would surely break in two."

Then they went still farther out of the town, and drove their geese into the country. And when they had come to the meadow, she sat down and unbound her hair which was like pure gold, and Conrad saw it and delighted in its brightness, and wanted to pluck out a few hairs. Then she said,

> "Blow, blow, thou gentle wind, I say,
> Blow Conrad's little hat away,
> And make him chase it here and there,
> Until I have braided all my hair,
> And bound it up again."

And there came such a violent wind that it blew Conrad's hat far away across country, and he was forced to run after it. When he came back, she had finished combing her hair and was putting it up again, and he could not get any of it. Then Conrad was angry, and would not speak to her, and thus they watched the geese until the evening, and then they went home.

Next day when they were driving the geese out through the dark gateway, the maiden said,

> "Alas, Falada, hanging there!"

Falada answered,

> "Alas, young Queen, how ill you fare!
> If this your tender mother knew,
> Her heart would surely break in two."

And she sat down again in the field and began to comb out her hair, and Conrad ran and tried to clutch it, so she said in haste,

> "Blow, blow, thou gentle wind, I say,
> Blow Conrad's little hat away,
> And make him chase it here and there,
> Until I have braided all my hair,
> And bound it up again."

Then the wind blew, and blew his little hat off his head and far away, and Conrad was forced to run after it, and when he came back, her hair had been put up a long time, and he could get none of it, and so they looked after their geese till evening came.

But in the evening after they had got home, Conrad went to the old

King, and said, "I won't tend the geese with that girl any longer!" "Why not?" inquired the aged King. "Oh, because she vexes me the whole day long." Then the aged King commanded him to relate what it was that she did to him. And Conrad said, "In the morning when we pass beneath the dark gateway with the flock, there is a sorry horse's head on the wall, and she says to it,

> 'Alas, Falada, hanging there!'

And the head replies,

> 'Alas, young Queen, how ill you fare!
> If this your tender mother knew,
> Her heart would surely break in two.' "

And Conrad went on to relate what happened on the goose pasture, and how when there he had to chase his hat.

The aged King commanded him to drive his flock out again next day, and as soon as morning came, he placed himself behind the dark gateway, and heard how the maiden spoke to the head of Falada, and then he, too, went into the country, and hid himself in the thicket in the meadow. Then he soon saw with his own eyes the goose-girl and the goose-boy bringing their flock, and how after a while she sat down and unplaited her hair, which shone with radiance. And soon she said,

> "Blow, blow, thou gentle wind, I say,
> Blow Conrad's little hat away,
> And make him chase it here and there,
> Until I have braided all my hair,
> And bound it up again."

Then came a blast of wind and carried off Conrad's hat, so that he had to run far away, while the maiden quietly went on combing and plaiting her hair, all of which the King observed. Then, quite unseen, he went away, and when the goose-girl came home in the evening, he called her aside, and asked why she did all these things. "I may not tell you that, and I dare not lament my sorrows to any human being, for I have sworn not to do so by the heaven which is above me; if I had not done that, I should have lost my life." He urged her and left her no peace, but he could draw nothing from her. Then said he, "If thou wilt not tell me anything, tell thy sorrows to the iron-stove there," and he went away. Then she crept into the iron-stove, and began to weep and lament, and emptied her whole heart, and said, "Here am I deserted by the whole world, and yet I am a King's daughter, and a false waiting-maid has by force brought me to such a pass that I have been compelled to put off my royal apparel, and she has taken my place with my bridegroom, and I have to perform menial service as a goose-girl. If my mother did but know that, her heart would break."

The aged King, however, was standing outside by the pipe of the stove, and was listening to what she said, and heard it. Then he came back again, and bade her come out of the stove. And royal garments were placed on her, and it was marvelous how beautiful she was! The aged King summoned his son, and revealed to him that he had got the false bride who was only a waiting-maid, but that the true one was standing there, as the sometime goose-girl. The young King rejoiced with all his heart when he saw her beauty and youth, and a great feast was made ready to which all the people and all good friends were invited. At the head of the table sat the bridegroom with the King's daughter at one side of him, and the waiting-maid on the other, but the waiting-maid was blinded, and did not recognize the princess in her dazzling array. When they had eaten and drunk, and were merry, the aged King asked the waiting-maid, as a riddle, what a person deserved who had behaved in such and such a way to her master, and at the same time related the whole story, and asked what sentence such a one merited. Then the false bride said, "She deserves no better fate than to be stripped entirely naked, and put in a barrel which is studded inside with pointed nails, and two white horses should be harnessed to it, which will drag her along through one street after another, till she is dead." "It is thou," said the aged King, "and thou hast pronounced thine own sentence, and thus shall it be done unto thee." And when the sentence had been carried out, the young King married his true bride, and both of them reigned over their kingdom in peace and happiness.

*Translated by Margaret Hunt*

# THE NECKLACE
# OF PRINCESS FIORIMONDE

## *Mary de Morgan*

Once there lived a King, whose wife was dead, but who had a most beautiful daughter—so beautiful that everyone thought she must be good as well, instead of which the Princess was really very wicked, and practised witchcraft and black magic which she had learned from an old witch who lived in a hut on the side of a lonely mountain. This old witch was wicked and hideous, and no one but the King's daughter knew that she lived there; but at night, when everyone else was asleep, the Princess, whose name was Fiorimonde, used to visit her by stealth to learn sorcery. It was only the witch's arts which had made Fiorimonde so beautiful that there was no one like her in the world, and in return the Princess helped her with all her tricks, and never told anyone she was there.

The time came when the King began to think he should like his daughter to marry, so he summoned his council and said, "We have no son to reign after our death, so we had best seek for a suitable prince to marry to our royal daughter and then, when we are too old, he shall be king in our stead." And all the council said he was very wise, and it would be well for the Princess to marry. So heralds were sent to all neighbouring kings and princes to say that the King would choose a husband for the Princess, who should be king after him. But when Fiorimonde heard this she wept with rage, for she knew quite well that if she had a husband he would find out how she went to visit the old witch, and would stop her practising magic, and then she would lose her beauty.

When night came, and everyone in the palace was fast asleep, the Princess went to her bedroom window and softly opened it. Then she took from her pocket a handful of peas and held them out of the window and chirruped low, and there flew down from the roof a small brown bird and sat upon her wrist and began to eat the peas. No sooner had it swallowed them than it began to grow and grow and grow till it was so big that the Princess could not hold it, but let it stand on the window-sill, and still it grew and grew and grew till it was as large as an ostrich. Then the Princess climbed out of the window and seated herself on the bird's back, and at once it flew straight away over the tops of the trees till it came to the mountain where the old witch dwelt, and stopped in front of the door of her hut.

The Princess jumped off, and muttered some words through the keyhole, when a croaking voice from within called,

"Why do you come to-night? Have I not told you I wished to be left alone for thirteen nights; why do you disturb me?"

"But I beg of you to let me in," said the Princess, "for I am in trouble and want your help."

"Come in then," said the voice; and the door flew open, and the Princess trod into the hut, in the middle of which, wrapped in a grey cloak which almost hid her, sat the witch. Princess Fiorimonde sat down near her, and told her her story. How the King wished her to marry, and had sent word to the neighbouring princes, that they might make offers for her.

"This is truly bad hearing," croaked the witch, "but we shall beat them yet; and you must deal with each Prince as he comes. Would you like them to become dogs, to come at your call, or birds, to fly in the air, and sing of your beauty, or will you make them all into beads, the beads of such a necklace as never woman wore before, so that they may rest upon your neck, and you may take them with you always?"

"The necklace! the necklace!" cried the Princess, clapping her hands with joy. "That will be best of all, to sling them upon a string and wear them around my throat. Little will the courtiers know whence come my new jewels."

"But this is a dangerous play," quoth the witch, "for, unless you are very careful, you yourself may become a bead and hang upon the string with the others, and there you will remain till someone cuts the string, and draws you off."

"Nay, never fear," said the Princess, "I will be careful, only tell me what to do, and I will have great princes and kings to adorn me, and all their greatness shall not help them."

Then the witch dipped her hand into a black bag which stood on the ground beside her, and drew out a long gold thread.

The ends were joined together, but no one could see the joins, and however much you pulled, it would not break. It would easily go over Fiorimonde's head, and the witch slipped it on her neck saying,

"Now mind, while this hangs here you are safe enough, but if once you join your fingers around the string you too will meet the fate of your lovers, and hang upon it yourself. As for the kings and princes who would marry you, all you have to do is to make them close their fingers around the chain, and at once they will be strung upon it as bright hard beads, and there they shall remain, till it is cut and they drop off."

"This is really delightful," cried the Princess; "and I am already quite impatient for the first to come that I may try."

"And now," said the witch, "since you are here, and there is yet time, we will have a dance, and I will summon the guests." So saying, she took from a corner a drum and a pair of drum-sticks, and going to the door, began to beat upon it. It made a terrible rattling. In a moment came flying through the air all sorts of forms. There were little dark elves with long tails, and goblins who chattered and laughed, and other witches who rode on broom-sticks. There was one wicked fairy in the form of a large cat, with bright green eyes, and another came sliding in like a long shining viper.

Then, when all had arrived, the witch stopped drumming, and, going to the middle of the hut, stamped on the floor, and a trap-door opened in the ground. The old witch stepped through it, and led the way down a narrow dark passage, to a large underground chamber, and all her strange guests followed, and here they all danced and made merry in a terrible way, but at first sound of cock-crow all the guests disappeared with a whiff, and the Princess hastened up the dark passage again, and out of the hut to where her big bird still waited for her, and mounting its back she flew home in a trice. Then, when she had stepped in at her bedroom window, she poured into a cup, from a small black bottle, a few drops of magic water, and gave it to the bird to drink, and as it sipped it grew smaller, and smaller, till at last it had quite regained its natural size, and hopped on to the roof as before, and the Princess shut her window, and got into bed, and fell asleep, and no one knew of her strange journey, or where she had been.

Next day Fiorimonde declared to her father the King, that she was quite willing to wed any prince he should fix upon as a husband for her, at which he was much pleased, and soon after informed her, that a young king was coming from over the sea to be her husband. He was king of a large rich country, and would take back his bride with him to his home. He was called King Pierrot. Great preparations were made for his arrival, and the Princess was decked in her finest array to greet him, and when he came all the courtiers said, "This is truly a proper husband for our beautiful Princess," for he was strong and handsome, with black hair, and eyes like sloes. King Pierrot was delighted with Fiorimonde's beauty, and was happy as the day is long; and all things went merrily till the evening before the marriage. A great feast was held, at which the Princess looked lovelier than ever dressed in a red gown, the colour of the inside of a rose, but she wore no jewels nor ornaments of any kind, save one shining gold string round her milk-white throat.

When the feast was done, the Princess stepped from her golden chair at her father's side, and walked softly into the garden, and stood under an elm-tree looking at the shining moon. In a few moments King Pierrot followed her, and stood beside her, looking at her and wondering at her beauty.

"To-morrow, then, my sweet Princess, you will be my Queen, and share all I possess. What gift would you wish me to give you on our wedding day?"

"I would have a necklace wrought of the finest gold and jewels to be found, and just the length of this gold cord which I wear around my throat," answered Princess Fiorimonde.

"Why do you wear that cord?" asked King Pierrot; "it has no jewel nor ornament about it."

"Nay, but there is no cord like mine in all the world," cried Fiorimonde, and her eyes sparkled wickedly as she spoke; "it is as light as a feather, but stronger than an iron chain. Take it in both hands and try to break it, that you may see how strong it is"; and King Pierrot took the cord in both hands to pull it hard; but no sooner were his fingers closed around it than he vanished like a puff of smoke, and on the cord appeared a bright, beautiful bead—so bright and beautiful as was never bead before—clear as crystal, but shining with all colours—green, blue, and gold.

Princess Fiorimonde gazed down at it and laughed aloud.

"Aha, my proud lover! are you there?" she cried with wicked glee; "my necklace bids fair to beat all others in the world," and she caressed the bead with the tips of her soft, white fingers, but was careful that they did not close round the string. Then she returned into the banqueting hall, and spoke to the King.

"Pray, sire," said she, "send someone at once to find King Pierrot, for, as he was talking to me a minute ago, he suddenly left me, and I am afraid lest I may have given him offence, or perhaps he is ill."

The King desired that the servants should seek for King Pierrot all over the grounds, and seek him they did, but nowhere was he to be found, and the old King looked offended.

"Doubtless he will be ready to-morrow in time for the wedding," quoth he, "but we are not best pleased that he should treat us in this way."

Princess Fiorimonde had a little maid called Yolande. She was a bright-faced girl with merry brown eyes, but she was not beautiful like Fiorimonde, and she did not love her mistress, for she was afraid of her, and suspected her of her wicked ways. When she undressed her that night she noticed the gold cord, and the one bright bead upon it, and as she combed the Princess's hair she looked over her shoulder into the looking-glass, and saw how she laughed, and how fondly she looked at the cord, and caressed the bead, again and again with her fingers.

"That is a wonderful bead on your Highness's cord," said Yolande, looking at its reflection in the mirror; "surely it must be a bridal gift from King Pierrot."

"And so it is, little Yolande," cried Fiorimonde, laughing merrily; "and the best gift he could give me. But I think one bead alone looks ugly and ungainly; soon I hope I shall have another, and another, and another, all as beautiful as the first."

Then Yolande shook her head, and said to herself, "This bodes no good."

Next morning all was prepared for the marriage, and the Princess was dressed in white satin and pearls with a long white lace veil over her, and a bridal wreath on her head, and she stood waiting among her grandly dressed ladies, who all said that such a beautiful bride had never been seen in the world before. But just as they were preparing to go down to the fine company in the hall, a messenger came in great haste summoning the Princess at once to her father the King, as he was much perplexed.

"My daughter," cried he, as Fiorimonde in all her bridal array entered the room where he sat alone, "what can we do? King Pierrot is nowhere to be found; I fear lest he may have been seized by robbers and basely murdered for his rich clothes, or carried away to some mountain and left there to starve. My soldiers are gone far and wide to seek him—and we shall hear of him ere day is done—but where there is no bridegroom there can be no bridal."

"Then let it be put off, my father," cried the Princess, "and to-morrow we shall know if it is for a wedding, or a funeral, we must dress"; and she pretended to weep, but even then could hardly keep from laughing.

So the wedding guests went away, and the Princess laid aside her bridal dress, and all waited anxiously for news of King Pierrot; and no news came. So at last everyone gave him up for dead, and mourned for him, and wondered how he had met his fate.

Princess Fiorimonde put on a black gown, and begged to be allowed to live in seclusion for one month in which to grieve for King Pierrot; but when she was again alone in her bedroom she sat before her looking-glass and laughed till tears ran down her cheeks; and Yolande watched her, and trembled, when she heard her laughter. She noticed, too, that beneath her black gown, the Princess still wore her gold cord, and did not move it night or day.

The month had barely passed away when the King came to his daughter, and announced that another suitor had presented himself, whom he should much like to be her husband. The Princess agreed quite obediently to all her father said; and it was arranged that the marriage should take place. This new prince was called Prince Hildebrandt. He came from a country far north, of which one day he would be king. He was tall, and fair, and strong, with flaxen hair and bright blue eyes. When Princess Fiorimonde saw his portrait she was much pleased, and said, "By all means let him come, and the sooner the better." So she put off her black clothes, and again great preparations were made for a wedding; and King Pierrot was quite forgotten.

Prince Hildebrandt came, and with him many fine gentlemen, and they brought beautiful gifts for the bride. The evening of his arrival all went well, and again there was a grand feast, and Fiorimonde looked so beautiful that Prince Hildebrandt was delighted; and this time she did not leave her father's side, but sat by him all the evening.

Early next morning at sunrise, when everyone was still sleeping, the Princess rose, and dressed herself in a plain white gown, and brushed all her hair over her shoulders, and crept quietly downstairs into the palace gardens; then she walked on till she came beneath the window of Prince Hildebrandt's room, and here she paused and began to sing a little song as sweet and joyous as a lark's. When Prince Hildebrandt heard it he got up and went to the window and looked out to see who sang, and when he saw Fiorimonde standing in the red sunrise-light, which made her hair look gold and her face rosy, he made haste to dress himself and go down to meet her.

"How, my Princess," cried he, as he stepped into the garden beside her. "This is indeed great happiness to meet you here so early. Tell me why do you come out at sunrise to sing by yourself?"

"I come that I may see the colours of the sky—red, blue, and gold," answered the Princess. "Look, there are no such colours to be seen anywhere, unless, indeed, it be in this bead which I wear here on my golden cord.

"What is that bead, and where did it come from?" asked Hildebrandt.

"It came from over the sea, where it shall never return again," answered the Princess. And again her eyes began to sparkle with eagerness, and she could scarcely conceal her mirth. "Lift the cord off my neck and look at it near, and tell me if you ever saw one like it."

Hildebrandt put out his hands and took hold of the cord, but no sooner were his fingers closed around it than he vanished, and a new bright bead was slung next to the first one on Fiorimonde's chain, and this one was even more beautiful than the other.

The Princess gave a long low laugh, quite terrible to hear.

"Oh, my sweet necklace," cried she, "how beautiful you are growing! I think I love you more than anything in the world besides." Then she went softly back to bed, without anyone hearing her, and fell sound asleep, and slept till Yolande came to tell her it was time for her to get up and dress for the wedding.

The Princess was dressed in gorgeous clothes, and only Yolande noticed that beneath her satin gown, she wore the golden cord, but now there were two beads upon it instead of one. Scarcely was she ready when the King burst into her room in a towering rage.

"My daughter," cried he, "there is a plot against us. Lay aside your bridal attire and think no more of Prince Hildebrandt, for he too has disappeared, and is nowhere to be found."

At this the Princess wept, and entreated that Hildebrandt should be sought for far and near, but she laughed to herself, and said, "Search where you will, yet you shall not find him"; and so again a great search was made, and when no trace of the Prince was found, all the palace was in an uproar.

The Princess again put off her bride's dress and clad herself in black, and sat alone, and pretended to weep, but Yolande, who watched her, shook her head, and said, "More will come and go before the wicked Princess has done her worst."

A month passed, in which Fiorimonde pretended to mourn for Hildebrandt, then she went to the King and said,

"Sire, I pray that you will not let people say that when any bridegroom comes to marry me, as soon as he has seen me he flies rather than be my husband. I beg that suitors may be summoned from far and near that I may not be left alone unwed."

The King agreed, and envoys were sent all the world over to bid any who would come and be the husband of Princess Fiorimonde. And come they did, kings and princes from south and north, east and west—King Adrian, Prince Sigbert, Prince Algar, and many more—but though all went well till the wedding morning, when it was time to go to church, no bridegroom was to be found. The old King was sadly frightened, and would fain have given up all hope of finding a husband for the Princess, but now she implored him, with tears in her eyes, not to let her be disgraced in this way. And so suitor after suitor continued to come, and now it was known, far and wide, that whoever came to ask for the hand of Princess Fiorimonde vanished, and was seen no more of men. The courtiers were afraid and whispered under their breath, "It is not all right, it cannot be"; but only Yolande noticed how the beads came upon the golden thread, till it was well-nigh covered, yet there always was room for one bead more.

So the years passed, and every year Princess Fiorimonde grew lovelier and lovelier, so that no one who saw her could guess how wicked she was.

In a far off country lived a young prince whose name was Florestan. He had a dear friend named Gervaise, whom he loved better than anyone in the world. Gervaise was tall, and broad, and stout of limb, and he loved Prince Florestan so well, that he would gladly have died to serve him.

It chanced that Prince Florestan saw a portrait of Princess Fiorimonde, and at once swore he would go to her father's court, and beg that he might have her for his wife, and Gervaise in vain tried to dissuade him.

"There is an evil fate about the Princess Fiorimonde," quoth he; "many have gone to marry her, but where are they now?"

"I don't know or care," answered Florestan, "but this is sure, that I will wed her and return here, and bring my bride with me."

So he set out for Fiorimonde's home, and Gervaise went with him with a heavy heart.

When they reached the court, the old King received them and welcomed them warmly, and he said to his courtiers, "Here is a fine young prince to whom we would gladly see our daughter wed. Let us hope that this time all will be well." But now Fiorimonde had grown so bold, that she scarcely tried to conceal her mirth.

"I will gladly marry him to-morrow, if he comes to the church," she said; "but if he is not there, what can I do?" and she laughed long and merrily, till those who heard her shuddered.

When the Princess's ladies came to tell her that Prince Florestan was arrived, she was in the garden, lying on the marble edge of a fountain, feeding the goldfish who swam in the water.

"Bid him come to me," she said, "for I will not go any more in state to meet any suitors, neither will I put on grand attire for them. Let him come and find me as I am, since all find it so easy to come and go." So her ladies told the prince that Fiorimonde waited for him near the fountain.

She did not rise when he came to where she lay, but his heart bounded with joy, for he had never in his life beheld such a beautiful woman.

She wore a thin soft white dress, which clung to her lithe figure. Her beautiful arms and hands were bare, and she dabbled with them in the water, and played with the fish. Her great blue eyes were sparkling with mirth, and were so beautiful, that no one noticed the wicked look hid in them; and on her neck lay the marvellous many-coloured necklace, which was itself a wonder to behold.

"You have my best greetings, Prince Florestan," she said. "And you, too, would be my suitor. Have you thought well of what you would do, since so many princes who have seen me have fled for ever, rather than marry me?" and as she spoke, she raised her white hand from the water, and held it out to the Prince, who stooped and kissed it, and scarcely knew how to answer her for bewilderment at her great loveliness.

Gervaise followed his master at a short distance, but he was ill at ease, and trembled for fear of what should come.

"Come, bid your friend leave us," said Fiorimonde, looking at Gervaise, "and sit beside me, and tell me of your home, and why you wish to marry me, and all pleasant things."

Florestan begged that Gervaise would leave them for a little, and he walked slowly away, in a very mournful mood.

He went on down the walks, not heeding where he was going, till he met Yolande, who stood beneath a tree laden with rosy apples, picking the fruit, and throwing it into a basket at her feet. He would have passed her in silence, but she stopped him, and said,

"Have you come with the new Prince? Do you love your master?"

"Ay, better than anyone else on the earth," answered Gervaise. "Why do you ask?"

"And where is he now?" said Yolande, not heeding Gervaise's question.

"He sits by the fountain with the beautiful Princess," said Gervaise.

"Then, I hope you have said goodbye to him well, for be assured you shall never see him again," said Yolande nodding her head.

"Why not, and who are you to talk like this?" asked Gervaise.

"My name is Yolande," answered she, "and I am Princess Fiorimonde's maid. Do you not know that Prince Florestan is the eleventh lover who has come to marry her, and one by one they have disappeared, and only I know where they are gone."

"And where are they gone?" cried Gervaise, "and why do you not tell the world, and prevent good men being lost like this?"

"Because I fear my mistress," said Yolande, speaking low and drawing near to him; "she is a sorceress, and she wears the brave kings and princes who come to woo her, strung upon a cord round her neck. Each one forms the bead of a necklace which she wears, both day and night. I have watched that necklace growing; first it was only an empty gold thread; then came King Pierrot, and when he disappeared the first bead appeared upon it. Then came Hildebrandt, and two beads were on the string instead of one; then followed Adrian, Sigbert, and Algar, and Cenred, and Pharamond, and Baldwyn, and Leofric, and Raoul, and all are gone, and ten beads hang upon the string, and to-night there will be eleven, and the eleventh will be your Prince Florestan."

"If this be so," cried Gervaise, "I will never rest till I have plunged my sword into Fiorimonde's heart"; but Yolande shook her head.

"She is a sorceress," she said, "and it might be hard to kill her; besides, that might not break the spell, and bring back the princes to life. I wish I could show you the necklace, and you might count the beads, and see if I do not speak the truth, but it is always about her neck, both night and day, so it is impossible."

"Take me to her room to-night when she is asleep, and let me see it there," said Gervaise.

"Very well, we will try," said Yolande; "but you must be very still, and make no noise, for if she wakes, remember it will be worse for us both."

When night came and all in the palace were fast asleep, Gervaise and Yolande met in the great hall, and Yolande told him that the Princess slumbered soundly.

"So now let us go," said she, "and I will show you the necklace on which Fiorimonde wears her lovers strung like beads, though how she transforms them I know not."

"Stay one instant, Yolande," said Gervaise, holding her back, as she would have tripped upstairs. "Perhaps, try how I may, I shall be beaten, and either die or become a bead like those who have come before me. But if I succeed, and rid the land of your wicked Princess, what will you promise me for a reward?"

"What would you have?" asked Yolande.

"I would have you say you will be my wife, and come back with me to my own land," said Gervaise.

"That I will promise gladly," said Yolande, kissing him, "but we must not speak or think of this till we have cut the cord from Fiorimonde's neck, and all her lovers are set free."

So they went softly up to the Princess's room, Yolande holding a small lantern, which gave only a dim light. There, in her grand bed, lay Princess Fiorimonde. They could just see her by the lantern's light, and she looked so beautiful that Gervaise began to think Yolande spoke falsely, when she said she was so wicked.

Her face was calm and sweet as a baby's; her hair fell in ruddy waves on the pillow; her rosy lips smiled, and the little dimples showed in her cheeks; her white soft hands were folded amidst the scented lace and linen of which the bed was made. Gervaise almost forgot to look at the glittering beads hung round her throat, in wondering at her loveliness, but Yolande pulled him by the arm.

"Do not look at her," she whispered softly, "since her beauty has cost dear already; look rather at what remains of those who thought her as fair as you do now; see here," and she pointed with her finger to each bead in turn.

"This was Pierrot, and this Hildebrandt, and these are Adrian, and Sigbert, and Algar, and Cenred, and that is Pharamond, and that Raoul, and last of all here is your own master Prince Florestan. Seek him now where you will and you will not find him, and you shall never see him again till the cord is cut and the charm broken."

"Of what is the cord made?" whispered Gervaise.

"It is of the finest gold," she answered. "Nay, do not you touch her lest she wake. I will show it to you." And Yolande put down the lantern and softly put out her hands to slip the beads aside, but as she did so, her fingers closed around the golden string, and directly she was gone. Another bead was added to the necklace, and Gervaise was alone with the sleeping Princess. He gazed about him in sore amazement and fear. He dared not call lest Fiorimonde should wake.

"Yolande," he whispered as loud as he dared, "Yolande where are you?" but no Yolande answered.

Then he bent down over the Princess and gazed at the necklace. Another bead was strung upon it next to the one to which Yolande had pointed as Prince Florestan. Again he counted them. "Eleven before, now there are twelve. Oh hateful Princess! I know now where go the brave kings and princes who came to woo you, and where, too, is my Yolande," and as he looked at the last bead, tears filled his eyes. It was brighter and clearer than the others, and of a warm red hue, like the red dress Yolande had worn. The Princess turned and laughed in her sleep, and at the sound of her laughter Gervaise was filled with horror and loathing. He crept shuddering from the room, and all night long sat up alone, plotting how he might defeat Fiorimonde, and set Florestan and Yolande free.

Next morning when Fiorimonde dressed she looked at her necklace and counted its beads, but she was much perplexed, for a new bead was added to the string.

"Who can have come and grasped my chain unknown to me?" she said to herself, and she sat and pondered for a long time. At last she broke into weird laughter.

"At any rate, whoever it was, is fitly punished," quoth she. "My brave necklace, you can take care of yourself, and if anyone tries to steal you, they will get their reward, and add to my glory. In truth I may sleep in peace, and fear nothing."

The day passed away and no one missed Yolande. Towards sunset the rain began to pour in torrents, and there was such a terrible thunderstorm that everyone was frightened. The thunder roared, the lightning gleamed flash after flash, every moment it grew fiercer and fiercer. The sky was so dark that, save for the lightning's light, nothing could be seen, but Princess Fiorimonde loved the thunder and lightning.

She sat in a room high up in one of the towers, clad in a black velvet dress, and she watched the lightning from the window, and laughed at each peal of thunder. In the midst of the storm a stranger, wrapped in a cloak, rode to the palace door, and the ladies ran to tell the Princess that a new prince had come to be her suitor. "And he will not tell his name," said they, "but says he hears that all are bidden to ask for the hand of Princess Fiorimonde, and he too would try his good fortune."

"Let him come at once," cried the Princess. "Be he prince or knave what care I? If princes all fly from me it may be better to marry a peasant."

So they led the newcomer up to the room where Fiorimonde sat. He was wrapped in a thick cloak, but he flung it aside as he came in, and showed how rich was his silken clothing underneath; and so well was he disguised, that Fiorimonde never saw that it was Gervaise, but looked at him, and thought she had never seen him before.

"You are most welcome, stranger prince, who has come through such lightning and thunder to find me," said she. "Is it true, then, that you wish to be my suitor? What have you heard of me?"

"It is quite true, Princess," said Gervaise. "And I have heard that you are the most beautiful woman in the world."

"And is that true also?" asked the Princess. "Look at me now, and see."

Gervaise looked at her and in his heart he said, "It is quite true, oh wicked Princess! There never was woman as beautiful as you, and never before did I hate a woman as I hate you now"; but aloud he said,

"No, Princess, that is not true; you are very beautiful, but I have seen a woman who is fairer than you for all that your skin looks ivory against your velvet dress, and your hair is like gold."

"A woman who is fairer than I?" cried Fiorimonde, and her breast began to heave and her eyes to sparkle with rage, for never before had she heard such a thing said. "Who are you who dares come and tell me of women more beautiful than I am?"

"I am a suitor who asks to be your husband, Princess," answered Gervaise, "but still I say I have seen a woman who was fairer than you."

"Who is she—where is she?" cried Fiorimonde, who could scarcely contain her anger. "Bring her here at once that I may see if you speak the truth."

"What will you give me to bring her to you?" said Gervaise. "Give me that necklace you wear on your neck, and then I will summon her in an instant"; but Fiorimonde shook her head.

"You have asked," said she, "for the only thing from which I cannot part," and then she bade her maids bring her her jewel-casket, and she drew out diamonds, and rubies, and pearls, and offered them, all or any, to Gervaise. The lightning shone on them and made them shine and flash, but he shook his head.

"No, none of these will do," quoth he. "You can see her for the necklace, but for nothing else."

"Take it off for yourself then," cried Fiorimonde, who now was so angry that she only wished to be rid of Gervaise in any way.

"No, indeed," said Gervaise, "I am no tire-woman, and should not know how to clasp and unclasp it"; and in spite of all Fiorimonde could say or do, he would not touch either her or the magic chain.

At night the storm grew even fiercer, but it did not trouble the Princess. She waited till all were asleep, and then she opened her bedroom window and chirruped softly to the little brown bird, who flew down from the roof at her call. Then she gave him a handful of seeds as before, and he grew and grew and grew till he was as large as an ostrich, and she sat upon his back and flew out through the air, laughing at the lightning and thunder which flashed and roared around her. Away they flew till they came to the old witch's cave, and here they found the witch sitting at her open door catching the lightning to make charms with.

"Welcome, my dear," croaked she, as Fiorimonde stepped from the bird; "here is a night we both love well. And how goes the necklace?—right merrily I see. Twelve beads already—but what is that twelfth?" and she looked at it closely.

"Nay, that is one thing I want you to tell me," said Fiorimonde, drying the rain from her golden hair. "Last night when I slept there were eleven, and this morning there are twelve; and I know not from whence comes the twelfth."

"It is no suitor," said the witch, "but from some young maid, that that bead is made. But why should you mind? It looks well with the others."

"Some young maid," said the Princess. "Then, it must be Cicely or Marybel, or Yolande, who would have robbed me of my necklace as I slept. But what care I? The silly wench is punished now, and so may all others be, who would do the same."

"And when will you get the thirteenth bead, and where will he come from?" asked the witch.

"He waits at the palace now," said Fiorimonde, chuckling. "And this is why I have to speak to you"; and then she told the witch of the stranger who had come in the storm, and of how he would not touch her necklace, nor take the cord in his hand, and how he said also that he knew a woman fairer than she.

"Beware, Princess, beware," cried the witch in a warning voice, as she listened. "Why should you heed tales of other women fairer than you? Have I not made you the most beautiful woman in the world, and can any others do more than I? Give no ear to what this stranger says or you shall rue it." But still the Princess murmured, and said she did not love to hear anyone speak of others as beautiful as she.

"Be warned in time," cried the witch, "or you will have cause to repent it. Are you so silly or so vain as to be troubled because a Prince says idly what you know is not true? I tell you do not listen to him, but let him be slung to your chain as soon as may be, and then he will speak no more." And then they talked together of how Fiorimonde could make Gervaise grasp the fatal string.

Next morning when the sun rose, Gervaise started off into the woods, and there he plucked acorns and haws, and hips, and strung them on to a string to form a rude necklace. This he hid in his bosom, and then went back to the palace without telling anyone.

When the Princess rose, she dressed herself as beautifully as she could, and braided her golden locks with great care, for this morning she meant her new suitor to meet his fate. After breakfast, she stepped into the garden, where the sun shone brightly, and all looked fresh after the storm. Here from the grass she picked up a golden ball, and began to play with it.

"Go to our new guest," cried she to her ladies, "and ask him to come here and play at ball with me." So they went, and soon they returned bringing Gervaise with them.

"Good morrow, prince," cried she. "Pray, come and try your skill at this game with me; and you," she said to her ladies, "do not wait to watch our play, but each go your way, and do what pleases you best." So they all went away, and left her alone with Gervaise.

"Well, prince," cried she as they began to play, "what do you think of me by morning light? Yesterday when you came it was so dark, with thunder and clouds, that you could scarcely see my face, but now that there is bright sunshine, pray look well at me, and see if you do not think me as beautiful as any woman on earth," and she smiled at Gervaise, and looked so lovely as she spoke, that he scarce knew how to answer her; but he remembered Yolande, and said,

"Doubtless you are very beautiful; then why should you mind my telling you that I have seen a woman lovelier than you?"

At this the Princess again began to be angry, but she thought of the witch's words and said,

"Then, if you think there is a woman fairer than I, look at my beads, and now, that you see their colours in the sun, say if you ever saw such jewels before."

"It is true I have never seen beads like yours, but I have a necklace here, which pleases me better"; and from his pocket he drew the haws and acorns, which he had strung together.

"What is that necklace, and where did you get it? Show it to me!" cried Fiorimonde; but Gervaise held it out of her reach, and said,

"I like my necklace better than yours, Princess; and, believe me, there is no necklace like mine in all the world."

"Why; is it a fairy necklace? What does it do? Pray give it to me!" cried Fiorimonde, trembling with anger and curiosity, for she thought, "Perhaps it has power to make the wearer beautiful; perhaps it was worn by the woman whom he thought more beautiful than I, and that is why she looked so fair."

"Come, I will make a fair exchange," said Gervaise. "Give me your necklace and you shall have mine, and when it is round your throat I will truthfully say that you are the fairest woman in the world; but first I must have your necklace."

"Take it, then," cried the Princess, who, in her rage and eagerness, forgot all else, and she seized the string of beads to lift it from her neck, but no sooner had she taken it in her hands than they fell with a rattle to the earth, and Fiorimonde herself was nowhere to be seen. Gervaise bent down over the necklace as it lay upon the grass, and, with a smile, counted thirteen beads; and he knew that the thirteenth was the wicked Princess, who had herself met the evil fate she had prepared for so many others.

"Oh, clever Princess!" cried he, laughing aloud, "you are not so very clever, I think, to be so easily outwitted." Then he picked up the necklace on the point of the sword and carried it, slung thereon, into the council chamber, where sat the King surrounded by statesmen and courtiers busy with state affairs.

"Pray, King," said Gervaise, "send someone to seek for Princess Fiorimonde. A moment ago she played with me at ball in the garden, and now she is nowhere to be seen."

The King desired that servants should seek her Royal Highness; but they came back saying she was not to be found.

"Then let me see if I cannot bring her to you; but first let those who have been longer lost than she, come and tell their own tale." And, so saying, Gervaise let the necklace slip from his sword on to the floor, and taking from his breast a sharp dagger, proceeded to cut the golden thread on which the beads were strung and as he clave it in two there came a mighty noise like a clap of thunder.

"Now"; cried he, "look, and see King Pierrot who was lost," and as he spoke he drew from the cord a bead, and King Pierrot, in his royal clothes, with his sword at his side, stood before them.

"Treachery!" he cried, but ere he could say more Gervaise had drawn off another bead, and Prince Hildebrandt appeared, and after him came Adrian, and Sigbert, and Algar, and Cenred, and Pharamond, and Baldwyn, and Leofric, and Raoul, and last of the princes, Gervaise's own dear master Florestan, and they all denounced Princess Fiorimonde and her wickedness.

"And now," cried Gervaise, "here is she who has helped to save you all," and he drew off the twelfth bead, and there stood Yolande in her red dress; and when he saw her Gervaise flung away his dagger and took her in his arms, and they wept for joy.

The King and all the courtiers sat pale and trembling, unable to speak for fear and shame. At length the King said with a deep groan,

"We owe you deep amends, O noble kings and princes! What punishment do you wish us to prepare for our most guilty daughter?" but here Gervaise stopped him and said,

"Give her no other punishment than what she has chosen for herself. See, here she is, the thirteenth bead upon the string; let no one dare to draw it off, but let this string be hung up where all people can see it and see the one bead, and know the wicked Princess is punished for her sorcery, so it will be a warning to others who would do like her."

So they lifted the golden thread with great care and hung it up outside the town-hall, and there the one bead glittered and gleamed in the sunlight, and all who saw it knew that it was the wicked Princess Fiorimonde who had justly met her fate.

Then all the kings and princess thanked Gervaise and Yolande, and loaded them with presents, and each went to his own land.

And Gervaise married Yolande, and they went back with Prince Florestan to their home, and all lived happily to the end of their lives.

## AUGUST

### *Algernon Charles Swinburne*

There were four red apples on the bough,
Half gold half red, that one might know
The blood was ripe inside the core;
The colour of the leaves was more
Like stems of yellow corn that grow
Through all the gold June meadow's floor.

The warm smell of the fruit was good
To feed on, and the split green wood,
With all its bearded lips and stains
Of mosses in the cloven veins,
Most pleasant, if one lay or stood
In sunshine or in happy rains.

There were four apples on the tree,
Red stained through gold, that all might see
The sun went warm from core to rind;
The green leaves made the summer blind
In that soft place they kept for me
With golden apples shut behind.

The leaves caught gold across the sun,
And where the bluest air begun
Thirsted for song to help the heat;
As I to feel my lady's feet
Draw close before the day were done
Both lips grew dry with dreams of it.

In the mute August afternoon
They trembled to some undertune
Of music in the silver air;
Great pleasure was it to be there
Till green turned duskier and the moon
Coloured the corn-sheaves like gold hair.

That August time it was delight
To watch the red moons wane to white
'Twixt grey seamed stems of apple-trees;
A sense of heavy harmonies
Grew on the growth of patient night,
More sweet than shapen music is.

But some three hours before the moon
The air, still eager from the noon,
Flagged after heat, not wholly dead;
Against the stem I leant my head;
The colour soothed me like a tune,
Green leaves all round the gold and red.

I lay there till the warm smell grew
More sharp, when flecks of yellow dew
Between the round ripe leaves that blurred
The rind with stain and wet; I heard
A wind that blew and breathed and blew,
Too weak to alter its one word.

The wet leaves next the gentle fruit
Felt smoother, and the brown tree-root
Felt the mould warmer: I too felt
(As water feels the slow gold melt
Right through it when the day burns mute)
The peace of time wherein love dwelt.

There were four apples on the tree,
Gold stained on red that all might see
The sweet blood filled them to the core:
The colour of her hair is more
Like stems of fair faint gold, that be
Mown from the harvest's middle floor.

# THE COURTSHIP OF THE YONGHY-BONGHY-BÒ

*Edward Lear*

## I

On the Coast of the Coromandel
Where the early pumpkins blow,
In the middle of the woods
   Lived the Yonghy-Bonghy-Bò.
Two old chairs, and half a candle,—
One old jug without a handle,—
     These were all his wordly goods:
     In the middle of the woods,
     These were all the wordly goods,
   Of the Yonghy-Bonghy-Bò,
   Of the Yonghy-Bonghy-Bò.

## II

Once, among the Bong-trees walking
   Where the early pumpkins blow,
     To a little heap of stones
   Came the Yonghy-Bonghy-Bò.
There he heard a Lady talking,
To some milk-white Hens of Dorking,—
     "'Tis the Lady Jingly Jones!
     "On that little heap of stones
     "Sits the Lady Jingly Jones!"
   Said the Yonghy-Bonghy-Bò,
   Said the Yonghy-Bonghy-Bò.

## III

"Lady Jingly! Lady Jingly!
   'Sitting where the pumpkins blow,

"Will you come and be my wife?"
Said the Yonghy-Bonghy-Bò.
"I am tired of living singly,—
"On this coast so wild and shingly,—
    "I'm a-weary of my life:
    "If you'll come and be my wife,
      "Quite serene would be my life!"—
Said the Yonghy-Bonghy-Bò,
Said the Yonghy-Bonghy-Bò.


## IV


"On this Coast of Coromandel,
  "Shrimps and watercresses grow,
    "Prawns are plentiful and cheap,"
Said the Yonghy-Bonghy-Bò.
"You shall have my Chairs and candle,
"And my jug without a handle!—
    "Gaze upon the rolling deep
    ("Fish is plentiful and cheap)
    "As the sea, my love is deep!"
Said the Yonghy-Bonghy-Bò,
Said the Yonghy-Bonghy-Bò.


## V


Lady Jingly answered sadly,
  And her tears began to flow,—
    "Your proposal comes too late,
  "Mr. Yonghy-Bonghy-Bò!
"I would be your wife most gladly!"
(Here she twirled her fingers madly,)
    "But in England I've a mate!
    "Yes! you've asked me far too late,
    "For in England I've a mate,
  "Mr. Yonghy-Bonghy-Bò!
  "Mr. Yonghy-Bonghy-Bò!"

## VI

"Mr. Jones—(his name is Handel,—
   "Handel Jones, Esquire, & Co.)
     "Dorking fowls delights to send,
   "Mr. Yonghy-Bonghy-Bò!
"Keep, oh! keep your chairs and candle,
"And your jug without a handle,—
     "I can merely be your friend!
     "—Should my Jones more Dorkings send,
   "I will give you three, my friend!
   "Mr. Yonghy-Bonghy-Bò!
   "Mr. Yonghy-Bonghy-Bò!"

## VII

"Though you've such a tiny body,
   "And your head so large doth grow,—
     "Though your hat may blow away,
   "Mr. Yonghy-Bonghy-Bò!
"Though you're such a Hoddy Doddy—
"Yet I wish that I could modi-
     "fy the words I needs must say!
     "Will you please to go away?
     "That is all I have to say—
   "Mr. Yonghy-Bonghy-Bò!
   "Mr. Yonghy-Bonghy-Bò!"

## VIII

Down the slippery slopes of Myrtle,
   Where the early pumpkins blow,
     To the calm and silent sea
   Fled the Yonghy-Bonghy-Bò.
There, beyond the Bay of Gurtle,
Lay a large and lively Turtle;—
     "You're the Cove," he said, "for me

"On your back beyond the sea,
"Turtle, you shall carry me!"
Said the Yonghy-Bonghy-Bò,
Said the Yonghy-Bonghy-Bò.


## IX

Through the silent-roaring ocean
    Did the Turtle swiftly go;
        Holding fast upon his shell
    Rode the Yonghy-Bonghy-Bò.
With a sad primæval motion
Towards the sunset isles of Boshen
        Still the Turtle bore him well.
        Holding fast upon his shell,
        "Lady Jingly Jones, farewell!"
Sang the Yonghy-Bonghy-Bò,
Sang the Yonghy-Bonghy-Bò.


## X

From the Coast of Coromandel,
    Did that Lady never go;
        On that heap of stones she mourns
    For the Yonghy-Bonghy-Bò.
On the Coast of Coromandel,
In his jug without a handle
        Still she weeps, and daily moans;
        On that little heap of stones
        To her Dorking Hens she moans,
    For the Yonghy-Bonghy-Bò,
    For the Yonghy-Bonghy-Bò.

## THE CROW AND THE PITCHER

### *Aesop*

A Crow, ready to die with thirst, flew with joy to a Pitcher, which he beheld at some distance. When he came, he found water in it indeed, but so near the bottom, that with all his stooping and straining he was not able to reach it. Then he endeavoured to overturn the Pitcher, that so at least he might be able to get a little of it. But his strength was not sufficient for this. At last seeing some pebbles lie near the place, he cast them one by one into the Pitcher; and thus, by degrees, raised the water up to the very brim, and satisfied his thirst.

*Translated by Samuel Croxall*

## THE BRIDE COMES TO YELLOW SKY

### *Stephen Crane*

#### I

The great Pullman was whirling onward with such dignity of motion that a glance from the window seemed simply to prove that the plains of Texas were pouring eastward. Vast flats of green grass, dull-hued spaces of mesquit and cactus, little groups of frame houses, woods of light and tender trees, all were sweeping into the east, sweeping over the horizon, a precipice.

A newly married pair had boarded this coach at San Antonio. The man's face was reddened from many days in the wind and sun, and a direct result of his new black clothes was that his brick-colored hands were constantly performing in a most conscious fashion. From time to time he looked down respectfully at his attire. He sat with a hand on each knee, like a man waiting in a barber's shop. The glances he devoted to other passengers were furtive and shy.

The bride was not pretty, nor was she very young. She wore a dress of blue cashmere, with small reservations of velvet here and there, and with steel buttons abounding. She continually twisted her head to regard her puff sleeves, very stiff, straight, and high. They embarrassed her. It was quite apparent that she had cooked, and that she expected to cook, dutifully. The blushes caused by the careless scrutiny of some passengers as she had entered the car were strange to see upon this plain, under-class countenance, which was drawn in placid, almost emotionless lines.

They were evidently very happy. "Ever been in a parlor-car before?" he asked, smiling with delight.

"No," she answered; "I never was. It's fine, ain't it?"

"Great! And then after a while we'll go forward to the diner, and get a big lay-out. Finest meal in the world. Charge a dollar."

"Oh, do they?" cried the bride. "Charge a dollar? Why, that's too much—for us—ain't it, Jack?"

"Not this trip, anyhow," he answered bravely. "We're going to go the whole thing."

Later he explained to her about the trains. "You see, it's a thousand miles from one end of Texas to the other; and this train runs right across it, and never stops but four times." He had the pride of an owner. He pointed out to her the dazzling fittings of the coach; and in truth her eyes opened wider as she contemplated the sea-green figured velvet, the shining brass, silver, and glass, the wood that gleamed as darkly brilliant as the surface of a pool of oil. At one end a bronze figure sturdily held a support for a separated chamber, and at convenient places on the ceiling were frescos in olive and silver.

To the minds of the pair, their surroundings reflected the glory of their marriage that morning in San Antonio; this was the environment of their new estate; and the man's face in particular beamed with an elation that made him appear ridiculous to the negro porter. This individual at times surveyed them from afar with an amused and superior grin. On other occasions he bullied them with skill in ways that did not make it exactly plain to them that they were being bullied. He subtly used all the manners of the most unconquerable kind of snobbery. He oppressed them; but of this oppression they had small knowledge, and they speedily forgot that infrequently a number of travelers covered them with stares of derisive enjoyment. Historically there was supposed to be something infinitely humorous in their situation.

"We are due in Yellow Sky at 3:42," he said, looking tenderly into her eyes.

"Oh, are we?" she said, as if she had not been aware of it. To evince surprise at her husband's statement was part of her wifely amiability. She took from a pocket a little silver watch; and as she held it before her, and stared at it with a frown of attention, the new husband's face shone.

"I bought it in San Anton' from a friend of mine," he told her gleefully.

"It's seventeen minutes past twelve," she said, looking up at him with a kind of shy and clumsy coquetry. A passenger, noting this play, grew excessively sardonic, and winked at himself in one of the numerous mirrors.

At last they went to the dining-car. Two rows of negro waiters, in glowing white suits, surveyed their entrance with the interest, and also the equanimity, of men who had been forewarned. The pair fell to the lot of a waiter who happened to feel pleasure in steering them through their meal. He viewed them with the manner of a fatherly pilot, his countenance radiant with benevolence. The patronage, entwined with the ordinary deference, was not plain to them. And yet, as they returned to their coach, they showed in their faces a sense of escape.

To the left, miles down a long purple slope, was a little ribbon of mist where moved the keening Rio Grande. The train was approaching it at an angle, and the apex was Yellow Sky. Presently it was apparent that, as the distance from Yellow Sky grew shorter, the husband became commensurately restless. His brick-red hands were more insistent in their prominence. Occasionally he was even rather absent-minded and far-away when the bride leaned forward and addressed him.

As a matter of truth, Jack Potter was beginning to find the shadow of a deed weigh upon him like a leaden slab. He, the town marshal of Yellow Sky, a man known, liked, and feared in his corner, a prominent person, had gone to San Antonio to meet a girl he believed he loved, and there, after the usual prayers, had actually induced her to marry him, without consulting Yellow Sky for any part of the transaction. He was now bringing his bride before an innocent and unsuspecting community.

Of course people in Yellow Sky married as it pleased them, in accordance with a general custom; but such was Potter's thought of his duty to his friends, or of their idea of his duty, or of an unspoken form which does not control men in these matters, that he felt he was heinous. He had committed an extraordinary crime. Face to face with this girl in San Antonio, and spurred by his sharp impulse, he had gone headlong over all the social hedges. At San Antonio he was like a man hidden in the dark. A knife to sever any friendly duty, any form, was easy to his hand in that remote city. But the hour of Yellow Sky—the hour of daylight—was approaching.

He knew full well that his marriage was an important thing to his town. It could only be exceeded by the burning of the new hotel. His friends could not forgive him. Frequently he had reflected on the advisability of telling them by telegraph, but a new cowardice had been upon him. He feared to do it. And now the train was hurrying him toward a scene of amazement, glee, and reproach. He glanced out of the window at the line of haze swinging slowly in toward the train.

Yellow Sky had a kind of brass band, which played painfully, to the delight of the populace. He laughed without heart as he thought of it. If the citizens could dream of his prospective arrival with his bride, they would parade the band at the station and escort them, amid cheers and laughing congratulations, to his adobe home.

He resolved that he would use all the devices of speed and plains-craft in making the journey from the station to his house. Once within that safe citadel, he could issue some sort of a vocal bulletin, and then not go among the citizens until they had time to wear off a little of their enthusiasm.

The bride looked anxiously at him. "What's worrying you, Jack?"

He laughed again. "I'm not worrying, girl; I'm only thinking of Yellow Sky."

She flushed in comprehension.

A sense of mutual guilt invaded their minds and developed a finer tenderness. They looked at each other with eyes softly aglow. But Potter often laughed the same nervous laugh; the flush upon the bride's face seemed quite permanent.

The traitor to the feelings of Yellow Sky narrowly watched the speeding landscape. "We're nearly there," he said.

Presently the porter came and announced the proximity of Potter's home. He held a brush in his hand, and, with all his airy superiority gone, he brushed Potter's new clothes as the latter slowly turned this way and that way. Potter fumbled out a coin and gave it to the porter, as he had seen others do. It was a heavy and muscle-bound business, as that of a man shoeing his first horse.

The porter took their bag, and as the train began to slow they moved forward to the hooded platform of the car. Presently the two engines and their long string of coaches rushed into the station of Yellow Sky.

"They have to take water here," said Potter, from a constricted throat and in mournful cadence, as one announcing death. Before the train stopped his eye had swept the length of the platform, and he was glad and astonished to see there was none upon it but the station-agent, who, with a slightly hurried and anxious air, was walking toward the water-tanks. When the train had halted, the porter alighted first, and placed in position a little temporary step.

"Come on, girl," said Potter, hoarsely. As he helped her down they each laughed on a false note. He took the bag from the negro, and bade his wife cling to his arm. As they slunk rapidly away, his hang-dog glance perceived that they were unloading the two trunks, and also that the station-agent, far ahead near the baggage-car, had turned and was running toward him, making gestures. He laughed, and groaned as he laughed, when he noted the first effect of his marital bliss upon Yellow Sky. He gripped his wife's arm firmly to his side, and they fled. Behind them the porter stood, chuckling fatuously.

## II

The California express on the Southern Railway was due at Yellow Sky in twenty one minutes. There were six men at the bar of the Weary Gentleman Saloon. One was a drummer, who talked a great deal and rapidly; three were Texans, who did not care to talk at that time; and two were Mexican sheep-herders, who did not talk as a general practice in the Weary Gentleman Saloon. The barkeeper's dog lay on the board walk that crossed in front of the door. His head was on his paws, and he glanced drowsily here and there with the constant vigilance of a dog that is kicked on occasion. Across the sandy street were some vivid green grass-plots, so wonderful in appearance, amid the sands that burned near them in a blazing sun, that they caused a doubt in the mind. They exactly resembled the grass mats used to represent lawns on the stage. At the cooler end of the railway station, a man without a coat sat in a tilted chair and smoked his pipe. The fresh-cut bank of the Rio Grande circled near the town, and there could be seen beyond it a great plum-colored plain of mesquit.

Save for the busy drummer and his companions in the saloon, Yellow Sky was dozing. The new-comer leaned gracefully upon the bar, and recited many tales with the confidence of a bard who has come upon a new field.

"—and at the moment that the old man fell down-stairs with the bureau in his arms, the old woman was coming up with two scuttles of coal, and of course—"

The drummer's tale was interrupted by a young man who suddenly appeared in the open door. He cried: "Scratchy Wilson's drunk, and has turned loose with both hands." The two Mexicans at once set down their glasses and faded out of the rear entrance of the saloon.

The drummer, innocent and jocular, answered: "All right, old man. S'pose he has? Come in and have a drink, anyhow."

But the information had made such an obvious cleft in every skull in the room that the drummer was obliged to see its importance. All had become instantly solemn. "Say," said he, mystified, "what is this?" His three companions made the introductory gesture of eloquent speech; but the young man at the door forestalled them.

"It means, my friend," he answered, as he came into the saloon, "that for the next two hours this town won't be a health resort."

The barkeeper went to the door, and locked and barred it; reaching out of the window, he pulled in heavy wooden shutters, and barred them. Immediately a solemn, chapel-like gloom was upon the place. The drummer was looking from one to another.

"But say," he cried, "what is this, anyhow? You don't mean there is going to be a gun-fight?"

"Don't know whether there'll be a fight or not," answered one man, grimly; "but there'll be some shootin'—some good shootin'."

The young man who had warned them waved his hand. "Oh, there'll be a fight fast enough, if any one wants it. Anybody can get a fight out there in the street. There's a fight just waiting."

The drummer seemed to be swayed between the interest of a foreigner and a perception of personal danger.

"What did you say his name was?" he asked.

"Scratchy Wilson," they answered in chorus.

"And will he kill anybody? What are you going to do? Does this happen often? Does he rampage around like this once a week or so? Can he break in that door?"

"No; he can't break down that door," replied the barkeeper. "He's tried it three times. But when he comes you'd better lay down on the floor, stranger. He's dead sure to shoot at it, and a bullet may come through."

Thereafter the drummer kept a strict eye upon the door. The time had not yet been called for him to hug the floor, but, as a minor precaution, he sidled near to the wall. "Will he kill anybody?" he said again.

The man laughed low and scornfully at the question.

"He's out to shoot, and he's out for trouble. Don't see any good in experimentin' with him."

"But what do you do in a case like this? What do you do?"

A man responded: "Why, he and Jack Potter—"

"But," in chorus the other men interrupted, "Jack Potter's in San Anton'."

"Well, who is he? What's he got to do with it?"

"Oh, he's the town marshal. He goes out and fights Scratchy when he gets on one of these tears."

"Wow!" said the drummer, mopping his brow. "Nice job he's got."

The voices had toned away to mere whisperings. The drummer wished to ask further questions, which were born of an increasing anxiety and bewilderment; but when he attempted them, the men merely looked at him in irritation and motioned him to remain silent. A tense waiting hush was upon them. In the deep shadows of the room their eyes shone as they listened for sounds from the street. One man made three gestures at the bar-keeper; and the latter, moving like a ghost, handed him a glass and a bottle. The man poured a full glass of whisky, and set down the bottle noiselessly. He gulped the whisky in a swallow, and turned again toward the door in immovable silence. The drummer saw that the barkeeper, without a sound, had taken a Winchester from beneath the bar. Later he saw this individual beckoning to him, so he tiptoed across the room.

"You better come with me back of the bar."

"No, thanks," said the drummer, perspiring; "I'd rather be where I can make a break for the back door."

Whereupon the man of bottles made a kindly but peremptory gesture. The drummer obeyed it, and, finding himself seated on a box with his head below the level of the bar, balm was laid upon his soul at sight of various zinc and copper fittings that bore a resemblance to armor-plate. The barkeeper took a seat comfortably upon an adjacent box.

"You see," he whispered, "this here Scratchy Wilson is a wonder with a gun—a perfect wonder; and when he goes on the war-trail, we hunt our holes—naturally. He's about the last one of the old gang that used to hang out along the river here. He's a terror when he's drunk. When he's sober he's all right—kind of simple—wouldn't hurt a fly—nicest fellow in town. But when he's drunk—whoo!"

There were periods of stillness. "I wish Jack Potter was back from San Anton'," said the barkeeper. "He shot Wilson up once,—in the leg,—and he would sail in and pull out the kinks in this thing."

Presently they heard from a distance the sound of a shot, followed by three wild yowls. It instantly removed a bond from the men in the darkened saloon. There was a shuffling of feet. They looked at each other. "Here he comes," they said.

## III

A man in a maroon-colored flannel shirt, which had been purchased for purposes of decoration, and made principally by some Jewish women on the East Side of New York, rounded a corner and walked into the middle of the main street of Yellow Sky. In either hand the man held a long, heavy, blue-black revolver. Often he yelled, and these cries rang through a semblance of a deserted village, shrilly flying over the roofs in a volume that seemed to have no relation to the ordinary vocal strength of a man. It was as if the surrounding stillness formed the arch of a tomb over him. These cries of ferocious challenge rang against walls of silence. And his boots had red tops with gilded imprints, of the kind beloved in winter by little sledding boys on the hillsides of New England.

The man's face flamed in a rage begot of whisky. His eyes, rolling, and yet keen for ambush, hunted the still doorways and windows. He walked with the creeping movement of the midnight cat. As it occurred to him, he roared menacing information. The long revolvers in his hands were as easy as straws; they were moved with an electric swiftness. The little fingers of each hand played sometimes in a musician's way. Plain from the low collar of the shirt, the cords of his neck straightened and sank, straightened and sank, as passion moved him. The only sounds were his terrible invitations. The calm adobes preserved their demeanor at the passing of this small thing in the middle of the street.

There was no offer of fight—no offer of fight. The man called to the sky. There were no attractions. He bellowed and fumed and swayed his revolvers here and everywhere.

The dog of the barkeeper of the Weary Gentleman Saloon had not appreciated the advance of events. He yet lay dozing in front of his master's door. At sight of the dog, the man paused and raised his revolver humor-ously. At sight of the man, the dog sprang up and walked diagonally away, with a sullen head, and growling. The man yelled, and the dog broke into a gallop. As it was about to enter an alley, there was a loud noise, a whistling, and something spat the ground directly before it. The dog screamed, and, wheeling in terror, galloped headlong in a new direction. Again there was a noise, a whistling, and sand was kicked viciously before it. Fear-stricken, the dog turned and flurried like an animal in a pen. The man stood laughing, his weapons at his hips.

Ultimately the man was attracted by the closed door of the Weary Gentleman Saloon. He went to it, and, hammering with a revolver, demanded drink.

The door remaining imperturbable, he picked a bit of paper from the walk, and nailed it to the framework with a knife. He then turned his back contemptuously upon this popular resort, and, walking to the opposite side of the street, and spinning there on his heel quickly and lithely, fired at the bit of paper. He missed it by a half-inch. He swore at himself, and went away. Later he comfortably fusilladed the windows of his most intimate friend. The man was playing with this town; it was a toy for him.

But still there was no offer of fight. The name of Jack Potter, his ancient antagonist, entered his mind, and he concluded that it would be a glad thing if he should go to Potter's house, and by bombardment induce him to come out and fight. He moved in the direction of his desire, chanting Apache scalp-music.

When he arrived at it, Potter's house presented the same still front as had the other adobes. Taking up a strategic position, the man howled a challenge. But this house regarded him as might a great stone god. It gave no sign. After a decent wait, the man howled further challenges, mingling with them wonderful epithets.

Presently there came the spectacle of a man churning himself into deepest rage over the immobility of a house. He fumed at it as the winter wind attacks a prairie cabin in the North. To the distance there should have gone the sound of a tumult like the fighting of two hundred Mexicans. As necessity bade him, he paused for breath or to reload his revolvers.


## IV

Potter and his bride walked sheepishly and with speed. Sometimes they laughed together shamefacedly and low.

"Next corner, dear," he said finally.

They both put forth the efforts of a pair walking bowed against a strong wind. Potter was about to raise a finger to point the first appearance of the new home when, as they circled the corner, they came face to face with a man in a maroon-colored shirt, who was feverishly pushing cartridges into a large revolver. Upon the instant the man dropped his revolver to the ground, and, like lightning, whipped another from its holster. The second weapon was aimed at the bridegroom's chest.

There was a silence. Potter's mouth seemed to be merely a grave for his tongue. He exhibited an instinct to at once loosen his arm from the woman's grip, and he dropped the bag to the sand. As for the bride, her face had gone as yellow as old cloth. She was a slave to hideous rites, gazing at the apparitional snake.

The two men faced each other at a distance of three paces. He of the revolver smiled and with a new and quiet ferocity.

"Tried to sneak up on me," he said. "Tried to sneak up on me!" His eyes grew more baleful. As Potter made a slight movement, the man thrust his revolver venomously forward. "No; don't you do it, Jack Potter. Don't you move a finger toward a gun just yet. Don't you move an eyelash. The time has come for me to settle with you, and I'm goin' to do it my own way, and loaf along with no interferin'. So if you don't want a gun bent on you, just mind what I tell you."

Potter looked at his enemy. "I ain't got a gun on me, Scratchy," he said. "Honest, I ain't." He was stiffening and steadying, but yet somewhere at the back of his mind a vision of the Pullman floated: the sea-green figured velvet, the shining brass, silver, and glass, the wood that gleamed as darkly brilliant as the surface of a pool of oil—all the glory of the marriage, the environment of the new estate. "You know I fight when it comes to fighting, Scratchy Wilson; but I ain't got a gun on me. You'll have to do all the shootin' yourself."

His enemy's face went livid. He stepped forward, and lashed his weapon to and fro before Potter's chest. "Don't you tell me you ain't got no gun on you, you whelp. Don't tell me no lie like that. There ain't a man in Texas ever seen you without no gun. Don't take me for no kid." His eyes blazed with light, and his throat worked like a pump.

"I ain't takin' you for no kid," answered Potter. His heels had not moved an inch backward. "I'm takin' you for a—fool. I tell you I ain't got a gun, and I ain't. If you're goin' to shoot me up, you better begin now; you'll never get a chance like this again."

So much enforced reasoning had told on Wilson's rage; he was calmer. "If you ain't got a gun, why ain't you got a gun?" he sneered. "Been to Sunday-school?"

"I ain't got a gun because I've just come from San Anton' with my wife. I'm married," said Potter. "And if I'd thought there was going to be any galoots like you prowling around when I brought my wife home, I'd had a gun, and don't you forget it."

"Married!" said Scratchy, not at all comprehending.

"Yes, married. I'm married," said Potter, distinctly.

"Married?" said Scratchy. Seemingly for the first time, he saw the drooping, drowning woman at the other man's side. "No!" he said. He was like a creature allowed a glimpse of another world. He moved a pace backward, and his arm, with the revolver, dropped to his side. "Is this the lady?" he asked.

"Yes; this is the lady," answered Potter.

There was another period of silence.

"Well," said Wilson at last, slowly, "I s'pose it's all off now."

"It's all off if you say so, Scratchy. You know I didn't make the trouble." Potter lifted his valise.

"Well, I 'low it's off, Jack," said Wilson. He was looking at the ground. "Married!" He was not a student of chivalry; it was merely that in the presence of this foreign condition he was a simple child of the earlier plains. He picked up his starboard revolver, and, placing both weapons in their holsters, he went away. His feet made funnel-shaped tracks in the heavy sand.

∾

# HUMPTY DUMPTY

## Lewis Carroll

However, the egg only got larger and larger, and more and more human: when she had come within a few yards of it, she saw that it had eyes and a nose and mouth; and, when she had come close to it, she saw clearly that it was HUMPTY DUMPTY himself. "It ca'n't be anybody else!" she said to herself. "I'm as certain of it, as if his name were written all over his face!"

It might have been written a hundred times, easily, on that enormous face. Humpty Dumpty was sitting, with his legs crossed like a Turk, on the top of a high wall—such a narrow one that Alice quite wondered how he could keep his balance—and, as his eyes were steadily fixed in the opposite direction, and he didn't take the least notice of her, she thought he must be a stuffed figure, after all.

"And how exactly like an egg he is!" she said aloud, standing with her hands ready to catch him, for she was every moment expecting him to fall.

"It's *very* provoking," Humpty Dumpty said after a long silence, looking away from Alice as he spoke, "to be called an egg—*very!*"

"I said you *looked* like an egg Sir," Alice gently explained. "And some eggs are very pretty, you know," she added, hoping to turn her remark into a sort of compliment.

"Some people," said Humpty Dumpty, looking away from her as usual, "have no more sense than a baby!"

Alice didn't know what to say to this: it wasn't at all like conversation, she thought, as he never said anything to *her;* in fact, his last remark was evidently addressed to a tree—so she stood and softly repeated to herself:—

> "*Humpty Dumpty sat on a wall:*
> *Humpty Dumpty had a great fall.*
> *All the King's horses and all the King's men*
> *Couldn't put Humpty Dumpty in his place again.*"

"That last line is much too long for the poetry," she added, almost out loud, forgetting that Humpty Dumpty would hear her.

"Don't stand chattering to yourself like that," Humpty Dumpty said, looking at her for the first time, "but tell me your name and your business."

"My *name* is Alice, but—"

"It's a stupid name enough!" Humpty Dumpty interrupted impatiently. "What does it mean?"

"*Must* a name mean something?" Alice asked doubtfully.

"Of course it must," Humpty Dumpty said with a short laugh: "*my* name means the shape I am—and a good handsome shape it is, too. With a name like yours, you might be any shape, almost."

"Why do you sit out here all alone?" said Alice, not wishing to begin an argument.

"Why, because there's nobody with me!" cried Humpty Dumpty. "Did you think I didn't know the answer to *that*? Ask another."

"Don't you think you'd be safer down on the ground?" Alice went on, not with any idea of making another riddle, but simply in her good-natured anxiety for the queer creature. "That wall is so *very* narrow!"

"What tremendously easy riddles you ask!" Humpty Dumpty growled out. "Of course I don't think so! Why, if ever I *did* fall off—which there"s no chance of—but *if* I did—" Here he pursed up his lips, and looked so solemn and grand that Alice could hardly help laughing. "*If* I *did* fall," he went on, "*the King has promised me*—ah, you may turn pale, if you like! You didn't think I was going to say that, did you? *The King has promised me — with his very own mouth*—to—to—"

"To send all his horses and all his men," Alice interrupted, rather unwisely.

"Now I declare that's too bad!" Humpty Dumpty cried, breaking into a sudden passion. "You've been listening at doors—and behind trees—and down chimneys—or you couldn't have known it!"

"I haven't, indeed!" Alice said very gently. "It's in a book."

"Ah, well! They may write such things in a *book*," Humpty Dumpty said in a calmer tone. "That's what you call a History of England, that is. Now, take a good look at me! I'm one that has spoken to a King, I am: mayhap you'll never see such another: and, to show you I'm not proud, you may shake hands with me!" And he grinned almost from ear to ear, as he leant forwards (and as nearly as possible fell off the wall in doing so) and offered Alice his hand. She watched him a little anxiously as she took it. "If he smiled much more the ends of his mouth might meet behind," she thought: "and then I don't know *what* would happen to his head! I'm afraid it would come off!"

"Yes, all his horses and all his men," Humpty Dumpty went on. "They'd pick me up again in a minute, *they* would! However, this conversation is going on a little too fast: let's go back to the last remark but one."

"I'm afraid I ca'n't quite remember it," Alice said, very politely.

"In that case we start afresh," said Humpty Dumpty, "and it's my turn to choose a subject—" ("He talks about it just as if it was a game!" thought Alice.) "So here's a question for you. How old did you say you were?"

Alice made a short calculation, and said "Seven years and six months."

"Wrong!" Humpty Dumpty exclaimed triumphantly. "You never said a word like it!"

"I thought you meant 'How old *are* you?'" Alice explained.

"If I'd meant that, I'd have said it," said Humpty Dumpty.

Alice didn't want to begin another argument, so she said nothing.

"Seven years and six months!" Humpty Dumpty repeated thoughtfully. "An uncomfortable sort of age. Now if you'd asked *my* advice, I'd have said 'Leave off at seven'—but it's too late now."

"I never ask advice about growing," Alice said indignantly.

"Too proud?" the other enquired.

Alice felt even more indignant at this suggestion. "I mean," she said, "that one ca'n't help growing older."

"*One* ca'n't, perhaps," said Humpty Dumpty; "but *two* can. With proper assistance, you might have left off at seven."

"What a beautiful belt you've got on!" Alice suddenly remarked. (They had had quite enough of the subject of age, she thought: and, if they really were to take turns in choosing subjects, it was *her* turn now.) "At least," she corrected herself on second thoughts, "a beautiful cravat, I should have said—no, a belt, I mean—I beg your pardon!" she added in dismay, for Humpty Dumpty looked thoroughly offended, and she began to wish she hadn't chosen that subject. "If only I knew," she thought to herself, "which was neck and which was waist!"

Evidently Humpty Dumpty was very angry, though he said nothing for a minute or two. When he *did* speak again, it was in a deep growl.

"It is a—*most—provoking*—thing," he said at last, "when a person doesn't know a cravat from a belt!"

"I know it's very ignorant of me," Alice said, in so humble a tone that Humpty Dumpty relented.

"It's a cravat, child, and a beautiful one, as you say. It's a present from the White King and Queen. There now!"

"Is it really?" said Alice, quite pleased to find that she *had* chosen a good subject, after all.

"They gave it me," Humpty Dumpty continued thoughtfully, as he crossed one knee over the other and clasped his hands round it, "they gave it me—for an un-birthday present."

"I beg your pardon?" Alice said with a puzzled air.

"I'm not offended," said Humpty Dumpty.

"I mean, what *is* an un-birthday present?"

"A present given when it isn't your birthday, of course."

Alice considered a little. "I like birthday presents best," she said at last.

"You don't know what you're talking about!" cried Humpty Dumpty. "How many days are there in a year?"

"Three hundred and sixty-five," said Alice.

"And how many birthdays have you?"

"One."

"And if you take one from three hundred and sixty-five, what remains?"

"Three hundred and sixty-four, of course."

Humpty Dumpty looked doubtful. "I'd rather see that done on paper," he said.

Alice couldn't help smiling as she took out her memorandum-book, and worked the sum for him:

$$\begin{array}{r} 365 \\ \underline{1} \\ 364 \\ \underline{\phantom{0}} \end{array}$$

Humpty Dumpty took the book, and looked at it carefully. "That seems to be done right—" he began.

"You're holding it upside down!" Alice interrupted.

"To be sure I was!" Humpty Dumpty said gaily, as she turned it round for him. "I thought it looked a little queer. As I was saying, that *seems* to be done right—though I haven't time to look it over thoroughly just now—and that shows that there are three hundred and sixty-four days when you might get un-birthday presents—"

"Certainly," said Alice.

"And only *one* for birthday presents, you know. There's glory for you!"

"I don't know what you mean by 'glory,'" Alice said.

Humpty Dumpty smiled contemptuously. "Of course you don't—till I tell you. I meant 'there's a nice knock-down argument for you!'"

"But 'glory' doesn't mean 'a nice knock-down argument,'" Alice objected.

"When *I* use a word," Humpty Dumpty said, in rather a scornful tone, "it means just what I choose it to mean—neither more nor less."

"The question is," said Alice, "whether you *can* make words mean so many different things."

"The question is," said Humpty Dumpty, "which is to be master—that's all."

Alice was too much puzzled to say anything; so after a minute Humpty Dumpty began again. "They've a temper, some of them—particularly verbs: they're the proudest—adjectives you can do anything with, but not verbs—however, *I* can manage the whole lot of them! Impenetrability! That's what *I* say!"

"Would you tell me, please," said Alice, "what that means?"

"Now you talk like a reasonable child," said Humpty Dumpty, looking very much pleased. "I meant by 'impenetrability' that we've had enough of that subject, and it would be just as well if you'd mention what you mean to do next, as I suppose you don't mean to stop here all the rest of your life."

"That's a great deal to make one word mean," Alice said in a thoughtful tone.

"When I make a word do a lot of work like that," said Humpty Dumpty, "I always pay it extra."

"Oh!" said Alice. She was too much puzzled to make any other remark.

"Ah, you should see 'em come round me of a Saturday night," Humpty Dumpty went on, wagging his head gravely from side to side, "for to get their wages, you know."

(Alice didn't venture to ask what he paid them with; and so you see I ca'n't tell *you*.)

"You seem very clever at explaining words, Sir," said Alice. "Would you kindly tell me the meaning of the poem called 'Jabberwocky'?"

"Let's hear it," said Humpty Dumpty. "I can explain all the poems that ever were invented—and a good many that haven't been invented just yet."

This sounded very hopeful, so Alice repeated the first verse:—

> *"'Twas brillig, and the slithy toves*
> *Did gyre and gimble in the wabe:*
> *All mimsy were the borogoves,*
> *And the mome raths outgrabe."*

"That's enough to begin with," Humpty Dumpty interrupted: "there are plenty of hard words there. *'Brillig'* means four o'clock in the afternoon—the time when you begin *broiling* things for dinner."

"That'll do very well," said Alice: "and *'slithy'*?"

"Well, *'slithy'* means 'lithe and slimy.' 'Lithe' is the same as 'active.' You see it's like a portmanteau—there are two meanings packed up into one word."

"I see it now," Alice remarked thoughtfully: "and what are *'toves'*?"

"Well, *'toves'* are something like badgers—they're something like lizards—and they're something like corkscrews."

"They must be very curious-looking creatures."

"They are that," said Humpty Dumpty: "also they make their nests under sun-dials—also they live on cheese."

"And what's to *'gyre'* and to *'gimble'*?"

"To *'gyre'* is to go round and round like a gyroscope. To *'gimble'* is to make holes like a gimblet."

"And *'the wabe'* is the grass-plot round a sun-dial, I suppose?" said Alice, surprised at her own ingenuity.

"Of course it is. It's called *'wabe,'* you know, because it goes a long way before it, and a long way behind it—"

"And a long way beyond it on each side," Alice added.

"Exactly so. Well then, *'mimsy'* is 'flimsy and miserable' (there's another portmanteau for you). And a *'borogove'* is a thin shabby-looking bird with its feathers sticking out all round—something like a live mop."

"And then *'mome raths'*?" said Alice. "I'm afraid I'm giving you a great deal of trouble."

"Well, a *'rath'* is a sort of green pig: but *'mome'* I'm not certain about.

I think it's short for 'from home'—meaning that they'd lost their way, you know."

"And what does '*outgrabe*' mean?"

"Well, '*outgribing*' is something between bellowing and whistling, with a kind of sneeze in the middle: however, you'll hear it done, maybe—down in the wood yonder—and, when you've once heard it, you'll be *quite* content. Who's been repeating all that hard stuff to you?"

"I read it in a book," said Alice. "But I *had* some poetry repeated to me much easier than that, by—Tweedledee, I think it was."

"As to poetry, you know," said Humpty Dumpty, stretching out one of his great hands, "I can repeat poetry as well as other folk, if it comes to that—"

"Oh, it needn't come to that!" Alice hastily said, hoping to keep him from beginning.

"The piece I'm going to repeat," he went on without noticing her remark, "was written entirely for your amusement."

Alice felt that in that case she really *ought* to listen to it; so she sat down, and said "Thank you" rather sadly.

> *"In winter, when the fields are white,*
> *I sing this song for your delight—*

only I don't sing it," he added, as an explanation.

"I see you don't," said Alice.

"If you can *see* whether I'm singing or not, you've sharper eyes than most," Humpty Dumpty remarked severely. Alice was silent.

> *"In spring, when woods are getting green,*
> *I'll try and tell you what I mean:"*

"Thank you very much," said Alice.

> *"In summer, when the days are long,*
> *Perhaps you'll understand the song:*
>
> *In autumn, when the leaves are brown,*
> *Take pen and ink, and write it down."*

"I will, if I can remember it so long," said Alice.

"You needn't go on making remarks like that," Humpty Dumpty said: "they're not sensible, and they put me out."

> *"I sent a message to the fish:*
> *I told them 'This is what I wish.'*
>
> *The little fishes of the sea,*
> *They sent an answer back to me.*
>
> *The little fishes' answer was*
> *'We cannot do it, Sir, because—'"*

"I'm afraid I don't quite understand," said Alice.
"It gets easier further on," Humpty Dumpty replied.

> *"I sent to them again to say*
> *'It will be better to obey.'*
>
> *The fishes answered, with a grin,*
> *'Why, what a temper you are in!'*
>
> *I told them once, I told them twice:*
> *They would not listen to advice.*
>
> *I took a kettle large and new,*
> *Fit for the deed I had to do.*
>
> *My heart went hop, my heart went thump:*
> *I filled the kettle at the pump.*
>
> *Then some one came to me and said*
> *'The little fishes are in bed.'*
>
> *I said to him, I said it plain,*
> *'Then you must wake them up again.'*
>
> *I said it very loud and clear:*
> *I went and shouted in his ear."*

Humpty Dumpty raised his voice almost to a scream as he repeated this verse, and Alice thought, with a shudder, "I wouldn't have been the messenger for *anything!*"

> *"But he was very stiff and proud:*
> *He said 'You needn't shout so loud!'*
>
> *And he was very proud and stiff:*
> *He said 'I'd go and wake them, if—'*
>
> *I took a corkscrew from the shelf:*
> *I went to wake them up myself.*
>
> *And when I found the door was locked,*
> *I pulled and pushed and kicked and knocked.*
>
> *And when I found the door was shut,*
> *I tried to turn the handle, but—"*

There was a long pause.

"Is that all?" Alice timidly asked.

"That's all," said Humpty Dumpty. "Good-bye."

This was rather sudden, Alice thought: but, after such a *very* strong hint that she ought to be going, she felt that it would hardly be civil to stay. So she got up, and held out her hand. "Good-bye, till we meet again!" she said as cheerfully as she could.

"I shouldn't know you again if we *did* meet," Humpty Dumpty replied in a discontented tone, giving her one of his fingers to shake: "you're so exactly like other people."

"The face is what one goes by, generally," Alice remarked in a thoughtful tone.

"That's just what I complain of," said Humpty Dumpty. "Your face is the same as everybody has—the two eyes, so—" (marking their places in the air with his thumb) "nose in the middle, mouth under. It's always the same. Now if you had the two eyes on the same side of the nose, for instance—or the mouth at the top—that would be *some* help."

"It wouldn't look nice," Alice objected. But Humpty Dumpty only shut his eyes, and said "Wait till you've tried."

Alice waited a minute to see if he would speak again, but, as he never opened his eyes or took any further notice of her, she said "Good-bye!" once more, and, getting no answer to this, she quietly walked away: but she couldn't help saying to herself, as she went, "Of all the unsatisfactory—" (she repeated this aloud, as it was a great comfort to have such a long word to say) "of all the unsatisfactory people I *ever* met—" She never finished the sentence, for at this moment a heavy crash shook the forest from end to end.

❧

# BOOK III

*Autumn*

# THE STAG LOOKING INTO THE WATER

## *Aesop*

A Stag that had been drinking at a clear spring, saw himself in the water; and, pleased with the prospect, stood afterwards for some time contemplating and surveying his shape and features, from head to foot. Ah! says he, what a glorious pair of branching horns are there! how gracefully do those antlers hang over my forehead, and give an agreeable turn to my whole face! If some other parts of my body were but proportionable to them, I would turn my back to nobody; but I have a set of such legs as really makes me ashamed to see them. People may talk what they please of their conveniences, and what great need we stand in of them, upon several occasions; but, for my part, I find them so very slender and unsightly, that I had as lief have none at all. While he was giving himself these airs, he was alarmed with the noise of some huntsmen and a pack of hounds, that had been just laid on upon the scent, and were making towards him. Away he flies in some consternation, and, bounding nimbly over the plain, threw dogs and men at a vast distance behind him. After which, taking a very thick copse, he had the ill-fortune to be entangled by his horns in a thicket, where he was held fast, till the hounds came in and pulled him down. Finding now how it was like to go with him, in the pangs of death, he is said to have uttered these words: Unhappy creature that I am! I am too late convinced, that what I prided myself in, has been the cause of my undoing; and what I so much disliked was the only thing that could have saved me.

*Translated by Samuel Croxall*

❧

# THE MOCK TURTLE'S STORY

## Lewis Carroll

"You ca'n't think how glad I am to see you again, you dear old thing!" said the Duchess, as she tucked her arm affectionately into Alice's, and they walked off together.

Alice was very glad to find her in such a pleasant temper, and thought to herself that perhaps it was only the pepper that had made her so savage when they met in the kitchen.

"When *I'm* a Duchess," she said to herself (not in a very hopeful tone, though), "I wo'n't have any pepper in my kitchen *at all*. Soup does very well without—Maybe it's always pepper that makes people hot-tempered," she went on, very much pleased at having found out a new kind of rule, "and vinegar that makes them sour—and camomile that makes them bitter—and—and barley-sugar and such things that make children sweet-tempered. I only wish people knew *that:* then they wouldn't be so stingy about it, you know—"

She had quite forgotten the Duchess by this time, and was a little startled when she heard her voice close to her ear. "You're thinking about something, my dear, and that makes you forget to talk. I ca'n't tell you just now what the moral of that is, but I shall remember it in a bit."

"Perhaps it hasn't one," Alice ventured to remark.

"Tut, tut, child!" said the Duchess. "Every thing's got a moral, if only you can find it." And she squeezed herself up closer to Alice's side as she spoke.

Alice did not much like her keeping so close to her: first, because the Duchess was *very* ugly; and secondly, because she was exactly the right height to rest her chin on Alice's shoulder, and it was an uncomfortably sharp chin. However, she did not like to be rude: so she bore it as well as she could.

"The game's going on rather better now," she said, by way of keeping up the conversation a little.

"'Tis so," said the Duchess: "and the moral of that is—'Oh, 'tis love, 'tis love, that makes the world go round!'"

"Somebody said," Alice whispered, "that it's done by everybody minding their own business!"

"Ah, well! It means much the same thing," said the Duchess, digging her sharp little chin into Alice's shoulder as she added "and the moral of *that* is—'Take care of the sense, and the sounds will take care of themselves.'"

"How fond she is of finding morals in things!" Alice thought to herself.

"I dare say you're wondering why I don't put my arm round your waist," the Duchess said, after a pause: "the reason is, that I'm doubtful about the temper of your flamingo. Shall I try the experiment?"

"He might bite," Alice cautiously replied, not feeling at all anxious to have the experiment tried.

"Very true," said the Duchess: "flamingoes and mustard both bite. And the moral of that is—'Birds of a feather flock together.'"

"Only mustard isn't a bird," Alice remarked.

"Right, as usual," said the Duchess: "what a clear way you have of putting things!"

"It's a mineral, I *think*," said Alice.

"Of course it is," said the Duchess, who seemed ready to agree to everything that Alice said: "there's a large mustard-mine near here. And the moral of that is—'The more there is of mine, the less there is of yours.'"

"Oh, I know!" exclaimed Alice, who had not attended to this last remark. "It's a vegetable. It doesn't look like one, but it is."

"I quite agree with you," said the Duchess; "and the moral of that is—'Be what you would seem to be'—or, if you'd like it put more simply—'Never imagine yourself not to be otherwise than what it might appear to others that what you were or might have been was not otherwise than what you had been would have appeared to them to be otherwise.'"

"I think I should understand that better," Alice said very politely, "if I had it written down: but I ca'n't quite follow it as you say it."

"That's nothing to what I could say if I chose," the Duchess replied, in a pleased tone.

"Pray don't trouble yourself to say it any longer than that," said Alice.

"Oh, don't talk about trouble!" said the Duchess. "I make you a present of everything I've said as yet."

"A cheap sort of present!" thought Alice. "I'm glad people don't give birthday-presents like that!" But she did not venture to say it out loud.

"Thinking again?" the Duchess asked, with another dig of her sharp little chin.

"I've a right to think," said Alice sharply, for she was beginning to feel a little worried.

"Just about as much right," said the Duchess, "as pigs have to fly; and the m——"

But here, to Alice's great surprise, the Duchess's voice died away, even in the middle of her favourite word "moral," and the arm that was linked into hers began to tremble. Alice looked up, and there stood the Queen in front of them, with her arms folded, frowning like a thunderstorm.

"A fine day, your Majesty!" the Duchess began in a low, weak voice.

"Now, I give you fair warning," shouted the Queen, stamping on the ground as she spoke; "either you or your head must be off, and that in about half no time! Take your choice!"

The Duchess took her choice, and was gone in a moment.

"Let's go on with the game," the Queen said to Alice; and Alice was too much frightened to say a word, but slowly followed her back to the croquet-ground.

The other guests had taken advantage of the Queen's absence, and were resting in the shade: however, the moment they saw her, they hurried back to the game, the Queen merely remarking that a moment's delay would cost them their lives.

All the time they were playing the Queen never left off quarreling with the other players, and shouting "Off with his head!" or "Off with her head!" Those whom she sentenced were taken into custody by the soldiers, who of course had to leave off being arches to do this, so that, by the end of half an hour or so, there were no arches left, and all the players, except the King, the Queen, and Alice, were in custody and under sentence of execution.

Then the Queen left off, quite out of breath, and said to Alice "Have you seen the Mock Turtle yet?"

"No," said Alice. "I don't even know what a Mock Turtle is."

"It's the thing Mock Turtle Soup is made from," said the Queen.

"I never saw one, or heard of one," said Alice.

"Come on, then," said the Queen, "and he shall tell you his history."

As they walked off together, Alice heard the King say in a low voice, to the company generally, "You are all pardoned." "Come, *that's* a good thing!" she said to herself, for she had felt quite unhappy at the number of executions the Queen had ordered.

They very soon came upon a Gryphon, lying fast asleep in the sun. "Up, lazy thing!" said the Queen, "and take this young lady to see the Mock Turtle, and to hear his history. I must go back and see after some executions I have ordered;" and she walked off, leaving Alice alone with the Gryphon. Alice did not quite like the look of the creature, but on the whole she thought it would be quite as safe to stay with it as to go after that savage Queen: so she waited.

The Gryphon sat up and rubbed its eyes: then it watched the Queen till she was out of sight: then it chuckled. "What fun!" said the Gryphon, half to itself, half to Alice.

"What *is* the fun?" said Alice.

"Why, *she,*" said the Gryphon. "It's all her fancy, that: they never executes nobody, you know. Come on!"

"Everybody says 'come on!' here," thought Alice, as she went slowly after it: "I never was so ordered about before, in all my life, never!"

They had not gone far before they saw the Mock Turtle in the distance, sitting sad and lonely on a little ledge of rock, and, as they came nearer, Alice could hear him sighing as if his heart would break. She pitied him deeply. "What is his sorrow?" she asked the Gryphon. And the Gryphon answered, very nearly in the same words as before, "It's all his fancy, that: he hasn't got no sorrow, you know. Come on!"

So they went up to the Mock Turtle, who looked at them with large eyes full of tears, but said nothing.

"This here young lady," said the Gryphon, "she wants for to know your history, she do."

"I'll tell it her," said the Mock Turtle in a deep, hollow tone. "Sit down, both of you, and don't speak a word till I've finished."

So they sat down, and nobody spoke for some minutes. Alice thought to herself "I don't see how he can *ever* finish, if he doesn't begin." But she waited patiently.

"Once," said the Mock Turtle at last, with a deep sigh, "I was a real Turtle."

These words were followed by a very long silence, broken only by an occasional exclamation of "Hjckrrh!" from the Gryphon, and the constant heavy sobbing of the Mock Turtle. Alice was very nearly getting up and saying "Thank you, Sir, for your interesting story," but she could not help thinking there *must* be more to come, so she sat still and said nothing.

"When we were little," the Mock Turtle went on at last, more calmly, though still sobbing a little now and then, "we went to school in the sea. The master was an old Turtle—we used to call him Tortoise—"

"Why did you call him Tortoise, if he wasn't one?" Alice asked.

"We called him Tortoise because he taught us," said the Mock Turtle angrily. "Really you are very dull!"

"You ought to be ashamed of yourself for asking such a simple question," added the Gryphon; and then they both sat silent and looked at poor Alice, who felt ready to sink into the earth. At last the Gryphon said to the Mock Turtle "Drive on, old fellow! Don't be all day about it!" and he went on in these words:—

"Yes, we went to school in the sea, though you mayn't believe it—"

"I never said I didn't!' interrupted Alice.

"You did," said the Mock Turtle.

"Hold your tongue!" added the Gryphon, before Alice could speak again. The Mock Turtle went on.

"We had the best of educations—in fact, we went to school every day—"

"*I've* been to a day-school, too," said Alice. "You needn't be so proud as all that."

"With extras?" asked the Mock Turtle, a little anxiously.

"Yes," said Alice: "we learned French and music."

"And washing?" said the Mock Turtle.

"Certainly not!" said Alice indignantly.

"Ah! Then yours wasn't a really good school," said the Mock Turtle in a tone of great relief. "Now, at *ours,* they had, at the end of the bill, 'French, music, *and washing*—extra.'"

"You couldn't have wanted it much," said Alice; "living at the bottom of the sea."

"I couldn't afford to learn it," said the Mock Turtle, with a sigh. "I only took the regular course."

"What was that?" inquired Alice.

"Reeling and Writhing, of course, to begin with," the Mock Turtle replied; "and then the different branches of Arithmetic—Ambition, Distraction, Uglification, and Derision."

"I never heard of 'Uglification,'" Alice ventured to say. "What is it?"

The Gryphon lifted up both its paws in surprise. "Never heard of uglifying!" it exclaimed. "You know what to beautify is, I suppose?"

"Yes," said Alice doubtfully: "it means—to—make—anything—prettier."

"Well, then," the Gryphon went on, "if you don't know what to uglify is, you *are* a simpleton."

Alice did not feel encouraged to ask any more questions about it: so she turned to the Mock Turtle, and said "What else had you to learn?"

"Well, there was Mystery," the Mock Turtle replied, counting off the subjects on his flappers,—"Mystery, ancient and modern, with Seaography: then Drawling—the Drawling-master was an old conger-eel, that used to come once a week: *he* taught us Drawling, Stretching, and Fainting in Coils."

"What was *that* like?" said Alice.

"Well, I ca'n't show it you, myself," the Mock Turtle said: "I'm too stiff. And the Gryphon never learnt it."

"Hadn't time," said the Gryphon: "I went to the Classical master, though. He was an old crab, *he* was."

"I never went to him," the Mock Turtle said with a sigh. "He taught Laughing and Grief, they used to say."

"So he did, so he did," said the Gryphon, sighing in his turn; and both creatures hid their faces in their paws.

"And how many hours a day did you do lessons?" said Alice, in a hurry to change the subject.

"Ten hours the first day," said the Mock Turtle: "nine the next, and so on."

"What a curious plan!" exclaimed Alice.

"That's the reason they're called lessons," the Gryphon remarked: "because they lessen from day to day."

This was quite a new idea to Alice, and she thought it over a little before she made her next remark. "Then the eleventh day must have been a holiday?"

"Of course it was," said the Mock Turtle.

"And how did you manage on the twelfth?" Alice went on eagerly.

"That's enough about lessons," the Gryphon interrupted in a very decided tone. "Tell her something about the games now."

∾

# THE FLOATING OLD MAN

### Edward Lear

There was an Old Man in a boat,
Who said, "I'm afloat! I'm afloat!"
When they said, "No! you ain't!" he was ready to faint,
That unhappy Old Man in a boat.

∾

# THE WOOD SO WILD

*Anonymous*

I must go walk the wood so wild,
    And wander here and there,
    In dread and deadly fear;
For where I trusted I am beguiled,
    And all for one.

Thus am I banished from my bliss
    By craft and false pretense,
    Faultless without offence,
And of return no certainty is,
    And all for love of one.

My bed shall be the greenwood tree,
    A tuft of brakes under my head,
    As if one from joy were fled;
Thus from my life day by day I flee,
    And all for one.

The running streams shall be my drink,
    Acorns shall be my food.
    Nothing may do me good,
But when of your beauty I do think,
    And all for love of one.

# THE PROBLEM OF THOR BRIDGE

*Arthur Conan Doyle*

Somewhere in the vaults of the bank of Cox and Co., at Charing Cross, there is a travel-worn and battered tin dispatch-box with my name, John H. Watson, M. D., Late Indian Army, painted upon the lid. It is crammed with papers, nearly all of which are records of cases to illustrate the curious problems which Mr. Sherlock Holmes had at various times to examine. Some, and not the least interesting, were complete failures, and as such will hardly bear narrating, since no final explanation is forthcoming. A problem without a solution may interest the student, but can hardly fail to annoy the casual reader. Among these unfinished tales is that of Mr. James Phillimore, who, stepping back into his own house to get his umbrella, was never more seen in this world. No less remarkable is that of the cutter *Alicia*, which sailed one spring morning into a small patch of mist from where she never again emerged, nor was anything further ever heard of herself and her crew. A third case worthy of note is that of Isadora Persano, the well-known journalist and duellist, who was found stark staring mad with a match box in front of him which contained a remarkable worm said to be unknown to science. Apart from these unfathomed cases, there are some which involve the secrets of private families to an extent which would mean consternation in many exalted quarters if it were thought possible that they might find their way into print. I need not say that such a breach of confidence is unthinkable, and that these records will be separated and destroyed now that my friend has time to turn his energies to the matter. There remain a considerable residue of cases of greater or less interest which I might have edited before had I not feared to give the public a surfeit which might react upon the reputation of the man whom above all others I revere. In some I was myself concerned and can speak as an eyewitness, while in others I was either not present or played so small a part that they could only be told as by a third person. The following narrative is drawn from my own experience.

It was a wild morning in October, and I observed as I was dressing how the last remaining leaves were being whirled from the solitary plane tree which graces the yard behind our house. I descended to breakfast prepared to find my companion in depressed spirits, for, like all great artists, he was easily impressed by his surroundings. On the contrary, I found that he had nearly finished his meal, and that his mood was particularly bright and joyous, with that somewhat sinister cheerfulness which was characteristic of his lighter moments.

"You have a case, Holmes?" I remarked.

"The faculty of deduction is certainly contagious, Watson," he answered. "It has enabled you to probe my secret. Yes, I have a case. After a month of trivialities and stagnation the wheels move once more."

"Might I share it?"

"There is little to share, but we may discuss it when you have consumed the two hard-boiled eggs with which our new cook has favoured us. Their condition may not be unconnected with the copy of the *Family Herald* which I observed yesterday upon the hall-table. Even so trivial a matter as cooking an egg demands an attention which is conscious of the passage of time and incompatible with the love romance in that excellent periodical."

A quarter of an hour later the table had been cleared and we were face to face. He had drawn a letter from his pocket.

"You have heard of Neil Gibson, the Gold King?" he said.

"You mean the American Senator?"

"Well, he was once Senator for some Western state, but is better known as the greatest gold-mining magnate in the world."

"Yes, I know of him. He has surely lived in England for some time. His name is very familiar."

"Yes, he bought a considerable estate in Hampshire some five years ago. Possibly you have already heard of the tragic end of his wife?"

"Of course. I remember it now. That is why the name is familiar. But I really know nothing of the details."

Holmes waved his hand towards some papers on a chair. "I had no idea that the case was coming my way or I should have had my extracts ready," said he. "The fact is that the problem, though exceedingly sensational, appeared to present no difficulty. The interesting personality of the accused does not obscure the clearness of the evidence. That was the view taken by the coroner's jury and also in the police-court proceedings. It is now referred to the Assizes at Winchester. I fear it is a thankless business. I can discover facts, Watson, but I cannot change them. Unless some entirely new and unexpected ones come to light I do not see what my client can hope for."

"Your client?"

"Ah, I forgot I had not told you. I am getting into your involved habit, Watson, of telling a story backward. You had best read this first."

The letter which he handed to me, written in a bold, masterful hand, ran as follows:

Claridge's Hotel, *October 3rd.*

Dear Mr. Sherlock Holmes:

I can't see the best woman God ever made go to her death without doing all that is possible to save her. I can't explain things—I can't even try to explain them, but I know beyond all doubt that Miss Dunbar is innocent. You know the facts—who doesn't? It has been the gossip of the country. And never a voice raised for her! It's the damned injustice of it all that makes me crazy. That woman has a heart that wouldn't let her kill a fly. Well, I'll come at eleven to-morrow and see if you can get some ray of light in the dark. Maybe I have a clue and don't know it. Anyhow, all I know and all I have and all I am are for your use if only you can save her. If ever in your life you showed your powers, put them now into this case.

Yours faithfully,
J. Neil Gibson.

"There you have it," said Sherlock Holmes, knocking out the ashes of his after-breakfast pipe and slowly refilling it. "That is the gentleman I await. As to the story, you have hardly time to master all these papers, so I must give it to you in a nutshell if you are to take an intelligent interest in the proceedings. This man is the greatest financial power in the world, and a man, as I understand, of most violent and formidable character. He married a wife, the victim of this tragedy, of whom I know nothing save that she was past her prime, which was the more unfortunate as a very attractive governess superintended the education of two young children. These are the three people concerned, and the scene is a grand old manor house, the centre of a historical English state. Then as to the tragedy. The wife was found in the grounds nearly half a mile from the house, late at night, clad in her dinner dress, with a shawl over her shoulders and a revolver bullet through her brain. No weapon was found near her and there was no local clue as to the murder. No weapon near her, Watson—mark that! The crime seems to have been committed late in the evening, and the body was found by a game-keeper about eleven o'clock, when it was examined by the police and by a doctor before being carried up to the house. Is this too condensed, or can you follow it clearly?"

"It is all very clear. But why suspect the governess?"

"Well, in the first place there is some very direct evidence. A revolver with one discharged chamber and a calibre which corresponded with the bullet was found on the floor of her wardrobe." His eyes fixed and he repeated in broken words, "On—the—floor—of—her—wardrobe." Then he sank into silence, and I saw that some train of thought had been set moving which I should be foolish to interrupt. Suddenly with a start he emerged into brisk life once more. "Yes, Watson, it was found. Pretty damning, eh? So the two juries thought. Then the dead woman had a note upon her making an appointment at that very place and signed by the governess. How's that? Finally there is the motive. Senator Gibson is an attractive person. If his wife dies, who more likely to succeed her than the young lady who had already by all accounts received pressing attentions from her employer? Love, fortune, power, all depending upon one middle-aged life. Ugly, Watson—very ugly!"

"Yes, indeed, Holmes."

"Nor could she prove an alibi. On the contrary, she had to admit that she was down near Thor Bridge—that was the scene of the tragedy—about that hour. She couldn't deny it, for some passing villager had seen her there."

"That really seems final."

"And yet, Watson—and yet! This bridge—a single broad span of stone with balustraded sides—carries the drive over the narrowest part of a long, deep, reed-girt sheet of water. Thor Mere it is called. In the mouth of the bridge lay the dead woman. Such are the main facts. But here, if I mistake not, is our client, considerably before his time."

Billy had opened the door, but the name which he announced was an unexpected one. Mr. Marlow Bates was a stranger to both of us. He was a thin, nervous wisp of a man with frightened eyes and a twitching, hesitating manner—a man whom my own professional eye would judge to be on the brink of an absolute nervous breakdown.

"You seem agitated, Mr. Bates," said Holmes. "Pray sit down. I fear I can only give you a short time, for I have an appointment at eleven."

"I know you have," our visitor gasped, shooting out short sentences like a man who is out of breath. "Mr. Gibson is coming. Mr. Gibson is my employer. I am manager of his estate. Mr. Holmes, he is a villain—an infernal villain."

"Strong language, Mr. Bates."

"I have to be emphatic, Mr. Holmes, for the time is so limited. I would not have him find me here for the world. He is almost due now. But I was so situated that I could not come earlier. His secretary, Mr. Ferguson, only told me this morning of his appointment with you."

"And you are his manager?"

"I have given him notice. In a couple of weeks I shall have shaken off his accursed slavery. A hard man, Mr. Holmes, hard to all about him. Those public charities are a screen to cover his private iniquities. But his wife was his chief victim. He was brutal to her—yes, sir, brutal! How she came by her death I do not know, but I am sure that he had made her life a misery to her. She was a creature of the tropics, a Brazilian by birth, as no doubt you know."

"No, it had escaped me."

"Tropical by birth and tropical by nature. A child of the sun and of passion. She had loved him as such women can love, but when her own physical charms had faded—I am told that they once were great—there was nothing to hold him. We all liked her and felt for her and hated him for the way that he treated her. But he is plausible and cunning. That is all I have to say to you. Don't take him at his face value. There is more behind. Now I'll go. No, no, don't detain me! He is almost due."

With a frightened look at the clock our strange visitor literally ran to the door and disappeared.

"Well! Well!" said Holmes after an interval of silence. "Mr. Gibson seems to have a nice loyal household. But the warning is a useful one and now we can only wait till the man himself appears."

Sharp at the hour we heard a heavy step upon the stairs, and the famous millionaire was shown into the room. As I looked upon him I understood not only the fears and dislike of his manager but also the execrations which so many business rivals have heaped upon his head. If I were a sculptor and desired to idealize the successful man of affairs, iron of nerve and leathery of conscience, I should choose Mr. Neil Gibson as my model. His tall, gaunt, craggy figure had a suggestion of hunger and rapacity. An Abraham Lincoln keyed to base uses instead of high ones would give some idea of the man. His face might have been chiselled in granite, hardset, craggy, remorseless, with deep lines upon it, the scars of many a crisis. Cold gray eyes, looking shrewdly out from under bristling brows, surveyed us each in turn. He bowed in perfunctory fashion as Holmes mentioned my name, and then with a masterful air of possession he drew a chair up to my companion and seated himself with his bony knees almost touching him.

"Let me say right here, Mr. Holmes," he began, "that money is nothing to me in this case. You can burn it if it's any use in lighting you to the truth. This woman is innocent and this woman has to be cleared, and it's up to you to do it. Name your figure!"

"My professional charges are upon a fixed scale," said Holmes coldly. "I do not vary them, save when I remit them altogether."

"Well, if dollars make no difference to you, think of the reputation. If you pull this off every paper in England and America will be booming you. You'll be the talk of two continents."

"Thank you. Mr. Gibson, I do not think that I am in need of booming. It may surprise you to know that I prefer to work anonymously, and that it is the problem itself which attracts me. But we are wasting time. Let us get down to the facts."

"I think that you will find all the main ones in the press reports. I don't know that I can add anything which will help you. But if there is anything you would wish more light upon—well, I am here to give it."

"Well, there is just one point."

"What is it?"

"What were the exact relations between you and Miss Dunbar?"

The Gold King gave a violent start and half rose from his chair. Then his massive calm came back to him.

"I suppose you are within your rights—and maybe doing your duty—in asking such a question, Mr. Holmes."

"We will agree to suppose so," said Holmes.

"Then I can assure you that our relations were entirely and always those of an employer towards a young lady whom he never conversed with, or ever saw, save when she was in the company of his children."

Holmes rose from his chair.

"I am a rather busy man, Mr. Gibson," said he, "and I have no time or taste for aimless conversations. I wish you good-morning."

Our visitor had risen also, and his great loose figure towered above Holmes. There was an angry gleam from under those bristling brows and a tinge of colour in the sallow cheeks.

"What the devil do you mean by this, Mr. Holmes? Do you dismiss my case?"

"Well, Mr. Gibson, at least I dismiss you. I should have thought my words were plain."

"Plain enough, but what's at the back of it? Raising the price on me, or afraid to tackle it, or what? I've a right to a plain answer."

"Well, perhaps you have," said Holmes. "I'll give you one. This case is quite sufficiently complicated to start with without the further difficulty of false information."

"Meaning that I lie."

"Well, I was trying to express it as delicately as I could, but if you insist upon the word I will not contradict you."

I sprang to my feet, for the expression upon the millionaire's face was fiendish in its intensity, and he had raised his great knotted fist. Holmes smiled languidly and reached his hand out for his pipe.

"Don't be noisy, Mr. Gibson. I find that after breakfast even the smallest argument is unsettling. I suggest that a stroll in the morning air and a little quiet thought will be greatly to your advantage."

With an effort the Gold King mastered his fury. I could not but admire him, for by a supreme self-command he had turned in a minute from a hot flame of anger to a frigid and contemptuous indifference.

"Well, it's your choice. I guess you know how to run your own business. I can't make you touch the case against your will. You've done yourself no good this morning, Mr. Holmes, for I have broken stronger men than you. No man ever crossed me and was the better for it."

"So many have said so, and yet here I am," said Holmes, smiling. "Well, good-morning, Mr. Gibson. You have a good deal yet to learn."

Our visitor made a noisy exit, but Holmes smoked in imperturbable silence with dreamy eyes fixed upon the ceiling.

"Any views, Watson?" he asked at last.

"Well, Holmes, I must confess that when I consider that this is a man who would certainly brush any obstacle from his path, and when I remember that his wife may have been an obstacle and an object of dislike, as that man Bates plainly told us, it seems to me—"

"Exactly. And to me also."

"But what were his relations with the governess, and how did you discover them?"

"Bluff, Watson, bluff! When I considered the passionate, unconventional, unbusinesslike tone of his letter and contrasted it with his self-contained manner and appearance, it was pretty clear that there was some deep emotion which centred upon the accused woman rather than upon the victim. We've got to understand the exact relations of those three people if we are to reach the truth. You saw the frontal attack which I made upon him, and how imperturbably he received it. Then I bluffed him by giving him the impression that I was absolutely certain, when in reality I was only extremely suspicious."

"Perhaps he will come back?"

"He is sure to come back. He *must* come back. He can't leave it where it is. Ha! isn't that a ring? Yes, there is his footstep. Well, Mr. Gibson, I was just saying to Dr. Watson that you were somewhat overdue."

The Gold King had reëntered the room in a more chastened mood than he had left it. His wounded pride still showed in his resentful eyes, but his common sense had shown him that he must yield if he would attain his end.

"I've been thinking it over, Mr. Holmes, and I feel that I have been hasty in taking your remarks amiss. You are justified in getting down to the facts, whatever they may be, and I think the more of you for it. I can assure you, however, that the relations between Miss Dunbar and me don't really touch this case."

"That is for me to decide, is it not?"

"Yes, I guess that is so. You're like a surgeon who wants every symptom before he can give his diagnosis."

"Exactly. That expresses it. And it is only a patient who has an object in deceiving his surgeon who would conceal the facts of his case."

"That may be so, but you will admit, Mr. Holmes, that most men would shy off a bit when they are asked point-blank what their relations with a woman may be—if there is really some serious feeling in the case. I guess most men have a little private reserve of their own in some corner of their souls where they don't welcome intruders. And you burst suddenly into it. But the object excuses you, since it was to try and save her. Well, the stakes are down and the reserve open, and you can explore where you will. What is it you want?"

"The truth."

The Gold King paused for a moment as one who marshals his thoughts. His grim, deep-lined face had become even sadder and more grave.

"I can give it to you in a very few words, Mr. Holmes," said he at last. "There are some things that are painful as well as difficult to say, so I won't go deeper than is needful. I met my wife when I was gold-hunting in Brazil. Maria Pinto was the daughter of a government official at Manaos, and she was very beautiful. I was young and ardent in those days, but even now, as I look back with colder blood and a more critical eye, I can see that she was rare and wonderful in her beauty. It was a deep rich nature, too, passionate, whole-hearted, tropical, ill-balanced, very different from the American women whom I had known. Well, to make a long story short, I loved her and I married her. It was only when the romance had passed—and it lingered for years—that I realized that we had nothing—absolutely nothing—in common. My love faded. If hers had faded also it might have been easier. But you know the wonderful way of women! Do what I might, nothing could turn her from me. If I have been harsh to her, even brutal as some have said, it has been because I knew that if I could kill her love, or if it turned to hate, it would be easier for both of us. But nothing changed her. She adored me in those English woods as she had adored me twenty years ago on the banks of the Amazon. Do what I might, she was as devoted as ever.

"Then came Miss Grace Dunbar. She answered our advertisement and became governess to our two children. Perhaps you have seen her portrait in the papers. The whole world has proclaimed that she also is a very beautiful woman. Now, I make no pretence to be more moral than my neighbours, and I will admit to you that I could not live under the same roof with such a woman and in daily contact with her without feeling a passionate regard for her. Do you blame me, Mr. Holmes?"

"I do not blame you for feeling it. I should blame you if you expressed it, since this young lady was in a sense under your protection."

"Well, maybe so," said the millionaire, though for a moment the reproof had brought the old angry gleam into his eyes. "I'm not pretending to be any better than I am. I guess all my life I've been a man that reached out his hand for what he wanted, and I never wanted anything more than the love and possession of that woman. I told her so."

"Oh, you did, did you?"

Holmes could look very formidable when he was moved.

"I said to her that if I could marry her I would, but that it was out of my power. I said that money was no object and that all I could do to make her happy and comfortable would be done."

"Very generous, I am sure," said Holmes with a sneer.

"See here, Mr. Holmes. I came to you on a question of evidence, not on a question of morals. I'm not asking for your criticism."

"It is only for the young lady's sake that I touch your case at all," said Holmes sternly. "I don't know that anything she is accused of is really worse than what you have yourself admitted, that you have tried to ruin a defenceless girl who was under your roof. Some of you rich men have to be taught that all the world cannot be bribed into condoning your offences."

To my surprise the Gold King took the reproof with equanimity.

"That's how I feel myself about it now. I thank God that my plans did not work out as I intended. She would have none of it, and she wanted to leave the house instantly."

"Why did she not?"

"Well, in the first place, others were dependent upon her, and it was no light matter for her to let them all down by sacrificing her living. When I had sworn—as I did—that she should never be molested again, she consented to remain. But there was another reason. She knew the influence she had over me, and that it was stronger than any other influence in the world. She wanted to use it for good."

"How?"

"Well, she knew something of my affairs. They are large, Mr. Holmes—large beyond the belief of an ordinary man. I can make or break—and it is usually break. It wasn't individuals only. It was communities, cities, even nations. Business is a hard game, and the weak go to the wall. I played the game for all it was worth. I never squealed myself, and I never cared if the other fellow squealed. But she saw it different. I guess she was right. She believed and said that a fortune for one man that was more than he needed should not be built on ten thousand ruined men who were left without the means of life. That was how she saw it, and I guess she could see past the dollars to something that was more lasting. She found that I listened to what she said, and she believed she was serving the world by influencing my actions. So she stayed—and then this came along."

"Can you throw any light upon that?"

The Gold King paused for a minute or more, his head sunk in his hands, lost in deep thought.

"It's very black against her. I can't deny that. And women lead an inward life and may do things beyond the judgment of a man. At first I was so rattled and taken aback that I was ready to think she had been led away in some extraordinary fashion that was clean against her usual nature. One explanation came into my head. I give it to you, Mr. Holmes, for what it is worth. There is no doubt that my wife was bitterly jealous. There is a soul-jealousy that can be as frantic as any body-jealousy, and though my wife had no cause—and I think she understood this—for the latter, she was aware that this English girl exerted an influence upon my mind and my acts that she herself never had. It was an influence for good, but that did not mend the matter. She was crazy with hatred, and the heat of the Amazon was always in her blood. She might have planned to murder Miss Dunbar—or we will say to threaten her with a gun and so frighten her into leaving us. Then there might have been a scuffle and the gun gone off and shot the woman who held it."

"That possibility had already occurred to me," said Holmes. "Indeed, it is the only obvious alternative to deliberate murder."

"But she utterly denies it."

"Well, that is not final—is it? One can understand that a woman placed in so awful a position might hurry home still in her bewilderment holding the revolver. She might even throw it down among her clothes, hardly knowing what she was doing, and when it was found she might try to lie her way out by a total denial, since all explanation was impossible. What is against such a supposition?"

"Miss Dunbar herself."

"Well, perhaps."

Holmes looked at his watch. "I have no doubt we can get the necessary permits this morning and reach Winchester by the evening train. When I have seen this young lady it is very possible that I may be of more use to you in the matter, though I cannot promise that my conclusions will necessarily be such as you desire."

There was some delay in the official pass, and instead of reaching Winchester that day we went down to Thor Place, the Hampshire estate of Mr. Neil Gibson. He did not accompany us himself, but we had the address of Sergeant Coventry, of the local police, who had first examined into the affair. He was a tall, thin, cadaverous man, with a secretive and mysterious manner which conveyed the idea that he knew or suspected a very great deal more than he dared say. He had a trick, too, of suddenly sinking his voice to a whisper as if he had come upon something of vital importance, though the information was usually commonplace enough. Behind these tricks of manner he soon showed himself to be a decent, honest fellow who was not too proud to admit that he was out of his depth and would welcome any help.

"Anyhow, I'd rather have you than Scotland Yard, Mr. Holmes," said he. "If the Yard gets called into a case, then the local loses all credit for success and may be blamed for failure. Now, you play straight, so I've heard."

"I need not appear in the matter at all," said Holmes to the evident relief of our melancholy acquaintance. "If I can clear it up I don't ask to have my name mentioned."

"Well, it's very handsome of you, I am sure. And your friend, Dr. Watson, can be trusted, I know. Now, Mr. Holmes, as we walk down to the place there is one question I should like to ask you. I'd breathe it to no soul but you." He looked round as though he hardly dare utter the words. "Don't you think there might be a case against Mr. Neil Gibson himself?"

"I have been considering that."

"You've not seen Miss Dunbar. She is a wonderful fine woman in every way. He may well have wished his wife out of the road. And these Americans are readier with pistols than our folk are. It was *his* pistol, you know."

"Was that clearly made out?"

"Yes, sir. It was one of a pair that he had."

"One of a pair? Where is the other?"

"Well, the gentleman has a lot of firearms of one sort and another. We never quite matched that particular pistol—but the box was made for two."

"If it was one of a pair you should surely be able to match it."

"Well, we have them all laid out at the house if you would care to look them over."

"Later, perhaps. I think we will walk down together and have a look at the scene of the tragedy."

This conversation had taken place in the little front room of Sergeant Coventry's humble cottage which served as the local police-station. A walk of half a mile or so across a wind-swept heath, all gold and bronze with the fading ferns, brought us to a side-gate opening into the grounds of the Thor Place estate. A path led us through the pheasant preserves, and then from a clearing we saw the widespread, half-timbered house, half Tudor and half Georgian, upon the crest of the hill. Beside us there was a long, reedy pool, constricted in the centre where the main carriage drive passed over a stone bridge, but swelling into small lakes on either side. Our guide paused at the mouth of this bridge, and he pointed to the ground.

"That was where Mrs. Gibson's body lay. I marked it by that stone."

"I understand that you were there before it was moved?"

"Yes, they sent for me at once."

"Who did?"

"Mr. Gibson himself. The moment the alarm was given and he had rushed down with others from the house, he insisted that nothing should be moved until the police should arrive."

"That was sensible. I gathered from the newspaper report that the shot was fired from close quarters."

"Yes, sir, very close."

"Near the right temple?"

"Just behind it, sir."

"How did the body lie?"

"On the back, sir. No trace of a struggle. No marks. No weapon. The short note from Miss Dunbar was clutched in her left hand."

"Clutched, you say?"

"Yes, sir, we could hardly open the fingers."

"That is of great importance. It excludes the idea that anyone could have placed the note there after death in order to furnish a false clue. Dear me! The note, as I remember, was quite short:

"I will be at Thor Bridge at nine o'clock.
                                    "G. Dunbar.

Was that not so?"

"Yes, sir."

"Did Miss Dunbar admit writing it?"

"Yes, sir."

"What was her explanation?"

"Her defence was reserved for the Assizes. She would say nothing."

"The problem is certainly a very interesting one. The point of the letter is very obscure, is it not?"

"Well, sir," said the guide, "it seemed, if I may be so bold as to say so, the only really clear point in the whole case."

Holmes shook his head.

"Granting that the letter is genuine and was really written, it was certainly received some time before—say one hour or two. Why, then, was this lady still clasping it in her left hand? Why should she carry it so carefully? She did not need to refer to it in the interview. Does it not seem remarkable?"

"Well, sir, as you put it, perhaps it does."

"I think I should like to sit quietly for a few minutes and think it out." He seated himself upon the stone ledge of the bridge, and I could see his quick gray eyes darting their questioning glances in every direction. Suddenly he sprang up again and ran across to the opposite parapet, whipped his lens from his pocket, and began to examine the stonework.

"This is curious," said he.

"Yes, sir, we saw the chip on the ledge. I expect it's been done by some passer-by."

The stonework was gray, but at this one point it showed white for a space not larger than a sixpence. When examined closely one could see that the surface was chipped as by a sharp blow.

"It took some violence to do that," said Holmes thoughtfully. With his cane he struck the ledge several times without leaving a mark. "Yes, it was a hard knock. In a curious place, too. It was not from above but from below, for you see that it is on the *lower* edge of the parapet."

"But it is at least fifteen feet from the body."

"Yes, it is fifteen feet from the body. It may have nothing to do with the matter, but it is a point worth noting. I do not think that we have anything more to learn here. There were no footsteps, you say?"

"The ground was iron hard, sir. There were no traces at all."

"Then we can go. We will go up to the house first and look over these weapons of which you speak. Then we shall get on to Winchester, for I should desire to see Miss Dunbar before we go farther."

Mr. Neil Gibson had not returned from town, but we saw in the house the neurotic Mr. Bates who had called upon us in the morning. He showed us with a sinister relish the formidable array of firearms of various shapes and sizes which his employer had accumulated in the course of an adventurous life.

"Mr. Gibson has his enemies, as anyone would expect who knew him and his methods," said he. "He sleeps with a loaded revolver in the drawer beside his bed. He is a man of violence, sir, and there are times when all of us are afraid of him. I am sure that the poor lady who has passed was often terrified."

"Did you ever witness physical violence towards her?"

"No, I cannot say that. But I have heard words which were nearly as bad—words of cold, cutting contempt, even before the servants."

"Our millionaire does not seem to shine in private life," remarked Holmes as we made our way to the station. "Well, Watson, we have come on a good many facts, some of them new ones, and yet I seem some way from my conclusion. In spite of the very evident dislike which Mr. Bates has to his employer, I gather from him that when the alarm came he was undoubtedly in his library. Dinner was over at 8:30 and all was normal up to then. It is true that the alarm was somewhat late in the evening, but the tragedy certainly occurred about the hour named in the note. There is no evidence at all that Mr. Gibson had been out of doors since his return from town at five o'clock. On the other hand, Miss Dunbar, as I understand it, admits that she had made an appointment to meet Mrs. Gibson at the bridge. Beyond this she would say nothing, as her lawyer had advised her to reserve her defence. We have several very vital questions to ask that young lady, and my mind will not be easy until we have seen her. I must confess that the case would seem to me to be very black against her if it were not for one thing."

"And what is that, Holmes?"

"The finding of the pistol in her wardrobe."

"Dear me, Holmes!" I cried, "that seemed to me to be the most damning incident of all."

"Not so, Watson. It had struck me even at my first perfunctory reading as very strange, and now that I am in closer touch with the case it is my only firm ground for hope. We must look for consistency. Where there is a want of it we must suspect deception."

"I hardly follow you."

"Well now, Watson, suppose for a moment that we visualize you in the character of a woman who, in a cold, premeditated fashion, is about to get rid of a rival. You have planned it. A note has been written. The victim has come. You have your weapon. The crime is done. It has been workmanlike and complete. Do you tell me that after carrying out so crafty a crime you would now ruin your reputation as a criminal by forgetting to fling your weapon into those adjacent reed-beds which would forever cover it, but you must needs carry it carefully home and put it in your own wardrobe, the very first place that would be searched? Your best friends would hardly call you a schemer, Watson, and yet I could not picture you doing anything so crude as that."

"In the excitement of the moment—"

"No, no, Watson, I will not admit that it is possible. Where a crime is coolly premeditated, then the means of covering it are coolly premeditated also. I hope, therefore, that we are in the presence of a serious misconception."

"But there is so much to explain."

"Well, we shall set about explaining it. When once your point of view is changed, the very thing which was so damning becomes a clue to the truth. For example, there is this revolver. Miss Dunbar disclaims all knowledge of it. On our new theory she is speaking truth when she says so. Therefore, it was placed in her wardrobe. Who placed it there? Someone who wished to incriminate her. Was not that person the actual criminal? You see how we come at once upon a most fruitful line of inquiry."

We were compelled to spend the night at Winchester, as the formalities had not yet been completed, but next morning, in the company of Mr. Joyce Cummings, the rising barrister who was entrusted with the defence, we were allowed to see the young lady in her cell. I had expected from all that we had heard to see a beautiful woman, but I can never forget the effect which Miss Dunbar produced upon me. It was no wonder that even the masterful millionaire had found in her something more powerful than himself—something which could control and guide him. One felt, too, as one looked at the strong, clear-cut, and yet sensitive face, that even should she be capable of some impetuous deed, none the less there was an innate nobility of character which would make her influence always for the good. She was a brunette, tall, with a noble figure and commanding presence, but her dark eyes had in them the appealing, helpless expression of the hunted creature who feels the nets around it, but can see no way out from the toils. Now, as she realized the presence and the help of my famous friend, there came a touch of colour in her wan cheeks and a light of hope began to glimmer in the glance which she turned upon us.

"Perhaps Mr. Neil Gibson has told you something of what occurred between us?" she asked in a low, agitated voice.

"Yes," Holmes answered, "you need not pain yourself by entering into that part of the story. After seeing you, I am prepared to accept Mr. Gibson's statement both as to the influence which you had over him and as to the innocence of your relations with him. But why was the whole situation not brought out in court?"

"It seemed to me incredible that such a charge could be sustained. I thought that if we waited the whole thing must clear itself up without our being compelled to enter into painful details of the inner life of the family. But I understand that far from clearing it has become even more serious."

"My dear young lady," cried Holmes earnestly, "I beg you to have no illusions upon the point. Mr. Cummings here would assure you that all the cards are at present against us, and that we must do everything that is possible if we are to win clear. It would be a cruel deception to pretend that you are not in very great danger. Give me all the help you can, then, to get at the truth."

"I will conceal nothing."

"Tell us, then, of your true relations with Mr. Gibson's wife."

"She hated me, Mr. Holmes. She hated me with all the fervour of her tropical nature. She was a woman who would do nothing by halves, and the measure of her love for her husband was the measure also of her hatred for me. It is probable that she misunderstood our relations. I would not wish to wrong her, but she loved so vividly in a physical sense that she could hardly understand the mental, and even spiritual, tie which held her husband to me, or imagine that it was only my desire to influence his power to good ends which kept me under his roof. I can see now that I was wrong. Nothing could justify me in remaining where I was a cause of unhappiness, and yet it is certain that the unhappiness would have remained even if I had left the house."

"Now, Miss Dunbar," said Holmes, "I beg you to tell us exactly what occurred that evening."

"I can tell you the truth so far as I know it, Mr. Holmes, but I am in a position to prove nothing, and there are points—the most vital points—which I can neither explain nor can I imagine any explanation."

"If you will find the facts, perhaps others may find the explanation."

"With regard, then, to my presence at Thor Bridge that night, I received a note from Mrs. Gibson in the morning. It lay on the table of the schoolroom, and it may have been left there by her own hand. It implored me to see her there after dinner, said she had something important to say to me, and asked me to leave an answer on the sundial in the garden, as she desired no one to be in our confidence. I saw no reason for such secrecy, but I did as she asked, accepting the appointment. She asked me to destroy her note and I burned it in the schoolroom grate. She was very much afraid of her husband, who treated her with a harshness for which I frequently reproached him, and I could only imagine that she acted in this way because she did not wish him to know of our interview."

"Yet she kept your reply very carefully?"

"Yes. I was surprised to hear that she had it in her hand when she died."

"Well, what happened then?"

"I went down as I had promised. When I reached the bridge she was waiting for me. Never did I realize till that moment how this poor creature hated me. She was like a mad woman—indeed, I think she *was* a mad woman, subtly mad with the deep power of deception which insane people may have. How else could she have met me with unconcern every day and yet had so raging a hatred of me in her heart? I will not say what she said. She poured her whole wild fury out in burning and horrible words. I did not even answer—I could not. It was dreadful to see her. I put my hands to my ears and rushed away. When I left her she was standing, still shrieking out her curses at me, in the mouth of the bridge."

"Where she was afterwards found?"

"Within a few yards from the spot."

"And yet, presuming that she met her death shortly after you left her, you heard no shot?"

"No, I heard nothing. But, indeed, Mr. Holmes, I was so agitated and horrified by this terrible outbreak that I rushed to get back to the peace of my own room, and I was incapable of noticing anything which happened."

"You say that you returned to your room. Did you leave it again before next morning?"

"Yes, when the alarm came that the poor creature had met her death I ran out with the others."

"Did you see Mr. Gibson?"

"Yes, he had just returned from the bridge when I saw him. He had sent for the doctor and the police."

"Did he seem to you much perturbed?"

"Mr. Gibson is a very strong, self-contained man. I do not think that he would ever show his emotions on the surface. But I, who knew him so well, could see that he was deeply concerned."

"Then we come to the all-important point. This pistol that was found in your room. Had you ever seen it before?"

"Never, I swear it."

"When was it found?"

"Next morning, when the police made their search."

"Among your clothes?"

"Yes, on the floor of my wardrobe under my dresses."

"You could not guess how long it had been there?"

"It had not been there the morning before."

"How do you know?"

"Because I tidied out the wardrobe."

"That is final. Then someone came into your room and placed the pistol there in order to inculpate you."

"It must have been so."

"And when?"

"It could only have been at meal-time, or else at the hours when I would be in the schoolroom with the children."

"As you were when you got the note?"

"Yes, from that time onward for the whole morning."

"Thank you, Miss Dunbar. Is there any other point which could help me in the investigation?"

"I can think of none."

"There was some sign of violence on the stonework of the bridge—a perfectly fresh chip just opposite the body. Could you suggest any possible explanation of that?"

"Surely it must be a mere coincidence."

"Curious, Miss Dunbar, very curious. Why should it appear at the very time of the tragedy, and why at the very place?"

"But what could have caused it? Only great violence could have such an effect."

Holmes did not answer. His pale, eager face had suddenly assumed that tense, far-away expression which I had learned to associate with the supreme manifestations of his genius. So evident was the crisis in his mind that none of us dared to speak, and we sat, barrister, prisoner, and myself, watching him in a concentrated and absorbed silence. Suddenly he sprang from his chair, vibrating with nervous energy and the pressing need for action.

"Come, Watson, come!" he cried.

"What is it, Mr. Holmes?"

"Never mind, my dear lady. You will hear from me, Mr. Cummings. With the help of the god of justice I will give you a case which will make England ring. You will get news by to-morrow, Miss Dunbar, and meanwhile take my assurance that the clouds are lifting and that I have every hope that the light of truth is breaking through."

It was not a long journey from Winchester to Thor Place, but it was long to me in my impatience, while for Holmes it was evident that it seemed endless; for, in his nervous restlessness, he could not sit still, but paced the carriage or drummed with his long, sensitive fingers upon the cushions beside him. Suddenly, however, as we neared our destination he seated himself opposite to me—we had a first-class carriage to ourselves—and laying a hand upon each of my knees he looked into my eyes with the peculiarly mischievous gaze which was characteristic of his more imp-like moods.

"Watson," said he, "I have some recollection that you go armed upon these excursions of ours."

It was as well for him that I did so, for he took little care for his own safety when his mind was once absorbed by a problem, so that more than once my revolver had been a good friend in need. I reminded him of the fact.

"Yes, yes, I am a little absent-minded in such matters. But have you your revolver on you?"

I produced it from my hip-pocket, a short, handy, but very serviceable little weapon. He undid the catch, shook out the cartridges, and examined it with care.

"It's heavy—remarkably heavy," said he.

"Yes, it is a solid bit of work."

He mused over it for a minute.

"Do you know, Watson," said he, "I believe your revolver is going to have a very intimate connection with the mystery which we are investigating."

"My dear Holmes, you are joking."

"No, Watson, I am very serious. There is a test before us. If the test comes off, all will be clear. And the test will depend upon the conduct of this little weapon. One cartridge out. Now we will replace the other five and put on the safety-catch. So! That increases the weight and makes it a better reproduction."

I had no glimmer of what was in his mind, nor did he enlighten me, but sat lost in thought until we pulled up in the little Hampshire station. We secured a ramshackle trap, and in a quarter of an hour were at the house of our confidential friend, the sergeant.

"A clue, Mr. Holmes? What is it?"

"It all depends upon the behaviour of Dr. Watson's revolver," said my friend. "Here it is. Now, officer, can you give me ten yards of string?"

The village shop provided a ball of stout twine.

"I think that this is all we will need," said Holmes. "Now, if you please, we will get off on what I hope is the last stage of our journey."

The sun was setting and turning the rolling Hampshire moor into a wonderful autumnal panorama. The sergeant, with many critical and incredulous glances, which showed his deep doubts of the sanity of my companion, lurched along beside us. As we approached the scene of the crime I could see that my friend under all his habitual coolness was in truth deeply agitated.

"Yes," he said in answer to my remark, "you have seen me miss my mark before, Watson. I have an instinct for such things, and yet it has sometimes played me false. It seemed a certainty when first it flashed across my mind in the cell at Winchester, but one drawback of an active mind is that one can always conceive alternative explanations which would make our scent a false one. And yet—and yet—Well, Watson, we can but try."

As he walked he had firmly tied one end of the string to the handle of the revolver. We had now reached the scene of the tragedy. With great care he marked out under the guidance of the policeman the exact spot where the body had been stretched. He then hunted among the heather and the ferns until he found a considerable stone. This he secured to the other end of his line of string, and he hung it over the parapet of the bridge so that it swung clear above the water. He then stood on the fatal spot, some distance from the edge of the bridge, with my revolver in his hand, the string being taut between the weapon and the heavy stone on the farther side.

"Now for it!" he cried.

At the words he raised the pistol to his head, and then let go his grip. In an instant it had been whisked away by the weight of the stone, had struck with a sharp crack against the parapet, and had vanished over the side into the water. It had hardly gone before Holmes was kneeling beside the stonework, and a joyous cry showed that he had found what he expected.

"Was there ever a more exact demonstration?" he cried. "See, Watson, your revolver has solved the problem!" As he spoke he pointed to a second chip of the exact size and shape of the first which had appeared on the under edge of the stone balustrade.

"We'll stay at the inn to-night," he continued as he rose and faced the astonished sergeant. "You will, of course, get a grappling-hook and you will easily restore my friend's revolver. You will also find beside it the revolver, string and weight with which this vindictive woman attempted to disguise her own crime and to fasten a charge of murder upon an innocent victim. You can let Mr. Gibson know that I will see him in the morning, when steps can be taken for Miss Dunbar's vindication."

Late that evening, as we sat together smoking our pipes in the village inn, Holmes gave me a brief review of what had passed.

"I fear, Watson," said he, "that you will not improve any reputation which I may have acquired by adding the case of the Thor Bridge mystery to your annals. I have been sluggish in mind and wanting in that mixture of imagination and reality which is the basis of my art. I confess that the chip in the stonework was a sufficient clue to suggest the true solution, and that I blame myself for not having attained it sooner.

"It must be admitted that the workings of this unhappy woman's mind were deep and subtle, so that it was no very simple matter to unravel her plot. I do not think that in our adventures we have ever come across a stranger example of what perverted love can bring about. Whether Miss Dunbar was her rival in a physical or in a merely mental sense seems to have been equally unforgivable in her eyes. No doubt she blamed this innocent lady for all those harsh dealings and unkind words with which her husband tried to repel her too demonstrative affection. Her first resolution was to end her own life. Her second was to do it in such a way as to involve her victim in a fate which was worse far than any sudden death could be.

"We can follow the various steps quite clearly, and they show a remarkable subtlety of mind. A note was extracted very cleverly from Miss Dunbar which would make it appear that she had chosen the scene of the crime. In her anxiety that it should be discovered she somewhat overdid it by holding it in her hand to the last. This alone should have excited my suspicions earlier than it did.

"Then she took one of her husband's revolvers—there was, as you saw, an arsenal in the house—and kept it for her own use. A similar one she concealed that morning in Miss Dunbar's wardrobe after discharging one barrel, which she could easily do in the woods without attracting attention. She then went down to the bridge where she had contrived this exceedingly ingenious method for getting rid of her weapon. When Miss Dunbar appeared she used her last breath in pouring out her hatred, and then, when she was out of hearing, carried out her terrible purpose. Every link is now in its place and the chain is complete. The papers may ask why the mere was not dragged in the first instance, but it is easy to be wise after the event, and in any case the expanse of a reed-filled lake is no easy matter to drag unless you have a clear perception of what you are looking for and where. Well, Watson, we have helped a remarkable woman, and also a formidable man. Should they in the future join their forces, as seems not unlikely, the financial world may find that Mr. Neil Gibson has learned something in that schoolroom of sorrow where our earthly lessons are taught."

∾

# WAKEFIELD

## *Nathaniel Hawthorne*

In some old magazine or newspaper, I recollect a story, told as truth, of a man—let us call him Wakefield—who absented himself for a long time, from his wife. The fact, thus abstractedly stated, is not very uncommon, nor—without a proper distinction of circumstances—to be condemned either as naughty or nonsensical. Howbeit, this, though far from the most aggravated, is perhaps the strangest instance, on record, of marital delinquency; and, moreover, as remarkable a freak as may be found in the whole list of human oddities. The wedded couple lived in London. The man, under pretence of going a journey, took lodgings in the next street to his own house, and there, unheard of by his wife or friends, and without the shadow of a reason for such self-banishment, dwelt upwards of twenty years. During that period, he beheld his home every day, and frequently the forlorn Mrs. Wakefield. And after so great a gap in his matrimonial felicity—when his death was reckoned certain, his estate settled, his name dismissed from memory, and his wife, long, long ago, resigned to her autumnal widowhood—he entered the door one evening, quietly, as from a day's absence, and became a loving spouse till death.

This outline is all that I remember. But the incident, though of the purest originality, unexampled, and probably never to be repeated, is one, I think, which appeals to the general sympathies of mankind. We know, each for himself, that none of us would perpetrate such a folly, yet feel as if some other might. To my own contemplations, at least, it has often recurred, always exciting wonder, but with a sense that the story must be true, and a conception of its hero's character. Whenever any subject so forcibly affects the mind, time is well spent in thinking of it. If the reader choose, let him do his own meditation; or if he prefer to ramble with me through the twenty years of Wakefield's vagary, I bid him welcome; trusting that there will be a pervading spirit and a moral, even should we fail to find them, done up neatly, and condensed into the final sentence. Thought has always its efficacy, and every striking incident its moral.

What sort of a man was Wakefield? We are free to shape out our own idea, and call it by his name. He was now in the meridian of life; his matrimonial affections, never violent, were sobered into a calm, habitual sentiment; of all husbands, he was likely to be the most constant, because a certain sluggishness would keep his heart at rest, wherever it might be placed. He was intellectual, but not actively so; his mind occupied itself in long and lazy musings, that tended to no purpose, or had not vigor to attain it; his thoughts were seldom so energetic as to seize hold of words. Imagination, in the proper meaning of the term, made no part of Wakefield's gifts. With a cold, but not depraved nor wandering heart, and a mind never feverish with riotous thoughts, nor perplexed with originality, who could have anticipated, that our friend would entitle himself to a foremost place among the doers of eccentric deeds? Had his acquaintances been asked, who was the man in London, the surest to perform nothing to-day which should be remembered on the morrow, they would have thought of Wakefield. Only the wife of his bosom might have hesitated. She, without having analyzed his character, was partly aware of a quiet selfishness, that had rusted into his inactive mind—of a peculiar sort of vanity, the most uneasy attribute about him—of a disposition to craft, which had seldom produced more positive effects than the keeping of petty secrets, hardly worth revealing—and, lastly, of what she called a little strangeness, sometimes, in the good man. This latter quality is indefinable, and perhaps non-existent.

Let us now imagine Wakefield bidding adieu to his wife. It is the dusk of an October evening. His equipment is a drab great coat, a hat covered with an oil-cloth, top-boots, an umbrella in one hand and a small portmanteau in the other. He has informed Mrs. Wakefield that he is to take the night-coach into the country. She would fain inquire the length of his journey, its object, and the probable time of his return; but, indulgent to his harmless love of mystery, interrogates him only by a look. He tells her not to expect him positively by the return coach, nor to be alarmed should he tarry three or four days; but, at all events, to look for him at supper on Friday evening. Wakefield himself, be it considered, has no suspicion of what is before him. He holds out his hand; she gives her own, and meets his parting kiss, in the matter-of-course way of a ten years' matrimony; and forth goes the middle-aged Mr. Wakefield, almost resolved to perplex his good lady by a whole week's absence. After the door has closed behind him, she perceives it thrust partly open, and a vision of her husband's face, through the aperture, smiling on her, and gone in a moment. For the time, this little incident is dismissed without a thought. But, long afterwards, when she has been more years a widow than a wife, that smile recurs, and flickers across all her reminiscences of Wakefield's visage. In her many musings, she surrounds the original smile with a multitude of fantasies, which make it strange and awful; as, for instance, if she imagines him in a coffin, that parting look is frozen on his pale features; or, if she dreams of him in Heaven, still his blessed spirit wears a quiet and crafty smile. Yet, for its sake, when all others have given him up for dead, she sometimes doubts whether she is a widow.

But, our business is with the husband. We must hurry after him, along the street, ere he lose his individuality, and melt into the great mass of London life. It would be vain searching for him there. Let us follow close at his heels, therefore, until, after several superfluous turns and doublings, we find him comfortably established by the fireside of a small apartment, previously bespoken. He is in the next street to his own, and at his journey's end. He can scarcely trust his good fortune, in having got thither unperceived—recollecting that, at one time, he was delayed by the throng, in the very focus of a lighted lantern; and, again, there were footsteps, that seemed to tread behind his own, distinct from the multitudinous tramp around him; and, anon, he heard a voice shouting afar, and fancied that it called his name. Doubtless, a dozen busy-bodies had been watching him, and told his wife the whole affair. Poor Wakefield! Little knowest thou thine own insignificance in this great world! No mortal eye but mine has traced thee. Go quietly to thy bed, foolish man; and, on the morrow, if thou wilt be wise, get thee home to good Mrs. Wakefield, and tell her the truth. Remove not thyself, even for a little week, from thy place in her chaste bosom. Were she, for a single moment, to deem thee dead, or lost, or lastingly divided from her, thou wouldst be woefully conscious of a change in thy true wife, forever after. It is perilous to make a chasm in human affections; not that they gape so long and wide—but so quickly close again!

Almost repenting of his frolic, or whatever it may be termed, Wakefield lies down betimes, and starting from his first nap, spreads forth his arms into the wide and solitary waste of the unaccustomed bed. "No"—thinks he, gathering the bed-clothes about him—"I will not sleep alone another night."

In the morning, he rises earlier than usual, and sets himself to consider what he really means to do. Such are his loose and rambling modes of thought, that he has taken this very singular step, with the consciousness of a purpose, indeed, but without being able to define it sufficiently for his own contemplation. The vagueness of the project, and the convulsive effort with which he plunges into the execution of it, are equally characteristic of a feeble-minded man. Wakefield sifts his ideas, however, as minutely as he may, and finds himself curious to know the progress of matters at home—how his exemplary wife will endure her widowhood, of a week; and, briefly, how the little sphere of creatures and circumstances, in which he was a central object, will be affected by his removal. A morbid vanity, therefore, lies nearest the bottom of the affair. But, how is he to attain his ends? Not, certainly, by keeping close in this comfortable lodging, where, though he slept and awoke in the next street to his home, he is as effectually abroad, as if the stage-coach had been whirling him away all night. Yet, should he reappear, the whole project is knocked in the head. His poor brains being hopelessly puzzled with this dilemma, he at length ventures out, partly resolving to cross the head of the street, and send one hasty glance towards his forsaken domicile. Habit—for he is a man of habits—takes him by the hand, and guides him, wholly unaware, to his own door, where, just at the critical moment, he is aroused by the scraping of his foot upon the step. Wakefield! whither are you going?

At that instant, his fate was turning on the pivot. Little dreaming of the doom to which his first backward step devotes him, he hurries away, breathless with agitation hitherto unfelt, and hardly dares turn his head, at the distant corner. Can it be, that nobody caught sight of him? Will not the whole household—the decent Mrs. Wakefield, the smart maid-servant, and the dirty little foot-boy—raise a hue-and-cry, through London streets, in pursuit of their fugitive lord and master? Wonderful escape! He gathers courage to pause and look homeward, but is perplexed with a sense of change about the familiar edifice, such as affects us all, when, after a separation of months or years, we again see some hill or lake, or work of art, with which we were friends, of old. In ordinary cases, this indescribable impression is caused by the comparison and contrast between our imperfect reminiscences and the reality. In Wakefield, the magic of a single night has wrought a similar transformation, because, in that brief period, a great moral change has been effected. But this is a secret from himself. Before leaving the spot, he catches a far and momentary glimpse of his wife, passing athwart the front window, with her face turned towards the head of the street. The crafty nincompoop takes to his heels, scared with the idea, that, among a thousand such atoms of mortality, her eye must have detected him. Right glad is his heart, though his brain be somewhat dizzy, when he finds himself by the coal-fire of his lodgings.

So much for the commencement of this long whim-wham. After the initial conception, and the stirring up of the man's sluggish temperament to put it in practice, the whole matter evolves itself in a natural train. We may suppose him, as the result of deep deliberation, buying a new wig, of reddish hair, and selecting sundry garments, in a fashion unlike his customary suit of brown, from a Jew's old-clothes bag. It is accomplished. Wakefield is another man. The new system being now established, a retrograde movement to the old would be almost as difficult as the step that placed him in his unparalleled position. Furthermore, he is rendered obstinate by a sulkiness, occasionally incident to his temper, and brought on, at present, by the inadequate sensation which he conceives to have been produced in the bosom of Mrs. Wakefield. He will not go back until she be frightened half to death. Well, twice or thrice has she passed before his sight, each time with a heavier step, a paler cheek, and more anxious brow; and, in the third week of his non-appearance, he detects a portent of evil entering the house, in the guise of an apothecary. Next day, the knocker is muffled. Towards nightfall, comes the chariot of a physician, and deposits its big-wigged and solemn burthen at Wakefield's door, whence, after a quarter of an hour's visit, he emerges, perchance the herald of a funeral. Dear woman! Will she die? By this time, Wakefield is excited to something like energy of feeling, but still lingers away from his wife's bedside, pleading with his conscience, that she must not be disturbed at such a juncture. If aught else restrains him, he does not know it. In the course of a few weeks, she gradually recovers; the crisis is over; her heart is sad, perhaps, but quiet; and, let him return soon or late, it will never be feverish for him again. Such ideas glimmer through the mist of Wakefield's mind, and render him indistinctly conscious, that an almost impassable gulf divides his hired apartment from his former home. "It is but in the next street!" he sometimes says. Fool! it is in another world. Hitherto, he has put off his return from one particular day to another; henceforward, he leaves the precise time undetermined. Not to-morrow—probably next week—pretty soon. Poor man! The dead have nearly as much chance of re-visiting their earthly homes, as the self-banished Wakefield.

Would that I had a folio to write, instead of an article of a dozen pages! Then might I exemplify how an influence, beyond our control, lays its strong hand on every deed which we do, and weaves its consequences into an iron tissue of necessity. Wakefield is spell-bound. We must leave him, for ten years or so, to haunt around his house, without once crossing the threshold, and to be faithful to his wife, with all the affection of which his heart is capable, while he is slowly fading out of hers. Long since, it must be remarked, he has lost the perception of singularity in his conduct.

Now for a scene! Amid the throng of a London street, we distinguish a man, now waxing elderly, with few characteristics to attract careless observers, yet bearing, in his whole aspect, the hand-writing of no common fate, for such as have the skill to read it. He is meagre; his low and narrow forehead is deeply wrinkled; his eyes, small and lustreless, sometimes wander apprehensively about him, but oftener seem to look inward.

He bends his head, but moves with an indescribable obliquity of gait, as if unwilling to display his full front to the world. Watch him, long enough to see what we have described, and you will allow, that circumstances—which often produce remarkable men from nature's ordinary handi-work—have produced one such here. Next, leaving him to sidle along the foot-walk, cast your eyes in the opposite direction, where a portly female, considerably in the wane of life, with a prayer-book in her hand, is proceeding to yonder church. She has the placid mien of settled widowhood. Her regrets have either died away, or have become so essential to her heart, that they would be poorly exchanged for joy. Just as the lean man and well conditioned woman are passing, a slight obstruction occurs, and brings these two figures directly in contact. Their hands touch; the pressure of the crowd forces her bosom against his shoulder; they stand, face to face, staring into each other's eyes. After a ten years' separation, thus Wakefield meets his wife!

The throng eddies away, and carries them asunder. The sober widow, resuming her former pace, proceeds to church, but pauses in the portal, and throws a perplexed glance along the street. She passes in, however, opening her prayer-book as she goes. And the man? With so wild a face, that busy and selfish London stands to gaze after him, he hurries to his lodgings, bolts the door, and throws himself upon the bed. The latent feelings of years break out; his feeble mind acquires a brief energy from their strength; all the miserable strangeness of his life is revealed to him at a glance; and he cries out, passionately—"Wakefield! Wakefield! You are mad!"

Perhaps he was so. The singularity of his situation must have so moulded him to itself, that, considered in regard to his fellow-creatures and the business of life, he could not be said to possess his right mind. He had contrived, or rather he had happened, to dissever himself from the world—to vanish—to give up his place and privileges with living men, without being admitted among the dead. The life of a hermit is nowise parallel to his. He was in the bustle of the city, as of old; but the crowd swept by, and saw him not; he was, we may figuratively say, always beside his wife, and at his hearth, yet must never feel the warmth of the one, nor the affection of the other. It was Wakefield's unprecedented fate, to retain his original share of human sympathies, and to be still involved in human interests, while he had lost his reciprocal influence on them. It would be a most curious speculation, to trace out the effect of such circumstances on his heart and intellect, separately, and in unison. Yet, changed as he was, he would seldom be conscious of it, but deem himself the same man as ever; glimpses of the truth, indeed, would come, but only for the moment; and still he would keep saying—"I shall soon go back!"—nor reflect, that he had been saying so for twenty years.

I conceive, also, that these twenty years would appear, in the retrospect, scarcely longer than the week to which Wakefield had at first limited his absence. He would look on the affair as no more than an interlude in the main business of his life. When, after a little while more, he should deem it time to re-enter his parlor, his wife would clap her hands for joy, on beholding the middle-aged Mr. Wakefield. Alas, what a mistake! Would Time but await the close of our favorite follies, we should be young men, all of us, and till Doom's Day.

One evening, in the twentieth year since he vanished, Wakefield is taking his customary walk towards the dwelling which he still calls his own. It is a gusty night of autumn, with frequent showers, that patter down upon the pavement, and are gone, before a man can put up his umbrella. Pausing near the house, Wakefield discerns, through the parlor-windows of the second floor, the red glow, and the glimmer and fitful flash, of a comfortable fire. On the ceiling, appears a grotesque shadow of good Mrs. Wakefield. The cap, the nose and chin, and the broad waist, form an admirable caricature, which dances, moreover, with the up-flickering and down-sinking blaze, almost too merrily for the shade of an elderly widow. At this instant, a shower chances to fall, and is driven, by the unmannerly gust, full into Wakefield's face and bosom. He is quite penetrated with its autumnal chill. Shall he stand, wet and shivering here, when his own hearth has a good fire to warm him, and his own wife will run to fetch the gray coat and small-clothes, which, doubtless, she has kept carefully in the closet of their bed-chamber? No! Wakefield is no such fool. He ascends the steps—heavily!—for twenty years have stiffened his legs, since he came down—but he knows it not. Stay, Wakefield! Would you go to the sole home that is left you? Then step into your grave! The door opens. As he passes in, we have a parting glimpse of his visage, and recognize the crafty smile, which was the precursor of the little joke, that he has ever since been playing off at his wife's expense. How unmercifully has he quizzed the poor woman! Well; a good night's rest to Wakefield!

This happy event—supposing it to be such—could only have occurred at an unpremeditated moment. We will not follow our friend across the threshold. He has left us much food for thought, a portion of which shall lend its wisdom to a moral; and be shaped into a figure. Amid the seeming confusion of our mysterious world, individuals are so nicely adjusted to a system, and systems to one another, and to a whole, that, by stepping aside for a moment, a man exposes himself to a fearful risk of losing his place forever. Like Wakefield, he may become, as it were, the Outcast of the Universe.

∽

# THE SPRING LOVER AND THE AUTUMN LOVER

## Lafcadio Hearn

This is a story of the youth of Yamato, when the gods still walked upon the Land of the Reed Plains and took pleasure in the fresh and waving rice-ears of the country-side.

There was a lady having in her something of earth and something of heaven. She was a king's daughter. She was augustly radiant and renowned. She was called the Dear Delight of the World, the Greatly Desired, the Fairest of the Fair. She was slender and strong, at once mysterious and gay, fickle yet faithful, gentle yet hard to please. The gods loved her, but men worshiped her.

The coming of the Dear Delight was on this wise. Prince Ama Boko had a red jewel of one of his enemies. The jewel was a peace-offering. Prince Ama Boko set it in a casket upon a stand. He said, "This is a jewel of price." Then the jewel was transformed into an exceeding fair lady. Her name was the Lady of the Red Jewel, and Prince Ama Boko took her to wife. There was born to them one only daughter, who was the Greatly Desired, the Fairest of the Fair.

It is true that eighty men of name came to seek her hand. Princes they were, and warriors, and deities. They came from near and they came from far. Across the Sea Path they came in great ships, white sails or creaking oars, with brave and lusty sailors. Through the forests dark and dangerous they made their way to the Princess, the Greatly Desired; or lightly, lightly they descended by way of the Floating Bridge in garments of glamour and silver-shod. They brought their gifts with them—gold, fair jewels upon a string, light garments of feathers, singing birds, sweet things to eat, silk cocoons, oranges in a basket. They brought minstrels and singers and dancers and tellers of tales to entertain the Princess, the Greatly Desired.

As for the Princess, she sat still in her white bower with her maidens about her. Passing rich was her robe, and ever and anon her maidens spread it afresh over the mats, set out her deep sleeves, or combed her long hair with a golden comb.

Round about the bower was a gallery of white wood, and here the suitors came and knelt in the presence of their liege lady.

Many and many a time the carp leapt in the garden fish-pond. Many and many a time a scarlet pomegranate flower fluttered and dropped from the tree. Many and many a time the lady shook her head and a lover went his way, sad and sorry.

Now it happened that the God of Autumn went to try his fortune with the Princess. He was a brave young man indeed. Ardent were his eyes; the color flamed in his dark cheek. He was girded with a sword that ten men could not lift. The chrysanthemums of autumn burned upon his coat in cunning broidery. He came and bent his proud head to the very ground before the Princess, then raised it and looked her full in the eyes. She opened her sweet red lips—waited—said nothing—but shook her head.

So the God of Autumn went forth from her presence, blinded with his bitter tears.

He found his younger brother, the God of Spring.

"How fares it with you, my brother?" said the God of Spring.

"Ill, ill indeed, for she will not have me. She is the proud lady. Mine is the broken heart."

"Ah, my brother!" said the God of Spring.

"You'd best come home with me, for all is over with us," said the God of Autumn.

But the God of Spring said, "I stay here."

"What," cried his brother, "is it likely, then, that she will take you if she'll have none of me? Will she love the smooth cheeks of a child and flout the man full grown? Will you go to her, brother? She'll laugh at you for your pains."

"Still I will go," said the God of Spring.

"A wager! A wager!" the God of Autumn cried. "I'll give you a cask of *saké* if you win her—*saké* for the merry feast of your wedding. If you lose her, the *saké* will be for me. I'll drown my grief in it."

"Well, brother," said the God of Spring, "I take the wager. You'll have your *saké* like enough indeed."

"And so I think," said the God of Autumn, and went his ways.

Then the young God of Spring went to his mother, who loved him.

"Do you love me, my mother?" he said.

She answered, "More than a hundred existences."

"Mother," he said, "get me for my wife the Princess, the Fairest of the Fair. She is called the Greatly Desired; greatly, oh, greatly, do I desire her."

"You love her, my son?" said his mother.

"More than a hundred existences," he said.

"Then lie down, my son, my best beloved, lie down and sleep, and I will work for you."

So she spread a couch for him, and when he was asleep she looked on him.

"Your face," she said, "is the sweetest thing in the world."

There was no sleep for her the live-long night. But she went swiftly to a place she knew of, where the wistaria drooped over a still pool. She plucked her sprays and tendrils and brought home as much as she could carry. The wistaria was white and purple, and you must know it was not yet in flower, but hidden in the unopened bud. From it she wove magically a robe. She fashioned sandals also, and a bow and arrows.

In the morning she waked the God of Spring.

"Come, my son," she said, "let me put this robe on you."

The God of Spring rubbed his eyes. "A sober suit for courting," he said. But he did as his mother bade him. And he bound the sandals on his feet, and slung the bow and the arrows in their quiver on his back.

"Will all be well, my mother?" he said.

"All will be well, beloved," she answered him.

So the God of Spring came before the Fairest of the Fair. And one of her maidens laughed and said:

"See, mistress, there comes to woo you today only a little plain boy, all in sober gray."

But the Fairest of the Fair lifted up her eyes and looked upon the God of Spring. And in the same moment the wistaria with which he was clothed burst into flower. He was sweet-scented, white and purple from head to heel.

The Princess rose from the white mats.

"Lord," she said, "I am yours if you will have me."

Hand in hand they went together to the mother of the God of Spring.

"Ah, my mother," he said, "what shall I do now? My brother the God of Autumn is angry with me. He will not give me the *saké* I have won from him in a wager. Great is his rage. He will seek to take our lives."

"Be still, beloved," said his mother, "and fear not."

She took a cane of hollow bamboo, and in the hollow she put salt and stones; and when she had wrapped the cane round with leaves, she hung it in the smoke of the fire. She said:

"The green leaves fade and die. So you must do, my eldest born, the God of Autumn. The stone sinks in the sea, so must you sink. You must sink, you must fail, like the ebb tide."

Now the tale is told, and all the world knows why Spring is fresh and merry and young, and Autumn the saddest thing that is.

❧

# GOBLIN MARKET

## *Christina Rossetti*

Morning and evening
Maids heard the goblins cry:
"Come buy our orchard fruits,
Come buy, come buy:
Apples and quinces,
Lemons and oranges,
Plump unpecked cherries,
Melons and raspberries,
Bloom-down-cheeked peaches,
Swart-headed mulberries,
Wild free-born cranberries,
Crab-apples, dewberries,
Pine-apples, blackberries,
Apricots, strawberries;—
All ripe together
In summer weather,—
Morns that pass by,
Fair eves that fly;
Come buy, come buy:
Our grapes fresh from the vine,
Pomegranates full and fine,
Dates and sharp bullaces,
Rare pears and greengages,
Damsons and bilberries,
Taste them and try:
Currants and gooseberries,

Bright-fire-like barberries,
Figs to fill your mouth,
Citrons from the South,
Sweet to tongue and sound to eye;
Come buy, come buy."

Evening by evening
Among the brookside rushes,
Laura bowed her head to hear,
Lizzie veiled her blushes:
Crouching close together
In the cooling weather,
With clasping arms and cautioning lips,
With tingling cheeks and finger tips.
"Lie close," Laura said,
Pricking up her golden head:
"We must not look at goblin men,
We must not buy their fruits:
Who knows upon what soil they fed
Their hungry thirsty roots?"
"Come buy," call the goblins
Hobbling down the glen.
"Oh," cried Lizzie, "Laura, Laura,
You should not peep at goblin men."
Lizzie covered up her eyes,
Covered close lest they should look;
Laura reared her glossy head,
And whispered like the restless brook:
"Look, Lizzie, look, Lizzie,
Down the glen tramp little men.
One hauls a basket,
One bears a plate,
One lugs a golden dish
Of many pounds weight.
How fair the vine must grow
Whose grapes are so luscious;
How warm the wind must blow
Thro' those fruit bushes."
"No," said Lizzie: "No, no, no;
Their offers should not charm us,

Their evil gifts would harm us."
She thrust a dimpled finger
In each ear, shut eyes and ran:
Curious Laura chose to linger
Wondering at each merchant man.
One had a cat's face,
One whisked a tail,
One tramped at a rat's pace,
One crawled like a snail,
One like a wombat prowled obtuse and furry,
One like a ratel tumbled hurry skurry.
She heard a voice like voice of doves
Cooing all together:
They sounded kind and full of loves
In the pleasant weather.

Laura stretched her gleaming neck
Like a rush-imbedded swan,
Like a lily from the beck,
Like a moonlit poplar branch,
Like a vessel at the launch
When its last restraint is gone.

Backwards up the mossy glen
Turned and trooped the goblin men,
With their shrill repeated cry,
"Come buy, come buy."
When they reached where Laura was
They stood stock still upon the moss,
Leering at each other,
Brother with queer brother;
Signalling each other,
Brother with sly brother.
One set his basket down,
One reared his plate;
One began to weave a crown
Of tendrils, leaves and rough nuts brown
(Men sell not such in any town);
One heaved the golden weight

Of dish and fruit to offer her:
"Come buy, come buy," was still their cry.
Laura stared but did not stir,
Longed but had no money:
The whisk-tailed merchant bade her taste
In tones as smooth as honey,
The cat-faced purr'd,
The rat-paced spoke a word
Of welcome, and the snail-paced even was heard;
One parrot-voiced and jolly
Cried "Pretty Goblin" still for "Pretty Polly;"—
One whistled like a bird.

But sweet-tooth Laura spoke in haste:
"Good folk, I have no coin;
To take were to purloin:
I have no copper in my purse,
I have no silver either,
And all my gold is on the furze
That shakes in windy weather
Above the rusty heather."
"You have much gold upon your head,"
They answered all together:
"Buy from us with a golden curl."
She clipped a precious golden lock,
She dropped a tear more rare than pearl,
Then sucked their fruit globes fair or red:
Sweeter than honey from the rock,
Stronger than man-rejoicing wine,
Clearer than water flowed that juice;
She never tasted such before,
How should it cloy with length of use?
She sucked and sucked and sucked the more
Fruits which that unknown orchard bore;
She sucked until her lips were sore;
Then flung the emptied rinds away
But gathered up one kernel-stone,
And knew not was it night or day
As she turned home alone.

Lizzie met her at the gate
Full of wise upbraidings:
"Dear, you should not stay so late,
Twilight is not good for maidens;
Should not loiter in the glen
In the haunts of goblin men.
Do you not remember Jeanie,
How she met them in the moonlight,
Took their gifts both choice and many,
Ate their fruits and wore their flowers
Plucked from bowers
Where summer ripens at all hours?
But ever in the moonlight
She pined and pined away;
Sought them by night and day,
Found them no more but dwindled and grew grey;
Then fell with the first snow,
While to this day no grass will grow
Where she lies low:
I planted daisies there a year ago
That never blow.
You should not loiter so."
"Nay, hush," said Laura:
"Nay, hush, my sister:
I ate and ate my fill,
Yet my mouth waters still;
Tomorrow night I will
Buy more:" and kissed her:
"Have done with sorrow;
I'll bring you plums tomorrow
Fresh on their mother twigs,
Cherries worth getting;
You cannot think what figs
My teeth have met in,
What melons icy-cold
Piled on a dish of gold
Too huge for me to hold,
What peaches with a velvet nap,
Pellucid grapes without one seed:
Odorous indeed must be the mead

Whereon they grow, and pure the wave they drink
With lilies at the brink,
And sugar-sweet their sap."
Golden head by golden head,
Like two pigeons in one nest
Folded in each other's wings,
They lay down in their curtained bed:
Like two blossoms on one stem,
Like two flakes of new-fall'n snow,
Like two wands of ivory
Tipped with gold for awful kings.
Moon and stars gazed in at them,
Wind sang to them lullaby,
Lumbering owls forbore to fly,
Not a bat flapped to and fro
Round their rest:
Cheek to cheek and breast to breast
Locked together in one nest.

Early in the morning
When the first cock crowed his warning,
Neat like bees, as sweet and busy,
Laura rose with Lizzie:
Fetched in honey, milked the cows,
Aired and set to rights the house,
Kneaded cakes of whitest wheat,
Cakes for dainty mouths to eat,
Next churned butter, whipped up cream,
Fed their poultry, sat and sewed;
Talked as modest maidens should:
Lizzie with an open heart,
Laura in an absent dream,
One content, one sick in part;
One warbling for the mere bright day's delight,
One longing for the night.

At length slow evening came:
They went with pitchers to the reedy brook;
Lizzie most placid in her look,
Laura most like a leaping flame.

They drew the gurgling water from its deep;
Lizzie plucked purple and rich golden flags,
Then turning homewards said: "The sunset flushes
Those furthest loftiest crags;
Come, Laura, not another maiden lags,
No wilful squirrel wags,
The beasts and birds are fast asleep."
But Laura loitered still among the rushes
And said the bank was steep.

And said the hour was early still,
The dew not fall'n, the wind not chill:
Listening ever, but not catching
The customary cry,
"Come buy, come buy,"
With its iterated jingle
Of sugar-baited words:
Not for all her watching
Once discerning even one goblin
Racing, whisking, tumbling, hobbling;
Let alone the herds
That used to tramp along the glen,
In groups or single,
Of brisk fruit-merchant men.
Till Lizzie urged, "O Laura, come;
I hear the fruit-call but I dare not look:
You should not loiter longer at this brook:
Come with me home.
The stars rise, the moon bends her arc,
Each glowworm winks her spark,
Let us get home before the night grows dark:
For clouds may gather
Tho' this is summer weather,
Put out the lights and drench us thro';
Then if we lost our way what should we do?"

Laura turned cold as stone
To find her sister heard that cry alone,
That goblin cry,
"Come buy our fruits, come buy."

Must she then buy no more such dainty fruit?
Must she no more such succous pasture find,
Gone deaf and blind?
Her tree of life drooped from the root:
She said not one word in her heart's sore ache;
But peering thro' the dimness, nought discerning,
Trudged home, her pitcher dripping all the way;
So crept to bed, and lay
Silent till Lizzie slept;
Then sat up in a passionate yearning,
And gnashed her teeth for baulked desire, and wept
As if her heart would break.

Day after day, night after night,
Laura kept watch in vain
In sullen silence of exceeding pain.
She never caught again the goblin cry:
"Come buy, come buy;"—
She never spied the goblin men
Hawking their fruits along the glen:
But when the noon waxed bright
Her hair grew thin and grey;
She dwindled, as the fair full moon doth turn
To swift decay and burn
Her fire away.

One day remembering her kernel-stone
She set it by a wall that faced the south;
Dewed it with tears, hoped for a root,
Watched for a waxing shoot,
But there came none;
It never saw the sun,
It never felt the trickling moisture run:
While with sunk eyes and faded mouth
She dreamed of melons, as a traveller sees
False waves in desert drouth
With shade of leaf-crowned trees,
And burns the thirstier in the sandful breeze.
She no more swept the house,
Tended the fowls or cows,

Fetched honey, kneaded cakes of wheat,
Brought water from the brook:
But sat down listless in the chimney-nook
And would not eat.

Tender Lizzie could not bear
To watch her sister's cankerous care
Yet not to share.
She night and morning
Caught the goblins' cry:
"Come buy our orchard fruits,
Come buy, come buy:"—
Beside the brook, along the glen,
She heard the tramp of goblin men,
The voice and stir
Poor Laura could not hear;
Longed to buy fruit to comfort her,
But feared to pay too dear.
She thought of Jeanie in her grave,
Who should have been a bride;
But who for joys brides hope to have
Fell sick and died
In her gay prime,
In earliest Winter time,
With the first glazing rime,
With the first snow-fall of crisp Winter time.
Till Laura dwindling
Seemed knocking at Death's door:
Then Lizzie weighed no more
Better and worse;
But put a silver penny in her purse,
Kissed Laura, crossed the heath with clumps of furze
At twilight, halted by the brook:
And for the first time in her life
Began to listen and look.

Laughed every goblin
When they spied her peeping:
Came towards her hobbling,
Flying, running, leaping,

Puffing and blowing,
Chuckling, clapping, crowing,
Clucking and gobbling,
Mopping and mowing,
Full of airs and graces,
Pulling wry faces,
Demure grimaces,
Cat-like and rat-like,
Ratel-and wombat-like,
Snail-paced in a hurry,
Parrot-voiced and whistler,
Helter skelter, hurry skurry,
Chattering like magpies,
Fluttering like pigeons,
Gliding like fishes,—
Hugged her and kissed her,
Squeezed and caressed her:
Stretched up their dishes,
Panniers, and plates:
"Look at our apples
Russet and dun,
Bob at our cherries,
Bite at our peaches,
Citrons and dates,
Grapes for the asking,
Pears red with basking
Out in the sun,
Plums on their twigs;
Pluck them and suck them,
Pomegranates, figs."—
"Good folk," said Lizzie,
Mindful of Jeanie:
"Give me much and many:"—
Held out her apron,
Tossed them her penny.
"Nay, take a seat with us,
Honour and eat with us,"
They answered grinning:
"Our feast is but beginning.
Night yet is early,

Warm and dew-pearly,
Wakeful and starry:
Such fruits as these
No man can carry;
Half their bloom would fly,
Half their dew would dry,
Half their flavour would pass by.
Sit down and feast with us,
Be welcome guest with us,
Cheer you and rest with us."—
"Thank you," said Lizzie: "But one waits
At home alone for me:
So without further parleying,
If you will not sell me any
Of your fruits tho' much and many,
Give me back my silver penny
I tossed you for a fee."—
They began to scratch their pates,
No longer wagging, purring,
But visibly demurring,
Grunting and snarling.
One called her proud,
Cross-grained, uncivil;
Their tones waxed loud,
Their looks were evil.
Lashing their tails
They trod and hustled her,
Elbowed and jostled her,
Clawed with their nails,
Barking, mewing, hissing, mocking,
Tore her gown and soiled her stocking,
Twitched her hair out by the roots,
Stamped upon her tender feet,
Held her hands and squeezed their fruits
Against her mouth to make her eat.
White and golden Lizzie stood,
Like a lily in a flood,—
Like a rock of blue-veined stone
Lashed by tides obstreperously,—

Like a beacon left alone
In a hoary roaring sea,
Sending up a golden fire,—
Like a fruit-crowned orange-tree
White with blossoms honey-sweet
Sore beset by wasp and bee,—
Like a royal virgin town
Topped with gilded dome and spire
Close beleaguered by a fleet
Mad to tug her standard down.

One may lead a horse to water,
Twenty cannot make him drink.
Tho' the goblins cuffed and caught her,
Coaxed and fought her,
Bullied and besought her,
Scratched her, pinched her black as ink,
Kicked and knocked her,
Mauled and mocked her,
Lizzie uttered not a word;
Would not open lip from lip
Lest they should cram a mouthful in:
But laughed in heart to feel the drip
Of juice that syrupped all her face,
And lodged in dimples of her chin,
And streaked her neck which quaked like curd.
At last the evil people
Worn out by her resistance
Flung back her penny, kicked their fruit
Along whichever road they took,
Not leaving root or stone or shoot;
Some writhed into the ground,
Some dived into the brook
With ring and ripple,
Some scudded on the gale without a sound,
Some vanished in the distance.

In a smart, ache, tingle,
Lizzie went her way;

Knew not was it night or day;
Sprang up the bank, tore thro' the furze,
Threaded copse and dingle,
And heard her penny jingle
Bouncing in her purse,
Its bounce was music to her ear.
She ran and ran
As if she feared some goblin man
Dogged her with gibe or curse
Or something worse:
But not one goblin skurried after,
Nor was she pricked by fear;
The kind heart made her windy-paced
That urged her home quite out of breath with haste
And inward laughter.

She cried "Laura," up the garden,
"Did you miss me?
Come and kiss me.
Never mind my bruises,
Hug me, kiss me, suck my juices
Squeezed from goblin fruits for you,
Goblin pulp and goblin dew.
Eat me, drink me, love me;
Laura, make much of me:
For your sake I have braved the glen
And had to do with goblin merchant men."

Laura started from her chair,
Flung her arms up in the air,
Clutched her hair:
"Lizzie, Lizzie, have you tasted
For my sake the fruit forbidden?
Must your light like mine be hidden,
Your young life like mine be wasted,
Undone in mine undoing
And ruined in my ruin,
Thirsty, cankered, goblin-ridden?"—
She clung about her sister,

Kissed and kissed and kissed her:
Tears once again
Refreshed her shrunken eyes,
Dropping like rain
After long sultry drouth;
Shaking with aguish fear, and pain,
She kissed and kissed her with a hungry mouth.
Her lips began to scorch,
That juice was wormwood to her tongue,
She loathed the feast:
Writhing as one possessed she leaped and sung,
Rent all her robe, and wrung
Her hands in lamentable haste,
And beat her breast.
Her locks streamed like the torch
Borne by a racer at full speed,
Or like the mane of horses in their flight,
Or like an eagle when she stems the light
Straight toward the sun,
Or like a caged thing freed,
Or like a flying flag when armies run.

Swift fire spread thro' her veins, knocked at her heart,
Met the fire smouldering there,
And overbore its lesser flame;
She gorged on bitterness without a name:
Ah! fool, to choose such part
Of soul-consuming care!
Sense failed in the mortal strife:
Like the watch-tower of a town
Which an earthquake shatters down,
Like a lightning-stricken mast,
Like a wind-uprooted tree
Spun about,
Like a foam-topped waterspout
Cast down headlong in the sea,
She fell at last;
Pleasure past and anguish past,
Is it death or is it life?

Life out of death.
That night long Lizzie watched by her,
Counted her pulse's flagging stir,
Felt for her breath,
Held water to her lips, and cooled her face
With tears and fanning leaves:
But when the first birds chirped about their eaves,
And early reapers plodded to the place
Of golden sheaves,
And dew-wet grass
Bowed in the morning winds so brisk to pass,
And new buds with new day
Opened of cup-like lilies on the stream,
Laura awoke as from a dream,
Laughed in the innocent old way,
Hugged Lizzie but not twice or thrice;
Her gleaming locks showed not one thread of grey,
Her breath was sweet as May
And light danced in her eyes.
Days, weeks, months, years
Afterwards, when both were wives
With children of their own;
Their mother-hearts beset with fears,
Their lives bound up in tender lives;
Laura would call the little ones
And tell them of her early prime,
Those pleasant days long gone
Of not-returning time:
Would talk about the haunted glen,
The wicked, quaint fruit-merchant men,
Their fruits like honey to the throat
But poison in the blood;
(Men sell not such in any town:)
Would tell them how her sister stood
In deadly peril to do her good,
And win the fiery antidote:
Then joining hands to little hands
Would bid them cling together,
"For there is no friend like a sister
In calm or stormy weather;

To cheer one on the tedious way,
To fetch one if one goes astray,
To lift one if one totters down,
To strengthen whilst one stands."

∾

# THE THREE STRANGERS

## *Thomas Hardy*

Among the few features of agricultural England which retain an appearance but little modified by the lapse of centuries, may be reckoned the long, grassy and furzy downs, coombs, or ewe-leases, as they are called according to their kind, that fill a large area of certain counties in the south and south-west. If any mark of human occupation is met with hereon, it usually takes the form of the solitary cottage of some shepherd.

Fifty years ago such a lonely cottage stood on such a down, and may possibly be standing there now. In spite of its loneliness, however, the spot, by actual measurement, was not three miles from a county-town: Yet that affected it little. Three miles of irregular upland, during the long inimical seasons, with their sleets, snows, rains, and mists, afford withdrawing space enough to isolate a Timon or a Nebuchadnezzar; much less, in fair weather, to please that less repellent tribe, the poets, philosophers, artists, and others who "conceive and meditate of pleasant things."

Some old earthen camp or barrow, some clump of trees, at least some starved fragment of ancient hedge is usually taken advantage of in the erection of these forlorn dwellings. But, in the present case, such a kind of shelter had been disregarded. Higher Crowstairs, as the house was called, stood quite detached and undefended. The only reason for its precise situation seemed to be the crossing of two footpaths at right angles hard by, which may have crossed there and thus for a good five hundred years. Hence the house was exposed to the elements on all sides. But, though the wind up here blew unmistakably when it did blow, and the rain hit hard whenever it fell, the various weathers of the winter season were not quite so formidable on the down as they were imagined to be by dwellers on low ground. The raw rimes were not so pernicious as in the hollows, and the frosts were scarcely so severe. When the shepherd and his family who tenanted the house were pitied for their sufferings from the exposure, they said that upon the whole they were less inconvenienced by "wuzzes and flames" (hoarses and phlegms) than when they had lived by the stream of a snug neighbouring valley.

The night of March 28, 182–, was precisely one of the nights that were wont to call forth these expressions of commiseration. The level rainstorm smote walls, slopes, and hedges like the clothyard shafts of Senlac and Crecy. Such sheep and outdoor animals as had no shelter stood with their buttocks to the winds; while the tails of little birds trying to roost on some scraggy thorn were blown inside-out like umbrellas. The gable-end of the cottage was stained with wet, and the eavesdroppings flapped against the wall. Yet never was commiseration for the shepherd more misplaced. For that cheerful rustic was entertaining a large party in glorification of the christening of his second girl.

The guests had arrived before the rain began to fall, and they were all now assembled in the chief or living-room of the dwelling. A glance into the apartment at eight o'clock on this eventful evening would have resulted in the opinion that it was as cosy and comfortable a nook as could be wished for in boisterous weather. The calling of its inhabitant was proclaimed by a number of highly-polished sheep-crooks without stems that were hung ornamentally over the fireplace, the curl of each shining crook varying from the antiquated type engraved in the patriarchal pictures of old family Bibles to the most approved fashion of the last local sheep-fair. The room was lighted by half-a-dozen candles, having wicks only a trifle smaller than the grease which enveloped them, in candlesticks that were never used but at high-days, holy-days, and family feats. The lights were scattered about the room, two of them standing on the chimney-piece. This position of candles was in itself significant. Candles on the chimney-piece always meant a party.

On the hearth, in front of a back-brand to give substance, blazed a fire of thorns, that crackled "like the laughter of the fool."

Nineteen persons were gathered here. Of these, five women, wearing gowns of various bright hues, sat in chairs along the wall; girls shy and not shy filled the window-bench; four men, including Charley Jake the hedge-carpenter, Elijah New the parish-clerk, and John Pitcher, a neighbouring dairyman, the shepherd's father-in-law, lolled in the settle; a young man and maid, who were blushing over tentative *pourparlers* on a life-companionship, sat beneath the corner-cupboard; and an elderly engaged man of fifty or upward moved restlessly about from spots where his betrothed was not to the spot where she was. Enjoyment was pretty general, and so much the more prevailed in being unhampered by conventional restrictions.

Absolute confidence in each other's good opinion begat perfect ease, while the finishing stroke of manner, amounting to a truly princely serenity, was lent to the majority by the absence of any expression or trait denoting that they wished to get on in the world, enlarge their minds, or do any eclipsing thing whatever—which nowadays so generally nips the bloom and *bon-homie* of all except the two extremes of the social scale.

Shepherd Fennel had married well, his wife being a dairyman's daughter from a vale at a distance, who brought fifty guineas in her pocket—and kept them there, till they should be required for ministering to the needs of a coming family. This frugal woman had been somewhat exercised as to the character that should be given to the gathering. A sit-still party had its advantages; but an undisturbed position of ease in chairs and settles was apt to lead on the men to such an unconscionable deal of toping that they would sometimes fairly drink the house dry. A dancing-party was the alternative; but this, while avoiding the foregoing objection on the score of good drink, had a counterbalancing disadvantage in the matter of good victuals, the ravenous appetites engendered by the exercise causing immense havoc in the buttery. Shepherdess Fennel fell back upon the intermediate plan of mingling short dances with short periods of talk and singing, so as to hinder any ungovernable rage in either. But this scheme was entirely confined to her own gentle mind: the shepherd himself was in the mood to exhibit the most reckless phases of hospitality.

The fiddler was a boy of those parts, about twelve years of age, who had a wonderful dexterity in jigs and reels, though his fingers were so small and short as to necessitate a constant shifting for the high notes, from which he scrambled back to the first position with sounds not of unmixed purity of tone. At seven the shrill tweedle-dee of this youngster had begun, accompanied by a booming ground-bass from Elijah New, the parish-clerk, who had thoughtfully brought with him his favourite musical instrument, the serpent. Dancing was instantaneous, Mrs. Fennel privately enjoining the players on no account to let the dance exceed the length of a quarter of an hour.

But Elijah and the boy in the excitement of their position quite forgot the injunction. Moreover, Oliver Giles, a man of seventeen, one of the dancers, who was enamoured of his partner, a fair girl of thirty-three rolling years, had recklessly handed a new crown-piece to the musicians, as a bribe to keep going as long as they had muscle and wind. Mrs. Fennel, seeing the steam begin to generate on the countenances of her guests, crossed over and touched the fiddler's elbow and put her hand on the serpent's mouth. But they took no notice, and fearing she might lose her character of genial hostess if she were to interfere too markedly, she retired and sat down helpless. And so the dance whizzed on with cumulative fury, the performers moving in their planet-like courses, direct and retrograde, from apogee to perigee, till the hand of the well-kicked clock at the bottom of the room had travelled over the circumference of an hour.

While these cheerful events were in course of enactment within Fennel's pastoral dwelling an incident having considerable bearing on the party had occurred in the gloomy night without. Mrs. Fennel's concern about the growing fierceness of the dance corresponded in point of time with the ascent of a human figure to the solitary hill of Higher Crowstairs from the direction of the distant town. This personage strode on through the rain without a pause, following the little-worn path which, further on in its course, skirted the shepherd's cottage.

It was nearly the time of full moon, and on this account, though the sky was lined with a uniform sheet of dripping cloud, ordinary objects out of doors were readily visible. The sad wan light revealed the lonely pedestrian to be a man of supple frame; his gait suggested that he had somewhat passed the period of perfect and instinctive agility, though not so far as to be otherwise than rapid of motion when occasion required. At a rough guess, he might have been about forty years of age. He appeared tall, but a recruiting sergeant, or other person accustomed to the judging of men's heights by the eye, would have discerned that this was chiefly owing to his gauntness, and that he was not more than five-feet-eight or nine.

Notwithstanding the regularity of his tread there was caution in it, as in that of one who mentally feels his way; and despite the fact that it was not a black coat nor a dark garment of any sort that he wore, there was something about him which suggested that he naturally belonged to the black-coated tribes of men. His clothes were of fustian, and his boots hobnailed, yet in his progress he showed not the mud-accustomed bearing of hobnailed and fustianed peasantry.

By the time that he had arrived abreast of the shepherd's premises the rain came down, or rather came along, with yet more determined violence. The outskirts of the little settlement partially broke the force of wind and rain, and this induced him to stand still. The most salient of the shepherd's domestic erections was an empty sty at the forward corner of his hedgeless garden, for in these latitudes the principle of masking the homelier features of your establishment by a conventional frontage was unknown. The traveller's eye was attracted to this small building by the pallid shine of the wet slates that covered it. He turned aside, and, finding it empty, stood under the pent-roof for shelter.

While he stood the boom of the serpent within the adjacent house, and the lesser strains of the fiddler, reached the spot as an accompaniment to the surging hiss of the flying rain on the sod, its louder beating on the cabbage-leaves of the garden, on the straw hackles of eight or ten beehives just discernible by the path, and its dripping from the eaves into a row of buckets and pans that had been placed under the walls of the cottage. For at Higher Crowstairs, as at all such elevated domiciles, the grand difficulty of housekeeping was an insufficiency of water; and a casual rainfall was utilized by turning out, as catchers, every utensil that the house contained. Some queer stories might be told of the contrivances for economy in suds and dish-waters that are absolutely necessitated in upland habitations during the droughts of summer. But at this season there were no such exigencies; a mere acceptance of what the skies bestowed was sufficient for an abundant store.

At last the notes of the serpent ceased and the house was silent. This cessation of activity aroused the solitary pedestrian from the reverie into which he had lapsed, and, emerging from the shed, with an apparently new intention, he walked up the path to the house-door. Arrived here, his first act was to kneel down on a large stone beside the row of vessels, and to drink a copious draught from one of them. Having quenched his thirst he rose and lifted his hand to knock, but paused with his eye upon the panel. Since the dark surface of the wood revealed absolutely nothing, it was evident that he must be mentally looking through the door, as if he wished to measure thereby all the possibilities that a house of this sort might include, and how they might bear upon the question of his entry.

In his indecision he turned and surveyed the scene around. Not a soul was anywhere visible. The garden-path stretched downward from his feet, gleaming like the track of a snail; the roof of the little well (mostly dry), the well-cover, the top rail of the garden-gate, were varnished with the same dull liquid glaze; while, far away in the vale, a faint whiteness of more than usual extent showed that the rivers were high in the meads. Beyond all this winked a few bleared lamplights through the beating drops—lights that denoted the situation of the county-town from which he had appeared to come. The absence of all notes of life in that direction seemed to clinch his intentions, and he knocked at the door.

Within, a desultory chat had taken the place of movement and musical sound. The hedge-carpenter was suggesting a song to the company, which nobody just then was inclined to undertake, so that the knock afforded a not unwelcome diversion.

"Walk in!" said the shepherd promptly.

The latch clicked upward, and out of the night our pedestrian appeared upon the door-mat. The shepherd arose, snuffed two of the nearest candles, and turned to look at him.

Their light disclosed that the stranger was dark in complexion and not unprepossessing as to feature. His hat, which for a moment he did not remove, hung low over his eyes, without concealing that they were large, open, and determined, moving with a flash rather than a glance round the room. He seemed pleased with his survey, and, baring his shaggy head, said, in a rich deep voice, "The rain is so heavy, friends, that I ask leave to come in and rest awhile."

"To be sure, stranger," said the shepherd. "And faith, you've been lucky in choosing your time, for we are having a bit of a fling for glad cause—though, to be sure, a man could hardly wish that glad cause to happen more than once a year."

"Nor less," spoke up a women. "For 'tis best to get your family over and done with, as soon as you can, so as to be all the earlier out of the fag o't."

"And what may be this glad cause?" asked the stranger.

"A birth and christening," said the shepherd.

The stranger hoped his host might not be made unhappy either by too many or too few of such episodes, and being invited by a gesture to a pull at the mug, he readily acquiesced. His manner, which, before entering, had been so dubious, was now altogether that of a careless and candid man.

"Late to be traipsing athwart this coomb—hey?" said the engaged man of fifty.

"Late it is, master, as you say.—I'll take a seat in the chimney-corner, if you have nothing to urge against it, ma'am; for I am a little moist on the side that was next the rain."

Mrs. Shepherd Fennel assented, and made room for the self-invited comer, who, having got completely inside the chimney-corner, stretched out his legs and his arms with the expansiveness of a person quite at home.

"Yes, I am rather cracked in the vamp," he said freely, seeing that the eyes of the shepherd's wife fell upon his boots, "and I am not well fitted either. I have had some rough times lately, and have been forced to pick up what I can get in the way of wearing, but I must find a suit better fit for working-days when I reach home."

"One of hereabouts?" she inquired.

"Not quite that—further up the country."

"I thought so. And so be I; and by your tongue you come from my neighbourhood."

"But you would hardly have heard of me," he said quickly. "My time would be long before yours, ma'am, you see."

This testimony to the youthfulness of his hostess had the effect of stopping her cross-examination.

"There is only one thing more wanted to make me happy," continued the new-comer. "And that is a little baccy, which I am sorry to say I am out of."

"I'll fill your pipe," said the shepherd.

"I must ask you to lend me a pipe likewise."

"A smoker, and no pipe about 'ee?"

"I have dropped it somewhere on the road."

The shepherd filled and handed him a new clay pipe, saying, as he did so, "Hand me your baccy-box—I'll fill that too, now I am about it."

The man went through the movement of searching his pockets.

"Lost that too?" said his entertainer, with some surprise.

"I am afraid so," said the man with some confusion. "Give it to me in a screw of paper." Lighting his pipe at the candle with a suction that drew the whole flame into the bowl, he resettled himself in the corner and bent his looks upon the faint steam from his damp legs, as if he wished to say no more.

Meanwhile the general body of guests had been taking little notice of this visitor by reason of an absorbing discussion in which they were engaged with the band about a tune for the next dance. The matter being settled, they were about to stand up when an interruption came in the shape of another knock at the door.

At sound of the same the man in the chimney-corner took up the poker and began stirring the brands as if doing it thoroughly were the one aim of his existence; and a second time the shepherd said, "Walk in!" In a moment another man stood upon the straw-woven door-mat. He too was a stranger.

This individual was one of a type radically different from the first. There was more of the commonplace in his manner, and a certain jovial cosmopolitanism sat upon his features. He was several years older than the first arrival, his hair being slightly frosted, his eyebrows bristly, and his whiskers cut back from his cheeks. His face was rather full and flabby, and yet it was not altogether a face without power. A few grog-blossoms marked the neighbourhood of his nose. He flung back his long drab great-coat, revealing that beneath it he wore a suit of cinder-gray shade throughout, large heavy seals, of some metal or other that would take a polish, dangling from his fob as his only personal ornament. Shaking the water-drops from his low-crowned glazed hat, he said, "I must ask for a few minutes' shelter, comrades, or I shall be wetted to my skin before I get to Casterbridge."

"Make yourself at home, master," said the shepherd, perhaps a trifle less heartily than on the first occasion. Not that Fennel had the least tinge of niggardliness in his composition; but the room was far from large, spare chairs were not numerous, and damp companions were not altogether desirable at close quarters for the women and girls in their bright-coloured gowns.

However, the second comer, after taking off his greatcoat, and hanging his hat on a nail in one of the ceiling-beams as if he had been specially invited to put it there, advanced and sat down at the table. This had been pushed so closely into the chimney-corner, to give all available room to the dancers, that its inner edge grazed the elbow of the man who had ensconced himself by the fire; and thus the two strangers were brought into close companionship. They nodded to each other by way of breaking the ice of unacquaintance, and the first stranger handed his neighbour the family mug—a huge vessel of brown ware, having its upper edge worn away like a threshold by the rub of whole generations of thirsty lips that had gone the way of all flesh, and bearing the following inscription burnt upon its rotund side in yellow letters:—

THERE IS NO FUN
UNTILL i CUM

The other man, nothing loth, raised the mug to his lips, and drank on, and on, and on—till a curious blueness overspread the countenance of the shepherd's wife, who had regarded with no little surprise the first stranger's free offer to the second of what did not belong to him to dispense.

"I knew it!" said the toper to the shepherd with much satisfaction. "When I walked up your garden before coming in, and saw the hives all of a row, I said to myself, 'Where there's bees there's honey, and where there's honey there's mead.' But mead of such a truly comfortable sort as this I really didn't expect to meet in my older days." He took yet another pull at the mug, till it assumed an ominous elevation.

"Glad you enjoy it!" said the shepherd warmly.

"It is goodish mead," assented Mrs. Fennel, with an absence of enthusiasm which seemed to say that it was possible to buy praise for one's cellar at too heavy a price. "It is trouble enough to make—and really I hardly think we shall make any more. For honey sells well, and we ourselves can make shift with a drop o' small mead and metheglin for common use from the comb-washings."

"O, but you'll never have the heart!" reproachfully cried the stranger in cinder-gray, after taking up the mug a third time and setting it down empty. "I love mead, when 'tis old like this, as I love to go to church o' Sundays or to relieve the needy any day of the week."

"He, ha, ha!" said the man in the chimney-corner, who, in spite of the taciturnity induced by the pipe of tobacco, could not or would not refrain from this slight testimony to his comrade's humour.

Now the old mead of those days, brewed of the purest first-year or maiden honey, four pounds to the gallon—with its due complement of white of eggs, cinnamon, ginger, cloves, mace, rosemary, yeast, and processes of working, bottling, and cellaring—tasted remarkably strong; but it did not taste so strong as it actually was. Hence, presently, the stranger in cinder-gray at the table, moved by its creeping influence, unbuttoned his waistcoat, threw himself back in his chair, spread his legs, and made his presence felt in various ways.

"Well, well, as I say," he resumed, "I am going to Casterbridge, and to Casterbridge I must go. I should have been almost there by this time; but the rain drove me into your dwelling, and I'm not sorry for it."

"You don't live in Casterbridge?" said the shepherd.

"Not as yet; though I shortly mean to move there."

"Going to set up in trade, perhaps?"

"No, no," said the shepherd's wife. "It is easy to see that the gentleman is rich, and don't want to work at anything."

The cinder-gray stranger paused, as if to consider whether he would accept that definition of himself. He presently rejected it by answering, "Rich is not quite the word for me, dame. I do work, and I must work. And even if I only get to Casterbridge by midnight I must begin work there at eight to-morrow morning. Yes, het or wet, blow or snow, famine or sword, my day's work to-morrow must be done."

"Poor man! Then, in spite o' seeming, you be worse off than we?" replied the shepherd's wife.

"'Tis the nature of my trade, men and maidens. 'Tis the nature of my trade more than my poverty. . . . But really and truly I must up and off, or I shan't get a lodging in the town." However, the speaker did not move, and directly added, "There's time for one more draught of friendship before I go; and I'd perform it at once if the mug were not dry."

"Here's a mug o' small," said Mrs. Fennel. "Small, we call it, though to be sure 'tis only the first wash o' the combs."

"No," said the stranger disdainfully. "I won't spoil your first kindness by partaking o' your second."

"Certainly not," broke in Fennel. "We don't increase and multiply every day, and I'll fill the mug again." He went away to the dark place under the stairs where the barrel stood. The shepherdess followed him.

"Why should you do this?" she said reproachfully, as soon as they were alone. "He's emptied it once, though it held enough for ten people; and now he's not contented wi' the small, but must needs call for more o' the strong! And a stranger unbeknown to any of us. For my part, I don't like the look o' the man at all."

"But he's in the house, my honey; and 'tis a wet night, and a christening. Daze it, what's a cup of mead more or less? There'll be plenty more next bee-burning."

"Very well—this time, then," she answered, looking wistfully at the barrel. "But what is the man's calling, and where is he one of, that he should come in and join us like this?"

"I don't know. I'll ask him again."

The catastrophe of having the mug drained dry at one pull by the stranger in cinder-gray was effectually guarded against this time by Mrs. Fennel. She poured out his allowance in a small cup, keeping the large one at a discreet distance from him. When he had tossed off his portion the shepherd renewed his inquiry about the stranger's occupation.

The latter did not immediately reply, and the man in the chimney-corner, with sudden demonstrativeness, said, "Anybody may know my trade—I'm a wheelwright."

"A very good trade for these parts," said the shepherd.

"And anybody may know mine—if they've the sense to find it out," said the stranger in cinder-gray.

"You may generally tell what a man is by his claws," observed the hedge-carpenter, looking at his own hands. "My fingers be as full of thorns as an old pin-cushion is of pins."

The hands of the man in the chimney-corner instinctively sought the shade, and he gazed into the fire as he resumed his pipe. The man at the table took up the hedge-carpenter's remark, and added smartly, "True; but the oddity of my trade is that, instead of setting a mark upon me, it sets a mark upon my customers."

No observation being offered by anybody in elucidation of this enigma the shepherd's wife once more called for a song. The same obstacles presented themselves as at the former time—one had no voice, another had forgotten the first verse. The stranger at the table, whose soul had now risen to a good working temperature, relieved the difficulty by exclaiming that, to start the company, he would sing himself. Thrusting one thumb into the arm-hole of his waistcoat, he waved the other hand in the air, and, with an extemporizing gaze at the shining sheep-crooks above the mantelpiece, began:—

> "O my trade it is the rarest one,
> > Simple shepherds all—
> My trade is a sight to see;
> For my customers I tie, and take them up on high,
> And waft 'em to a far countree!"

The room was silent when he had finished the verse—with one exception, that of the man in the chimney-corner, who, at the singer's word, "Chorus!" joined him in a deep bass voice of musical relish—

> "And waft 'em to a far countree!"

Oliver Giles, John Pitcher the dairyman, the parish-clerk, the engaged man of fifty, the row of young women against the wall, seemed lost in thought not of the gayest kind. The shepherd looked meditatively on the ground, the shepherdess gazed keenly at the singer, and with some suspicion; she was doubting whether this stranger were merely singing an old song from recollection, or was composing one there and then for the occasion. All were as perplexed at the obscure revelation as the guests at Belshazzar's Feast, except the man in the chimney-corner, who quietly said, "Second verse, stranger," and smoked on.

The singer thoroughly moistened himself from his lips inwards, and went on with the next stanza as requested:—

> "My tools are but common ones,
> > Simple shepherds all—
> My tools are no sight to see:
> A little hempen string, and a post whereon to swing,
> Are implements enough for me!"

Shepherd Fennel glanced round. There was no longer any doubt that the stranger was answering his question rhythmically. The guests one and all started back with suppressed exclamations. The young woman engaged to the man of fifty fainted half-way, and would have proceeded, but finding him wanting in alacrity for catching her she sat down trembling.

"O, he's the——!" whispered the people in the background, mentioning the name of an ominous public officer. "He's come to do it! 'Tis to be at Casterbridge jail to-morrow—the man for sheep-stealing—the poor clock-maker we heard of, who used to live away at Shottsford and had no work to do—Timothy Summers, whose family were a-starving, and so he went out of Shottsford by the high-road, and took a sheep in open daylight, defying the farmer and the farmer's wife and the farmer's lad, and every man jack among 'em. He" (and they nodded towards the stranger of the deadly trade) "is come from up the country to do it because there's not enough to do in his own county-town, and he's got the place here now our own county man's dead; he's going to live in the same cottage under the prison wall."

The stranger in cinder-gray took no notice of this whispered string of observations, but again wetted his lips. Seeing that his friend in the chimney-corner was the only one who reciprocated his joviality in any way, he held out his cup towards that appreciative comrade, who also held out his own. They clinked together, the eyes of the rest of the room hanging upon the singer's actions. He parted his lips for the third verse; but at that moment another knock was audible upon the door. This time the knock was faint and hesitating.

The company seemed scared; the shepherd looked with consternation towards the entrance, and it was with some effort that he resisted his alarmed wife's deprecatory glance, and uttered for the third time the welcoming words, "Walk in!"

The door was gently opened, and another man stood upon the mat. He, like those who had preceded him, was a stranger. This time it was a short, small personage, of fair complexion, and dressed in a decent suit of dark clothes.

"Can you tell me the way to ———?" he began: when, gazing round the room to observe the nature of the company amongst whom he had fallen, his eyes lighted on the stranger in cinder-gray. It was just at the instant when the latter, who had thrown his mind into his song with such a will that he scarcely heeded the interruption, silenced all whispers and inquiries by bursting into his third verse:—

"To-morrow is my working day,
　　Simple shepherds all—

To-morrow is a working day for me:
For the farmer's sheep is slain, and the lad who did it ta 'en,
And on his soul may God ha' merc-y!"

The stranger in the chimney-corner, waving cups with the singer so
heartily that his mead splashed over on the hearth, repeated in his bass voice
as before:—

"And on his soul may God ha' merc-y!"

All this time the third stranger had been standing in the doorway. Finding now that he did not come forward or go on speaking, the guests particularly regarded him. They noticed to their surprise that he stood before
them the picture of abject terror—his knees trembling, his hand shaking so
violently that the door-latch by which he supported himself rattled audibly:
his white lips were parted, and his eyes fixed on the merry officer of justice
in the middle of the room. A moment more and he had turned, closed the
door, and fled.

"What a man can it be?" said the shepherd.

The rest, between the awfulness of their late discovery and the odd conduct of this third visitor, looked as if they knew not what to think, and said
nothing. Instinctively they withdrew further and further from the grim
gentleman in their midst, whom some of them seemed to take for the Prince
of Darkness himself, till they formed a remote circle, an empty space of floor
being left between them and him—

"... circulus, cujus centrum diabolus."

The room was so silent—though there were more than twenty people
in it—that nothing could be heard but the patter of the rain against the
window-shutters, accompanied by the occasional hiss of a stray drop that
fell down the chimney into the fire, and the steady puffing of the man in
the corner, who had now resumed his pipe of long clay.

The stillness was unexpectedly broken. The distant sound of a gun
reverberated through the air—apparently from the direction of the county-
town.

"Be jiggered!" cried the stranger who had sung the song, jumping up.

"What does that mean?" asked several.

"A prisoner escaped from the jail—that's what it means."

All listened. The sound was repeated, and none of them spoke but the man in the chimney-corner, who said quietly, "I've often been told that in this county they fire a gun at such times; but I never heard it till now."

"I wonder if it is *my* man?" murmured the personage in cinder-gray.

"Surely it is !" said the shepherd involuntarily. "And surely we've zeed him! That little man who looked in at the door by now, and quivered like a leaf when he zeed ye and heard your song!"

"His teeth chattered, and the breath went out of his body," said the dairyman.

"And his heart seemed to sink within him like a stone," said Oliver Giles.

"And he bolted as if he'd been shot at," said the hedge-carpenter.

"True—his teeth chattered, and his heart seemed to sink; and he bolted as if he'd been shot at," slowly summed up the man in the chimney-corner.

"I didn't notice it," remarked the hangman.

"We were all a-wondering what made him run off in such a fright," faltered one of the women against the wall, "and now 'tis explained!"

The firing of the alarm-gun went on at intervals, low and sullenly, and their suspicions became a certainty. The sinister gentleman in cinder-gray roused himself. "Is there a constable here?" he asked, in thick tones. "If so, let him step forward."

The engaged man of fifty stepped quavering out from the wall, his betrothed beginning to sob on the back of the chair.

"You are a sworn constable?"

"I be, sir."

"Then pursue the criminal at once, with assistance, and bring him back here. He can't have gone far."

"I will, sir, I will—when I've got my staff. I'll go home and get it, and come sharp here, and start in a body."

"Staff!—never mind your staff; the man'll be gone!"

"But I can't do nothing without my staff—can I, William, and John, and Charles Jake? No; for there's the king's royal crown a painted on en in yaller and gold, and the lion and the unicorn, so as when I raise en up and hit my prisoner, 'tis made a lawful blow thereby. I wouldn't 'tempt to take up a man without my staff—no, not I. If I hadn't the law to gie me courage, why, instead o' my taking up him he might take up me!"

"Now, I'm a king's man myself, and can give you authority enough for this," said the formidable officer in gray. "Now then, all of ye, be ready. Have ye any lanterns?"

"Yes—have ye any lanterns?—I demand it!" said the constable.

"And the rest of you able-bodied—"

"Able-bodied men—yes—the rest of ye!" said the constable.

"Have you some good stout staves and pitchforks—"

"Staves and pitchforks—in the name o' the law! And take 'em in yer hands and go in quest, and do as we in authority tell ye!"

Thus aroused, the men prepared to give chase. The evidence was, indeed, though circumstantial, so convincing, that but little argument was needed to show the shepherd's guests that after what they had seen it would look very much like connivance if they did not instantly pursue the unhappy third stranger, who could not as yet have gone more than a few hundred yards over such uneven country.

A shepherd is always well provided with lanterns; and, lighting these hastily, and with hurdle-staves in their hands, they poured out of the door, taking a direction along the crest of the hill, away from the town, the rain having fortunately a little abated.

Disturbed by the noise, or possibly by unpleasant dreams of her baptism, the child who had been christened began to cry heart-brokenly in the room overhead. These notes of grief came down through the chinks of the floor to the ears of the women below, who jumped up one by one, and seemed glad of the excuse to ascend and comfort the baby, for the incidents of the last half-hour greatly oppressed them. Thus in the space of two or three minutes the room on the ground-floor was deserted quite.

But it was not for long. Hardly had the sound of footsteps died away when a man returned round the corner of the house from the direction the pursuers had taken. Peeping in at the door, and seeing nobody there, he entered leisurely. It was the stranger of the chimney-corner, who had gone out with the rest. The motive of his return was shown by his helping himself to a cut piece of skimmer-cake that lay on a ledge beside where he had sat, and which he had apparently forgotten to take with him. He also poured out half a cup more mead from the quantity that remained, ravenously eating and drinking these as he stood. He had not finished when another figure came in just as quietly—his friend in cinder-gray.

"O—you here?" said the latter, smiling. "I thought you had gone to help in the capture." And this speaker also revealed the object of his return by looking solicitously round for the fascinating mug of old mead.

"And I thought you had gone," said the other, continuing his skimmer-cake with some effort.

"Well, on second thoughts, I felt there were enough without me," said the first confidentially, "and such a night as it is, too. Besides, 'tis the business o' the Government to take care of its criminals—not mine."

"True; so it is. And I felt as you did, that there were enough without me."

"I don't want to break my limbs running over the humps and hollows of this wild country."

"Nor I neither, between you and me."

"These shepherd-people are used to it—simple-minded souls, you know, stirred up to anything in a moment. They'll have him ready for me before the morning, and no trouble to me at all."

"They'll have him, and we shall have saved ourselves all labour in the matter."

"True, true. Well, my way is to Casterbridge; and 'tis as much as my legs will do to take me that far. Going the same way?"

"No, I am sorry to say! I have to get home over there" (he nodded indefinitely to the right), "and I feel as you do, that it is quite enough for my legs to do before bedtime."

The other had by this time finished the mead in the mug, after which, shaking hands heartily at the door, and wishing each other well, they went their several ways.

In the meantime the company of pursuers had reached the end of the hog's-back elevation which dominated this part of the down. They had decided on no particular plan of action; and, finding that the man of the baleful trade was no longer in their company, they seemed quite unable to form any such plan now. They descended in all directions down the hill, and straightway several of the party fell into the snare set by Nature for all misguided midnight ramblers over this part of the cretaceous formation. The "lanchets," or flint slopes, which belted the escarpment at intervals of a dozen yards, took the less cautious ones unawares, and losing their footing on the rubbly steep they slid sharply downwards, the lanterns rolling from their hands to the bottom, and there lying on their sides till the horn was scorched through.

When they had again gathered themselves together the shepherd, as the man who knew the country best, took the lead, and guided them round these treacherous inclines. The lanterns, which seemed rather to dazzle their eyes and warn the fugitive than to assist them in the exploration, were extinguished, due silence was observed; and in this more rational order they plunged into the vale. It was a grassy, briery, moist defile, affording some shelter to any person who had sought it; but the party perambulated it in vain, and ascended on the other side. Here they wandered apart, and after an interval closed together again to report progress. At the second time of closing in they found themselves near a lonely ash, the single tree on this part of the coomb, probably sown there by a passing bird some fifty years before. And here, standing a little to one side of the trunk, as motionless as the trunk itself, appeared the man they were in quest of, his outline being well defined against the sky beyond. The band noiselessly drew up and faced him.

"Your money or your life!" said the constable sternly to the still figure.

"No, no," whispered John Pitcher. "'Tisn't our side ought to say that. That's the doctrine of vagabonds like him, and we be on the side of the law."

"Well, well," replied the constable impatiently; "I must say something, mustn't I? and if you had all the weight o' this undertaking upon your mind, perhaps you'd say the wrong thing too!—Prisoner at the bar, surrender, in the name of the Father—the Crown, I mane!"

The man under the tree seemed now to notice them for the first time, and, giving them no opportunity whatever for exhibiting their courage, he strolled slowly towards them. He was, indeed, the little man, the third stranger; but his trepidation had in a great measure gone.

"Well, travellers," he said, "did I hear ye speak to me?"

"You did: you've got to come and be our prisoner at once!" said the constable. "We arrest'ee on the charge of not biding in Casterbridge jail in a decent proper manner to be hung to-morrow morning. Neighbours, do your duty, and seize the culpet!"

On hearing the charge the man seemed enlightened, and, saying not another word, resigned himself with preternatural civility to the search-party, who, with their staves in their hands, surrounded him on all sides, and marched him back towards the shepherd's cottage.

It was eleven o'clock by the time they arrived. The light shining from the open door, a sound of men's voices within, proclaimed to them as they approached the house that some new events had arisen in their absence. On entering they discovered the shepherd's living-room to be invaded by two officers from Casterbridge jail, and a well-known magistrate who lived at the nearest country-seat, intelligence of the escape having become generally circulated.

"Gentlemen," said the constable, "I have brought back your man—not without risk and danger; but every one must do his duty! He is inside this circle of able-bodied persons, who have lent me useful aid, considering their ignorance of Crown work. Men, bring forward your prisoner!" And the third stranger was led to the light.

"Who is this?" said one of the officials.

"The man," said the constable.

"Certainly not," said the turnkey; and the first corroborated his statement.

"But how can it be otherwise?" asked the constable. "Or why was he so terrified at sight o' the singing instrument of the law who sat there?" Here he related the strange behaviour of the third stranger on entering the house during the hangman's song.

"Can't understand it," said the officer coolly. "All I know is that it is not the condemned man. He's quite a different character from this one; a gauntish fellow, with dark hair and eyes, rather good-looking, and with a musical bass voice that if you heard it once you'd never mistake as long as you lived."

"Why, souls—'twas the man in the chimney-corner!"

"Hey—what?" said the magistrate, coming forward after inquiring particulars from the shepherd in the background. "Haven't you got the man after all?"

"Well, sir," said the constable, "he's the man we were in search of, that's true; and yet he's not the man we were in search of. For the man we were in search of was not the man we wanted, sir, if you understand my every-day way; for 'twas the man in the chimney-corner!"

"A pretty kettle of fish altogether!" said the magistrate. "You had better start for the other man at once."

The prisoner now spoke for the first time. The mention of the man in the chimney-corner seemed to have moved him as nothing else could do. "Sir," he said, stepping forward to the magistrate, "take no more trouble about me. The time is come when I may as well speak. I have done nothing; my crime is that the condemned man is my brother. Early this afternoon I left home at Shottsford to tramp it all the way to Casterbridge jail to bid him farewell. I was benighted, and called here to rest and ask the way. When I opened the door I saw before me the very man, my brother, that I thought to see in the condemned cell at Casterbridge. He was in this chimney-corner; and jammed close to him, so that he could not have got out if he had tried, was the executioner who'd come to take his life, singing a song about it and not knowing that it was his victim who was close by, joining in to save appearances. My brother threw a glance of agony at me, and I knew he meant, 'Don't reveal what you see; my life depends on it.' I was so terror-struck that I could hardly stand, and, not knowing what I did, I turned and hurried away."

The narrator's manner and tone had the stamp of truth, and his story made a great impression on all around.

"And do you know where your brother is at the present time?" asked the magistrate.

"I do not. I have never seen him since I closed this door."

"I can testify to that, for we've been between ye ever since," said the constable.

"Where does he think to fly to?—what is his occupation?"

"He's a watch-and-clock-maker, sir."

"'A said 'a was a wheelwright—a wicked rogue," said the constable.

"The wheels of clocks and watches he meant, no doubt," said Shepherd Fennel. "I thought his hands were palish for's trade."

"Well, it appears to me that nothing can be gained by retaining this poor man in custody," said the magistrate; "your business lies with the other, unquestionably."

And so the little man was released off-hand; but he looked nothing the less sad on that account, it being beyond the power of magistrate or constable to raze out the written troubles in his brain, for they concerned another whom he regarded with more solicitude than himself. When this was done, and the man had gone his way, the night was found to be so far advanced that it was deemed useless to renew the search before the next morning.

Next day, accordingly, the quest for the clever sheep-stealer became general and keen, to all appearance at least. But the intended punishment was cruelly disproportioned to the transgression, and the sympathy of a great many country-folk in that district was strongly on the side of the fugitive. Moreover, his marvellous coolness and daring in hob-and-nobbing with the hangman, under the unprecedented circumstances of the shepherd's party, won their admiration. So that it may be questioned if all those who ostensibly made themselves so busy in exploring woods and fields and lanes were quite so thorough when it came to the private examination of their own lofts and outhouses. Stories were afloat of a mysterious figure being occasionally seen in some old overgrown trackway or other, remote from turnpike roads; but when a search was instituted in any of these suspected quarters nobody was found. Thus the days and weeks passed without tidings.

In brief, the bass-voiced man of the chimney-corner was never recaptured. Some said that he went across the sea, others that he did not, but buried himself in the depths of a populous city. At any rate, the gentleman in cinder-gray never did his morning's work at Casterbridge, nor met anywhere at all, for business purposes, the genial comrade with whom he had passed an hour of relaxation in the lonely house on the slope of the coomb.

The grass has long been green on the graves of Shepherd Fennel and his frugal wife; the guests who made up the christening party have mainly followed their entertainers to the tomb; the baby in whose honour they all had met is a matron in the sere and yellow leaf. But the arrival of the three strangers at the shepherd's that night, and the details connected therewith, is a story as well known as ever in the country about Higher Crowstairs.

&

# HOW MUCH LAND DOES A MAN NEED?

## *Leo Tolstoy*

### I

An elder sister came to visit her younger sister in the country. The elder was married to a tradesman in town, the younger to a peasant in the village. As the sisters sat over their tea talking, the elder began to boast of the advantages of town life: saying how comfortably they lived there, how well they dressed, what fine clothes her children wore, what good things they ate and drank, and how she went to the theatre, promenades, and entertainments.

The younger sister was piqued, and in turn disparaged the life of a tradesman, and stood up for that of a peasant.

"I would not change my way of life for yours," said she. "We may live roughly, but at least we are free from anxiety. You live in better style than we do, but though you often earn more than you need, you are very likely to lose all you have. You know the proverb, 'Loss and gain are brothers twain.' It often happens that people who are wealthy one day are begging their bread the next. Our way is safer. Though a peasant's life is not a fat one, it is a long one. We shall never grow rich, but we shall always have enough to eat."

The elder sister said sneeringly:

"Enough? Yes, if you like to share with the pigs and the calves! What do you know of elegance or manners! However much your goodman may slave, you will die as you are living—on a dung heap—and your children the same."

"Well, what of that?" replied the younger. "Of course our work is rough and coarse. But, on the other hand, it is sure, and we need not bow to any one. But you, in your towns, are surrounded by temptations; to-day all may be right, but to-morrow the Evil One may tempt your husband with cards, wine, or women, and all will go to ruin. Don't such things happen often enough?"

Pahóm, the master of the house, was lying on the top of the stove and he listened to the women's chatter.

"It is perfectly true," thought he. "Busy as we are from childhood tilling mother earth, we peasants have no time to let any nonsense settle in our heads. Our only trouble is that we haven't land enough. If I had plenty of land, I shouldn't fear the Devil himself!"

The women finished their tea, chatted a while about dress, and then cleared away the tea-things and lay down to sleep.

But the Devil had been sitting behind the stove, and had heard all that was said. He was pleased that the peasant's wife had led her husband into boasting, and that he had said that if he had plenty of land he would not fear the Devil himself.

"All right," thought the Devil. "We will have a tussle. I'll give you land enough; and by means of that land I will get you into my power."

## II

Close to the village there lived a lady, a small land-owner who had an estate of about three hundred acres.* She had always lived on good terms with the peasants until she engaged as her steward an old soldier, who took to burdening the people with fines. However careful Pahóm tried to be, it happened again and again that now a horse of his got among the lady's oats, now a cow strayed into her garden, now his calves found their way into her meadows—and he always had to pay a fine.

Pahóm paid up, but grumbled, and going home in a temper, was rough with his family. All through that summer, Pahóm had much trouble because of this steward, and he was even glad when winter came and the cattle had to be stabled. Though he grudged the fodder when they could no longer graze on the pasture-land, at least he was free from anxiety about them.

In the winter the news got about that the lady was going to sell her land and that the keeper of the inn on the high road was bargaining for it. When the peasants heard this they were very much alarmed.

"Well," thought they, "if the innkeeper gets the land, he will worry us with fines worse than the lady's steward. We all depend on that estate."

---

*120 *desyatíns*. The *desyatína* is properly 2.7 acres but in this story round numbers are used.

So the peasants went on behalf of their Commune, and asked the lady not to sell the land to the innkeeper, offering her a better price for it themselves. The lady agreed to let them have it. Then the peasants tried to arrange for the Commune to buy the whole estate, so that it might be held by them all in common. They met twice to discuss it, but could not settle the matter; the Evil One sowed discord among them and they could not agree. So they decided to buy the land individually, each according to his means; and the lady agreed to this plan as she had to the other.

Presently Pahóm heard that a neighbour of his was buying fifty acres, and that the lady had consented to accept one half in cash and to wait a year for the other half. Pahóm felt envious.

"Look at that," thought he, "the land is all being sold, and I shall get none of it." So he spoke to his wife.

"Other people are buying," said he, "and we must also buy twenty acres or so. Life is becoming impossible. That steward is simply crushing us with his fines."

So they put their heads together and considered how they could manage to buy it. They had one hundred rúbles laid by. They sold a colt and one half of their bees, hired out one of their sons as a labourer and took his wages in advance; borrowed the rest from a brother-in-law, and so scraped together half the purchase money.

Having done this, Pahóm chose out a farm of forty acres, some of it wooded, and went to the lady to bargain for it. They came to an agreement, and he shook hands with her upon it and paid her a deposit in advance. Then they went to town and signed the deeds; he paying half the price down, and undertaking to pay the remainder within two years.

So now Pahóm had land of his own. He borrowed seed, and sowed it on the land he had bought. The harvest was a good one, and within a year he had managed to pay off his debts both to the lady and to his brother-in-law. So he became a landowner, ploughing and sowing his own land, making hay on his own land, cutting his own trees, and feeding his cattle on his own pasture. When he went out to plough his fields, or to look at his growing corn, or at his grass-meadows, his heart would fill with joy. The grass that grew and the flowers that bloomed there seemed to him unlike any that grew elsewhere. Formerly, when he had passed by that land, it had appeared the same as any other land, but now it seemed quite different.

## III

So Pahóm was well-contented, and everything would have been right if the neighbouring peasants would only not have trespassed on his corn-fields and meadows. He appealed to them most civilly, but they still went on: now the Communal herdsmen would let the village cows stray into his meadows, then horses from the night pasture would get among his corn. Pahóm turned them out again and again, and forgave their owners, and for a long time he forbore to prosecute any one. But at last he lost patience and complained to the District Court. He knew it was the peasants' want of land, and no evil intent on their part, that caused the trouble, but he thought:

"I cannot go on overlooking it or they will destroy all I have. They must be taught a lesson."

So he had them up, gave them one lesson, and then another, and two or three of the peasants were fined. After a time Pahóm's neighbours began to bear him a grudge for this, and would now and then let their cattle on to his land on purpose. One peasant even got into Pahóm's wood at night and cut down five young lime trees for their bark. Pahóm passing through the wood one day noticed something white. He came nearer and saw the stripped trunks lying on the ground, and close by stood the stumps where the trees had been. Pahóm was furious.

"If he had only cut one here and there it would have been bad enough," thought Pahóm, "but the rascal has actually cut down a whole clump. If I could only find out who did this, I would pay him out."

He racked his brains as to who it could be. Finally he decided: "It must be Simon—no one else could have done it." So he went to Simon's homestead to have a look round, but he found nothing, and only had an angry scene. However, he now felt more certain than ever that Simon had done it, and he lodged a complaint. Simon was summoned. The case was tried, and retried, and at the end of it all Simon was acquitted, there being no evidence against him. Pahóm felt still more aggrieved, and let his anger loose upon the Elder and the Judges.

"You let thieves grease your palms," said he. "If you were honest folk yourselves you would not let a thief go free."

So Pahóm quarrelled with the Judges and with his neighbours. Threats to burn his building began to be uttered. So though Pahóm had more land, his place in the Commune was much worse than before.

About this time a rumour got about that many people were moving to new parts.

"There's no need for me to leave my land," thought Pahóm. "But some of the others might leave our village and then there would be more room for us. I would take over their land myself and make my estate a bit bigger. I could then live more at ease. As it is, I am still too cramped to be comfortable."

One day Pahóm was sitting at home when a peasant, passing through the village, happened to call in. He was allowed to stay the night, and supper was given him. Pahóm had a talk with this peasant and asked him where he came from. The stranger answered that he came from beyond the Vólga, where he had been working. One word led to another, and the man went on to say that many people were settling in those parts. He told how some people from his village had settled there. They had joined the Commune, and had had twenty-five acres per man granted them. The land was so good, he said, that the rye sown on it grew as high as a horse, and so thick that five cuts of a sickle made a sheaf. One peasant, he said, had brought nothing with him but his bare hands, and now he had six horses and two cows of his own.

Pahóm's heart kindled with desire. He thought:

"Why should I suffer in this narrow hole, if one can live so well elsewhere? I will sell my land and my homestead here, and with the money I will start afresh over there and get everything new. In this crowded place one is always having trouble. But I must first go and find out all about it myself."

Towards summer he got ready and started. He went down the Vólga on a steamer to Samára, then walked another three hundred miles on foot, and at last reached the place. It was just as the stranger had said. The peasants had plenty of land: every man had twenty-five acres of Communal land given him for his use, and any one who had money could buy, besides, at two shillings an acre* as much good freehold land as he wanted.

Having found out all he wished to know, Pahóm returned home as autumn came on, and began selling off his belongings. He sold his land at a profit, sold his homestead and all his cattle, and withdrew from membership of the Commune. He only waited till the spring, and then started with his family for the new settlement.

---

*Three rúbles per *desyatína*.

## IV

As soon as Pahóm and his family reached their new abode, he applied for admission into the Commune of a large village. He stood treat to the Elders and obtained the necessary documents. Five shares of Communal land were given him for his own and his sons' use: that is to say—125 acres (not all together, but in different fields) besides the use of the Communal pasture. Pahóm put up the buildings he needed, and bought cattle. Of the Communal land alone he had three times as much as at his former home, and the land was good corn-land. He was ten times better off than he had been. He had plenty of arable land and pasturage, and could keep as many head of cattle as he liked.

At first, in the bustle of building and settling down, Pahóm was pleased with it all, but when he got used to it he began to think that even here he had not enough land. The first year, he sowed wheat on his share of the Communal land and had a good crop. He wanted to go on sowing wheat, but had not enough Communal land for the purpose, and what he had already used was not available; for in those parts wheat is only sown on virgin soil or on fallow land. It is sown for one or two years, and then the land lies fallow till it is again over-grown with prairie grass. There were many who wanted such land and there was not enough for all; so that people quarrelled about it. Those who were better off wanted it for growing wheat, and those who were poor wanted it to let to dealers, so that they might raise money to pay their taxes. Pahóm wanted to sow more wheat, so he rented land from a dealer for a year. He sowed much wheat and had a fine crop, but the land was too far from the village—the wheat had to be carted more than ten miles. After a time Pahóm noticed that some peasant-dealers were living on separate farms and were growing wealthy; and he thought:

"If I were to buy some freehold land and have a homestead on it, it would be a different thing altogether. Then it would all be nice and compact."

The question of buying freehold land recurred to him again and again.

He went on in the same way for three years, renting land and sowing wheat. The seasons turned out well and the crops were good, so that he began to lay money by. He might have gone on living contentedly, but he grew tired of having to rent other people's land every year, and having to scramble for it. Wherever there was good land to be had, the peasants would rush for it and it was taken up at once, so that unless you were sharp about it you got none. It happened in the third year that he and a dealer together rented a piece of pasture-land from some peasants; and they had already ploughed it up, when there was some dispute and the peasants went to law about it, and things fell out so that the labour was all lost.

"If it were my own land," thought Pahóm, "I should be independent, and there would not be all this unpleasantness."

So Pahóm began looking out for land which he could buy; and he came across a peasant who had bought thirteen hundred acres, but having got into difficulties was willing to sell again cheap. Pahóm bargained and haggled with him, and at last they settled the price at 1,500 rúbles, part in cash and part to be paid later. They had all but clinched the matter when a passing dealer happened to stop at Pahóm's one day to get a feed for his horses. He drank tea with Pahóm and they had a talk. The dealer said that he was just returning from the land of the Bashkírs, far away, where he had bought thirteen thousand acres of land, all for 1,000 rúbles. Pahóm questioned him further, and the tradesman said:

"All one need do is to make friends with the chiefs. I gave away about one hundred rúbles worth of silk robes and carpets, besides a case of tea, and I gave wine to those who would drink it; and I got the land for less than a penny an acre."* And he showed Pahóm the title-deeds, saying:

"The land lies near a river, and the whole prairie is virgin soil."

Pahóm plied him with questions, and the tradesman said:

"There is more land there than you could cover if you walked a year, and it all belongs to the Bashkírs. They are as simple as sheep, and land can be got almost for nothing."

"There now," thought Pahóm, "with my one thousand rúbles, why should I get only thirteen hundred acres, and saddle myself with a debt besides? If I take it out there, I can get more than ten times as much for the money."

V

Pahóm inquired how to get to the place, and as soon as the tradesman had left him, he prepared to go there himself. He left his wife to look after the homestead, and started on his journey taking his man with him. They

*Five *kopéks* for a *desyatína*.

stopped at a town on their way and bought a case of tea, some wine, and other presents, as the tradesman had advised. On and on they went until they had gone more than three hundred miles, and on the seventh day they came to a place where the Bashkírs had pitched their tents. It was all just as the tradesman had said. The people lived on the steppes, by a river, in felt-covered tents. They neither tilled the ground, nor ate bread. Their cattle and horses grazed in herds on the steppe. The colts were tethered behind the tents, and the mares were driven to them twice a day. The mares were milked, and from the milk kumiss was made. It was the women who prepared kumiss, and they also made cheese. As far as the men were concerned, drinking kumiss and tea, eating mutton, and playing on their pipes, was all they cared about. They were all stout and merry, and all the summer long they never thought of doing any work. They were quite ignorant, and knew no Russian, but were good-natured enough.

As soon as they saw Pahóm, they came out of their tents and gathered round their visitor. An interpreter was found, and Pahóm told them he had come about some land. The Bashkírs seemed very glad; they took Pahóm and led him into one of the best tents, where they made him sit on some down cushions placed on a carpet, while they sat round him. They gave him some tea and kumiss, and had a sheep killed, and gave him mutton to eat. Pahóm took presents out of his cart and distributed them among the Bashkírs, and divided the tea amongst them. The Bashkírs were delighted. They talked a great deal among themselves, and then told the interpreter to translate.

"They wish to tell you," said the interpreter, "that they like you, and that it is our custom to do all we can to please a guest and to repay him for his gifts. You have given us presents, now tell us which of the things we possess please you best, that we may present them to you."

"What pleases me best here," answered Pahóm, "is your land. Our land is crowded and the soil is exhausted; but you have plenty of land and it is good land. I never saw the like of it."

The interpreter translated. The Bashkírs talked among themselves for a while. Pahóm could not understand what they were saying, but saw that they were much amused and that they shouted and laughed. Then they were silent and looked at Pahóm while the interpreter said:

"They wish me to tell you that in return for your presents they will gladly give you as much land as you want. You have only to point it out with your hand and it is yours."

The Bashkírs talked again for a while and began to dispute. Pahóm asked what they were disputing about, and the interpreter told him that some of them thought they ought to ask their Chief about the land and not act in his absence, while others thought there was no need to wait for his return.


## VI


While the Bashkírs were disputing, a man in a large fox-fur cap appeared on the scene. They all became silent and rose to their feet. The interpreter said, "This is our Chief himself."

Pahóm immediately fetched the best dressing-gown and five pounds of tea, and offered these to the Chief. The Chief accepted them, and seated himself in the place of honour. The Bashkírs at once began telling him something. The Chief listened for a while, then made a sign with his head for them to be silent, and addressing himself to Pahóm, said in Russian:

"Well, let it be so. Choose whatever piece of land you like; we have plenty of it."

"How can I take as much as I like?" thought Pahóm. "I must get a deed to make it secure, or else they may say, "It is yours," and afterwards may take it away again."

"Thank you for your kind words," he said aloud. "You have much land, and I only want a little. But I should like to be sure which bit is mine. Could it not be measured and made over to me? Life and death are in God's hands. You good people give it to me, but your children might wish to take it away again."

"You are quite right," said the Chief. "We will make it over to you."

"I heard that a dealer had been here," continued Pahóm, "and that you gave him a little land, too, and signed title-deeds to that effect. I should like to have it done in the same way."

The Chief understood.

"Yes," replied he, "that can be done quite easily. We have a scribe, and we will go to town with you and have the deed properly sealed."

"And what will be the price?" asked Pahóm.

"Our price is always the same: one thousand rúbles a day."

Pahóm did not understand.

"A day? What measure is that? How many acres would that be?"

"We do not know how to reckon it out," said the Chief. "We sell it by the day. As much as you can go round on your feet in a day is yours, and the price is one thousand rúbles a day."

Pahóm was surprised.

"But in a day you can get round a large tract of land," he said.

The Chief laughed.

"It will all be yours!" said he. "But there is one condition: If you don't return on the same day to the spot whence you started, your money is lost."

"But how am I to mark the way that I have gone?"

"Why, we shall go to any spot you like, and stay there. You must start from that spot and make your round, taking a spade with you. Wherever you think necessary, make a mark. At every turning, dig a hole and pile up the turf; then afterwards we will go round with a plough from hole to hole. You may make as large a circuit as you please, but before the sun sets you must return to the place you started from. All the land you cover will be yours."

Pahóm was delighted. It was decided to start early next morning. They talked a while, and after drinking some more kumiss and eating some more mutton, they had tea again, and then the night came on. They gave Pahóm a feather-bed to sleep on, and the Bashkírs dispersed for the night, promising to assemble the next morning at day-break and ride out before sunrise to the appointed spot.

## VII

Pahóm lay on the feather-bed, but could not sleep. He kept thinking about the land.

"What a large tract I will mark off!" thought he. "I can easily do thirty-five miles in a day. The days are long now, and within a circuit of thirty-five miles what a lot of land there will be! I will sell the poorer land, or let it to peasants, but I'll pick out the best and farm it. I will buy two ox-teams, and hire two more labourers. About a hundred and fifty acres shall be plough-land, and I will pasture cattle on the rest."

Pahóm lay awake all night, and dozed off only just before dawn. Hardly were his eyes closed when he had a dream. He thought he was lying in that same tent and heard somebody chuckling outside. He wondered who it could be, and rose and went out, and he saw the Bashkír Chief sitting in front of the tent holding his sides and rolling about with laughter. Going nearer to the Chief, Pahóm asked: "What are you laughing at?" But he saw that it was no longer the Chief, but the dealer who had recently stopped at his house and had told him about the land. Just as Pahóm was going to ask, "Have you been here long?" he saw that it was not the dealer, but the peasant who had come up from the Vólga, long ago, to Pahóm's old home. Then he saw that it was not the peasant either, but the Devil himself with hoofs and horns, sitting there and chuckling, and before him lay a man barefoot, prostrate on the ground, with only trousers and a shirt on. And Pahóm dreamt that he looked more attentively to see what sort of a man it was that was lying there, and he saw that the man was dead, and that it was himself! He awoke horror-struck.

"What things one does dream," thought he.

Looking round he saw through the open door that the dawn was breaking.

"It's time to wake them up," thought he. "We ought to be starting."

He got up, roused his man (who was sleeping in his cart), bade him harness; and went to call the Bashkírs.

"It's time to go to the steppe to measure the land," he said.

The Bashkírs rose and assembled, and the Chief came too. Then they began drinking kumiss again, and offered Pahóm some tea, but he would not wait.

"If we are to go, let us go. It is high time," said he.


## VIII


The Bashkírs got ready and they all started: some mounted on horses, and some in carts. Pahóm drove in his own small cart with his servant and took a spade with him. When they reached the steppe, the morning red was beginning to kindle. They ascended a hillock (called by the Bashkírs a *shikhan*) and dismounting from their carts and their horses, gathered in one spot. The Chief came up to Pahóm and stretching out his arm towards the plain:

"See," said he, "all this, as far as your eye can reach, is ours. You may have any part of it you like."

Pahóm's eyes glistened: it was all virgin soil, as flat as the palm of your hand, as black as the seed of a poppy, and in the hollows different kinds of grasses grew breast high.

The Chief took off his fox-fur cap, placed it on the ground and said:

"This will be the mark. Start from here, and return here again. All the land you go round shall be yours."

Pahóm took out his money and put it on the cap. Then he took off his outer coat, remaining in his sleeveless under-coat. He unfastened his girdle and tied it tight below his stomach, put a little bag of bread into the breast of his coat, and tying a flask of water to his girdle, he drew up the tops of his boots, took the spade from his man, and stood ready to start. He considered for some moments which way he had better go—it was tempting everywhere.

"No matter," he concluded, "I will go towards the rising sun."

He turned his face to the east, stretched himself, and waited for the sun to appear above the rim.

"I must lose no time," he thought, "and it is easier walking while it is still cool."

The sun's rays had hardly flashed above the horizon, before Pahóm, carrying the spade over his shoulder, went down into the steppe.

Pahóm started walking neither slowly nor quickly. After having gone a thousand yards he stopped, dug a hole, and placed pieces of turf one on another to make it more visible. Then he went on; and now that he had walked off his stiffness he quickened his pace. After a while he dug another hole.

Pahóm looked back. The hillock could be distinctly seen in the sunlight, with the people on it, and the glittering tyres of the cart-wheels. At a rough guess Pahóm concluded that he had walked three miles. It was growing warmer; he took off his under-coat, flung it across his shoulder, and went on again. It had grown quite warm now; he looked at the sun, it was time to think of breakfast.

"The first shift is done, but there are four in a day, and it is too soon yet to turn. But I will just take off my boots," said he to himself.

He sat down, took off his boots, stuck them into his girdle, and went on. It was easy walking now.

"I will go on for another three miles," thought he, "and then turn to the left. This spot is so fine, that it would be a pity to lose it. The further one goes, the better the land seems."

He went straight on for a while, and when he looked round, the hillock was scarcely visible and the people on it looked like black ants, and he could just see something glistening there in the sun.

"Ah," thought Pahóm, "I have gone far enough in this direction, it is time to turn. Besides I am in a regular sweat, and very thirsty."

He stopped, dug a large hole, and heaped up pieces of turf. Next he untied his flask, had a drink, and then turned sharply to the left. He went on and on; the grass was high, and it was very hot.

Pahóm began to grow tired: he looked at the sun and saw that it was noon.

"Well," he thought, "I must have a rest."

He sat down, and ate some bread and drank some water; but he did not lie down, thinking that if he did he might fall asleep. After sitting a little while, he went on again. At first he walked easily: the food had strengthened him; but it had become terribly hot and he felt sleepy, still he went on, thinking: "An hour to suffer, a life-time to live."

He went a long way in this direction also, and was about to turn to the left again, when he perceived a damp hollow: "It would be a pity to leave that out," he thought. "Flax would do well there." So he went on past the hollow, and dug a hole on the other side of it before he turned the corner. Pahóm looked towards the hillock. The heat made the air hazy: it seemed to be quivering, and through the haze the people on the hillock could scarcely be seen.

"Ah!" thought Pahóm, "I have made the sides too long; I must make this one shorter." And he went along the third side, stepping faster. He looked at the sun: it was nearly half-way to the horizon, and he had not yet done two miles of the third side of the square. He was still ten miles from the goal.

"No," he thought, "though it will make my land lop-sided, I must hurry back in a straight line now. I might go too far, and as it is I have a great deal of land."

So Pahóm hurriedly dug a hole, and turned straight towards the hillock.

## IX

Pahóm went straight towards the hillock, but he now walked with difficulty. He was done up with the heat, his bare feet were cut and bruised, and his legs began to fail. He longed to rest, but it was impossible if he meant to get back before sunset. The sun waits for no man, and it was sinking lower and lower.

"Oh dear," he thought, "if only I have not blundered trying for too much! What if I am too late?"

He looked towards the hillock and at the sun. He was still far from his goal, and the sun was already near the rim.

Pahóm walked on and on; it was very hard walking but he went quicker and quicker. He pressed on, but was still far from the place. He began running, threw away his coat, his boots, his flask, and his cap, and kept only the spade which he used as a support.

"What shall I do," he thought again, "I have grasped too much and ruined the whole affair. I can't get there before the sun sets."

And this fear made him still more breathless. Pahóm went on running, his soaking shirt and trousers stuck to him and his mouth was parched. His breast was working like a blacksmith's bellows, his heart was beating like a hammer, and his legs were giving way as if they did not belong to him. Pahóm was seized with terror lest he should die of the strain.

Though afraid of death, he could not stop. "After having run all that way they will call me a fool if I stop now," thought he. And he ran on and on, and drew near and heard the Bashkírs yelling and shouting to him, and their cries inflamed his heart still more. He gathered his last strength and ran on.

The sun was close to the rim, and cloaked in mist looked large, and red as blood. Now, yes now, it was about to set! The sun was quite low, but he was also quite near his aim. Pahóm could already see the people on the hillock waving their arms to hurry him up. He could see the fox-fur cap on the ground and the money on it, and the Chief sitting on the ground holding his sides. And Pahóm remembered his dream.

"There is plenty of land," thought he, "but will God let me live on it? I have lost my life, I have lost my life! I shall never reach that spot!"

Pahóm looked at the sun, which had reached the earth: one side of it had already disappeared. With all his remaining strength he rushed on, bending his body forward so that his legs could hardly follow fast enough to keep him from falling. Just as he reached the hillock it suddenly grew dark. He looked up—the sun had already set! He gave a cry: "All my labour has been in vain," thought he, and was about to stop, but he heard the Bashkírs still shouting, and remembered that though to him, from below, the sun seemed to have set, they on the hillock could still see it. He took a long breath and ran up the hillock. It was still light there. He reached the top and saw the cap. Before it sat the Chief laughing and holding his sides. Again Pahóm remembered his dream, and he uttered a cry: his legs gave way beneath him, he fell forward and reached the cap with his hands.

"Ah, that's a fine fellow!" exclaimed the Chief. "He has gained much land!"

Pahóm's servant came running up and tried to raise him, but he saw that blood was flowing from his mouth. Pahóm was dead!

The Bashkírs clicked their tongues to show their pity.

His servant picked up the spade and dug a grave long enough for

Pahóm to lie in, and buried him in it. Six feet from his head to his heels was all he needed.

*Translated by Louise and Aylmer Maude*

∾

# ALI THE PERSIAN'S STORY OF THE KURD SHARPER

## *The Arabian Nights*

The Khalif Haroun er Reshid, being more than commonly restless one night, sent for his Vizier and said to him, "O Jaafer, I am sore wakeful and heavy at heart to-night, and I desire of thee what may cheer my spirit and ease me of my oppression." "O Commander of the Faithful," answered Jaafer, "I have a friend, by name Ali the Persian, who hath store of tales and pleasant stories, such as lighten the heart and do away care." "Fetch him to me," said the Khalif. "I hear and obey," replied Jaafer and going out from before him, sent for Ali the Persian and said to him, "The Commander of the Faithful calls for thee." "I hear and obey," answered Ali and followed the Vizier into the presence of the Khalif, who bade him be seated and said to him, "O Ali, my heart is heavy within me this night and I hear that thou hast great store of tales and anecdotes; so I desire of thee that thou let me hear what will relieve my oppression and gladden my melancholy." "O Commander of the Faithful," said he, "shall I tell thee what I have seen with my eyes or what I have heard with my ears?" "An thou have seen aught [worth telling]," replied the Khalif, "let me hear that." "Know then, O Commander of the Faithful," said Ali, "that some years ago I left this my native city of Baghdad on a journey, having with me a boy who carried a light wallet. Presently, we came to a certain city, where, as I was buying and selling, a rascally thief of a Kurd fell on me and seized my wallet, saying, 'This is my bag, and all that is in it is my property.' Thereupon, 'Ho, Muslims all,' cried I, 'deliver me from the hand of the vilest of oppressors!' But they all said, 'Come, both of you, to the Cadi and submit yourselves to his judgment." I agreed to this and we both presented ourselves before the Cadi, who said, 'What brings you hither and what is your case?' Quoth I, 'We are men at difference, who appeal to thee and submit ourselves to thy judgment.' 'Which of you is the complainant?' asked the Cadi. So the Kurd came forward and said, 'God preserve our lord the Cadi! Verily, this bag is my bag and all that is in it is my property. It was lost from me and I found it with this man.' 'When didst thou lose it?' asked the Cadi. 'But yesterday,' replied the Kurd; 'and I passed a sleepless night by reason of its loss.' 'If it be thy bag,' said the Cadi, 'tell me what is in it.' Quoth the Kurd, 'There were in my bag two silver styles and eye-powders and a handkerchief, and I had laid therein two gilt cups and two candlesticks. Moreover it contained two tents and two platters and two hooks and a cushion and two leather rugs and two ewers and a brass tray and two basins and a cooking-pot and two water-jars and a ladle and a sacking-needle and a she-cat and two bitches and a wooden trencher and two sacks and two saddles and a gown and two fur pelisses and a cow and two calves and a she-goat and two sheep and an ewe and two lambs and two green pavilions and a camel and two she-camels and a she-buffalo and two bulls and a lioness and two lions and a she-bear and two foxes and a mattress and two couches and an upper chamber and two saloons and a portico and two ante-rooms and a kitchen with two doors and a company of Kurds who will testify that the bag is mine.' Then said the Cadi to me, 'And thou, what sayst thou?' So I came forward, O Commander of the Faithful (and indeed the Kurd's speech had bewildered me) and said, 'God advance our lord the Cadi! There was nothing in this my wallet, save a little ruined house and another without a door and a dog-kennel and a boys' school and youths playing dice and tents and tent-poles and the cities of Bassora and Baghdad and the palace of Sheddad ben Aad and a smith's forge and a fishing net and cudgels and pickets and girls and boys and a thousand pimps, who will testify that the bag is my bag.' When the Kurd heard my words, he wept and wailed and said, 'O my lord the Cadi, my bag is known and what is in it is renowned; therein are castles and citadels and cranes and beasts of prey and men playing chess and draughts. Moreover, in this my bag is a brood-mare and two colts and a stallion and two blood-horses and two long lances and a lion and two hares and a city and two villages and a courtesan and two sharking pimps and a catamite and two gallows-birds and a blind man and two dogs and a cripple and two lameters and a priest and two deacons and a patriarch and two monks and a Cadi and two assessors, who will testify that the bag is my bag.' Quoth the Cadi to me, 'And what sayst thou, O Ali?' So, O Commander of the Faithful, being filled with rage, I came forward and said, 'God keep our lord the Cadi! I had in this my wallet a coat of mail and a broadsword and armouries and a thousand fighting rams and a sheep-fold and a thousand barking dogs and gardens and vines and flowers and sweet herbs and figs and apples and pictures and statues and flagons and goblets and fair-faced slave-girls and singing-women and marriage-feasts and tumult and clamour and great tracts of land and brothers of success and a company of daybreak-raiders, with swords and spears and bows and arrows, and true friends and dear ones and intimates and comrades and men imprisoned for punishment and cup-companions and a drum and flutes and flags and banners and boys and girls and brides, in all their wedding bravery, and singing-girls and five Abyssinian women and three Hindi and four women of Medina and a score of Greek girls and half a hundred Turkish and threescore and ten Persian girls and fourscore Kurd and fourscore and ten Georgian women and Tigris and Euphrates and a fowling net and a flint and steel and Many-Columned Irem and a thousand rogues and pimps and horse-courses and stables and mosques and baths and a builder and a carpenter and a plank and a nail and a black slave, with a pair of recorders, and a captain and a caravan-leader and towns and cities and a hundred thousand dinars and Cufa and Ambar and twenty chests full of stuffs and twenty store-houses for victual and Gaza and Askalon and from Damietta to Essouan and the palace of Kisra Anoushirwan and the kingdom of Solomon and from Wadi Numan to the land of Khorassan and Balkh and Ispahan and from India to the Soudan. Therein also (may God prolong the life of our lord the Cadi!) are doublets and cloths and a thousand sharp razors to shave the Cadi's chin, except he fear my resentment and adjudge the bag to be mine.'

"When the Cadi heard what I and the Kurd avouched, he was confounded and said, 'I see ye are none other than two pestilent atheistical fellows, who make sport of Cadis and magistrates and stand not in fear of reproach. Never did any tell or hear tell of aught more extraordinary than that which ye pretend. By Allah, from China to Shejreh umm Ghailan, nor from Fars to the Soudan, nor from Wadi Numan to Khorassan, was ever heard or credited the like of what ye avouch! Is this bag a bottomless sea or the Day of Resurrection, that shall gather together the just and unjust?' Then he bade open the bag; so I opened it and behold, there was in it bread and a lemon and cheese and olives. So I threw it down before the Kurd and went away."

When the Khalif heard Ali's story, he laughed till he fell backward and made him a handsome present.

*Translated by John Payne*

# A LEAVE-TAKING

## *Algernon Charles Swinburne*

Let us go hence, my songs; she will not hear.
Let us go hence together without fear;
Keep silence now, for singing-time is over,
And over all old things and all things dear.
She loves not you nor me as all we love her.
Yea, though we sang as angels in her ear,
      She would not hear.

Let us rise up and part; she will not know.
Let us go seaward as the great winds go,
Full of blown sand and foam; what help is here?
There is no help, for all these things are so,
And all the world is bitter as a tear.
And how these things are, though ye strove to show,
      She would not know.

Let us go hence and rest; she will not love.
We gave love many dreams and days to keep,
Flowers without scent, and fruits that would not grow,
Saying, "If thou wilt, thrust in thy sickle and reap."
All is reaped now; no grass is left to mow;
And we that sowed, though all we fell on sleep,
      She would not weep.

Let us go hence and rest; she will not love.
She shall not hear us if we sing hereof,
Nor see love's ways, how sore they are and steep.
Come hence, let be, lie still; it is enough.
Love is a barren sea, bitter and deep;
And though she saw all heaven in flower above,
      She would not love.

Let us give up, go down; she will not care.
Though all the stars made gold of all the air,

And the sea moving saw before it move
One moon-flower making all the foam-flowers fair;
Though all those waves went over us, and drove
Deep down the stifling lips and drowning hair,
        She would not care.

Let us go hence, go hence; she will not see.
Sing all once more together; surely she,
She, too, remembering days and words that were,
Will turn a little toward us, sighing; but we,
We are hence, we are gone, as though we had not been there.
Nay, and though all men seeing had pity on me,
        She would not see.

## THE UNQUIET GRAVE

*Anonymous*

"The wind doth blow to-day, my love,
    And a few small drops of rain;
I never had but one true love,
    In cold grave she was lain.

"I'll do as much for my true love
    As any young man may;
I'll sit and mourn all at her grave
    For a twelvemonth and a day."

The twelvemonth and a day being up,
    The dead began to speak:
"Oh who sits weeping on my grave,
    And will not let me sleep?"

"'Tis I, my love, sits on your grave,
    And will not let you sleep;

For I crave one kiss of your clay-cold lips,
 And that is all I seek."


"You crave one kiss of my clay-cold lips;
 But my breath smells earthy strong;
If you have one kiss of my clay-cold lips,
 Your time will not be long.


"'Tis down in yonder garden green,
 Love, where we used to walk,
The finest flower that ere was seen
 Is withered to a stalk.


"The stalk is withered dry, my love,
 So will our hearts decay;
So make yourself content, my love,
 Till God calls you away."

       ॐ


# AUTUMN

## *John Clare*


The thistle down's flying, though the winds are all
  still,
On the green grass now lying, now mounting the
  hill,
The spring from the fountain now boils like a pot;
Through stones past the counting it bubbles red-
  hot.


The ground parched and cracked is like overbaked
  bread,
The greensward all wracked is, bents dried up and
  dead.

The fallow fields glitter like water indeed,
And gossamers twitter, flung from weed unto weed.

Hill tops like hot iron glitter bright in the sun,
And the rivers we're eying burn to gold as they run;
Burning hot is the ground, liquid gold is the air;
Whoever looks round sees Eternity there.

ꙮ

## "THIS IS THE KEY OF THE KINGDOM"

*Anonymous*

This is the Key of the Kingdom
In that Kingdom is a city;
In that city is a town;
In that town there is a street;
In that street there winds a lane;
In that lane there is a yard;
In that yard there is a house;
In that house there waits a room;
In that room an empty bed;
And on that bed a basket—
A Basket of Sweet Flowers:
*Of Flowers, of Flowers;*
*A Basket of Sweet Flowers.*

Flowers in a Basket;
Basket on the bed;
Bed in the chamber;
Chamber in the house;
House in the weedy yard;
Yard in the winding lane;
Lane in the broad street;
Street in the high town;
Town in the city;

City in the Kingdom—
This is the Key of the Kingdom.
*Of the Kingdom this is the Key.*

∾

# THE DONG WITH A LUMINOUS NOSE

*Edward Lear*

When awful darkness and silence reign
Over the great Gromboolian plain,
   Through the long, long wintry nights;—
When the angry breakers roar
As they beat on the rocky shore;—
   When Storm-clouds brood on the towering heights
Of the Hills of the Chankly Bore:—

Then, through the vast and gloomy dark,
There moves what seems a fiery spark,
   A lonely spark with silvery rays
   Piercing the coal-black night,—
   A Meteor strange and bright:—
Hither and thither the vision strays,
   A single lurid light.

Slowly it wanders,—pauses,—creeps,—
Anon it sparkles,—flashes and leaps;
And ever as onward it gleaming goes
A light on the Bong-tree stems it throws.
And those who watch at that midnight hour
From Hall or Terrace, or lofty Tower,
Cry, as the wild light passes along,—
    "The Dong!—the Dong!
  "The wandering Dong through the forest goes!
    "The Dong! the Dong!
  "The Dong with a luminous Nose!"

Long years ago
The Dong was happy and gay,
Till he fell in love with a Jumbly Girl
Who came to those shores one day,
For the Jumblies came in a sieve, they did,—
Landing at eve near the Zemmery Fidd
Where the Oblong Oysters grow,
And the rocks are smooth and gray.
And all the woods and the valleys rang
With the Chorus they daily and nightly sang,—
*"Far and few, far and few,*
*Are the lands where the Jumblies live;*
*Their heads are green, and their hands are blue*
*And they went to sea in a sieve."*

Happily, happily passed those days!
While the cheerful Jumblies staid;
They danced in circlets all night long,
To the plaintive pipe of the lively Dong,
In moonlight, shine, or shade.
For day and night he was always there
By the side of the Jumbly Girl so fair,
With her sky-blue hands, and her sea-green hair.
Till the morning came of that hateful day
When the Jumblies sailed in their sieve away,
And the Dong was left on the cruel shore
Gazing—gazing for evermore,—
Ever keeping his weary eyes on
That pea-green sail on the far horizon,—
Singing the Jumbly Chorus still
As he sate all day on the grassy hill,—
*"Far and few, far and few,*
*Are the lands where the Jumblies live;*
*Their heads are green, and their hands are blue,*
*And they went to sea in a sieve."*

But when the sun was low in the West,
The Dong arose and said;—
—"What little sense I once possessed

Has quite gone out of my head!"—
And since that day he wanders still
By lake and forest, marsh and hill,
Singing—"O somewhere, in valley or plain
"Might I find my Jumbly Girl again!
"For ever I'll seek by lake and shore
"Till I find my Jumbly Girl once more!"

    Playing a pipe with silvery squeaks,
    Since then his Jumbly Girl he seeks,
    And because by night he could not see,
    He gathered the bark of the Twangum Tree
        On the flowery plain that grows.
        And he wove him a wondrous Nose,—
    A Nose as strange as a Nose could be!
Of vast proportions and painted red,
And tied with cords to the back of his head.
    —In a hollow rounded space it ended
    With a luminous Lamp within suspended,
        All fenced about
        With a bandage stout
        To prevent the wind from blowing it out;—
    And with holes all round to send the light,
    In gleaming rays on the dismal night.

And now each night, and all night long,
Over those plains still roams the Dong;
And above the wail of the Chimp and Snipe
You may hear the squeak of his plaintive pipe
While ever he seeks, but seeks in vain
To meet with his Jumbly Girl again;
Lonely and wild—all night he goes,—
The Dong with a luminous Nose!
And all who watch at the midnight hour,
From Hall or Terrace, or lofty Tower,
Cry, as they trace the Meteor bright,
Moving along through the dreary night,—
    "This is the hour when forth he goes,
"The Dong with a luminous Nose!

"Yonder—over the plain he goes;
    He goes!
  "He goes;
"The Dong with a luminous Nose!"

&#8766;

## "WEEP YOU NO MORE, SAD FOUNTAINS"

*Anonymous*

Weep you no more, sad fountains;
    What need you flow so fast?
Look how the snowy mountains
    Heaven's sun doth gently waste.
      But my sun's heavenly eyes
        View not your weeping,
        That now lies sleeping
      Softly, now softly lies
        Sleeping.

Sleep is a reconciling,
    A rest that peace begets:
Doth not the sun rise smiling
    When fair at even he sets?
      Rest you then, rest, sad eyes,
        Melt not in weeping,
        While she lies sleeping
      Softly, now softly lies
        Sleeping.

&#8766;

## "WILL YOU WALK A LITTLE FASTER?"

### Lewis Carroll

"Will you walk a little faster?" said a
  whiting to a snail.
"There's a porpoise close behind us, and he's
  treading on my tail.
See how eagerly the lobsters and the turtles
  all advance!
They are waiting on the shingle—will you
  come and join the dance?
Will you, won't you, will you, won't you,
  will you join the dance?
Will you, won't you, will you, won't you,
  won't you join the dance?

"You can really have no notion how delightful
  it will be,
When they take us up and throw us, with the
  lobsters, out to sea!"
But the snail replied, "Too far, too far!" and
  gave a look askance—
Said he thanked the whiting kindly, but
  he would not join the dance.
Would not, could not, would not, could not,
  would not join the dance.
Would not, could not, would not, could not,
  could not join the dance.

"What matters it how far we go?" his scaly
  friend replied.
"There is another shore, you know, upon the
  other side.
The further off from England the nearer is to
  France—
Then turn not, pale beloved snail, but come and
  join the dance.

Will you, won't you, will you, won't you,
will you join the dance?
Will you, won't you, will you, won't you,
won't you join the dance?"

❧

# THE TWO POTS

## Aesop

An Earthen Pot, and one of Brass, standing together upon the river's brink, were both carried away by the flowing in of the tide. The Earthen Pot showed some uneasiness, as fearing he should be broken; but his companion of Brass bid him be under no apprehension, for that he would take care of him. O, replies the other, keep as far off as ever you can, I entreat you; it is you I am most afraid of: for, whether the stream dashes you against me, or me against you, I am sure to be the sufferer; and therefore I beg of you do not let us come near one another.

*Translated by Samuel Croxall*

❧

# FEATHERTOP

## A MORALIZED LEGEND

## Nathaniel Hawthorne

"Dickon," cried Mother Rigby, "a coal for my pipe!" The pipe was in the old dame's mouth, when she said these words. She had thrust it there after filling it with tobacco, but without stooping to light it at the hearth; where, indeed, there was no appearance of a fire having been kindled, that morning. Forthwith, however, as soon as the order was given, there was an intense red glow out of the bowl of the pipe, and a whiff of smoke from

Mother Rigby's lips. Whence the coal came, and how brought thither by an invisible hand, I have never been able to discover.

"Good!" quoth Mother Rigby, with a nod of her head. "Thank ye, Dickon! And now for making this scarecrow. Be within call, Dickon, in case I need you again."

The good woman had risen thus early (for, as yet, it was scarcely sunrise) in order to set about making a scarecrow, which she intended to put in the middle of her corn-patch. It was now the latter week of May, and the crows and black-birds had already discovered the little, green, rolled-up leaf of the Indian corn, just peeping out of the soil. She was determined, therefore, to contrive as lifelike a scarecrow as ever was seen, and to finish it immediately, from top to toe, so that it should begin its sentinel's duty that very morning. Now, Mother Rigby (as everybody must have heard) was one of the most cunning and potent witches in New England, and might, with very little trouble, have made a scarecrow ugly enough to frighten the minister himself. But, on this occasion, as she had awakened in an uncommonly pleasant humor, and was further dulcified by her pipe of tobacco, she resolved to produce something fine, beautiful, and splendid, rather than hideous and horrible.

"I don't want to set up a hobgoblin in my own corn-patch and almost at my own door-step," said Mother Rigby to herself, puffing out a whiff of smoke. "I could do it if I pleased; but I'm tired of doing marvellous things, and so I'll keep within the bounds of every-day business, just for variety's sake. Besides, there's no use in scaring the little children, for a mile round-about, though 'tis true I'm a witch!"

It was settled, therefore, in her own mind, that the scarecrow should represent a fine gentleman of the period, so far as the materials at hand would allow. Perhaps it may be as well to enumerate the chief of the articles that went to the composition of this figure.

The most important item of all, probably, although it made so little show, was a certain broomstick, on which Mother Rigby had taken many an airy gallop at midnight, and which now served the scarecrow by way of a spinal column, or, as the unlearned phrase it, a backbone. One of its arms was a disabled flail, which used to be wielded by Goodman Rigby, before his spouse worried him out of this troublesome world; the other, if I mistake not, was composed of the pudding-stick and a broken rung of a chair, tied loosely together at the elbow. As for its legs, the right was a hoe-handle, and the left, an undistinguished and miscellaneous stick from the wood-pile. Its lungs, stomach, and other affairs of that kind, were nothing better than a meal-bag stuffed with straw. Thus, we have made out the skeleton and entire corporosity of the scarecrow, with the exception of its head; and this was admirably supplied by a somewhat withered and shrivelled pumpkin in which Mother Rigby cut two holes for the eyes and a slit for the mouth, leaving a bluish-colored knob, in the middle, to pass for a nose. It was really quite a respectable face.

"I've seen worse ones on human shoulders, at any rate," said Mother Rigby. "And many a fine gentleman has a pumpkin-head, as well as my scarecrow!"

But the clothes, in this case, were to be the making of the man. So the good old woman took down from a peg an ancient plum-colored coat, of London make, and with relics of embroidery on its seams, cuffs, pocket-flaps, and button-holes, but lamentably worn and faded, patched at the elbows, tattered at the skirts, and threadbare all over. On the left breast was a round hole, whence either a star of nobility had been rent away, or else the hot heart of some former wearer had scorched it through and through. The neighbors said, that this rich garment belonged to the Black Man's wardrobe, and that he kept it at Mother Rigby's cottage for the convenience of slipping it on, whenever he wished to make a grand appearance at the governor's table. To match the coat, there was a velvet waistcoat of very ample size, and formerly embroidered with foliage, that had been as brightly golden as the maple-leaves in October, but which had now quite vanished out of the substance of the velvet. Next came a pair of scarlet breeches, once worn by the French governor of Louisbourg, and the knees of which had touched the lower step of the throne of Louis le Grand. The Frenchman had given these small-clothes to an Indian powwow, who parted with them to the old witch for a gill of strong-waters, at one of their dances in the forest. Furthermore, Mother Rigby produced a pair of silk stockings and put them on the figure's legs, where they showed as unsubstantial as a dream, with the wooden reality of the two sticks making itself miserably apparent through the holes. Lastly, she put her dead husband's wig on the bare scalp of the pumpkin, and surmounted the whole with a rusty three-cornered hat, in which was stuck the longest tail-feather of a rooster.

Then the old dame stood the figure up in a corner of her cottage, and chuckled to behold its yellow semblance of a visage, with its knobby little nose thrust into the air. It had a strangely self-satisfied aspect, and seemed to say—"Come look at me!"

"And you are well worth looking at—that's a fact!" quoth Mother Rigby, in admiration at her own handiwork. "I've made many a puppet, since I've been a witch; but methinks this is the finest of them all. 'Tis almost too good for a scarecrow. And, by the by, I'll just fill a fresh pipe of tobacco, and then take him out to the corn-patch."

While filling her pipe, the old woman continued to gaze with almost motherly affection at the figure in the corner. To say the truth—whether it were chance, or skill, or downright witchcraft—there was something wonderfully human in this ridiculous shape, bedizened with its tattered finery; and as for the countenance, it appeared to shrivel its yellow surface into a grin—a funny kind of expression, betwixt scorn and merriment, as if it understood itself to be a jest at mankind. The more Mother Rigby looked, the better she was pleased.

"Dickon," cried she, sharply, "another coal for my pipe!"

Hardly had she spoken, than, just as before, there was a red glowing coal on the top of the tobacco. She drew in a long whiff, and puffed it forth again into the bar of morning sunshine, which struggled through the one dusty pane of her cottage window. Mother Rigby always liked to flavor her pipe with a coal of fire from the particular chimney-corner, whence this had been brought. But where that chimney-corner might be, or who brought the coal from it—further than that the invisible messenger seemed to respond to the name of Dickon—I cannot tell.

"That puppet yonder," thought Mother Rigby, still with her eyes fixed on the scarecrow, "is too good a piece of work to stand all summer in a corn-patch, frightening away the crows and blackbirds. He's capable of better things. Why, I've danced with a worse one, when partners happened to be scarce, at our witch meetings in the forest! What if I should let him take his chance among the other men of straw and empty fellows, who go bustling about the world?"

The old witch took three or four more whiffs of her pipe, and smiled.

"He'll meet plenty of his brethren, at every street-corner!" continued she. "Well; I didn't mean to dabble in witchcraft to-day, further than the lighting of my pipe; but a witch I am, and a witch I'm likely to be, and there's no use trying to shirk it. I'll make a man of my scarecrow, were it only for the joke's sake!"

While muttering these words, Mother Rigby took the pipe from her own mouth, and thrust it into the crevice which represented the same feature in the pumpkin-visage of the scarecrow.

"Puff, darling, puff!" said she. "Puff away, my fine fellow! Your life depends on it!"

This was a strange exhortation, undoubtedly, to be addressed to a mere thing of sticks, straw, and old clothes, with nothing better than a shrivelled pumpkin for a head; as we know to have been the scarecrow's case.

Nevertheless, as we must carefully hold in remembrance, Mother Rigby was a witch of singular power and dexterity; and, keeping this fact duly before our minds, we shall see nothing beyond credibility in the remarkable incidents of our story. Indeed, the great difficulty will be at once got over, if we can only bring ourselves to believe, that, as soon as the old dame bade him puff, there came a whiff of smoke from the scarecrow's mouth. It was the very feeblest of whiffs, to be sure; but it was followed by another and another, each more decided than the preceding one.

"Puff away, my pet! Puff away, pretty one!" Mother Rigby kept repeating, with her pleasantest smile. "It is the breath of life to ye; and that you may take my word for!"

Beyond all question, the pipe was bewitched. There must have been a spell, either in the tobacco, or in the fiercely glowing coal that so mysteriously burned on top of it, or in the pungently aromatic smoke, which exhaled from the kindled weed. The figure, after a few doubtful attempts, at length blew forth a volley of smoke, extending all the way from the obscure corner into the bar of sunshine. There it eddied and melted away among the motes of dust. It seemed a convulsive effort; for the two or three next whiffs were fainter, although the coal still glowed, and threw a gleam over the scarecrow's visage. The old witch clapt her skinny palms together, and smiled encouragingly upon her handiwork. She saw that the charm worked well. The shrivelled, yellow face, which heretofore had been no face at all, had already a thin, fantastic haze, as it were, of human likeness, shifting to-and-fro across it; sometimes vanishing entirely, but growing more perceptible than ever, with the next whiff from the pipe. The whole figure, in like manner, assumed a show of life, such as we impart to ill-defined shapes among the clouds, and half-deceive ourselves with the pastime of our own fancy.

If we must needs pry closely into the matter, it may be doubted whether there was any real change, after all, in the sordid, worn-out, worthless, and ill-joined substance of the scarecrow; but merely a spectral illusion, and a cunning effect of light and shade, so colored and contrived as to delude the eyes of most men. The miracles of witchcraft seem always to have had a very shallow subtlety; and, at least, if the above explanation do not hit the truth of the process, I can suggest no better.

"Well puffed, my pretty lad!" still cried old Mother Rigby. "Come; another good, stout whiff; and let it be with might and main! Puff for thy life, I tell thee! Puff out of the very bottom of thy heart; if any heart thou hast, or any bottom to it! Well done, again! Thou didst suck in that mouthfull, as if for the pure love of it."

And then the witch beckoned to the scarecrow, throwing so much magnetic potency into her gesture, that it seemed as if it must inevitably be obeyed, like the mystic call of the load-stone, when it summons the iron.

"Why lurkest thou in the corner, lazy one?" said she. "Step forth! Thou hast the world before thee!"

Upon my word, if the legend were not one which I heard on my grandmother's knee, and which had established its place among things credible before my childish judgment could analyze its probability, I question whether I should have the face to tell it now!

In obedience to Mother Rigby's word, and extending its arm as if to reach her outstretched hand, the figure made a step forward—a kind of hitch and jerk, however, rather than a step—then tottered, and almost lost its balance. What could the witch expect? It was nothing, after all, but a scarecrow, stuck upon two sticks. But the strong-willed old beldam scowled, and beckoned, and flung the energy of her purpose so forcibly at this poor combination of rotten wood, and musty straw, and ragged garments, that it was compelled to show itself a man, in spite of the reality of things. So it stept into the bar of sunshine. There it stood—poor devil of a contrivance that it was!—with only the thinnest vesture of human similitude about it, through which was evident the stiff, ricketty, incongruous, faded, tattered, good-for-nothing patchwork of its substance, ready to sink in a heap upon the floor, as conscious of its own unworthiness to be erect. Shall I confess the truth? At its present point of vivification, the scarecrow reminds me of some of the lukewarm and abortive characters, composed of heterogeneous materials, used for the thousandth time, and never worth using, with which romance-writers (and myself, no doubt, among the rest) have so over-peopled the world of fiction.

But the fierce old hag began to get angry and show a glimpse of her diabolic nature (like a snake's head peeping with a hiss out of her bosom) at this pusillanimous behavior of the thing, which she had taken the trouble to put together.

"Puff away, wretch!" cried she wrathfully. "Puff, puff, puff, thou thing of straw and emptiness!—thou rag or two!—thou meal bag!—thou pumpkin-head!—thou nothing!—where shall I find a name vile enough to call thee by! Puff, I say, and suck in thy fantastic life along with the smoke; else I snatch the pipe from thy mouth, and hurl thee where that red coal came from!"

Thus threatened, the unhappy scarecrow had nothing for it, but to puff away for dear life. As need was, therefore, it applied itself lustily to the pipe, and sent forth such abundant vollies of tobacco-smoke that the small cottage-kitchen became all vaporous. The one sunbeam struggled mistily through, and could but imperfectly define the image of the cracked and dusty window-pane on the opposite wall. Mother Rigby, meanwhile, with one brown arm akimbo and the other stretched towards the figure, loomed grimly amid the obscurity, with such port and expression as when she was wont to heave a ponderous nightmare on her victims, and stand at the bed-side to enjoy their agony. In fear and trembling did this poor scarecrow puff. But its efforts, it must be acknowledged, served an excellent purpose; for, with each successive whiff, the figure lost more and more of its dizzy and perplexing tenuity, and seemed to take denser substance. Its very garments, moreover, partook of the magical change, and shone with the gloss of novelty, and glistened with the skilfully embroidered gold that had long ago been rent away. And, half-revealed among the smoke, a yellow visage bent its lustreless eyes on Mother Rigby.

At last, the old witch clenched her fist, and shook it at the figure. Not that she was positively angry, but merely acting on the principle—perhaps untrue, or not the only truth, though as high a one as Mother Rigby could be expected to attain—that feeble and torpid natures, being incapable of better inspiration, must be stirred up by fear. But, here was the crisis. Should she fail in what she now sought to effect, it was her ruthless purpose to scatter the miserable simulacre into its original elements.

"Thou hast a man's aspect," said she sternly. "Have also the echo and mockery of a voice! I bid thee speak!"

The scarecrow gasped, struggled, and at length emitted a murmur, which was so incorporated with its smoky breath that you could scarcely tell whether it were indeed a voice, or only a whiff of tobacco. Some narrators of this legend hold the opinion, that Mother Rigby's conjurations, and the fierceness of her will, had compelled a familiar spirit into the figure, and that the voice was his.

"Mother," mumbled the poor, stifled voice, "be not so awful with me! I would fain speak; but being without wits, what can I say?"

"Thou canst speak, darling, canst thou?" cried Mother Rigby, relaxing her grim countenance into a smile. "And what shalt thou say, quoth-a! Say, indeed! Art thou of the brotherhood of the empty skull, and demandest of me what thou shalt say? Thou shalt say a thousand things, and saying them a thousand times over, thou shalt still have said nothing! Be not afraid, I tell thee! When thou comest into the world (whither I purpose sending thee, forthwith) thou shalt not lack the wherewithal to talk. Talk! Why, thou shalt babble like a mill-stream, if thou wilt. Thou hast brains enough for that, I trow!"

"At your service, mother," responded the figure.

"And was well said, my pretty one!" answered Mother Rigby. "Then thou spakest like thyself, and meant nothing. Thou shalt have a hundred such set phrases, and five hundred to the boot of them. And now, darling I have taken so much pains with thee, and thou art so beautiful, that, by my troth, I love thee better than my witch's puppet in the world; and I've made them of all sorts—clay, wax, straw, sticks, night-fog, morning-mist, sea-foam, and chimney-smoke! But thou art the very best. So give heed to what I say!"

"Yes, kind mother," said the figure, "with all my heart!"

"With all thy heart!" cried the old witch, setting her hands to her sides, and laughing loudly. "Thou hast such a pretty way of speaking! With all thy heart! And thou didst put thy hand to the left side of thy waistcoat, as if thou really hadst one!"

So now, in high good-humor with this fantastic contrivance of hers, Mother Rigby told the scarecrow that it must go and play its part in the great world, where not one man in a hundred, she affirmed, was gifted with more real substance than itself. And, that he might hold up his head with the best of them, she endowed him, on the spot, with an unreckonable amount of wealth. It consisted partly of a gold mine in Eldorado, and of ten thousand shares in a broken bubble, and of half a million acres of vineyard at the North pole, and of a castle in the air and a chateau in Spain, together with all the rents and income therefrom accruing. She further made over to him the cargo of a certain ship, laden with salt of Cadiz, which she herself, by her necromantic arts, had caused to founder, ten years before, in the deepest of mid-ocean. If the salt were not dissolved, and could be brought to market, it would fetch a pretty penny among the fishermen. That he might not lack ready money, she gave him a copper farthing, of Birmingham manufacture, being all the coin she had about her, and likewise a great deal of brass, which she applied to his forehead, thus making it yellower than ever.

"With that brass alone," quoth Mother Rigby, "thou canst pay thy way all over the earth. Kiss me, pretty darling! I have done my best for thee."

Furthermore, that the adventurer might lack no possible advantage towards a fair start in life, this excellent old dame gave him a token, by which he was to introduce himself to a certain magistrate, member of the council, merchant, and elder of the church (the four capacities constituting but one man) who stood at the head of society in the neighboring metropolis. The token was neither more nor less than a single word, which Mother Rigby whispered to the scarecrow, and which the scarecrow was to whisper to the merchant.

"Gouty as the old fellow is, he'll run thy errands for thee, when once thou hast given him that word in his ear," said the old witch. "Mother Rigby knows the worshipful Justice Gookin, and the worshipful justice knows Mother Rigby!"

Here the witch thrust her wrinkled face close to the puppet's, chuckling irrepressibly, and fidgetting all through her system, with delight at the idea which she meant to communicate.

"The worshipful Master Gookin," whispered she, "hath a comely maiden to his daughter! And hark ye, my pet! Thou hast a fair outside, and a pretty wit enough of thine own. Yea; a pretty wit enough! Thou wilt think better of it, when thou hast seen more of other people's wits. Now, with thy outside and thy inside, thou art the very man to win a young girl's heart. Never doubt it! I tell thee it shall be so. Put but a bold face on the matter, sigh, smile, flourish thy hat, thrust forth thy leg like a dancing-master, put thy right hand to the left side of thy waistcoat—and pretty Polly Gookin is thine own!"

All this while, the new creature had been sucking in and exhaling the vapory fragrance of his pipe, and seemed now to continue this occupation as much for the enjoyment which it afforded, as because it was an essential condition of his existence. It was wonderful to see how exceedingly like a human being it behaved. Its eyes (for it appeared to possess a pair) were bent on Mother Rigby, and at suitable junctures, it nodded or shook its head. Neither did it lack words proper for the occasion—"Really! Indeed! Pray tell me! Is it possible! Upon my word! By no means! Oh! Ah! Hem!"—and other such weighty utterances as imply attention, inquiry, acquiescence, or dissent, on the part of the auditor. Even had you stood by, and seen the scarecrow made, you could scarcely have resisted the conviction that it perfectly understood the cunning counsels, which the old witch poured into its counterfeit of an ear. The more earnestly it applied its lips to the pipe, the more distinctly was its human likeness stamped among visible realities; the more sagacious grew its expression; the more lifelike its gestures and movements, and the more intelligibly audible its voice. Its garments, too, glistened so much the brighter with an illusory magnificence. The very pipe, in which burned the spell of all this wonderwork, ceased to appear as a smoke-blackened earthen stump, and became a meerschaum, with painted bowl and amber mouth-piece.

It might be apprehended, however, that, as the life of the illusion seemed identical with the vapor of the pipe, it would terminate simultaneously with the reduction of the tobacco to ashes. But the beldam foresaw the difficulty.

"Hold thou the pipe, my precious one," said she, "while I fill it for thee again."

It was sorrowful to behold how the fine gentleman began to fade back into a scarecrow, while Mother Rigby shook the ashes out of the pipe, and proceeded to replenish it from her tobacco-box.

"Dickon," cried she, in her high, sharp tone, "another coal for this pipe!"

No sooner said than the intensely red speck of fire was glowing within the pipe-bowl; and the scarecrow, without waiting for the witch's bidding, applied the tube to its lips, and drew in a few short, convulsive whiffs, which soon, however, became regular and equable.

"Now, mine own heart's darling," quoth Mother Rigby, "whatever may happen to thee, thou must stick to thy pipe. Thy life is in it; and that, at least, thou knowest well, if thou knowest naught besides. Stick to thy pipe, I say! Smoke, puff, blow thy cloud; and tell the people, if any question be made, that it is for thy health, and that so the physician orders thee to do. And, sweet one, when thou shalt find thy pipe getting low, go apart into some corner, and (first filling thyself with smoke) cry sharply—'Dickon, a fresh pipe of tobacco!' and—'Dickon, another coal for my pipe!'—and have it into thy pretty mouth, as speedily as may be. Else, instead of a gallant gentleman in a gold-laced coat, thou wilt be but a jumble of sticks, and tattered clothes, and a bag of straw, and a withered pumpkin! Now depart, my treasure, and good luck go with thee!"

"Never fear, mother!" said the figure, in a stout voice, and sending forth a courageous whiff of smoke. "I will thrive, if an honest man and a gentleman may!"

"Oh, thou wilt be the death of me!" cried the old witch, convulsed with laughter. "That was well said! If an honest man and a gentleman may! Thou playest thy part to perfection. Get along with thee for a smart fellow; and I will wager on thy head, as a man of pith and substance, with a brain, and what they call a heart, and all else that a man should have, against any other thing on two legs. I hold myself a better witch than yesterday, for thy sake. Did not I make thee? And I defy any witch in New England to make such another! Here; take my staff along with thee!"

The staff, though it was but a plain oaken stick, immediately took the aspect of a gold-headed cane.

"That gold-head has as much sense in it as thine own," said Mother Rigby, "and it will guide thee straight to worshipful Master Gookin's door. Get thee gone, my pretty pet, my darling, my precious one, my treasure; and if any ask thy name, it is Feathertop. For thou hast a feather in thy hat, and I have thrust a handfull of feathers into the hollow of thy head, and thy wig, too, is of the fashion they call Feathertop—so be Feathertop thy name!"

And, issuing from the cottage, Feathertop strode manfully towards town. Mother Rigby stood at the threshold, well pleased to see how the sunbeams glistened on him, as if all his magnificence were real, and how diligently and lovingly he smoked his pipe, and how handsomely he walked, in spite of a little stiffness of his legs. She watched him, until out of sight, and threw a witch-benediction after her darling, when a turn of the road snatched him from her view.

Betimes in the forenoon, when the principal street of the neighboring town was just at its acme of life and bustle, a stranger of very distinguished figure was seen on the side-walk. His port, as well as his garments, betokened nothing short of nobility. He wore a richly embroidered plum-colored coat, a waistcoat of costly velvet, magnificently adorned with golden foliage, a pair of splendid scarlet breeches, and the finest and glossiest of white silk stockings. His head was covered with a peruque, so daintily powdered and adjusted that it would have been sacrilege to disorder it with a hat; which, therefore (and it was a gold-laced hat, set off with a snowy feather) he carried beneath his arm. On the breast of his coat glistened a star. He managed his gold-headed cane with an airy grace, peculiar to the fine gentleman of the period; and, to give the highest possible finish to his equipment, he had lace ruffles at his wrists, of a most ethereal delicacy, sufficiently avouching how idle and aristocratic must be the hands which they half concealed.

It was a remarkable point in the accoutrement of this brilliant personage, that he held in his left hand a fantastic kind of a pipe, with an exquisitely painted bowl, and an amber mouth-piece. This he applied to his lips, as often as every five or six paces, and inhaled a deep whiff of smoke, which, after being retained a moment in his lungs, might be seen to eddy gracefully from his mouth and nostrils.

As may well be supposed, the street was all a-stir to find out the stranger's name.

"It is some great nobleman, beyond question," said one of the townspeople. "Do you see the star at his breast?"

"Nay; it is too bright to be seen," said another. "Yes; he must needs be a nobleman, as you say. But, by what conveyance, think you, can his lordship have voyaged or travelled hither? There has been no vessel from the old country for a month past; and if he have arrived overland from the southward, pray where are his attendants and equipage?"

"He needs no equipage to set off his rank," remarked a third. "If he came among us in rags, nobility would shine through a hole in his elbow. I never saw such dignity of aspect. He has the old Norman blood in his veins, I warrant him!"

"I rather take him to be a Dutchman, or one of your High Germans," said another citizen. "The men of those countries have always the pipe at their mouths."

"And so has a Turk," answered his companion. "But, in my judgment, this stranger hath been bred at the French court, and hath there learned politeness and grace of manner, which none understand so well as the nobility of France. That gait, now! A vulgar spectator might deem it stiff—he might call it a hitch and jerk—but, to my eye, it hath an unspeakable majesty, and must have been acquired by constant observation of the deportment of the Grand Monarque. The stranger's character and office are evident enough. He is a French ambassador, come to treat with our rulers about the cession of Canada."

"More probably a Spaniard," said another, "and hence his yellow complexion. Or, most likely, he is from the Havana, or from some port on the Spanish Main, and comes to make investigation about the piracies which our Governor is thought to connive at. Those settlers in Peru and Mexico have skins as yellow as the gold which they dig out of their mines."

"Yellow or not," cried a lady, "he is a beautiful man!—so tall—so slender!—such a fine, noble face, with so well-shaped a nose, and all that delicacy of expression about the mouth! And, bless me, how bright his star is! It positively shoots out flames!"

"So do your eyes, fair lady!" said the stranger, with a bow, and a flourish of his pipe; for he was just passing at the instant. "Upon my honor, they have quite dazzled me!"

"Was ever so original and exquisite a compliment?" murmured the lady, in an ecstasy of delight.

Amid the general admiration, excited by the stranger's appearance, there were only two dissenting voices. One was that of an impertinent cur, which, after snuffing at the heels of the glistening figure, put its tail between its legs and skulked into its master's back-yard, vociferating an execrable howl. The other dissentient was a young child, who squalled at the fullest stretch of his lungs, and babbled some unintelligible nonsense about a pumpkin.

Feathertop, meanwhile, pursued his way along the street. Except for the few complimentary words to the lady, and, now and then, a slight inclination of the head, in requital of the profound reverences of the by-standers, he seemed wholly absorbed in his pipe. There needed no other proof of his rank and consequence, than the perfect equanimity with which he comported himself, while the curiosity and admiration of the town swelled almost into clamor around him. With a crowd still gathering behind his footsteps, he finally reached the mansion-house of the worshipful Justice Gookin, entered the gate, ascended the steps of the front-door, and knocked. In the interim, before his summons was answered, the stranger was observed to shake the ashes out of his pipe.

"What did he say, in that sharp voice?" inquired one of the spectators.

"Nay, I know not," answered his friend. "But the sun dazzles my eyes strangely! How dim and faded his lordship looks, all of a sudden! Bless my wits, what is the matter with me!"

"The wonder is," said the other, "that his pipe (which was out only an instant ago) should be all a-light again, and with the reddest coal I ever saw! There is something mysterious about this stranger. What a whiff of smoke was that! Dim and faded, do you call him? Why, as he turns about, the star on his breast is all a-blaze."

"It is, indeed," said his companion; "and it will go near to dazzle pretty Polly Gookin, whom I see peeping at it out of the chamber-window."

The door being now opened, Feathertop turned to the crowd, made a stately bend of his body, like a great man acknowledging the reverence of the meaner sort, and vanished into the house. There was a mysterious kind of a smile, if it might not better be called a grin or grimace, upon his visage; but of all the throng that beheld him, not an individual appears to have possessed insight enough to detect the illusive character of the stranger, except a little child and a cur-dog.

Our legend here loses somewhat of its continuity, and, passing over the preliminary explanation between Feathertop and the merchant, goes in quest of the pretty Polly Gookin. She was a damsel of a soft, round figure, with light hair and blue eyes, and a fair rosy face, which seemed neither very shrewd nor very simple. This young lady had caught a glimpse of the glistening stranger, while standing at the threshold, and had forthwith put on a laced cap, a string of beads, her finest kerchief, and her stiffest damask petticoat, in preparation for the interview. Hurrying from her chamber to the parlor, she had ever since been viewing herself in the large looking-glass, and practising pretty airs—now a smile, now a ceremonious dignity of aspect, and now a softer smile than the former—kissing her hand, likewise, tossing her head, and managing her fan; while, within the mirror, an unsubstantial little maid repeated every gesture, and did all the foolish things that Polly did, but without making her ashamed of them. In short, it was the fault of pretty Polly's ability, rather than her will, if she failed to be as complete an artifice as the illustrious Feathertop himself; and when she thus tampered with her own simplicity, the witch's phantom might well hope to win her.

No sooner did Polly hear her father's gouty footsteps approaching the parlor-door, accompanied with the stiff clatter of Feathertop's high-heeled shoes, than she seated herself bolt upright, and innocently began warbling a song.

"Polly! Daughter Polly!" cried the old merchant. "Come hither, child!"

Master Gookin's aspect, as he opened the door, was doubtful and troubled.

"This gentleman," continued he, presenting the stranger, "is the Chevalier Feathertop—nay, I beg his pardon, my Lord Feathertop!—who hath brought me a token of remembrance from an ancient friend of mine. Pay your duty to his lordship, child, and honor him as his quality deserves."

After these few words of introduction, the worshipful magistrate immediately quitted the room. But, even in that brief moment (had the fair Polly glanced aside at her father, instead of devoting herself wholly to the brilliant guest) she might have taken warning of some mischief nigh at hand. The old man was nervous, fidgety, and very pale. Purposing a smile of courtesy, he had deformed his face with a sort of galvanic grin, which, when Feathertop's back was turned, he exchanged for a scowl; at the same time shaking his fist, and stamping his gouty foot—an incivility which brought its retribution along with it. The truth appears to have been, that Mother Rigby's word of introduction, whatever it might be, had operated far more on the rich merchant's fears, than on his good-will. Moreover, being a man of wonderfully acute observation, he had noticed that the painted figures, on the bowl of Feathertop's pipe, were in motion. Looking more closely, he became convinced, that these figures were a party of little demons, each duly provided with horns and a tail, and dancing hand in hand, with gestures of diabolical merriment, round the circumference of the pipe-bowl. As if to confirm his suspicions, while Master Gookin ushered his guest along a dusky passage, from his private room to the parlor, the star on Feathertop's breast had scintillated actual flames, and threw a flickering gleam upon the wall, the ceiling, and the floor.

With such sinister prognostics manifesting themselves on all hands, it is not to be marvelled at that the merchant should have felt that he was committing his daughter to a very questionable acquaintance. He cursed, in his secret soul, the insinuating elegance of Feathertop's manners, as this brilliant personage bowed, smiled, put his hand on his heart, inhaled a long whiff from his pipe, and enriched the atmosphere with the smoky vapor of a fragrant and visible sigh. Gladly would poor Master Gookin have thrust his dangerous guest into the street. But there was a constraint and terror within him. This respectable old gentleman, we fear, at an earlier period of life, had given some pledge or other to the Evil Principle, and perhaps was now to redeem it by the sacrifice of his daughter.

It so happened that the parlor-door was partly of glass, shaded by a silken curtain, the folds of which hung a little awry. So strong was the merchant's interest in witnessing what was to ensue between the fair Polly and the gallant Feathertop, that, after quitting the room, he could by no means refrain from peeping through the crevice of the curtain.

But there was nothing very miraculous to be seen; nothing—except the trifles previously noticed—to confirm the idea of a supernatural peril, environing the pretty Polly. The stranger, it is true, was evidently a thorough and practised man of the world, systematic and self-possessed, and therefore the sort of person to whom a parent ought not to confide a simple young girl, without due watchfulness for the result. The worthy magistrate, who had been conversant with all degrees and qualities of mankind, could not but perceive that every motion and gesture of the distinguished Feathertop came in its proper place; nothing had been left rude or native in him; a well-digested conventionalism had incorporated itself thoroughly with his substance, and transformed him into a work of art. Perhaps it was this peculiarity that invested him with a species of ghastliness and awe. It is the effect of anything completely and consummately artificial, in human shape, that the person impresses us as an unreality, and as having hardly pith enough to cast a shadow upon the floor. As regarded Feathertop, all this resulted in a wild, extravagant, and fantastical impression, as if his life and being were akin to the smoke that curled upward from his pipe.

But pretty Polly Gookin felt not thus. The pair were now promenading the room; Feathertop with his dainty stride, and no less dainty grimace; the girl with a native maidenly grace, just touched, not spoiled, by a slightly affected manner, which seemed caught from the perfect artifice of her companion. The longer the interview continued, the more charmed was pretty Polly, until, within the first quarter of an hour (as the old magistrate noted by his watch) she was evidently beginning to be in love. Nor need it have been witchcraft that subdued her in such a hurry; the poor child's heart, it may be, was so very fervent, that it melted her with its own warmth, as reflected from the hollow semblance of a lover. No matter what Feathertop said, his words found depth and reverberation in her ear; no matter what he did, his action was heroic to her eye. And, by this time, it is to be supposed, there was a blush on Polly's cheek, a tender smile about her mouth, and a liquid softness in her glance; while the star kept coruscating on Feathertop's breast, and the little demons careered, with more frantic merriment than ever, about the circumference of his pipe-bowl. Oh, pretty Polly Gookin, why should these imps rejoice so madly that a silly maiden's heart was about to be given to a shadow! Is it so unusual a misfortune?— so rare a triumph?

By and by, Feathertop paused, and throwing himself into an imposing attitude, seemed to summon the fair girl to survey his figure, and resist him longer, if she could. His star, his embroidery, his buckles, glowed, at that instant, with unutterable splendor; the picturesque hues of his attire took a richer depth of coloring; there was a gleam and polish over his whole presence, betokening the perfect witchery of well-ordered manners. The maiden raised her eyes, and suffered them to linger upon her companion with a bashful and admiring gaze. Then, as if desirous of judging what value her own simple comeliness might have, side by side with so much brilliancy, she cast a glance towards the full-length looking-glass, in front of which they happened to be standing. It was one of the truest plates in the world, and incapable of flattery. No sooner did the images, therein reflected, meet Polly's eye, than she shrieked, shrank from the stranger's side, gazed at him, for a moment, in the wildest dismay, and sank insensible upon the floor. Feathertop, likewise, had looked towards the mirror, and there beheld, not the glittering mockery of his outside show, but a picture of the sordid patchwork of his real composition, stript of all witchcraft.

The wretched simulacrum! We almost pity him. He threw up his arms, with an expression of despair, that went farther than any of his previous manifestations, towards vindicating his claims to be reckoned human. For perchance the only time, since this so often empty and deceptive life of mortals began its course, an Illusion had seen and fully recognized itself.

Mother Rigby was seated by her kitchen-hearth, in the twilight of this eventful day, and had just shaken the ashes out of a new pipe, when she heard a hurried tramp along the road. Yet it did not seem so much the tramp of human footsteps, as the clatter of sticks or the rattling of dry bones.

"Ha!" thought the old witch. "What step is that? Whose skeleton is out of its grave now, I wonder!"

A figure burst headlong into the cottage-door. It was Feathertop! His pipe was still a-light; the star still flamed upon his breast; the embroidery still glowed upon his garments; nor had he lost, in any degree or manner that could be estimated, the aspect that assimilated him with our mortal-brotherhood. But yet, in some indescribable way (as is the case with all that has deluded us, when once found out) the poor reality was felt beneath the cunning artifice.

"What has gone wrong?" demanded the witch. "Did yonder snuffling hypocrite thrust my darling from his door? The villain! I'll set twenty fiends to torment him, till he offer thee his daughter on his bended knees!"

"No, mother," said Feathertop despondingly, "it was not that!"

"Did the girl scorn my precious one?" asked Mother Rigby, her fierce eyes glowing like two coals of Tophet. "I'll cover her face with pimples! Her nose shall be as red as the coal in thy pipe! Her front teeth shall drop out! In a week hence, she shall not be worth thy having!"

"Let her alone, mother!" answered poor Feathertop. "The girl was half-won; and methinks a kiss from her sweet lips might have made me altogether human! But," he added, after a brief pause, and then a howl of self-contempt, "I've seen myself, mother!—I've seen myself for the wretched, ragged, empty thing I am! I'll exist no longer!"

Snatching the pipe from his mouth, he flung it with all his might against the chimney, and, at the same instant, sank upon the floor, a medley of straw and tattered garments, with some sticks protruding from the heap; and a shrivelled pumpkin in the midst. The eye-holes were now lustreless; but the rudely-carved gap, that just before had been a mouth, still seemed to twist itself into a despairing grin, and was so far human.

"Poor fellow!" quoth Mother Rigby, with a rueful glance at the relics of her ill-fated contrivance. "My poor, dear, pretty Feathertop! There are thousands upon thousands of coxcombs and charlatans in the world, made up of just such a jumble of worn-out, forgotten, and good-for-nothing trash, as he was! Yet they live in fair repute, and never see themselves for what they are! And why should my poor puppet be the only one to know himself, and perish for it?"

While thus muttering, the witch had filled a fresh pipe of tobacco, and held the stem between her fingers, as doubtful whether to thrust it into her own mouth or Feathertop's.

"Poor Feathertop!" she continued. "I could easily give him another chance, and send him forth again to-morrow. But, no! his feelings are too tender; his sensibilities too deep. He seems to have too much heart to bustle for his own advantage, in such an empty and heartless world. Well, well! I'll make a scarecrow of him, after all. 'Tis an innocent and a useful vocation, and will suit my darling well; and if each of his human brethren had as fit a one, 'twould be the better for mankind; and as for this pipe of tobacco, I need it more than he!"

So saying, Mother Rigby put the stem between her lips. "Dickon!" cried she, in her high, sharp tone, "another coal for my pipe!"

∽

# THE RECESSIONAL

## Saki

Clovis sat in the hottest zone but two of a Turkish bath, alternately inert in statuesque contemplation and rapidly manœuvring a fountain-pen over the pages of a note-book.

"Don't interrupt me with your childish prattle," he observed to Bertie van Tahn, who had slung himself languidly into a neighbouring chair and looked conversationally inclined; "I'm writing deathless verse."

Bertie looked interested.

"I say, what a boon you would be to portrait painters if you really got to be notorious as a poetry writer. If they couldn't get your likeness hung in the Academy as 'Clovis Sangrail, Esq., at work on his latest poem,' they could slip you in as a Study of the Nude or Orpheus descending into Jermyn Street. They always complain that modern dress handicaps them, whereas a towel and a fountain-pen—"

"It was Mrs. Packletide's suggestion that I should write this thing," said Clovis, ignoring the bypaths to fame that Bertie van Tahn was pointing out to him. "You see, Loona Bimberton had a Coronation Ode accepted by the *New Infancy,* a paper that has been started with the idea of making the *New Age* seem elderly and hidebound. 'So clever of you, dear Loona,' the Packletide remarked when she had read it; 'of course, any one could write a Coronation Ode, but no one else would have thought of doing it.' Loona protested that these things were extremely difficult to do, and gave us to understand that they were more or less the province of a gifted few. Now the Packletide has been rather decent to me in many ways, a sort of financial ambulance, you know, that carries you off the field when you're hard hit, which is a frequent occurrence with me, and I've no use whatever for Loona Bimberton, so I chipped in and said I could turn out that sort of stuff by the square yard if I gave my mind to it. Loona said

I couldn't, and we got bets on, and between you and me I think the money's fairly safe. Of course, one of the conditions of the wager is that the thing has to be published in something or other, local newspapers barred; but Mrs. Packletide has endeared herself by many little acts of thoughtfulness to the editor of the *Smoky Chimney,* so if I can hammer out anything at all approaching the level of the usual Ode output we ought to be all right. So far I'm getting along so comfortably that I begin to be afraid that I must be one of the gifted few."

"It's rather late in the day for a Coronation Ode, isn't it?" said Bertie.

"Of course," said Clovis; "this is going to be a Durbar Recessional, the sort of thing that you can keep by you for all time if you want to."

"Now I understand your choice of a place to write it in," said Bertie van Tahn, with the air of one who has suddenly unravelled a hitherto obscure problem; "you want to get the local temperature."

"I came here to get freedom from the inane interruptions of the mentally deficient," said Clovis, "but it seems I asked too much of fate."

Bertie van Tahn prepared to use his towel as a weapon of precision, but reflecting that he had a good deal of unprotected coast-line himself, and that Clovis was equipped with a fountain-pen as well as a towel, he relapsed pacifically into the depths of his chair.

"May one hear extracts from the immortal work?" he asked. "I promise that nothing that I hear now shall prejudice me against borrowing a copy of the *Smoky Chimney* at the right moment."

"It's rather like casting pearls into a trough," remarked Clovis pleasantly, "but I don't mind reading you bits of it. It begins with a general dispersal of the Durbar participants:

> " 'Back to their homes in Himalayan heights
> The stale pale elephants of Cutch Behar
> Roll like great galleons on a tideless sea—' "

"I don't believe Cutch Behar is anywhere near the Himalayan region," interrupted Bertie. "You ought to have an atlas on hand when you do this sort of thing; and why stale and pale?"

"After the late hours and the excitement, of course," said Clovis; "and I said their *homes* were in the Himalayas. You can have Himalayan elephants in Cutch Behar, I suppose, just as you have Irish-bred horses running at Ascot."

"You said they were going back to the Himalayas," objected Bertie.

"Well, they would naturally be sent home to recuperate. It's the usual thing out there to turn elephants loose in the hills, just as we put horses out to grass in this country."

Clovis could at least flatter himself that he had infused some of the reckless splendour of the East into his mendacity.

"Is it all going to be in blank verse?" asked the critic.

"Of course not; 'Durbar' comes at the end of the fourth line."

"That seems so cowardly; however, it explains why you pitched on Cutch Behar."

"There is more connection between geographical place-names and poetical inspiration than is generally recognized; one of the chief reasons why there are so few really great poems about Russia in our language is that you can't possibly get a rhyme to names like Smolensk and Tobolsk and Minsk."

Clovis spoke with the authority of one who has tried.

"Of course, you could rhyme Omsk with Tomsk," he continued; "in fact, they seem to be there for that purpose, but the public wouldn't stand that sort of thing indefinitely."

"The public will stand a good deal," said Bertie malevolently, "and so small a proportion of it knows Russian that you could always have an explanatory footnote asserting that the last three letters in Smolensk are not pronounced. It's quite as believable as your statement about putting elephants out to grass in the Himalayan range."

"I've got rather a nice bit," resumed Clovis with unruffled serenity, "giving an evening scene on the outskirts of a jungle village:

> " 'Where the coiled cobra in the gloaming gloats,
> And prowling panthers stalk the wary goats.' "

"There is practically no gloaming in tropical countries," said Bertie indulgently; "but I like the masterly reticence with which you treat the cobra's motive for gloating. The unknown is proverbially the uncanny. I can picture nervous readers of the *Smoky Chimney* keeping the light turned on in their bedrooms all night out of sheer sickening uncertainty as to *what* the cobra might have been gloating about."

"Cobras gloat naturally," said Clovis, "just as wolves are always ravening from mere force of habit, even after they've hopelessly overeaten themselves. I've got a fine bit of colour painting later on," he added, "where I describe the dawn coming up over the Brahma-putra river:

" 'The amber dawn-drenched East with sun-shafts kissed,
Stained sanguine apricot and amethyst,
O'er the washed emerald of the mango groves
Hangs in a mist of opalescent mauves,
While painted parrot-flights impinge the haze
With scarlet, chalcedon and chrysoprase.' "

"I've never seen the dawn come up over the Brahma-putra river," said Bertie, "so I can't say if it's a good description of the event, but it sounds more like an account of an extensive jewel robbery. Anyhow, the parrots give a good useful touch of local colour. I suppose you've introduced some tigers into the scenery? An Indian landscape would have rather a bare, unfinished look without a tiger or two in the middle distance."

"I've got a hen-tiger somewhere in the poem," said Clovis, hunting through his notes. "Here she is:

" 'The tawny tigress 'mid the tangled teak
Drags to her purring cubs' enraptured ears
The harsh death-rattle in the pea-fowl's beak,
A jungle lullaby of blood and tears.' "

Bertie van Tahn rose hurriedly from his recumbent position and made for the glass door leading into the next compartment.

"I think your idea of home life in the jungle is perfectly horrid," he said. "The cobra was sinister enough, but the improvised rattle in the tiger-nursery is the limit. If you're going to make me turn hot and cold all over I may as well go into the steam room at once."

"Just listen to this line," said Clovis; "it would make the reputation of any ordinary poet:

" 'and overhead
The pendulum-patient Punkah, parent of stillborn breeze.' "

"Most of your readers will think 'punkah' is a kind of iced drink or half-time at polo," said Bertie, and disappeared into the steam.

The *Smoky Chimney* duly published the "Recessional," but it proved to be its swan song, for the paper never attained to another issue.

Loona Bimberton gave up her intention of attending the Durbar and went into a nursing-home on the Sussex Downs. Nervous breakdown after a particularly strenuous season was the usually accepted explanation, but there are three or four people who know that she never really recovered from the dawn breaking over the Brahma-putra river.

❧

## "I LOVED A LASS"

### George Wither

I loved a lass, a fair one,
　As fair as e'er was seen;
She was indeed a rare one,
　Another Sheba Queen:
But, fool as then I was,
　I thought she loved me too:
But now, alas! she has left me,
　*Falero, lero, loo!* . . .

And as abroad we walkèd
　As lovers' fashion is,
Oft as we sweetly talkèd
　The sun would steal a kiss.
The wind upon her lips
　Likewise most sweetly blew;
But now, alas! she has left me,
　*Falero, lero, loo!*

Many a merry meeting
　My love and I have had;
She was my only sweeting,
　She made my heart full glad;
The tears stood in her eyes
　Like to the morning dew:
But now, alas! she has left me,
　*Falero, lero, loo!*

Her cheeks were like the cherry,
    Her skin was white as snow;
When she was blithe and merry
    She angel-like did show;
Her waist exceeding small,
    The fives did fit her shoe:
But now, alas! she's left me,
    *Falero, lero, loo!*

In summer time or winter
    She had her heart's desire;
I still did scorn to stint her
    From sugar, sack, or fire;
The world went round about,
    No cares we ever knew:
But now, alas! she's left me,
    *Falero, lero, loo!* . . .

No riches now can raise me,
    No want make me despair;
No misery amaze me,
    Nor yet for want I care.
I have lost a world itself,
    My earthly heaven, adieu,
Since she, alas! hath left me,
    *Falero, lero, loo.* . . .

❧

# "THE SPLENDOUR FALLS
ON CASTLE WALLS"

*Alfred, Lord Tennyson*

The splendour falls on castle walls
    And snowy summits old in story:
The long light shakes across the lakes,

And the wild cataract leaps in glory.
Blow, bugle, blow, set the wild echoes flying,
Blow, bugle; answer, echoes, dying, dying, dying.

O hark, O hear! how thin and clear,
    And thinner, clearer, farther going!
O sweet and far from cliff and scar
    The horns of Elfland faintly blowing!
Blow, let us hear the purple glens replying:
Blow, bugle; answer, echoes, dying, dying, dying.

O love, they die in yon rich sky,
    They faint on hill or field or river:
Our echoes roll from soul to soul,
    And grow for ever and for ever.
Blow, bugle, blow, set the wild echoes flying,
And answer, echoes, answer, dying, dying, dying.

## "SO, WE'LL GO NO MORE A-ROVING"

*George Gordon, Lord Byron*

So, we'll go no more a-roving
    So late into the night,
Though the heart be still as loving,
    And the moon be still as bright.

For the sword outwears its sheath,
    And the soul wears out the breast,
And the heart must pause to breathe,
    And love itself have rest.

Though the night was made for loving,
    And the day returns too soon,

Yet we'll go no more a-roving
By the light of the moon.

∾

# THE DALLIANCE OF THE EAGLES

*Walt Whitman*

Skirting the river road, (my forenoon walk, my rest,)
Skyward in air a sudden muffled sound, the dalliance of
 the eagles,
The rushing amorous contact high in space together,
The clinching interlocking claws, a living, fierce,
 gyrating wheel,
Four beating wings, two beaks, a swirling mass tight
 grappling,
In tumbling turning clustering loops, straight
 downward falling,
Till o'er the river pois'd, the twain yet one, a moment's
 lull,
A motionless still balance in the air, then parting,
 talons loosing,
Upward again on slow-firm pinions slanting, their
 separate diverse flight,
She hers, he his, pursuing.

∾

# NOVEMBER

## *Robert Bridges*

The lonely season in lonely lands, when fled
Are half the birds, and mists lie low, and the sun
Is rarely seen, nor strayeth far from his bed;
The short days pass unwelcomed one by one.

   Out by the ricks the mantled engine stands
Crestfallen, deserted,—for now all hands
Are told to the plough,—and ere it is dawn appear
The teams following and crossing far and near,
As hour by hour they broaden the brown bands
Of the striped fields; and behind them firk and
      prance
The heavy rooks, and daws grey-pated dance:
As awhile, surmounting a crest, in sharp outline
(A miniature of toil, a gem's design,)
They are pictured, horses and men, or now near by
Above the lane they shout lifting the share,
By the trim hedgerow bloom'd with purple air;
Where, under the thorns, dead leaves in huddle lie
Packed by the gales of Autumn, and in and out
The small wrens glide
With a happy note of cheer,
And yellow amorets flutter above and about,
Gay, familiar in fear.

   And now, if the night shall be cold, across the sky
Linnets and twites, in small flocks helter-skelter,
All the afternoon to the gardens fly,
From thistle-pastures hurrying to gain the shelter
Of American rhododendron or cherry-laurel:
And here and there, near chilly setting of sun,
In an isolated tree a congregation
Of starlings chatter and chide,

Thickset as summer leaves, in garrulous quarrel:
Suddenly they hush as one,—
The tree top springs,—
And off, with a whirr of wings,
They fly by the score
To the holly-thicket, and there with myriads more
Dispute for the roosts; and from the unseen nation
A babel of tongues, like running water unceasing,
Makes live the wood, the flocking cries increasing,
Wrangling discordantly, incessantly,
While falls the night on them self-occupied;
The long dark night, that lengthens slow,
Deepening with Winter to starve grass and tree,
And soon to bury in snow
The Earth, that, sleeping 'neath her frozen stole,
Shall dream a dream crept from the sunless pole
Of how her end shall be.

∾

# DRINKING SONG

## *John Still*

Back and side go bare, go bare,
    Both foot and hand go cold;
But belly, God send thee good ale enough;
    Whether it be new or old!

I cannot eat but little meat; my stomach is not good;
But, sure I think that I can drink with him that wears a
        hood.
Though I go bare; take ye no care, I am nothing a-cold;
I stuff my skin so full within of jolly good ale and old.
    Back and side go bare, go bare,
        Both foot and hand go cold;
    But belly, God send thee good ale enough;
        Whether it be new or old!

I love no roast but a nut-brown toast, and a crab laid in
the fire;
A little bread shall do me stead! much bread I do not
desire;
No frost, nor snow, no wind, I trow, can hurt me if I
would;
I am so wrapped, and throughly lapped of jolly good ale
and old!
Back and side go bare, go bare,
Both foot and hand go cold;
But belly, God send thee good ale enough;
Whether it be new or old!

And Tyb my Wife, that as her life loveth well good ale to
seek,
Full oft drinks she, till ye may see the tears run down her
cheek;
Then doth she troll to me the bowl, even as a Malt Worm
should;
And saith, "Sweet Heart! I took my part of this jolly good
ale and old!"
Back and side go bare, go bare,
Both foot and hand go cold;
But belly, God send thee good ale enough;
Whether it be new or old!

Now let them drink till they nod and wink, even as Good
Fellows should do,
They shall not miss to have the bliss good ale doth bring
men to.
And all poor souls that have scoured bowls, or have them
lustily trolled,
God save the lives of them and their Wives, whether they
be young or old!
Back and side go bare, go bare,
Both foot and hand go cold;
But belly, God send thee good ale enough;
Whether it be new or old!

# LOVE WILL FIND OUT THE WAY

*Anonymous*

Over the mountains
    And under the waves,
Under the fountains
    And under the graves;
Under floods that are deepest,
    Which Neptune obey,
Over rocks that are steepest,
    Love will find out the way.

When there is no place
    For the glow-worm to lie,
Where there is no space
    For receipt of a fly;
Where the midge dares not venture
    Lest herself fast she lay,
If Love come, he will enter
    And will find out the way.

You may esteem him
    A child for his might;
Or you may deem him
    A coward from his flight:
But if she whom Love doth honour
    Be conceal'd from the day—
Set a thousand guards upon her,
    Love will find out the way.

Some think to lose him
    By having him confined;
And some do suppose him,
    Poor heart! to be blind;
But if ne'er so close ye wall him,
    Do the best that you may,

Blind Love, if so you call him,
    Will find out his way.

You may train the eagle
    To stoop to your fist;
Or you may inveigle
    The Phoenix of the east;
The lioness, ye may move her
    To give over her prey;
But you'll ne'er stop a lover—
    He will find out his way.

If the earth it should part him,
    He would gallop it o'er;
If the seas should o'erthwart him,
    He would swim to the shore;
Should his Love become a swallow,
    Through the air to stray,
Love will lend wings to follow,
    And will find out the way.

There is no striving
    To cross his intent;
There is no contriving
    His plots to prevent;
But if once the message greet him
    That his True Love doth stay,
If Death should come and meet him,
    Love will find out the way!

# MY CAT JEOFFRY

## Christopher Smart

For I will consider my Cat Jeoffry.
For he is the servant of the Living God duly and daily
      serving him.
For at the first glance of the glory of God in the East he
      worships in his way.
For is this done by wreathing his body seven times round
      with elegant quickness.
For then he leaps up to catch the musk, which is the bless-
      ing of God upon his prayer.
For he rolls upon the prank to work it in.
For having done duty and received blessing he begins to
      consider himself.
For this he performs in ten degrees.
For first he looks upon his fore-paws to see if they are
      clean.
For secondly he kicks up behind to clear away there.
For thirdly he works it upon stretch with the fore-paws
      extended.
For fourthly he sharpens his paws by wood.
For fifthly he washes himself.
For Sixthly he rolls upon wash.
For Seventhly he fleas himself, that he may not be in-
      terrupted upon the beat.
For Eighthly he rubs himself against a post.
For Ninthly he looks up for his instructions.
For Tenthly he goes in quest of food.
For having considered God and himself he will consider
      his neighbour.
For if he meets another cat he will kiss her in kindness.
For when he takes his prey he plays with it to give it a
      chance.
For one mouse in seven escapes by his dallying.
For when his day's work is done his business more properly
      begins.

For he keeps the Lord's watch in the night against the
    adversary.
For he counteracts the powers of darkness by his electrical
    skin & glaring eyes.
For he counteracts the Devil, who is death, by brisking
    about the life.
For in his morning orisons he loves the sun and the sun
    loves him.
For he is of the tribe of Tiger.
For the Cherub Cat is a term of the Angel Tiger.
For he has the subtlety and hissing of a serpent, which in
    goodness he suppresses.
For he will not do destruction if he is well-fed, neither will
    he spit without provocation.
For he purrs in thankfulness, when God tells him he's a
    good Cat.
For he is an instrument for the children to learn benevo-
    lence upon.
For every house is incompleat without him & a blessing
    is lacking in the spirit.
For the Lord commanded Moses concerning the cats at
    the departure of the Children of Israel from
    Egypt.
For every family had one cat at least in the bag.
For the English Cats are the best in Europe.
For he is the cleanest in the use of his fore-paws of any
    quadrupede.
For the dexterity of his defence is an instance of the love
    of God to him exceedingly.
For he is the quickest to his mark of any creature.
For he is tenacious of his point.
For he is a mixture of gravity and waggery.
For he knows that God is his Saviour.
For there is nothing sweeter than his peace when at rest.
For there is nothing brisker than his life when in motion.
For he is of the Lord's poor and so indeed is he called by
    benevolence perpetually—Poor Jeoffry! poor
    Jeoffry! the rat has bit thy throat.
For I bless the name of the Lord Jesus that Jeoffry is
    better.

For the divine spirit comes about his body to sustain it
        in compleat cat.
For his tongue is exceeding pure so that it has in purity
        what it wants in musick.
For he is docile and can learn certain things.
For he can set up with gravity which is patience upon
        approbation.
For he can fetch and carry, which is patience in employ-
        ment.
For he can jump over a stick which is patience upon proof
        positive.
For he can spraggle upon waggle at the word of command.
For he can jump from an eminence into his master's
        bosom.
For he can catch the cork and toss it again.
For he is hated by the hypocrite and miser.
For the former is afraid of detection.
For the latter refuses the charge.
For he camels his back to bear the first notion of business.
For he is good to think on, if a man would express himself
        neatly.
For he made a great figure in Egypt for his signal services.
For he killed the Icneumon-rat very pernicious by land.
For his ears are so acute that they sting again.
For from this proceeds the passing quickness of his at-
        tention.
For by stroking him I have found out electricity.
For I perceived God's light about him both wax and fire.
For the Electrical fire is the spiritual substance, which
        God sends from heaven to sustain the
        bodies both of man and beast.
For God has blessed him in the variety of his movements.
For, tho' he cannot fly, he is an excellent clamberer.
For his motions upon the face of the earth are more than
        any other quadrupede.
For he can tread to all the measures upon the musick.
For he can swim for life.
For he can creep.

## THE WHITE ISLAND

*Robert Herrick*

In this world, the Isle of Dreams,
    While we sit by sorrow's streams,
Tears and terrors are our themes,
      Reciting:

But when once from hence we fly,
More and more approaching nigh
Unto young eternity,
      Uniting—
In that whiter Island, where
Things are evermore sincere;
Candour here, and lustre there,
      Delighting:—
There no monstrous fancies shall
Out of hell an horror call
To create, or cause at all
      Affrighting:
There, in calm and cooling sleep,
We our eyes shall never steep,
But eternal watch shall keep,
      Attending
Pleasures such as shall pursue
Me immortalized, and you;
And fresh joys, as never too
      Have ending.

## DEATH AND CUPID

### Aesop

Cupid, one sultry summer's noon, tired with play and faint with heat, went into a cool grotto to repose himself, which happened to be the cave of Death. He threw himself carelessly down on the floor, and his quiver turning topsy-turvy, all the arrows fell out, and mingled with those of Death, which lay scattered up and down the place. When he awoke, he gathered them up as well as he could; but they were so intermingled, that though he knew the certain number, he could not rightly distinguish them; from which it happened, that he took up some of the arrows which belonged to Death, and left several of his own in the room of them. This is the cause that we, now and then, see the hearts of the old and decrepid transfixed with the bolts of love; and with equal grief and surprise, behold the youthful, blooming part of our species smitten with the darts of Death.

*Translated by Samuel Croxall*

∾

## "WHO HAS SEEN THE WIND?"

### Christina Rossetti

Who has seen the wind?
  Neither I nor you:
But when the leaves hang trembling
  The wind is passing thro'.

Who has seen the wind?
  Neither you nor I:
But when the trees bow down their heads
  The wind is passing by.

∾

# BOOK IV

# Winter

# THE RED SHOES

## Hans Christian Andersen

There was once a little girl, very pretty and delicate, but so poor that in summer-time she went barefoot, and in winter wore large wooden shoes, so that her little ankles grew quite red and sore.

In the village dwelt the shoemaker's mother; she sat down one day, and made out of some old pieces of red cloth a pair of little shoes; they were clumsy enough certainly, but they fitted the little girl tolerably well, and she gave them to her. The little girl's name was Karen.

It was the day of her mother's funeral when the red shoes were given to Karen; they were not at all suitable for mourning, but she had no others, and in them she walked with bare legs behind the miserable straw-bier.

Just then a large old carriage rolled by; in it sat a large old lady; she looked at the little girl and pitied her, and she said to the priest, "Give me the little girl, and I will take care of her."

And Karen thought it was all for the sake of the red shoes that the old lady had taken this fancy to her; but the old lady said they were frightful, and they were burnt. And Karen was dressed very neatly; she was taught to read and to work; and people told her she was pretty, but the Mirror said, "Thou art more than pretty, thou art beautiful!"

It happened one day that the Queen travelled through that part of the country, with her little daughter, the Princess; and all the people, Karen amongst them, crowded in front of the palace, whilst the little Princess stood, dressed in white, at a window, for every one to see her. She wore neither train nor gold crown; but on her feet were pretty red morocco shoes, much prettier ones, indeed, than those the shoemaker's mother had made for little Karen. Nothing in the world could be compared to these red shoes!

Karen was now old enough to be confirmed; she was to have both new frock and new shoes. The rich shoemaker in the town took the measure of her little foot. Large glass cases, full of neat shoes and shining boots, were fixed round the room; however, the old lady's sight was not very good, and, naturally enough, she had not so much pleasure in looking at them as Karen had. Amongst the shoes was a pair of red ones, just like those worn by the

Princess. How gay they were! and the shoemaker said, they had been made for a count's daughter, but had not quite fitted her.

"They are of polished leather," said the old lady; "see how they shine!"

"Yes, they shine beautifully!" exclaimed Karen. And as the shoes fitted her, they were bought, but the old lady did not know that they were red, for she would never have suffered Karen to go to confirmation in red shoes. But Karen did so.

Everybody looked at her feet, and as she walked up the nave to the chancel, it seemed to her that even the antique sculptured figures on the monuments, with their stiff ruffs and long black robes, fixed their eyes on her red shoes; of them only she thought when the Bishop laid his hand on her head, when he spoke of Holy Baptism, of her covenant with God, and how that she must now be a full-grown Christian. The organ sent forth its deep, solemn tones; the children's sweet voices mingled with those of the choristers, but Karen still thought only of her red shoes.

That afternoon, when the old lady was told that Karen had worn red shoes at her confirmation, she was much vexed, and told Karen that they were quite unsuitable, and that henceforward, whenever she went to church, she must wear black shoes, were they ever so old.

Next Sunday was the Communion-day; Karen looked first at the red shoes, then at the black ones, then at the red again, and—put them on.

It was beautiful, sunshiny weather; Karen and the old lady walked to church through the corn-fields; the path was very dusty.

At the church-door stood an old soldier; he was leaning on crutches, and had a marvellously long beard, not white, but reddish-hued, and he bowed almost to the earth, and asked the old lady if he might wipe the dust off her shoes. And Karen put out her little foot also. "Oh, what pretty dancing-shoes!" quoth the old soldier; "take care, and mind you do not let them slip off when you dance;" and he passed his hands over them.

The old lady gave the soldier a halfpenny, and then went with Karen into church.

And every one looked at Karen's red shoes; and all the carved figures, too, bent their gaze upon them; and when Karen knelt before the altar, the red shoes still floated before her eyes; she thought of them, and of them only, and she forgot to join in the hymn of praise,—she forgot to repeat "Our Father."

At last all the people came out of church, and the old lady got into her carriage. Karen was just lifting her foot to follow her, when the old soldier standing in the porch exclaimed, "Only look, what pretty dancing-shoes!" And Karen could not help it, she felt she must make a few of her dancing-steps; and after she had once begun, her feet continued to move, just as though the shoes had received power over them; she danced round the churchyard—she could not stop—the coachman was obliged to run after her—he took hold of her and lifted her into the carriage, but the feet still continued to dance, so as to kick the good old lady most cruelly. At last the shoes were taken off, and the feet had rest.

And now the shoes were put away in a press, but Karen could not help going to look at them every now and then.

The old lady lay ill in bed; the doctor said she could not live much longer; she certainly needed careful nursing, and who should be her nurse and constant attendant but Karen? But there was to be a grand ball in the town; Karen was invited; she looked at the old lady, who was almost dying, she looked at the red shoes—she put them on; there could be no harm in doing that, at least; she went to the ball, and began to dance.

But when she wanted to move to the right, the shoes bore her to the left; and when she would dance up the room, the shoes danced down the room, danced down the stairs, through the streets, and through the gates of the town. Dance she did, and dance she must, straight out into the dark wood.

Something all at once shone through the trees! she thought at first it must be the moon's bright face, shining blood red through the night mists; but no, it was the old soldier with the red beard—he sat there, nodding at her, and repeating, "Only look, what pretty dancing-shoes!"

She was very much frightened, and tried to throw off her red shoes, but could not unclasp them. She hastily tore off her stockings; but the shoes she could not get rid of—they had, it seemed, grown on to her feet. Dance she did, and dance she must, over field and meadow, in rain and in sunshine, by night and by day—by night! that was most horrible! She danced into the lonely churchyard, but the dead there danced not—they were at rest: she would fain have sat down on the poor man's grave, where the bitter tansy grew, but for her there was neither rest nor respite. She danced past the open church-door; there she saw an Angel, clad in long white robes, and with wings that reached from his shoulders to the earth; his countenance was grave and stern, and in his hand he held a broad glittering sword.

"Dance shalt thou," said he; "dance on, in thy red shoes, till thou art pale and cold, and thy skin shrinks and crumples up like a skeleton's! Dance shalt thou still, from door to door; and wherever proud, vain children live, thou shalt knock, so that they may hear thee and fear! Dance shalt thou, dance on—"

"Mercy!" cried Karen; but she heard not the Angel's answer, for the shoes carried her through the gate, into the fields, along highways and by-ways, and still she must dance.

One morning she danced past a door she knew well; she heard psalm-singing from within, and presently a coffin strewn with flowers, was borne out. Then Karen knew that the good old lady was dead, and she felt herself a thing forsaken by all mankind, and accursed by the Angel of God.

Dance she did, and dance she must, even through the dark night; the shoes bore her continually over thorns and briers, till her limbs were torn and bleeding. Away she danced over the heath to a little solitary house; she knew that the headsman dwelt there, and she tapped with her fingers against the panes, crying,—

"Come out! come out!—I cannot come in to you, I am dancing."

And the headsman replied, "Surely thou knowest not who I am. I cut off the heads of wicked men, and my axe is very sharp and keen."

"Cut not off my head!" said Karen; "for then I could not live to repent of my sin; but cut off my feet with the red shoes."

And then she confessed to him all her sin, and the headsman cut off her feet with the red shoes on them; but even after this the shoes still danced away with those little feet over the fields, and into the deep forests.

And the headsman made her a pair of wooden feet, and hewed down some boughs to serve her as crutches, and he taught her the psalm which is always repeated by criminals, and she kissed the hand that had guided the axe, and went her way over the heath.

"Now I have certainly suffered quite enough through the red shoes," thought Karen; "I will go to church and let people see me once more!" and she went as fast as she could to the church-porch; but as she approached it, the red shoes danced before her, and she was frightened and turned back.

All that week through she endured the keenest anguish and shed many bitter tears; however, when Sunday came, she said to herself, "Well, I must have suffered and striven enough by this time; I dare say I am quite as good as many of those who are holding their heads so high in church." So she took courage and went there, but she had not passed the churchyard-gate before she saw the red shoes again dancing before her, and in great terror she again turned back, and more deeply than ever bewailed her sin.

She then went to the pastor's house, and begged that some employment might be given her, promising to work diligently and do all she could; she did not wish for any wages, she said, she only wanted a roof to shelter her, and to dwell with good people. And the pastor's wife had pity on her, and took her into her service. And Karen was grateful and industrious. Every evening she sat silently listening to the pastor, while he read the Holy Scriptures aloud. All the children loved her, but when she heard them talk about dress and finery, and about being as beautiful as a queen, she would sorrowfully shake her head.

Again Sunday came, all the pastor's household went to church, and they asked her if she would not go too, but she sighed and looked with tears in her eyes upon her crutches.

When they were all gone, she went into her own little lowly chamber— it was but just large enough to contain a bed and a chair—and there she sat down with her psalm-book in her hand; and whilst she was meekly and devoutly reading in it, the wind wafted the tones of the organ from the church into her room, and she lifted up her face to heaven and prayed, with tears, "Oh, God, help me!"

Then the sun shone brightly, so brightly!—and behold! close before her stood the white-robed Angel of God, the same whom she had seen on that night of horror at the church-porch, but his hand wielded not now, as then, a sharp, threatening sword,—he held a lovely green bough, full of roses. With this he touched the ceiling, which immediately rose to a great height, a bright gold star sparkling in the spot where the Angel's green bough had touched it. And he touched the walls, whereupon the room widened, and Karen saw the organ, the old monuments, and the congregation all sitting in their richly-carved seats and singing from their psalm-books.—

For the church had come home to the poor girl in her little narrow chamber, or rather the chamber had grown, as it were, into the church; she sat with the rest of the pastor's household, and when the psalm was ended, they looked up and nodded to her, saying, "Thou didst well to come, Karen!"

"This is mercy!" said she.

And the organ played again, and the children's voices in the choir mingled so sweetly and plaintively with it!—The bright sunbeams streamed warmly through the windows upon Karen's seat; her heart was so full of sunshine, of peace and gladness, that it broke; her soul flew upon a sunbeam to her Father in heaven, where not a look of reproach awaited her—not a word was breathed of the Red Shoes.

*Translated by Caroline Peachey*

ॐ

# THE SIGNAL-MAN

## *Charles Dickens*

"Halloa! Below there!"

When he heard a voice thus calling to him, he was standing at the door of his box, with a flag in his hand, furled round its short pole. One would have thought, considering the nature of the ground, that he could not have doubted from what quarter the voice came; but, instead of looking up to where I stood on the top of the steep cutting nearly over his head, he turned himself about, and looked down the Line. There was something remarkable in his manner of doing so, though I could not have said for my life what. But I know it was remarkable enough to attract my notice, even though his figure was foreshortened and shadowed, down in the deep trench, and mine was high above him, so steeped in the glow of an angry sunset, that I had shaded my eyes with my hand before I saw him at all.

"Halloa! Below!"

From looking down the Line, he turned himself about again, and, raising his eyes, saw my figure high above him.

"Is there any path by which I can come down and speak to you?"

He looked up at me without replying, and I looked down at him without pressing him too soon with a repetition of my idle question. Just then there came a vague vibration in the earth and air, quickly changing into a violent pulsation, and an on-coming rush that caused me to start back, as though it had force to draw me down. When such vapour as rose to my height from this rapid train had passed me, and was skimming away over the landscape, I looked down again, and saw him refurling the flag he had shown while the train went by.

I repeated my inquiry. After a pause, during which he seemed to regard me with fixed attention, he motioned with his rolled-up flag towards a point on my level, some two or three hundred yards distant. I called down to him, "All right!" and made for that point. There, by dint of looking closely about me, I found a rough zigzag descending path notched out, which I followed.

The cutting was extremely deep, and unusually precipitate. It was made through a clammy stone, that became oozier and wetter as I went down. For these reasons, I found the way long enough to give me time to recall a sin-

gular air of reluctance or compulsion with which he had pointed out the
path.

When I came down low enough upon the zigzag descent to see him
again, I saw that he was standing between the rails on the way by which the
train had lately passed, in an attitude as if he were waiting for me to
appear. He had his left hand at his chin, and that left elbow rested on his
right hand, crossed over his breast. His attitude was one of such expectation
and watchfulness, that I stopped a moment, wondering at it.

I resumed my downward way, and stepping out upon the level of the
railroad, and drawing nearer to him, saw that he was a dark sallow man,
with a dark beard and rather heavy eyebrows. His post was in as solitary
and dismal a place as ever I saw. On either side, a dripping-wet wall of
jagged stone, excluding all view but a strip of sky; the perspective one way
only a crooked prolongation of this great dungeon; the shorter perspective
in the other direction terminating in a gloomy red light, and the gloomier
entrance to a black tunnel, in whose massive architecture there was a barbarous, depressing, and forbidding air. So little sun-light ever found its way
to this spot, that it had an earthy, deadly smell; and so much cold wind
rushed through it, that it struck chill to me, as if I had left the natural
world.

Before he stirred, I was near enough to him to have touched him. Not
even then removing his eyes from mine, he stepped back one step, and
lifted his hand.

This was a lonesome post to occupy (I said), and it had riveted my attention when I looked down from up yonder. A visitor was a rarity, I should
suppose; not an unwelcome rarity, I hoped? In me he merely saw a man
who had been shut up within narrow limits all his life, and who, being at
last set free, had a newly-awakened interest in these great works. To such
purpose I spoke to him; but I am far from sure of the terms I used; for,
besides that I am not happy in opening any conversation, there was something in the man that daunted me.

He directed a most curious look towards the red light near the tunnel's mouth, and looked all about it, as if something were missing from it,
and then looked at me.

That light was part of his charge? Was it not?

He answered in a low voice, "Don't you know it is?"

The monstrous thought came into my mind, as I perused the fixed
eyes and the saturnine face, that this was a spirit, not a man. I have specu-
lated since whether there may have been infection in his mind.

In my turn, I stepped back. But, in making the action, I detected in his eyes some latent fear of me. This put the monstrous thought to flight.

"You look at me," I said, forcing a smile, "as if you had a dread of me."

"I was doubtful," he returned, "whether I had seen you before."

"Where?"

He pointed to the red light he had looked at.

"There?" I said.

Intently watchful of me, he replied (but without sound), "Yes."

"My good fellow, what should I do there? However, be that as it may, I never was there, you may swear."

"I think I may," he rejoined. "Yes; I am sure I may."

His manner cleared, like my own. He replied to my remarks with readiness, and in well-chosen words. Had he much to do there? Yes; that was to say, he had enough responsibility to bear; but exactness and watchfulness were what was required of him, and of actual work—manual labour—he had next to none. To change that signal, to trim those lights, and to turn this iron handle now and then, was all he had to do under that head. Regarding those many long and lonely hours of which I seemed to make so much, he could only say that the routine of his life had shaped itself into that form, and he had grown used to it. He had taught himself a language down here,—if only to know it by sight, and to have formed his own crude ideas of its pronunciation, could be called learning it. He had also worked at fractions and decimals, and tried a little algebra; but he was, and had been as a boy, a poor hand at figures. Was it necessary for him when on duty always to remain in that channel of damp air, and could he never rise into the sunshine from between those high stone walls? Why, that depended upon times and circumstances. Under some conditions there would be less upon the Line than under others, and the same held good as to certain hours of the day and night. In bright weather he did choose occasions for getting a little above these lower shadows; but, being at all times liable to be called by his electric bell, and at such times listening for it with redoubled anxiety, the relief was less than I would suppose.

He took me into his box, where there was a fire, a desk for an official book in which he had to make certain entries, a telegraphic instrument with its dial, face, and needles, and the little bell of which he had spoken. On my trusting that he would excuse the remark that he had been well educated, and (I hoped I might say without offence), perhaps educated above that station, he observed that instances of slight incongruity in such wise would rarely be found wanting among large bodies of men; that he had heard it was so in workhouses, in the police force, even in that last desperate resource, the army; and that he knew it was so, more or less, in any great railway staff. He had been, when young (if I could believe it, sitting in that hut,—he scarcely could), a student of natural philosophy, and had attended lectures; but he had run wild, misused his opportunities, gone down, and never risen again. He had no complaint to offer about that. He had made his bed, and he lay upon it. It was far too late to make another.

All that I have here condensed he said in a quiet manner, with his grave dark regards divided between me and the fire. He threw in the word "Sir" from time to time, and especially when he referred to his youth,—as though to request me to understand that he claimed to be nothing but what I found him. He was several times interrupted by the little bell, and had to read off messages and send replies. Once he had to stand without the door, and display a flag as a train passed, and make some verbal communication to the driver. In the discharge of his duties, I observed him to be remarkably exact and vigilant, breaking off his discourse at a syllable, and remaining silent until what he had to do was done.

In a word, I should have set this man down as one of the safest of men to be employed in that capacity, but for the circumstance that while he was speaking to me he twice broke off with a fallen colour, turned his face towards the little bell when it did NOT ring, opened the door of the hut (which was kept shut to exclude the unhealthy damp), and looked out towards the red light near the mouth of the tunnel. On both of those occasions, he came back to the fire with the inexplicable air upon him which I had remarked, without being able to define, when we were so far asunder.

Said I, when I rose to leave him, "You almost make me think that I have met with a contented man."

(I am afraid I must acknowledge that I said it to lead him on.)

"I believe I used to be so," he rejoined in the low voice in which he had first spoken; "but I am troubled, sir, I am troubled."

He would have recalled the words of he could. He had said them, however, and I took them up quickly.

"With what? What is you trouble?"

"It is difficult to impart, sir. It is very, very difficult to speak of. If ever you make me another visit, I will try to tell you."

"But I expressly intend to make you another visit. Say, when shall it be?"

"I go off early in the morning, and I shall be on again at ten to-morrow night, sir."

"I will come at eleven."

He thanked me, and went out at the door with me. "I'll show my white light, sir," he said in his peculiar low voice, "till you have found the way up. When you have found it, don't call out! And when you are at the top, don't call out!"

His manner seemed to make the place strike colder to me, but I said no more than, "Very well."

"And when you come down to-morrow night, don't call out! Let me ask you a parting question. What made you cry, 'Halloa! Below there!' to-night?"

"Heaven knows," said I. "I cried something to that effect— —"

"Not to that effect, sir. Those were the very words. I know them well."

"Admit those were the very words. I said them, no doubt, because I saw you below."

"For no other reason?"

"What other reason could I possibly have?"

"You had no feeling that they were conveyed to you in any supernatural way?"

"No."

He wished me good night, and held up his light. I walked by the side of the down Line of rails (with a very disagreeable sensation of a train coming behind me) until I found the path. It was easier to mount than to descend, and I got back to my inn without any adventure.

Punctual to my appointment, I placed my foot on the first notch of the zigzag next night as the distant clocks were striking eleven. He was waiting for me at the bottom, with his white light on. "I have not called out," I said when we came close together; "may I speak now?" "By all means, sir." "Good night, then, and here's my hand." "Good night, sir, and here's mine." With that we walked side by side to his box, entered it, closed the door, and sat down by the fire.

"I have made up my mind, sir," he began, bending forward as soon as we were seated, and speaking in a tone but a little above a whisper, "that you shall not have to ask me twice what troubles me. I took you for some one else yesterday evening. That troubles me."

"That mistake?"

"No. That some one else."

"Who is it?"

"I don't know."

"Like me?"

"I don't know. I never saw the face. The left arm is across the face, and the right arm is waved,—violently waved. This way."

I followed his action with my eyes, and it was the action of an arm gesticulating, with the utmost passion and vehemence, "For God's sake, clear the way"

"One moonlight night," said the man, "I was sitting here, when I heard a voice cry, 'Halloa! Below there!' I started up, looked from that door, and saw this Some one else standing by the red light near the tunnel, waving as I just now showed you. The voice seemed hoarse with shouting, and it cried, 'Look out! Look out!' And then again, 'Halloa! Below there! Look out!' I caught up my lamp, turned it on red, and ran towards the figure, calling, 'What's wrong? What has happened? Where?' It stood just outside the blackness of the tunnel. I advanced so close upon it that I wondered at its keeping the sleeve across its eyes. I ran right up at it, and had my hand stretched out to pull the sleeve away, when it was gone."

"Into the tunnel?" said I.

"No. I ran on into the tunnel, five hundred yards. I stopped, and held my lamp above my head, and saw the figures of the measured distance, and saw the wet stains stealing down the walls and trickling through the arch. I ran out again faster than I had run in (for I had a mortal abhorrence of the place upon me), and I looked all round the red light with my own red light, and I went up the iron ladder to the gallery atop of it, and I came down again, and ran back here. I telegraphed both ways, 'An alarm has been given. Is anything wrong?' The answer came back, both ways, 'All well.'"

Resisting the slow touch of a frozen finger tracing out my spine, I showed him how that this figure must be a deception of his sense of sight; and how that figures, originating in disease of the delicate nerves that minister to the functions of the eye, were known to have often troubled patients, some of whom had become conscious of the nature of their affliction, and had even proved it by experiments upon themselves. "As to an imaginary cry," said I, "do but listen for a moment to the wind in this unnatural valley while we speak so low, and to the wild harp it makes of the telegraph wires!"

That was all very well, he returned, after we had sat listening for awhile, and he ought to know something of the wind and the wires,—he who so often passed long winter nights there, alone and watching. But he would beg to remark that he had not finished.

I asked his pardon, and he slowly added these words, touching my arm:

"Within six hours after the Appearance, the memorable accident on this Line happened, and within ten hours the dead and wounded were brought along through the tunnel over the spot where the figure had stood."

A disagreeable shudder crept over me, but I did my best against it. It was not to be denied, I rejoined, that this was a remarkable coincidence, calculated deeply to impress his mind. But it was unquestionable that remarkable coincidences did continually occur, and they must be taken into account in dealing with such a subject. Though to be sure I must admit, I added (for I thought I saw that he was going to bring the objection to bear upon me), men of common sense did not allow much for coincidences in making the ordinary calculations of life.

He again begged to remark that he had not finished.

I again begged his pardon for being betrayed into interruptions.

"This," he said, again laying his hand upon my arm, and glancing over his shoulder with hollow eyes, "was just a year ago. Six or seven months passed, and I had recovered from the surprise and shock, when one morning, as the day was breaking, I, standing at the door, looked towards the red light, and saw the spectre again." He stopped with a fixed look at me.

"Did it cry out?"

"No. It was silent."

"Did it wave its arm?"

"No. It leaned against the shaft of the light, with both hands before the face. Like this."

Once more I followed his action with my eyes. It was an action of mourning. I have seen such an attitude in stone figures on tombs.

"Did you go up to it?"

"I came in and sat down, partly to collect my thoughts, partly because it had turned me faint. When I went to the door again, daylight was above me, and the ghost was gone."

"But nothing followed? Nothing came of this?"

He touched me on the arm with his forefinger twice or thrice giving a ghastly nod each time:

"That very day, as a train came out of the tunnel, I noticed at a carriage window on my side, what looked like a confusion of hands and heads, and something waved. I saw it just in time to signal the driver, Stop! He shut off, and put his brake on, but the train drifted past here a hundred and fifty yards or more. I ran after it, and, as I went along, heard terrible screams and cries. A beautiful young lady had died instantaneously in one of the compartments, and was brought in here, and laid down on this floor between us."

Involuntarily I pushed my chair back, as I looked from the boards at which he pointed to himself.

"True, sir. True. Precisely as it happened, so I tell it you."

I could think of nothing to say to any purpose, and my mouth was very dry. The wind and the wires took up the story with a long lamenting wail.

He resumed. "Now, sir, mark this, and judge how my mind is troubled. The spectre came back a week ago. Ever since, it has been there, now and again, by fits and starts."

"At the light?"

"At the Danger-light."

"What does it seem to do?"

He repeated, if possible with increased passion and vehemence, that former gesticulation of, "For God's sake, clear the way!"

Then he went on. "I have no peace or rest for it. It calls to me, for many minutes together, in an agonised manner, 'Below there! Look out! Look out!' It stands waving to me. It rings my little bell——"

I caught at that. "Did it ring your bell yesterday evening when I was here, and you went to the door?"

"Twice."

"Why, see," said I, "how your imagination misleads you! My eyes were on the bell, and my ears were open to the bell, and, if I am a living man, it did NOT ring at those times. No, nor at any other time, except when it was rung in the natural course of physical things by the station communicating with you."

He shook his head. "I have never made a mistake as to that yet, sir. I have never confused the spectre's ring with the man's. The ghost's ring is a strange vibration in the bell that it derives from nothing else, and I have not asserted that the bell stirs to the eye. I don't wonder that you failed to hear it. But *I* heard it."

"And did the spectre seem to be there when you looked out?"

"It WAS there."

"Both times?"

He repeated firmly: "Both times."

"Will you come to the door with me, and look for it now?"

He bit his under lip as though he were somewhat unwilling, but arose. I opened the door, and stood on the step, while he stood in the doorway. There was the Danger-light. There was the dismal mouth of the tunnel. There were the high, wet stone walls of the cutting. There were the stars above them.

"Do you see it?" I asked him, taking particular note of his face. His eyes were prominent and strained, but not very much more so, perhaps, than my own had been when I had directed them earnestly towards the same spot.

"No," he answered. "It is not there."

"Agreed," said I.

We went in again, shut the door, and resumed our seats. I was think-ing how best to improve this advantage, if it might be called one, when he took up the conversation in such a matter-of-course way, so assuming that there could be no serious question of fact between us, that I felt myself placed in the weakest of positions.

"By this time you will fully understand, sir," he said, "that what trou-bles me so dreadfully is the question, What does the spectre mean?"

I was not sure, I told him, that I did fully understand.

"What is its warning against?" he said, ruminating, with his eyes on the fire, and only by times turning them on me. "What is the danger? Where is the danger? There is danger overhanging somewhere on the Line. Some dreadful calamity will happen. It is not to be doubted this third time, after what has gone before. But surely this is a cruel haunting of *me*. What can *I* do?"

He pulled out his handkerchief, and wiped the drops from his heated forehead.

"If I telegraph Danger on either side of me, or on both, I can give no reason for it," he went on, wiping the palms of hands. "I should get into trouble, and do no good. They would think I was mad. This is the way it would work,—Message: 'Danger! Take care!' Answer: 'What Danger Where?' Message: 'Don't know. But, for God's sake, take care!' They would displace me. What else could they do?"

His pain of mind was most pitiable to see. It was the mental torture of a conscientious man, oppressed beyond endurance by an unintelligible responsibility involving life.

"When it first stood under the Danger-light," he went on putting his dark hair back from his head, and drawing his hands outward across and across his temples in an extremity feverish distress, "why not tell me where that accident was to happen,—if it must happen? Why not tell me how it could be averted,—if it could have been averted? When on its sec-ond coming it hid its face, why not tell me, instead, 'She going to die. Let them keep her at home'? If it came, on those two occasions, only to show me that its warnings were true, and so to prepare me for the third, why not warn me plainly now? And I, Lord help me! A mere poor signal-man on this solitary station! Why not go to somebody with credit to be believed, and power to act?"

When I saw him in this state, I saw that for the poor man's sake, as well as for the public safety, what I had to do for the time was to compose his mind. Therefore, setting aside all question of reality or unreality between us, I represented to him that whoever thoroughly discharged his duty must do well, and that at least it was his comfort that he understood his duty, though he did not understand these confounding Appearances. In this effort I succeeded far better than in the attempt to reason him out of his conviction. He became calm; the occupations incidental to his post as the night advanced began to make larger demands on his attention: and I left him at two in the morning. I had offered to stay through the night, but he would not hear of it.

That I more than once looked back at the red light as I ascended the pathway, that I did not like the red light, and that I should have slept but poorly if my bed had been under it, I see no reason to conceal. Nor did I like the two sequences of the accident and the dead girl. I see no reason to conceal that either.

But what ran most in my thoughts was the consideration, how ought I to act, having become the recipient of this disclosure? I had proved the man to be intelligent, vigilant, painstaking, and exact; but how long might he remain so, in his state of mind? Though in a subordinate position, still he held a most important trust, and would I (for instance) like to stake my own life on the chances of his continuing to execute it with precision?

Unable to overcome a feeling that there would be something treacherous in my communicating what he had told me to his superiors in the Company, without first being plain with himself and proposing a middle course to him, I ultimately resolved to offer to accompany him (otherwise keeping his secret for the present) to the wisest medical practitioner we could hear of in those parts, and to take his opinion. A change in his time of duty would come round next night, he had apprised me, and he would be off an hour or two after sunrise, and on again soon after sunset. I had appointed to return accordingly.

Next evening was a lovely evening, and I walked out early to enjoy it. The sun was not yet quite down when I traversed the field-path near the top of the deep cutting. I would extend my walk for an hour, I said to myself, half an hour on and half an hour back, and it would then be time to go to my signal-man's box.

Before pursuing my stroll, I stepped to the brink, and mechanically looked down, from the point from which I had first seen him. I cannot describe the thrill that seized upon me when close at the mouth of the tunnel, I saw the appearance of a man, with his left sleeve across his eyes, passionately waving his right arm.

The nameless horror that oppressed me passed in a moment, for in a moment I saw that this appearance of a man was a man indeed, and that there was a little group of other men, standing at a short distance, to whom he seemed to be rehearsing the gesture he made. The Danger-light was not yet lighted. Against its shaft, a little low hut, entirely new to me, had been made of some wooden supports and tarpaulin. It looked no bigger than a bed.

With an irresistible sense that something was wrong,—with a flashing self-reproachful fear that fatal mischief had come of my leaving the man there, and causing no one to be sent to overlook or correct what he did,—I descended the notched path with all the speed I could make.

"What is the matter?" I asked the men.

"Signal-man killed this morning, sir."

"Not the man belonging to that box?"

"Yes, sir."

"Not the man I know?"

"You will recognise him, sir, if you knew him," said the man who spoke for the others, solemnly uncovering his own head, and raising an end of the tarpaulin, "for his face is quite composed."

"Oh, how did this happen, how did this happen?" I asked, turning from one to another as the hut closed in again.

"He was cut down by an engine, sir. No man in England knew his work better. But somehow he was not clear of the outer rail. It was just at broad day. He had struck the light, and had the lamp in his hand. As the engine came out of the tunnel, his back was towards her, and she cut him down. That man drove her, and was showing how it happened. Show the gentleman, Tom."

The man, who wore a rough dark dress, stepped back to his former place at the mouth of the tunnel.

"Coming round the curve in the tunnel, sir," he said, "I saw him at the end, like as if I saw him down a perspective-glass. There was no time to check speed, and I knew him to be very careful. As he didn't seem to take heed of the whistle, I shut it off when we were running down upon him, and called to him as loud as I could call."

"What did you say?"

"I said, 'Below there! Look out! Look out! For God's sake, clear the way!'"

I started.

"Ah! it was a dreadful time, sir. I never left off calling to him. I put this arm before my eyes not to see, and I waved this arm to the last; but it was no use."

\*   \*   \*

Without prolonging the narrative to dwell on any one of its curious circumstances more than on any other, I may, in closing it, point out the coincidence that the warning of the Engine-Driver included, not only the words which the unfortunate Signal-man had repeated to me as haunting him, but also the words which I myself—not he—had attached, and that only in my own mind, to the gesticulation he had imitated.

∽

# A MERRY NOTE

## William Shakespeare

When Icicles hang by the wall,
    And Dick the shepherd blows his nail,
And Tom bears Logs into the hall,
    And Milk comes frozen home in pail:
When blood is nipped, and ways be foul,
Then nightly sings the staring Owl,
        Tu-whit to-who
      A merry note,
While greasy Joan doth skim the pot.

When all aloud the wind doth blow,
    And coughing drowns the Parson's saw;
And birds sit brooding in the snow,
    And Marian's nose looks red and raw;
When roasted Crabs hiss in the bowl,
Then nightly sings the staring Owl,
        Tu-whit to-who
      A merry note,
While greasy Joan doth skim the pot.

∽

## "BLOW, BLOW, THOU WINTER WIND"

*William Shakespeare*

Blow, blow, thou winter wind,
Thou art not so unkind
    As man's ingratitude;
Thy tooth is not so keen,
Because thou art not seen,
    Although thy breath be rude.
Heigh ho! sing heigh ho, unto the green holly,
Most friendship is feigning, most Loving mere folly:
    Then heigh ho, the holly,
    This Life is most jolly.

Freeze, freeze, thou bitter sky,
That dost not bite so nigh
    As benefits forgot;
Though thou the waters warp,
Thy sting is not so sharp,
    As friend remembered not.
Heigh ho! sing heigh ho! unto the green holly,
Most friendship is feigning, most Loving mere folly:
    Then heigh ho, the holly,
    This Life is most jolly.

## THE LION OF WINTER

*William Shakespeare*

Now the hungry Lion roars,
And the Wolf behowls the Moon:
Whiles the heavy ploughman snores,
All with weary task fordone.

Now that wasted brands do glow,
Whil'st the stritch-owl scritching loud,
Puts the wretch that lies in woe
In remembrance of a shroud.
Now it is the time of night
That the graves, all gaping wide,
Every one lets forth his spright,
In the Church-way paths to glide.
And we Fairies, that do run,
By the triple *Hecate*'s team,
From the presence of the Sun,
Following darkness like a dream,
Now are frolic; not a Mouse
Shall disturb this hallowed house.
I am sent with broom before,
To sweep the dust behind the door.

Through the house give glimmering light,
By the dead and drowsie fire;
Every Elf and Fairy spright
Hop as light as bird from briar! . . .

## DIRGE IN WOODS

*George Meredith*

A wind sways the pines,
          And below
Not a breath of wild air;
Still as the mosses that glow
On the flooring and over the lines
Of the roots here and there
The pine-tree drops its dead;
They are quiet, as under the sea.
Overhead, overhead
Rushes life in a race,

As the clouds the clouds chase;
And we go,
And we drop like the fruits of the tree,
Even we,
Even so.

❧

# A WINTRY SONNET

*Christina Rossetti*

A Robin said: The Spring will never come,
  And I shall never care to build again.
A Rosebush said: These frosts are wearisome,
  My sap will never stir for sun or rain.
The half Moon said: These nights are fogged and slow,
  I neither care to wax nor care to wane.
The Ocean said: I thirst from long ago,
  Because earth's rivers cannot fill the main.—
When Springtime came, red Robin built a nest,
  And trilled a lover's song in sheer delight.
  Grey hoarfrost vanished, and the Rose with might
  Clothed her in leaves and buds of crimson core.
The dim Moon brightened. Ocean sunned his crest,
  Dimpled his blue, yet thirsted evermore.

❧

## SONG

### *Christina Rossetti*

When I am dead, my dearest,
 Sing no sad songs for me;
Plant thou no roses at my head,
 Nor shady cypress tree:
Be the green grass above me
 With showers and dewdrops wet;
And if thou wilt, remember,
 And if thou wilt, forget.

I shall not see the shadows,
 I shall not feel the rain;
I shall not hear the nightingale
 Sing on, as if in pain:
And dreaming through the twilight
 That doth not rise nor set,
Haply I may remember,
 And haply may forget.

∾

## THE SILVER SWAN

### *Orlando Gibbons*

The silver swan, who living had no note
When death approached unlocked her silent throat;
Leaning her breast against the reedy shore,
Thus sung her first and last, and sung no more:
Farewell, all joys; O death, come close mine eyes;
More geese than swans now live, more fools than wise.

∾

## NIGHTMARE

### *William Schwenk Gilbert*

When you're lying awake with a dismal headache,
    and repose is taboo'd by anxiety,
I conceive you may use any language you choose to
    indulge in, without impropriety;
For your brain is on fire—the bedclothes conspire of
    usual slumber to plunder you:
First your counterpane goes, and uncovers your toes,
    and your sheet slips demurely from under you;
Then the blanketing tickles—you feel like mixed
    pickles—so terribly sharp is the pricking,
And you're hot, and you're cross, and you tumble
    and toss till there's nothing 'twixt you and the
    ticking.
Then the bedclothes all creep to the ground in a heap,
    and you pick 'em all up in a tangle;
Next your pillow resigns and politely declines to
    remain at its usual angle!
Well, you get some repose in the form of a doze, with
    hot eye-balls and head ever aching,
But your slumbering teems with such horrible dreams
    that you'd very much better be waking;
For you dream you are crossing the Channel, and
    tossing about in a steamer from Harwich—
Which is something between a large bathing machine
    and a very small second-class carriage—
And you're giving a treat (penny ice and cold meat)
    to a party of friends and relations—
They're a ravenous horde—and they all come on
    board at Sloane Square and South Kensington
    Stations.
And bound on that journey you find your attorney
    (who started that morning from Devon);
He's a bit undersized, and you don't feel surprised
    when he tells you he's only eleven.

Well, you're driving like mad with this singular lad
      (by-the-bye the ship's now a four-wheeler),
And you're playing round games, and he calls you
      bad names when you tell him that "ties pay the
      dealer";
But this you can't stand, as you throw up your hand,
      and you find you're as cold as an icicle,
In your shirt and your socks (the black silk with gold
      clocks), crossing Salisbury Plain on a bicycle:
And he and the crew are on bicycles too—which
      they've somehow or other invested in—
And he's telling the tars, all the particu*lars* of a com-
      pany he's interested in—
It's a scheme of devices, to get at low prices all goods
      from cough mixtures to cables
(Which tickled the sailors) by treating retailers, as
      though they were all vege*ta*bles—
You get a good spadesman to plant a small trades-
      man (first take off his boots with a boot-
      tree),
And his legs will take root, and his fingers will shoot,
      and they'll blossom and bud like a fruit-tree—
From the greengrocer tree you get grapes and green-
      pea, cauliflower, pineapple, and cranberries,
While the pastrycook plant, cherry brandy will grant,
      apple puffs, and three-corners, and Banburys—
The shares are a penny, and ever so many are taken
      by Rothschild and Baring,
And just as a few are allotted to you, you awake with
      a shudder despairing—
You're a regular wreck, with a crick in your neck,
      and no wonder you snore, for your head's on
      the floor, and you've needles and pins from
      your soles to your shins, and your flesh is a-creep,
      for your left leg's asleep, and you've cramp in
      your toes, and a fly on your nose, and some fluff
      in your lung, and a feverish tongue, and a thirst
      that's intense, and a general sense that you
      haven't been sleeping in clover;
But the darkness has passed, and it's daylight at

last, and the night has been long—ditto ditto
my song—and thank goodness they're both of
them over!

༚

# WITCHES' LOAVES

## O. Henry

Miss Martha Meacham kept the little bakery on the corner (the one where
you go up three steps, and the bell tinkles when you open the door).

Miss Martha was forty, her bank-book showed a credit of two thousand
dollars, and she possessed two false teeth and a sympathetic heart. Many
people have married whose chances to do so were much inferior to Miss
Martha's.

Two or three times a week a customer came in in whom she began to
take an interest. He was a middle-aged man, wearing spectacles and a
brown beard trimmed to a careful point.

He spoke English with a strong German accent. His clothes were
worn and darned in places, and wrinkled and baggy in others. But he
looked neat, and had very good manners.

He always bought two loaves of stale bread. Fresh bread was five
cents a loaf. Stale ones were two for five. Never did he call for anything but
stale bread.

Once Miss Martha saw a red and brown stain on his fingers. She was
sure then that he was an artist and very poor. No doubt he lived in a garret,
where he painted pictures and ate stale bread and thought of the good things
to eat in Miss Martha's bakery.

Often when Miss Martha sat down to her chops and light rolls and
jam and tea she would sigh, and wish that the gentle-mannered artist
might share her tasty meal instead of eating his dry crust in that draughty
attic. Miss Martha's heart, as you have been told, was a sympathetic one.

In order to test her theory as to his occupation, she brought from her
room one day a painting that she had bought at a sale, and set it against the
shelves behind the bread counter.

It was a Venetian scene. A splendid marble palazzo (so it said on the picture) stood in the foreground—or rather forewater. For the rest there were gondolas (with the lady trailing her hand in the water), clouds, sky, and chiaroscuro in plenty. No artist could fail to notice it.

Two days afterward the customer came in.

"Two loafs of stale bread, if you blease."

"You haf here a fine bicture, madame," he said while she was wrapping up the bread.

"Yes?" says Miss Martha, revelling in her own cunning. "I do so admire art and" (no, it would not do to say "artists" thus early) "and paintings," she substituted. "You think it is a good picture?"

"Der halace," said the customer, "is not in good drawing. Der bairspective of it is not true. Goot morning, madame."

He took his bread, bowed, and hurried out.

Yes, he must be an artist. Miss Martha took the picture back to her room.

How gentle and kindly his eyes shone behind his spectacles! What a broad brow he had! To be able to judge perspective at a glance—and to live on stale bread! But genius often has to struggle before it is recognized.

What a thing it would be for art and perspective if genius were backed by two thousand dollars in bank, a bakery, and a sympathetic heart to— But these were day-dreams, Miss Martha.

Often now when he came he would chat for a while across the show-case. He seemed to crave Miss Martha's cheerful words.

He kept on buying stale bread. Never a cake, never a pie, never one of her delicious Sally Lunns.

She thought he began to look thinner and discouraged. Her heart ached to add something good to eat to his meagre purchase, but her courage failed at the act. She did not dare affront him. She knew the pride of artists.

Miss Martha took to wearing her blue-dotted silk waist behind the counter. In the back room she cooked a mysterious compound of quince seeds and borax. Ever so many people use it for the complexion.

One day the customer came in as usual, laid his nickel on the show-case, and called for his stale loaves. While Miss Martha was reaching for them there was a great tooting and clanging, and a fire-engine came lumbering past.

The customer hurried to the door to look, as any one will. Suddenly inspired, Miss Martha seized the opportunity.

On the bottom shelf behind the counter was a pound of fresh butter that the dairyman had left ten minutes before. With bread knife Miss Martha made a deep slash in each of the stale loaves, inserted a generous quantity of butter, and pressed the loaves tight again.

When the customer turned once more she was tying the paper around them.

When he had gone, after an unusually pleasant little chat, Miss Martha smiled to herself, but not without a slight fluttering of the heart.

Had she been too bold? Would he take offense? But surely not. There was no language of edibles. Butter was no emblem of unmaidenly forwardness.

For a long time that day her mind dwelt on the subject. She imagined the scene when he should discover her little deception.

He would lay down his brushes and palette. There would stand his easel with the picture he was painting in which the perspective was beyond criticism.

He would prepare for his luncheon of dry bread and water. He would slice into a loaf—ah!

Miss Martha blushed. Would he think of the hand that placed it there as he ate? Would he—

The front door bell jangled viciously. Somebody was coming in, making a great deal of noise.

Miss Martha hurried to the front. Two men were there. One was a young man smoking a pipe—a man she had never seen before. The other was her artist.

His face was very red, his hat was on the back of his head, his hair was wildly rumpled. He clinched his two fists and shook them ferociously at Miss Martha. *At Miss Martha.*

*"Dummkopf!"* he shouted with extreme loudness; and then *"Tausendonfer!"* or something like it in German.

The young man tried to draw him away.

"I vill not go," he said angrily, "else I shall told her."

He made a bass drum of Miss Martha's counter.

"You haf shpoilt me," he cried, his blue eyes blazing behind his spectacles. "I vill tell you. You vas von *meddlingsome old cat!*"

Miss Martha leaned weakly against the shelves and laid one hand on her blue-dotted silk waist. The young man took the other by the collar.

"Come on," he said, "you've said enough." He dragged the angry one out at the door to the sidewalk, and then came back.

"Guess you ought to be told, ma'am," he said, "what the row is about.

That's Blumberger. He's an architectural draftsman. I work in the same office with him.

"He's been working hard for three months drawing a plan for a new city hall. It was a prize competition. He finished inking the lines yesterday. You know, a draftsman always makes his drawing in pencil first. When it's done he rubs out the pencil lines with handfuls of stale bread crumbs. That's better than India rubber.

"Blumberger's been buying the bread here. Well, to-day—well, you know, ma'am, that butter isn't—well, Blumberger's plan isn't good for anything now except to cut up into railroad sandwiches."

Miss Martha went into the back room. She took off the blue-dotted silk waist and put on the old brown serge she used to wear. Then she poured the quince seed and borax mixture out of the window into the ash can.

∾

# THE HORLA, OR MODERN GHOSTS

## Guy de Maupassant

*May 8.* What a beautiful day! I have spent all the morning lying in the grass in front of my house, under the enormous plantain tree which covers it, and shades and shelters the whole of it. I like this part of the country and I am fond of living here because I am attached to it by deep roots, profound and delicate roots which attach a man to the soil on which his ancestors were born and died, which attach him to what people think and what they eat, to the usages as well as to the food, local expressions, the peculiar language of the peasants, to the smell of the soil, of the villages and of the atmosphere itself.

I love my house in which I grew up. From my windows I can see the Seine which flows by the side of my garden, on the other side of the road, almost through my grounds, the great wide Seine, which goes to Rouen and Havre, and which is covered with boats passing to and fro.

On the left, down yonder, lies Rouen, that large town with its blue roofs, under its pointed, Gothic towers. They are innumerable, delicate or broad, dominated by the spire of the cathedral, and full of bells which sound through the blue air on fine mornings, sending their sweet and distant iron clang, to me; their metallic sound which the breeze wafts in my direction, now stronger and now weaker, according as the wind is stronger or lighter.

What a delicious morning it was!

About eleven o'clock, a long line of boats drawn by a steam-tug, as big as a fly, and which scarcely puffed while emitting its thick smoke, passed my gate.

After two English schooners, whose red flag fluttered towards the sky, there came a magnificent Brazilian three-master; it was perfectly white and wonderfully clean and shining. I saluted it, I hardly know why, except that the sight of the vessel gave me great pleasure.

*May 12.* I have had a slight feverish attack for the last few days, and I feel ill, or rather I feel low-spirited.

Whence do these mysterious influences come, which change our happiness into discouragement, and our self-confidence into diffidence? One might almost say that the air, the invisible air, is full of unknowable Forces, whose mysterious presence we have to endure. I wake up in the best spirits, with an inclination to sing in my throat. Why? I go down by the side of the water, and suddenly, after walking a short distance, I return home wretched, as if some misfortune were awaiting me there. Why? Is it a cold shiver which, passing over my skin, has upset my nerves and given me low spirits? Is it the form of the clouds, or the color of the sky, or the color of the surrounding objects which is so changeable, which have troubled my thoughts as they passed before my eyes? Who can tell? Everything that surrounds us, everything that we see without looking at it, everything that we touch without knowing it, everything that we handle without feeling it, all that we meet without clearly distinguishing it, has a rapid, surprising and inexplicable effect upon us and upon our organs, and through them on our ideas and on our heart itself.

How profound that mystery of the Invisible is! We cannot fathom it with our miserable senses, with our eyes which are unable to perceive what is either too small or too great, too near to, or too far from us; neither the inhabitants of a star nor of a drop of water . . . with our ears that deceive us, for they transmit to us the vibrations of the air in sonorous notes. They are fairies who work the miracle of changing that movement into noise, and by that metamorphosis give birth to music, which makes the mute agitation of nature musical . . . with our sense of smell which is smaller than that of a dog . . . with our sense of taste which can scarcely distinguish the age of a wine!

Oh! If we only had other organs which would work other miracles in our favor, what a number of fresh things we might discover around us!

*May 16.*    I am ill, decidedly! I was so well last month! I am feverish, horribly feverish, or rather I am in a state of feverish enervation, which makes my mind suffer as much as my body. I have without ceasing that horrible sensation of some danger threatening me, that apprehension of some coming misfortune or of approaching death, that presentiment which is, no doubt, an attack of some illness which is still unknown, which germinates in the flesh and in the blood.

*May 18.*    I have just come from consulting my medical man, for I could no longer get any sleep. He found that my pulse was high, my eyes dilated, my nerves highly strung, but no alarming symptoms. I must have a course of shower baths and of bromide of potassium.

*May 25.*    No change! My state is really very peculiar. As the evening comes on, an incomprehensible feeling of disquietude seizes me, just as if night concealed some terrible menace towards me. I dine quickly, and then try to read, but I do not understand the words, and can scarcely distinguish the letters. Then I walk up and down my drawing-room, oppressed by a feeling of confused and irresistible fear, the fear of sleep and fear of my bed.

About ten o'clock I go up to my room. As soon as I have got in I double lock, and bolt it: I am frightened . . . of what? Up till the present time I have been frightened of nothing . . . I open my cupboards, and look under my bed; I listen . . . I listen . . . to what? How strange it is that a simple feeling of discomfort, impeded or heightened circulation, perhaps the irritation of a nervous thread, a slight congestion, a small disturbance in the imperfect and delicate functions of our living machinery, can turn the most light-hearted of men into a melancholy one, and make a coward of the bravest? Then, I go to bed, and I wait for sleep as a man might wait for the executioner. I wait for its coming with dread, and my heart beats and my legs tremble, while my whole body shivers beneath the warmth of the bedclothes, until the moment when I suddenly fall asleep, as one would throw oneself into a pool of stagnant water in order to drown oneself. I do not feel as I used to do formerly, this perfidious sleep which is close to me and watching me, which is going to seize me by the head, to close my eyes and annihilate me, coming over me.

I sleep—a long time—two or three hours perhaps—then a dream—no—a nightmare lays hold on me. I feel that I am in bed and asleep . . . I feel it and I know it . . . and I feel also that somebody is coming close to me, is looking at me, touching me, is getting on to my bed, is kneeling on my chest, is taking my neck between his hands and squeezing it . . . squeezing it with all his might in order to strangle me.

I struggle, bound by that terrible powerlessness which paralyzes us in our dreams; I try to cry out—but I cannot; I want to move—I cannot; I try, with the most violent efforts and out of breath, to turn over and throw off this being which is crushing and suffocating me—I cannot!

And then suddenly, I wake up, shaken and bathed in perspiration; I light a candle and find that I am alone, and after that crisis, which occurs every night, I at length fall asleep and slumber tranquilly till morning.

*June 2.* My state has grown worse. What is the matter with me? The bromide does me no good, and the shower baths have no effect whatever. Sometimes, in order to tire myself out, though I am fatigued enough already, I go for a walk in the forest of Roumare. I used to think at first that the fresh light and soft air, impregnated with the odor of herbs and leaves, would instill new blood into my veins and impart fresh energy to my heart. I turned into a broad ride in the wood, and then I turned towards La Bouille, through a narrow path, between two rows of exceedingly tall trees, which placed a thick, green, almost black roof between the sky and me.

A sudden shiver ran through me, not a cold shiver, but a shiver of agony, and so I hastened my steps, uneasy at being alone in the wood, frightened stupidly and without reason, at the profound solitude. Suddenly it seemed to me as if I were being followed, that somebody was walking at my heels, close, quite close to me, near enough to touch me.

I turned round suddenly, but I was alone. I saw nothing behind me except the straight, broad ride, empty and bordered by high trees, horribly empty; on the other side it also extended until it was lost in the distance, and looked just the same, terrible.

I closed my eyes. Why? And then I began to turn round on one heel very quickly, just like a top. I nearly fell down, and opened my eyes; the trees were dancing round me and the earth heaved; I was obliged to sit down. Then, ah! I no longer remembered how I had come! What a strange idea! What a strange, strange idea! I did not the least know. I started off to the right, and got back into the avenue which had led me into the middle of the forest.

*June 3.* I have had a terrible night. I shall go away for a few weeks, for no doubt a journey will set me up again.

*July 2.* I have come back, quite cured, and have had a most delightful trip into the bargain. I have been to Mont Saint-Michel, which I had not seen before.

What a sight, when one arrives as I did, at Avranches towards the end of the day! The town stands on a hill, and I was taken into the public garden at the extremity of the town. I uttered a cry of astonishment. An extraordinarily large bay lay extended before me, as far as my eyes could reach, between two hills which were lost to sight in the mist; and in the middle of this immense yellow bay, under a clear, golden sky, a peculiar hill rose up, somber and pointed in the midst of the sand. The sun had just disappeared, and under the still flaming sky the outline of that fantastic rock stood out, which bears on its summit a fantastic monument.

At daybreak I went to it. The tide was low as it had been the night before, and I saw that wonderful abbey rise up before me as I approached it. After several hours walking, I reached the enormous mass of rocks which supports the little town, dominated by the great church. Having climbed the steep and narrow street, I entered the most wonderful Gothic building that has ever been built to God on earth, as large as a town, full of low rooms which seem buried beneath vaulted roofs, and lofty galleries supported by delicate columns.

I entered this gigantic granite jewel which is as light as a bit of lace, covered with towers, with slender belfries to which spiral staircases ascend, and which raise their strange heads that bristle with chimeras, with devils, with fantastic animals, with monstrous flowers, and which are joined together by finely carved arches, to the blue sky by day, and to the black sky by night.

When I had reached the summit, I said to the monk who accompanied me: "Father, how happy you must be here!" And he replied: "It is very windy, Monsieur"; and so we began to talk while watching the rising tide, which ran over the sand and covered it with a steel cuirass.

And then the monk told me stories, all the old stories belonging to the place, legends, nothing but legends.

One of them struck me forcibly. The country people, those belonging to the Mornet, declare that at night one can hear talking going on in the sand, and then that one hears two goats bleat, one with a strong, the other with a weak voice. Incredulous people declare that it is nothing but the cry of the sea birds, which occasionally resembles bleatings, and occasionally human lamentations; but belated fishermen swear that they have met an old shepherd, whose head, which is covered by his cloak, they can never see, wandering on the downs, between two tides, round the little town placed so far out of the world, and who is guiding and walking before them, a he-goat with a man's face, and a she-goat with a woman's face, and both of them with white hair; and talking incessantly, quarreling in a strange language, and then suddenly ceasing to talk in order to bleat with all their might.

"Do you believe it?" I asked the monk. "I scarcely know," he replied, and I continued: "If there are other beings besides ourselves on this earth, how comes it that we have not known it for so long a time, or why have you not seen them? How is it that I have not seen them?" He replied: "Do we see the hundred thousandth part of what exists? Look here; there is the wind, which is the strongest force in nature, which knocks down men, and blows down buildings, uproots trees, raises the sea into mountains of water, destroys cliffs and casts great ships onto the breakers; the wind which kills, which whistles, which sighs, which roars,—have you ever seen it, and can you see it? It exists for all that, however!"

I was silent before this simple reasoning. That man was a philosopher, or perhaps a fool; I could not say which exactly, so I held my tongue. What he had said, had often been in my own thoughts.

*July 3.*   I have slept badly; certainly there is some feverish influence here, for my coachman is suffering in the same way as I am. When I went back home yesterday, I noticed his singular paleness, and I asked him: "What is the matter with you, Jean?" "The matter is that I never get any rest, and my nights devour my days. Since your departure, Monsieur, there has been a spell over me."

However, the other servants are all well, but I am very frightened of having another attack, myself.

*July 4.*   I am decidedly taken again; for my old nightmares have returned. Last night I felt somebody leaning on me who was sucking my life from between my lips with his mouth. Yes, he was sucking it out of my neck, like a leech would have done. Then he got up, satiated, and I woke up, so beaten, crushed and annihilated that I could not move. If this continues for a few days, I shall certainly go away again.

*July 5.*   Have I lost my reason? What has happened, what I saw last night is so strange, that my head wanders when I think of it!

As I do now every evening, I had locked my door, and then, being thirsty, I drank half a glass of water, and I accidentally noticed that the water-bottle was full up to the cut-glass stopper.

Then I went to bed and fell into one of my terrible sleeps, from which I was aroused in about two hours by a still more terrible shock.

Picture to yourself a sleeping man who is being murdered and who wakes up with a knife in his chest, and who is rattling in his throat, covered with blood, and who can no longer breathe and is going to die and does not understand anything at all about it—there it is.

Having recovered my senses, I was thirsty again, so I lit a candle and went to the table on which my water-bottle was. I lifted it up and tilted it over my glass, but nothing came out. It was empty! It was completely empty! At first I could not understand it at all, and then suddenly I was seized by such a terrible feeling that I had to sit down, or rather I fell into a chair! Then I sprang up with a bound to look about me, and then I sat down again, overcome by astonishment and fear, in front of the transparent crystal bottle! I looked at it with fixed eyes, trying to conjecture, and my hands trembled! Somebody had drunk the water, but who? I? I without any doubt. It could surely only be I? In that case I was a somnambulist. I lived, without knowing it, that double mysterious life which makes us doubt whether there are not two beings in us, or whether a strange, unknowable and invisible being does not at such moments, when our soul is in a state of torpor, animate our captive body which obeys this other being, as it does us ourselves, and more than it does ourselves.

Oh! Who will understand my horrible agony? Who will understand the emotion of a man who is sound in mind, wide awake, full of sound sense, and who looks in horror at the remains of a little water that has disappeared while he was asleep, through the glass of a water-bottle! And I remained there until it was daylight, without venturing to go to bed again.

*July 6.* I am going mad. Again all the contents of my water-bottle have been drunk during the night;—or rather, I have drunk it!

But is it I? Is it I? Who could it be? Who? Oh! God! Am I going mad? Who will save me?

*July 10.* I have just been through some surprising ideals. Decidedly I am mad! And yet! . . .

On July 6, before going to bed, I put some wine, milk, water, bread and strawberries on my table. Somebody drank—I drank—all the water and a little of the milk, but neither the wine, bread nor the strawberries were touched.

On the seventh of July I renewed the same experiment, with the same results, and on July 8, I left out the water and the milk and nothing was touched.

Lastly, on July 9 I put only water and milk on my table, taking care to wrap up the bottles in white muslin and to tie down the stoppers. Then I rubbed my lips, my beard and my hands with pencil lead, and went to bed.

Irresistible sleep seized me, which was soon followed by a terrible awakening. I had not moved, and my sheets were not marked. I rushed to the table. The muslin round the bottles remained intact; I undid the string, trembling with fear. All the water had been drunk, and so had the milk! Ah! Great God! . . .

I must start for Paris immediately.

*July 12.* Paris. I must have lost my head during the last few days! I must be the plaything of my enervated imagination, unless I am really a somnambulist, or that I have been brought under the power of one of those influences which have been proved to exist, but which have hitherto been inexplicable, which are called suggestions. In any case, my mental state bordered on madness, and twenty-four hours of Paris sufficed to restore me to my equilibrium.

Yesterday after doing some business and paying some visits which instilled fresh and invigorating mental air into me, I wound up my evening at the *Théâtre-Français*. A play by Alexandre Dumas the Younger was being acted, and his active and powerful mind completed my cure. Certainly solitude is dangerous for active minds. We require men who can think and can talk, around us. When we are alone for a long time, we people space with phantoms.

I returned along the boulevards to my hotel in excellent spirits. Amid the jostling of the crowd I thought, not without irony, of my terrors and surmises of the previous week, because I believed, yes, I believed, that an invisible being lived beneath my roof. How weak our head is, and how quickly it is terrified and goes astray, as soon as we are struck by a small, incomprehensible fact.

Instead of concluding with these simple words: "I do not understand because the cause escapes me," we immediately imagine terrible mysteries and supernatural powers.

*July 14.* *Fête* of the Republic. I walked through the streets, and the crackers and flags amused me like a child. Still it is very foolish to be merry on a fixed date, by a Government decree. The populace, an imbecile flock of sheep, now steadily patient, and now in ferocious revolt. Say to it: "Amuse yourself," and it amuses itself. Say to it: "Go and fight with your neighbor," and it goes and fights. Say to it: "Vote for the Emperor," and it votes for the Emperor, and then say to it: "Vote for the Republic," and it votes for the Republic.

Those who direct it are also stupid; but instead of obeying men, they obey principles, which can only be stupid, sterile and false, for the very reason that they are principles, that is to say, ideas which are considered as certain and unchangeable, in this world where one is certain of nothing, since light is an illusion and noise is an illusion.

*July 16.* I saw some things yesterday that troubled me very much.

I was dining with my cousin Madame Sablé, whose husband is colonel of the 76th Chasseurs at Limoges. There were two young women there, one of whom had married a medical man, Dr. Parent, who devotes himself a great deal to nervous diseases and the extraordinary manifestations to which at this moment experiments in hypnotism and suggestion give rise.

He related to us at some length the remarkable results obtained by English scientists and the doctors of the medical school at Nancy, and the facts which he adduced, appeared to me so strange, that I declared that I was altogether incredulous.

"We are," he declared, "on the point of discovering one of the most important secrets of nature, I mean to say, one of its most important secrets on this earth, for there are certainly some which are of a different kind of importance up in the stars, yonder. Ever since man has thought, since he has been able to express and write down his thoughts, he has felt himself close to a mystery which is impenetrable to his coarse and imperfect senses, and he endeavors to supplement the want of power of his organs, by the efforts of his intellect. As long as that intellect still remained in its elementary stage, this intercourse with invisible spirits, assumed forms which were commonplace though terrifying. Thence sprang the popular belief in the supernatural, the legends of wandering spirits, of fairies, of gnomes, ghosts, I might even say the legend of God, for our conceptions of the workman-creator, from whatever religion they may have come down to us, are certainly the most mediocre, the stupidest and the most unacceptable inventions that ever sprang from the frightened brain of any human creatures. Nothing is truer than what Voltaire says: "God made man in His own image, but man has certainly paid Him back again.""

"But for rather more than a century, men seem to have had a presentiment of something new. Mesmer and some others have put us on an unexpected track, and especially within the last two or three years, we have arrived at really surprising results."

My cousin, who is also very incredulous, smiled, and Dr. Parent said to her: "Would you like me to try and send you to sleep, Madame?" "Yes, certainly."

She sat down in an easy-chair, and he began to look at her fixedly, so as to fascinate her. I suddenly felt myself somewhat uncomfortable, with a beating heart and a choking feeling in my throat. I saw that Madame Sablé's eyes were growing heavy, her mouth twitched and her bosom heaved, and at the end of ten minutes she was asleep.

"Stand behind her," the doctor said to me, and so I took a seat behind her. He put a visiting-card into her hands, and said to her: "This is a looking-glass; what do you see in it?" And she replied: "I see my cousin." "What is he doing?" "He is twisting his moustache." "And now?" "He is taking a photograph out of his pocket." "Whose photograph is it?" "His own."

That was true, and that photograph had been given me that same evening at the hotel.

"What is his attitude in this portrait?" "He is standing up with his hat in his hand."

So she saw on that card, on that piece of white pasteboard, as if she had seen it in a looking-glass.

The young women were frightened, and exclaimed: "That is quite enough! Quite, quite enough!"

But the doctor said to her authoritatively: "You will get up at eight o'clock to-morrow morning; then you will go and call on your cousin at his hotel and ask him to lend you five thousands francs which your husband demands of you, and which he will ask for when he sets out on his coming journey."

Then he woke her up.

On returning to my hotel, I thought over this curious *séance* and I was assailed by doubts, not as to my cousin's absolute and undoubted good faith, for I had known her as well as if she had been my own sister ever since she was a child, but as to a possible trick on the doctor's part. Had not he, per-haps, kept a glass hidden in his hand, which he showed to the young woman in her sleep, at the same time as he did the card? Professional con-jurors do things which are just as singular.

So I went home and to bed, and this morning, at about half past eight, I was awakened by my footman, who said to me: "Madame Sablé has asked to see you immediately, Monsieur," so I dressed hastily and went to her.

She sat down in some agitation, with her eyes on the floor, and without raising her veil she said to me: "My dear cousin, I am going to ask a great favor of you." "What is it, cousin?" "I do not like to tell you, and yet I must. I am in absolute want of five thousand francs." "What, you?" "Yes, I, or rather my husband, who has asked me to procure the money for him."

I was so stupefied that I stammered out my answers. I asked myself whether she had not really been making fun of me with Dr. Parent, if it were not merely a very well-acted farce which had been got up beforehand. On looking at her attentively, however, my doubts disappeared. She was trembling with grief, so painful was this step to her, and I was sure that her throat was full of sobs.

I knew that she was very rich and so I continued: "What! Has not your husband five thousand francs at his disposal! Come, think. Are you sure that he commissioned you to ask me for them?"

She hesitated for a few seconds, as if she were making a great effort to search her memory, and then she replied: "Yes . . . yes, I am quite sure of it." "He has written to you?"

She hesitated again and reflected, and I guessed the torture of her thoughts. She did not know. She only knew that she was to borrow five thousand francs of me for her husband. So she told a lie. "Yes, he has written to me." "When pray? You did not mention it to me yesterday." "I received his letter this morning." "Can you show it me?" "No; no . . . no . . . it contained private matters . . . things too personal to ourselves . . . I burnt it." "So your husband runs into debt?"

She hesitated again, and then murmured: "I do not know." Thereupon I said bluntly: "I have not five thousand francs at my disposal at this moment, my dear cousin."

She uttered a kind of a cry as if she were in pain and said: "Oh! oh! I beseech you, I beseech you to get them for me . . ."

She got excited and clasped her hands as if she were praying to me! I heard her voice change its tone; she wept and stammered, harassed and dominated by the irresistible order that she had received.

"Oh! oh! I beg you to . . . if you knew what I am suffering . . . I want them to-day."

I had pity on her: "You shall have them by and by, I swear to you." "Oh! thank you! thank you! How kind you are."

I continued: "Do you remember what took place at your house last night?" "Yes." "Do you remember that Dr. Parent sent you to sleep?" "Yes." "Oh! Very well then; he ordered you to come to me this morning to borrow five thousand francs, and at this moment you are obeying that suggestion."

She considered for a few moments, and then replied: "But as it is my husband who wants them . . ."

For a whole hour I tried to convince her, but could not succeed, and when she had gone I went to the doctor. He was just going out, and he listened to me with a smile, and said: "Do you believe now?" "Yes, I cannot help it." "Let us go to your cousin's."

She was already dozing on a couch, overcome with fatigue. The doctor felt her pulse, looked at her for some time with one hand raised towards her eyes which she closed by degrees under the irresistible power of this magnetic influence, and when she was asleep, he said:

"Your husband does not require the five thousand francs any longer! You must, therefore, forget that you asked your cousin to lend them to you, and, if he speaks to you about it, you will not understand him."

Then he woke her up, and I took out a pocketbook and said: "Here is what you asked me for this morning, my dear cousin." But she was so surprised, that I did not venture to persist; nevertheless, I tried to recall the circumstance to her, but she denied it vigorously, thought that I was making fun of her, and in the end, very nearly lost her temper.

There! I have just come back, and I have not been able to eat any lunch, for this experiment has altogether upset me.

*July 19.*   Many people to whom I have told the adventure, have laughed at me. I no longer know what to think. The wise man says: Perhaps?

*July 21.*   I dined at Bougival, and then I spent the evening at a boatmen's ball. Decidedly everything depends on place and surroundings. It would be the height of folly to believe in the supernatural on the *île de la Grenouillière** . . . but on the top of Mont Saint-Michel? . . . and in India? We are terribly under the influence of our surroundings. I shall return home next week.

*July 30.*   I came back to my own house yesterday. Everything is going on well.

*August 2.*   Nothing new. It is splendid weather, and I spent my days in watching the Seine flow past.

*August 4.*   Quarrels among my servants. They declare that the glasses are broken in the cupboards at night. The footman accuses the cook, who accuses the needle woman, who accuses the other two. Who is the culprit? A clever person, to be able to tell.

*August 6.*   This time, I am not mad. I have seen . . . I have seen . . . I have seen! . . . I can doubt no longer . . . I have seen it! . . .

I was walking at two o'clock among my rose trees, in the full sunlight . . . in the walk bordered by autumn roses which are beginning to fall. As I stopped to look at a *Géant de Bataille,* which had three splendid blooms, I distinctly saw the stalk of one of the roses bend, close to me, as if an invisible hand had bent it, and then break, as if that hand had picked it! Then the flower raised itself, following the curve which a hand would have described in carrying it towards a mouth, and it remained suspended in the transparent air, all alone and motionless, a terrible red spot, three yards from my eyes. In desperation I rushed at it to take it! I found nothing; it had disappeared. Then I was seized with furious rage against myself, for it is not allowable for a reasonable and serious man to have such hallucinations.

*Frog-island

But was it a hallucination? I turned round to look for the stalk, and I found it immediately under the bush, freshly broken, between two other roses which remained on the branch, and I returned home then, with a much disturbed mind; for I am certain now, as certain as I am of the alternation of day and night, that there exists close to me an invisible being that lives on milk and on water, which can touch objects, take them and change their places; which is, consequently, endowed with a material nature, although it is imperceptible to our senses, and which lives as I do, under my roof. . . .

*August 7.* I slept tranquilly. He drank the water out of my decanter, but did not disturb my sleep.

I ask myself whether I am mad. As I was walking just now in the sun by the riverside, doubts as to my own sanity arose in me; not vague doubts such as I have had hitherto, but precise and absolute doubts. I have seen mad people, and I have known some who have been quite intelligent, lucid, even clear-sighted in every concern of life, except on one point. They spoke clearly, readily, profoundly on everything, when suddenly their thoughts struck upon the breakers of their madness and broke to pieces there, and were dispersed and foundered in that furious and terrible sea, full of bounding waves, fogs and squalls, which is called *madness*.

I certainly should think that I was mad, absolutely mad, if I were not conscious, did not perfectly know my state, if I did not fathom it by analyzing it with the most complete lucidity. I should, in fact, be a reasonable man who was laboring under a hallucination. Some unknown disturbance must have been excited in my brain, one of those disturbances which physiologists of the present day try to note and to fix precisely, and that disturbance must have caused a profound gulf in my mind and in the order and logic of my ideas. Similar phenomena occur in the dreams which lead us through the most unlikely phantasmagoria, without causing us any surprise, because our verifying apparatus and our sense of control has gone to sleep, while our imaginative faculty wakes and works. Is it not possible that one of the imperceptible keys of the cerebral finger-board has been paralyzed in me? Some men lose the recollection of proper names, or of verbs or of numbers or merely of dates, in consequence of an accident. The localization of all the particles of thought has been proved nowadays; what then would there be surprising in the fact that my faculty of controlling the unreality of certain hallucinations should be destroyed for the time being!

I thought of all this as I walked by the side of the water. The sun was shining brightly on the river and made earth delightful, while it filled my looks with love for life, for the swallows, whose agility is always delightful in my eyes, for the plants by the riverside, whose rustling is a pleasure to my ears.

By degrees, however, an inexplicable feeling of discomfort seized me. It seemed to me as if some unknown force were numbing and stopping me, were preventing me from going further and were calling me back. I felt that painful wish to return which oppresses you when you have left a beloved invalid at home, and when you are seized by a presentiment that he is worse.

I, therefore, returned in spite of myself, feeling certain that I should find some bad news awaiting me, a letter or a telegram. There was nothing, however, and I was more surprised and uneasy than if I had had another fantastic vision.

*August 8.*    I spent a terrible evening, yesterday. He does not show himself any more, but I feel that he is near me, watching me, looking at me, penetrating me, dominating me and more redoubtable when he hides himself thus, than if he were to manifest his constant and invisible presence by supernatural phenomena. However, I slept.

*August 9.*    Nothing, but I am afraid.

*August 10.*    Nothing; what will happen to-morrow?

*August 11.*    Still nothing; I cannot stop at home with this fear hanging over me and these thoughts in my mind; I shall go away.

*August 12.*    Ten o'clock at night. All day long I have been trying to get away, and have not been able. I wished to accomplish this simple and easy act of liberty—go out—get into my carriage in order to go to Rouen—and I have not been able to do it. What is the reason?

*August 13.*    When one is attacked by certain maladies, all the springs of our physical being appear to be broken, all our energies destroyed, all our muscles relaxed, our bones to have become as soft as our flesh, and our blood as liquid as water. I am experiencing that condition in my moral being in a strange and distressing manner. I have no longer any strength, any courage, any self-control, nor even any power to set my own will in motion. I have no power left to *will* anything, but some one does it for me and I obey.

*August 14.*    I am lost! Somebody possesses my soul and governs it! Somebody orders all my acts, all my movements, all my thoughts. I am no longer anything in myself, nothing except an enslaved and terrified spectator of all the things which I do. I wish to go out; I cannot. He does not wish to, and so I remain, trembling and distracted in the armchair in which he keeps me sitting. I merely wish to get up and to rouse myself, so as to think that I am still master of myself: I cannot! I am riveted to my chair, and my chair adheres to the ground in such a manner that no force could move us.

Then suddenly, I must, I must go to the bottom of my garden to pick some strawberries and eat them, and I go there. I pick the strawberries and I eat them! Oh! my God! my God! Is there a God? If there be one, deliver me! save me! succor me! Pardon! Pity! Mercy! Save me! Oh! what sufferings! what torture! what horror!

*August 15.*   Certainly this is the way in which my poor cousin was possessed and swayed, when she came to borrow five thousand francs of me. She was under the power of a strange will which had entered into her, like another soul, like another parasitic and ruling soul. Is the world coming to an end?

But who is he, this invisible being that rules me? This unknowable being, this rover of a supernatural race?

Invisible beings exist, then! How is it then that since the beginning of the world they have never manifested themselves in such a manner precisely as they do to me? I have never read anything which resembles what goes on in my house. Oh! If I could only leave it, if I could only go away and flee, so as never to return. I should be saved, but I cannot.

*August 16.*   I managed to escape to-day for two hours, like a prisoner who finds the door of his dungeon accidentally open. I suddenly felt that I was free and that he was far away, and so I gave orders to put the horses in as quickly as possible, and I drove to Rouen. Oh! How delightful to be able to say to a man who obeyed you: "Go to Rouen!"

I made him pull up before the library, and I begged them to lend me Dr. Herrmann Herestauss's treatise on the unknown inhabitants of the ancient and modern world.

Then, as I was getting into my carriage, I intended to say: "To the railway station!" but instead of this I shouted,—I did not say, but I shouted— in such a loud voice that all the passers-by turned round: "Home!" and I fell back onto the cushion of my carriage, overcome by mental agony. He had found me out and regained possession of me.

*August 17.*   Oh! What a night! what a night! And yet it seems to me that I ought to rejoice. I read until one o'clock in the morning! Herestauss, Doctor of Philosophy and Theogony, wrote the history and the manifestations of all those invisible beings which hover around man, or of whom he dreams. He describes their origin, their domains, their power; but none of them resembles the one which haunts me. One might say that man, ever since he has thought, has had a foreboding of, and feared a new being, stronger than himself, his successor in this world, and that, feeling him near, and not being able to foretell the nature of that master, he has, in his terror, created the whole race of hidden beings, of vague phantoms born of fear.

Having, therefore, read until one o'clock in the morning, I went and sat down at the open window, in order to cool my forehead and my thoughts, in the calm night air. It was very pleasant and warm! How I should have enjoyed such a night formerly!

There was no moon, but the stars darted out their rays in the dark heavens. Who inhabits those worlds? What forms, what living beings, what animals are there yonder? What do those who are thinkers in those distant worlds know more than we do? What can they do more than we can? What do they see which we do not know? Will not one of them, some day or other, traversing space, appear on our earth to conquer it, just as the Norsemen formerly crossed the sea in order to subjugate nations more feeble than themselves?

We are so weak, so unarmed, so ignorant, so small, we who live on this particle of mud which turns round in a drop of water.

I fell asleep, dreaming thus in the cool night air, and then, having slept for about three quarters of an hour, I opened my eyes without moving, awakened by I know not what confused and strange sensation. At first I saw nothing, and then suddenly it appeared to me as if a page of a book which had remained open on my table, turned over of its own accord. Not a breath of air had come in at my window, and I was surprised and waited. In about four minutes, I saw, I saw, yes I saw with my own eyes another page lift itself up and fall down on the others, as if a finger had turned it over. My armchair was empty, appeared empty, but I knew that he was there, he, and sitting in my place, and that he was reading. With a furious bound, the bound of an enraged wild beast that wishes to disembowel its tamer, I crossed my room to seize him, to strangle him, to kill him! . . . But before I could reach it, my chair fell over as if somebody had run away from me . . . my table rocked, my lamp fell and went out, and my window closed as if some thief had been surprised and had fled out into the night, shutting it behind him.

So he had run away: he had been afraid: he, afraid of me!

So . . . so . . . to-morrow . . . or later . . . some day or other . . . I should be able to hold him in my clutches and crush him against the ground! Do not dogs occasionally bite and strangle their masters?

*August 18.*   I have been thinking the whole day long. Oh! yes, I will obey him, follow his impulses, fulfill all his wishes, show myself humble, submissive, a coward. He is the stronger; but an hour will come . . .

*August 19.*   I know, . . . I know . . . I know all! I have just read the following in the *Revue du Monde Scientifique:* "A curious piece of news comes to us from Rio de Janeiro. Madness, an epidemic of madness, which may be compared to that contagious madness which attacked the people of Europe in the Middle Ages, is at this moment raging in the Province of San-Paulo. The frightened inhabitants are leaving their houses, deserting their villages, abandoning their land, saying that they are pursued, possessed, governed like human cattle by invisible, though tangible beings, a species of vampire, which feed on their life while they are asleep, and who, besides, drink water and milk without appearing to touch any other nourishment.

"Professor Don Pedro Henriques, accompanied by several medical savants, has gone to the Province of San-Paulo, in order to study the origin and the manifestations of this surprising madness on the spot, and to propose such measures to the Emperor as may appear to him to be most fitted to restore the mad population to reason."

Ah! Ah! I remember now that fine Brazilian three-master which passed in front of my windows as it was going up the Seine, on the 8th of last May! I thought it looked so pretty, so white and bright! That Being was on board of her, coming from there, where its race sprang from. And it saw me! It saw my house which was also white, and he sprang from the ship onto the land. Oh! Good heavens!

Now I know, I can divine. The reign of man is over, and he has come. He whom disquieted priests exorcised, whom sorcerers evoked on dark nights, without yet seeing him appear, to whom the presentiments of the transient masters of the world lent all the monstrous or graceful forms of gnomes, spirits, genii, fairies and familiar spirits. After the coarse conceptions of primitive fear, more clear-sighted men foresaw it more clearly. Mesmer divined him, and ten years ago physicians accurately discovered the nature of his power, even before he exercised it himself. They played with that weapon of their new Lord, the sway of a mysterious will over the human soul, which had become enslaved. They called it magnetism, hypnotism, suggestion . . . what do I know? I have seen them amusing themselves like impudent children with this horrible power! Woe to us! Woe to man! He has come, the . . . the . . . what does he call himself . . . the . . . I fancy that he is shouting out his name to me and I do not hear him . . . the . . . yes . . . he is shouting it out . . . I am listening . . . I cannot . . . repeat . . . it . . . Horla . . . I have heard . . . the Horla, . . . it is he . . . the Horla . . . he has come! . . .

Ah! the vulture has eaten the pigeon, the wolf has eaten the lamb; the lion has devoured the buffalo with sharp horns; man has killed the lion with an arrow, with a sword, with gunpowder; but the Horla will make of man what we have made of the horse and of the ox: his chattel, his slave and his food, by the men power of his will. Woe to us!

But, nevertheless, the animal sometimes revolts and kills the man who has subjugated it. . . . I should also like . . . I shall be able to . . . but I must know him, touch him, see him! Learned men say that beasts' eyes, as they differ from ours, do not distinguish like ours do. . . . And my eye cannot distinguish this newcomer who is oppressing me.

Why? Oh! Now I remember the words of the monk at Mont Saint-Michel: "Can we see the hundred thousandth part of what exists? Look here; there is the wind, which is the strongest force in nature, which knocks men, and blows down buildings, uproots trees, raises the sea into mountains of water, destroys cliffs and casts great ships onto the breakers; the wind which kills, which whistles, which sighs, which roars,—have you ever seen it, and can you see it? It exists for all that, however!"

And I went on thinking: my eyes are so weak, so imperfect, that they do not even distinguish hard bodies, if they are as transparent as glass! . . . If a glass without tinfoil behind it were to bar my way, I should run into it, just like a bird which has flown into a room breaks its head against the windowpanes. A thousand things, moreover, deceive him and lead him astray. How should it then be surprising that he cannot perceive a fresh body which is traversed by the light.

A new being! Why not? It was assuredly bound to come! Why should we be the last? We do not distinguish it, like all the others created before us? The reason is, that its nature is more perfect, its body finer and more finished than ours, that ours is so weak, so awkwardly conceived, encumbered with organs that are always tired, always on the strain like locks that are too complicated, which lives like a plant and like a beast, nourishing itself with difficulty on air, herbs and flesh, an animal machine, which is a prey to maladies, to malformations, to decay; broken-winded, badly regulated, simple and eccentric, ingeniously badly made, a coarse and a delicate work, the outline of a being which might become intelligent and grand.

We are only a few, so few in this world, from the oyster up to man. Why should there not be one more, when once that period is accomplished which separates the successive apparitions from all the different species?

Why not one more? Why not, also, other trees with immense, splendid flowers, perfuming whole regions? Why not other elements besides fire, air, earth and water? There are four, only four, those nursing fathers of various beings! What a pity! Why are they not forty, four hundred, four thousand! How poor everything is, how mean and wretched! grudgingly given, dryly invented, clumsily made! Ah! the elephant and the hippopotamus, what grace! And the camel, what elegance!

But, the butterfly you will say, a flying flower! I dream of one that should be as large as a hundred worlds, with wings whose shape, beauty, colors and motion I cannot even express. But I see it . . . it flutters from star to star, refreshing them and perfuming them with the light and harmonious breath of its flight! . . . And the people up there look at it as it passes in an ecstasy of delight! . . .

What is the matter with me? It is he, the Horla, who haunts me, and who makes me think of these foolish things! He is within me, he is becoming my soul; I shall kill him!

*August 19.*   I shall kill him. I have seen him! Yesterday I sat down at my table and pretended to write very assiduously. I knew quite well that he would come prowling round me, quite close to me, so close that I might perhaps be able to touch him, to seize him. And then! . . . then I should have the strength of desperation; I should have my hands, my knees, my chest, my forehead, my teeth to strangle him, to crush him, to bite him, to tear him to pieces. And I watched for him with all my overexcited organs.

I had lighted my two lamps and the eight wax candles on my mantelpiece, as if, by this light, I could have discovered him.

My bed, my old oak bed with its columns was opposite to me; on my right was the fireplace; on my left the door, which was carefully closed, after I had left it open for some time, in order to attract him; behind me was a very high wardrobe with a looking-glass in it, which served me to dress by every day, and in which I was in the habit of looking at myself from head to foot every time I passed it.

So I pretended to be writing in order to deceive him, for he also was watching me, and suddenly I felt, I was certain that he was reading over my shoulder, that he was there, almost touching my ear.

I got up so quickly, with my hands extended, that I almost fell. Eh! well? . . . It was as bright as at midday, but I did not see myself in the glass! . . . It was empty, clear, profound, full of light! But my figure was not reflected in it . . . and I, I was opposite to it! I saw the large, clear glass from top to bottom, and I looked at it with unsteady eyes; and I did not dare to advance; I did not venture to make a movement, nevertheless, feeling perfectly that he was there, but that he would escape me again, he whose imperceptible body had absorbed my reflection.

How frightened I was! And then suddenly I began to see myself through a mist in the depths of the looking-glass, in a mist as it were through a sheet of water; and it seemed to me as if this water were flowing slowly from left to right, and making my figure clearer every moment. It was like the end of an eclipse. Whatever it was that hid me, did not appear to possess any clearly defined outlines, but a sort of opaque transparency, which gradually grew clearer.

At last I was able to distinguish myself completely, as I do every day when I look at myself.

I had seen it! And the horror of it remained with me, and makes me shudder even now.

*August 20.*    How could I kill it, as I could not get hold of it? Poison? But it would see me mix it with the water; and then, would our poisons have any effect on its impalpable body? No . . . no . . . no doubt about the matter . . . Then? . . . then? . . .

*August 21.*    I sent for a blacksmith from Rouen, and ordered iron shutters of him for my room, such as some private hotels in Paris have on the ground floor, for fear of thieves, and he is going to make me a similar door as well. I have made myself out as a coward, but I do not care about that! . . .

*September 10.*    Rouen, Hotel Continental. It is done; . . . it is done. . . . But is he dead? My mind is thoroughly upset by what I have seen.

Well, then, yesterday, the locksmith having put on the iron shutters and door, I left everything open until midnight, although it was getting cold.

Suddenly I felt that he was there, and joy, mad joy took possession of me. I got up softly, and I walked to the right and left for sometime, so that he might not guess anything; then I took off my boots and put on my slippers carelessly; then I fastened the iron shutters and going back to the door quickly I double-locked it with a padlock, putting the key into my pocket.

Suddenly I noticed that he was moving restlessly round me, that in his turn he was frightened and was ordering me to let him out. I nearly yielded, though I did not yet, but putting my back to the door, I half opened, just enough to allow me to go out backwards, and as I am very tall, my head touched the lintel. I was sure that he had not been able to escape, and I shut him up quite alone, quite alone. What happiness! I had him fast. Then I ran downstairs; in the drawing-room, which was under my bedroom, I took the two lamps and I poured all the oil onto the carpet, the furniture, everywhere; then I set the fire to it and made my escape, after having carefully double-locked the door.

I went and hid myself at the bottom of the garden, in a clump of laurel bushes. How long it was! how long it was! Everything was dark, silent, motionless, not a breath of air and not a star, but heavy banks of clouds which one could not see, but which weighed, oh! so heavily on my soul.

I looked at my house and waited. How long it took! I already began to think that the fire had gone out of its own accord, or that he had extinguished it, when one of the lower windows gave way under the violence of the flames, and a long, soft, caressing sheet of red flame mounted up the white wall, and kissed it as high as the roof. The light fell onto the trees, the branches, and the leaves, and a shiver of fear pervaded them also! The birds awoke; a dog began to howl, and it seemed to me as if the day were breaking! Almost immediately two other windows flew into fragments, and I saw that the whole of the lower part of my house was nothing but a terrible furnace. But a cry, a horrible, shrill, heart-rending cry, a woman's cry, sounded through the night, and two garret windows were opened! I had forgotten the servants! I saw the terror-struck faces, and their frantically waving arms! . . .

Then, overwhelmed with horror, I set off to run to the village, shouting: "Help! help! fire! fire! I met some people who were already coming onto the scene, and I went back with them to see!

By this time the house was nothing but a horrible and a magnificent funeral pile, a monstrous funeral pile which lit up the whole country, a funeral pile where men were burning, and where he was burning also, He, He, my prisoner, that new Being, the new master, the Horla!

Suddenly the whole roof fell in between the walls, and a volcano of flames darted up to the sky. Through all the windows which opened onto that furnace, I saw the flames darting, and I thought that he was there, in that kiln, dead.

Dead? perhaps? . . . His body? Was not his body, which was transparent, indestructible by such means as would kill ours?

If he was not dead? . . . Perhaps time alone has power over that Invisible and Redoubtable Being. Why this transparent, unrecognizable body, this body belonging to a spirit, if it also had to fear ills, infirmities and premature destruction?

Premature destruction? All human terror springs from that! After man the Horla. After him who can die every day, at any hour, at any moment, by any accident, he came who was only to die at his own proper hour and minute, because he had touched the limits of his existence!

No . . . no . . . without any doubt . . . he is not dead . . . Then . . . then . . . I suppose I must kill myself! . . .

*Translator unknown; perhaps edited by Arthur Symons*

# SIR PATRICK SPENCE

*Anonymous*

The king sits in Dumferling toune,
    Drinking the blude-reid wine:
"O whar will I get ae guid sailor,
    To sail this schip of mine?"

Up and spak an eldlern knicht,
    Sat at the king's richt kne;
"Sir Patrick Spence is the best sailor
    That sails upon the se."

The king has written a braid letter,
    And signed it wi' his hand,
And sent it to Sir Patrick Spence,
    Was walking on the sand.

The first line that Sir Patrick red,
    A loud lauch lauched he;
The next line that Sir Patrick red,
    The teir blinded his ee.

"O wha is this has done this deid,
    This ill deid don to me,
To send me out this time o' the yeir,
    To sail upon the se!

"Mak haste, mak haste, my mirry men all,
    Our guid schip sails the morne."
"O say na sae, my master deir,
    Fir I feir a deadlie storme.

"Late, late eyestreen I saw the new moone
    Wi' the auld moone in hir arme,
And I feir, I feir, my deir master,
    That we will cum to harme."

O our Scots nobles were richt laith*
   To weet† their cork-heil'd schoone;
Bot lang owre†† a' the play wer playd,
   Thair hats they swam aboone.

O lang, lang may their ladies sit
   Wi' thair fans into their hand
Or eir they se Sir Patrick Spence
   Cum sailing to the land.

O lang, lang may the ladies stand,
   Wi' thair gold kems in their hair,
Waiting for thair ain deir lords,
   For they'll se thame no mair.

Haf owre, haf owre to Aberdour,
   It's fiftie fadom deip,
And thair lies guid Sir Patrick Spence,
   Wi' the Scots lords at his feit.

ℰ

# A HELEN OF KIRCONNELL

### *Anonymous*

. . . I wish I were where Helen lies,
Night and day on me she cries;
O that I were where Helen lies
   On fair Kirconnell lea!

Curst be the heart that thought the thought,
And curst the hand that fired the shot,

*Right
†Wet
††But long ere

When in my arms burd Helen dropt,
    And died for sake o' me!

O think na but my heart was sair
When my love dropt down and spake nae mair;
I laid her down wi' meikle care
    On fair Kirconnell lea.

As I went down the water-side,
None but my foe to be my guide,
None but my foe to be my guide,
    On fair Kirconnell lea;

I lighted down, my sword to draw,
I hackèd him in pieces sma',
I hackèd him in pieces sma',
    For her that died for me.

O Helen fair, beyond compare,
I'll make a garland of thy hair
Shall bind my heart for evermair,
    Until the day I die.

O that I were where Helen lies,
Night and day on me she cries;
Out of my bed she bids me rise,
    Says, "Haste and come to me!"

O Helen fair! O Helen chaste!
If I were with thee, I were blest,
Where thou lies low and takes thy rest
    On fair Kirconnell lea.

I wish my grave were growing green,
A winding-sheet drawn ower my een,
And I in Helen's arms lying,
    On fair Kirconnell lea.

I wish I were where Helen lies,
Night and day on me she cries;

And I am weary of the skies,
 Since my love died for me.

ಌ


## "I KNOW A LITTLE GARDEN-CLOSE"

### *William Morris*


I know a little garden-close
Set thick with lily and red rose,
Where I would wander if I might
From dewy dawn to dewy night,
And have one with me wandering.

And though within it no birds sing,
And though no pillared house is there,
And though the apple boughs are bare
Of fruit and blossom, would to God,
Her feet upon the green grass trod,
And I beheld them as before.

There comes a murmur from the shore,
And in the close two fair streams are,
Drawn from the purple hills afar,
Drawn down unto the restless sea;
Dark hills whose heath-bloom feeds no bee,
Dark shores no ship has ever seen,
Tormented by the billows green
Whose murmur comes unceasingly
Unto the place for which I cry.

For which I cry both day and night,
For which I let slip all delight,
Whereby I grow both deaf and blind,
Careless to win, unskilled to find,
And quick to lose what all men seek.

Yet tottering as I am, and weak,
Still have I left a little breath
To seek within the jaws of death
An entrance to that happy place,
To seek the unforgotten face,
Once seen, once kissed, once reft from me
Anight the murmuring of the sea.

∾

# NIGHT

## William Blake

The sun descending in the west,
The evening star does shine;
The birds are silent in their nest,
And I must seek for mine.
 The moon, like a flower,
 In heaven's high bower,
 With silent delight
 Sits and smiles on the night.

Farewell green fields and happy groves,
Where flocks have took delight.
Where lambs have nibbled, silent moves
The feet of angels bright;
 Unseen they pour blessing,
 And joy without ceasing,
 On each bud and blossom,
 And each sleeping bosom.

They look in every thoughtless nest,
Where birds are covered warm;
They visit caves of every beast;
To keep them all from harm.
 If they see any weeping,
 That should have been sleeping,

They pour sleep on their head,
And sit down by their bed.

When wolves and tygers howl for prey,
They pitying stand and weep;
Seeking to drive their thirst away,
And keep them from the sheep.
But if they rush dreadful,
The angels, most heedful,
Receive each mild spirit,
New worlds to inherit.

And there the lion's ruddy eyes
Shall flow with tears of gold,
And pitying the tender cries,
And walking round the fold,
Saying, "Wrath, by his meekness,
And, by his health, sickness
Is driven away
From our immortal day.

"And now beside thee, bleating lamb,
I can lie down and sleep;
Or think on Him who bore thy name,
Graze after thee and weep.
For, washed in life's river,
My bright mane for ever
Shall shine like the gold,
As I guard o'er the fold."

## SNOW-FLAKES

*Henry Wadsworth Longfellow*

Out of the bosom of the Air,
    Out of the cloud-folds of her garments shaken,
Over the woodlands brown and bare,
    Over the harvest-fields forsaken,
        Silent, and soft, and slow,
        Descends the snow.

Even as our cloudy fancies take
    Suddenly shape in some divine expression,
Even as the troubled heart doth make
    In the white countenance confession,
        The troubled sky reveals
        The grief it feels.

This is the poem of the air,
    Slowly in silent syllables recorded;
This is the secret of despair,
    Long in its cloudy bosom hoarded.
        Now whispered and revealed
        To wood and field.

❧

## SNOWSTORM

*John Clare*

I

What a night! The wind howls, hisses, and but stops
To howl more loud, while the snow volley keeps
Incessant batter at the window-pane,

Making our comforts feel as sweet again;
And in the morning, when the tempest drops,
At every cottage door mountainous heaps
Of snow lie drifted, that all entrance stops
Until the besom<sup>*</sup> and the shovel gain
The path, and leave a wall on either side.
The shepherd, rambling valleys white and wide,
With new sensations his old memory fills,
When hedges left at night, no more descried,
Are turned to one white sweep of curving hills,
And trees turned bushes half their bodies hide.


## II


The boy that goes to fodder with surprise
Walks o'er the gate he opened yesternight.
The hedges all have vanished from his eyes;
E'en some tree-tops the sheep could reach to bite.
The novel scene engenders new delight,
And, though with cautious steps his sports begin,
He bolder shuffles the huge hills of snow,
Till down he drops and plunges to the chin,
And struggles much and oft escape to win—
Then turns and laughs but dare not further go;
For deep the grass and bushes lie below,
Where little birds that soon at eve went in
With heads tucked in their wings now pine for day
And little feel boys o'er their heads can stray.

***

*Broom

# THE SNOWSTORM

*Ralph Waldo Emerson*

Announced by all the trumpets of the sky,
Arrives the snow, and, driving o'er the fields,
Seems nowhere to alight: the whited air
Hides hills and woods, the river, and the heaven,
And veils the farm-house at the garden's end.
The sled and traveller stopped, the courier's feet
Delayed, all friends shut out, the housemates sit
Around the radiant fireplace, enclosed
In a tumultuous privacy of storm.

Come see the north wind's masonry.
Out of an unseen quarry evermore
Furnished with tile, the fierce artificer
Curves his white bastions with projected roof
Round every windward stake, or tree, or door.
Speeding, the myriad-handed, his wild work
So fanciful, so savage, nought cares he
For number or proportion. Mockingly,
On coop or kennel he hangs Parian wreaths;
A swan-like form invests the hidden thorn;
Fills up the farmer's lane from wall to wall,
Maugre the farmer's sighs; and at the gate
A tapering turret overtops the work.
And when his hours are numbered, and the world
Is all his own, retiring, as he were not,
Leaves, when the sun appears, astonished Art
To mimic in slow structures, stone by stone,
Built in an age, the mad wind's night-work,
The frolic architecture of the snow.

## LONDON SNOW

### *Robert Bridges*

When men were all asleep the snow came flying,
In large white flakes falling on the city brown,
Stealthily and perpetually settling and loosely lying,
　Hushing the latest traffic of the drowsy town;
Deadening, muffling, stifling its murmurs failing;
Lazily and incessantly floating down and down:
　Silently sifting and veiling road, roof and railing;
Hiding difference, making unevenness even,
Into angles and crevices softly drifting and sailing.
　All night it fell, and when full inches seven
It lay in the depth of its uncompacted lightness,
The clouds blew off from a high and frosty heaven;
　And all woke earlier for the unaccustomed brightness
Of the winter dawning, the strange unheavenly glare:
The eye marvelled— marvelled at the dazzling whiteness;
　The ear hearkened to the stillness of the solemn air;
No sound of wheel rumbling nor of foot falling,
And the busy morning cries came thin and spare.
　Then boys I heard, as they went to school, calling,
They gathered up the crystal manna to freeze
Their tongues with tasting, their hands with snowballing;
　Or rioted in a drift, plunging up to the knees;
Or peering up from under the white-mossed wonder,
"O look at the trees!" they cried, "O look at the trees!"
　With lessened load a few carts creak and blunder,
Following along the white deserted way,
A country company long dispersed asunder:
　When now already the sun, in pale display
Standing by Paul's high dome, spread forth below
His sparkling beams, and awoke the stir of the day.
　For now doors open, and war is waged with the snow;
And trains of sombre men, past tale of number,
Tread long brown paths, as toward their toil they go:
　But even for them awhile no cares encumber

Their minds diverted; the daily word is unspoken,
The daily thoughts of labour and sorrow slumber
At the sight of the beauty that greets them, for the charm
they have broken.

❧

# BITS OF STRAW

## John Clare

I peeled bits of straw and I got switches too
From the grey peeling willow as idlers do,
And I switched at the flies as I sat all alone
Till my flesh, blood, and marrow was turned to dry bone.
My illness was love, though I knew not the smart,
But the beauty of love was the blood of my heart.
Crowded places, I shunned them as noises too rude
And fled to the silence of sweet solitude,
Where the flower in green darkness buds, blossoms, and fades,
Unseen of all shepherds and flower-loving maids—
The hermit bees find them but once and away;
There I'll bury alive and in silence decay.
I looked on the eyes of fair women too long,
Till silence and shame stole the use of my tongue:
When I tried to speak to her I'd nothing to say,
So I turned myself round and she wandered away.
When she got too far off, why, I'd something to tell,
So I sent sighs behind her and walked to my cell.
Willow switches I broke and peeled bits of straws,
Ever lonely in crowds, in nature's own laws—
My ball-room the pasture, my music the bees,
My drink was the fountain, my church the tall trees.
Who ever would love or be tied to a wife
When it makes a man mad all the days of his life?

❧

# THE BELL-TOWER

## *Herman Melville*

In the south of Europe, nigh a once frescoed capital, now with dank mould cankering its bloom, central in a plain, stands what, at distance, seems the black mossed stump of some immeasurable pine, fallen, in forgotten days, with Anak and the Titan.

As all along where the pine tree falls, its dissolution leaves a mossy mound—last-flung shadow of the perished trunk; never lengthening, never lessening; unsubject to the fleet falsities of the sun; shade immutable, and true gauge which cometh by prostration—so westward from what seems the stump, one steadfast spear of lichened ruin veins the plain.

From that tree-top, what birded chimes of silver throats had rung. A stone pine; a metallic aviary in its crown: the Bell-Tower, built by the great mechanician, the unblest foundling, Bannadonna.

Like Babel's, its base was laid in a high hour of renovated earth, following the second deluge, when the waters of the Dark Ages had dried up, and once more the green appeared. No wonder that, after so long and deep submersion, the jubilant expectation of the race should, as with Noah's sons, soar into Shinar aspiration.

In firm resolve, no man in Europe at that period went beyond Bannadonna. Enriched through commerce with the Levant, the state in which he lived voted to have the noblest Bell-Tower in Italy. His repute assigned him to be architect.

Stone by stone, month by month, the tower rose. Higher, higher; snail-like in pace, but torch or rocket in its pride.

After the masons would depart, the builder, standing alone upon its ever-ascending summit, at close of every day, saw that he overtopped still higher walls and trees. He would tarry till a late hour there, wrapped in schemes of other and still loftier piles. Those who of saints' days thronged the spot—hanging to the rude poles of scaffolding, like sailors on yards, or bees on boughs, unmindful of lime and dust, and falling chips of stone— their homage not the less inspirited him to self-esteem.

At length the holiday of the Tower came. To the sound of viols, the climax-stone slowly rose in air, and, amid the firing of ordnance, was laid by Bannadonna's hands upon the final course. Then mounting it, he stood erect, alone, with folded arms, gazing upon the white summits of blue inland Alps, and whiter crests of bluer Alps off-shore—sights invisible from the plain. Invisible, too, from thence was that eye he turned below, when, like the cannon booms, came up to him the people's combustions of applause.

That which stirred them so was, seeing with what serenity the builder stood three hundred feet in air, upon an unrailed perch. This none but he durst do. But his periodic standing upon the pile, in each stage of its growth—such discipline had its last result.

Little remained now but the bells. These, in all respects, must correspond with their receptacle.

The minor ones were prosperously cast. A highly enriched one followed, of a singular make, intended for suspension in a manner before unknown. The purpose of this bell, its rotary motion, and connection with the clock-work, also executed at the time, will, in the sequel, receive mention.

In the one erection, bell-tower and clock-tower were united, though, before that period, such structures had commonly been built distinct; as the Campanile and Torre del 'Orologio of St. Mark to this day attest.

But it was upon the great state-bell that the founder lavished his more daring skill. In vain did some of the less elated magistrates here caution him; saying that though truly the tower was Titanic, yet limit should be set to the dependent weight of its swaying masses. But undeterred, he prepared his mammoth mould, dented with mythological devices; kindled his fires of balsamic firs; melted his tin and copper, and, throwing in much plate, contributed by the public spirit of the nobles, let loose the tide.

The unleashed metals bayed like hounds. The workmen shrunk. Through their fright, fatal harm to the bell was dreaded. Fearless as Shadrach, Bannadonna, rushing through the glow, smote the chief culprit with his ponderous ladle. From the smitten part, a splinter was dashed into the seething mass, and at once was melted in.

Next day a portion of the work was heedfully uncovered. All seemed right. Upon the third morning, with equal satisfaction, it was bared still lower. At length, like some old Theban king, the whole cooled casting was disinterred. All was fair except in one strange spot. But as he suffered no one to attend him in these inspections, he concealed the blemish by some preparation which none knew better to devise.

The casting of such a mass was deemed no small triumph for the caster; one, too, in which the state might not scorn to share. The homicide was overlooked. By the charitable that deed was but imputed to sudden transports of esthetic passion, not to any flagitious quality. A kick from an Arabian charger; not sign of vice, but blood.

His felony remitted by the judge, absolution given him by the priest, what more could even a sickly conscience have desired.

Honoring the tower and its builder with another holiday, the republic witnessed the hoisting of the bells and clockwork amid shows and pomps superior to the former.

Some months of more than usual solitude on Bannadonna's part ensued. It was not unknown that he was engaged upon something for the belfry, intended to complete it, and surpass all that had gone before. Most people imagined that the design would involve a casting like the bells. But those who thought they had some further insight, would shake their heads, with hints, that not for nothing did the mechanician keep so secret. Meantime, his seclusion failed not to invest his work with more or less of that sort of mystery pertaining to the forbidden.

Ere long he had a heavy object hoisted to the belfry, wrapped in a dark sack or cloak—a procedure sometimes had in the case of an elaborate piece of sculpture, or statue, which, being intended to grace the front of a new edifice, the architect does not desire exposed to critical eyes, till set up, finished, in its appointed place. Such was the impression now. But, as the object rose, a statuary present observed, or thought he did, that it was not entirely rigid, but was, in a manner, pliant. At last, when the hidden thing had attained its final height, and, obscurely seen from below, seemed almost of itself to step into the belfry, as if with little assistance from the crane, a shrewd old blacksmith present ventured the suspicion that it was but a living man. This surmise was thought a foolish one, while the general interest failed not to augment.

Not without demur from Bannadonna, the chief-magistrate of the town, with an associate—both elderly men—followed what seemed the image up the tower. But, arrived at the belfry, they had little recompense. Plausibly entrenching himself behind the conceded mysteries of his art, the mechanician withheld present explanation. The magistrates glanced toward the cloaked object, which, to their surprise, seemed now to have changed its attitude, or else had before been more preplexingly concealed by the violent muffling action of the wind without. It seemed now seated upon some sort of frame, or chair, contained within the domino. They observed that nigh the top, in a sort of square, the web of the cloth, either from accident or design, had its warp partly withdrawn, and the cross threads plucked out here and there, so as to form a sort of woven grating.

Whether it were the low wind or no, stealing through the stone lattice-work, or only their own perturbed imaginations, is uncertain, but they thought they discerned a slight sort of fitful, spring-like motion, in the domino. Nothing, however incidental or insignificant, escaped their uneasy eyes. Among other things, they pried out, in a corner, an earthen cup, partly corroded and partly encrusted, and one whispered to the other, that this cup was just such a one as might, in mockery, be offered to the lips of some brazen statue, or, perhaps, still worse.

But, being questioned, the mechanician said, that the cup was simply used in his founder's business, and described the purpose; in short, a cup to test the condition of metals in fusion. He added, that it had got into the belfry by the merest chance.

Again, and again, they gazed at the domino, as at some suspicious incognito at a Venetian mask. All sorts of vague apprehensions stirred them. They even dreaded lest, when they should descend, the mechanician, though without a flesh and blood companion, for all that, would not be left alone.

Affecting some merriment at their disquietude, he begged to relieve them, by extending a coarse sheet of workman's canvas between them and the object.

Meantime he sought to interest them in his other work; nor, now that the domino was out of sight, did they long remain insensible to the artistic wonders lying round them; wonders hitherto beheld but in their unfinished state; because, since hoisting the bells, none but the caster had entered within the belfry. It was one trait of his, that, even in details, he would not let another do what he could, without too great loss of time, accomplish for himself. So, for several preceding weeks, what ever hours were unemployed in his secret design, had been devoted to elaborating the figures on the bells.

The clock-bell, in particular, now drew attention. Under a patient chisel, the latent beauty of its enrichments, before obscured by the cloudings incident to casting, that beauty in its shyest grace, was now revealed. Round and round the bell, twelve figures of gay girls, garlanded, hand-in-hand, danced in a choral ring—the embodied hours.

"Bannadonna," said the chief, "this bell excels all else. No added touch could here improve. Hark!" hearing a sound, "was that the wind?"

"The wind, Excellenza," was the light response. "But the figures, they are not yet without their faults. They need some touches yet. When those are given, and the—block yonder," pointing towards the canvas screen, "when Haman there, as I merrily call him,—him? *it,* I mean—when

Haman is fixed on this, his lofty tree, then, gentlemen, will I be most happy to receive you here again."

The equivocal reference to the object caused some return of restlessness. However, on their part, the visitors forbore further allusion to it, unwilling, perhaps, to let the foundling see how easily it lay within his plebeian art to stir the placid dignity of nobles.

"Well, Bannadonna," said the chief, "how long ere you are ready to set the clock going, so that the hour shall be sounded? Our interest in you, not less than in the work itself, makes us anxious to be assured of your success. The people, too,—why, they are shouting now. Say the exact hour when you will be ready."

"To-morrow, Excellenza, if you listen for it,—or should you not, all the same—strange music will be heard. The stroke of one shall be the first from yonder bell," pointing to the bell adorned with girls and garlands, "that stroke shall fall there, where the hand of Una clasps Dua's. The stroke of one shall sever that loved clasp. To-morrow, then, at one o'clock, as struck here, precisely here," advancing and placing his finger upon the clasp, "the poor mechanic will be most happy once more to give you liege audience, in this his littered shop. Farewell till then, illustrious magnificoes, and hark ye for your vassal's stroke."

His still, Vulcanic face hiding its burning brightness like a forge, he moved with ostentatious deference towards the scuttle, as if so far to escort their exit. But the junior magistrate, a kind-hearted man, troubled at what seemed to him a certain sardonical disdain, lurking beneath the foundling's humble mien, and in Christian sympathy more distressed at it on his account than on his own, dimly surmising what might be the final fate of such a cynic solitaire, nor perhaps uninfluenced by the general strangeness of surrounding things, this good magistrate had glanced sadly, sideways from the speaker, and thereupon his foreboding eye had started at the expression of the unchanging face of the Hour Una.

"How is this, Bannadonna?" he lowly asked, "Una looks unlike her sisters."

"In Christ's name, Bannadonna," impulsively broke in the chief, his attention, for the first attracted to the figure, by his associate's remark, "Una's face looks just like that of Deborah, the prophetess, as painted by the Florentine, Del Fonca."

"Surely, Bannadonna," lowly resumed the milder magistrate, "you meant the twelve should wear the same jocundly abandoned air. But see, the smile of Una seems but a fatal one. This different."

While his mild associate was speaking, the chief glanced, inquiringly, from him to the caster, as if anxious to mark how the discrepancy would be accounted for. As the chief stood, his advanced foot was on the scuttle's curb.

Bannadonna spoke:

"Excellenza, now that, following your keener eye, I glance upon the face of Una, I do, indeed perceive some little variance. But look all round the bell, and you will find no two faces entirely correspond. Because there is a law in art—but the cold wind is rising more; these lattices are but a poor defense. Suffer me, magnificoes, to conduct you, at least, partly on your way. Those in whose well-being there is a public stake, should be heedfully attended."

"Touching the look of Una, you were saying, Bannadonna, that there was a certain law in art," observed the chief, as the three now descended the stone shaft, "pray, tell me, then—."

"Pardon; another time, Excellenza;—the tower is damp."

"Nay, I must rest, and hear it now. Here,—here is a wide landing, and through this leeward slit, no wind, but ample light. Tell us of your law; and at large."

"Since, Excellenza, you insist, know that there is a law in art, which bars the possibility of duplicates. Some years ago, you may remember, I graved a small seal for your republic, bearing, for its chief device, the head of your own ancestor, its illustrious founder. It becoming necessary, for the customs' use, to have innumerable impressions for bales and boxes, I graved an entire plate, containing one hundred of the seals. Now, though, indeed, my object was to have those hundred heads identical, and though, I dare say, people think them so, yet, upon closely scanning an uncut impression from the plate, no two of those five-score faces, side by side, will be found alike. Gravity is the air of all; but, diversified in all. In some, benevolent; in some, ambiguous; in two or three, to a close scrutiny, all but incipiently malign, the variation of less than a hair's breadth in the linear shadings round the mouth sufficing to all this. Now, Excellenza, transmute that general gravity into joyousness, and subject it to twelve of those variations I have described, and tell me, will you not have my hours here, and Una one of them? But I like—."

"Hark! is that—a footfall above?"

"Mortar, Excellenza; sometimes it drops to the belfry-floor from the arch where the stone-work was left undressed. I must have it seen to. As I was about to say: for one, I like this law forbidding duplicates. It evokes fine personalities. Yes, Excellenza, that strange, and—to you—uncertain smile, and those fore-looking eyes of Una, suit Bannadonna very well."

"Hark!—sure we left no soul above?"

"No soul, Excellenza; rest assured, no *soul*.—Again the mortar."

"It fell not while we were there."

"Ah, in your presence, it better knew its place, Excellenza," blandly bowed Bannadonna.

"But, Una," said the milder magistrate, "she seemed intently gazing on you; one would have almost sworn that she picked you out from among us three."

"If she did, possibly, it might have been her finer apprehension, Excellenza."

"How, Bannadonna? I do not understand you."

"No consequence, no consequence, Excellenza—but the shifted wind is blowing through the slit. Suffer me to escort you on; and then, pardon, but the toiler must to his tools."

"It may be foolish, Signor," said the milder magistrate, as, from the third landing, the two now went down unescorted, "but, somehow, our great mechanician moves me strangely. Why, just now, when he so superciliously replied, his walk seemed Sisera's, God's vain foe, in Del Fonca's painting. And that young, sculptured Deborah, too. Ay, and that—."

"Tush, tush, Signor!" returned the chief. "A passing whim. Deborah?—Where's Jael, pray?"

"Ah," said the other, as they now stepped upon the sod, "Ah, Signor, I see you leave your fears behind you with the chill and gloom; but mine, even in this sunny air, remain. Hark!"

It was a sound from just within the tower door, whence they had emerged. Turning, they saw it closed.

"He has slipped down and barred us out," smiled the chief; "but it is his custom."

Proclamation was now made, that the next day, at one hour after meridian, the clock would strike, and—thanks to the mechanician's powerful art—with unusual accompaniments. But what those should be, none as yet could say. The announcement was received with cheers.

By the looser sort, who encamped about the tower all night, lights were seen gleaming through the topmost blindwork, only disappearing with the morning sun. Strange sounds, too, were heard, or were thought to be, by those whom anxious watching might not have left mentally undisturbed—sounds, not only of some ringing implement, but also—so they said—half-suppressed screams and plainings, such as might have issued from some ghostly engine, overplied.

Slowly the day drew on; part of the concourse chasing the weary time with songs and games, till, at last, the great blurred sun rolled, like a football, against the plain.

At noon, the nobility and principal citizens came from the town in cavalcade, a guard of soldiers, also, with music, the more to honor the occasion.

Only one hour more. Impatience grew. Watches were held in hands of feverish men, who stood, now scrutinizing their small dial-plates, and then, with neck thrown back, gazing toward the belfry, as if the eye might foretell that which could only be made sensible to the ear; for, as yet, there was no dial to the tower-clock.

The hour hands of a thousand watches now verged within a hair's breadth of the figure 1. A silence, as of the expectation of some Shiloh, pervaded the swarming plain. Suddenly a dull, mangled sound—naught ringing in it; scarcely audible, indeed, to the outer circles of the people—that dull sound dropped heavily from the belfry. At the same moment, each man stared at his neighbor blankly. All watches were upheld. All hour-hands were at—had passed—the figure 1. No bellstroke from the tower. The multitude became tumultuous.

Waiting a few moments, the chief magistrate, commanding silence, hailed the belfry, to know what thing unforeseen had happened there.

No response.

He hailed again and yet again.

All continued hushed.

By his order, the soldiers burst in the tower-door; when, stationing guards to defend it from the now surging mob, the chief, accompanied by his former associate, climbed the winding stairs. Half-way up, they stopped to listen. No sound. Mounting faster, they reached the belfry; but, at the threshold, started at the spectacle disclosed. A spaniel, which, unbeknown to them, had followed them thus far, stood shivering as before some unknown monster in a brake: or, rather, as if it snuffed footsteps leading to some other world. Bannadonna lay, prostrate and bleeding, at the base of the bell which was adorned with girls and garlands. He lay at the feet of the hour Una; his head coinciding, in a vertical line, with her left hand, clasped by the hour Dua. With downcast face impending over him, like Jael over nailed Sisera in the tent, was the domino; now no more becloaked.

It had limbs, and seemed clad in a scaly mail, lustrous as a dragon-beetle's. It was manacled, and its clubbed arms were uplifted, as if, with its manacles, once more to smite its already smitten victim. One advanced foot of it was inserted beneath the dead body, as if in the act of spurning it.

Uncertainty falls on what now followed.

It were but natural to suppose that the magistrates would, at first, shrink from immediate personal contact with what they saw. At the least, for a time, they would stand in involuntary doubt; it may be, in more or less of horrified alarm. Certain it is, that an arquebuss was called for from below. And some add, that its report, followed by a fierce whiz, as of the sudden snapping of a main-spring, with a steely din, as if a stack of sword-blades should be dashed upon a pavement, these blended sounds came ringing to the plain, attracting every eye far upward to the belfry, whence, through the lattice-work, thin wreaths of smoke were curling.

Some averred that it was the spaniel, gone mad by fear, which was shot. This, others denied. True it was, the spaniel never more was seen; and, probably, for some unknown reason, it shared the burial now to be related of the domino. For, whatever the preceding circumstances may have been, the first instinctive panic over, or else all ground of reasonable fear removed, the two magistrates, by themselves, quickly rehooded the figure in the dropped cloak wherein it had been hoisted. The same night, it was secretly lowered to the ground, smuggled to the beach, pulled far out to sea, and sunk. Nor to any after urgency, even in free convivial hours, would the twain ever disclose the full secrets of the belfry.

From the mystery unavoidably investing it, the popular solution of the foundling's fate involved more or less supernatural agency. But some few less unscientific minds pretended to find little difficulty in otherwise accounting for it. In the chain of circumstantial inferences drawn, there may, or may not, have been some absent or defective links. But, as the explanation in question is the only one which tradition has explicitly preserved, in dearth of better, it will here be given. But, in the first place, it is requisite to present the supposition entertained as to the entire motive and mode, with their origin, of the secret design of Bannadonna; the minds above-mentioned assuming to penetrate as well into his soul as into the event. The disclosure will indirectly involve reference to peculiar matters, none of the clearest, beyond the immediate subject.

At that period, no large bell was made to sound otherwise than as at present, by agitation of a tongue within, by means of ropes, or percussion from without, either from cumbrous machinery, or stalwart watchmen, armed with heavy hammers, stationed in the belfry, or in sentry-boxes on the open roof, according as the bell was sheltered or exposed.

It was from observing these exposed bells, with their watchmen, that the foundling, as was opined, derived the first suggestion of his scheme. Perched on a great mast or spire, the human figure, viewed from below, undergoes such a reduction in its apparent size, as to obliterate its intelligent features. It evinces no personality. Instead of bespeaking volition, its gestures rather resemble the automatic ones of the arms of a telegraph.

Musing, therefore, upon the purely Punchinello aspect of the human figure thus beheld, it had indirectly occurred to Bannadonna to devise some metallic agent, which should strike the hour with its mechanic hand, with even greater precision than the vital one. And, moreover, as the vital watchman on the roof, sallying from his retreat at the given periods, walked to the bell with uplifted mace, to smite it, Bannadonna had resolved that his invention should likewise possess the power of locomotion, and, along with that, the appearance, at least, of intelligence and will.

If the conjectures of those who claimed acquaintance with the intent of Bannadonna be thus far correct, no unenterprising spirit could have been his. But they stopped not here; intimating that though, indeed, his design had, in the first place, been prompted by the sight of the watchman, and confined to the devising of a subtle substitute for him: yet, as is not seldom the case with projectors, by insensible gradations, proceeding from comparatively pigmy aims to Titanic ones, the original scheme had, in its anticipated eventualities, at last, attained to an unheard of degree of daring. He still bent his efforts upon the locomotive figure for the belfry, but only as a partial type of an ulterior creature, a sort of elephantine helot, adapted to further, in a degree scarcely to be imagined, the universal conveniences and glories of humanity; supplying nothing less than a supplement to the Six Days' Work; stocking the earth with a new serf, more useful than the ox, swifter than the dolphin, stronger than the lion, more cunning than the ape, for industry an ant, more fiery than serpents, and yet, in patience, another ass. All excellences of all God-made creatures, which served man, were here to receive advancement, and then to be combined in one. Talus was to have been the all-accomplished helot's name. Talus, iron slave to Bannadonna, and, through him, to man.

Here, it might well be thought that, were these last conjectures as to the foundling's secrets not erroneous, then must he have been hopelessly infected with the craziest chimeras of his age; far outgoing Albert Magus and Cornelius Agrippa. But the contrary was averred. However marvelous his design, however apparently transcending not alone the bounds of human invention, but those of divine creation, yet the proposed means to be employed were alleged to have been confined within the sober forms of sober reason. It was affirmed that, to a degree of more than skeptic scorn, Bannadonna had been without sympathy for any of the vain-glorious irrationalities of his time. For example, he had not concluded, with the visionaries among the metaphysicians, that between the finer mechanic forces and the ruder animal vitality some germ of correspondence might prove discoverable. As little did his scheme partake of the enthusiasm of some natural philosophers, who hoped, by physiological and chemical inductions, to arrive at a knowledge of the source of life, and so qualify themselves to manufacture and improve upon it. Much less had he aught in common with the tribe of alchemists, who sought, by a species of incantations, to evoke some surprising vitality from the laboratory. Neither had he imagined, with certain sanguine theosophists, that, by faithful adoration of the Highest, unheard-of powers would be vouchsafed to man. A practical materialist, what Bannadonna had aimed at was to have been reached, not by logic, not by crucible, not by conjuration, not by altars; but by plain vice-bench and hammer. In short, to solve nature, to steal into her, to intrigue beyond her, to procure some one else to bind her to his hand;—these, one and all, had not been his objects; but, asking no favors from any element or any being, of himself, to rival her, outstrip her, and rule her. He stooped to conquer. With him, common sense was theurgy; machinery, miracle; Prometheus, the heroic name for machinist; man, the true God.

Nevertheless, in his initial step, so far as the experimental automaton for the belfry was concerned, he allowed fancy some little play; or, perhaps, what seemed his fancifulness was but his utilitarian ambition collaterally extended. In figure, the creature for the belfry should not be likened after the human pattern, nor any animal one, nor after the ideals, however wild, of ancient fable, but equally in aspect as in organism be an original production; the more terrible to behold, the better.

Such, then, were the suppositions as to the present scheme, and the reserved intent. How, at the very threshold, so unlooked for a catastrophe overturned all, or rather, what was the conjecture here, is now to be set forth.

It was thought that on the day preceding the fatality, his visitors having left him, Bannadonna had unpacked the belfry image, adjusted it, and placed it in the retreat provided—a sort of sentry-box in one corner of the belfry; in short, throughout the night, and for some part of the ensuing morning, he had been engaged in arranging everything connected with the domino; the issuing from the sentry-box each sixty minutes; sliding along a grooved way, like a railway; advancing to the clock-bell, with uplifted manacles; striking it at one of the twelve junctions of the four-and-twenty hands; then wheeling, circling the bell, and retiring to its post, there to bide for another sixty minutes, when the same process was to be repeated; the bell, by a cunning mechanism, meantime turning on its vertical axis, so as to present, to the descending mace, the clasped hands of the next two figures, when it would strike two, three, and so on, to the end. The musical metal in this time-bell being so managed in the fusion, by some art, perishing with its originator, that each of the clasps of the four-and-twenty hands should give forth its own peculiar resonance when parted.

But on the magic metal, the magic and metallic stranger never struck but that one stroke, drove but that one nail, severed but that one clasp, by which Bannadonna clung to his ambitious life. For, after winding up the creature in the sentry-box, so that, for the present, skipping the intervening hours, it should not emerge till the hour of one, but should then infallibly emerge, and, after deftly oiling the grooves whereon it was to slide, it was surmised that the mechanician must then have hurried to the bell, to give his final touches to its sculpture. True artist, he here became absorbed; and absorption still further intensified, it may be, by his striving to abate that strange look of Una; which, though, before others, he had treated with such unconcern, might not, in secret, have been without its thorn.

And so, for the interval, he was oblivious of his creature; which, not oblivious of him, and true to its creation, and true to its heedful winding up, left its post precisely at the given moment; along its well-oiled route, slid noiselessly towards its mark; and, aiming at the hand of Una, to ring one clangorous note, dully smote the intervening brain of Bannadonna, turned backwards to it; the manacled arms then instantly up-springing to their hovering poise. The falling body clogged the thing's return; so there it stood, still impending over Bannadonna, as if whispering some post-mortem terror. The chisel lay dropped from the hand, but beside the hand; the oil-flask spilled across the iron track.

In his unhappy end, not unmindful of the rare genius of the mechanician, the republic decreed him a stately funeral. It was resolved that the great bell—the one whose casting had been jeopardized through the timidity of the ill-starred workman—should be rung upon the entrance of the bier into the cathedral. The most robust man of the country round was assigned the office of bell-ringer.

But as the pall-bearers entered the cathedral porch, naught but a broken and disastrous sound, like that of some lone Alpine land-slide, fell from the tower upon their ears. And then, all was hushed.

Glancing backwards, they saw the groined belfry crashed sideways in. It afterwards appeared that the powerful peasant, who had the bell-rope in charge, wishing to test at once the full glory of the bell, had swayed down upon the rope with one concentrate jerk. The mass of quaking metal, too ponderous for its frame, and strangely feeble somewhere at its top, loosed from its fastening, tore sideways down, and tumbling in one sheer fall, three hundred feet to the soft sward below, buried itself inverted and half out of sight.

Upon its disinterment, the main fracture was found to have started from a small spot in the ear; which, being scraped, revealed a defect, deceptively minute, in the casting; which defect must subsequently have been pasted over with some unknown compound.

The remolten metal soon reassumed its place in the tower's repaired superstructure. For one year the metallic choir of birds sang musically in its belfry-bough-work of sculptured blinds and traceries. But on the first anniversary of the tower's completion—at early dawn, before the concourse had surrounded it—an earthquake came; one loud crash was heard. The stone-pine, with all its bower of songsters, lay overthrown upon the plain.

So the blind slave obeyed its blinder lord; but, in obedience, slew him. So the creator was killed by the creature. So the bell was too heavy for the tower. So the bell's main weakness was where man's blood had flawed it. And so pride went before the fall.

## IN THE DARK

### E. Nesbit

It may have been a form of madness. Or it may be that he really was what is called haunted. Or it may—though I don't pretend to understand how—have been the development, through intense suffering, of a sixth sense in a very nervous, highly-strung nature. Something certainly led him where They were. And to him They were all one.

He told me the first part of the story, and the last part of it I saw with my own eyes.

### I

Haldane and I were friends even in our school-days. What first brought us together was our common hatred of Visger, who came from our part of the country. His people knew our people at home, so he was put on to us when he came. He was the most intolerable person, boy and man, that I have ever known. He would not tell a lie. And that was all right. But he didn't stop at that. If he were asked whether any other chap had done anything—been out of bounds, or up to any sort of lark—he would always say, "I don't know, sir, but I believe so." He never did know—we took care of that. But what he believed was always right. I remember Haldane twisting his arm to say how he knew about that cherry-tree business, and he only said, "I don't know—I just feel sure. And I was right, you see." What can you do with a boy like that?

We grew up to be men. At least Haldane and I did. Visger grew up to be a prig. He was a vegetarian and a teetotaler, and an all-wooler and a Christian Scientist, and all the things that prigs are—but he wasn't a common prig. He knew all sorts of things that he oughtn't to have known, that he *couldn't* have known in any ordinary decent way. It wasn't that he found things out. He just knew them. Once, when I was very unhappy, he came into my rooms—we were all in our last year at Oxford—and talked about things I hardly knew myself. That was really why I went to India that winter. It was bad enough to be unhappy, without having that beast knowing all about it.

I was away over a year. Coming back, I thought a lot about how jolly it would be to see old Haldane again. If I thought about Visger at all, I wished he was dead. But I didn't think about him much.

I did want to see Haldane. He was always such a jolly chap—gay, and kindly, and simple, honourable, upright, and full of practical sympathies. I longed to see him, to see the smile in his jolly blue eyes, looking out from the net of wrinkles that laughing had made round them, to hear his jolly laugh, and feel the good grip of his big hand. I went straight from the docks to his chambers in Gray's Inn, and I found him cold, pale, anaemic, with dull eyes and a limp hand, and pale lips that smiled without mirth, and uttered a welcome without gladness.

He was surrounded by a litter of disordered furniture and personal effects half packed. Some big boxes stood corded, and there were cases of books, filled and waiting for the enclosing boards to be nailed on.

"Yes, I'm moving," he said. "I can't stand these rooms. There's something rum about them—something devilish rum. I clear out tomorrow."

The autumn dusk was filling the corners with shadows. "You got the furs," I said, just for something to say, for I saw the big case that held them lying corded among the others.

"Furs?" he said. "Oh yes. Thanks awfully. Yes. I forgot about the furs." He laughed, out of politeness, I suppose, for there was no joke about the furs. They were many and fine—the best I could get for money, and I had seen them packed and sent off when my heart was very sore. He stood looking at me, and saying nothing.

"Come out and have a bit of dinner," I said as cheerfully as I could.

"Too busy," he answered, after the slightest possible pause, and a glance round the room—"look here—I'm awfully glad to see you—If you'd just slip over and order in dinner—I'd go myself—only—Well, you see how it is."

I went. And when I came back, he had cleared a space near the fire, and moved his big gate-table into it. We dined there by candle light. I tried to be amusing. He, I am sure, tried to be amused. We did not succeed, either of us. And his haggard eyes watched me all the time, save in those fleeting moments when, without turning his head, he glanced back over his shoulder into the shadows that crowded round the little lighted place where we sat.

When we had dined and the man had come and taken away the dishes, I looked at Haldane very steadily, so that he stopped in a pointless anecdote, and looked interrogation at me.

"Well?" I said

"You're not listening," he said petulantly. "What's the matter?"

"That's what you'd better tell me," I said.

He was silent, gave one of those furtive glances at the shadows, and stooped to stir the fire to—I knew it—a blaze that must light every corner of the room.

"You're all to pieces," I said cheerfully. "What have you been up to? Wine? Cards? Speculation? A woman? If you won't tell me, you'll have to tell your doctor. Why, my dear chap, you're a wreck."

"You're a comfortable friend to have about the place," he said, and smiled a mechanical smile not at all pleasant to see.

"I'm the friend you want, I think," said I. "Do you suppose I'm blind? Something's gone wrong and you've taken to something. Morphia, perhaps? And you've brooded over the thing till you've lost all sense of proportion. Out with it, old chap. I bet you a dollar it's not so bad as you think it."

"If I could tell you—or tell anyone," he said slowly, "it wouldn't be so bad as it is. If I could tell anyone, I'd tell you. And even as it is, I've told you more than I've told anyone else."

I could get nothing more out of him. But he pressed me to stay—would have given me his bed and made himself a shake-down, he said. But I had engaged my room at the Victoria, and I was expecting letters. So I left him, quite late—and he stood on the stairs, holding a candle over the bannisters to light me down.

When I went back next morning, he was gone. Men were moving his furniture into a big van with Somebody's Pantechnicon painted on it in big letters.

He had left no address with the porter, and had driven off in a hansom with two portmanteaux—to Waterloo, the porter thought.

Well, a man has a right to the monopoly of his own troubles, if he chooses to have it. And I had troubles of my own that kept me busy.


## II


It was more than a year later that I saw Haldane again. I had got rooms in the Albany by this time, and he turned up there one morning, very early indeed—before breakfast in fact. And if he looked ghastly before, he now looked almost ghostly. His face looked as though it had worn thin, like an oyster shell that has for years been cast up twice a day by the sea on a shore all pebbly. His hands were thin as bird's claws, and they trembled like caught butterflies.

I welcomed him with enthusiastic cordiality and pressed breakfast on him. This time, I decided, I would ask no questions. For I saw that none were needed. He would tell me. He intended to tell me. He had come here to tell me, and for nothing else.

I lit the spirit lamp—I made coffee and small talk for him, and I ate and drank, and waited for him to begin. And it was like this that he began:

"I am going," he said, "to kill myself—oh, don't be alarmed,"—I suppose I had said or looked something—"I shan't do it here, or now. I shall do it when I have to—when I can't bear it any longer. And I want some one to know why. I don't want to feel that I'm the only living creature who does know. And I can trust you, can't I?"

I murmured something reassuring.

"I should like you, if you don't mind, to give me your word, that you won't tell a soul what I'm going to tell you, as long as I'm alive. Afterwards . . . you can tell whom you please."

I gave him my word.

He sat silent looking at the fire. Then he shrugged his shoulders.

"It's extraordinary how difficult it is to say it," he said, and smiled. "The fact is—you know that beast, George Visger."

"Yes," I said. "I haven't seen him since I came back. Some one told me he'd gone to some island or other to preach vegetarianism to be cannibals. Anyhow, he's out of the way, bad luck to him."

"Yes," said Haldane, "he's out of the way. But he's not preaching anything. In point of fact, he's dead."

"Dead?" was all I could think of to say.

"Yes," said he; "it's not generally known, but he is."

"What did he die of?" I asked, not that I cared. The bare fact was good enough for me.

"You know what an interfering chap he always was. Always knew everything. Heart to heart talks—and have everything open and above board. Well, he interfered between me and some one else—told her a pack of lies."

"Lies?"

"Well, the *things* were true, but he made lies of them the way he told them—*you* know." I did. I nodded. "And she threw me over. And she died. And we weren't even friends. And I couldn't see her—before—I couldn't even . . . Oh, my God . . . But I went to the funeral. He was there. They'd asked *him*. And then I came back to my rooms. And I was sitting there, thinking. And he came up."

"He would do. It's just what he would do. The beast! I hope you kicked him out."

"No, I didn't. I listened to what he'd got to say. He came to say, No doubt it was all for the best. And he hadn't known the things he told her. He'd only guessed. He'd guessed right, damn him. What right had he to guess right? And he said it was all for the best, because, besides that, there was madness in my family. He'd found that out too—"

"And is there?"

"If there is, I didn't know it. And that was why it was all for the best. So then I said, "There wasn't any madness in my family before, but there is now," and I got hold of his throat. I am not sure whether I meant to kill him; I ought to have meant to kill him. Anyhow, I did kill him. What did you say?"

I had said nothing. It is not easy to think at once of the tactful and suitable thing to say, when your oldest friend tells you that he is a murderer.

"When I could get my hands out of his throat—it was as difficult as it is to drop the handles of a galvanic battery—he fell in a lump on the hearth-rug. And I saw what I'd done. How is it that murderers ever get found out?"

"They're careless, I suppose," I found myself saying, "they lose their nerve."

"I didn't,' he said. "I never was calmer, I sat down in the big chair and looked at him, and thought it all out. He was just off to that island—I knew that. He'd said good-bye to every one. He'd told me that. There was no blood to get rid of—or only a touch at the corner of his slack mouth. He wasn't going to travel in his own name because of interviewers. Mr. Somebody Something's luggage would be unclaimed and his cabin empty. No one would guess that Mr. Somebody Something was Sir George Visger, F.R.S. It was all as plain as plain. There was nothing to get rid of, but the man. No weapon, no blood—and I got rid of him all right."

"How?"

He smiled cunningly.

"No, no," he said; "that's where I draw the line. It's not that I doubt your word, but if you talked in your sleep, or had a fever or anything. No, no. As long as you don't know where the body is, don't you see, I'm all right. Even if you could prove that I've said all this—which you can't—it's only the wanderings of my poor unhinged brain. See?"

I saw. And I was sorry for him. And I did not believe that he had killed Visger. He was not the sort of man who kills people. So I said:

"Yes, old chap, I see. Now look here. Let's go away together, you and I—travel a bit and see the world, and forget all about that beastly chap."

His eyes lighted up at that.

"Why," he said, "you understand. You don't hate me and shrink from me. I wish I'd told you before—you know—when you came and I was packing all my sticks. But it's too late now."

"Too late? Not a bit of it," I said. "Come, we'll pack our traps and be off tonight—out into the unknown, don't you know."

"That's where *I'm* going," he said. "You wait. When you've heard what's been happening to me, you won't be so keen to go travelling about with me."

"But you've told me what's been happening to you," I said, and the more I thought about what he had told me, the less I believed it.

"No," he said, slowly, "no—I've told you what happened to *him*. What happened to me is quite different. Did I tell you what his last words were? Just when I was coming at him. Before I'd got his throat, you know. He said, 'Look out. You'll never to able to get rid of the body—Besides, anger's sinful.' You know that way he had, like a tract on its hind legs. So afterwards I got thinking of that. But I didn't think of it for a year. Because I did get rid of his body all right. And then I was sitting in that comfortable chair, and I thought, 'Hullo, it must be about a year now, since that—' and I pulled out my pocket-book and went to the window to look at a little almanack I carry about—it was getting dusk—and sure enough it was a year, to the day. And then I remembered what he'd said. And I said to myself, 'Not much trouble about getting rid of *your* body, you brute.' And then I looked at the hearth-rug and—Ah!" he screamed suddenly and very loud—"I can't tell you—no, I can't."

My man opened the door—he wore a smooth face over his wriggling curiosity. "Did you call, sir?"

"Yes," I lied. "I want you to take a note to the bank, and wait for an answer."

When he was got rid of, Haldane said: "Where was I?—"

"You were just telling me what happened after you looked at the almanack. What was it?"

"Nothing much," he said, laughing softly, "oh, nothing much—only that I glanced at the hearth-rug—and there *he* was—the man I'd killed a year before. Don't try to explain, or I shall lose my temper. The door was shut. The windows were shut. He hadn't been there a minute before. And he was there then. That's all."

Hallucination was one of the words I stumbled among.

"Exactly what I thought," he said triumphantly, "but—I touched it. It was quite real. Heavy, you know, and harder than live people are somehow, to the touch—more like a stone thing covered with kid the hands were, and the arms like a marble statue in a blue serge suit. Don't you hate men who wear blue serge suits?"

"There are hallucinations of touch too," I found myself saying.

"Exactly what I thought," said Haldane more triumphant than ever, "but there are limits, you know—limits. So then I thought someone had got him out—the real him—and stuck him there to frighten me—while my back was turned, and I went to the place where I'd hidden him, and he was there—ah!—just as I'd left him. Only . . . it was a year ago. There are two of him there now."

"My dear chap," I said, "this is simply comic."

"Yes," he said, "it is amusing. I find it so myself. Especially in the night when I wake up and think of it. I hope I shan't die in the dark, Winston: That's one of the reasons why I think I shall have to kill myself. I could be sure then of not dying in the dark."

"Is *that* all?" I asked, feeling sure that it must be.

"No," said Haldane at once. "That's *not* all. He's come back to me again. In a railway carriage it was. I'd been asleep. When I woke up, there he was lying on the seat opposite me. Looked just the same. I pitched him out on the line in Red Hill Tunnel. And if I see him again, I'm going out myself. I can't stand it. It's too much. I'd sooner go. Whatever the next world's like, there aren't things in it like that. We leave them here, in graves and boxes and . . . You think I'm mad. But I'm not. You can't help me—no one can help me. He *knew,* you see. He said I shouldn't be able to get rid of the body. And I can't get rid of it. I can't. I can't. He knew. He always did know things that he *couldn't* know. But I'll cut his game short. After all, I've got the ace of trumps, and I play it on his next trick. I give you my word of honour, Winston, that I'm not mad."

"My dear old man," I said, "I don't think you're mad. But I do think your nerves are very much upset. Mine are a bit, too. Do you know why I went to India? It was because of you and her. I couldn't stay and see it, though I wished for your happiness and all that; you know I did. And when I came back, she . . . and you . . . Let's see it out together," I said. "You won't keep fancying things if you've got me to talk to. And I always said you weren't half a bad old duffer."

"She liked you," he said.

"Oh, yes," I said, "she liked me."

## III

That was how we came to go abroad together. I was full of hope for him. He'd always been such a splendid chap—so sane and strong. I couldn't believe that he was gone mad, gone for ever, I mean, so that he'd never come right again. Perhaps my own trouble made it easy for me to see things not quite straight. Anyway, I took him away to recover his mind's health, exactly as I should have taken him away to get strong after a fever. And the madness seemed to pass away, and in a month or two we were perfectly jolly, and I thought I had cured him. And I was very glad because of that old friendship of ours, and because she had loved him and liked me.

We never spoke of Visger. I thought he had forgotten all about him. I thought I understood how his mind, over-strained by sorrow and anger, had fixed on the man he hated, and woven a nightmare web of horror round that detestable personality. And I had got the whip hand of my own trouble. And we were as jolly as sandboys together all those months.

And we came to Bruges at last in our travels, and Bruges was very full, because of the Exhibition. We could only get one room and one bed. So we tossed for the bed, and the one who lost the toss was to make the best of the night in the arm-chair. And the bed-clothes we were to share equitably.

We spent the evening at a *café chantant* and finished at a beer hall, and it was late and sleepy when we got back to the Grande Vigne. I took our key from its nail in the concierge's room, and we went up. We talked awhile, I remember, of the town, and the belfry, and the Venetian aspect of the canals by moonlight, and then Haldane got into bed, and I made a chrysalis of myself with my share of the blankets and fitted the tight roll into the arm-chair. I was not at all comfortable, but I was compensatingly tired, and I was nearly asleep when Haldane roused me up to tell me about his will.

"I've left everything to you, old man," he said. "I know I can trust you to see to everything."

"Quite so," said I, "and if you don't mind, we'll talk about it in the morning."

He tried to go on about it, and about what a friend I'd been, and all that, but I shut him up and told him to go to sleep. But no. He wasn't comfortable, he said. And he'd got a thirst like a lime kiln. And he'd noticed that there was no water-bottle in the room. "And the water in the jug's like pale soup," he said.

"Oh, all right," said I. "Light your candle and go and get some water, then, in Heaven's name, and let me get to sleep."

But he said, "No—you light it. I don't want to get out of bed in the dark. I might—I might step on something, mightn't I—or walk into something that wasn't there when I got into bed."

"Rot," I said, "walk into your grandmother." But I lit the candle all the same. He sat up in bed and looked at me—very pale—with his hair all tumbled from the pillow, and his eyes blinking and shining.

"That's better," he said. And then, "I say—look here. Oh—yes—I see. It's all right. Queer how they mark the sheets here. Blest if I didn't think it was blood, just for the minute."

The sheet was marked, not at the corner, as sheets are marked at home, but right in the middle where it turns down, with big, red, cross-stitching.

"Yes, I see," I said, "it is a queer place to mark it."

"It's queer letters do have on it," he said. "G.V."

"Grande Vigne," I said. "What letters do you expect them to mark things with? Hurry up."

"You come too," he said. "Yes, it does stand for Grande Vigne, of course. I wish you'd come down too, Winston."

"I'll *go* down," I said and turned with the candle in my hand.

He was out of bed and close to me in a flash.

"No," said he, "I don't want to stay alone in the dark."

He said it just as a frightened child might have done.

"All right then, come along," I said. And we went. I tried to make some joke, I remember, about the length of his hair, and the cut of his pyjamas—but I was sick with disappointment. For it was almost quite plain to me, even then, that all my time and trouble had been thrown away, and that he wasn't cured after all. We went down as quietly as we could, and got a carafe of water from the long bare dining table in the salle-à-manger. He got hold of my arm at first, and then he got the candle away from me, and went very slowly, shading the light with his hand, and looking very carefully all about, as though he expected to see something that he wanted very desperately not to see. And of course, I knew what that something was. I didn't like the way he was going on. I can't at all express how deeply I didn't like it. And he looked over his shoulder every now and then, just as he did that first evening after I came back from India.

The thing got on my nerves so that I could hardly find the way back to our room. And when we got there, I give you my word, I more than half expected to see what *he* had expected to see—that, or something like that, on the hearth-rug. But of course there was nothing.

I blew out the light and tightened my blankets round me—I'd been trailing them after me in our expedition. And I was settled in my chair when Haldane spoke.

"You've got all the blankets," he said.

"No, I haven't," said I, "only what I've always had."

"I can't find mine then," he said and I could hear his teeth chattering. "And I'm cold. I'm . . . For God's sake, light the candle. Light it. Light it. Something horrible . . ."

And I couldn't find the matches.

"Light the candle, light the candle," he said, and his voice broke, as a boy's does sometimes in chapel. "If you don't he'll come to me. It is so easy to come at any one in the dark. Oh Winston, light the candle, for the love of God! I can't die in the dark."

"I am lighting it," I said savagely, and I was feeling for the matches on the marble-topped chest of drawers, on the mantelpiece—everywhere but on the round centre table where I'd put them. "You're not going to die. Don't be a fool," I said. "It's all right. I'll get a light in a second."

He said, "It's cold. It's cold. It's cold," like that, three times. And then he screamed aloud, like a woman—like a child—like a hare when the dogs have got it. I had heard him scream like that once before.

"What is it?" I cried, hardly less loud. "For God's sake, hold your noise. What is it?"

There was an empty silence. Then, very slowly:

"It's Visger," he said. And he spoke thickly, as through some stifling veil.

"Nonsense. Where?" I asked, and my hand closed on the matches as he spoke.

"Here," he screamed sharply, as though he had torn the veil away, "here, beside me. In the bed."

I got the candle alight. I got across to him.

He was crushed in a heap at the edge of the bed. Stretched on the bed beyond him was a dead man, white and very cold.

Haldane had died in the dark.

It was all so simple.

We had come to the wrong room. The man the room belonged to was there, on the bed he had engaged and paid for before he died of heart disease, earlier in the day. A French *commis-voyageur* representing soap and perfumery; his name, Félix Leblanc.

Later, in England, I made cautious enquiries. The body of a man had been found in the Red Hill Tunnel—a haberdasher man named Simmons, who had drunk spirits of salts, owing to the depression of trade. The bottle was clutched in his dead hand.

For reasons that I had, I took care to have a police inspector with me when I opened the boxes that came to me by Haldane's will. One of them was the big box, metal lined, in which I had sent him the skins from India—for a wedding present, God help us all!

It was closely soldered.

Inside were the skins of beasts? No. The bodies of two men. One was identified, after some trouble, as that of a hawker of pens in city offices—subject to fits. He had died in one, it seemed. The other body was Visger's right enough.

Explain it as you like. I offered you, if you remember, a choice of explanations before I began the story. I have not yet found the explanation that can satisfy me.

## THE HAG

*Robert Herrick*

The Hag is astride,
This night for to ride;
The Devil and she together:
Through thick, and through thin,
Now out, and then in,
Though ne'r so foul be the weather.

A Thorn or a Burr
She takes for a Spur:
With a lash of a Bramble she rides now,
Through Brakes and through Briars,
O're Ditches, and Mires,
She follows the Spirit that guides now.

No Beast, for his food,
Dares now range the wood;
But hushed in his lair he lies lurking:
While mischiefs, by these,
On Land and on Seas,
At noon of Night are a working.

The storm will arise,
And trouble the skies;
This night, and more for the wonder,
The ghost from the Tomb
Affrighted shall come,
Called out by the clap of the Thunder.

## A SPELL

*John Dryden*

Choose the darkest part o' the grove,
Such as ghosts at noon-day love.
Dig a trench, and dig it nigh
Where the bones of Laius lie;
Altars raised of turf or stone,
Will th' infernal pow'rs have none.
Answer me, if this be done?
           *'Tis done.*
Is the sacrifice made fit?
Draw her backward to the pit:
Draw the barren heifer back;
Barren let her be, and black.
Cut the curled hair that grows
Full betwixt her horns and brows:
And turn your faces from the sun;
Answer me, if this be done?
           *'Tis done.*
Pour in blood, and blood like wine,
To Mother Earth and Proserpine:
Mingle milk into the stream:
Feast the ghosts that love the stream;
Snatch a brand from funeral pile:
Toss it in, to make them boil:
And turn your faces from the sun;
Answer me, if this be done?
           *'Tis done.*

## THE OLD GHOST

*Thomas Lovell Beddoes*

Over the water an old ghost strode
    To a churchyard on the shore,
And over him the waters had flowed
    A thousand years or more,
And pale and wan and weary
    Looked never a sprite as he;
For it's lonely and it's dreary
    The ghost of a body to be
    That has mouldered away in the sea.

Over the billows the old ghost stepped,
    And the winds in mockery sung;
For the bodiless ghost would fain have wept
    Over the maiden that lay so young
    'Mong the thistles and toadstools so hoary.
    And he begged of the waves a tear,
But they shook upwards their moonlight glory,
    And the shark looked on with a sneer
    At his yearning desire and agony.

❧

## SORROW

*Aubrey de Vere*

When I was young, I said to Sorrow,
"Come I will play with thee"—
He is near me now all day;
And at night returns to say,
"I will come again to-morrow,
I will come and stay with thee."

Through the woods we walk together;
His soft footsteps rustle nigh me.
To shield an unregarded head,
He hath built a wintry shed;
And all night in rainy weather,
I hear his gentle breathings by me.

∾

# LUKE HAVERGAL

*Edwin Arlington Robinson*

Go to the western gate, Luke Havergal,
There where the vines cling crimson on the wall,
And in the twilight wait for what will come.
The leaves will whisper there of her, and some,
Like flying words, will strike you as they fall;
But go, and if you listen she will call.
Go to the western gate, Luke Havergal—
Luke Havergal.

No, there is not a dawn in eastern skies
To rift the fiery night that's in your eyes;
But there, where western glooms are gathering,
The dark will end the dark, if anything:
God slays Himself with every leaf that flies,
And hell is more than half of paradise.
No, there is not a dawn in eastern skies—
In eastern skies.

Out of a grave I come to tell you this,
Out of a grave I come to quench the kiss
That flames upon your forehead with a glow
That blinds you to the way that you must go.
Yes, there is yet one way to where she is,
Bitter, but one that faith may never miss.

Out of a grave I come to tell you this—
To tell you this.

There is the western gate, Luke Havergal,
There are the crimson leaves upon the wall.
Go, for the winds are tearing them away,—
Nor think to riddle the dead words they say,
Nor any more to feel them as they fall;
But go, and if you trust her she will call.
There is the western gate, Luke Havergal—
Luke Havergal.

❧

# DIRGE

*Thomas Lovell Beddoes*

We do lie beneath the grass
    In the moonlight, in the shade
Of the yew-tree. They that pass
    Hear us not. We are afraid
        They would envy our delight,
        In our graves by glow-worm night.
Come follow us, and smile as we;
    We sail to the rock in the ancient waves,
Where the snow falls by thousands into the sea,
    And the drowned and the shipwrecked have
        happy graves.

❧

## THE TWO SPIRITS

*Percy Bysshe Shelley*

### FIRST SPIRIT

O thou, who plumed with strong desire
    Wouldst float above the earth, beware!
A Shadow tracks thy flight of fire—
    Night is coming!
    Bright are the regions of the air,
And among the winds and beams
    It were delight to wander there—
    Night is coming!

### SECOND SPIRIT

The deathless stars are bright above;
    If I would cross the shade of night,
Within my heart is the lamp of love,
    And that is day!
    And the moon will smile with gentle light
On my golden plumes where'er they move;
    The meteors will linger round my flight,
    And make night day.

### FIRST SPIRIT

But if the whirlwinds of darkness waken
    Hail, and lightning, and stormy rain;
See, the bounds of the air are shaken—
    Night is coming!
    The red swift clouds of the hurricane
Yon declining sun have overtaken,
    The clash of the hail sweeps over the plain—
    Night is coming.

## SECOND SPIRIT

I see the light, and I hear the sound;
    I'll sail on the flood of the tempest dark,
With the calm within and the light around
        Which makes night day:
    And thou, when the gloom is deep and stark,
Look from thy dull earth, slumber-bound,
    My moon-like flight thou then mayst mark
        On high, far away.

---

Some say there is a precipice
    Where one vast pine is frozen to ruin
O'er piles of snow and chasms of ice
        Mid Alpine mountains;
    And that the languid storm pursuing
That winged shape, for ever flies
    Round those hoar branches, aye renewing
        Its aëry fountains.
Some say when nights are dry and clear,
    And the death-dews sleep on the morass,
Sweet whispers are heard by the traveller,
        Which make night day:
    And a silver shape like his early love doth pass
Upborne by her wild and glittering hair,
    And when he awakes on the fragrant grass,
        He finds night day.

☙

## THE PHANTOM-WOOER

*Thomas Lovell Beddoes*

A ghost, that loved a lady fair,
Ever in the starry air
    Of midnight at her pillow stood;
And, with a sweetness skies above
The luring words of human love,
    Her soul the phantom wooed.
Sweet and sweet is their poisoned note,
The little snakes of silver throat,
In mossy skulls that nest and lie,
Ever singing "die, oh! die."

Young soul put off your flesh, and come
With me into the quiet tomb,
    Our bed is lovely, dark, and sweet;
The earth will swing us, as she goes,
Beneath our coverlid of snows,
    And the warm leaden sheet.
Dear and dear is their poisoned note,
The little snakes of silver throat,
In mossy skulls that nest and lie,
Ever singing "die, oh! die."

## THE PORTENT

*Herman Melville*

Hanging from the beam,
    Slowly swaying (such the law),
Gaunt the shadow on your green,
    Shenandoah!

The cut is on the crown
(Lo, John Brown),
And the stabs shall heal no more.

Hidden in the cap
          Is the anguish none can draw;
So your future veils its face,
          Shenandoah!
But the streaming beard is shown
(Weird John Brown),
The meteor of the war.

❧

# WILLIAM WILSON

## Edgar Allan Poe

*What say of it? what say [of]* CONSCIENCE *grim,*
*That spectre in my path?*
          *Chamberlayne's Pharronida.*

Let me call myself, for the present, William Wilson. The fair page now lying before me need not be sullied with my real appellation. This has been already too much an object for the scorn—for the horror—for the detestation of my race. To the uttermost regions of the globe have not the indignant winds bruited its unparalleled infamy? Oh, outcast of all outcasts most abandoned!—to the earth art thou not forever dead? to its honors, to its flowers, to its golden aspirations?—and a cloud, dense, dismal, and limitless, does it not hang eternally between thy hopes and heaven?

I would not, if I could, here or to-day, embody a record of my later years of unspeakable misery, and unpardonable crime. This epoch—these later years—took unto themselves a sudden elevation in turpitude, whose origin alone it is my present purpose to assign. Men usually grow base by degrees. From me, in an instant, all virtue dropped bodily as a mantle. From comparatively trivial wickedness I passed, with the stride of a giant, into more than the enormities of an Elah-Gabalus. What chance—what one event brought this evil thing to pass, bear with me while I relate.

Death approaches; and the shadow which foreruns him has thrown a softening influence over my spirit. I long, in passing through the dim valley, for the sympathy—I had nearly said for the pity—of my fellow men. I would fain have them believe that I have been, in some measure, the slave of circumstances beyond human control. I would wish them to seek out for me, in the details I am about to give, some little oasis of *fatality* amid a wilderness of error. I would have them allow—what they cannot refrain from allowing—that, although temptation may have erewhile existed as great, man was never *thus,* at least, tempted before—certainly, never *thus* fell. And is it therefore that he has never thus suffered? Have I not indeed been living in a dream? And am I not now dying a victim to the horror and the mystery of the wildest of all sublunary visions?

I am the descendant of a race whose imaginative and easily excitable temperament has at all times rendered them remarkable; and, in my earliest infancy, I gave evidence of having fully inherited the family character. As I advanced in years it was more strongly developed; becoming, for many reasons, a cause of serious disquietude to my friends, and of positive injury to myself. I grew self-willed, addicted to the wildest caprices, and a prey to the most ungovernable passions. Weak-minded, and beset with constitutional infirmities akin to my own, my parents could do but little to check the evil propensities which distinguished me. Some feeble and ill-directed efforts resulted in complete failure on their part, and, of course, in total triumph on mine. Thenceforward my voice was a household law; and at an age when few children have abandoned their leading-strings, I was left to the guidance of my own will, and became, in all but name, the master of my own actions.

My earliest recollections of a school-life, are connected with a large, rambling, Elizabethan house, in a misty-looking village of England, where were a vast number of gigantic and gnarled trees, and where all the houses were excessively ancient. In truth, it was a dream-like and spirit-soothing place, that venerable old town. At this moment, in fancy, I feel the refreshing chilliness of its deeply-shadowed avenues, inhale the fragrance of its thousand shrubberies, and thrill anew with undefinable delight, at the deep hollow note of the church-bell, breaking, each hour, with sullen and sudden roar, upon the stillness of the dusky atmosphere in which the fretted Gothic steeple lay imbedded and asleep.

It gives me, perhaps, as much of pleasure as I can now in any manner experience, to dwell upon minute recollections of the school and its concerns. Steeped in misery as I am—misery, alas! only too real—I shall be pardoned for seeking relief, however slight and temporary, in the weakness of a few rambling details. These, moreover, utterly trivial, and even ridiculous in themselves, assume, to my fancy, adventitious importance, as connected with a period and a locality when and where I recognise the first ambiguous monitions of the destiny which afterwards so fully overshadowed me. Let me then remember.

The house, I have said, was old and irregular. The grounds were extensive, and a high and solid brick wall, topped with a bed of mortar and broken glass, encompassed the whole. This prison-like rampart formed the limit of our domain; beyond it we saw but thrice a week—once every Saturday afternoon, when, attended by two ushers, we were permitted to take brief walks in a body through some of the neighbouring fields—and twice during Sunday, when we were paraded in the same formal manner to the morning and evening service in the one church of the village. Of this church the principal of our school was pastor. With how deep a spirit of wonder and perplexity was I wont to regard him from our remote pew in the gallery, as, with step solemn and slow, he ascended the pulpit! This reverend man, with countenance so demurely benign, with robes so glossy and so clerically flowing, with wig so minutely powdered, so rigid and so vast,—could this be he who, of late, with sour visage, and in snuffy habiliments, administered, ferule in hand, the Draconian laws of the academy? Oh, gigantic paradox, too utterly monstrous for solution!

At an angle of the ponderous wall frowned a more ponderous gate. It was riveted and studded with iron bolts, and surmounted with jagged iron spikes. What impressions of deep awe did it inspire! It was never opened save for the three periodical egressions and ingressions already mentioned; then, in every creak of its mighty hinges, we found a plenitude of mystery— a world of matter for solemn remark, or for more solemn meditation.

The extensive enclosure was irregular in form, having many capacious recesses. Of these, three or four of the largest constituted the play-ground. It was level, and covered with fine hard gravel. I well remember it had no trees, nor benches, nor anything similar within it. Of course it was in the rear of the house. In front lay a small parterre, planted with box and other shrubs; but through this sacred division we passed only upon rare occasions indeed—such as a first advent to school or final departure thence, or perhaps, when a parent or friend having called for us, we joyfully took our way home for the Christmas or Midsummer holy-days.

But the house!—how quaint an old building was this!—to me how veritably a palace of enchantment! There was really no end to its windings— to its incomprehensible subdivisions. It was difficult, at any given time, to say with certainty upon which of its two stories one happened to be. From

each room to every other there were sure to be found three or four steps
either in ascent or descent. Then the lateral branches were innumerable—
inconceivable—and so returning in upon themselves, that our most exact
ideas in regard to the whole mansion were not very far different from those
with which we pondered upon infinity. During the five years of my residence here, I was never able to ascertain with precision, in what remote
locality lay the little sleeping apartment assigned to myself and some eigh-
teen or twenty other scholars.

The school-room was the largest in the house—I could not help thinking, in the world. It was very long, narrow, and dismally low, with pointed
Gothic windows and a ceiling of oak. In a remote and terror-inspiring
angle was a square enclosure of eight or ten feet, comprising the *sanctum,*
"during hours," of our principal, the Reverend Dr. Bransby. It was a solid
structure, with massy door, sooner than open which in the absence of the
"Dominie," we would all have willingly perished by the *peine forte et dure.*
In other angles were two other similar boxes, far less reverenced, indeed,
but still greatly matters of awe. One of these was the pulpit of the "classical" usher, one of the "English and mathematical." Interspersed about
the room, crossing and recrossing in endless irregularity, were innumerable
benches and desks, black, ancient, and time-worn, piled desperately with
much-bethumbed books, and so beseamed with initial letters, names at full
length, grotesque figures, and other multiplied efforts of the knife, as to
have entirely lost what little of original form might have been their portion
in days long departed. (A huge bucket with water stood at one extremity
of the room, and a clock of stupendous dimensions at the other.)

Encompassed by the massy walls of this venerable academy, I passed,
yet not in tedium or disgust, the years of the third lustrum of my life. The
teeming brain of childhood requires no external world of incident to
occupy or amuse it; and the apparently dismal monotony of a school was
replete with more intense excitement than my riper youth has derived
from luxury, or my full manhood from crime. Yet I must believe that my
first mental development had in it much of the uncommon—even much of
the *outré.* Upon mankind at large the events of very early existence rarely
leave in mature age any definite impression. All is gray shadow—a weak
and irregular remembrance—an indistinct regathering of feeble pleasures
and phantasmagoric pains. With me this is not so. In childhood I must
have felt with the energy of a man what I now find stamped upon memory
in lines as vivid, as deep, and as durable as the *exergues* of the Carthaginian
medals.

Yet in fact—in the fact of the world's view—how little was there to remember! The morning's awakening, the nightly summons to bed; the connings, the recitations; the periodical half-holidays, and perambulations; the play-ground, with its broils, its pastimes, its intrigues;—these, by a mental sorcery long forgotten, were made to involve a wilderness of sensation, a world of rich incident, an universe of varied emotion, of excitement the most passionate and spirit-stirring. *"Oh, le bon temps, que ce siècle de fer!"*

In truth, the ardor, the enthusiasm, and the imperiousness of my disposition, soon rendered me a marked character among my schoolmates, and by slow, but natural gradations, gave me an ascendancy over all not greatly older than myself;—over all with a single exception. This exception was found in the person of a scholar, who, although no relation, bore the same Christian and surname as myself;—a circumstance, in fact, little remarkable; for, notwithstanding a noble descent, mine was one of those everyday appellations which seem, by prescriptive right, to have been, time out of mind, the common property of the mob. In this narrative I have therefore designated myself as William Wilson,—a fictitious title not very dissimilar to the real. My namesake alone, of those who in school phraseology constituted "our set," presumed to compete with me in the studies of the class—in the sports and broils of the play-ground—to refuse implicit belief in my assertions, and submission to my will—indeed, to interfere with my arbitrary dictation in any respect whatsoever. If there is on earth a supreme and unqualified despotism, it is the despotism of a master mind in boyhood over the less energetic spirits of its companions.

Wilson's rebellion was to me a source of the greatest embarrassment;—the more so as, in spite of the bravado with which in public I made a point of treating him and his pretensions, I secretly felt that I feared him, and could not help thinking the equality which he maintained so easily with myself, a proof of his true superiority; since not to be overcome cost me a perpetual struggle. Yet this superiority—even this equality—was in truth acknowledged by no one but myself; our associates, by some unaccountable blindness, seemed not even to suspect it. Indeed, his competition, his resistance, and especially his impertinent and dogged interference with my purposes, were not more pointed than private. He appeared to be destitute alike of the ambition which urged, and of the passionate energy of mind which enabled me to excel. In his rivalry he might have been supposed actuated solely by a whimsical desire to thwart, astonish, or mortify myself; although there were times when I could not help observing, with a feeling made up of wonder, abasement, and pique, that he mingled with his injuries, his insults, or his contradictions, a certain most inappropriate, and assuredly most unwelcome *affectionateness* of manner. I could only conceive this singular behavior to arise from a consummate self-conceit assuming the vulgar airs of patronage and protection.

Perhaps it was this latter trait in Wilson's conduct, conjoined with our identity of name, and the mere accident of our having entered the school upon the same day, which set afloat the notion that we were brothers, among the senior classes in the academy. These do not usually inquire with much strictness into the affairs of their juniors. I have before said, or should have said, that Wilson was not, in the most remote degree, connected with my family. But assuredly if we *had* been brothers we must have been twins; for, after leaving Dr. Bransby's, I casually learned that my namesake was born on the nineteenth of January, 1813—and this is a somewhat remarkable coincidence; for the day is precisely that of my own nativity.

It may seem strange that in spite of the continual anxiety occasioned me by the rivalry of Wilson, and his intolerable spirit of contradiction, I could not bring myself to hate him altogether. We had, to be sure, nearly every day a quarrel in which, yielding me publicly the palm of victory, he, in some manner, contrived to make me feel that it was he who had deserved it; yet a sense of pride on my part, and a veritable dignity on his own, kept us always upon what are called "speaking terms," while there were many points of strong congeniality in our tempers, operating to awake in me a sentiment which our position alone, perhaps, prevented from ripening into friendship. It is difficult, indeed, to define, or even to describe, my real feelings towards him. They formed a motley and heterogeneous admixture;— some petulant animosity, which was not yet hatred, some esteem, more respect, much fear, with a world of uneasy curiosity. To the moralist it will be unnecessary to say, in addition, that Wilson and myself were the most inseparable of companions.

It was no doubt the anomalous state of affairs existing between us, which turned all my attacks upon him (and they were many, either open or covert) into the channel of banter or practical joke (giving pain while assuming the aspect of mere fun) rather than into a more serious and determined hostility. But my endeavours on this head were by no means uniformly successful, even when my plans were the most wittily concocted; for my namesake had much about him, in character, of that unassuming and quiet austerity which, while enjoying the poignancy of its own jokes, has no heel of Achilles in itself, and absolutely refuses to be laughed at. I could find, indeed, but one vulnerable point, and that, lying in a personal peculiarity, arising, perhaps, from constitutional disease, would have been spared by any antagonist less at his wit's end than myself;—my rival had a weakness in the faucial or guttural organs, which precluded him from raising his voice at any time *above a very low whisper.* Of this defect I did not fail to take what poor advantage lay in my power.

Wilson's retaliations in kind were many; and there was one form of his practical wit that disturbed me beyond measure. How his sagacity first discovered at all that so petty a thing would vex me, is a question I never could solve; but, having discovered, he habitually practised the annoyance. I had always felt aversion to my uncourtly patronymic, and its very common, if not plebeian prænomen. The words were venom in my ears; and when, upon the day of my arrival, a second William Wilson came also to the academy, I felt angry with him for bearing the name, and doubly disgusted with the name because a stranger bore it, who would be the cause of its twofold repetition, who would be constantly in my presence, and whose concerns, in the ordinary routine of the school business, must inevitably, on account of the detestable coincidence, be often confounded with my own.

The feeling of vexation thus engendered grew stronger with every circumstance tending to show resemblance, moral or physical, between my rival and myself. I had not then discovered the remarkable fact that we were of the same age; but I saw that we were of the same height, and I perceived that we were even singularly alike in general contour of person and outline of feature. I was galled, too, by the rumor touching a relationship, which had grown current in the upper forms. In a word, nothing could more seriously disturb me (although I scrupulously concealed such disturbance) than any allusion to a similarity of mind, person, or condition existing between us. But, in truth, I had no reason to believe that (with the exception of the matter of relationship, and in the case of Wilson himself) this similarity had ever been made a subject of comment, or even observed at all by our schoolfellows. That *he* observed it in all its bearings, and as fixedly as I, was apparent; but that he could discover in such circumstances so fruitful a field of annoyance, can only be attributed, as I said before, to his more than ordinary penetration.

His cue, which was to perfect an imitation of myself, lay both in words and in actions; and most admirably did he play his part. My dress it was an easy matter to copy; my gait and general manner were, without difficulty, appropriated; in spite of his constitutional defect, even my voice did not escape him. My louder tones were, of course, unattempted, but then the key, it was identical; *and his singular whisper, it grew the very echo of my own.*

How greatly this most exquisite portraiture harassed me (for it could not justly be termed a caricature) I will not now venture to describe. I had but one consolation—in the fact that the imitation, apparently, was noticed by myself alone, and that I had to endure only the knowing and strangely sarcastic smiles of my namesake himself. Satisfied with having produced in my bosom the intended effect, he seemed to chuckle in secret over the sting he had inflicted, and was characteristically disregardful of the public applause which the success of his witty endeavours might have so easily elicited. That the school, indeed, did not feel his design, perceive its accomplishment, and participate in his sneer, was, for many anxious months, a riddle I could not resolve. Perhaps the *gradation* of his copy rendered it not so readily perceptible; or, more possibly, I owed my security to the masterly air of the copyist, who, disdaining the letter (which in a painting is all the obtuse can see) gave but the full spirit of his original for my individual contemplation and chagrin.

I have already more than once spoken of the disgusting air of patronage which he assumed toward me, and of his frequent officious interference with my will. This interference often took the ungracious character of advice; advice not openly given, but hinted or insinuated. I received it with a repugnance which gained strength as I grew in years. Yet, at this distant day, let me do him the simple justice to acknowledge that I can recall no occasion when the suggestions of my rival were on the side of those errors or follies so usual to his immature age and seeming inexperience; that his moral sense, at least, if not his general talents and worldly wisdom, was far keener than my own; and that I might, to-day, have been a better, and thus a happier man, had I less frequently rejected the counsels embodied in those meaning whispers which I then but too cordially hated and too bitterly despised.

As it was, I at length grew restive in the extreme under his distasteful supervision, and daily resented more and more openly what I considered his intolerable arrogance. I have said that, in the first years of our connexion as schoolmates, my feelings in regard to him might have been easily ripened into friendship: but, in the latter months of my residence at the academy, although the intrusion of his ordinary manner had, beyond doubt, in some measure, abated, my sentiments, in nearly similar proportion, partook very much of positive hatred. Upon one occasion he saw this, I think, and afterwards avoided, or made a show of avoiding me.

It was about the same period, if I remember aright, that, in an altercation of violence with him, in which he was more than usually thrown off his guard, and spoke and acted with an openness of demeanor rather foreign to his nature, I discovered, or fancied I discovered, in his accent, his air, and general appearance, a something which first startled, and then deeply interested me, by bringing to mind dim visions of my earliest infancy—

wild, confused and thronging memories of a time when memory herself was yet unborn. I cannot better describe the sensation which oppressed me than by saying that I could with difficulty shake off the belief of my having been acquainted with the being who stood before me, at some epoch very long ago—some point of the past even infinitely remote. The delusion, however, faded rapidly as it came; and I mention it at all but to define the day of the last conversation I there held with my singular namesake.

The huge old house, with its countless subdivisions, had several large chambers communicating with each other, where slept the greater number of the students. There were, however (as must necessarily happen in a building so awkwardly planned) many little nooks or recesses, the odds and ends of the structure; and these the economic ingenuity of Dr. Bransby had also fitted up as dormitories; although, being the merest closets, they were capable of accommodating but a single individual. One of these small apartments was occupied by Wilson.

One night, about the close of my fifth year at the school, and immediately after the altercation just mentioned, finding every one wrapped in sleep, I arose from bed, and, lamp in hand, stole through a wilderness of narrow passages from my own bedroom to that of my rival. I had long been plotting one of those ill-natured pieces of practical wit at his expense in which I had hitherto been so uniformly unsuccessful. It was my intention, now, to put my scheme in operation, and I resolved to make him feel the whole extent of the malice with which I was imbued. Having reached his closet, I noiselessly entered, leaving the lamp, with a shade over it, on the outside. I advanced a step, and listened to the sound of his tranquil breathing. Assured of his being asleep, I returned, took the light, and with it again approached the bed. Close curtains were around it, which, in the prosecution of my plan, I slowly and quietly withdrew, when the bright rays fell vividly upon the sleeper, and my eyes, at the same moment, upon his countenance. I looked;—and a numbness, an iciness of feeling instantly pervaded my frame. My breast heaved, my knees tottered, my whole spirit became possessed with an objectless yet intolerable horror. Gasping for breath, I lowered the lamp in still nearer proximity to the face. Were these—*these* the lineaments of William Wilson? I saw, indeed, that they were his, but I shook as if with a fit of the ague in fancying they were not. What *was* there about them to confound me in this manner? I gazed;—while my brain reeled with a multitude of incoherent thoughts. Not thus he appeared—assuredly not *thus*—in the vivacity of his waking hours. The same name! the same contour of person! the same day of arrival at the academy! And then his dogged and meaningless imitation of my gait, my voice, my habits, and my manner! Was it, in truth, within the bounds of human possibility, that *what I now saw* was the result, merely, of the habitual practice of this sarcastic imitation? Awe-stricken, and with a creeping shudder, I extinguished the lamp, passed silently from the chamber, and left, at once, the halls of that old academy, never to enter them again.

After a lapse of some months, spent at home in mere idleness, I found myself a student at Eton. The brief interval had been sufficient to enfeeble my remembrance of the events at Dr. Bransby's, or at least to effect a material change in the nature of the feelings with which I remembered them. The truth—the tragedy—of the drama was no more. I could now find room to doubt the evidence of my senses; and seldom called up the subject at all but with wonder at the extent of human credulity, and a smile at the vivid force of the imagination which I hereditarily possessed. Neither was this species of scepticism likely to be diminished by the character of the life I led at Eton. The vortex of thoughtless folly into which I there so immediately and so recklessly plunged, washed away all but the froth of my past hours, engulfed at once every solid or serious impression, and left to memory only the veriest levities of a former existence.

I do not wish, however, to trace the course of my miserable profligacy here—a profligacy which set at defiance the laws, while it eluded the vigilance of the institution. Three years of folly, passed without profit, had but given me rooted habits of vice, and added, in a somewhat unusual degree, to my bodily stature, when, after a week of soulless dissipation, I invited a small party of the most dissolute students to a secret carousal in my chambers. We met at a late hour of the night; for our debaucheries were to be faithfully protracted until morning. The wine flowed freely, and there were not wanting other and perhaps more dangerous seductions; so that the grey dawn had already faintly appeared in the east, while our delirious extravagance was at its height. Madly flushed with cards and intoxication, I was in the act of insisting upon a toast of more than wonted profanity, when my attention was suddenly diverted by the violent, although partial unclosing of the door of the apartment, and by the eager voice of a servant from without. He said that some person, apparently in great haste, demanded to speak with me in the hall.

Wildly excited with wine, the unexpected interruption rather delighted than surprised me. I staggered forward at once, and a few steps brought me to the vestibule of the building. In this low and small room there hung no lamp; and now no light at all was admitted, save that of the exceedingly feeble dawn which made its way through the semi-circular window. As I put my foot over the threshold, I became aware of the figure of a youth about my own height, and habited in a white kerseymere morning frock, cut in the novel fashion of the one I myself wore at the moment. This the faint light enabled me to perceive; but the features of his face I could not distinguish. Upon my entering he strode hurriedly up to me, and, seizing me by the arm with a gesture of petulant impatience, whispered the words "William Wilson!" in my ear.

I grew perfectly sober in an instant.

There was that in the manner of the stranger, and in the tremulous shake of his uplifted finger, as he held it between my eyes and the light, which filled me with unqualified amazement; but it was not this which had so violently moved me. It was the pregnancy of solemn admonition in the singular, low, hissing utterance; and, above all, it was the character, the tone, *the key,* of those few, simple, and familiar, yet *whispered* syllables, which came with a thousand thronging memories of by-gone days, and struck upon my soul with the shock of a galvanic battery. Ere I could recover the use of my senses he was gone.

Although this event failed not of a vivid effect upon my disordered imagination, yet was it evanescent as vivid. For some weeks, indeed, I busied myself in earnest inquiry, or was wrapped in a cloud of morbid speculation. I did not pretend to disguise from my perception the identity of the singular individual who thus perseveringly interfered with my affairs, and harassed me with his insinuated counsel. But who and what was this Wilson?—and whence came he?—and what were his purposes? Upon neither of these points could I be satisfied; merely ascertaining, in regard to him, that a sudden accident in his family had caused his removal from Dr. Bransby's academy on the afternoon of the day in which I myself had eloped. But in a brief period I ceased to think upon the subject; my attention being all absorbed in a contemplated departure for Oxford. Thither I soon went; the uncalculating vanity of my parents furnishing me with an outfit and annual establishment, which would enable me to indulge at will in the luxury already so dear to my heart,—to vie in profuseness of expenditure with the haughtiest heirs of the wealthiest earldoms in Great Britain.

Excited by such appliances to vice, my constitutional temperament broke forth with redoubled ardor, and I spurned even the common restraints of decency in the mad infatuation of my revels. But it were absurd to pause in the detail of my extravagance. Let it suffice, that among spendthrifts I out-Heroded Herod, and that, giving name to a multitude of novel follies, I added no brief appendix to the long catalogue of vices then usual in the most dissolute university of Europe.

It could hardly be credited, however, that I had, even here, so utterly fallen from the gentlemanly estate, as to seek acquaintance with the vilest arts of the gambler by profession, and, having become an adept in his despicable science, to practise it habitually as a means of increasing my already enormous income at the expense of the weak-minded among my fellow-collegians. Such, nevertheless, was the fact. And the very enormity of this offence against all manly and honourable sentiment proved, beyond doubt, the main if not the sole reason of the impunity with which it was committed. Who, indeed, among my most abandoned associates, would not rather have disputed the clearest evidence of his senses, than have suspected of such courses, the gay, the frank, the generous William Wilson—the noblest and most liberal commoner at Oxford—him whose follies (said his parasites) were but the follies of youth and unbridled fancy—whose errors but inimitable whim—whose darkest vice but a careless and dashing extravagance?

I had been now two years successfully busied in this way, when there came to the university a young *parvenu* nobleman, Glendinning—rich, said report, as Herodes Atticus—his riches, too, as easily acquired. I soon found him of weak intellect, and, of course, marked him as a fitting subject for my skill. I frequently engaged him in play, and contrived, with the gambler's usual art, to let him win considerable sums, the more effectually to entangle him in my snares. At length, my schemes being ripe, I met him (with the full intention that this meeting should be final and decisive) at the chambers of a fellow-commoner (Mr. Preston) equally intimate with both, but who, to do him justice, entertained not even a remote suspicion of my design. To give to this a better colouring, I had contrived to have assembled a party of some eight or ten, and was solicitously careful that the introduction of cards should appear accidental, and originate in the proposal of my contemplated dupe himself. To be brief upon a vile topic, none of the low finesse was omitted, so customary upon similar occasions that it is a just matter for wonder how any are still found so besotted as to fall its victim.

We had protracted our sitting far into the night, and I had at length effected the manœuvre of getting Glendinning as my sole antagonist. The game, too, was my favorite *écarté*. The rest of the company, interested in the extent of our play, had abandoned their own cards, and were standing around us as spectators. The *parvenu,* who had been induced by my artifices in the early part of the evening, to drink deeply, now shuffled, dealt, or played, with a wild nervousness of manner for which his intoxication, I thought, might partially, but could not altogether account. In a very short period he had become my debtor to a large amount, when, having taken a long draught of port, he did precisely what I had been coolly anticipating— he proposed to double our already extravagant stakes. With a well-feigned show of reluctance, and not until after my repeated refusal had seduced him into some angry words which gave a color of *pique* to my compliance, did I finally comply. The result, of course, did but prove how entirely the prey was in my toils; in less than an hour he had quadrupled his debt. For some time his countenance had been losing the florid tinge lent it by the wine; but now, to my astonishment, I perceived that it had grown to a pallor truly fearful. I say to my astonishment. Glendinning had been represented to my eager inquiries as immeasurably wealthy; and the sums which he had as yet lost, although in themselves vast, could not, I supposed, very seriously annoy, much less so violently affect him. That he was overcome by the wine just swallowed, was the idea which most readily presented itself; and, rather with a view to the preservation of my own character in the eyes of my associates, than from any less interested motive, I was about to insist, peremptorily, upon a discontinuance of the play, when some expressions at my elbow from among the company, and an ejaculation evincing utter despair on the part of Glendinning, gave me to understand that I had effected his total ruin under circumstances which, rendering him an object for the pity of all, should have protected him from the ill offices even of a fiend.

What now might have been my conduct it is difficult to say. The pitiable condition of my dupe had thrown an air of embarrassed gloom over all; and, for some moments, a profound silence was maintained, during which I could not help feeling my cheeks tingle with the many burning glances of scorn or reproach cast upon me by the less abandoned of the party. I will even own that an intolerable weight of anxiety was for a brief instant lifted from my bosom by the sudden and extraordinary interruption which ensued. The wide, heavy folding doors of the apartment were all at once thrown open, to their full extent, with a vigorous and rushing impetuosity that extinguished, as if by magic, every candle in the room. Their light, in dying, enabled us just to perceive that a stranger had entered, about my own height, and closely muffled in a cloak. The darkness, however, was now total; and we could only *feel* that he was standing in our midst. Before any one of us could recover from the extreme astonishment into which this rudeness had thrown all, we heard the voice of the intruder.

"Gentlemen," he said, in a low, distinct, and never-to-be-forgotten *whisper* which thrilled to the very marrow of my bones, "Gentlemen, I make no apology for this behaviour, because in thus behaving, I am but fulfilling a duty. You are, beyond doubt, uninformed of the true character of the person who has to-night won at *écarté* a large sum of money from Lord Glendinning. I will therefore put you upon an expeditious and decisive plan of obtaining this very necessary information. Please to examine, at your leisure, the inner linings of the cuff of his left sleeve, and the several little packages which may be found in the somewhat capacious pockets of his embroidered morning owrapper."

While he spoke, so profound was the stillness that one might have heard a pin drop upon the floor. In ceasing, he departed at once, and as abruptly as he had entered. Can I—shall I describe my sensations?—must I say that I felt all the horrors of the damned? Most assuredly I had little time given for reflection. Many hands roughly seized me upon the spot, and lights were immediately reprocured. A search ensued. In the lining of my sleeve were found all the court cards essential in *écarté,* and, in the pockets of my wrapper, a number of packs, fac-similes of those used at our sittings, with the single exception that mine were of the species called, technically, *arrondées;* the honours being slightly convex at the ends, the lower cards slightly convex at the sides. In this disposition, the dupe who cuts, as customary, at the length of the pack, will invariably find that he cuts his antagonist an honor; while the gambler, cutting at the breadth, will, as certainly, cut nothing for his victim which may count in the records of the game.

Any burst of indignation upon this discovery would have affected me less than the silent contempt, or the sarcastic composure, with which it was received.

"Mr. Wilson," said our host, stooping to remove from beneath his feet an exceedingly luxurious cloak of rare furs, "Mr. Wilson, this is your property." (The weather was cold; and, upon quitting my own room, I had thrown a cloak over my dressing wrapper, putting it off upon reaching the scene of play.) "I presume it is supererogatory to seek here (eyeing the folds of the garment with a bitter smile) for any farther evidence of your skill. Indeed, we have had enough. You will see the necessity, I hope, of quitting Oxford—at all events, of quitting instantly my chambers."

Abased, humbled to the dust as I then was, it is probable that I should have resented this galling language by immediate personal violence, had not my whole attention been at the moment arrested by a fact of the most startling character. The cloak which I had worn was of a rare description of fur; how rare, how extravagantly costly, I shall not venture to say. Its fashion, too, was of my own fantastic invention; for I was fastidious to an absurd degree of coxcombry, in matters of this frivolous nature. When, therefore, Mr. Preston reached me that which he had picked up upon the floor, and near the folding doors of the apartment, it was with an astonishment nearly bordering upon terror, that I perceived my own already hanging on my arm (where I had no doubt unwittingly placed it) and that the one presented me was but its exact counterpart in every, in even the minutest possible particular. The singular being who had so disastrously exposed me, had been muffled, I remembered, in a cloak; and none had been worn at all by any of the members of our party with the exception of myself. Retaining some presence of mind, I took the one offered me by Preston; placed it, unnoticed, over my own; left the apartment with a resolute scowl of defiance; and, next morning ere dawn of day, commenced a hurried journey from Oxford to the continent, in a perfect agony of horror and of shame.

*I fled in vain.* My evil destiny pursued me as if in exultation, and proved, indeed, that the exercise of its mysterious dominion had as yet only begun. Scarcely had I set foot in Paris ere I had fresh evidence of the detestable interest taken by this Wilson in my concerns. Years flew, while I experienced no relief. Villain!—at Rome, with how untimely, yet with how spectral an officiousness, stepped he in between me and my ambition! At Vienna, too—at Berlin—and at Moscow! Where, in truth, had I *not* bitter cause to curse him within my heart? From his inscrutable tyranny did I at length flee, panic-stricken, as from a pestilence; and to the very ends of the earth *I fled in vain.*

And again, and again, in secret communion with my own spirit, would I demand the questions "Who is he?—whence came he?—and what are his objects?" But no answer was there found. And then I scrutinized, with a minute scrutiny, the forms, and the methods, and the leading traits of his impertinent supervision. But even here there was very little upon which to base a conjecture. It was noticeable, indeed, that, in no one of the multiplied instances in which he had of late crossed my path, had he so crossed it except to frustrate those schemes, or to disturb those actions, which, if fully carried out, might have resulted in bitter mischief. Poor justification this, in truth, for an authority so imperiously assumed! Poor indemnity for natural rights of self-agency so pertinaciously, so insultingly denied!

I had also been forced to notice that my tormentor, for a very long period of time (while scrupulously and with miraculous dexterity maintaining his whim of an identity of apparel with myself) had so contrived it, in the execution of his varied interference with my will, that I saw not, at any moment, the features of his face. Be Wilson what he might, *this,* at least, was but the veriest of affectation, or of folly. Could he, for an instant, have supposed that, in my admonisher at Eton—in the destroyer of my honour at Oxford,—in him who thwarted my ambition at Rome, my revenge at Paris, my passionate love at Naples, or what he falsely termed my avarice in Egypt,—that in this, my arch-enemy and evil genius, I could fail to recognise the William Wilson of my school boy days,—the namesake, the companion, the rival,—the hated and dreaded rival at Dr. Bransby's? Impossible!—But let me hasten to the last eventful scene of the drama.

Thus far I had succumbed supinely to this imperious domination. The sentiment of deep awe with which I habitually regarded the elevated character, the majestic wisdom, the apparent omnipresence and omnipotence of Wilson, added to a feeling of even terror, with which certain other traits in his nature and assumptions inspired me, had operated, hitherto, to impress me with an idea of my own utter weakness and helplessness, and to suggest an implicit, although bitterly reluctant submission to his arbitrary will. But, of late days, I had given myself up entirely to wine; and its maddening influence upon my hereditary temper rendered me more and more impatient of control. I began to murmur,—to hesitate,—to resist. And was it only fancy which induced me to believe that, with the increase of my own firmness, that of my tormentor underwent a proportional diminution? Be this as it may, I now began to feel the inspiration of a burning hope, and at length nurtured in my secret thoughts a stern and desperate resolution that I would submit no longer to be enslaved.

It was at Rome, during the Carnival of 18  , that I attended a masquerade in the palazzo of the Neapolitan Duke Di Broglio. I had indulged more freely than usual in the excesses of the wine-table; and now the suffocating atmosphere of the crowded rooms irritated me beyond endurance. The difficulty, too, of forcing my way through the mazes of the company contributed not a little to the ruffling of my temper; for I was anxiously seeking (let me not say with what unworthy motive) the young, the gay, the beautiful wife of the aged and doting Di Broglio. With a too unscrupulous confidence she had previously communicated to me the secret of the costume in which she would be habited, and now, having caught a glimpse of her person, I was hurrying to make my way into her presence.—At this moment I felt a light hand placed upon my shoulder, and that everremembered, low, damnable *whisper* within my ear.

In an absolute frenzy of wrath, I turned at once upon him who had thus interrupted me, and seized him violently by the collar. He was attired, as I had expected, in a costume altogether similar to my own; wearing a Spanish cloak of blue velvet, begirt about the waist with a crimson belt sustaining a rapier. A mask of black silk entirely covered his face.

"Scoundrel!" I said, in a voice husky with rage, while every syllable I uttered seemed as new fuel to my fury, "scoundrel! impostor! accursed villain! you shall not—you *shall not* dog me unto death! Follow me, or I stab you where you stand!"—and I broke my way from the ball-room into a small ante-chamber adjoining—dragging him unresistingly with me as I went.

Upon entering, I thrust him furiously from me. He staggered against the wall, while I closed the door with an oath, and commanded him to draw. He hesitated but for an instant; then, with a slight sigh, drew in silence, and put himself upon his defence.

The contest was brief indeed. I was frantic with every species of wild excitement, and felt within my single arm the energy and power of a multitude. In a few seconds I forced him by sheer strength against the wainscoting, and thus, getting him at mercy, plunged my sword, with brute ferocity, repeatedly through and through his bosom.

At that instant some person tried the latch of the door. I hastened to prevent an intrusion, and then immediately returned to my dying antagonist. But what human language can adequately portray *that* astonishment, *that* horror which possessed me at the spectacle then presented to view? The brief moment in which I averted my eyes had been sufficient to produce, apparently, a material change in the arrangements at the upper or farther end of the room. A large mirror,—so at first it seemed to me in my confusion—now stood where none had been perceptible before; and, as I stepped up to it in extremity of terror, mine own image, but with features all pale and dabbled in blood, advanced to meet me with a feeble and tottering gait.

Thus it appeared, I say, but was not. It was my antagonist—it was Wilson, who then stood before me in the agonies of his dissolution. His mask and cloak lay, where he had thrown them, upon the floor. Not a thread in all his raiment—not a line in all the marked and singular lineaments of his face which was not, even in the most absolute identity, *mine own!*

It was Wilson; but he spoke no longer in a whisper, and I could have fancied that I myself was speaking while he said:

*"You have conquered, and I yield. Yet, henceforward art thou also dead—dead to the World, to Heaven and to Hope! In me didst thou exist—and, in my death, see by this image, which is thine own, how utterly thou hast murdered thyself."*

∾

# THE QUEEN OF SPADES

## Alexander Pushkin

*The Queen of Spades signifies secret ill-will.*
NEW FORTUNE-TELLER

I

*When bleak was the weather,*
*The friends came together*
*To play.*
*The stakes, they were doubled;*
*The sly ones, untroubled,*
*Were gay.*
*They all had their innings,*
*And chalked up their winnings,*
*And so*
*They kept busy together*
*Throughout the bleak weather,*
*Oho!*

There was a card party at the rooms of Narumov of the Horse Guards. The long winter night passed away imperceptibly, and it was five o'clock in the morning before the company sat down to supper. Those who had won, ate with a good appetite; the others sat staring absently at their empty plates. When the champagne appeared, however, the conversation became more animated, and all took a part in it.

"And how did you fare, Surin?" asked the host.

"Oh, I lost, as usual. I must confess that I am unlucky: I never raise the original stakes, I always keep cool, I never allow anything to put me out, and yet I always lose!"

"And you have never been tempted? You have never staked on several cards in succession? . . . Your firmness astonishes me."

"But what do you think of Hermann?" said one of the guests, pointing to a young engineer. "He has never had a card in his hand in his life, he has never in his life doubled the stake, and yet he sits here till five o'clock in the morning watching our play."

"Play interests me very much," said Hermann: "but I am not in the position to sacrifice the necessary in the hope of winning the superfluous."

"Hermann is a German: he is prudent—that is all!" observed Tomsky. "But if there is one person that I cannot understand, it is my grandmother, the Countess Anna Fedotovna."

"How? What?" cried the guests.

"I cannot understand," continued Tomsky, "how it is that my grandmother does not punt."

"What is there remarkable about an old lady of eighty not gambling?" said Narumov.

"Then you know nothing about her?"

"No, really; haven't the faintest idea."

"Oh! then listen. You must know that, about sixty years ago, my grandmother went to Paris, where she created quite a sensation. People used to run after her to catch a glimpse of '*la Vénus moscovite.*' Richelieu courted her, and my grandmother maintains that he almost blew out his brains in consequence of her cruelty. At that time ladies used to play faro. On one occasion at the Court, she lost a very considerable sum to the Duke of Orleans. On returning home, my grandmother removed the patches from her face, took off her hoops, informed my grandfather of her loss at the gaming table, and ordered him to pay the money. My deceased grandfather, as far as I remember, was a sort of butler to my grandmother. He dreaded her like fire; but, on hearing of such a heavy loss, he almost went out of his mind; he calculated the various sums she had lost, and pointed out to her that in six months she had spent half a million, that neither their Moscow nor Saratov estates were near Paris, and finally refused point-blank to pay the debt. My grandmother slapped his face and slept by herself as a sign of her displeasure. The next day she sent for her husband, hoping that this domestic punishment had produced an effect upon him, but she found him inflexible. For the first time in her life, she condescended to offer reasons and explanations. She thought she could convince him by pointing out to him that there are debts and debts, and that there is a great difference between a Prince and a coachmaker. But it was all in vain, grandfather was in revolt. He said 'no,' and that was all. My grandmother did not know what to do. She was on friendly terms with a very remarkable man. You have heard of Count St. Germain, about whom so many marvelous stories are told. You know that he represented himself as the Wandering Jew, as the discoverer of the elixir of life, of the philosopher's stone, and so forth. Some laughed at him as a charlatan; but Casanova, in his memoirs, says that he was a spy. But be that as it may, St. Germain, in spite of the mystery surrounding him, was a man of decent appearance and had an amiable manner in company. Even to this day my grandmother is in love with him, and becomes quite angry if anyone speaks disrespectfully of him. My grandmother knew that St. Germain had large sums of money at his disposal. She resolved to have recourse to him, and she wrote a letter to him asking him to come to her without delay. The queer old man immediately waited upon her and found her overwhelmed with grief. She described to him in the blackest colors the barbarity of her husband, and ended by declaring that she placed all her hopes in his friendship and graciousness.

"St. Germain reflected.

" 'I could advance you the sum you want,' said he; 'but I know that you would not rest easy until you had paid me back, and I should not like to bring fresh troubles upon you. But there is another way of getting out of your difficulty: you can win back your money.'

" 'But, my dear Count,' replied my grandmother, 'I tell you that we haven't any money left.'

" 'Money is not necessary,' replied St. Germain. 'Be pleased to listen to me.'

"Then he revealed to her a secret, for which each of us would give a good deal . . ."

The young gamblers listened with increased attention. Tomsky lit his pipe, pulled at it, and continued:

"That same evening my grandmother went to Versailles *au jeu de la Reine.* The Duke of Orleans kept the bank; my grandmother excused herself in an offhanded manner for not having yet paid her debt, by inventing some little story, and then began to play against him. She chose three cards and played them one after the other: all three won at the start and my grandmother recovered all that she had lost."

"Mere chance!" said one of the guests.

"A fairy tale!" observed Hermann.

"Perhaps they were marked cards!" said a third.

"I do not think so," replied Tomsky gravely.

"What!" said Narumov. "You have a grandmother who knows how to hit upon three lucky cards in succession, and you have never yet succeeded in getting the secret of it out of her?"

"That's the deuce of it!" replied Tomsky. "She had four sons, one of whom was my father; all four are desperate gamblers, and yet not to one of them did she ever reveal her secret, although it would not have been a bad thing either for them or for me. But this is what I heard from my uncle, Count Ivan Ilyich, and he assured me, on his honor, that it was true. The late

Chaplitzky—the same who died in poverty after having squandered millions—once lost, in his youth, about three hundred thousand rubles—to Zorich, if I remember rightly. He was in despair. My grandmother, who was always very hard on extravagant young men, took pity, however, upon Chaplitzky. She mentioned to him three cards, telling him to play them one after the other, at the same time exacting from him a solemn promise that he would never play cards again as long as he lived. Chaplitzky then went to his victorious opponent, and they began a fresh game. On the first card he staked fifty thousand rubles and won at once; he doubled the stake and won again, doubled it again, and won, not only all he had lost, but something over and above that. . . .

"But it is time to go to bed: it is a quarter to six already."

And indeed it was already beginning to dawn; the young men emptied their glasses and then took leave of one another.

## II

*—Il paraît que monsieur est
décidément pour les suivantes.
—Que voulez-vous, madame? Elles
sont plus fraîches.*

SOCIETY TALK

The old Countess X. was seated in her dressing room in front of her looking glass. Three maids stood around her. One held a small pot of rouge, another a box of hairpins, and the third a tall cap with bright red ribbons. The Countess had no longer the slightest pretensions to beauty—hers had faded long ago—but she still preserved all the habits of her youth, dressed in strict accordance with the fashion of the seventies, and made as long and as careful a toilette as she would have done sixty years previously. Near the window, at an embroidery frame, sat a young lady, her ward.

"Good morning, *Grand'maman,*" said a young officer, entering the room. "*Bonjour, Mademoiselle Lise. Grand'maman,* I have a favor to ask of you."

"What is it, Paul?"

"I want you to let me introduce one of my friends to you, and to allow me to bring him to the ball on Friday."

"Bring him direct to the ball and introduce him to me there. Were you at N.'s yesterday?"

"Yes; everything went off very pleasantly, and dancing kept up until five o'clock. How beautiful Mme. Yeletzkaya was!"

"But, my dear, what is there beautiful about her? You should have seen her grandmother, Princess Darya Petrovna! By the way, she must have aged very much, Princess Darya Petrovna."

"How do you mean, aged?" cried Tomsky thoughtlessly. "She died seven years ago."

The young lady raised her head and made a sign to the young man. He then remembered that the old Countess was never to be informed of the death of any of her contemporaries, and he bit his lip. But the Countess heard the news with the greatest indifference.

"Died!" said she. "And I did not know it. We were appointed maids of honor at the same time, and when we were being presented, the Empress..."

And the Countess for the hundredth time related the anecdote to her grandson.

"Come, Paul," said she, when she had finished her story, "help me to get up. Lizanka, where is my snuffbox?"

And the Countess with her three maids went behind a screen to finish her toilette. Tomsky was left alone with the young lady.

"Who is the gentleman you wish to introduce to the Countess?" asked Lizaveta Ivanovna in a whisper.

"Narumov. Do you know him?"

"No. Is he in the army or is he a civilian?"

"In the army."

"Is he in the Engineers?"

"No, in the Cavalry. What made you think that he was in the Engineers?"

The young lady smiled, but made no reply.

"Paul," cried the Countess, from behind the screen, "send me some new novel, only, pray, not the kind they write nowadays."

"What do you mean, *Grand'maman?*"

"That is, a novel, in which the hero strangles neither his father nor his mother, and in which there are no drowned bodies. I have a great horror of them."

"There are no such novels nowadays. Would you like a Russian one?"

"Are there any Russian novels? Send me one, my dear, please send me one!"

"Good-bye, *Grand'maman:* I am in a hurry. .... Good-bye, Lizaveta Ivanovna. What, then, made you think that Narumov was in the Engineers?"

And Tomsky withdrew from the dressing room.

Lizaveta Ivanovna was left alone: she laid aside her work and began to look out of the window. A few moments afterwards, from behind a corner house on the other side of the street, a young officer appeared. A deep blush covered her cheeks; she took up her work again and bent her head over the frame. At the same moment the Countess returned, completely dressed.

"Order the carriage, Lizaveta," said she; "we will go out for a drive."

Lizaveta arose from the frame and began to put away her work.

"What is the matter with you, my dear, are you deaf?" cried the Countess. "Order the carriage to be got ready at once."

"I will do so this moment," replied the young lady, and ran into the anteroom.

A servant entered and gave the Countess some books from Prince Pavel Alexandrovich.

"Tell him that I am much obliged to him," said the Countess. "Lizaveta! Lizaveta! Where are you running to?"

"I am going to dress."

"There is plenty of time, my dear. Sit down here. Open the first volume and read aloud to me."

Her companion took the book and read a few lines.

"Louder," said the Countess. "What is the matter with you, my dear? Have you lost your voice? Wait—give me that footstool—a little nearer—that will do!"

Lizaveta read two more pages. The Countess yawned.

"Put the book down," said she. "What a lot of nonsense! Send it back to Prince Pavel with my thanks. . . . But where is the carriage?"

"The carriage is ready," said Lizaveta, looking out into the street.

"How is it that you are not dressed?" said the Countess. "I must always wait for you. It is intolerable, my dear!"

Liza hastened to her room. She had not been there two minutes, before the Countess began to ring with all her might. The three maids came running in at one door and the valet at another.

"How is it that you don't come when I ring for you?" said the Countess. "Tell Lizaveta Ivanovna that I am waiting for her."

Lizaveta returned with her hat and cloak on.

"At last you are here!" said the Countess. "But why such an elaborate toilette? Whom do you intend to captivate? What sort of weather is it? It seems rather windy."

"No, Your Ladyship, it is very calm," replied the valet.

"You always speak thoughtlessly. Open the window. So it is: windy and bitterly cold. Unharness the horses. Lizaveta, we won't go out—there was no need for you to deck yourself out like that."

"And that's my life!" thought Lizaveta Ivanovna.

And, in truth, Lizaveta Ivanovna was a very unfortunate creature. "It is bitter to eat the bread of another," says Dante, "and hard to climb his stair." But who can know what the bitterness of dependence is so well as the poor companion of an old lady of quality? The Countess X. had by no means a bad heart, but she was capricious, like a woman who had been spoiled by the world, as well as avaricious and sunk in cold egoism, like all old people who are no longer capable of affection, and whose thoughts are with the past and not the present. She participated in all the vanities of the great world, went to balls, where she sat in a corner, painted and dressed in old-fashioned style, like an ugly but indispensable ornament of the ball-room; the guests on entering approached her and bowed profoundly, as if in accordance with a set ceremony, but after that nobody took any further notice of her. She received the whole town at her house, and observed the strictest etiquette, although she could no longer recognize people. Her numerous domestics, growing fat and old in her antechamber and servants' hall, did just as they liked, and vied with each other in robbing the moribund old woman. Lizaveta Ivanovna was the martyr of the household. She poured tea, and was reprimanded for using too much sugar; she read novels aloud to the Countess, and the faults of the author were visited upon her head; she accompanied the Countess in her walks, and was held answerable for the weather or the state of the pavement. A salary was attached to the post, but she very rarely received it, although she was expected to dress like everybody else, that is to say, like very few indeed. In society she played the most pitiable role. Everybody knew her, and nobody paid her any attention. At balls she danced only when a partner was wanted, and ladies would only take hold of her arm when it was necessary to lead her out of the room to attend to their dresses. She had a great deal of *amour propre,* and felt her position keenly, and she looked about her with impatience for a deliverer to come to her rescue; but the young men, calculating in their giddiness, did not condescend to pay her any attention, although Lizaveta Ivanovna was a hundred times prettier than the bare-faced and cold-hearted marriageable girls around whom they hovered. Many a time did she quietly slink away from the dull and elegant drawing room, to go and cry in her own poor little room, in which stood a screen, a chest of drawers, a looking glass and a painted bedstead, and where a tallow candle burned feebly in a copper candlestick.

One morning—this was about two days after the card party described at the beginning of this story, and a week previous to the scene at which we have just assisted—Lizaveta Ivanovna was seated near the window at her embroidery frame, when, happening to look out into the street, she caught sight of a young officer of the Engineers, standing motionless with his eyes fixed upon her window. She lowered her head and went on again with her work. About five minutes afterward she looked out again—the young officer was still standing in the same place. Not being in the habit of coquetting with passing officers, she did not continue to gaze out into the street, but went on sewing for a couple of hours, without raising her head. Dinner was announced. She rose up and began to put her embroidery away, but glancing casually out the window, she perceived the officer again. This seemed to her very strange. After dinner she went to the window with a certain feeling of uneasiness, but the officer was no longer there—and she thought no more about him.

A couple of days afterwards, just as she was stepping into the carriage with the Countess, she saw him again. He was standing close to the entrance, with his face half concealed by his beaver collar, his black eyes flashing beneath his hat. Lizaveta felt alarmed, though she knew not why, and she trembled as she seated herself in the carriage.

On returning home, she hastened to the window—the officer was standing in his accustomed place, with his eyes fixed upon her. She drew back, a prey to curiosity and agitated by a feeling which was quite new to her.

From that time on not a day passed without the young officer making his appearance under the window at the customary hour. A spontaneous relationship was established between them. Sitting in her place at work, she would feel his approach; and raising her head, she would look at him longer and longer each day. The young man seemed to be very grateful to her for it: she saw with the sharp eye of youth, how a sudden flush covered his pale cheeks each time that their glances met. By the end of the week she smiled at him. . . .

When Tomsky asked permission of his grandmother the Countess to present one of his friends to her, the young girl's heart beat violently. But hearing that Narumov was not an engineer, but in the Horse Guards, she regretted that by her indiscreet question, she had betrayed her secret to the volatile Tomsky.

Hermann was the son of a Russified German, from whom he had inherited a small fortune. Being firmly convinced of the necessity of insuring his independence, Hermann did not touch even the interest on his capital, but lived on his pay, without allowing himself the slightest luxury. Moreover, he was reserved and ambitious, and his companions rarely had an opportunity of making merry at the expense of his excessive parsimony. He had strong passions and an ardent imagination, but his firmness of disposition preserved him from the ordinary errors of youth. Thus, though a gambler at heart, he never touched a card, for he considered his position did not allow him—as he said—"to risk the necessary in the hope of winning the superfluous," yet he would sit for nights together at the card table and follow with feverish excitement the various turns of the game.

The story of the three cards had produced a powerful impression upon his imagination, and all night long he could think of nothing else. "If only," he thought to himself the following evening, as he wandered through St. Petersburg, "if only the old Countess would reveal her secret to me! If she would only tell me the names of the three winning cards! Why should I not try my fortune? I must get introduced to her and win her favor—perhaps become her lover. . . . But all that will take time, and she is eighty-seven years old: she might be dead in a week, in a couple of days even! . . . And the story itself: is it credible? . . . No! Prudence, moderation and work: those are my three winning cards, that is what will increase my capital threefold, sevenfold, and procure for me ease and independence."

Musing in this manner, he walked on until he found himself in one of the principal streets of St. Petersburg, in front of a house of old-fashioned architecture. The street was blocked with carriages; one after the other they rolled up in front of the illuminated entrance. Every minute there emerged from the coaches the shapely foot of a young beauty, a spurred boot, a striped stocking above a diplomatic shoe. Fur coats and cloaks whisked past the majestic porter.

Hermann stopped. "Whose house is this?" he asked the watchman at the corner.

"The Countess X.'s," replied the watchman.

Hermann trembled. The strange story of the three cards again presented itself to his imagination. He began walking up and down before the house, thinking of its owner and her marvelous gift. Returning late to his modest lodging, he could not go to sleep for a long time, and when at last he did doze off, he could dream of nothing but cards, green tables, piles of banknotes and heaps of gold coins. He played card after card, firmly turning down the corners, and won uninterruptedly, raking in the gold and filling his pockets with the notes. Waking up late the next morning, he sighed over the loss of his imaginary wealth, then went out again to wander about the streets, and found himself once more in front of the Countess's house. Some unknown power seemed to draw him thither. He stopped and began to stare at the windows. In one of these he saw the head of a black-haired woman, which was bent probably over some book or handwork. The head was raised. Hermann saw a fresh-cheeked face and a pair of black eyes. That moment decided his fate.


# III

*Vous m'écrivez, mon ange, des lettres de*
*quatre pages plus vite que je ne puis les lire.*
A CORRESPONDENCE

Lizaveta Ivanovna had scarcely taken off her hat and cloak, when the Countess sent for her and again ordered the carriage. The vehicle drew up before the door, and they prepared to take their seats. Just at the moment when two footmen were assisting the old lady into the carriage, Lizaveta saw her engineer close beside the wheel; he grasped her hand; alarm caused her to lose her presence of mind, and the young man disappeared— but not before leaving a letter in her hand. She concealed it in her glove, and during the whole of the drive she neither saw nor heard anything. It was the custom of the Countess, when out for an airing in her carriage to be constantly asking such questions as: "Who was that person that met us just now? What is the name of this bridge? What is written on that signboard?" On this occasion, however, Lizaveta returned such vague and absurd answers, that the Countess became angry with her.

"What is the matter with you, my dear?" she exclaimed. "Have you taken leave of your senses, or what is it? Do you not hear me or understand what I say? . . . Heaven be thanked, I am still in my right mind and speak plainly enough!"

Lizaveta Ivanovna did not hear her. On returning home she ran to her room, and drew the letter out of her glove: it was not sealed. Lizaveta read it. The letter contained a declaration of love; it was tender, respectful, and copied word for word from a German novel. But Lizaveta did not not know anything of the German language, and she was quite delighted with the letter.

For all that, it troubled her exceedingly. For the first time in her life she was entering into secret and intimate relations with a young man. His boldness horrified her. She reproached herself for her imprudent behavior, and knew not what to do. Should she cease to sit at the window and, by assuming an appearance of indifference toward him, put a check upon the young officer's desire to pursue her further? Should she send his letter back to him, or should she answer him in a cold and resolute manner? There was nobody to whom she could turn in her perplexity, for she had neither female friend nor adviser. . . . At length she resolved to reply to him.

She sat down at her little writing table, took pen and paper, and began to think. Several times she began her letter, and then tore it up: the way she had expressed herself seemed to her either too indulgent or too severe. At last she succeeded in writing a few lines with which she felt satisfied.

"I am convinced," she wrote, "that your intentions are honorable, and that you do not wish to offend me by any imprudent action, but our acquaintance should not have begun in such a manner. I return you your letter, and I hope that I shall never have any cause to complain of undeserved disrespect."

The next day, as soon as Hermann made his appearance, Lizaveta rose from her embroidery, went into the drawing room, opened the wicket and threw the letter into the street, trusting to the young officer's alertness.

Hermann hastened forward, picked it up and then repaired to a confectioner's shop. Breaking the seal of the envelope, he found inside it his own letter and Lizaveta's reply. He had expected this, and he returned home, very much taken up with his intrigue.

Three days afterward, a bright-eyed young girl from a milliner's establishment brought Lizaveta a letter. Lizaveta opened it with great uneasiness, fearing that it was a demand for money, when suddenly she recognized Hermann's handwriting.

"You have made a mistake, my dear," said she; "this letter is not for me."

"Oh, yes, it is for you," replied the pert girl, without concealing a sly smile. "Have the goodness to read it."

Lizaveta glanced at the letter. Hermann requested an interview.

"It cannot be," said Lizaveta Ivanovna, alarmed both at the haste with which he had made his request, and the manner in which it had been transmitted. "This letter is certainly not for me."

And she tore it into fragments.

"If the letter was not for you, why have you torn it up?" said the girl. "I should have given it back to the person who sent it."

"Be good enough, my dear," said Lizaveta, disconcerted by this remark, "not to bring me any more letters in future, and tell the person who sent you that he ought to be ashamed. . . ."

But Hermann was not the man to be thus put off. Every day Lizaveta received from him a letter, sent now in this way, now in that. They were no longer translated from the German. Hermann wrote them under the inspiration of passion, and spoke in his own language, and they bore full testimony to the inflexibility of his desire and the disordered condition of his uncontrollable imagination. Lizaveta no longer thought of sending them back to him: she became intoxicated with them and began to reply to them, and little by little her answers became longer and more affectionate. At last she threw out of the window to him the following letter:

"This evening there is going to be a ball at the X. Embassy. The Countess will be there. We shall remain until two o'clock. This is your opportunity of seeing me alone. As soon as the Countess is gone, the servants will very probably go out, and there will be nobody left but the porter, but he, too, usually retires to his lodge. Come at half past eleven. Walk straight upstairs. If you meet anybody in the anteroom, ask if the Countess is at home. If you are told she is not, there will be nothing left for you to do but to go away and return another time. But it is most probable that you will meet nobody. The maidservants all sit together in one room. On leaving the anteroom, turn to the left, and walk straight on until you reach the Countess' bedroom. In the bedroom, behind a screen, you will find two small doors: the one on the right leads to a study, which the Countess never enters; the one on the left leads to a corridor, at the end of which is a narrow winding staircase; this leads to my room."

Hermann quivered like a tiger, as he waited for the appointed time. At ten o'clock in the evening he was already in front of the Countess' house. The weather was terrible; the wind was howling; the sleety snow fell in large flakes; the lamps emitted a feeble light, the streets were deserted; from time to time a sledge, drawn by a sorry-looking hack, passed by, the driver on the lookout for a belated fare. Hermann stood there wearing nothing but his jacket, yet he felt neither the wind nor the snow.

At last the Countess' carriage drew up. Hermann saw two footmen carry out in their arms the bent form of the old lady, wrapped in sables, and immediately behind her, clad in a light mantle, and with a wreath of fresh flowers on her head, followed Lizaveta. The door was closed. The carriage rolled away heavily through the yielding snow. The porter shut the street door; the windows became dark.

Hermann began walking up and down near the deserted house; at length he stopped under a lamp, and glanced at his watch: it was twenty minutes past eleven. He remained standing under the lamp, his eyes fixed upon the watch, impatiently waiting for the remaining minutes to pass. At half past eleven precisely, Hermann ascended the steps of the house, and made his way into the brightly illuminated vestibule. The porter was not there. Hermann ran up the stairs, opened the door of the anteroom and saw a footman sitting asleep in an antique soiled armchair, under a lamp. With a light firm step Hermann walked past him. The reception room and the drawing room were in semi-darkness. They were lit feebly by a lamp in the anteroom.

Hermann entered the bedroom. Before an ikon case, filled with ancient ikons, a golden sanctuary lamp was burning. Armchairs, upholstered in faded brocade, and sofas, the gilding of which was worn off and which were piled with down cushions, stood in melancholy symmetry around the room, the walls of which were hung with China silk. On the wall hung two portraits painted in Paris by Madame Lebrun. One of them represented a plump, pink-cheeked man of about forty in a light green uniform and with a star on his breast; the other—a beautiful young woman, with an aquiline nose, curls at her temples, and a rose in her powdered hair. In all the corners stood porcelain shepherds and shepherdesses, clocks from the workshop of the celebrated Leroy, boxes, roulettes, fans, and the various gewgaws for ladies that were invented at the end of the last century, together with Montgolfier's balloon and Mesmer's magnetism. Hermann stepped behind the screen. Behind it stood a little iron bed; on the right was the door which led to the study; on the left—the other which led to the corridor. He opened the latter, and saw the little winding staircase which led to the room of the poor ward. . . . But he retraced his steps and entered the dark study.

The time passed slowly. All was still. The clock in the drawing room struck twelve; in all the rooms, one clock after another marked the hour, and everything was quiet again. Hermann stood leaning against the cold stove. He was calm; his heart beat regularly, like that of a man resolved upon a dangerous but inevitable undertaking. The clock struck one, then two; and he heard the distant rumbling of carriage wheels. In spite of himself, excitement seized him. The carriage drew near and stopped. He heard the sound of the carriage step being let down. All was bustle within the house. The servants were running hither and thither, voices were heard, and the house was lit up. Three antiquated chambermaids entered the bedroom, and they were shortly afterwards followed by the Countess who, more dead than alive, sank into an armchair. Hermann peeped through a chink. Lizaveta Ivanovna passed close by him, and he heard her hurried steps as she hurried up her staircase. For a moment his heart was assailed by something like remorse, but the emotion was only transitory. He stood petrified.

The Countess began to undress before her looking glass. Her cap, decorated with roses, was unpinned, and then her powdered wig was removed from off her white and closely cropped head. Hairpins fell in showers around her. Her yellow satin dress, embroidered with silver, fell down at her swollen feet.

Hermann witnessed the repulsive mysteries of her toilette; at last the Countess was in her nightcap and nightgown, and in this costume, more suitable to her age, she appeared less hideous and terrifying.

Like all old people in general, the Countess suffered from sleeplessness. Having undressed, she seated herself at the window in an armchair and dismissed her maids. The candles were taken away, and once more the room was lit only by the sanctuary lamp. The Countess sat there looking quite yellow, moving her flaccid lips and swaying from side to side. Her dull eyes expressed complete vacancy of mind, and, looking at her, one would have thought that the rocking of her body was not voluntary, but was produced by the action of some concealed galvanic mechanism.

Suddenly the deathlike face changed incredibly. The lips ceased to move, the eyes became animated: before the Countess stood a stranger.

"Do not be alarmed, for Heaven's sake, do not be alarmed!" said he in a low but distinct voice. "I have no intention of doing you any harm, I have only come to ask a favor of you."

The old woman looked at him in silence, as if she had not heard what he had said. Hermann thought that she was deaf, and, bending down toward her ear, he repeated what he had said. The old woman remained silent as before.

"You can insure the happiness of my life," continued Hermann, "and it will cost you nothing. I know that you can name three cards in succession—"

Hermann stopped. The Countess appeared now to understand what was asked of her; she seemed to be seeking words with which to reply.

"It was a joke," she replied at last. "I swear it was only a joke."

"This is no joking matter," replied Hermann angrily. "Remember Chaplitzky, whom you helped to win back what he had lost."

The Countess became visibly uneasy. Her features expressed strong emotion, but she soon lapsed into her former insensibility.

"Can you not name me these three winning cards?" continued Hermann.

The Countess remained silent; Hermann continued: "For whom are you preserving your secret? For your grandsons? They are rich enough without it; they do not know the worth of money. Your cards would be of no use to a spendthrift. He who cannot preserve his paternal inheritance, will die in want, even though he had a demon at his service. I am not a man of that sort; I know the value of money. Your three cards will not be wasted on me. Come!"

He paused and tremblingly awaited her reply. The Countess remained silent; Hermann fell upon his knees.

"If your heart has ever known the feeling of love," said he, "if you remember its rapture, if you have ever smiled at the cry of your new-born child, if your breast has ever throbbed with any human feeling, I entreat you by the feelings of a wife, a lover, a mother, by all that is most sacred in life, not to reject my plea. Reveal to me your secret. Of what use is it to you? ... Maybe it is connected with some terrible sin, the loss of eternal bliss, some bargain with the devil. . . . Consider—you are old; you have not long to live—I am ready to take your sins upon my soul. Only reveal to me your secret. Remember that the happiness of a man is in your hands, that not only I, but my children, grandchildren, and great-grandchildren, will bless your memory and reverence it as something sacred. . . ."

The old woman answered not a word.

Hermann rose to his feet.

"You old witch!" he exclaimed, clenching his teeth. "Then I will make you answer!"

With these words he drew a pistol from his pocket.

At the sight of the pistol, the Countess for the second time exhibited strong emotion. She shook her head and raised her hands as if to protect herself from the shot . . . then she fell backward and remained motionless.

"Come, an end to this childish nonsense!" said Hermann, taking hold of her hand. "I ask you for the last time: will you tell me the names of your three cards, or will you not?"

The Countess made no reply. Hermann perceived that she was dead!

## IV

*7 mai, 18—*
*Homme sans moeurs et sans religion!*
A CORRESPONDENCE

Lizaveta Ivanovna was sitting in her room, still in her ball dress, lost in deep thought. On returning home, she had hastily dismissed the sleepy maid, who reluctantly came forward to assist her, saying that she would undress herself, and with a trembling heart had gone up to her own room, hoping to find Hermann there, but yet desiring not to find him. At the first glance she convinced herself that he was not there, and she thanked her fate for the obstacle which had prevented their meeting. She sat down without undressing, and began to recall to mind all the circumstances which in so short a time had carried her so far. It was not three weeks since the time when she had first seen the young man from the window—and she already was in correspondence with him, and he had succeeded in inducing her to grant him a nocturnal tryst! She knew his name only through his having written it at the bottom of some of his letters; she had never spoken to him, had never heard his voice, and had never heard anything of him until that evening. But, strange to say, that very evening at the ball, Tomsky, being piqued with the young Princess Pauline N., who, contrary to her usual custom, did not flirt with him, wished to revenge himself by assuming an air of indifference: he therefore engaged Lizaveta Ivanovna and danced an endless mazurka with her. All the time he kept teasing her about her partiality for officers in the Engineers; he assured her that he knew far more than she could have supposed, and some of his jests were so happily aimed, that Lizaveta thought several times that her secret was known to him.

"From whom have you learned all this?" she asked, smiling.

"From a friend of a person very well known to you," replied Tomsky, "from a very remarkable man."

"And who is this remarkable man?"

"His name is Hermann."

Lizaveta made no reply; but her hands and feet turned to ice.

"This Hermann," continued Tomsky, "is a truly romantic character. He has the profile of a Napoleon, and the soul of a Mephistopheles. I believe that he has at least three crimes upon his conscience. . . . How pale you are!"

"I have a headache. . . . But what did this Hermann—or whatever his name is—tell you?"

"Hermann is very much dissatisfied with his friend: he says that in his place he would act very differently. . . . I even think that Hermann himself has designs upon you; at least, he listens not indifferently to his friend's enamored exclamations."

"But where has he seen me?"

"In church, perhaps; or promenading—God alone knows where. It may have been in your room, while you were asleep, for he is capable of it."

Three ladies approaching him with the question: *"Oubli ou regret?"* interrupted the conversation, which had become so tantalizingly interesting to Lizaveta.

The lady chosen by Tomsky was the Princess Pauline herself. She succeeded in effecting a reconciliation with him by making an extra turn in the dance and managing to delay resuming her seat. On returning to his place, Tomsky thought no more either of Hermann or Lizaveta. She longed to renew the interrupted conversation, but the mazurka came to an end, and shortly afterwards the old Countess took her departure.

Tomsky's words were nothing more than the small talk of the mazurka, but they sank deep into the soul of the young dreamer. The portrait, sketched by Tomsky, agreed with the picture she had formed in her own mind, and that image, rendered commonplace by current novels, terrified and fascinated her imagination. She was now sitting with her bare arms crossed and her head, still adorned with flowers, was bowed over her half-uncovered breast. Suddenly the door opened and Hermann entered. She shuddered.

"Where have you been?" she asked in a frightened whisper.

"In the old Countess' bedroom," replied Hermann. "I have just left her. The Countess is dead."

"My God! What are you saying?"

"And I am afraid," added Hermann, "that I am the cause of her death."

Lizaveta looked at him, and Tomsky's words found an echo in her soul: "This man has at least three crimes upon his conscience!" Hermann sat down by the window near her, and related all that had happened.

Lizaveta listened to him in terror. So all those passionate letters, those ardent demands, this bold obstinate pursuit—all this was not love! Money—that was what his soul yearned for! She could not satisfy his desire and make him happy! The poor girl had been nothing but the blind accomplice of a robber, of the murderer of her aged benefactress! . . . She wept bitter tears of belated, agonized repentance. Hermann gazed at her in silence: his heart, too, was tormented, but neither the tears of the poor girl, nor the wonderful charm of her beauty, enhanced by her grief, could produce any impression upon his hardened soul. He felt no pricking of conscience at the thought of the dead old woman. One thing only horrified him: the irreparable loss of the secret which he had expected would bring him wealth.

"You are a monster!" said Lizaveta at last.

"I did not wish her death," replied Hermann: "my pistol is not loaded."

Both grew silent.

The day began to dawn. Lizaveta extinguished her candle: a pale light illumined her room. She wiped her tear-stained eyes and raised them toward Hermann: he was sitting on the window sill, with his arms folded and frowning fiercely. In this attitude he bore a striking resemblance to the portrait of Napoleon. This resemblance struck even Lizaveta Ivanovna.

"How shall I get you out of the house?" said she at last. "I thought of conducting you down the secret staircase, but in that case it would be necessary to go through the Countess' bedroom, and I am afraid."

"Tell me how to find this secret staircase—I will go alone."

Lizaveta arose, took from her drawer a key, handed it to Hermann and gave him the necessary instructions. Hermann pressed her cold, unresponsive hand, kissed her bowed head, and left the room.

He descended the winding staircase, and once more entered the Countess' bedroom. The dead old woman sat as if petrified; her face expressed profound tranquillity. Hermann stopped before her, and gazed long and earnestly at her, as if he wished to convince himself of the terrible reality; at last he entered the study, felt behind the tapestry for the door, and then began to descend the dark staircase, agitated by strange emotions. "At this very hour," thought he, "some sixty years ago, a young gallant, who has long been moldering in his grave, may have stolen down this very staircase, perhaps coming from the very same bedroom, wearing an embroidered caftan, with his hair dressed *à l'oiseau royal* and pressing to his heart his three-cornered hat, and the heart of his aged mistress has only today ceased to beat. . . ."

At the bottom of the staircase Hermann found a door, which he opened with the same key, and found himself in a corridor which led him into the street.

## V

*That night the deceased Baroness von W. appeared to me. She was clad all in white and said to me: "How are you, Mr. Councilor?"*

SWEDENBORG

Three days after the fatal night, at nine o'clock in the morning, Hermann repaired to the Convent of——, where the burial service for the deceased Countess was to be held. Although feeling no remorse, he could not altogether stifle the voice of conscience, which kept repeating to him: "You are the murderer of the old woman!" While he had little true faith, he was very superstitious; and believing that the dead Countess might exercise an evil influence on his life, he resolved to be present at her funeral in order to ask her pardon.

The church was full. It was with difficulty that Hermann made his way through the crowd. The coffin stood on a sumptuous catafalque under a velvet baldachin. The deceased lay within it, her hands crossed upon her breast, and wearing a lace cap and a white satin gown. Around the catafalque stood the members of her household: the servants in black caftans, with armorial ribbons upon their shoulders, and candles in their hands; the relatives—children, grandchildren, and great-grandchildren—in deep mourning.

Nobody wept; tears would have been *une affectation*. The Countess was so old that her death could have surprised nobody, and her relatives had long looked upon her as not among the living. A famous preacher delivered the funeral oration. In simple and touching words he described the peaceful passing away of the saintly woman whose long life had been a serene, moving preparation for a Christian end. "The angel of death found her," said the preacher, "engaged in pious meditation and waiting for the midnight bridegroom."

The service concluded in an atmosphere of melancholy decorum. The relatives went forward first to bid farewell to the deceased. Then followed the numerous acquaintances, who had come to render the last homage to her who for so many years had participated in their frivolous amusements. After these followed the members of the Countess' household. The last of these was the old housekeeper who was of the same age as the deceased. Two young women led her forward, supporting her by the arms. She had not strength enough to bow down to the ground—she was the only one to shed a few tears and kiss the cold hand of her mistress.

Hermann now resolved to approach the coffin. He bowed down to the ground and for several minutes lay on the cold floor, which was strewn with fir boughs; at last he arose, as pale as the deceased Countess herself, ascended the steps of the catafalque and bent over the corpse. . . . At that moment it seemed to him that the dead woman darted a mocking look at him and winked with one eye. Hermann started back, took a false step and fell to the ground. He was lifted up. At the same moment Lizaveta Ivanovna was carried into the vestibule of the church in a faint. This episode disturbed for some minutes the solemnity of the gloomy ceremony. Among the congregation arose a muffled murmur, and the lean chamberlain, a near relative of the deceased, whispered in the ear of an Englishman who was standing near him, that the young officer was a natural son of the Countess, to which the Englishman coldly replied: "Oh!"

During the whole of that day, Hermann was exceedingly perturbed. Dining in an out-of-the-way restaurant, he drank a great deal of wine, contrary to his usual custom, in the hope of allaying his inward agitation. But the wine only served to excite his imagination still more. On returning home, he threw himself upon his bed without undressing, and fell into a deep sleep.

When he woke up it was already night, and the moon was shining into the room. He looked at his watch: it was a quarter to three. Sleep had left him; he sat down upon his bed and thought of the funeral of the old Countess.

At that moment somebody in the street looked in at his window, and immediately passed on again. Hermann paid no attention to this incident. A few moments afterward he heard the door of the anteroom open. Hermann thought that it was his orderly, drunk as usual, returning from some nocturnal expedition, but presently he heard footsteps that were unknown to him: somebody was shuffling softly across the floor in slippers. The door opened, and a woman, dressed in white, entered the room. Hermann mistook her for his old nurse, and wondered what could bring her there at that hour of the night. But the white woman glided rapidly across the room and stood before him—and Hermann recognized the Countess!

"I have come to you against my will," she said in a firm voice: "but I have been ordered to grant your request. Three, seven, ace will win for you if played in succession, but only on these conditions: that you do not play more than one card in twenty-four hours, and that you never play again during the rest of your life. I forgive you my death, on condition that you marry my ward, Lizaveta Ivanovna."

With these words she turned round very quietly, walked with a shuffling gait toward the door and disappeared. Hermann heard the street door bang, and he saw someone look in at him through the window again.

For a long time Hermann could not recover himself. Then he went into the next room. His orderly was asleep upon the floor, and he had much difficulty in waking him. The orderly was drunk as usual, and nothing could be got out of him. The street door was locked. Hermann returned to his room, lit his candle, and set down an account of his vision.

## VI

*"Attendez!"*
*"How dare you say* attendez *to me?"*
*"Your Excellency, I said: 'Attendez, sir.'"*

Two fixed ideas can no more exist together in the moral world than two bodies can occupy one and the same place in the physical world. "Three, seven, ace" soon drove out of Hermann's mind the thought of the dead Countess. "Three, seven, ace" were perpetually running through his head and continually on his lips. If he saw a young girl, he would say: "How slender she is! Quite like the three of hearts." If anybody asked: "What is the time?" he would reply: "Five minutes to seven." Every stout man that he saw reminded him of the ace. "Three, seven, ace" haunted him in his sleep, and assumed all possible shapes. The three bloomed before him in the form of a magnificent flower, the seven was represented by a Gothic portal, and the ace became transformed into a gigantic spider. One thought alone occupied his whole mind — to make use of the secret which he had purchased so dearly. He thought of applying for a furlough so as to travel abroad. He wanted to go to Paris and force fortune to yield a treasure to him in the public gambling houses there. Chance spared him all this trouble.

There was in Moscow a society of wealthy gamblers, presided over by the celebrated Chekalinsky, who had passed all his life at the card table and had amassed millions, accepting bills of exchange for his winnings and paying his losses in ready money. His long experience secured for him the confidence of his companions, and his open house, his famous cook, and his agreeable and cheerful manner gained for him the respect of the public. He came to St. Petersburg. The young men of the capital flocked to his rooms, forgetting balls for cards, and preferring the temptations of faro to the seductions of flirting. Narumov conducted Hermann to Chekalinsky's residence.

They passed through a suite a magnificent rooms, filled with courteous attendants. Several generals and privy counselors were playing whist; young men were lolling carelessly upon the velvet-covered sofas, eating ices and smoking pipes. In the drawing room, at the head of a long table, around which crowded about a score of players, sat the master of the house keeping the bank. He was a man of about sixty years of age, of a very dignified appearance; his head was covered with silvery-white hair; his full, florid countenance expressed good nature, and his eyes twinkled with a perpetual smile. Narumov introduced Hermann to him. Chekalinsky shook him by the hand in a friendly manner, requested him not to stand on ceremony, and then went on dealing.

The game lasted a long time. On the table lay more than thirty cards. Chekalinsky paused after each throw, in order to give the players time to arrange their cards and note down their losses, listened politely to their requests, and more politely still, straightened out the corners of cards that some absent-minded player's hand had turned down. At last the game was finished. Chekalinsky shuffled the cards and prepared to deal again.

"Allow me to play a card," said Hermann, stretching our his hand from behind a stout gentleman who was punting.

Chekalinsky smiled and bowed silently, as a sign of acquiescence. Narumov laughingly congratulated Hermann on ending his long abstention from cards, and wished him a lucky beginning.

"Here goes!" said Hermann, writing the figure with chalk on the back of his card.

"How much, sir?" asked the banker, screwing up his eyes. "Excuse me, I cannot see quite clearly."

"Forty-seven thousand," replied Hermann.

At these words every head in the room turned suddenly round, and all eyes were fixed upon Hermann.

"He has taken leave of his senses!" thought Narumov.

"Allow me to observe," said Chekalinsky, with his eternal smile, "that that is a very high stake; nobody here has ever staked more than two hundred and seventy-five rubles at a time."

"Well," retorted Hermann, "do you accept my card or not?"

Chekalinsky bowed with the same look of humble acquiescence.

"I only wish to inform you," said he, "that enjoying the full confidence of my partners, I can only play for ready money. For my own part, I am, of course, quite convinced that your word is sufficient, but for the sake of order, and because of the accounts, I must ask you to put the money on your card."

Hermann drew from his pocket a banknote and handed it to Chekalinsky, who, after examining it in a cursory manner, placed it on Hermann's card.

He began to deal. On the right a nine turned up, and on the left a three.

"I win!" said Hermann, showing his card.

A murmur of astonishment arose among the players. Chekalinsky frowned, but the smile quickly returned to his face.

"Do you wish me to settle with you?" he said to Hermann.

"If you please," replied the latter.

Chekalinsky drew from his pocket a number of banknotes and paid up at once. Hermann took his money and left the table. Narumov could not recover from his astonishment. Hermann drank a glass of lemonade and went home.

The next evening he again appeared at Chekalinsky's. The host was dealing. Hermann walked up to the table; the punters immediately made room for him. Chekalinsky greeted him with a gracious bow.

Hermann waited for the next game, took a card and placed upon it his forty-seven thousand rubles, together with his winnings of the previous evening.

Chekalinsky began to deal. A knave turned up on the right, a seven on the left.

Hermann showed his seven.

There was a general exclamation. Chekalinsky was obviously disturbed, but he counted out the ninety-four thousand rubles and handed them over to Hermann, who pocketed them in the coolest manner possible and immediately left the house.

The next evening Hermann appeared again at the table. Everyone was expecting him. The generals and privy counselors left their whist in order to watch such extraordinary play. The young officers jumped up from their sofas, and even the servants crowded into the room. All pressed round Hermann. The other players left off punting, impatient to see how it would end. Hermann stood at the table and prepared to play alone against the pale but still smiling Chekalinsky. Each opened a new pack of cards. Chekalinsky shuffled. Hermann took a card and covered it with a pile of banknotes. It was like a duel. Deep silence reigned.

Chekalinsky began to deal; his hands trembled. On the right a queen turned up, and on the left an ace.

"Ace wins!" cried Hermann, showing his card.

"Your queen has lost," said Chekalinsky sweetly.

Hermann started; instead of an ace, there lay before him the queen of spades! He could not believe his eyes, nor could he understand how he had made such a mistake.

At that moment it seemed to him that the queen of spades screwed up her eyes and sneered. He was struck by the remarkable resemblance. . . .

"The old woman!" he exclaimed, in terror.

Chekalinsky gathered up his winnings. For some time Hermann remained perfectly motionless. When at last he left the table, the room buzzed with loud talk.

"Splendidly punted!" said the players. Chekalinsky shuffled the cards afresh, and the game went on as usual.

## CONCLUSION

Hermann went out of his mind. He is now confined in room Number 17 of the Obukhov Hospital. He never answers any questions, but he constantly mutters with unusual rapidity: "Three, seven, ace! Three, seven, queen!"

Lizaveta Ivanovna has married a very amiable young man, a son of the former steward of the old Countess. He is a civil servant, and has a considerable fortune. Lizaveta is bringing up a poor relative.

Tomsky has been promoted to the rank of captain, and is marrying Princess Pauline.

*Translated by T. Keane*

∾

## ALL SOULS'

*Edith Wharton*

Queer and inexplicable as the business was, on the surface it appeared fairly simple—at the time, at least; but with the passing of years, and owing to there not having been a single witness of what happened except Sara Clayburn herself, the stories about it have become so exaggerated, and often so ridiculously inaccurate, that it seems necessary that someone connected with the affair, though not actually present—I repeat that when it happened my cousin was (or thought she was) quite alone in her house—should record the few facts actually known.

In those days I was often at Whitegates (as the place had always been called)—I was there, in fact, not long before, and almost immediately after, the strange happenings of those thirty-six hours. Jim Clayburn and his widow were both my cousins, and because of that, and of my intimacy with them, both families think I am more likely than anybody else to be able to get at the facts, as far as they can be called facts, and as anybody can get at them. So I have written down, as clearly as I could, the gist of the various talks I had with cousin Sara, when she could be got to talk—it wasn't often—about what occurred during that mysterious weekend.

I read the other day in a book by a fashionable essayist that ghosts went out when electric light came in. What nonsense! The writer, though he is fond of dabbling, in a literary way, in the supernatural, hasn't even reached the threshold of his subject. As between turreted castles patrolled by headless victims with clanking chains, and the comfortable suburban house with a refrigerator and central heating where you feel, as soon as you're in it, *that there's something wrong,* give me the latter for sending a chill down the spine! And, by the way, haven't you noticed that it's generally not the high-strung and imaginative who see ghosts, but the calm matter-of-fact people who don't believe in them, and are sure they wouldn't mind if they did see one? Well, that was the case with Sara Clayburn and her house. The house, in spite of its age—it was built, I believe, about 1780—was open, airy, high-ceilinged, with electricity, central heating and all the modern appliances: and its mistress was—well, very much like her house. And, anyhow, this isn't exactly a ghost story and I've dragged in the analogy only as a way of showing you what kind of woman my cousin was, and how unlikely it would have seemed that what happened at Whitegates should have happened just there—or to her.

When Jim Clayburn died the family all thought that, as the couple had no children, his widow would give up Whitegates and move either to New York or Boston—for being of good Colonial stock, with many relatives and friends, she would have found a place ready for her in either. But Sara Clayburn seldom did what other people expected, and in this case she did exactly the contrary; she stayed at Whitegates.

"What, turn my back on the old house—tear up all the family roots, and go and hang myself up in a bird-cage flat in one of those new skyscrapers in Lexington Avenue, with a bunch of chickweed and a cuttlefish to replace my good Connecticut mutton? No, thank you. Here I belong, and here I stay till my executors hand the place over to Jim's next-of-kin—that stupid fat Presley boy. . . . Well, don't let's talk about him. But I tell you what—I'll keep him out of here as long as I can." And she did—for being still in the early fifties when her husband died, and a muscular, resolute figure of a woman, she was more than a match for the fat Presley boy, and attended his funeral a few years ago, in correct mourning, with a faint smile under her veil.

Whitegates was a pleasant hospitable-looking house, on a height overlooking the stately windings of the Connecticut River; but it was five or six miles from Norrington, the nearest town, and its situation would certainly have seemed remote and lonely to modern servants. Luckily, however, Sara Clayburn had inherited from her mother-in-law two- or three-old stand-bys who seemed as much a part of the family tradition as the roof they lived under; and I never heard of her having any trouble in her domestic arrangements.

The house, in Colonial days, had been foursquare, with four spacious rooms on the ground floor, an oak-floored hall dividing them, the usual kitchen extension at the back, and a good attic under the roof. But Jim's grandparents, when interest in the "Colonial" began to revive, in the early eighties, had added two wings, at right angles to the south front, so that the old "circle" before the front door became a grassy court, enclosed on three sides, with a big elm in the middle. Thus the house was turned into a roomy dwelling, in which the last three generations of Clayburns had exercised a large hospitality; but the architect had respected the character of the old house, and the enlargement made it more comfortable without lessening its simplicity. There was a lot of land about it, and Jim Clayburn, like his fathers before him, farmed it, not without profit, and played a considerable and respected part in state politics. The Clayburns were always spoken of as a "good influence" in the county, and the townspeople were glad when they learned that Sara did not mean to desert the place—"though it must be lonesome, winters, living all alone up there atop of that hill"—they remarked as the days shortened, and the first snow began to pile up under the quadruple row of elms along the common.

Well, if I've given you a sufficiently clear idea of Whitegates and the Clayburns—who shared with their old house a sort of reassuring orderliness and dignity—I'll efface myself, and tell the tale, not in my cousin's words, for they were too confused and fragmentary, but as I built it up gradually out of her half-avowals and nervous reticences. If the thing happened at all—and I must leave you to judge of that—I think it must have happened in this way. . . .

I

The morning had been bitter, with a driving sleet—though it was only the last day of October—but after lunch a watery sun showed for a while through banked-up woolly clouds, and tempted Sara Clayburn out. She was an energetic walker, and given, at that season, to tramping three or four miles along the valley road, and coming back by way of Shaker's wood. She had made her usual round, and was following the main drive to the house when she overtook a plainly-dressed woman walking in the same direction. If the scene had not been so lonely—the way to Whitegates at the end of an autumn day was not a frequented one—Mrs. Clayburn might not have paid any attention to the woman, for she was in no way noticeable; but when she caught up with the intruder my cousin was surprised to find that she was a stranger—for the mistress of Whitegates prided herself on knowing, at least by sight, most of her country neighbors. It was almost dark, and the woman's face was hardly visible, but Mrs. Clayburn told me she recalled her as middle-aged, plain and rather pale.

Mrs. Clayburn greeted her, and then added: "You're going to the house?"

"Yes, ma'am," the woman answered, in a voice that the Connecticut Valley in old days would have called "foreign," but that would have been unnoticed by ears used to the modern multiplicity of tongues. "No, I couldn't say where she came from," Sara always said. "What struck me as queer was that I didn't know her."

She asked the woman, politely, what she wanted, and the woman answered: "Only to see one of the girls." The answer was natural enough, and Mrs. Clayburn nodded and turned off from the drive to the lower part of the gardens, so that she saw no more of the visitor then or afterward. And, in fact, a half hour later something happened which put the stranger entirely out of her mind. The brisk and light-footed Mrs. Clayburn, as she approached the house, slipped on a frozen puddle, turned her ankle and lay suddenly helpless.

Price, the butler, and Agnes, the dour old Scottish maid whom Sara had inherited from her mother-in-law, of course knew exactly what to do. In no time they had their mistress stretched out on a lounge, and Dr. Selgrove had been called up from Norrington. When he arrived, he ordered Mrs. Clayburn to bed, did the necessary examining and bandaging, and shook his head over her ankle, which he feared was fractured. He thought, however, that if she would swear not to get up, or even shift the position of her leg, he could spare her the discomfort of putting it in plaster. Mrs. Clayburn agreed, the more promptly as the doctor warned her that any rash movement would prolong her immobility. Her quick imperious nature made the prospect trying, and she was annoyed with herself for having been so clumsy. But the mischief was done, and she immediately thought what an opportunity she would have for going over her accounts and catching up with her correspondence. So she settled down resignedly in her bed.

"And you won't miss much, you know, if you have to stay there a few days. It's beginning to snow, and it looks as if we were in for a good spell of it," the doctor remarked, glancing through the window as he gathered up his implements. "Well, we don't often get snow here as early as this; but winter's got to begin sometime," he concluded philosophically. At the door he stopped to add: "You don't want me to send up a nurse from Norrington? Not to nurse you, you know; there's nothing much to do till I see you again. But this is a pretty lonely place when the snow begins, and I thought maybe—"

Sara Clayburn laughed. "Lonely? With my old servants? You forget how many winters I've spent here alone with them. Two of them were with me in my mother-in-law's time."

"That's so," Dr. Selgrove agreed. "You're a good deal luckier than most people, that way. Well, let me see; this is Saturday. We'll have to let the inflammation go down before we can X-ray you. Monday morning, first thing, I'll be here with the X-ray man. If you want me sooner, call me up." And he was gone.

## II

The foot at first, had not been very painful; but toward the small hours Mrs. Clayburn began to suffer. She was a bad patient, like most healthy and active people. Not being used to pain she did not know how to bear it, and the hours of wakefulness and immobility seemed endless. Agnes, before leaving her, had made everything as comfortable as possible. She had put a jug of lemonade within reach, and had even (Mrs. Clayburn thought it odd afterward) insisted on bringing in a tray with sandwiches and a thermos of tea. "In case you're hungry in the night, madam."

"Thank you; but I'm never hungry in the night. And I certainly shan't be tonight—only thirsty. I think I'm feverish."

"Well, there's the lemonade, madam."

"That will do. Take the other things away, please." (Sara had always hated the sight of unwanted food "messing about" in her room.)

"Very well, madam. Only you might—"

"Please take it away," Mrs. Clayburn repeated irritably.

"Very good, madam." But as Agnes went out, her mistress heard her set the tray down softly on a table behind the screen which shut off the door.

"Obstinate old goose!" she thought, rather touched by the old woman's insistence.

Sleep, once it had gone, would not return, and the long black hours moved more and more slowly. How late the dawn came in November! "If only I could move my leg," she grumbled.

She lay still and strained her ears for the first steps of the servants. Whitegates was an early house, its mistress setting the example; it would surely not be long now before one of the women came. She was tempted to ring for Agnes, but refrained. The woman had been up late, and this was Sunday morning, when the household was always allowed a little extra time. Mrs. Clayburn reflected restlessly: "I was a fool not to let her leave the tea beside the bed, as she wanted to. I wonder if I could get up and get it?" But she remembered the doctor's warning, and dared not move. Anything rather than risk prolonging her imprisonment. . . .

Ah, there was the stable clock striking. How loud it sounded in the snowy stillness! One—two—three—four—five. . . .

What? Only five? Three hours and a quarter more before she could hope to hear the door handle turned. . . . After a while she dozed off again, uncomfortably.

Another sound aroused her. Again the stable clock. She listened. But the room was still in deep darkness, and only six strokes fell. . . . She thought of reciting something to put her to sleep; but she seldom read poetry, and being naturally a good sleeper, she could not remember any of the usual devices against insomnia. The whole of her leg felt like lead now. The bandages had grown terribly tight—her ankle must have swollen. . . . She lay staring at the dark windows, watching for the first glimmer of dawn. At last she saw a pale filter of daylight through the shutters. One by one the objects between the bed and the window recovered first their outline, then their bulk, and seemed to be stealthily regrouping themselves, after goodness knows what secret displacements during the night. Who that has lived in an old house could possibly believe that the furniture in it stays still all night? Mrs. Clayburn almost fancied she saw one little slender-legged table slipping hastily back into its place.

"It knows Agnes is coming, and it's afraid," she thought whimsically. Her bad night must have made her imaginative for such nonsense as that about the furniture had never occurred to her before. . . .

At length, after hours more, as it seemed, the stable clock struck eight. Only another quarter of an hour. She watched the hand moving slowly across the face of the little clock beside her bed ... ten minutes ... five ... only five! Agnes was as punctual as destiny ... in two minutes now she would come. The two minutes passed, and she did not come. Poor Agnes—she had looked pale and tired the night before. She had overslept herself, no doubt—or perhaps she felt ill, and would send the housemaid to replace her. Mrs. Clayburn waited.

She waited half an hour; then she reached up to the bell at the head of the bed. Poor old Agnes—her mistress felt guilty about waking her. But Agnes did not appear—and after a considerable interval Mrs. Clayburn, now with a certain impatience, rang again. She rang once; twice; three times—but still no one came.

Once more she waited; then she said to herself: "There must be something wrong with the electricity." Well—she could find out by switching on the bed lamp at her elbow (how admirably the room was equipped with every practical appliance!). She switched it on—but no light came. Electric current cut off; and it was Sunday, and nothing could be done about it till the next morning. Unless it turned out to be just a burnt-out fuse, which Price could remedy. Well, in a moment now some one would surely come to her door.

It was nine o'clock before she admitted to herself that something uncommonly strange must have happened in the house. She began to feel a nervous apprehension; but she was not the woman to encourage it. If only she had had the telephone put in her room, instead of out on the landing! She measured mentally the distance to be traveled, remembered Dr. Selgrove's admonition, and wondered if her broken ankle would carry her there. She dreaded the prospect of being put in plaster, but she had to get to the telephone, whatever happened.

She wrapped herself in her dressing gown, found a walking stick, and, resting heavily on it, dragged herself to the door. In her bedroom the careful Agnes had closed and fastened the shutters, so that it was not much lighter there than at dawn; but outside in the corridor the cold whiteness of the snowy morning seemed almost reassuring. Mysterious things—dreadful things—were associated with darkness; and here was the wholesome prosaic daylight come again to banish them. Mrs. Clayburn looked about her and listened. Silence. A deep nocturnal silence in that daylit house, in which five people were presumably coming and going about their work. It was certainly strange. ... She looked out of the window, hoping to see someone crossing the court or coming along the drive. But no one was in sight, and the snow seemed to have the place to itself: a quiet steady snow. It was still falling, with a business-like regularity, muffling the outer world in layers on layers of thick white velvet, and intensifying the silence within. A noiseless world—were people so sure that absence of noise was what they wanted? Let them first try a lonely country house in a November snowstorm!

She dragged herself along the passage to the telephone. When she unhooked the receiver she noticed that her hand trembled.

She rang up the pantry—no answer. She rang again. Silence—more silence! It seemed to be piling itself up like the snow on the roof and in the gutters. Silence. How many people that she knew had any idea what silence was—and how loud it sounded when you really listened to it?

Again she waited: then she rang up "Central." No answer. She tried three times. After that she tried the pantry again. . . . The telephone was cut off, then; like the electric current. Who was at work downstairs, isolating her thus from the world? Her heart began to hammer. Luckily there was a chair near the telephone, and she sat down to recover her strength—or was it her courage?

Agnes and the housemaid slept in the nearest wing. She would certainly get as far as that when she had pulled herself together. Had she the courage—? Yes, of course she had. She had always been regarded as a plucky woman; and had so regarded herself. But this silence—

It occurred to her that by looking from the window of a neighboring bathroom she could see the kitchen chimney. There ought to be smoke coming from it at that hour; and if there were she thought she would be less afraid to go on. She got as far as the bathroom and looking through the window saw that no smoke came from the chimney. Her sense of loneliness grew more acute. Whatever had happened belowstairs must have happened before the morning's work had begun. The cook had not had time to light the fire, the other servants had not yet begun their round. She sank down on the nearest chair, struggling against her fears. What next would she discover if she carried on her investigations?

The pain in her ankle made progress difficult; but she was aware of it now only as an obstacle to haste. No matter what it cost her in physical suffering, she must find out what was happening belowstairs—or had happened. But first she would go to the maid's room. And if that were empty—well, somehow she would have to get herself downstairs.

She limped along the passage, and on the way steadied herself by resting her hand on a radiator. It was stone-cold. Yet in that well-ordered house in winter the central heating, though damped down at night, was never allowed to go out, and by eight in the morning a mellow warmth pervaded the rooms. The icy chill of the pipes startled her. It was the chauffeur who looked after the heating—so he too was involved in the mystery, whatever it was, as well as the house servants. But this only deepened the problem.

### III

At Agnes's door Mrs. Clayburn paused and knocked. She expected no answer, and there was none. She opened the door and went in. The room was dark and very cold. She went to the window and flung back the shutters; then she looked slowly around, vaguely apprehensive of what she might see. The room was empty but what frightened her was not so much its emptiness as its air of scrupulous and undisturbed order. There was no sign of anyone having lately dressed in it—or undressed the night before. And the bed had not been slept in.

Mrs. Clayburn leaned against the wall for a moment; then she crossed the floor and opened the cupboard. That was where Agnes kept her dresses; and the dresses were there, neatly hanging in a row. On the shelf above were Agnes's few and unfashionable hats, rearrangements of her mistress's old ones. Mrs. Clayburn, who knew them all, looked at the shelf, and saw that one was missing. And so was also the warm winter coat she had given to Agnes the previous winter.

The woman was out, then; had gone out, no doubt, the night before, since the bed was unslept in, the dressing and washing appliances untouched. Agnes, who never set foot out of the house after dark, who despised the movies as much as she did the wireless, and could never be persuaded that a little innocent amusement was a necessary element in life, had deserted the house on a snowy winter night, while her mistress lay upstairs, suffering and helpless! Why had she gone, and where had she gone? When she was undressing Mrs. Clayburn the night before, taking her orders, trying to make her more comfortable, was she already planning this mysterious nocturnal escape? Or had something—the mysterious and dreadful Something for the clue of which Mrs. Clayburn was still groping—occurred later in the evening, sending the maid downstairs and out of doors into the bitter night? Perhaps one of the men at the garage—where the chauffeur and gardener lived—had been suddenly taken ill, and someone had run up to the house for Agnes. Yes—that must be the explanation. . . . Yet how much it left unexplained.

Next to Agnes's room was the linen room; beyond that was the housemaid's door. Mrs. Clayburn went to it and knocked. "Mary!" No one answered, and she went in. The room was in the same immaculate order as her maid's, and here too the bed was unslept in, and there were no signs of dressing or undressing. The two women had no doubt gone out together— gone where?

More and more the cold unanswering silence of the house weighed down on Mrs. Clayburn. She had never thought of it as a big house, but now, in this snowy winter light, it seemed immense, and full of ominous corners around which one dared not look.

Beyond the housemaid's room were the back stairs. It was the nearest way down, and every step that Mrs. Clayburn took was increasingly painful; but she decided to walk slowly back, the whole length of the passage, and go down by the front stairs. She did not know why she did this; but she felt that at the moment she was past reasoning, and had better obey her instinct.

More than once she had explored the ground floor alone in the small hours, in search of unwonted midnight noises; but now it was not the idea of noises that frightened her, but that inexorable and hostile silence, the sense that the house had retained in full daylight its nocturnal mystery, and was watching her as she was watching it, that in entering those empty orderly rooms she might be disturbing some unseen confabulation on which beings of flesh-and-blood had better not intrude.

The broad oak stairs were beautifully polished, and so slippery that she had to cling to the rail and let herself down tread by tread. And as she descended, the silence descended with her—heavier, denser, more absolute. She seemed to feel its steps just behind her, softly keeping time with hers. It had a quality she had never been aware of in any other silence, as though it were not merely an absence of sound, a thin barrier between the ear and the surging murmur of life just beyond, but an impenetrable substance made out of the worldwide cessation of all life and all movement.

Yes, that was what laid a chill on her: the feeling that there was no limit to this silence, no outer margin, nothing beyond it. By this time she had reached the foot of the stairs and was limping across the hall to the drawing room. Whatever she found there, she was sure, would be mute and lifeless; but what would it be? The bodies of her dead servants, mown down by some homicidal maniac? And what if it were her turn next—if he were waiting for her behind the heavy curtains of the room she was about to enter? Well, she must find out—she must face whatever lay in wait. Not impelled by bravery—the last drop of courage had oozed out of her—but because anything, anything was better than to remain shut up in that snowbound house without knowing whether she was alone in it or not, "I must find that out, I must find that out," she repeated to herself in a sort of meaningless sing-song.

The cold outer light flooded the drawing room. The shutters had not been closed, nor the curtains drawn. She looked about her. The room was empty, and every chair in its usual place. Her armchair was pushed up by the chimney, and the cold hearth was piled with the ashes of the fire at which she had warmed herself before starting on her ill-fated walk. Even her empty coffee cup stood on a table near the armchair. It was evident that the servants had not been in the room since she had left it the day before after luncheon. And suddenly the conviction entered into her that, as she found the drawing room, so she would find the rest of the house; cold, orderly—and empty. She would find nothing, she would find no one. She no longer felt any dread of ordinary human dangers lurking in those dumb spaces ahead of her. She knew she was utterly alone under her own roof. She sat down to rest her aching ankle, and looked slowly about her.

There were the other rooms to be visited, and she was determined to go through them all—but she knew in advance that they would give no answer to her question. She knew it, seemingly, from the quality of the silence which enveloped her. There was no break, no thinnest crack in it anywhere. It had the cold continuity of the snow which was still falling steadily outside.

She had no idea how long she waited before nerving herself to continue her inspection. She no longer felt the pain in her ankle, but was only conscious that she must not bear her weight on it, and therefore moved very slowly, supporting herself on each piece of furniture in her path. On the ground floor no shutter had been closed, no curtain drawn, and she progressed without difficulty from room to room: the library, her morning room, the dining room. In each of them, every piece of furniture was in its usual place. In the dining room, the table had been laid for her dinner of the previous evening, and the candelabra, with candles unlit, stood reflected in the dark mahogany. She was not the kind of woman to nibble a poached egg on a tray when she was alone, but always came down to the dining room, and had what she called a civilized meal.

The back premises remained to be visited. From the dining room she entered the pantry, and there too everything was in irreproachable order. She opened the door and looked down the back passage with its neat linoleum floor covering. The deep silence accompanied her; she still felt it moving watchfully at her side, as though she were its prisoner and it might throw itself upon her if she attempted to escape. She limped on toward the kitchen. That of course would be empty too, and immaculate. But she must see it.

She leaned a minute in the embrasure of a window in the passage. "It's like the 'Mary Celeste'—a 'Mary Celeste' on *terra firma*," she thought, recalling the unsolved sea mystery of her childhood. "No one ever knew what happened on board the 'Mary Celeste.' And perhaps no one will ever know what has happened here. Even I shan't know."

At the thought her latent fear seemed to take on a new quality. It was like an icy liquid running through every vein, and lying in a pool about her heart. She understood now that she had never before known what fear was, and that most of the people she had met had probably never known either. For this sensation was something quite different. . . .

It absorbed her so completely that she was not aware how long she remained leaning there. But suddenly a new impulse pushed her forward, and she walked on toward the scullery. She went there first because there was a service slide in the wall, through which she might peep into the kitchen without being seen; and some indefinable instinct told her that the kitchen held the clue to the mystery. She still felt strongly that whatever had happened in the house must have its source and center in the kitchen.

In the scullery, as she had expected, everything was clean and tidy. Whatever had happened, no one in the house appeared to have been taken by surprise; there was nowhere any sign of confusion or disorder. "It looks as if they'd known beforehand, and put everything straight," she thought. She glanced at the wall facing the door, and saw that the slide was open. And then, as she was approaching it, the silence was broken. A voice was speaking in the kitchen—a man's voice, low but emphatic, and which she had never heard before.

She stood still, cold with fear. But this fear was again a different one. Her previous terrors had been speculative, conjectural, a ghostly emanation of the surrounding silence. This was a plain everyday dread of evildoers. Oh, God, why had she not remembered her husband's revolver, which ever since his death had lain in a drawer in her room?

She turned to retreat across the smooth slippery floor but halfway her stick slipped from her, and crashed down on the tiles. The noise seemed to echo on and on through the emptiness, and she stood still, aghast. Now that she had betrayed her presence, flight was useless. Whoever was beyond the kitchen door would be upon her in a second. . . .

But to her astonishment the voice went on speaking. It was as though neither the speaker nor his listeners had heard her. The invisible stranger spoke so low that she could not make out what he was saying, but the tone was passionately earnest, almost threatening. The next moment she realized that he was speaking in a foreign language, a language unknown to her. Once more her terror was surmounted by the urgent desire to know what was going on, so close to her yet unseen. She crept to the slide, peered cautiously through into the kitchen, and saw that it was as orderly and empty as the other rooms. But in the middle of the carefully scoured table stood a portable wireless, and the voice she heard came out of it. . . .

She must have fainted then, she supposed; at any rate she felt so weak and dizzy that her memory of what next happened remained indistinct. But in the course of time she groped her way back to the pantry, and there found a bottle of spirits—brandy or whisky, she could not remember which. She found a glass, poured herself a stiff drink, and while it was flushing through her veins, managed, she never knew with how many shuddering delays, to drag herself through the deserted ground floor, up the stairs, and down the corridor to her own room. There, apparently, she fell across the threshold, again unconscious. . . .

When she came to, she remembered, her first care had been to lock herself in; then to recover her husband's revolver. It was not loaded, but she found some cartridges, and succeeded in loading it. Then she remembered that Agnes, on leaving her the evening before, had refused to carry away the tray with the tea and sandwiches, and she fell on them with a sudden hunger. She recalled also noticing that a flask of brandy had been put beside the thermos, and being vaguely surprised. Agnes's departure, then, had been deliberately planned, and she had known that her mistress, who never touched spirits, might have need of a stimulant before she returned. Mrs. Clayburn poured some of the brandy into her tea, and swallowed it greedily.

After that (she told me later) she remembered that she had managed to start a fire in her grate, and after warming herself, had got back into her bed, piling on it all the coverings she could find. The afternoon passed in a haze of pain, out of which there emerged now and then a dim shape of fear—the fear that she might lie there alone and untended till she died of cold, and of the terror of her solitude. For she was sure by this time that the house was empty—completely empty, from garret to cellar. She knew it was so, she could not tell why; but again she felt that it must be because of the peculiar quality of the silence—the silence which had dogged her steps wherever she went, and was now folded down on her like a pall. She was sure that the nearness of any other human being, however dumb and secret, would have made a faint crack in the texture of that silence, flawed it as a sheet of glass is flawed by a pebble thrown against it. . . .

## IV

"Is that easier?" the doctor asked, lifting himself from bending over her ankle. He shook his head disapprovingly. "Looks to me as if you'd disobeyed orders—eh? Been moving about, haven't you? And I guess Dr. Selgrove told you to keep quiet till he saw you again, didn't he?"

The speaker was a stranger, whom Mrs. Clayburn knew only by name. Her own doctor had been called away that morning to the bedside of an old patient in Baltimore, and had asked this young man, who was beginning to be known at Norrington, to replace him. The newcomer was shy, and somewhat familiar, as the shy often are, and Mrs. Clayburn decided that she did not much like him. But before she could convey this by the tone of her reply (and she was past mistress of the shades of disapproval) she heard Agnes speaking—yes, Agnes, the same, the usual Agnes, standing behind the doctor, neat and stern-looking as ever. "Mrs. Clayburn must have got up and walked about in the night instead of ringing for me, as she'd ought to," Agnes intervened severely.

This was too much! In spite of the pain, which was now exquisite, Mrs. Clayburn laughed. "Ringing for you? How could I, with the electricity cut off?"

"The electricity cut off?" Agnes's surprise was masterly. "Why, when was it cut off?" She pressed her finger on the bell beside the bed, and the call tinkled through the quiet room. "I tried that bell before I left you last night, madam, because if there'd been anything wrong with it I'd have come and slept in the dressing room sooner than leave you here alone."

Mrs. Clayburn lay speechless, staring up at her. "Last night? But last night I was all alone in the house."

Agnes's firm features did not alter. She folded her hands resignedly across her trim apron. "Perhaps the pain's made you a little confused, madam." She looked at the doctor, who nodded.

"The pain in your foot must have been pretty bad," he said.

"It was," Mrs. Clayburn replied. "But it was nothing to the horror of being left alone in this empty house since the day before yesterday, with the heat and the electricity cut off, and the telephone not working."

The doctor was looking at her in evident wonder. Agnes's sallow face flushed slightly, but only as if in indignation at an unjust charge. "But, madam, I made up your fire with my own hands last night—and look, it's smoldering still. I was getting ready to start it again just now, when the doctor came."

"That's so. She was down on her knees before it," the doctor corroborated.

Again Mrs. Clayburn laughed. Ingeniously as the tissue of lies was being woven about her, she felt she could still break through it. "I made up the fire myself yesterday—there was no one else to do it," she said, addressing the doctor, but keeping her eyes on her maid. "I got up twice to put on more coal, because the house was like a sepulcher. The central heating must have been out since Saturday afternoon."

At this incredible statement Agnes's face expressed only a polite distress; but the new doctor was evidently embarrassed at being drawn into an unintelligible controversy with which he had no time to deal. He said he had brought the X-ray photographer with him, but that the ankle was too much swollen to be photographed at present. He asked Mrs. Clayburn to excuse his haste, as he had all Dr. Selgrove's patients to visit besides his own, and promised to come back that evening to decide whether she could be X-rayed then, and whether, as he evidently feared, the ankle would have to be put in plaster. Then, handing his prescriptions to Agnes, he departed.

Mrs. Clayburn spent a feverish and suffering day. She did not feel well enough to carry on the discussion with Agnes; she did not ask to see the other servants. She grew drowsy, and understood that her mind was confused with fever. Agnes and the housemaid waited on her as attentively as usual, and by the time the doctor returned in the evening her temperature had fallen; but she decided not to speak of what was on her mind until Dr. Selgrove reappeared. He was to be back the following evening; and the new doctor preferred to wait for him before deciding to put the ankle in plaster—though he feared this was now inevitable.


# V


That afternoon Mrs. Clayburn had me summoned by telephone, and I arrived at Whitegates the following day. My cousin, who looked pale and nervous, merely pointed to her foot, which had been put in plaster, and thanked me for coming to keep her company. She explained that Dr. Selgrove had been taken suddenly ill in Baltimore, and would not be back for several days, but that the young man who replaced him seemed fairly competent. She made no allusion to the strange incidents I have set down, but I felt at once that she had received a shock which her accident, however painful, could not explain.

Finally, one evening, she told me the story of her strange weekend, as it had presented itself to her unusually clear and accurate mind, and as I have recorded it above. She did not tell me this till several weeks after my arrival; but she was still upstairs at the time, and obliged to divide her days between her bed and a lounge. During those endless intervening weeks, she told me, she had thought the whole matter over: and though the events of the mysterious thirty-six hours were still vivid to her, they had already lost something of their haunting terror, and she had finally decided not to reopen the question with Agnes, or to touch on it in speaking to the other servants. Dr. Selgrove's illness had been not only serious but prolonged. He had not yet returned, and it was reported that as soon as he was well enough he would go on a West Indian cruise, and not resume his practice at Norrington till the spring. Dr. Selgrove, as my cousin was perfectly aware, was the only person who could prove that thirty-six hours had elapsed between his visit and that of his successor; and the latter, a shy young man, burdened by the heavy additional practice suddenly thrown on his shoulders, told me (when I risked a little private talk with him) that in the haste of Dr. Selgrove's departure the only instructions he had given about Mrs. Clayburn were summed up in the brief memorandum: "Broken ankle. Have X-rayed."

Knowing my cousin's authoritative character, I was surprised at her decision not to speak to the servants of what had happened; but on think-ing it over I concluded she was right. They were all exactly as they had been before that unexplained episode: efficient, devoted, respectful and respectable. She was dependent on them and felt at home with them, and she evidently preferred to put the whole matter out of her mind, as far as she could. She was absolutely certain that something strange had happened in her house, and I was more than ever convinced that she had received a shock which the accident of a broken ankle was not sufficient to account for; but in the end I agreed that nothing was to be gained by cross-questioning the servants or the new doctor.

I was at Whitegates off and on that winter and during the following summer, and when I went home to New York for good early in October I left my cousin in her old health and spirits. Dr. Selgrove had been ordered to Switzerland for the summer, and this further postponement of his return to his practice seemed to have put the happenings of the strange weekend out of her mind. Her life was going on as peacefully and normally as usual, and I left her without anxiety, and indeed without a thought of the mystery, which was now nearly a year old.

I was living then in a small flat in New York by myself, and I had hardly settled into it when, very late one evening—on the last day of

October—I heard my bell ring. As it was my maid's evening out, and I was alone, I went to the door myself, and on the threshold, to my amazement, I saw Sara Clayburn. She was wrapped in a fur cloak, with a hat drawn down over her forehead, and a face so pale and haggard that I saw something dreadful must have happened to her. "Sara," I gasped, not knowing what I was saying, "where in the world have you come from at this hour?"

"From Whitegates. I missed the last train and came by car." She came in and sat down on the bench near the door. I saw that she could hardly stand, and sat down beside her, putting my arm about her. "For heaven's sake, tell me what's happened."

She looked at me without seeming to see me. "I telephoned to Nixon's and hired a car. It took me five hours and a quarter to get here." She looked about her. "Can you take me in for the night? I've left my luggage downstairs."

"For as many nights as you like. But you look so ill—"

She shook her head. "No; I'm not ill. I'm only frightened—deathly frightened," she repeated in a whisper.

Her voice was so strange, and the hands I was pressing between mine were so cold, that I drew her to her feet and led her straight to my little guest room. My flat was in an old-fashioned building, not many stories high, and I was on more human terms with the staff than is possible in one of the modern Babels. I telephoned down to have my cousin's bags brought up, and meanwhile I filled a hot water bottle, warmed the bed, and got her into it as quickly as I could. I had never seen her as unquestioning and submissive, and that alarmed me even more than her pallor. She was not the woman to let herself be undressed and put to bed like a baby; but she submitted without a word, as though aware that she had reached the end of her tether.

"It's good to be here," she said in a quieter tone, as I tucked her up and smoothed the pillows. "Don't leave me yet, will you—not just yet."

"I'm not going to leave you for more than a minute—just to get you a cup of tea," I reassured her; and she lay still. I left the door open, so that she could hear me stirring about in the little pantry across the passage, and when I brought her the tea she swallowed it gratefully, and a little color came into her face. I sat with her in silence for some time; but at last she began: "You see it's exactly a year—"

I should have preferred to have her put off till the next morning whatever she had to tell me; but I saw from her burning eyes that she was determined to rid her mind of what was burdening it, and that until she had done so it would be useless to proffer the sleeping draft I had ready.

"A year since what?" I asked stupidly, not yet associating her precipitate arrival with the mysterious occurrences of the previous year at Whitegates.

She looked at me in surprise. "A year since I met that woman. Don't you remember—the strange woman who was coming up the drive the afternoon when I broke my ankle? I didn't think of it at the time, but it was on All Souls' eve that I met her."

Yes, I said, I remembered that it was.

"Well—and this is All Souls' eve, isn't it? I'm not as good as you are on Church dates, but I thought it was."

"Yes. This is All Souls' eve."

"I thought so. . . . Well, this afternoon I went out for my usual walk. I'd been writing letters, and paying bills, and didn't start till late; not till it was nearly dusk. But it was a lovely clear evening. And as I got near the gate, there was the woman coming in—the same woman . . . going toward the house. . . ."

I pressed my cousin's hand, which was hot and feverish now. "If it was dusk, could you be perfectly sure it was the same woman?" I asked.

"Oh, perfectly sure, the evening was so clear. I knew her and she knew me; and I could see she was angry at meeting me. I stopped her and asked: 'Where are you going?' just as I had asked her last year. And she said, in the same queer half-foreign voice: 'Only to see one of the girls,' as she had before. Then I felt angry all of a sudden, and I said: 'You shan't set foot in my house again. Do you hear me? I order you to leave.' And she laughed; yes, she laughed—very low, but distinctly. By that time it had got quite dark, as if a sudden storm was sweeping up over the sky, so that though she was so near me I could hardly see her. We were standing by the clump of hemlocks at the turn of the drive, and as I went up to her, furious at her impertinence, she passed behind the hemlocks, and when I followed her she wasn't there. . . . No; I swear to you she wasn't there. . . . And in the darkness I hurried back to the house, afraid that she would slip by me and get there first. And the queer thing was that as I reached the door the black cloud vanished, and there was the transparent twilight again. In the house everything seemed as usual, and the servants were busy about their work; but I couldn't get it out of my head that the woman, under the shadow of that cloud, had somehow got there before me." She paused for breath, and began again. "In the hall I stopped at the telephone and rang up Nixon, and told him to send me a car at once to go to New York, with a man he knew to drive me. And Nixon came with the car himself. . . ."

Her head sank back on the pillow and she looked at me like a fright-ened child. "It was good of Nixon," she said.

"Yes; it was very good of him. But when they saw you leaving—the servants, I mean. . . ."

"Yes. Well, when I got upstairs to my room I rang for Agnes. She came, looking just as cool and quiet as usual. And when I told her I was starting for New York in half an hour—I said it was on account of a sudden busi-ness call—well, then her presence of mind failed her for the first time. She forgot to look surprised, she even forgot to make an objection—and you know what an objector Agnes is. And as I watched her I could see a little secret spark of relief in her eyes, though she was so on her guard. And she just said: 'Very well, madam,' and asked me what I wanted to take with me. Just as if I were in the habit of dashing off to New York after dark on an autumn night to meet a business engagement! No, she made a mistake not to show any surprise—and not even to ask me why I didn't take my own car. And her losing her head in that way frightened me more than anything else. For I saw she was so thankful I was going that she hardly dared speak, for fear she should betray herself, or I should change my mind."

After that Mrs. Clayburn lay a long while silent, breathing less unrest-fully; and at last she closed her eyes, as though she felt more at ease now that she had spoken, and wanted to sleep. As I got up quietly to leave her, she turned her head a little and murmured: "I shall never go back to Whitegates again." Then she shut her eyes and I saw that she was falling asleep.

I have set down above, I hope without omitting anything essential, the record of my cousin's strange experience as she told it to me. Of what hap-pened at Whitegates that is all I can personally vouch for. The rest—and of course there is a rest—is pure conjecture; and I give it only as such.

My cousin's maid, Agnes, was from the isle of Skye, and the Hebrides, as everyone knows, are full of the supernatural—whether in the shape of ghostly presences, or the almost ghostlier sense of unseen watchers peopling the long nights of those stormy solitudes. My cousin, at any rate, always regarded Agnes as the—perhaps unconscious, at any rate irresponsible—channel through which communications from the other side of the veil reached the submissive household at Whitegates. Though Agnes had been with Mrs. Clayburn for a long time without any peculiar incident reveal-ing this affinity with the unknown forces, the power to communicate with them may all the while have been latent in the woman, only awaiting a kindred touch; and that touch may have been given by the unknown vis-itor whom my cousin, two years in succession, had met coming up the drive at Whitegates on the eve of All Souls'. Certainly the date bears out my hypothesis; for I suppose that, even in this unimaginative age, a few people still remember that All Souls' eve is the night when the dead can walk—and when, by the same token, other spirits, piteous or malevolent, are also freed from the restrictions which secure the earth to the living on the other days of the year.

If the recurrence of this date is more than a coincidence—and for my part I think it is—then I take it that the strange woman who twice came up the drive at Whitegates on All Souls' eve was either a "fetch," or else, more probably, and more alarmingly, a living woman inhabited by a witch. The history of witchcraft, as is well known, abounds in such cases, and such a messenger might well have been delegated by the powers who rule in these matters to summon Agnes and her fellow servants to a midnight "Coven" in some neighboring solitude. To learn what happens at Covens, and the reason of the irresistible fascination they exercise over the timorous and superstitious, one need only address oneself to the immense body of literature dealing with these mysterious rites. Anyone who has once felt the faintest curiosity to assist at a Coven apparently soon finds the curiosity increase to desire, the desire to an uncontrollable longing, which, when the opportunity presents itself, breaks down all inhibitions; for those who have once taken part in a Coven will move heaven and earth to take part again.

Such is my—conjectural—explanation of the strange happenings at Whitegates. My cousin always said she could not believe that incidents which might fit into the desolate landscape of the Hebrides could occur in the cheerful and populous Connecticut Valley; but if she did not believe, she at least feared—such moral paradoxes are not uncommon—and though she insisted that there must be some natural explanation of the mystery, she never returned to investigate it.

"No, no," she said with a little shiver, whenever I touched on the subject of her going back to Whitegates, "I don't want ever to risk seeing that woman again. . . ." And she never went back.

ॐ

# THE CARRION CROW

*Thomas Lovell Beddoes*

Old Adam, the carrion crow,
   The old crow of Cairo;
He sat in the shower, and let it flow
   Under his tail and over his crest;
     And through every feather
     Leaked the wet weather;
   And the bough swung under his nest;
For his beak it was heavy with marrow.
     Is that the wind dying? Oh no;
     It's only two devils, that blow
     Through a murderer's bones, to and fro,
     In the ghosts' moonshine.

Ho! Eve, my grey carrion wife,
   When we have supped on kings' marrow,
Where shall we drink and make merry our life?
   Our nest it is queen Cleopatra's skull,
     'Tis cloven and cracked,
     And battered and hacked,
   But with tears of blue eyes it is full:
Let us drink then, my raven of Cairo.
     Is that the wind dying? O no;
     It's only two devils, that blow
     Through a murderer's bones, to and fro,
     In the ghosts' moonshine.

ॐ

## BADGER

### *John Clare*

When midnight comes a host of dogs and men
Go out and track the badger to his den,
And put a sack within the hole, and lie
Till the old grunting badger passes by.
He comes and hears—they let the strongest loose.
The old fox hears the noise and drops the goose.
The poacher shoots and hurries from the cry,
And the old hare half wounded buzzes by.
They get a forked stick to bear him down
And clap the dogs and take him to the town,
And bait him all the day with many dogs,
And laugh and shout and fright the scampering hogs.
He runs along and bites at all he meets:
They shout and hollo down the noisy streets.

He turns about to face the loud uproar
And drives the rebels to their very door.
The frequent stone is hurled where'er they go;
When badgers fight, then every one's a foe.
The dogs are clapt and urged to join the fray;
The badger turns and drives them all away.
Though scarcely half as big, demure and small,
He fights with dogs for hours and beats them all.
The heavy mastiff, savage in the fray,
Lies down and licks his feet and turns away.
The bulldog knows his match and waxes cold,
The badger grins and never leaves his hold.
He drives the crowd and follows at their heels
And bites them through—the drunkard swears and reels.

The frighted women take the boys away,
The blackguard laughs and hurries on the fray.
He tries to reach the woods, an awkward race,
But sticks and cudgels quickly stop the chase.

He turns agen and drives the noisy crowd
And beats the many dogs in noises loud.
He drives away and beats them every one,
And then they loose them all and set them on.
He falls as dead and kicked by boys and men,
Then starts and grins and drives the crowd agen;
Till kicked and torn and beaten out he lies
And leaves his hold and cackles, groans, and dies.

❧

# THE EAGLE

## Alfred, Lord Tennyson

He clasps the crag with crooked hands;
Close to the sun in lonely lands,
Ringed with the azure world, he stands.

The wrinkled sea beneath him crawls;
He watches from his mountain walls,
And like a thunderbolt he falls.

❧

# MARIANA

## Alfred, Lord Tennyson

With blackest moss the flower-plots
    Were thickly crusted, one and all:
The rusted nails fell from the knots
    That held the pear to the gable-wall.
The broken sheds look'd sad and strange:
    Unlifted was the clinking latch:
    Weeded and worn the ancient thatch

Upon the lonely moated grange.
      She only said, "My life is dreary,
         He cometh not," she said:
      She said, "I am aweary, aweary,
         I would that I were dead!"

Her tears fell with the dews at even;
      Her tears fell ere the dews were dried;
She could not look on the sweet heaven,
      Either at morn or eventide.
After the flitting of the bats,
      When thickest dark did trance the sky,
      She drew her casement-curtain by,
And glanced athwart the glooming flats.
      She only said, "The night is dreary,
         He cometh not," she said;
      She said, "I am aweary, aweary,
         I would that I were dead!"

Upon the middle of the night,
      Waking she heard the night-fowl crow:
The cock sung out an hour ere light:
      From the dark fen the oxen's low
Came to her: without hope of change,
      In sleep she seem'd to walk forlorn,
      Till cold winds woke the gray-eyed morn
About the lonely moated grange.
      She only said, "The day is dreary,
         He cometh not," she said;
      She said, "I am aweary, aweary,
         I would that I were dead!"

About a stone-cast from the wall
      A sluice with blacken'd waters slept,
And o'er it many, round and small,
      The cluster'd marish-mosses crept.
Hard by a poplar shook alway,
      All silver-green with gnarled bark:
      For leagues no other tree did mark
The level waste, the rounding gray.

She only said, "My life is dreary,
      He cometh not," she said;
She said, "I am aweary, aweary,
      I would that I were dead!"


And ever when the moon was low,
      And the shrill winds were up and away,
In the white curtain, to and fro,
      She saw the gusty shadow sway.
But when the moon was very low,
      And wild winds bound within their cell,
      The shadow of the poplar fell
Upon her bed, across her brow.
      She only said, "The night is dreary,
            He cometh not," she said;
      She said, "I am aweary, aweary,
            I would that I were dead!"


All day within the dreamy house,
      The doors upon their hinges creak'd;
The blue fly sung in the pane; the mouse
      Behind the mouldering wainscot shriek'd,
Or from the crevice peer'd about.
      Old faces glimmer'd thro' the doors,
      Old footsteps trod the upper floors,
Old voices call'd her from without.
      She only said, "My life is dreary,
            He cometh not," she said;
      She said, "I am aweary, aweary,
            I would that I were dead!"


The sparrow's chirrup on the roof,
      The slow clock ticking, and the sound
Which to the wooing wind aloof
      The poplar made, did all confound
Her sense; but most she loathed the hour
      When the thick-moted sunbeam lay
      Athwart the chambers, and the day
Was sloping toward his western bower.
      Then said she, "I am very dreary,

He will not come," she said;
She wept, "I am aweary, aweary,
O God, that I were dead!"

~

## THE KRAKEN

*Alfred, Lord Tennyson*

Below the thunders of the upper deep;
Far far beneath in the abysmal sea,
His ancient, dreamless, uninvited sleep
The Kraken sleepeth: faintest sunlights flee
About his shadowy sides: above him swell
Huge sponges of millennial growth and height;
And far away into the sickly light,
From many a wondrous grot and secret cell
Unnumber'd and enormous polypi
Winnow with giant fins the slumbering green.
There he hath lain for ages and will lie
Battening upon huge seaworms in his sleep,
Until the latter fire shall heat the deep;
Then once by men and angels to be seen,
In roaring he shall rise and on the surface die.

~

# THE REMARKABLE CASE
# OF DAVIDSON'S EYES

## H. G. Wells

## I

The transitory mental aberration of Sidney Davidson, remarkable enough
in itself, is still more remarkable if Wade's explanation is to be credited. It
sets one dreaming of the oddest possibilities of inter-communication in the
future, of spending an intercalary five minutes on the other side of the
world, or being watched in our most secret operations by unsuspected eyes.
It happened that I was the immediate witness of Davidson's seizure, and so
it falls naturally to me to put the story upon paper.

When I say that I was the immediate witness of his seizure, I mean that
I was the first on the scene. The thing happened at the Harlow Technical
College, just beyond the Highgate Archway. He was alone in the larger laboratory when the thing happened. I was in a smaller room, where the balances are, writing up some notes. The thunderstorm had completely upset
my work, of course. It was just after one of the louder peals that I thought
I heard some glass smash in the other room. I stopped writing, and turned
round to listen. For a moment I heard nothing; the hail was playing the
devil's tattoo on the corrugated zinc of the roof. Then came another sound,
a smash—no doubt of it this time. Something heavy had been knocked off
the bench. I jumped up at once and went and opened the door leading into
the big laboratory.

I was surprised to hear a queer sort of laugh, and saw Davidson standing unsteadily in the middle of the room, with a dazzled look on his face.
My first impression was that he was drunk. He did not notice me. He was
clawing out at something invisible a yard in front of his face. He put out his
hand, slowly, rather hesitatingly, and then clutched nothing. "What's come
to it?" he said. He held up his hands to his face, fingers spread out. "Great
Scott!" he said. The thing happened three or four years ago, when every one
swore by that personage. Then he began raising his feet clumsily, as though
he had expected to find them glued to the floor.

"Davidson!" cried I. "What's the matter with you?" He turned round
in my direction and looked about for me. He looked over me and at me
and on either side of me, without the slightest sign of seeing me. "Waves,"

he said; "and a remarkably neat schooner. I'd swear that was Bellow's voice. *Hallo!*" He shouted suddenly at the top of his voice.

I thought he was up to some foolery. Then I saw littered about his feet the shattered remains of the best of our electrometers. "What's up, man?" said I. "You've smashed the electrometer!"

"Bellows again!" said he. "Friends left, if my hands are gone. Something about electrometers. Which way *are* you, Bellows?" He suddenly came staggering towards me. "The damned stuff cuts like butter," he said. He walked straight into the bench and recoiled. "None so buttery that!" he said, and stood swaying.

I felt scared. "Davidson," said I, "what on earth's come over you?"

He looked round him in every direction. "I could swear that was Bellows. Why don't you show yourself like a man, Bellows?"

It occurred to me that he must be suddenly struck blind. I walked round the table and laid my hand upon his arm. I never saw a man more startled in my life. He jumped away from me, and came round into an attitude of self-defence, his face fairly distorted with terror. "Good God!" he cried. "What was that?"

"It's I—Bellows. Confound it, Davidson!"

He jumped when I answered him and stared—how can I express it?—right through me. He began talking, not to me, but to himself. "Here in broad daylight on a clear beach. Not a place to hide in." He looked about him wildly. "Here! I'm *off*." He suddenly turned and ran headlong into the big electro-magnet— so violently that, as we found afterwards, he bruised his shoulder and jawbone cruelly. At that he stepped back a pace, and cried out with almost a whimper, "What, in Heaven's name, has come over me?" He stood, blanched with terror and trembling violently, with his right arm clutching his left, where that had collided with the magnet.

By that time I was excited and fairly scared. "Davidson," said I, "don't be afraid."

He was startled at my voice, but not so excessively as before. I repeated my words in as clear and as firm a tone as I could assume. "Bellows," he said, "is that you?"

"Can't you see it's me?"

He laughed. "I can't even see it's myself. Where the devil are we?"

"Here," said I, "in the laboratory."

"The laboratory!" he answered in a puzzled tone, and put his hand to his forehead. "I *was* in the laboratory— till that flash came, but I'm hanged if I'm there now. What ship is that?"

"There's no ship," said I. "Do be sensible, old chap."

"No ship," he repeated, and seemed to forget my denial forthwith. "I suppose," said he slowly, "we're both dead. But the rummy part is I feel just as though I still had a body. Don't get used to it all at once, I suppose. The old shop was struck by lightning, I suppose. Jolly quick thing, Bellows— eh?"

"Don't talk nonsense. You're very much alive. You are in the laboratory, blundering about. You've just smashed a new electrometer. I don't envy you when Boyce arrives."

He stared away from me towards the diagrams of cryohydrates. "I must be deaf," said he. "They've fired a gun, for there goes the puff of smoke, and I never heard a sound."

I put my hand on his arm again, and this time he was less alarmed. "We seem to have a sort of invisible bodies," said he. "By Jove! there's a boat coming round the headland. It's very much like the old life after all—in a different climate."

I shook his arm. "Davidson," I cried, "wake up!"

## II

It was just then that Boyce came in. So soon as he spoke Davidson exclaimed: "Old Boyce! Dead too! What a lark!" I hastened to explain that Davidson was in a kind of somnambulistic trance. Boyce was interested at once. We both did all we could to rouse the fellow out of his extraordinary state. He answered our questions, and asked us some of his own, but his attention seemed distracted by his hallucination about a beach and a ship. He kept interpolating observations concerning some boat and the davits, and sails filling with the wind. It made one feel queer, in the dusky laboratory, to hear him saying such things.

He was blind and helpless. We had to walk him down the passage, one at each elbow, to Boyce's private room, and while Boyce talked to him there, and humoured him about this ship idea, I went along the corridor and asked old Wade to come and look at him. The voice of our Dean sobered him a little, but not very much. He asked where his hands were, and why he had to walk about up to his waist in the ground. Wade thought over him a long time—you know how he knits his brows—and then made him feel the couch, guiding his hands to it. "That's a couch," said Wade. "The couch in the private room of Professor Boyce. Horse-hair stuffing."

Davidson felt about, and puzzled over it, and answered presently that he could feel it all right, but he couldn't see it.

"What *do* you see?" asked Wade. Davidson said he could see nothing but a lot of sand and broken-up shells. Wade gave him some other things to feel, telling him what they were, and watching him keenly.

"The ship is almost hull down," said Davidson presently, *apropos* of nothing.

"Never mind the ship," said Wade. "Listen to me, Davidson. Do you know what hallucination means?"

"Rather," said Davidson.

"Well, everything you see is hallucinatory."

"Bishop Berkeley," said Davidson.

"Don't mistake me," said Wade. "You are alive and in this room of Boyce's. But something has happened to your eyes. You cannot see; you can feel and hear, but not see. Do you follow me?"

"It seems to me that I see too much." Davidson rubbed his knuckles into his eyes. "Well?" he said.

"That's all. Don't let it perplex you. Bellows here and I will take you home in a cab."

"Wait a bit." Davidson thought. "Help me to sit down," said he presently; "and now—I'm sorry to trouble you—but will you tell me all that over again?"

Wade repeated it very patiently. Davidson shut his eyes, and pressed his hands upon his forehead. "Yes," said he. "It's quite right. Now my eyes are shut I know you're right. That's you, Bellows, sitting by me on the couch. I'm in England again. And we're in the dark."

Then he opened his eyes. "And there," said he, "is the sun just rising, and the yards of the ship, and a tumbled sea, and a couple of birds flying. I never saw anything so real. And I'm sitting up to my neck in a bank of sand."

He bent forward and covered his face with his hands. Then he opened his eyes again. "Dark sea and sunrise! And yet I'm sitting on a sofa in old Boyce's room! . . . God help me!"


III


That was the beginning. For three weeks this strange affection of Davidson's eyes continued unabated. It was far worse than being blind. He was absolutely helpless, and had to be fed like a newly-hatched bird, and led about and undressed. If he attempted to move, he fell over things or struck himself against walls or doors. After a day or so he got used to hearing our voices without seeing us, and willingly admitted he was at home, and that Wade was right in what he told him. My sister, to whom he was engaged, insisted on coming to see him, and would sit for hours every day while he talked about this beach of his. Holding her hand seemed to comfort him immensely. He explained that when we left the College and drove home—he lived in Hampstead village—it appeared to him as if we drove right through a sandhill—it was perfectly black until he emerged again—and through rocks and trees and solid obstacles, and when he was taken to his own room it made him giddy and almost frantic with the fear of falling, because going upstairs seemed to lift him thirty or forty feet above the rocks of his imaginary island. He kept saying he should smash all the eggs. The end was that he had to be taken down into his father's consulting room and laid upon a couch that stood there.

He described the island as being a bleak kind of place on the whole, with very little vegetation, except some peaty stuff, and a lot of bare rock. There were multitudes of penguins, and they made the rocks white and disagreeable to see. The sea was often rough, and once there was a thunderstorm, and he lay and shouted at the silent flashes. Once or twice seals pulled up on the beach, but only on the first two or three days. He said it was very funny the way in which the penguins used to waddle right through him, and how he seemed to lie among them without disturbing them.

I remember one odd thing, and that was when he wanted very badly to smoke. We put a pipe in his hands—he almost poked his eye out with it—and lit it. But he couldn't taste anything. I've since found it's the same with me—I don't know if it's the usual case—that I cannot enjoy tobacco at all unless I can see the smoke.

But the queerest part of his vision came when Wade sent him out in a bath-chair to get fresh air. The Davidsons hired a chair, and got that deaf and obstinate dependant of theirs, Widgery, to attend to it. Widgery's ideas of healthy expeditions were peculiar. My sister, who had been to the Dogs' Home, met them in Camden Town, towards King's Cross, Widgery trotting along complacently, and Davidson, evidently most distressed, trying in his feeble, blind way to attract Widgery's attention.

He positively wept when my sister spoke to him. "Oh, get me out of this horrible darkness!" he said, feeling for her hand. "I must get out of it, or I shall die." He was quite incapable of explaining what was the matter, but my sister decided he must go home, and presently, as they went uphill towards Hampstead, the horror seemed to drop from him. He said it was good to see the stars again, though it was then about noon and a blazing day.

"It seemed," he told me afterwards, "as if I was being carried irresistibly towards the water. I was not very much alarmed at first. Of course it was night there—a lovely night."

"Of course?" I asked, for that struck me as odd.

"Of course," said he. "It's always night there when it is day here. . . . Well, we went right into the water, which was calm and shining under the moonlight—just a broad swell that seemed to grow broader and flatter as I came down into it. The surface glistened just like a skin—it might have been empty space underneath for all I could tell to the contrary. Very slowly, for I rode slanting into it, the water crept up to my eyes. Then I went under and the skin seemed to break and heal again about my eyes. The moon gave a jump up in the sky and grew green and dim, and fish, faintly glowing, came darting round me—and things that seemed made of luminous glass; and I passed through a tangle of seaweeds that shone with an oily lustre. And so I drove down into the sea, and the stars went out one by one, and the moon grew greener and darker, and the seaweed became a luminous purple-red. It was all very faint and mysterious, and everything seemed to quiver. And all the while I could hear the wheels of the bath-chair creaking, and the footsteps of people going by, and a man in the distance selling the special *Pall Mall.*

"I kept sinking down deeper and deeper into the water. It became inky black about me, not a ray from above came down into that darkness, and the phosphorescent things grew brighter and brighter. The snaky branches of the deeper weeds flickered like the flames of spirit-lamps; but, after a time, there were no more weeds. The fishes came staring and gaping towards me, and into me and through me, I never imagined such fishes before. They had lines of fire along the sides of them as though they had been outlined with a luminous pencil. And there was a ghastly thing swimming backwards with a lot of twining arms. And then I saw, coming very slowly towards me through the gloom, a hazy mass of light that resolved itself as it drew nearer into multitudes of fishes, struggling and darting round something that drifted. I drove on straight towards it, and presently I saw in the midst of the tumult, and by the light of the fish, a bit of splintered spar looming over me, and a dark hull tilting over, and some glowing phosphorescent forms that were shaken and writhed as the fish bit at them. Then it was I began to try to attract Widgery's attention. A horror came upon me. Ugh! I should have driven right into those half-eaten—things. If your sister had not come! They had great holes in them, Bellows, and . . . Never mind. But it was ghastly!"

## IV

For three weeks Davidson remained in this singular state, seeing what at the time we imagined was an altogether phantasmal world, and stone blind to the world around him. Then, one Tuesday, when I called I met old Davidson in the passage. "He can see his thumb!" the old gentleman said, in a perfect transport. He was struggling into his overcoat. "He can see his thumb, Bellows!" he said, with the tears in his eyes. "The lad will be all right yet."

I rushed in to Davidson. He was holding up a little book before his face, and looking at it and laughing in a weak kind of way.

"It's amazing," said he. "There's a kind of patch come there." He pointed with his finger. "I'm on the rocks as usual, and the penguins are staggering and flapping about as usual, and there's been a whale showing every now and then, but it's got too dark now to make him out. But put something *there,* and I see it—I do see it. It's very dim and broken in places, but I see it all the same, like a faint spectre of itself. I found it out this morning while they were dressing me. It's like a hole in this infernal phantom world. Just put your hand by mine. No—not there. Ah! Yes! I see it. The base of your thumb and a bit of cuff! It looks like the ghost of a bit of your hand sticking out of the darkling sky. Just by it there's a group of stars like a cross coming out."

From that time Davidson began to mend. His account of the change, like his account of the vision, was oddly convincing. Over patches of his field of vision, the phantom world grew fainter, grew transparent, as it were, and through these translucent gaps he began to see dimly the real world about him. The patches grew in size and number, ran together and spread until only here and there were blind spots left upon his eyes. He was able to get up and steer himself about, feed himself once more, read, smoke, and behave like an ordinary citizen again. At first it was very confusing for him to have these two pictures overlapping each other like the changing views of a lantern, but in a little while he began to distinguish the real from the illusory.

At first he was unfeignedly glad, and seemed only too anxious to complete his cure by taking exercise and tonics. But as that odd island of his began to fade away from him, he became queerly interested in it. He wanted particularly to go down in the deep sea again, and would spend half his time wandering about the low-lying parts of London, trying to find the water-logged wreck he had seen drifting. The glare of real daylight

very soon impressed him so vividly as to blot out everything of his shadowy
world, but of a night-time, in a darkened room, he could still see the
white-splashed rocks of the island, and the clumsy penguins staggering to
and fro. But even these grew fainter and fainter, and, at last, soon after he
married my sister, he saw them for the last time.


V


And now to tell of the queerest thing of all. About two years after his cure
I dined with the Davidsons, and after dinner a man named Atkins called
in. He is a lieutenant in the Royal Navy, and a pleasant, talkative man. He
was on friendly terms with my brother-in-law, and was soon on friendly
terms with me. It came out that he was engaged to Davidson's cousin, and
incidentally he took out a kind of pocket photograph case to show us a new
rendering of his *fiancée*. "And, by-the-by," said he, "here's the old *Fulmar*."

Davidson looked at it casually. Then suddenly his face lit up. "Good
heavens!" said he. "I could almost swear—"

"What?" said Atkins.

"That I had seen that ship before."

"Don't see how you can have. She hasn't been out of the South Seas
for six years, and before then—"

"But," began Davidson, and then, "Yes—that's the ship I dreamt of;
I'm sure that's the ship I dreamt of. She was standing off an island that
swarmed with penguins, and she fired a gun."

"Good Lord!" said Atkins, who had now heard the particulars of the
seizure. "How the deuce could you dream that?"

And then, bit by bit, it came out that on the very day Davidson was
seized, H.M.S. *Fulmar* had actually been off a little rock to the south of
Antipodes Island. A boat had landed overnight to get penguins' eggs, had
been delayed, and a thunderstorm drifting up, the boat's crew had waited
until the morning before rejoining the ship. Atkins had been one of them,
and he corroborated word for word, the descriptions Davidson had given
of the island and the boat. There is not the slightest doubt in any of our
minds that Davidson has really seen the place. In some unaccountable way,
while he moved hither and thither in London, his sight moved hither and
thither in a manner that corresponded, about this distant island. *How* is
absolutely a mystery.

That completes the remarkable story of Davidson's eyes. It's perhaps
the best authenticated case in existence of real vision at a distance. Expla-

nation there is none forthcoming, except what Professor Wade has thrown out. But his explanation invokes the Fourth Dimension, and a dissertation on theoretical kinds of space. To talk of there being 'a kink in space' seems mere nonsense to me; it may be because I am no mathematician. When I said that nothing would alter the fact that the place is eight thousand miles away, he answered that two points might be a yard away on a sheet of paper, and yet be brought together by bending the paper round. The reader may grasp his argument, but I certainly do not. His idea seems to be that Davidson, stooping between the poles of the big electro-magnet, had some extraordinary twist given to his retinal elements through the sudden change in the field of force due to the lightning.

He thinks, as a consequence of this, that it may be possible to live visually in one part of the world, while one lives bodily in another. He has even made some experiments in support of his views; but, so far, he had simply succeeded in blinding a few dogs. I believe that is the net result of his work, though I have not seen him for some weeks. Latterly I have been so busy with my work in connection with the Saint Pancras installation that I have had little opportunity of calling to see him. But the whole of his theory seems fantastic to me. The facts concerning Davidson stand on an altogether different footing, and I can testify personally to the accuracy of every detail I have given.

∾

# THE NOSE

## Nikolai Gogol

## I

An extraordinarily strange incident took place in Petersburg on the 25th of March. The barber, Ivan Yakovlevitch, who lives in the Voznesensky Prospect (his surname is lost, and nothing more appears even on his signboard, where a gentleman is depicted with his cheeks covered with soapsuds, together with an inscription "also lets blood")—the barber Ivan Yakovlevitch woke up rather early and was aware of a smell of hot bread. Raising himself in bed he saw his spouse, a rather portly lady who was very fond of drinking coffee, engaged in taking out of the oven some freshly-baked loaves.

"I won't have coffee to-day, Praskovya Osipovna," said Ivan Yakovlevitch; "instead I should like some hot bread with onion." (The fact is that Ivan Yakovlevitch would have liked both, but he knew that it was utterly impossible to ask for two things at once, for Praskovya Osipovna greatly disliked such caprices.)

"Let the fool have bread, so much the better for me," thought his spouse to herself; "there will be an extra cup of coffee left," and she flung one loaf on the table.

For the sake of propriety Ivan Yakovlevitch put a tail coat over his shirt, and, sitting down to the table, sprinkled with salt and prepared two onions, took a knife in his hand and, making a solemn face, set to work to cut the bread. After dividing the loaf into two halves he looked into the middle of it—and to his amazement saw there something that looked white. Ivan Yakovlevitch scooped at it carefully with his knife and felt it with his finger: "It's solid," he said to himself. "Whatever can it be?"

He thrust in his finger and drew it out—it was a nose! . . . Ivan Yakovlevitch's hand dropped with astonishment, he rubbed his eyes and felt it: it actually was a nose, and, what's more, it looked to him somehow familiar. A look of horror came into Ivan Yakovlevitch's face. But that horror was nothing to the indignation with which his wife was overcome.

"Where have you cut that nose off, you brute?" she cried wrathfully. "You scoundrel, you drunkard, I'll go to the police myself to tell of you! You ruffian! Here I have heard from three men that when you are shaving them you pull at their noses till you almost tug them off."

But Ivan Yakovlevitch was more dead than alive: he perceived that the nose was no other than that of Kovalyov, the collegiate assessor, whom he shaved every Wednesday and every Sunday.

"Stay, Praskovya Osipovna! I'll wrap it up in a rag and put it in a corner. Let it stay there for a bit; I'll return it later on."

"I won't hear of it! As though I would allow a stray nose to lie about in my room. You dried-up biscuit! To be sure, he can do nothing but sharpen his razors on the strop, but soon he won't be fit to do his duties at all, the gad-about, the good-for-nothing! As though I were going to answer to the police for you. . . . Oh, you sloven, you stupid blockhead. Away with it, away with it! Take it where you like! Don't let me set eyes on it again!"

Ivan Yakovlevitch stood as though utterly crushed. He thought and thought, and did not know what to think. "The devil only knows how it happened," he said at last, scratching behind his ear. "Did I come home drunk last night or not? I can't say for certain now. But from all signs and tokens it must be a thing quite unheard of, for bread is a thing that is baked, while a nose is something quite different. I can't make head or tail of it." Ivan Yakovlevitch sank into silence. The thought that the police might make a search there for the nose and throw the blame of it on him reduced him to complete prostration. Already the red collar, beautifully embroidered with silver, the sabre, hovered before his eyes, and he trembled all over. At last he got his breeches and his boots, pulled on these wretched objects, and, accompanied by the stern upbraidings of Praskovya Osipovna, wrapped the nose in a rag and went out into the street.

He wanted to thrust it out of sight somewhere, under a gate, or somehow accidentally to drop it and then turn off into a side street, but as ill-luck would have it he kept coming upon some one he knew, who would at once begin by asking: "Where are you going?" or "Whom are you going to shave so early?" so that Ivan Yakovlevitch could never find a good moment. Another time he really did drop it, but a sentry pointed to it with his halberd from a long way off, saying as he did so: "Pick it up, you have dropped something!" and Ivan Yakovlevitch was obliged to pick up the nose and put it in his pocket. He was overcome by despair, especially as the number of people in the street was continually increasing as the shops and stalls began to open.

He made up his mind to go to St. Isaac's Bridge in the hope of being able to fling it into the Neva. . . . But I am rather in fault for not having hitherto said anything about Ivan Yakovlevitch, a worthy man in many respects.

Ivan Yakovlevitch, like every self-respecting Russian workman, was a terrible drunkard, and though every day he shaved other people's chins, his own went for ever unshaven. Ivan Yakovlevitch's tail coat (he never wore any other shape) was piebald, that is, it was black dappled all over with brown and yellow and grey; the collar was shiny, and instead of three buttons there was only one hanging on a thread. Ivan Yakovlevitch was a great cynic, and when Kovalyov the collegiate assessor said to him while he was being shaved: "Your hands always stink, Ivan Yakovlevitch," the latter would reply with the question: "What should make them stink?" "I can't tell, my good man, but they do stink," the collegiate assessor would say, and, taking a pinch of snuff, Ivan Yakovlevitch lathered him for it on his cheeks and under his nose and behind his ears and under his beard—in fact wherever he chose.

The worthy citizen found himself by now on St. Isaac's Bridge. First of all he looked about him, then bent over the parapet as though to look under the bridge to see whether there were a great number of fish racing by, and stealthily flung in the rag with the nose. He felt as though with it a heavy weight had rolled off his back. Ivan Yakovlevitch actually grinned. Instead of going to shave the chins of government clerks, he repaired to an establishment bearing the inscription "Tea and refreshments" and asked for a glass of punch, when he suddenly observed at the end of the bridge a police inspector of respectable appearance with full whiskers, with a three-cornered hat and a sword. He turned cold, and meanwhile the inspector beckoned to him and said: "Come this way, my good man."

Ivan Yakovlevitch, knowing the etiquette, took off his hat some way off and, as he approached, said: "I wish your honour good health."

"No, no, old fellow, I am not 'your honour': tell me what you were about, standing on the bridge?"

"Upon my soul, sir, I was on my way to shave my customers, and I was only looking to see whether the current was running fast."

"That's a lie, that's a lie! You won't get off with that. Kindly answer!"

"I am ready to shave you, gracious sir, two or even three times a week with no conditions whatever," answered Ivan Yakovlevitch.

"No, my friend, that is nonsense; I have three barbers to shave me and they think it a great honour, too. But be so kind as to tell me what you were doing there?"

Ivan Yakovlevitch turned pale . . . but the incident is completely veiled in obscurity, and absolutely nothing is known of what happened next.


## II


Kovalyov the collegiate assessor woke up early next morning and made the sound "brrrr . . ." with the lips as he always did when he woke up, though he could not himself have explained the reason for his doing so. Kovalyov stretched and asked for a little looking-glass that was standing on the table. He wanted to look at a pimple which had come out upon his nose on the previous evening, but to his great astonishment there was a completely flat space where his nose should have been. Kovalyov in a fright asked for some water and a towel to rub his eyes: there really was no nose. He began feeling with his hand, and pinched himself to see whether he was still asleep: it appeared that he was not asleep. The collegiate assessor jumped out of bed, he shook himself—there was still no nose. . . . He ordered his clothes to be given him at once and flew off straight to the head police-master.

But meanwhile we must say a word about Kovalyov in order that the reader may have some idea of what kind of collegiate assessor he was. Collegiate assessors who receive that title through learned diplomas cannot be compared with those who are created collegiate assessors in the Caucasus. They are two quite different species. The learned collegiate assessors . . . But Russia is such a wonderful country that, if you say a word about one collegiate assessor, all the collegiate assessors from Riga to Kamchatka would certainly take it to themselves; and it is the same, of course, with all grades and titles. Kovalyov was a collegiate assessor from the Caucasus. He had only been of that rank for the last two years, and so could not forget it for a moment; and to give himself greater weight and dignity he did not call himself simply collegiate assessor but always spoke of himself as a major. "Listen, my dear," he would usually say when he met in the street a woman selling shirt-fronts, "you go to my house; I live in Sadovoy Street; just ask, does Major Kovalyov live here? Any one will show you." If he met some prepossessing little baggage he would give her besides a secret instruction, adding: "You ask for Major Kovalyov's flat, my love." For this reason we will for the future speak of him as the major.

Major Kovalyov was in the habit of walking every day up and down the Nevsky Prospect. The collar of his shirt-front was always extremely clean and well starched. His whiskers were such as one may see nowadays on provincial and district surveyors, on architects and army doctors, also on those employed on special commissions and in general on all such men as have full ruddy cheeks and are very good hands at a game of boston: these whiskers start from the middle of the cheek and go straight up to the nose. Major Kovalyov used to wear a number of cornelian seals, some with crests on them and others on which were carved Wednesday, Thursday, Monday, and so on. Major Kovalyov had come to Petersburg on business, that is, to look for a post befitting his rank: if he were successful, the post of a vice-governor, and failing that the situation of an executive clerk in some prominent department. Major Kovalyov was not averse to matrimony, but only on condition he could find a bride with a fortune of two hundred thousand. And so the reader may judge for himself what was the major's position when he saw, instead of a nice-looking, well-proportioned nose, an extremely stupid level space.

As ill-luck would have it, not a cab was to be seen in the street, and he was obliged to walk, wrapping himself in his cloak and hiding his face in his handkerchief, as though his nose were bleeding. "But perhaps it was my imagination: it's impossible I could have been so silly as to lose my nose," he thought, and went into a confectioner's on purpose to look at himself in the looking-glass. Fortunately there was no one in the shop: some boys were sweeping the floor and putting all the chairs straight; others with sleepy faces were bringing in hot turnovers on trays: yesterday's papers covered with coffee stains were lying about on the tables and chairs. "Well, thank God, there is nobody here," he thought; "now I can look." He went timidly up to the mirror and looked. "What the devil's the meaning of it? how nasty!" he commented, spitting. "If only there had been something instead of a nose, but there is nothing! . . ."

Biting his lips, he went out of the confectioner's with annoyance, and resolved, contrary to his usual practice, not to look or smile at any one. All at once he stood as though rooted to the spot before the door of a house. Something inexplicable took place before his eyes: a carriage was stopping at the entrance; the carriage door flew open; a gentleman in uniform, bending down, sprang out and ran up the steps. What was the horror and at the same time amazement of Kovalyov when he recognised that this was his own nose! At this extraordinary spectacle it seemed to him that everything was heaving before his eyes; he felt that he could scarcely stand; but he made up his mind, come what may, to await the gentleman's return to the carriage, and he stood trembling all over as though in fever. Two minutes later the nose actually did come out. He was in a gold-laced uniform with a big stand-up collar; he had on chamois-leather breeches, at his side was a sword. From his plumed hat it might be gathered that he was of the rank of a civil councillor. Everything showed that he was going somewhere to pay a visit. He looked to both sides, called to the coachman to open the carriage door, got in and drove off.

Poor Kovalyov almost went out of his mind; he did not know what to think of such a strange occurrence. How was it possible for a nose—which had only yesterday been on his face and could neither drive nor walk—to be in uniform! He ran after the carriage, which luckily did not go far, but stopped before the entrance to the bazaar.

He hurried in that direction, made his way through a row of old beggar women with their faces tied up and two chinks in place of their eyes at whom he used to laugh so merrily. There were not many people about. Kovalyov felt so upset that he could not make up his mind what to do, and looked for the gentleman up and down the street; at last he saw him standing before a shop. The nose was hiding his face completely in a high stand-up collar and was surveying some goods in the shop window with the utmost attention.

"How am I to approach him?" thought Kovalyov. "One can see by everything—from his uniform, from his hat—that he is a civil councillor. The devil only knows how to do it!"

He began by coughing at his side; but the nose never changed his position for a minute.

"Sir," said Kovalyov, inwardly forcing himself to speak confidently. "Sir. . . ."

"What do you want?" answered the nose, turning round.

"It seems . . . strange to me, sir. . . . You ought to know your proper place, and all at once I find you, where? . . . You will admit . . ."

"Excuse me, I cannot understand what you are talking about. . . . Explain."

"How am I to explain to him?" thought Kovalyov, and plucking up his courage he began: "Of course I . . . I am a major, by the way. For me to go about without a nose you must admit is improper. An old woman selling peeled oranges on Voskresensky Bridge may sit there without a nose; but having prospects of obtaining . . . and being besides acquainted with a great many ladies in the families of Tchehtarev the civil councillor and others . . . You can judge for yourself . . . I don't know, sir (at this point Major Kovalyov shrugged his shoulders) . . . excuse me . . . if you look at the matter in accordance with the principles of duty and honour . . . you can understand of yourself . . ."

"I don't understand a word," said the nose. "Explain it more satisfactorily."

"Sir," said Kovalyov, with a sense of his own dignity, "I don't know how to understand your words. The matter appears to me perfectly obvious . . . either you wish . . . Why, you are my own nose!"

The nose looked at the major and his eyebrows slightly quivered.

"You are mistaken, sir, I am an independent individual. Moreover, there can be no sort of close relations between us. I see, sir, from the buttons of your uniform, you must be serving in a different department." Saying this the nose turned away.

Kovalyov was utterly confused, not knowing what to do or even what to think. Meanwhile they heard the agreeable rustle of a lady's dress: an elderly lady was approaching, all decked out in lace, and with her a slim lady in a white dress which looked very charming on her slender figure, in a straw-coloured hat as light as a pastry puff. Behind them stood, opening his snuff-box, a tall footman with big whiskers and quite a dozen collars.

Kovalyov came nearer, pulled out the cambric collar of his shirt-front, arranged the seals on his gold watch-chain, and, smiling from side to side, turned his attention to the ethereal lady who, like a spring flower, faintly swayed forward and put her white hand with its half-transparent fingers to her brow. The smile on Kovalyov's face broadened when he saw under the hat her round, dazzlingly white chin and part of her cheek flushed with the hues of the first spring rose; but all at once he skipped away as though he had been scalded. He recollected that he had absolutely nothing on his face in place of a nose, and tears oozed from his eyes. He turned away to tell the gentleman in uniform straight out that he was only pretending to be a civil councillor, that he was a rogue and a scoundrel, and that he was nothing else than his own nose. . . . But the nose was no longer there; he had managed to gallop off, probably again to call on some one.

This reduced Kovalyov to despair. He went back and stood for a minute or two under the colonnade, carefully looking in all directions to see whether the nose was anywhere about. He remembered very well that there was a plume in his hat and gold lace on his uniform; but he had not noticed his greatcoat nor the colour of his carriage, nor his horses, nor even whether he had a footman behind him and if so in what livery. Moreover, such numbers of carriages were driving backwards and forwards and at such a speed that it was difficult even to distinguish them; and if he had distinguished one of them he would have had no means of stopping it. It was a lovely, sunny day. There were masses of people on the Nevsky; ladies were scattered like a perfect cataract of flowers all over the pavement from Politseysky to the Anitchkin Bridge. Here he saw coming towards him an upper-court councillor of his acquaintance whom he used to call "lieutenant-colonel," particularly if he were speaking to other people. There he saw Yaryzhkin, a head clerk in the senate, a great friend of his, who always lost points when he went eight at boston. And here was another major who had received the rank of assessor in the Caucasus, beckoning to him. . . .

"Ah, deuce take it," said Kovalyov. "Hi, cab! drive straight to the police-master's."

Kovalyov got into a cab and shouted to the driver:

"Drive like a house on fire."

"Is the police-master at home?" he cried, going into the entry.

"No," answered the porter, "he has only just gone out."

"Well, I declare!"

"Yes," added the porter, "and he has not been gone so long: if you had come but a tiny minute earlier you might have found him."

Kovalyov, still keeping the handkerchief over his face, got into the cab and shouted in a voice of despair: "Drive on."

"Where?" asked the cabman.

"Drive straight on!"

"How straight on? Here's the turning, is it to right or to left?"

This question pulled Kovalyov up and forced him to think again. In his position he ought first of all to address himself to the department of law and order, not because it had any direct connection with the police but because the intervention of the latter might be far more rapid than any help he could get in other departments. To seek satisfaction from the higher officials of the department in which the nose had announced himself as serving would have been injudicious, since from the nose's own answers he had been able to perceive that nothing was sacred to that man and that he might tell lies in this case too, just as he had lied in declaring that he had never seen him before. And so Kovalyov was on the point of telling the cabman to drive to the police station, when again the idea occurred to him that this rogue and scoundrel who had at their first meeting behaved in such a shameless way might seize the opportunity and slip out of the town—and then all his searches would be in vain, or might be prolonged, which God forbid, for a whole month. At last it seemed that Heaven itself directed him. He decided to go straight to a newspaper office and without loss of time to publish a circumstantial description of the nose, so that any one meeting it might at once present it to him or at least let him know where it was. And so, deciding upon this course, he told the cabman to drive to the newspaper office, and all the way never ceased pommelling him with his fist on the back, saying as he did so, "Quicker, you rascal; make haste, you knave!"

"Ugh, sir!" said the cabman, shaking his head and flicking with the reins at the horse, whose coat was as long as a lapdog's. At last the droshky stopped and Kovalyov ran panting into a little reception room where a grey-headed clerk in spectacles, wearing an old tailcoat, was sitting at a table and with a pen between his teeth was counting over some coppers he had before him.

"Who receives inquiries here?" cried Kovalyov. "Ah, good day!"

"I wish you good day," said the grey-headed clerk, raising his eyes for a moment and then dropping them again on the money lying in heaps on the table.

"I want to insert an advertisement. . . ."

"Allow me to ask you to wait a minute," the clerk pronounced, with one hand noting a figure on the paper and with the finger of his left hand moving two beads on the reckoning board. A flunkey with braid on his livery and a rather clean appearance, which betrayed that he had at some time served in an aristocratic family, was standing at the table with a written paper in his hand and thought fit to display his social abilities: "Would you believe it, sir, that the little cur is not worth eighty kopecks; in fact I wouldn't give eight for it, but the countess is fond of it—my goodness, she is fond of it, and here she will give a hundred roubles to any one who finds it! To speak politely, as you and I are speaking now, people's tastes are quite incompatible: when a man's a sportsman then he'll keep a setter or a poodle; he won't mind giving five hundred or a thousand so long as it is a good dog."

The worthy clerk listened to this with a significant air, and at the same time was reckoning the number of letters in the advertisement brought him. Along the sides of the room stood a number of old women, shop-boys, and house-porters who had brought advertisements. In one it was announced that a coachman of sober habits was looking for a situation; in the next a second-hand carriage brought from Paris in 1814 was offered for sale; next a maid-servant, aged nineteen, experienced in laundry work and also competent to do other work, was looking for a situation; a strong droshky with only one spring broken was for sale; a spirited, young, dappled grey horse, only seventeen years old, for sale; a new consignment of turnip and radish seed from London; a summer villa with all conveniences, stabling for two horses, and a piece of land that might well be planted with fine birches and pine trees; there was also an appeal to those wishing to purchase old boot-soles, inviting such to come for the same every day between eight o'clock in the morning and three o'clock in the afternoon. The room in which all this company was assembled was a small one and the air in it was extremely thick, but the collegiate assessor Kovalyov was incapable of noticing the stench both because he kept his handkerchief over his face and because his nose was goodness knows where.

"Dear sir, allow me to ask you . . . my case is very urgent," he said at last impatiently.

"In a minute, in a minute! . . . Two roubles, forty-three kopecks! . . . This minute! One rouble and sixty-four kopecks!" said the grey-headed gentleman, flinging the old women and house-porters the various documents they had brought. "What can I do for you?" he said at last, turning to Kovalyov.

"I want to ask . . ." said Kovalyov. "Some robbery or trickery has occurred; I cannot make it out at all. I only want you to advertise that any one who brings me the scoundrel will receive a handsome reward."

"Allow me to ask what is your surname?"

"No, why put my surname? I cannot give it you! I have a large circle of acquaintances: Madame Tchehtarev, wife of a civil councillor, Pelageya Grigoryevna Podtatchin, widow of an officer . . . they will find out. God forbid! You can simply put: 'a collegiate assessor,' or better still, 'a person of major's rank.' "

"Is the runaway your house-serf, then?"

"A house-serf indeed! that would not be so great a piece of knavery! It's my nose . . . has run away from me . . . my own nose."

"H'm, what a strange surname! And is it a very large sum this Mr. Nosov has robbed you of?"

"Nosov! . . . you are on the wrong tack. It is my nose, my own nose that has disappeared, I don't know where. The devil wanted to have a joke at my expense."

"But in what way did it disappear? There is something I can't quite understand."

"And indeed, I can't tell you how it happened; the point is that now it is driving about the town, calling itself a civil councillor. And so I beg you to announce that any one who catches him must bring him at once to me as quickly as possible. Only think, really, how can I get on without such a conspicuous part of my person. It's not like a little toe, the loss of which I could hide in my boot and no one could say whether it was there or not. I go on Thursdays to Madame Tchehtatrev's; Pelageya Grigoryevna Podtatchin, an officer's widow, and her very pretty daughter are great friends of mine; and you can judge for yourself what a fix I am in now. . . . I can't possibly show myself now. . . ."

The clerk pondered, a fact which was manifest from the way he compressed his lips.

"No, I can't put an advertisement like that in the paper," he said at last, after a long silence.

"What? Why not?"

"Well. The newspaper might lose its reputation. If every one is going to write that his nose has run away, why . . . As it is, they say we print lots of absurd things and false reports."

"But what is there absurd about this? I don't see anything absurd in it."

"You fancy there is nothing absurd in it? But last week, now, this was what happened. A government clerk came to me just as you have; he brought an advertisement, it came to two roubles seventy-three kopecks, and all the advertisement amounted to was that a poodle with a black coat had strayed. You wouldn't think that there was anything in that, would you? But it turned out to be a lampoon on some one: the poodle was the cashier of some department, I don't remember which."

"But I am not asking you to advertise about poodles but about my own nose; that is almost the same as about myself."

"No, such an advertisement I cannot insert."

"But since my nose really is lost!"

"If it is lost that is a matter for the doctor. They say there are people who can fit you with a nose of any shape you like. But I observe you must be a gentleman of merry disposition and are fond of having your joke."

"I swear as God is holy! If you like, since it has come to that, I will show you."

"I don't want to trouble you," said the clerk, taking a pinch of snuff. "However, if it is no trouble," he added, moved by curiosity, "it might be desirable to have a look."

The collegiate assessor took the handkerchief from his face. "It really is extremely strange," said the clerk, "the place is perfectly flat, like a freshly fried pancake. Yes, it's incredibly smooth."

"Will you dispute it now? You see for yourself I must advertise. I shall be particularly grateful to you and very glad this incident has given me the pleasure of your acquaintance."

The major, as may be seen, made up his mind on this occasion to resort to a little flattery.

"To print such an advertisement is, of course, not such a very great matter," said the clerk. "But I do not foresee any advantage to you from it. If you do want to, put it in the hands of some one with a skilful pen, describe it as a rare freak of nature, and publish the little article in the *Northern Bee*" (at this point he once more took a pinch of snuff) "for the benefit of youth" (at this moment he wiped his nose), "or anyway as a matter of general interest."

The collegiate assessor felt quite hopeless. He dropped his eyes and looked at the bottom of the paper where there was an announcement of an entertainment; his face was ready to break into a smile as he saw the name of a pretty actress, and his hand went to his pocket to feel whether he had a five-rouble note there, for an officer of his rank ought, in Kovalyov's opinion, to have a seat in the stalls; but the thought of his nose spoilt it all.

Even the clerk seemed touched by Kovalyov's difficult position. Desirous of relieving his distress in some way, he thought it befitting to express his sympathy in a few words: "I am really very much grieved that such an incident should have occurred to you. Wouldn't you like a pinch of snuff? it relieves headache and dissipates depression; even in intestinal trouble it is of use." Saying this the clerk offered Kovalyov his snuff-box, rather neatly opening the lid with a portrait of a lady in a hat on it.

This unpremeditated action drove Kovalyov out of all patience.

"I can't understand how you can think fit to make a joke of it," he said angrily; "don't you see that I am without just what I need for sniffing! The devil take your snuff! I can't bear the sight of it now, not merely your miserable Berezina stuff but even if you were to offer me rappee itself!" Saying this he walked out of the newspaper office, deeply mortified, and went in the direction of the local police superintendent.

Kovalyov walked in at the very moment when he was stretching and clearing his throat and saying: "Ah, I should enjoy a couple of hours' nap!" And so it might be foreseen that the collegiate assessor's visit was not very opportune. The police superintendent was a great patron of all arts and manufactures; but the paper note he preferred to everything. "That is a thing," he used to say, "there is nothing better than that thing; it does not ask for food, it takes up little space, there is always room for it in the pocket, and if you drop it, it does not break."

The police superintendent received Kovalyov rather coldly and said that after dinner was not the time to make an enquiry, that nature itself had ordained that man should rest a little after eating (the collegiate assessor could see from this that the sayings of the ancient sages were not unfamiliar to the local superintendent), and that a respectable man does not have his nose pulled off.

This was adding insult to injury. It must be said that Kovalyov was very easily offended. He could forgive anything whatever said about himself, but could never forgive insult to his rank or his calling. He was even of the opinion that any reference to officers of the higher ranks might be allowed to pass in stage plays, but that no attack ought to be made on those of a lower grade. The reception given him by the local superintendent so disconcerted him that he tossed his head and said with an air of dignity and a slight gesticulation of surprise: "I must observe that after observations so insulting on your part I can add nothing more . . ." and went out.

He went home hardly conscious of the ground under his feet. But now it was dusk. His lodgings seemed to him melancholy or rather utterly disgusting after all these unsuccessful efforts. Going into his entry he saw his valet, Ivan, lying on his dirty leather sofa; he was spitting on the ceiling and rather successfully aiming at the same spot. The nonchalance of his servant enraged him; he hit him on the forehead with his hat, saying: "You pig, you are always doing something stupid."

Ivan leapt up and rushed headlong to help him off with his cloak.

Going into his room, weary and dejected, the major threw himself into an easy chair, and at last, after several sighs, said:—

"My God, my God! Why has this misfortune befallen me? If I had lost an arm or a leg—anyway it would have been better; but without a nose a man is goodness knows what: neither fish nor fowl nor human being, good for nothing but to fling out of window! And if only it had been cut off in battle or in a duel, or if I had been the cause of it myself, but, as it is, it is lost for no cause or reason, it is lost for nothing, absolutely nothing! But no, it cannot be," he added after a moment's thought; "it's incredible that a nose should be lost. It must be a dream or an illusion. Perhaps by some mistake I drank instead of water the vodka I use to rub my chin after shaving. Ivan, the fool, did not remove it and very likely I took it." To convince himself that he was not drunk, the major pinched himself so painfully that he shrieked. The pain completely convinced him that he was living and acting in real life. He slowly approached the looking-glass and at first screwed up his eyes with the idea that maybe his nose would appear in its proper place; but at the same minute sprang back, saying: "What a caricature."

It really was incomprehensible; if a button had been lost or a silver spoon or a watch or anything similar—but to have lost this, and in one's own flat too! . . . Thinking over all the circumstances, Major Kovalyov reached the supposition that what might be nearest the truth was that the person responsible for this could be no other than Madame Podtatchin, who wanted him to marry her daughter. He himself liked flirting with her, but avoided a definite engagement. When the mother had informed him directly that she wished for the marriage, he had slyly put her off with his compliments, saying that he was still young, that he must serve for five years so as to be exactly forty-two. And that Madame Podtatchin had therefore made up her mind, probably out of revenge, to ruin him, and had hired for the purpose some peasant witches, because it was impossible to suppose that the nose had been cut off in any way; no one had come into his room; the barber Ivan Yakovlevitch had shaved him on Wednesday, and all Wednesday and even all Thursday his nose had been all right—that he remembered and was quite certain about; besides, he would have felt pain, and there could have been no doubt that the wound could not have healed so soon and been as flat as a pancake. He formed various plans in his mind: either to summon Madame Podtatchin formally before the court or to go to her himself and tax her with it. These reflections were interrupted by a light which gleamed through all the cracks of the door and let him know that a candle had been lighted in the entry by Ivan. Soon Ivan himself appeared, holding it before him and lighting up the whole room. Kovalyov's first movement was to snatch up his handkerchief and cover the place where yesterday his nose had been, that his really stupid servant might not gape at the sight of anything so peculiar in his master.

Ivan had hardly time to retreat to his lair when there was the sound of an unfamiliar voice in the entry, pronouncing the words: "Does the collegiate assessor Kovalyov live here?"

"Come in, Major Kovalyov is here," said Kovalyov, jumping up hurriedly and opening the door.

There walked in a police officer of handsome appearance, with whiskers neither too fair nor too dark, and rather fat cheeks, the very one who at the beginning of our story was standing at the end of St. Isaac's Bridge.

"You have been pleased to lose your nose, sir?"

"That is so."

"It is now found."

"What are you saying?" cried Major Kovalyov. He could not speak for joy. He gazed open-eyed at the police officer standing before him, on whose full lips and cheeks the flickering light of the candle was brightly reflected. "How?"

"By a strange chance: he was caught almost on the road. He had already taken his seat in the diligence and was intending to go to Riga, and had already taken a passport in the name of a government clerk. And the strange thing is that I myself took him for a gentleman at first, but fortunately I had my spectacles with me and I soon saw that it was a nose. You know I am short-sighted. And if you stand before me I only see that you have a face, but I don't notice your nose or your beard or anything. My mother-in-law, that is my wife's mother, doesn't see anything either."

Kovalyov was beside himself with joy. "Where? Where? I'll run at once."

"Don't disturb yourself. Knowing that you were in need of it I brought it along with me. And the strange thing is that the man who has had the most to do with the affair is a rascal of a barber in the Voznesensky Street, who is now in custody. I have long suspected him of drunkenness and thieving, and only the day before yesterday he carried off a strip of buttons from one shop. Your nose is exactly as it was." With this the police officer put his hand in his pocket and drew out the nose just as it was.

"That's it!" Kovalyov cried. "That's certainly it. You must have a cup of tea with me this evening."

"I should look upon it as a great pleasure, but I can't possibly manage it: I have to go from here to the penitentiary. . . . How the prices of all provisions are going up! . . . At home I have my mother-in-law, that is my wife's mother, and my children, the eldest particularly gives signs of great promise, he is a very intelligent child; but we have absolutely no means for his education. . . ."

For some time after the policeman's departure the collegiate assessor remained in a state of bewilderment, and it was only a few minutes later that he was capable of feeling and understanding again: he was reduced to such stupefaction by this unexpected good fortune. He took the recovered nose carefully in his two hands, holding them together like a cup, and once more examined it attentively.

"Yes, that's it, it's certainly it," said Major Kovalyov. "There's the pimple that came out on the left side yesterday." The major almost laughed aloud with joy.

But nothing in this world is of long duration, and so his joy was not so great the next moment; and the moment after, it was still less, and in the end he passed imperceptibly into his ordinary frame of mind, just as a circle on the water caused by a falling stone gradually passes away into the unbroken smoothness of the surface. Kovalyov began to think, and reflected that the business was not finished yet; the nose was found, but it had to be put on, fixed in its proper place.

"And what if it won't stick?" Asking himself this question, the major turned pale.

With a feeling of irrepressible terror he rushed to the table and moved the looking-glass forward that he might not put the nose on crooked. His hands trembled. Cautiously and circumspectly he replaced it in its former position. Oh horror, the nose would not stick on! . . . He put it to his lips, slightly warmed it with his breath, and again applied it to the flat space between his two cheeks; but nothing would make the nose keep on.

"Come, come, stick on, you fool!" he said to it; but the nose seemed made of wood and fell on the table with a strange sound as though it were a cork. The major's face worked convulsively.

"Is it possible that it won't grow on again?" But, however often he applied it to the proper place, the attempt was as unsuccessful as before.

He called Ivan and sent him for a doctor who tenanted the best flat on the first storey of the same house. The doctor was a handsome man, he had magnificent pitch-black whiskers, a fresh and healthy wife, ate fresh apples in the morning and kept his mouth extraordinarily clean, rinsing it out for nearly three-quarters of an hour every morning and cleaning his teeth with five different sorts of brushes. The doctor appeared immediately. Asking how long ago the trouble had occurred, he took Major Kovalyov by the chin and with his thumb gave him a flip on the spot where the nose had been, making the major jerk back his head so abruptly that he knocked the back of it against the wall. The doctor said that that did not matter, and, advising him to move a little away from the wall, he told him to bend his head round first to the right, and feeling the place where the nose had been, said, "H'm!" Then he told him to turn his head round to the left side and again said "H'm!" And in conclusion he gave him again a flip with his thumb, so that Major Kovalyov threw up his head like a horse when his teeth are being looked at. After making this experiment the doctor shook his head and said:—

"No, it's impossible. You had better stay as you are, for it may be made much worse. Of course, it might be stuck on; I could stick it on for you at once, if you like; but I assure you it would be worse for you."

"That's a nice thing to say! How can I stay without a nose?" said Kovalyov. "Things can't possibly be worse than now. It's simply beyond everything. Where can I show myself with such a caricature of a face? I have a good circle of acquaintances. To-day, for instance, I ought to be at two evening parties. I know a great many people; Madame Tchehtarev, the wife of a civil councillor, Madame Podtatchin, an officer's widow . . . though after the way she has behaved, I'll have nothing more to do with her except through the police. Do me a favour," Kovalyov went on in a supplicating voice; "is there no means of sticking it on? Even if it were not neatly done, so long as it would keep on; I could even hold it on with my hand at critical moments. I wouldn't dance in any case for fear of a rash movement upsetting it. As for remuneration for your services, you may be assured that as far as my means allow . . ."

"Believe me," said the doctor, in a voice neither loud nor low but persuasive and magnetic, "that I never work from mercenary motives; that is opposed to my principles and my science. It is true that I accept a fee for my visits, but that is simply to avoid wounding my patients by refusing it. Of course I could replace your nose; but I assure you on my honour, since you do not believe my word, that it will be much worse for you. You had better wait for the action of nature itself. Wash it frequently with cold water, and I assure you that even without a nose you will be just as healthy as with one. And I advise you to put the nose in a bottle, in spirits or, better still, put two tablespoonfuls of sour vodka on it and heated vinegar—and then you might get quite a sum of money for it. I'd even take it myself, if you don't ask too much for it."

"No, no, I wouldn't sell it for anything," Major Kovalyov cried in despair; "I'd rather it were lost than that!"

"Excuse me!" said the doctor, bowing himself out. "I was trying to be of use to you. . . . Well, there is nothing for it! Anyway, you see that I have done my best." Saying this the doctor walked out of the room with a majestic air. Kovalyov did not notice his face, and, almost lost to consciousness, saw nothing but the cuffs of his clean and snow-white shirt peeping out from the sleeves of his black tail-coat.

Next day he decided, before lodging a complaint with the police, to write to Madame Podtatchin to see whether she would consent to return him what was needful without a struggle. The letter was as follows:—

Dear Madam,
    Alexandra Grigoryevna.
    I cannot understand this strange conduct on your part. You may rest assured that you will gain nothing by what you have done, and you will not get a step nearer forcing me to marry your daughter. Believe me, that business in regard to my nose is no secret, no more than it is that you and no other are the person chiefly responsible. The sudden parting of the same from its natural position, its flight and masquerading, at one time in the form of a government clerk and finally in its own shape, is nothing else than the consequence of the sorceries practised by you or by those who are versed in the same honourable arts as you are. For my part I consider it my duty to warn you, if the above-mentioned nose is not in its proper place to-day, I shall be obliged to resort to the assistance and protection of the law.
    I have, however, with complete respect to you, the honour to be
Your respectful servant,<br>Platon Kovalyov.

Dear Sir,
    Platon Kuzmitch!
    Your letter greatly astonished me. I must frankly confess that I did not expect it, especially in regard to your unjust reproaches. I assure you I have never received the government clerk of whom you speak in my house, neither in masquerade nor in his own attire. It is true that Filipp Ivanovitch Potantchikov has been to see me, and although, indeed, he is asking me for my daughter's hand and is a well conducted, sober man of great learning, I have never encouraged his hopes. You make some reference to your nose also. If you wish me to understand by that that you imagine that I meant to make a long nose at you, that is, to give you a formal refusal, I am surprised that you should speak of such a thing when, as you know perfectly well,

I was quite of the opposite way of thinking, and if you are courting my daughter with a view to lawful matrimony I am ready to satisfy you immediately, seeing that has always been the object of my keenest desires, in the hope of which I remain always ready to be of service to you.

Alexandra Podtatchin.

"No," said Kovalyov to himself after reading the letter, "she really is not to blame. It's impossible. The letter is written as it could not be written by any one guilty of a crime." The collegiate assessor was an expert on this subject, as he had been sent several times to the Caucasus to conduct investigations. "In what way, by what fate, has this happened? Only the devil could make it out!" he said at last, letting his hands fall to his sides.

Meanwhile the rumours of this strange occurrence were spreading all over the town, and of course not without especial additions. Just at that time the minds of all were particularly interested in the marvellous: experiments in the influence of magnetism had been attracting public attention only recently. Moreover, the story of the dancing chair in Konyushenny Street was still fresh, and so there is nothing to be surprised at in the fact that people were soon beginning to say that the nose of a collegiate assessor called Kovalyov was walking along the Nevsky Prospect at exactly three in the afternoon. Numbers of inquisitive people flocked there every day. Somebody said that the nose was in Yunker's shop—and near Yunker's there was such a crowd and such a crush that the police were actually obliged to intervene. One speculator, a man of dignified appearance with whiskers, who used to sell all sorts of cakes and tarts at the doors of the theatres, made purposely some very strong wooden benches, which he offered to the curious to stand on, for eighty kopecks each. One very worthy colonel left home earlier on account of it, and with a great deal of trouble made his way through the crowd; but to his great indignation, instead of the nose, he saw in the shop windows the usual woollen vest and a lithograph depicting a girl pulling up her stocking while a foppish young man, with a waist-coat with revers and a small beard, peeps at her from behind a tree; a picture which had been hanging in the same place for more than ten years. As he walked away he said with vexation: "How can people be led astray by such stupid and incredible stories!" Then rumour would have it that it was not on the Nevsky Prospect but in the Tavritchesky Park that Major Kovalyov's nose took its walks abroad; that it had been there for ever so long; that, even when Hozrev-Mirza used to live there, he was greatly surprised at this strange freak of nature. Several students from the Academy of Surgery made their way to the park. One worthy lady of high rank wrote a letter to the superintendent of the park asking him to show her children this rare phenomenon with, if possible, an explanation that should be edifying and instructive for the young.

All the gentlemen who invariably attend social gatherings and like to amuse the ladies were extremely thankful for all these events, for their stock of anecdotes was completely exhausted. A small group of worthy and well-intentioned persons were greatly displeased. One gentleman said with indignation that he could not understand how in the present enlightened age people could spread abroad these absurd inventions, and that he was surprised that the government took no notice of it. This gentleman, as may be seen, belonged to the number of those who would like the government to meddle in everything, even in their daily quarrels with their wives. After this . . . but here again the whole adventure is lost in fog, and what happened afterwards is absolutely unknown.

## III

What is utterly nonsensical happens in the world. Sometimes there is not the slightest resemblance to truth about it: all at once that very nose which had been driving about the place in the form of a civil councillor, and had made such a stir in the town, turned up again as though nothing had happened, in its proper place, that is, precisely between the two cheeks of Major Kovalyov. This took place on the seventh of April. Waking up and casually glancing into the looking-glass, he sees—his nose! puts up his hands, actually his nose! "Aha!" said Kovalyov, and in his joy he almost danced a jig barefoot about his room; but the entrance of Ivan checked him. He ordered the latter to bring him water at once, and as he washed he glanced once more into the looking-glass—the nose! As he wiped himself with the towel he glanced again into the looking-glass—the nose!

"Look, Ivan, I fancy I have a pimple on my nose," he said, while he thought: "How dreadful if Ivan says 'No, indeed, sir, there's no pimple and, indeed, there is no nose either!' "

But Ivan said: "There is nothing, there is no pimple: your nose is quite clear!"

"Good, dash it all!" the major said to himself, and he snapped his fingers.

At that moment Ivan Yakovlevitch the barber peeped in at the door, but as timidly as a cat who has just been beaten for stealing the bacon.

"Tell me first: are your hands clean?" Kovalyov shouted to him while he was still some way off.

"Yes."

"You are lying!"

"Upon my word, they are clean, sir."

"Well, mind now."

Kovalyov sat down. Ivan Yakovlevitch covered him up with a towel, and in one instant with the aid of his brushes had smothered the whole of his beard and part of his cheek in cream, like that which is served at merchants' name-day parties.

"My eye!" Ivan Yakovlevitch said to himself, glancing at the nose and then turning his customer's head on the other side and looking at it sideways. "There it is, sure enough. What can it mean?" He went on pondering, and for a long while he gazed at the nose. At last, lightly, with a cautiousness which may well be imagined, he raised two fingers to take it by the tip. Such was Ivan Yakovlevitch's system.

"Now, now, now, mind!" cried Kovalyov. Ivan Yakovlevitch let his hands drop, and was flustered and confused as he had never been confused before. At last he began circumspectly tickling him with the razor under his beard, and, although it was difficult and not at all handy for him to shave without holding on to the olfactory portion of the face, yet he did at last somehow, pressing his rough thumb into his cheek and lower jaw, overcome all difficulties, and finish shaving him.

When it was all over, Kovalyov at once made haste to dress, took a cab, and drove to the confectioner's shop. Before he was inside the door he shouted: "Waiter, a cup of chocolate!" and at the same instant peeped at himself in the looking-glass. The nose was there. He turned round gaily and, with a satirical air, slightly screwing up his eyes, looked at two military men, one of whom had a nose hardly bigger than a waistcoat button. After that he set off for the office of the department, in which he was urging his claims to a post as vice-governor or, failing that, the post of an executive clerk. After crossing the waiting-room he glanced at the mirror; the nose was there. Then he drove to see another collegiate assessor or major, who was much given to making fun of people, and to whom he often said in reply to various sharp observations: "There you are, I know you, you are as sharp as a pin!" On the way he thought: "If even the major does not split with laughter when he sees me, then it is a sure sign that everything is in its place." But the sarcastic collegiate assessor said nothing. "Good, good, dash it all!" Kovalyov thought to himself. On the way he met Madame Podtatchin with her daughter; he was profuse in his bows to them and was greeted with exclamations of delight—so there could be nothing amiss with him, he thought. He conversed with them for a long time and, taking out his snuff-box, purposely put a pinch to each nostril while he said to himself: "So much for you, you petticoats, you hens! but I am not going to marry your daughter all the same. Just simply *par amour*—I daresay!"

And from that time forth Major Kovalyov promenaded about, as though nothing had happened, on the Nevsky Prospect, and at the theatres and everywhere. And the nose, too, as though nothing had happened, sat on his face without even a sign of coming off at the sides. And after this Major Kovalyov was always seen in a good humour, smiling, resolutely pursuing all the pretty ladies, and even on one occasion stopping before a shop in the Gostiny Dvor and buying the ribbon of some order, I cannot say with what object, since he was not himself a cavalier of any order.

So this is the strange event that occurred in the Northern capital of our spacious empire! Only now, on thinking it all over, we perceive that there is a great deal that is improbably in it. Apart from the fact that it certainly is strange for a nose supernaturally to leave its place and to appear in various places in the guise of a civil councillor—how was it that Kovalyov did not grasp that he could not advertise about his nose in a newspaper office? I do not mean to say that I should think it too expensive to advertise: that is nonsense, and I am by no means a mercenary person: but is unseemly, awkward, not nice! And again: how did the nose come into the loaf, and how about Ivan Yakovlevitch himself? . . . no, that I cannot understand, I am absolutely unable to understand it! But what is stranger, what is more uncomprehensible than anything is that authors can choose such subjects. I confess that is quite beyond my grasp, it really is . . . No, no! I cannot understand it at all. In the first place, it is absolutely without profit to the fatherland; in the second place . . . but in the second place, too, there is no profit. I really do not know what to say of it. . . .

And yet, with all that, though of course one may admit the first point, the second and the third . . . may even . . . but there, are there not inconsequences everywhere?—and yet, when you think it over, there really is something in it. Whatever any one may say, such things do happen—not often, but they do happen.

*Translated by Constance Garnett*

# THE SONG OF TRIUMPHANT LOVE

*Ivan Turgenev*

This is what I read in an old Italian manuscript:—

## I

About the middle of the sixteenth century there were living in Ferrara (it was at that time flourishing under the sceptre of its magnificent arch-dukes, the patrons of the arts and poetry) two young men, named Fabio and Muzzio. They were of the same age, and of near kinship, and were scarcely ever apart; the warmest affection had united them from early childhood . . . the similarity of their positions strengthened the bond. Both belonged to old families; both were rich, independent, and without family ties; tastes and inclinations were alike in both. Muzzio was devoted to music, Fabio to painting. They were looked upon with pride by the whole of Ferrara, as ornaments of the court, society, and town. In appearance, however, they were not alike, thought both were distinguished by a grace-ful, youthful beauty. Fabio was taller, fair of face and flaxen of hair, and he had blue eyes. Muzzio, on the other hand, had a swarthy face and black hair, and in his dark brown eyes there was not the merry light, nor on his lips the genial smile of Fabio; his thick eyebrows overhung narrow eyelids, while Fabio's golden eyebrows formed delicate half-circles on his pure, smooth brow. In conversation, too, Muzzio was less animated. For all that, the two friends were both alike looked on with favour by ladies, as well they might be, being models of chivalrous courtliness and generosity.

At the same time there was living in Ferrara a girl named Valeria. She was considered one of the greatest beauties in the town, though it was very seldom possible to see her, as she led a retired life, and never went out except to church, and on great holidays for a walk. She lived with her mother, a widow of noble family, though of small fortune, who had no other children. In every one whom Valeria met she inspired a sensation of involuntary admiration, and an equally involuntary tenderness and respect, so modest was her mien, so little, it seemed, was she aware of all the power of her own charms. Some, it is true, found her a little pale; her eyes, almost always downcast, expressed a certain shyness, even timidity; her lips rarely smiled,

and then only faintly; her voice scarcely any one had heard. But the rumour
went that it was most beautiful, and that, shut up in her own room, in the
early morning when everything still slumbered in the town, she loved to
sing old songs to the sound of the lute, on which she used to play herself. In
spite of her pallor, Valeria was blooming with health; and even old people,
as they gazed on her, could not but think, "Oh, how happy the youth for
whom that pure maiden bud, still enfolded in its petals, will one day open
into full flower!"

## II

Fabio and Muzzio saw Valeria for the first time at a magnificent public fes-
tival, celebrated at the command of the Archduke of Ferrara, Ercol, son of
the celebrated Lucrezia Borgia, in honour of some illustrious grandees who
had come from Paris on the invitation of the Archduchess, daughter of the
French king Louis XII. Valeria was sitting beside her mother on an elegant
tribune, built after a design of Palladio, in the principal square of Ferrara,
for the most honourable ladies in the town. Both Fabio and Muzzio fell passionately in love with her on that day; and, as they never had any secrets
from each other, each of them soon knew what was passing in his friend's
heart. They agreed together that both should try to get to know Valeria; and
if she should deign to choose one of them, the other should submit without
a murmur to her decision. A few weeks later, thanks to the excellent
renown they deservedly enjoyed, they succeeded in penetrating into the
widow's house, difficult though it was to obtain an entry to it; she permitted them to visit her. From that time forward they were able almost every
day to see Valeria and to converse with her; and every day the passion kindled in the hearts of both young men grew stronger and stronger. Valeria,
however, showed no preference for either of them, though their society was
obviously agreeable to her. With Muzzio, she occupied herself with music;
but she talked more with Fabio, with him she was less timid. At last, they
resolved to learn once for all their fate, and sent a letter to Valeria, in which
they begged her to be open with them, and to say to which she would be
ready to give her hand. Valeria showed this letter to her mother, and
declared that she was willing to remain unmarried, but if her mother
considered it time for her to enter upon matrimony, then she would marry
whichever one her mother's choice should fix upon. The excellent widow
shed a few tears at the thought of parting from her beloved child; there was,
however, no good ground for refusing the suitors, she considered both of

them equally worthy of her daughter's hand. But, as she secretly preferred Fabio, and suspected that Valeria liked him the better, she fixed upon him. The next day Fabio heard of his happy fate, while all that was left for Muzzio was to keep his word, and submit.

And this he did; but to be the witness of the triumph of his friend and rival was more than he could do. He promptly sold the greater part of his property, and collecting some thousands of ducats, he set off on a far journey to the East. As he said farewell to Fabio, he told him that he should not return till he felt that the last traces of passion had vanished from his heart. It was painful to Fabio to part from the friend of his childhood and youth. . . . but the joyous anticipation of approaching bliss soon swallowed up all other sensations, and he gave himself up wholly to the transports of successful love.

Shortly after, he celebrated his nuptials with Valeria, and only then learnt the full worth of the treasure it had been his fortune to obtain. He had a charming villa, shut in by a shady garden, a short distance from Ferrara; he moved thither with his wife and her mother. Then a time of happiness began for them. Married life brought out in a new and enchanting light all the perfections of Valeria. Fabio became an artist of distinction—no longer a mere amateur, but a real master. Valeria's mother rejoiced, and thanked God as she looked upon the happy pair. Four years flew by unperceived, like a delicious dream. One thing only was wanting to the young couple, one lack they mourned over as a sorrow: they had no children . . . but they had not given up all hope of them. At the end of the fourth year they were overtaken by a great, this time a real sorrow; Valeria's mother died after an illness of a few days.

Many tears were shed by Valeria; for a long time she could not accustom herself to her loss. But another year went by; life again asserted its rights and flowed along its old channel. And behold, one fine summer evening, unexpected by every one, Muzzio returned to Ferrara.

## III

During the whole space of five years that had elapsed since his departure no one had heard anything of him; all talk about him had died away, as though he had vanished from the face of the earth. When Fabio met his friend in one of the streets of Ferrara he almost cried out aloud, first in alarm and then in delight, and he at once invited him to his villa. There happened to be in his garden there a spacious pavilion, apart from the house; he proposed to his friend that he should establish himself in this pavilion. Muzzio readily agreed and moved thither the same day together with his servant, a dumb Malay—dumb but not deaf, and indeed, to judge by the alertness of his expression, a very intelligent man. . . . His tongue had been cut out. Muzzio brought with him dozens of boxes, filled with treasures of all sorts collected by him in the course of his prolonged travels. Valeria was delighted at Muzzio's return; and he greeted her with cheerful friendliness, but composure; it could be seen in every action that he had kept the promise given to Fabio. During the day he completely arranged everything in order in his pavilion; aided by his Malay, he unpacked the curiosities he had brought; rugs, silken stuffs, velvet and brocaded garments, weapons, goblets, dishes and bowls, decorated with enamel, things made of gold and silver, and inlaid with pearl and turquoise, carved boxes of jasper and ivory, cut bottles, spices, incense, skins of wild beasts, and feathers of unknown birds, and a number of other things, the very use of which seemed mysterious and incomprehensible. Among all these precious things there was a rich pearl necklace, bestowed upon Muzzio by the king of Persia for some great and secret service; he asked permission of Valeria to put this necklace with his own hand about her neck; she was struck by its great weight and a sort of strange heat in it . . . it seemed to burn to her skin. In the evening after dinner as they sat on the terrace of the villa in the shade of the oleanders and laurels, Muzzio began to relate his adventures. He told of the distant lands he had seen, of cloud-topped mountains and deserts, rivers like seas; he told of immense buildings and temples, of trees a thousand years old, of birds and flowers of the colours of the rainbow: he named the cities and the peoples he had visited . . . their very names seemed like a fairly tale. The whole East was familiar to Muzzio; he had traversed Persia, Arabia, where the horses are nobler and more beautiful than any other living creatures; he had penetrated into the very heart of India, where the race of men grow like stately trees; he had reached the boundaries of China and Thibet, where the living god, called the Grand Llama, dwells on earth in the guise of a silent man with narrow eyes. Marvellous were his tales. Both Fabio and Valeria listened to him as if enchanted. Muzzio's features had really changed very little; his face, swarthy from childhood, had grown darker still, burnt under the rays of a hotter sun, his eyes seemed more deepset than before—and that was all; but the expression of his face had become different: concentrated and dignified, it never showed more life when he recalled the dangers he had encountered by night in forests that resounded with the roar of tigers or by day on solitary ways where savage fanatics lay in wait for travellers, to slay them in honour of their iron goddess who demands human sacrifices. And Muzzio's voice had grown deeper and more even; his hands, his whole body had lost the freedom of gesture peculiar to the Italian race. With the aid of his servant, the obsequiously alert Malay, he showed his hosts a few of the feats he had learnt from the Indian Brahmins. Thus for instance, having first hidden himself behind a curtain, he suddenly appeared sitting in the air cross-legged, the tips of his fingers pressed lightly on a bamboo cane placed vertically, which astounded Fabio not a little and positively alarmed Valeria. . . . "Isn't he a sorcerer?" was her thought. When he proceeded, piping on a little flute, to call some tame snakes out of a covered basket, where their dark flat heads with quivering tongues appeared under a particoloured cloth, Valeria was terrified and begged Muzzio to put away these loathsome horrors as soon as possible. At supper Muzzio regaled his friends with wine of Shiraz from a round long-necked flagon; it was of extraordinary fragrance and thickness, of a golden colour with a shade of green in it, and it shone with a strange brightness as it was poured into the tiny jasper goblets. In taste it was unlike European wines: it was very sweet and spicy, and, drunk slowly in small draughts, produced a sensation of pleasant drowsiness in all the limbs. Muzzio made both Fabio and Valeria drink a goblet of it, and he drank one himself. Bending over her goblet he murmured something, moving his fingers as he did so. Valeria noticed this; but as in all Muzzio's doings, in his whole behaviour, there was something strange and out of the common, she only thought, "Can he have adopted some new faith in India, or is that the custom there?" Then after a short silence she asked him: "Had he persevered with music during his travels?" Muzzio, in reply, bade the Malay bring his Indian violin. It was like those of to-day, but instead of four strings it had only three, the upper part of it was covered with a bluish snake-skin, and the slender bow of reed was in the form of a half-moon, and on its extreme end glittered a pointed diamond.

Muzzio played first some mournful airs, national songs as he told them, strange and even barbarous to an Italian ear; the sound of the metallic strings was plaintive and feeble. But when Muzzio began the last song, it suddenly gained force and rang out tunefully and powerfully; the passionate melody flowed out under the wide sweeps of the bow, flowed out, exquisitely twisting and coiling like the snake that covered the violin-top; and such fire, such triumphant bliss glowed and burned in this melody that Fabio and Valeria felt wrung to the heart and tears came into their eyes; . . . while Muzzio, his head bent, and pressed close to the violin, his cheeks pale, his eyebrows drawn together into a single straight line, seemed still more concentrated and solemn; and the diamond at the end of the bow flashed sparks of light as though it too were kindled by the fire of the divine song. When Muzzio had finished, and still keeping fast the violin between his chin and his shoulder, dropped the hand that held the bow, "What is that? What is that you have been playing to us?" cried Fabio. Valeria uttered not a word—but her whole being seemed echoing her husband's question. Muzzio laid the violin on the table—and slightly tossing back his hair, he said with a polite smile: "That—that melody . . . that song I heard once in the island of Ceylon. That song is known there among the people as the song of happy, triumphant love." "Play it again," Fabio was murmuring. "No; it can't be played again," answered Muzzio. "Besides, it is now too late. Signora Valeria ought to be at rest; and it's time for me too . . . I am weary." During the whole day Muzzio had treated Valeria with respectful simplicity, as a friend of former days, but as he went out he clasped her hand very tightly, squeezing his fingers on her palm, and looking so intently into her face that though she did not raise her eyelids, she yet felt the look on her suddenly flaming cheeks. She said nothing to Muzzio, but jerked away her hand, and when he was gone, she gazed at the door through which he had passed out. She remembered how she had been a little afraid of him even in old days . . . and now she was overcome by perplexity. Muzzio went off to his pavilion: the husband and wife went to their bedroom.

## IV

Valeria did not quickly fall asleep; there was a faint and languid fever in her blood and a slight ringing in her ears . . . from that strange wine, as she supposed, and perhaps too from Muzzio's stories, from his playing on the violin . . . towards morning she did at last fall asleep, and she had an extraordinary dream.

She dreamt that she was going into a large room with a low ceiling . . . Such a room she had never seen in her life. All the walls were covered with tiny blue tiles with gold lines on them; slender carved pillars of alabaster supported the marble ceiling; the ceiling itself and the pillars seemed half transparent . . . a pale rosy light penetrated from all sides into the room, throwing a mysterious and uniform light on all the objects in it; brocaded cushions lay on a narrow rug in the very middle of the floor, which was smooth as a mirror. In the corners almost unseen were smoking lofty censers, of the shape of monstrous beasts; there was no window anywhere; a door hung with a velvet curtain stood dark and silent in a recess in the wall. And suddenly this curtain slowly glided, moved aside . . . and in came Muzzio. He bowed, opened his arms, laughed. . . . His fierce arms enfolded Valeria's waist; his parched lips burned her all over. . . . She fell backwards on the cushions.

Moaning with horror, after long struggles, Valeria awaked. Still not realising where she was and what was happening to her, she raised herself on her bed, looked round. . . . A tremor ran over her whole body. . . . Fabio was lying beside her. He was asleep; but his face in the light of the brilliant full moon looking in at the window was pale as a corpse's . . . it was sadder than a dead face. Valeria waked her husband, and directly he looked at her. "What is the matter?" he cried. "I had—I had a fearful dream," she whispered, still shuddering all over.

But at that instant from the direction of the pavilion came floating powerful sounds, and both Fabio and Valeria recognised the melody Muzzio had played to them, calling it the song of blissful triumphant love. Fabio looked in perplexity at Valeria . . . she closed her eyes, turned away, and both holding their breath, heard the song out to the end. As the last note died away, the moon passed behind a cloud, it was suddenly dark in the room. . . . Both the young people let their heads sink on their pillows without exchanging a word, and neither of them noticed when the other fell asleep.

V

The next morning Muzzio came in to breakfast; he seemed happy and greeted Valeria cheerfully. She answered him in confusion—stole a glance at him—and felt frightened at the sight of that serene happy face, those piercing and inquisitive eyes. Muzzio was beginning again to tell some story . . . but Fabio interrupted him at the first word.

"You could not sleep, I see, in your new quarters. My wife and I heard you playing last night's song."

"Yes! Did you hear it?" said Muzzio. "I played it indeed; but I had been asleep before that, and I had a wonderful dream too."

Valeria was on the alert. "What sort of dream?" asked Fabio.

"I dreamed," answered Muzzio, not taking his eyes off Valeria, "I was entering a spacious apartment with a ceiling decorated in Oriental fashion, carved columns supported the roof, the walls were covered with tiles, and though there were neither windows nor lights, the whole room was filled with a rosy light, just as though it were all built of transparent stone. In the corners, Chinese censers were smoking, on the floor lay brocaded cushions along a narrow rug. I went in through a door covered with a curtain, and at another door just opposite appeared a woman whom I once loved. And so beautiful she seemed to me, that I was all aflame with my old love. . . ."

Muzzio broke off significantly. Valeria sat motionless, and only gradually she turned white . . . and she drew her breath more slowly.

"Then," continued Muzzio, "I waked up and played that song."

"But who was that woman?" said Fabio.

"Who was she? The wife of an Indian—I met her in the town of Delhi. . . . She is not alive now—she died."

"And her husband?" asked Fabio, not knowing why he asked the question.

"Her husband, too, they say is dead. I soon lost sight of them both."

"Strange!" observed Fabio. "My wife too had an extraordinary dream last night"—Muzzio gazed intently at Valeria—"which she did not tell me," added Fabio.

But at this point Valeria got up and went out of the room. Immediately after breakfast, Muzzio too went away, explaining that he had to be in Ferrara on business, and that he would not be back before the evening.


# VI

A few weeks before Muzzio's return, Fabio had begun a portrait of his wife, depicting her with the attributes of Saint Cecilia. He had made considerable advance in his art; the renowned Luini, a pupil of Leonardo da Vinci, used to come to him at Ferrara, and while aiding him with his own counsels, pass on also the precepts of his great master. The portrait was almost completely finished; all that was left was to add a few strokes to the face, and Fabio might well be proud of his creation. After seeing Muzzio off on his way to Ferrara, he turned into his studio, where Valeria was usually waiting for him; but he did not find her there; he called her, she did not respond. Fabio was overcome by a secret uneasiness; he began looking for her. She was nowhere in the house; Fabio ran into the garden, and there in one of the more secluded walks he caught sight of Valeria. She was sitting on a seat, her head drooping on to her bosom and her hands folded upon her knees; while behind her, peeping out of the dark green of a cypress, a marble satyr, with a distorted malignant grin on his face, was putting his pouting lips to a Pan's pipe. Valeria was visibly relieved at her husband's appearance, and to his agitated questions she replied that she had a slight headache, but that it was of no consequence, and she was ready to come to sit to him. Fabio led her to the studio, posed her, and took up his brush; but to his great vexation, he could not finish the face as he would have liked to. And not because it was somewhat pale and looked exhausted . . . no; but the pure, saintly expression, which he liked so much in it, and which had given him the idea of painting Valeria as Saint Cecilia, he could not find in it that day. He flung down the brush at last, told his wife he was not in the mood for work, and that he would not prevent her from lying down, as she did not look at all well, and put the canvas with its face to the wall. Valeria agreed with him that she ought to rest, and repeating her complaints of a headache, withdrew into her bedroom.

Fabio remained in the studio. He felt a strange confused sensation incomprehensible to himself. Muzzio's stay under his roof, to which he, Fabio, had himself urgently invited him, was irksome to him. And not that he was jealous—could any one have been jealous of Valeria!—but he did not recognise his former comrade in his friend. All that was strange, unknown and new that Muzzio had brought with him from those distant lands—and which seemed to have entered into his very flesh and blood—all these magical feats, songs, strange drinks, this dumb Malay, even the spicy fragrance diffused by Muzzio's garments, his hair, his breath—all this inspired in Fabio a sensation akin to distrust, possibly even to timidity. And why did that Malay waiting at table stare with such disagreeable intentness at him, Fabio? Really any one might suppose that he understood Italian. Muzzio had said of him that in losing his tongue, this Malay had made a great sacrifice, and in return he was now possessed of great power. What sort of power? and how could he have obtained it at the price of his tongue? All this was very strange! very incomprehensible! Fabio went into his wife's room; she was lying on the bed, dressed, but was not asleep. Hearing his steps, she started, then again seemed delighted to see him just as in the garden. Fabio sat down beside the bed, took Valeria by the hand, and after a short silence, asked her, "What was the extraordinary dream that had frightened her so the previous night? And was it the same sort at all as the dream Muzzio had described?" Valeria crimsoned and said hurriedly: "O! no! no! I saw . . . a sort of monster which was trying to tear me to pieces." "A monster? in the shape of a man?" asked Fabio. "No, a beast . . . a beast!" Valeria turned away and hid her burning face in the pillows. Fabio held his wife's hand some time longer; silently he raised it to his lips, and withdrew.

Both the young people passed that day with heavy hearts. Something dark seemed hanging over their heads . . . but what it was, they could not tell. They wanted to be together, as though some danger threatened them; but what to say to one another they did not know. Fabio made an effort to take up the portrait, and to read Ariosto, whose poem had appeared not long before in Ferrara, and was now making a noise all over Italy; but nothing was of any use. . . . Late in the evening, just at suppertime, Muzzio returned.

## VII

He seemed composed and cheerful—but he told them little; he devoted himself rather to questioning Fabio about their common acquaintances, about the German war, and the Emperor Charles: he spoke of his own desire to visit Rome, to see the new Pope. He again offered Valeria some Shiraz wine, and on her refusal, observed as though to himself, "Now it's not needed, to be sure." Going back with his wife to their room, Fabio soon fell asleep; and waking up an hour later, felt a conviction that no one was sharing his bed; Valeria was not beside him. He got up quickly and at the same instant saw his wife in her night attire coming out of the garden into the room. The moon was shining brightly, though not long before a light rain had been falling. With eyes closed, with an expression of mysterious horror on her immovable face, Valeria approached the bed, and feeling for it with her hands stretched out before her, lay down hurriedly and in silence. Fabio turned to her with a question, but she made no reply; she seemed to be asleep. He touched her, and felt on her dress and on her hair drops of rain, and on the soles of her bare feet, little grains of sand. Then he leapt up and ran into the garden through the half-open door. The crude brilliance of the moon wrapt every object in light. Fabio looked about him, and perceived on the sand of the path prints of two pairs of feet—one pair were bare; and these prints led to a bower of jasmine, on one side, between the pavilion and the house. He stood still in perplexity, and suddenly once more he heard the strains of the song he had listened to the night before. Fabio shuddered, ran into the pavilion. . . . Muzzio was standing in the middle of the room playing on the violin. Fabio rushed up to him.

"You have been in the garden, your clothes are wet with rain."

"No . . . I don't know . . . I think . . . I have not been out. . . ." Muzzio answered slowly, seeming amazed at Fabio's entrance and his excitement.

Fabio seized him by the hand. "And why are you playing that melody again? Have you had a dream again?"

Muzzio glanced at Fabio with the same look of amazement, and said nothing.

"Answer me!"

> "'The moon stood high like a round shield . . .
> Like a snake, the river shines . . . ,
> The friend's awake, the foe's asleep . . .
> The bird is in the falcon's clutches . . . Help!'"

muttered Muzzio, humming to himself as though in delirium.

Fabio stepped back two paces, stared at Muzzio, pondered a moment . . . and went back to the house, to his bedroom.

Valeria, her head sunk on her shoulder and her hands hanging lifelessly, was in a heavy sleep. He could not quickly awaken her . . . but directly she saw him, she flung herself on his neck, and embraced him convulsively; she was trembling all over. "What is the matter, my precious, what is it?" Fabio kept repeating, trying to soothe her. But she still lay lifeless on his breast. "Ah, what fearful dreams I have!" she whispered, hiding her face against him. Fabio would have questioned her . . . but she only shuddered. The window-panes were flushed with the early light of morning when at last she fell asleep in his arms.


## VIII

The next day Muzzio disappeared from early morning, while Valeria informed her husband that she intended to go away to a neighbouring monastery, where lived her spiritual father, an old and austere monk, in whom she placed unbounded confidence. To Fabio's inquiries she replied, that she wanted by confession to relieve her soul, which was weighed down by the exceptional impressions of the last few days. As he looked upon Valeria's sunken face, and listened to her faint voice, Fabio approved of her plan; the worthy Father Lorenzo might give her valuable advice, and might disperse her doubts. . . . Under the escort of four attendants, Valeria set off to the monastery, while Fabio remained at home, and wandered about the garden till his wife's return, trying to comprehend what had happened to her, and a victim to constant fear and wrath, and the pain of undefined suspicions. . . . More than once he went up to the pavilion; but

Muzzio had not returned, and the Malay gazed at Fabio like a statue, obsequiously bowing his head, with a well-dissembled—so at least it seemed to Fabio—smile on his bronzed face. Meanwhile, Valeria had in confession told everything to her priest, not so much with shame as with horror. The priest heard her attentively, gave her his blessing, absolved her from her involuntary sin, but to himself he thought: "Sorcery, the arts of the devil ... the matter can't be left so," ... and he returned with Valeria to her villa, as though with the aim of completely pacifying and reassuring her. At the sight of the priest Fabio was thrown into some agitation; but the experienced old man had thought out beforehand how he must treat him. When he was left alone with Fabio, he did not of course betray the secrets of the confessional, but he advised him if possible to get rid of the guest they had invited to their house, as by his stories, his songs, and his whole behaviour he was troubling the imagination of Valeria. Moreover, in the old man's opinion, Muzzio had not, he remembered, been very firm in the faith in former days, and having spent so long a time in lands unenlightened by the truths of Christianity, he might well have brought thence the contagion of false doctrine, might even have become conversant with secret magic arts; and, therefore, though long friendship had indeed its claims, still a wise prudence pointed to the necessity of separation. Fabio fully agreed with the excellent monk. Valeria was even joyful when her husband reported to her the priest's counsel; and sent on his way with the cordial good-will of both the young people, loaded with good gifts for the monastery and the poor, Father Lorenzo returned home.

Fabio intended to have an explanation with Muzzio immediately after supper; but his strange guest did not return to supper. Then Fabio decided to defer his conversation with Muzzio until the following day; and both the young people retired to rest.

## IX

Valeria soon fell asleep; but Fabio could not sleep. In the stillness of the night, everything he had seen, everything he had felt presented itself more vividly; he put to himself still more insistently questions to which as before he could find no answer. Had Muzzio really become a sorcerer, and had he not already poisoned Valeria? She was ill ... but what was her disease? While he lay, his head in his hand, holding his feverish breath, and given up to painful reflection, the moon rose again upon a cloudless sky; and together with its beams, through the half-transparent window-panes, there began, from the direction of the pavilion—or was it Fabio's fancy?—to come a breath, like a light, fragrant current . . . then an urgent, passionate murmur was heard . . . and at that instant he observed that Valeria was beginning faintly to stir. He started, looked; she rose up, slid first one foot, then the other out of the bed, and like one bewitched of the moon, her sightless eyes fixed lifelessly before her, her hands stretched out, she began moving towards the garden! Fabio instantly ran out of the other door of the room, and running quickly round the corner of the house, bolted the door that led into the garden. . . . He had scarcely time to grasp at the bolt, when he felt some one trying to open the door from the inside, pressing against it . . . again and again . . . and then there was the sound of piteous passionate moans. . . .

"But Muzzio has not come back from the town," flashed through Fabio's head, and he rushed to the pavilion . . .

What did he see?

Coming towards him, along the path dazzlingly lighted up by the moon's rays, was Muzzio, he too moving like one moonstruck, his hands held out before him, and his eyes open but unseeing. . . . Fabio ran up to him, but he, not heeding him, moved on, treading evenly, step by step, and his rigid face smiled in the moonlight like the Malay's. Fabio would have called him by his name . . . but at that instant he heard, behind him in the house, the creaking of a window. . . . He looked round. . . .

Yes, the window of the bedroom was open from top to bottom, and putting one foot over the sill, Valeria stood in the window . . . her hands seemed to be seeking Muzzio . . . she seemed striving all over towards him. . . .

Unutterable fury filled Fabio's breast with a sudden inrush. "Accursed sorcerer!" he shrieked furiously, and seizing Muzzio by the throat with one hand, with the other he felt for the dagger in his girdle, and plunged the blade into his side up to the hilt.

Muzzio uttered a shrill scream, and clapping his hand to the wound, ran staggering back to the pavilion. . . . But at the very same instant when Fabio stabbed him, Valeria screamed just as shrilly, and fell to the earth like grass before the scythe.

Fabio flew to her, raised her up, carried her to the bed, began to speak to her. . . .

She lay a long time motionless, but at last she opened her eyes, heaved a deep, broken, blissful sigh, like one just rescued from imminent death, saw her husband, and twining her arms about his neck, crept close to him. "You, you, it is you," she faltered. Gradually her hands loosened their hold, her head sank back, and murmuring with a blissful smile, "Thank God, it is all over. . . . But how weary I am!" she fell into a sound but not heavy sleep.

X

Fabio sank down beside her bed, and never taking his eyes off her pale and sunken, but already calmer, face, began reflecting on what had happened . . . and also on how he ought to act now. What steps was he to take? If he had killed Muzzio—and remembering how deeply the dagger had gone in, he could have no doubt of it—it could not be hidden. He would have to bring it to the knowledge of the archduke, of the judges . . . but how explain, how describe such an incomprehensible affair? He, Fabio, had killed in his own house his own kinsman, his dearest friend? They will inquire, What for? on what ground? . . . But if Muzzio were not dead? Fabio could not endure to remain longer in uncertainty, and satisfying himself that Valeria was asleep, he cautiously got up from his chair, went out of the house, and made his way to the pavilion. Everything was still in it; only in one window a light was visible. With a sinking heart he opened the outer door (there was still the print of blood-stained fingers on it, and there were black drops of gore on the sand of the path), passed through the first dark room . . . and stood still on the threshold, overwhelmed with amazement.

In the middle of the room, on a Persian rug, with a brocaded cushion under his head, and all his limbs stretched out straight, lay Muzzio, covered with a wide, red shawl with a black pattern on it. His face, yellow as wax, with closed eyes and bluish eyelids, was turned towards the ceiling, no breathing could be discerned: he seemed a corpse. At his feet knelt the Malay, also wrapt in a red shawl. He was holding in his left hand a branch of some unknown plant, like a fern, and bending slightly forward, was gazing fixedly at his master. A small torch fixed on the floor burnt with a greenish flame, and was the only light in the room. The flame did not flicker nor smoke. The Malay did not stir at Fabio's entry, he merely turned his eyes upon him, and again bent them upon Muzzio. From time to time he raised and lowered the branch, and waved it in the air, and his dumb lips slowly parted and moved as though uttering soundless words. On the floor between the Malay and Muzzio lay the dagger, with which Fabio had stabbed his friend; the Malay struck one blow with the branch on the blood-stained blade. A minute passed . . . another. Fabio approached the

Malay, and stooping down to him, asked in an undertone, "Is he dead?" The Malay bent his head from above downwards, and disentangling his right hand from his shawl, he pointed imperiously to the door. Fabio would have repeated his question, but the gesture of the commanding hand was repeated, and Fabio went out, indignant and wondering, but obedient.

He found Valeria sleeping as before, with an even more tranquil expression on her face. He did not undress, but seated himself by the window, his head in his hand, and once more sank into thought. The rising sun found him still in the same place. Valeria had not waked up.

## XI

Fabio intended to wait till she awakened, and then to set off to Ferrara, when suddenly some one tapped lightly at the bedroom door. Fabio went out, and saw his old steward, Antonio. "Signor," began the old man, "the Malay has just informed me that Signor Muzzio has been taken ill, and wishes to be moved with all his belongings to the town; and that he begs you to let him have servants to assist in packing his things; and that at dinner-time you would send pack-horses, and saddle-horses, and a few attendants for the journey. Do you allow it?" "The Malay informed you of this?" asked Fabio. "In what manner? Why, he is dumb." "Here, signor, is the paper on which he wrote all this in our language, and very correctly." "And Muzzio, you say, is ill?" "Yes, he is very ill, and can see no one." "Have they sent for a doctor?" "No. The Malay forbade it." "And was it the Malay wrote you this?" "Yes, it was he." Fabio did not speak for a moment. "Well, then, arrange it all," he said at last. Antonio withdrew.

Fabio looked after his servant in bewilderment. "Then, he is not dead?" he thought . . . and he did not know whether to rejoice or to be sorry. "Ill?" But a few hours ago it was a corpse he had looked upon!

Fabio returned to Valeria. She waked up and raised her head. The husband and wife exchanged a long look full of significance. "He is gone?" Valeria said suddenly. Fabio shuddered. "How gone? Do you mean . . ." "Is he gone away?" she continued. A load fell from Fabio's heart. "Not yet; but he is going to-day." "And I shall never, never see him again?" "Never." "And these dreams will not come again?" "No." Valeria again heaved a sigh of relief; a blissful smile once more appeared on her lips. She held out both hands to her husband. "And we will never speak of him, never, do you hear, my dear one? And I will not leave my room till he is gone. And do you now send me my maids . . . but stay: take away that thing!" she pointed to the pearl necklace, lying on a little bedside table, the necklace given her by Muzzio, "and throw it at once into our deepest well. Embrace me. I am your Valeria; and do not come in to me till . . . he has gone." Fabio took the necklace—the pearls he fancied looked tarnished—and did as his wife had directed. Then he fell to wandering about the garden, looking from a distance at the pavilion, about which the bustle of preparations for departure was beginning. Servants were bringing out boxes, loading the horses . . . but the Malay was not among them. An irresistible impulse drew Fabio to look once more upon what was taking place in the pavilion. He recollected that there was at the back a secret door, by which he could reach the inner room where Muzzio had been lying in the morning. He stole round to this door, found it unlocked, and, parting the folds of a heavy curtain, turned a faltering glance upon the room within.

## XII

Muzzio was not now lying on the rug. Dressed as though for a journey, he sat in an arm-chair, but seemed a corpse, just as on Fabio's first visit. His torpid head fell back on the chair, and his outstretched hands hung lifeless, yellow, and rigid on his knees. His breast did not heave. Near the chair on the floor, which was strewn with dried herbs, stood some flat bowls of dark liquid, which exhaled a powerful, almost suffocating, odour, the odour of musk. Around each bowl was coiled a small snake of brazen hue, with golden eyes that flashed from time to time; while directly facing Muzzio, two paces from him, rose the long figure of the Malay, wrapt in a mantle of many-coloured brocade, girt round the waist with a tiger's tail, with a high hat of the shape of a pointed tiara on his head. But he was not motionless: at one moment he bowed down reverently, and seemed to be praying, at the next he drew himself up to his full height, even rose on tiptoe; then, with a rhythmic action, threw wide his arms, and moved them persistently in the direction of Muzzio, and seemed to threaten or command him, frowning and stamping with his foot. All these actions seemed to cost him great effort, even to cause him pain: he breathed heavily, the sweat streamed down his face. All at once he sank down to the ground, and drawing in a full breath, with knitted brow and immense effort, drew his clenched hands towards him, as though he were holding reins in them . . . and to the indescribable horror of Fabio, Muzzio's head slowly left the back of the chair, and moved forward, following the Malay's hands. . . . The Malay let them fall, and Muzzio's head fell heavily back again; the Malay repeated his movements, and obediently the head repeated them after him. The dark liquid in the bowls began boiling; the bowls themselves began to resound with a faint bell-like note, and the brazen snakes coiled freely about each of them. Then the Malay took a step forward, and raising his eyebrows and opening his eyes immensely wide, he bowed his head to Muzzio ... and the eyelids of the dead man quivered, parted uncertainly, and under them could be seen the eyeballs, dull as lead. The Malay's face was radiant with triumphant pride and delight, a delight almost malignant; he opened his mouth wide, and from the depths of his chest there broke out with effort a prolonged howl.... Muzzio's lips parted too, and a faint moan quivered on them in response to that inhuman sound....

But at this point Fabio could endure it no longer; he imagined he was present at some devilish incantation! He too uttered a shriek and rushed out, running home, home as quick as possible, without looking round, repeating prayers and crossing himself as he ran.

## XIII

Three hours later, Antonio came to him with the announcement that everything was ready, the things were packed, and Signor Muzzio was preparing to start. Without a word in answer to his servant, Fabio went out on to the terrace, whence the pavilion could be seen. A few pack-horses were grouped before it; a powerful raven horse, saddled for two riders, was led up to the steps, where servants were standing bare-headed, together with armed attendants. The door of the pavilion opened, and supported by the Malay, who wore once more his ordinary attire, appeared Muzzio. His face was death-like, and his hands hung like a dead man's—but he walked ... yes, positively walked, and, seated on the charger, he sat upright and felt for and found the reins. The Malay put his feet in the stirrups, leaped up behind him on the saddle, put his arm round him, and the whole party started. The horses moved at a walking pace, and when they turned round before the house, Fabio fancied that in Muzzio's dark face there gleamed two spots of white.... Could it be he had turned his eyes upon him? Only the Malay bowed to him ... ironically, as ever.

Did Valeria see all this? The blinds of her windows were drawn ... but it may be she was standing behind them.

## XIV

At dinner-time she came into the dining-room, and was very quiet and affectionate; she still complained, however, of weariness. But there was no agitation about her now, none of her former constant bewilderment and secret dread; and when, the day after Muzzio's departure, Fabio set to work again on her portrait, he found in her features the pure expression, the momentary eclipse of which had so troubled him . . . and his brush moved lightly and faithfully over the canvas.

The husband and wife took up their old life again. Muzzio vanished for them as though he had never existed. Fabio and Valeria were agreed, as it seemed, not to utter a syllable referring to him, not to learn anything of his later days; his fate remained, however, a mystery for all. Muzzio did actually disappear, as though he had sunk into the earth. Fabio one day thought it his duty to tell Valeria exactly what had taken place on that fatal night . . , but she probably divined his intention, and she held her breath, half-shutting her eyes, as though she were expecting a blow. . . . And Fabio understood her; he did not inflict that blow upon her.

One fine autumn day, Fabio was putting the last touches to his picture of his Cecilia; Valeria sat at the organ, her fingers straying at random over the keys. . . . Suddenly, without her knowing it, from under her hands came the first notes of that song of triumphant love which Muzzio had once played; and at the same instant, for the first time since her marriage, she felt within her the throb of a new palpitating life. . . . Valeria started, stopped. . . .

What did it mean? Could it be . . .

At this word the manuscript ended.

*Translated by Constance Garnett*

❧

# THE WALRUS AND THE CARPENTER

## *Lewis Carroll*

"The sun was shining on the sea,
　　Shining with all his might:
He did his very best to make
　　The billows smooth and bright—
And this was odd, because it was
　　The middle of the night.

The moon was shining sulkily,
　　Because she thought the sun
Had got no business to be there
　　After the day was done—
'It's very rude of him,' she said,
　　'To come and spoil the fun!'

The sea was wet as wet could be,
　　The sands were dry as dry.
You could not see a cloud, because
　　No cloud was in the sky:
No birds were flying overhead—
　　There were no birds to fly.

The Walrus and the Carpenter
　　Were walking close at hand:
They wept like anything to see
　　Such quantities of sand:
'If this were only cleared away,'
　　They said, 'it would be grand!'

'If seven maids with seven mops
　　Swept it for half a year,
Do you suppose,' the Walrus said,
　　'That they could get it clear?'
'I doubt it,' said the Carpenter,
　　And shed a bitter tear.

'O Oysters, come and walk with us!'
  The Walrus did beseech.
'A pleasant walk, a pleasant talk,
  Along the briny beach:
We cannot do with more than four,
  To give a hand to each.'

The eldest Oyster looked at him,
  But never a word he said:
The eldest Oyster winked his eye,
  And shook his heavy head—
Meaning to say he did not choose
  To leave the oyster-bed.

But four young Oysters hurried up,
  All eager for the treat:
Their coats were brushed, their faces washed,
  Their shoes were clean and neat—
And this was odd, because, you know,
  They hadn't any feet.

Four other Oysters followed them,
  And yet another four;
And thick and fast they came at last,
  And more, and more, and more—
All hopping through the frothy waves,
  And scrambling to the shore.

The Walrus and the Carpenter
  Walked on a mile or so,
And then they rested on a rock
  Conveniently low:
And all the little Oysters stood
  And waited in a row.

'The time has come,' the Walrus said,
  'To talk of many things:
Of shoes—and ships—and sealing wax—
  Of cabbages—and kings—
And why the sea is boiling hot—
  And whether pigs have wings.'

'But wait a bit,' the Oysters cried,
    'Before we have our chat;
For some of us are out of breath,
    And all of us are fat!'
'No hurry!' said the Carpenter.
    They thanked him much for that.

'A loaf of bread,' the Walrus said,
    'Is what we chiefly need:
Pepper and vinegar besides
    Are very good indeed—
Now, if you're ready, Oysters dear,
    We can begin to feed.'

'But not on us!' the Oysters cried,
    Turning a little blue.
'After such kindness, that would be
    A dismal thing to do!'
'The night is fine,' the Walrus said.
    'Do you admire the view?

'It was so kind of you to come!
    And you are very nice!'
The Carpenter said nothing but
    'Cut us another slice.
I wish you were not quite so deaf—
    I've had to ask you twice!'

'It seems a shame,' the Walrus said,
    'To play them such a trick.
After we've brought them out so far,
    And made them trot so quick!'
The Carpenter said nothing but
'The butter's spread too thick!'

'I weep for you,' the Walrus said:
    'I deeply sympathize.'
With sobs and tears he sorted out
    Those of the largest size,

Holding his pocket-handkerchief
Before his streaming eyes.

'O Oysters,' said the Carpenter,
    'You've had a pleasant run!
Shall we be trotting home again?'
    But answer came there none—
And this was scarcely odd, because
    They'd eaten every one."

❧

# A NOISELESS PATIENT SPIDER

## *Walt Whitman*

A noiseless patient spider,
I mark'd where on a little promontory it stood isolated,
Mark'd how to explore the vacant vast surrounding,
It launch'd forth filament, filament, filament, out of
        itself,
Ever unreeling them, ever tirelessly speeding them.

And you O my soul where you stand,
Surrounded, detached, in measureless oceans of space,
Ceaselessly musing, venturing, throwing, seeking the
        spheres to connect them,
Till the bridge you will need be form'd, till the ductile
        anchor hold,
Till the gossamer thread you fling catch somewhere,
        O my soul.

❧

# UP-HILL

## Christina Rossetti

Does the road wind up-hill all the way?
　　Yes, to the very end.
Will the day's journey take the whole long day?
　　From morn to night, my friend.

But is there for the night a resting-place?
　　A roof for when the slow dark hours begin.
May not the darkness hide it from my face?
　　You cannot miss that inn.

Shall I meet other wayfarers at night?
　　Those who have gone before.
Then must I knock, or call when just in sight?
　　They will not keep you standing at that door.

Shall I find comfort, travel-sore and weak?
　　Of labour you shall find the sum.
Will there be beds for me and all who seek?
　　Yea, beds for all who come.

# AUTHOR INDEX

# TITLE INDEX